*Against All
Things Ending*

The Last Chronicles of Thomas Covenant

The Runes of the Earth

Fatal Revenant

The Second Chronicles of Thomas Covenant

The Wounded Land

The One Tree

White Gold Wielder

The Chronicles of Thomas Covenant the Unbeliever

Lord Foul's Bane

The Illearth War

The Power That Preserves

Stephen R. Donaldson

G. P. Putnam's Sons
New York

Against All Things Ending

The Last Chronicles of Thomas Covenant

BOOK THREE

G. P. PUTNAM'S SONS
Publishers Since 1838
Published by the Penguin Group
Penguin Group (USA) Inc., 375 Hudson Street, New York, New York 10014, USA •
Penguin Group (Canada), 90 Eglinton Avenue East, Suite 700, Toronto, Ontario M4P 2Y3,
Canada (a division of Pearson Penguin Canada Inc.) • Penguin Books Ltd, 80 Strand,
London WC2R 0RL, England • Penguin Ireland, 25 St Stephen's Green, Dublin 2,
Ireland (a division of Penguin Books Ltd) • Penguin Group (Australia), 250 Camberwell
Road, Camberwell, Victoria 3124, Australia (a division of Pearson Australia Group
Pty Ltd) • Penguin Books India Pvt Ltd, 11 Community Centre, Panchsheel Park,
New Delhi–110 017, India • Penguin Group (NZ), 67 Apollo Drive, Rosedale,
North Shore 0632, New Zealand (a division of Pearson New Zealand Ltd) •
Penguin Books (South Africa) (Pty) Ltd, 24 Sturdee Avenue, Rosebank,
Johannesburg 2196, South Africa

Penguin Books Ltd, Registered Offices: 80 Strand, London WC2R 0RL, England

Library of Congress Cataloging-in-Publication Data

Donaldson, Stephen R.
  Against all things ending / Stephen R. Donaldson.
      p.   cm.—(The last chronicles of Thomas Covenant; bk.3)
  ISBN 978-0-399-15678-6
  1. Covenant, Thomas (Fictitious character)—Fiction.   I. Title
  PS3554.O469A74   2010   2010023390
  813'.54—dc22

Printed in the United States of America
10 9 8 7 6 5 4 3 2 1

Book design by Meighan Cavanaugh

to Perry Donaldson:

a daughter to make a man proud

Acknowledgments

The help that I've received while working on "The Last Chronicles of Thomas Covenant" in general, and on *Against All Things Ending* in particular, deserves more gratitude than I can properly express. Both John Eccker and Robyn Butler have been invaluable: diligent, generous beyond all expectation, and—when necessary—relentless. In addition, their valiant efforts to think well of even my worst prose have a certain fey charm.

For entirely different reasons, I want to thank Christopher Merchant. This book could not have been written without his particular involvement.

And the whole concept of "thanks" would be meaningless if it did not include Jennifer Dunstan, who lifts me up.

Contents

What Has Gone Before

"The Chronicles of Thomas Covenant the Unbeliever"

As a young man—a novelist, happily married, with an infant son, Roger—Thomas Covenant is inexplicably stricken with leprosy. In a leprosarium, where the last two fingers of his right hand are amputated, he learns that leprosy is incurable. As it progresses, it produces numbness, often killing its victims by leaving them unaware of injuries which then become infected. Medications arrest the progress of Covenant's affliction; but he is taught that his only real hope of survival lies in protecting himself obsessively from any form of damage.

Horrified by his illness, he returns to his home on Haven Farm, where his wife, Joan, has abandoned and divorced him in order to protect their son from exposure.

Other blows to his emotional stability follow. Fearing the mysterious nature of his illness, the people around him cast him in the traditional role of the leper: a pariah, outcast and unclean. In addition, he discovers that he has become impotent—and unable to write. Grimly he struggles to go on living; but as the pressure of his loneliness mounts, he begins to experience prolonged episodes of unconsciousness, during which he appears to have adventures in a magical realm known only as "the Land."

In the Land, physical and emotional health are tangible forces, made palpable by an eldritch energy called Earthpower. Because vitality and beauty are concrete qualities, as plain to the senses as size and color, the well-being of the physical world has become the guiding precept of the Land's people. When Covenant first encounters them, in *Lord Foul's Bane*, they greet him as the reincarnation of an ancient hero, Berek

Halfhand, because he, too, has lost half of his hand. Also he possesses a white gold ring—his wedding band—which they know to be a talisman of great power, able to wield "the wild magic that destroys peace."

Shortly after he first appears in the Land, Covenant's leprosy and impotence disappear, cured by Earthpower; and this, he knows, is impossible. Indeed, the mere idea that he possesses some form of magical power threatens his ability to sustain the stubborn disciplines on which his survival depends. Therefore he chooses to interpret his translation to the Land as a dream or hallucination. He responds to his welcome and health with Unbelief: the harsh, dogged assertion that the Land is not real.

Because of his Unbelief, his initial reactions to the people and wonders of the Land are at best dismissive, at worst despicable. At one point, overwhelmed by sensations he can neither accept nor control, and certain that his experiences are not real, he rapes Lena, a young girl who has befriended him. However, the people of the Land decline to punish or reject him for his actions. As Berek Halfhand reborn, he is beyond judgment. And there is an ancient prophecy concerning the white gold wielder: "With the one word of truth or treachery, / he will save or damn the Earth." Covenant's new companions in the Land know that they cannot make his choices for him. They can only hope that he will eventually follow Berek's example by saving the Land.

At first, such forbearance achieves little, although Covenant cannot deny that he is moved by the ineffable beauties of this world, as well as by the kindness of its people. During his travels, however, first with Lena's mother, Atiaran, then with the Giant Saltheart Foamfollower, and finally with the Lords of Revelstone, he learns enough of the history of the Land to understand what is at stake.

The Land has an ancient enemy, Lord Foul the Despiser, who dreams of destroying the Arch of Time—thereby destroying not only the Land but the entire Earth—in order to escape what he perceives to be a prison. Against this evil stands the Council of Lords, men and women who have dedicated their lives to nurturing the health of the Land, to studying the lost lore and wisdom of Berek and his long-dead descendants, and to opposing Despite.

Unfortunately these Lords possess only a small fraction of the power of their predecessors. The Staff of Law, Berek's primary instrument of Earthpower, has been hidden from them. And the lore of Law and Earthpower seems inherently inadequate to defeat Lord Foul. Wild magic rather than Law is the crux of Time. Without it, the Arch cannot be destroyed; but neither can it be defended.

Hence both the Lords and the Despiser seek Thomas Covenant's allegiance. The Lords attempt to win his aid with courage and compassion: the Despiser, through manipulation. And in this contest Covenant's Unbelief appears to place him on the side of the Despiser.

Nevertheless Covenant cannot deny his reaction to the Land's apparent transcendence. And as he is granted more and more friendship by the Lords and denizens of the Land, he finds that he is now dismayed by his earlier violence toward Lena. He faces an insoluble conundrum: the Land cannot be real, yet it feels entirely real. His heart responds to its loveliness—and that response has the potential to kill him by undermining his necessary habits of wariness and hopelessness.

Trapped within this contradiction, he attempts to escape through a series of unspoken bargains. In *Lord Foul's Bane*, he grants the Lords his passive support, hoping that this will enable him to avoid accepting the possibilities—the responsibilities—of his white gold ring. And at first his hopes are realized. The Lords find the lost Staff of Law; their immediate enemy, one of Lord Foul's servants, is defeated; and Covenant himself is released from the Land.

Back in his real world, however, he discovers that he has in fact gained nothing. Indeed, his plight has worsened: he remains a leper; and his experience of friendship and magic in the Land has weakened his ability to endure his outcast loneliness on Haven Farm. When he is translated to the Land a second time, in *The Illearth War*, he knows that he must devise a new bargain.

During his absence, the Land's plight has worsened as well. Decades have passed in the Land; and in that time Lord Foul has gained and mastered the Illearth Stone, an ancient bane of staggering power. With it, the Despiser has created an army which now marches to overwhelm the Lords of Revelstone. Although the Lords hold the Staff of Law, they lack sufficient might to withstand the evil horde. They need the strength of wild magic.

Other developments also tighten the grip of Covenant's dilemma. The Council is now led by High Lord Elena, his daughter by his rape of Lena. With her, he begins to experience the real consequences of his violence: it is clear to him—if to no one else— that she is not completely sane. In addition, the army of the Lords is led by a man named Hile Troy, who appears to have come to the Land from Covenant's own world. Troy's presence radically erodes Covenant's self-protective Unbelief.

Now more than ever Covenant feels that he must resolve his conundrum. Again he posits a bargain. He will give the defenders of the Land his active support. Specifically he will join Elena on a quest to discover the source of EarthBlood, the most concentrated form of Earthpower. But in return he will continue to deny that his ring holds any power. He will accept no responsibility for the ultimate fate of the Land.

This time, however, the results of his bargain are disastrous. Using the Illearth Stone, Lord Foul slaughters the Giants of Seareach. Hile Troy is only able to defeat the Despiser's army by giving his soul to Caerroil Wildwood, the Forestal of Garroting Deep. And Covenant's help enables Elena to find the EarthBlood, which she uses to sever one of the necessary boundaries between life and death. Her instability leads her to think that the dead will have more power against Lord Foul than the living. But she is terribly wrong; and in the resulting catastrophe both she and the Staff of Law are lost.

Covenant returns to his real world knowing that his attempts to resolve his dilemma have served the Despiser.

Nearly broken by his failures, he visits the Land once more in *The Power That Preserves*, where he discovers the full cost of his actions. Dead, his daughter now serves Lord Foul, using the Staff of Law to wreak havoc. Her mother, Lena, has lost her mind. And the defenders of the Land are besieged by an army too vast and powerful to be defeated.

Covenant still has no solution to his conundrum: only wild magic can save the Land, yet he cannot afford to accept its reality. However, sickened at heart by Lena's madness, and by the imminent ruin of the Land, he resolves to confront the Despiser himself. He has no hope of defeating Lord Foul, but he would rather sacrifice himself for the sake of an unreal yet magical place than preserve his outcast life in his real world.

Before he can reach the Despiser, however, he must first face dead Elena and the Staff of Law. He cannot oppose her; yet she defeats herself when her attack on him draws an overwhelming response from his ring—a response which also destroys the Staff.

Accompanied only by his old friend, the Giant Saltheart Foamfollower, Covenant finally gains his confrontation with Lord Foul and the Illearth Stone. Facing the full force of the Despiser's savagery and malice, he at last finds the solution to his conundrum, "the eye of the paradox": the point of balance between accepting that the Land is real and insisting that it is not. On that basis, he is able to combat Lord Foul by using the dire might of the Illearth Stone to trigger the wild magic of his ring. With that power, he shatters both the Stone and Lord Foul's home, thereby ending the threat of the Despiser's evil.

When he returns to his own world for the last time, he learns that his newfound balance benefits him there as well. He knows now that the reality or unreality of the Land is less important than his love for it; and this insight gives him the strength to face his life as a pariah without fear or bitterness.

"The Second Chronicles of Thomas Covenant"

For ten years after the events of *The Power That Preserves*, Covenant lives alone on Haven Farm, writing novels. He is still an outcast, but he has one friend, Dr. Julius Berenford. Then, however, two damaged women enter his life.

His ex-wife, Joan, returns to him, violently insane. Leaving Roger with her parents, she has spent some time in a commune which has dedicated itself to the service of

Despite, and which has chosen Covenant to be the victim of its evil. Hoping to spare anyone else the hazards of involvement, Covenant attempts to care for Joan alone.

When Covenant refuses aid, Dr. Berenford enlists Dr. Linden Avery, a young physician whom he has recently hired. Like Joan, she has been badly hurt, although in entirely different ways. As a young girl, she was locked in a room with her father while he committed suicide. And as a teenager, she killed her mother, an act of euthanasia to which she felt compelled by her mother's illness and pain. Loathing death, Linden has become a doctor in a haunted attempt to erase her past.

At Dr. Berenford's urging, she intrudes on Covenant's treatment of his ex-wife. When members of Joan's commune attack Haven Farm, seeking Covenant's death, Linden attempts to intervene, but she is struck down before she can save him. As a result, she accompanies him when he is returned to the Land.

During Covenant's absence, several thousand years have passed, and the Despiser has regained his power. As before, he seeks to use Covenant's wild magic in order to break the Arch of Time and escape his prison. In *The Wounded Land*, however, Covenant and Linden soon learn that Lord Foul has fundamentally altered his methods. Instead of relying on armies and warfare to goad Covenant, the Despiser has devised an attack on the natural Law which gives the Land its beauty and health.

The overt form of this attack is the Sunbane, a malefic corona around the sun which produces extravagant surges of fertility, rain, drought, and pestilence in mad succession. So great is the Sunbane's power and destructiveness that it has come to dominate all life in the Land. Yet the Sunbane is not what it appears to be. And its organic virulence serves primarily to mask Lord Foul's deeper manipulations.

He has spent centuries corrupting the Council of Lords. That group now rules over the Land as the Clave; and it is led by a Raver, one of the Despiser's most ancient and potent servants. The Clave extracts blood from the people of the Land to feed the Banefire, an enormous blaze which purportedly hinders the Sunbane, but which actually increases it.

However, the hidden purpose of the Clave and the Banefire is to inspire from Covenant an excessive exertion of wild magic. And toward that end, another Raver afflicts Covenant with a venom intended to cripple his control over his power. When the venom has done its work, Covenant will be unable to defend the Land without unleashing so much force that he destroys the Arch.

As for Linden Avery, Lord Foul intends to use her loathing of death against her. She alone is gifted or cursed with the health-sense which once informed and guided all the people of the Land by enabling them to perceive physical and emotional health directly. For that reason, she is uniquely vulnerable to the malevolence of the Sunbane, as well as to the insatiable malice of the Ravers. The manifest evil into which she has been plunged threatens the core of her identity.

Linden's health-sense accentuates her potential as a healer. However, it also gives her the capacity to possess other people; to reach so deeply into them that she can control their actions. By this means, Lord Foul intends to cripple her morally: he seeks to transform her into a woman who will possess Covenant in order to misuse his power. Thus she will give the Despiser what he wants even if Covenant does not.

And if those ploys fail, Lord Foul has other stratagems in place to achieve his ends.

Horrified in their separate ways by what has been done to the Land, Covenant and Linden wish to confront the Clave in Revelstone; but on their own, they cannot survive the complex perils of the Sunbane. Fortunately they gain the help of two villagers, Sunder and Hollian. Sunder and Hollian have lived with the Sunbane all their lives, and their experience enables Covenant and Linden to avoid ruin as they travel.

But Linden, Sunder, and Hollian are separated from Covenant near a region known as Andelain, captured by the Clave while he enters Andelain alone. It was once the most beautiful and Earthpowerful place in the Land; and he now discovers that it alone remains intact, defended from the Sunbane by the last Forestal, Caer-Caveral, who was formerly Hile Troy. There Covenant encounters his Dead, the spectres of his long-gone friends. They offer him advice and guidance for the struggle ahead. And they give him a gift: a strange ebony creature named Vain, an artificial being created for a hidden purpose by ur-viles, former servants of the Despiser.

Aided by Waynhim, benign relatives—and ancient enemies—of the ur-viles, Covenant hastens toward Revelstone to rescue his friends. When he encounters the Clave, he learns the cruelest secret of the Sunbane: it was made possible by his destruction of the Staff of Law thousands of years ago. Desperate to undo the harm which he has unwittingly caused, he risks wild magic in order to free Linden, Sunder, and Hollian, as well as a number of *Haruchai*, powerful warriors who at one time served the Council of Lords.

With his friends, Vain, and a small group of *Haruchai*, Covenant then sets out to locate the One Tree, the wood from which Berek originally fashioned the Staff of Law. Covenant hopes to devise a new Staff with which to oppose the Clave and the Sunbane.

Traveling eastward, toward the Sunbirth Sea, Covenant and his companions encounter a party of Giants, seafaring beings from the homeland of the lost Giants of Seareach. One of them, Cable Seadreamer, has had a vision of a terrible threat to the Earth, and the Giants have sent out a Search to discover the danger.

Convinced that this threat is the Sunbane, Covenant persuades the Search to help him find the One Tree; and in *The One Tree*, Covenant, Linden, Vain, and several *Haruchai* set sail aboard the Giantship Starfare's Gem, leaving Sunder and Hollian to rally the people of the Land against the Clave.

The quest for the One Tree takes Covenant and Linden first to the land of the

Elohim, cryptic beings of pure Earthpower who appear to understand and perhaps control the destiny of the Earth. The *Elohim* agree to reveal the location of the One Tree, but they exact a price: they cripple Covenant's mind, enclosing his consciousness in a kind of stasis, purportedly to protect the Earth from his growing power, but in fact to prevent him from carrying out Vain's unnamed purpose. Guided now by Linden's determination rather than Covenant's, the Search sets sail for the Isle of the One Tree.

Unexpectedly, however, they are joined by one of the *Elohim*, Findail, who has been Appointed to bear the consequences if Vain's purpose does not fail.

Linden soon finds that she is unable to free Covenant's mind without possessing him, which she fears to do, knowing that she may unleash his power. When she and all of her companions are imprisoned in *Bhrathairealm*, however, she succeeds at restoring his consciousness—much to Findail's dismay. Covenant then fights and masters a Sandgorgon, a fierce monster of the Great Desert. The creature's rampage through *Bhrathairealm* enables Covenant, Linden, and their companions to escape.

At last, Starfare's Gem reaches the Isle of the One Tree, where one of the *Haruchai*, Brinn, contrives to replace the Tree's Guardian. But when Covenant, Linden, and their companions approach their goal, they learn that they have been misled by the Despiser—and by the *Elohim*. Covenant's attempt to obtain wood for a new Staff of Law begins to rouse the Worm of the World's End. Once awakened, the Worm will accomplish Lord Foul's release from Time.

At the cost of his own life, Seadreamer succeeds at making Linden aware of the true danger. She in turn is able to forestall Covenant. Nevertheless the Worm has been disturbed, and its restlessness forces the Search to flee as the Isle sinks into the sea, taking the One Tree beyond reach.

Defeated, the Search sets course for the Land in *White Gold Wielder*. Covenant now believes that he has no alternative except to confront the Clave directly, to quench the Banefire, and then to battle the Despiser; and Linden is determined to aid him, in part because she has come to love him, and in part because she fears his unchecked wild magic.

With great difficulty, they eventually reach Revelstone, where they are rejoined by Sunder, Hollian, and several *Haruchai*. Together the Land's few defenders give battle to the Clave. After a fierce struggle, the companions corner the Raver that commands the Clave. There Seadreamer's brother, Grimmand Honninscrave, with the help of a Sandgorgon, sacrifices his life in order to make possible the "rending" of the Raver. As a result, the Sandgorgon gains a scrap of the Raver's sentience. Then Covenant flings himself into the Banefire, using its dark theurgy to transform the venom in his veins so that he can quench the Banefire without threatening the Arch. The Sunbane remains, but its evil no longer grows.

When the Clave has been dispersed, and Revelstone has been cleansed, Covenant and Linden turn toward Mount Thunder, where the Despiser now resides. As they travel, still followed by Vain and Findail, Linden's fears mount. She realizes that Covenant does not mean to fight Lord Foul. That contest, Covenant believes, will unleash enough force to destroy Time. Afraid that he will surrender to the Despiser, Linden prepares herself to possess him again, although she now understands that possession is a great evil.

Yet when she and Covenant finally face Lord Foul, deep within the Wightwarrens of Mount Thunder, she is possessed herself by a Raver; and her efforts to win free of that dark spirit's control leave her unwilling to interfere with Covenant's choices. As she has feared, he does surrender, giving Lord Foul his ring. But when the Despiser turns wild magic against Covenant, slaying his body, the altered venom is burned out of Covenant's spirit, and he becomes a being of pure wild magic, able to sustain the Arch despite the fury of Lord Foul's attacks. Eventually the Despiser expends so much of his own essence that he effectively defeats himself; and Covenant's ring falls to Linden.

Meanwhile, she has gleaned an understanding of Vain's purpose—and of Findail's Appointed role. Vain is pure structure, Findail, pure fluidity. Using Covenant's ring, Linden melds the two beings into a new Staff of Law. Then, guided by her health-sense and her physician's instincts, she reaches out with the restored power of Law to erase the Sunbane and begin the healing of the Land.

When she is done, Linden fades from the Land and returns to her own world, where she finds that Covenant is indeed dead. Yet she now holds his wedding ring. And when Dr. Berenford comes looking for her, she discovers that her time with Covenant and her own victories have transformed her. She is now truly Linden Avery the Chosen, as she was called in the Land: she can choose to live her old life in an entirely new way.

"The Last Chronicles of Thomas Covenant"

In Book One, *The Runes of the Earth*, ten years have passed for Linden Avery; and in that time, her life has changed. She has adopted a son, Jeremiah, now fifteen, who was horribly damaged during her first translation to the Land, losing half of his right hand and—apparently—all ordinary use of his mind. He displays a peculiar genius: he is able to build astonishing structures out of such toys as Tinkertoys and Legos. But in every other way, he is entirely unreactive. Nonetheless Linden is devoted to him, giving him all of her frustrated love for Thomas Covenant and the Land.

In addition, she has become the Chief Medical Officer of a local psychiatric hospital, where Covenant's ex-wife, Joan, is now a patient. For a time, Joan's condition resembles a vegetative catatonia. But then she starts to punish herself, punching her temple incessantly in an apparent effort to bring about her own death. Only the restoration of her white gold wedding band calms her, although it does not altogether prevent her violence.

As the story begins, Roger Covenant has reached twenty-one, and has come to claim custody of his mother: custody which Linden refuses, in part because she has no legal authority to release Joan, and in part because she does not trust Roger. To this setback, Roger responds by kidnapping his mother at gunpoint. And when Linden goes to the hospital to deal with the aftermath of Roger's attack, Roger captures Jeremiah as well.

Separately Linden and the police locate Roger, Joan, and Jeremiah. But while Linden confronts Roger, Joan is struck by lightning, and Roger opens fire on the police. In the ensuing fusillade, Linden, Roger, and Jeremiah are cut down; and Linden finds herself once again translated to the Land, where Lord Foul's disembodied voice informs her that he has gained possession of her son.

As before, several thousand years have passed in the Land, and everything that Linden knew has changed. The Land has been healed, restored to its former loveliness and potency. Now, however, it is ruled by Masters, *Haruchai* who have dedicated themselves to the suppression of all magical knowledge and power. And their task is simplified by an eerie smog called Kevin's Dirt, which blinds the people of the Land—as well as Linden—to the wealth of Earthpower all around them.

Yet the Land is threatened by perils which the Masters cannot defeat. *Caesures*—disruptions of time—wreak havoc, appearing and disappearing randomly as Joan releases insane blasts of wild magic. In addition, one of the *Elohim* has visited the Land, warning of dangers which include various monsters—and an unnamed *half-hand*. And the new Staff of Law that Linden created at the end of *White Gold Wielder* has been lost.

Desperate to locate and rescue Jeremiah, Linden soon acquires companions, both willing and reluctant: Anele, an ancient, Earthpowerful, and blind madman who claims that he is "the hope of the Land," and whose insanity varies with the surfaces—stone, dirt, grass—on which he stands; Liand, a naïve young man from Mithil Stonedown; Stave, a Master who distrusts Linden, and wishes to imprison Anele; a small group of ur-viles, artificial creatures that were at one time among Lord Foul's most dire minions; and a band of Ramen, the human servants of the Ranyhyn, Earthpowerful horses that once inhabited the Land. Among the Ramen, Linden discovers that the Ranyhyn intend to aid her in her search for her son. And she meets Esmer, the tormented and powerful descendant of the lost *Haruchai* Cail and the corrupted *Elohim* Kastenessen.

From Esmer, Linden learns the nature of the *caesures*. She is told that the ur-viles intend to protect her from betrayal by Esmer. And she finds that Anele knows where the Staff of Law was lost thousands of years ago.

Because she has no power except Covenant's ring, which she is only able to use with great difficulty—because she has no idea where Lord Foul has taken Jeremiah—and because she fears that she will not be able to travel the Land against the opposition of the Masters—Linden decides to risk entering a *caesure*. She hopes that it will take her into the past, to the time when her Staff of Law was lost, and that Anele will then be able to guide her to the Staff. Accompanied by Anele, Liand, Stave, the ur-viles, and three Ramen—the Manethrall Mahrtiir and his two Cords, Bhapa and Pahni—Linden rides into the temporal chaos of Joan's power.

Thanks to the theurgy of the ur-viles, and to the guidance of the Ranyhyn, she and her companions emerge from the *caesure* more than three thousand years in their past, where they find that the Staff has been hidden and protected by a group of Waynhim. When she reclaims the Staff, however, she is betrayed by Esmer: using powers inherited from Kastenessen, he brings a horde of Demondim out of the Land's deep past to assail her. The Demondim are monstrous beings, the makers of the ur-viles and Waynhim, and they attack with both their own fierce lore and the baleful energy of the Illearth Stone, which they siphon through a *caesure* from an era before Thomas Covenant's first visit to the Land.

Fearing that the attack of the Demondim will damage the integrity of the Land's history, Linden uses Covenant's ring to create a *caesure* of her own. That disruption of time carries her, all of her companions, and the Demondim to her natural present. To her surprise, however, her *caesure* deposits her and everyone with her before the gates of Revelstone, the seat of the Masters. While the Masters fight a hopeless battle against the Demondim, she and her companions enter the ambiguous sanctuary of Lord's Keep.

In Revelstone, Linden meets Handir, called the Voice of the Masters: their leader. And she encounters the Humbled, Galt, Branl, and Clyme: three *Haruchai* who have been maimed to resemble Thomas Covenant, and whose purpose is to embody the moral authority of the Masters. Cared for by a mysterious—and oddly comforting—woman named the Mahdoubt, Linden tries to imagine how she can persuade the Masters to aid her search for Jeremiah, and for the salvation of the Land. However, when she confronts Handir, the Humbled, and other Masters, all of her arguments are turned aside. Although the Masters are virtually helpless against the Demondim, they refuse to countenance Linden's desires. Only Stave elects to stand with her: an act of defiance for which he is punished and spurned by his kinsmen.

The confrontation ends abruptly when news comes that riders are approaching Revelstone. From the battlements, Linden sees four Masters racing to reach Lord's Keep ahead of the Demondim. With the Masters are Thomas Covenant and Jeremiah. And Jeremiah has emerged enthusiastically from his unreactive passivity.

In *Fatal Revenant*, the arrival of Covenant and Jeremiah brings turmoil. They are tangibly present and powerful, able to evade the forces of the Demondim. Yet they give no satisfactory account of their presence. And they refuse to let Linden touch them: they refuse to acknowledge her love. Instead they insist on being sequestered until they are ready to talk to her.

Meanwhile the Demondim mass at the gates, apparently preparing the evil of the Illearth Stone to destroy Revelstone. But they do not attack.

Profoundly shaken, Linden retreats alone to the plateau above Lord's Keep to await Covenant's summons. There she calls for Esmer, hoping that he will hear her—and that he will answer her questions. When he manifests himself, however, he surprises her by bringing more creatures out of the Land's distant past: a band of ur-viles and a smaller number of Waynhim who have joined together to serve Linden. Cryptically Esmer informs her that the creatures have prepared "manacles." And he reveals that the Demondim besieging Revelstone are now working in concert with Kastenessen. But he avoids Linden's other questions. Instead, for no apparent reason, he tells her that she "must be the first to drink of the EarthBlood."

When Esmer vanishes, Covenant's summons comes. Linden meets with Covenant and Jeremiah in their chambers—an encounter which only exacerbates her distress. Covenant speaks primarily in non sequiturs and evasions, although he insists that he knows how to save the Land. At the same time, Jeremiah pleads with Linden to trust his companion: he considers Covenant his friend. Feeling both rejected and suspicious, Linden refuses when Covenant asks for his white gold ring. In response, Covenant demands that she join him on the plateau, where he will show her how he intends to save the Land.

Linden complies. She knows no other way to discover why and how her loved ones have changed. Instead of revealing their intentions for the Land, however, Covenant and Jeremiah create a portal which snatches her away from her present. Without transition, she finds herself with Covenant and Jeremiah ten millennia in the Land's past, during the time of Berek Halfhand's last wars before he became the first of the High Lords.

They are near the dire forest of Garroting Deep—and they are far from the place and time that Covenant and Jeremiah sought. Instead they have been deflected from their destination by a man called the Theomach, who appears to have a mystical relationship with time. He is one of the Insequent, a race of humans who pursue arcane knowledge and power in complete isolation from each other: a race whose only shared trait, apparently, is a loathing for the *Elohim*. The Theomach interfered with Covenant and Jeremiah because he believed that their intentions were too dangerous—and because he wished to frustrate any interference by the *Elohim*.

The result, however, is that Linden, Covenant, and Jeremiah stand in the dead of winter many brutal leagues from *Melenkurion* Skyweir, where Covenant and Jeremiah hope to use the EarthBlood and the Power of Command to defeat Lord Foul permanently. They are too close to Garroting Deep; and they have no warm clothing or supplies. In desperation, Linden decides to approach Berek for help. Accompanied by the Theomach, Covenant, and Jeremiah, she wins the future High Lord's trust by healing many of his injured—and by introducing him to his own newborn health-sense.

Afterward the Theomach accomplishes his own purpose by persuading Berek to accept him as a guide and teacher. To show his good faith, he speaks the Seven Words. They are a mighty invocation of Earthpower which Linden has never heard before.

With supplies and horses provided by Berek Halfhand, Linden, Covenant, and Jeremiah begin the arduous trip along the Last Hills toward *Melenkurion* Skyweir. But when the exhausted mounts start to die, Covenant and Jeremiah transport Linden to the Skyweir through a series of spatial portals. On a plateau below the towering mountain, Jeremiah reveals the magic of his talent for constructs. With the right materials, he is able to devise "doors": doors from one place to another; doors that bypass time; doors between realities. Building a door shaped like a large wooden box, he conveys himself, Covenant, and Linden deep into *Melenkurion* Skyweir, to the hidden caves of the EarthBlood.

Covenant is now ready to exert the Power of Command. But Linden drinks first, remembering Esmer's counsel. She then uses her Command to expose the secrets of her companions.

At once, a glamour is dispelled. Covenant shows his true form: he is Roger Covenant, not Thomas, and he despises all that his father loves. His right hand wields immense power: it is Kastenessen's, grafted onto him to give him magicks which he does not naturally possess. And on Jeremiah's back rides one of the *croyel*, a succubus that both feeds from and strengthens its host. The sentience that Jeremiah has demonstrated is the *croyel*'s, not his own. Gloating, Roger explains that he and the *croyel* aspire to become gods when the Arch of Time falls. Bringing Linden into the past—and bringing her here—was an attempt to trick her into performing some action which would irretrievably violate the Land's history, thereby causing the Arch to crumble. So far, she has avoided that danger. But now she is trapped ten thousand years in the Land's past and cannot escape.

A terrible battle follows, during which the Staff of Law turns black. Using her Staff and the Seven Words to draw on the EarthBlood, Linden forces Roger and her possessed son to retreat. While an earthquake splits *Melenkurion* Skyweir, however, Roger and Jeremiah escape Linden and the past, leaving her stranded.

The experience transforms Linden. Assured of her own inadequacy, she now believes that only Thomas Covenant can accomplish what must be done. At the same time, her determination to save Jeremiah becomes even stronger—and more unscrupulous.

After an encounter with Caerroil Wildwood, the Forestal of Garroting Deep, who engraves her Staff with runes to make it more powerful, she is rescued from the past by the Mahdoubt. Here the Mahdoubt is revealed as one of the Insequent. When Linden is returned to Revelstone and her friends in her proper time, she learns that Liand has acquired a piece of *orcrest*, a stone capable of channeling Earthpower in various ways. She also hears that a stranger has single-handedly destroyed the entire horde of the Demondim.

Meeting this stranger, she finds that he is the Harrow, yet another Insequent. He covets both her Staff and Covenant's ring, and he has the power to take them by emptying her mind, depriving her of will. However, the Mahdoubt intervenes. Violating the fundamental ethics which govern the Insequent, she opposes the Harrow and defeats him, winning from him the promise that he will not wrest the Staff of Law and Covenant's ring from Linden by force: a victory which costs the Mahdoubt her own life. After assuring Linden that he will gain his desires by other means later, the Harrow disappears.

The next day, Linden, her friends, and the three Humbled summon Ranyhyn and ride away from Revelstone. Because she still has no idea where Jeremiah is hidden, or how to rescue him, her stated intention is to reach Andelain and consult with the Dead, as Covenant once did long ago. For reasons which she does not explain, she also hopes to recover High Lord Loric's *krill*, an eldritch dagger forged to wield quantities of power too great for any unaided mortal.

Along the way, she and her companions come upon a Woodhelven, a tree-village, which has been destroyed by a *caesure*: a *caesure* controlled by Esmer as a weapon against the Harrow. From them, she learns that the Harrow knows where Jeremiah has been hidden—and that Esmer intends to prevent the Insequent from revealing his secret. At the same time, Roger Covenant attacks with an army of Cavewights. Like Esmer, Roger desires the Harrow's death. In the ensuing battle, Linden's company is soon overwhelmed. Frantic, she takes a wild gamble: she tries to summon a Sandgorgon, a savage monster that once aided Covenant against the Clave. Six Sandgorgons charge into the fight, routing Roger and the Cavewights, and allowing the Harrow to escape with his life.

Later Linden hears that a large number of Sandgorgons have come to the Land, driven by the rent remnants of a Raver's malign spirit. In Covenant's name, they answered Linden's call. But now they have repaid their debt to him. They seek a new outlet for their own savage hungers, and for the Raver's malice.

When Linden and her companions have done what they can for the homeless tree-villagers, they ride on to Salva Gildenbourne, a great forest which encircles most of Andelain. There they encounter a party of Giants, Swordmainnir, all women except for one deranged man, Longwrath, who is their prisoner. When the Giants and Linden's company reach a place of comparative safety, they stop to rest and exchange tales.

The leader of the Giants, Rime Coldspray, the Ironhand, explains that Longwrath is a Swordmain who has been possessed by a *geas*: some external force drives him to kill an unnamed woman. With nine of her fellow Swordmainnir, the Ironhand has been following him across the seas, seeking the cause or purpose of his *geas*. After acquiring an apparently powerful sword, he has led the Giants to the Land. Here it becomes clear that the woman he feels coerced to kill is Linden herself.

To protect Linden, and for the sake of Linden's old friendship with the Giants of the Search, the Swordmainnir agree to accompany her to Andelain. But during the next day, they are assailed by the *skurj*, fiery worm-like monsters that serve Kastenessen. Two of the Giants are killed. Yet Liand saves the company by using his *orcrest* to summon a thunderstorm. The downpour forces the *skurj* underground, and the surviving companions are able to flee once more.

At last, they reach the safety of Andelain. The sacred Hills are warded by the Wraiths, small candle-flame sprites that repulse evil by drawing power from the awakened *krill*. Thus protected, the companions hasten to find the place where Covenant and Linden left the *krill* long ago.

During the dark of the moon, however, the company meets the Harrow again. Indirectly he has offered Linden a bargain: if she surrenders the Staff of Law and Covenant's ring, he will take her to Jeremiah. But while he taunts Linden, Infelice, the monarch of the *Elohim*, appears. She argues passionately against the Harrow—and against everything that Linden intends to do. Yet Linden ignores both Infelice and the Harrow as she approaches the *krill*.

There the Dead begin to arrive. While the four original High Lords observe, Caer-Caveral and High Lord Elena escort Thomas Covenant's spectre. Yet the Lords and the last Forestal and Covenant himself refuse to speak. None of them answer Linden.

Driven to the last extremity, Linden raises all of her power from both her Staff and Covenant's ring, and commits their contradictory magicks to the *krill*. With the *krill*, she cuts through the Laws of Life and Death until she succeeds at resurrecting Covenant; drawing his spirit out of the Arch of Time; restoring his slain body.

Yet power on such a scale has vast consequences. Resurrecting Covenant, Linden Avery also awakens the Worm of the World's End.

Part One

∞

"to achieve the ruin
of the Earth"

1.

The Burden of Too Much Time

Thomas Covenant knelt on the rich grass of Andelain as though he had fallen there from the distance of eons. He was full of the heavens and time. He had spent uncounted millennia among the essential strictures of creation, participating in every manifestation of the Arch: he had been as inhuman as the stars, and as alone. He had seen everything, known everything—and had labored to preserve it. From the first dawn of the Earth to the ripening of Earthpower in the Land—from the deepest roots of mountains to the farthest constellations—he had witnessed and understood and served. Across the ages, he had wielded his singular self in defense of Law and life.

But now he could not contain such illimitable vistas. Linden had made him mortal again. His mere flesh and bone refused to hold his power and knowledge, his span of comprehension. With every beat of his forgotten heart, intimations of eternity were expelled. They oozed from his new skin like sweat, and were lost.

Still he held more than he could endure. The burden of too much time was as profound as orogeny: it subjected his ordinary mind to pressures akin to those which caused earthquakes; tectonic shifts. His compelled transubstantiation left him frangible. As the structure of what he had known and understood and thought and desired failed, moment after unaccustomed moment, the sentience that had sustained him across uncounted ages became riddled with fault-lines and potential slippage.

In some fashion which was not yet awareness or true sensation, he recognized that he was surrounded by needs; by people and spectres who had gathered to witness Linden's choices. Dark against the benighted heavens, broad-boughed trees defined the hollow where he knelt among Andelain's hills. But their shadows paled in the fervid gleaming of Loric's *krill*, bright with wild magic—and in the ghostly luminescence of the four High Lords whose presence formed the boundaries of Covenant's crisis, and of Linden Avery's.

Towering and majestic, the Dead Lords stood timeless as sentinels at the points of the compass to observe, and perhaps to judge, the long consequences of their own lives. Berek and Damelon, Loric and Kevin: Covenant knew them—or had known them—as intimately as they knew themselves. He felt Berek's empathy, Damelon's concern, Loric's chagrin, Kevin's vehement repudiation. He comprehended their presence. They had been summoned by the same urgency which had brought him to this night, drawn and escorted by the Law-Breakers.

But when he regarded the spirits of the Lords—briefly, briefly, between one wrenching heartbeat and the next—he found that he was no longer one of them; one with them. Their thoughts had become as alien and immemorial as the speech of mountains.

Each throb of blood in his veins bereft him of himself.

Caer-Caveral and Elena he comprehended as well. They remained behind him on the slope of the hollow, Caer-Caveral wreathed in the austere self-sacrifice of his centuries as Andelain's Forestal, Elena heart-rent and grieving at the cost of the misplaced faith which had led her, unwilling, into the Despiser's service. The Law-Breakers might have had the stature of the High Lords—the grandeur and might of Berek and Damelon, the severe valor of Loric, the anguish of Kevin—but they had been diminished by their chosen deaths; their deliberate participation in the severances which had made possible Covenant's return to mortality. Now they had completed their purpose. They stood back, leaving Covenant to lose himself among his flaws.

Had he been able to do so, he might have acknowledged Infelice, not because he esteemed the self-absorbed surquedry of the *Elohim*, but because he understood the doom which Linden had wrought for them. Of the peoples of the Earth, the *Elohim* would be the first to suffer extermination. The havoc which would extinguish all of the world's glories would begin with them.

The Harrow he perceived in glimpses like the flickering of a far signal-fire. But he had already forgotten the warning that those glimpses should have conveyed. His human vision was blurred as if he were weeping, shedding tears of knowledge and power. Terrible futures hinged upon the Insequent, as they did upon Anele: Covenant saw that. Yet their import had dripped into the fissures of his dwindling mind, or had seeped away like blood.

The losses which Linden had forced him to bear surpassed his strength. They could not be endured. And still they grew, depriving him by increments of everything that death and purified wild magic and the Arch of Time had enabled. With every lived moment, fractures spread deeper into his soul.

The Worm of the World's End was coming. It was holocaust incarnate. He seemed to feel its hot breath on the nape of the Earth's neck.

The *Haruchai* he knew, and the Ranyhyn, and the Ramen, although their names had fled from him. Of the people who had once been the Bloodguard, and once his friends, he remembered only sorrow. In the name of their ancient pride and humiliation, they had made commitments with no possible outcome except bereavement. Now three of them had been maimed so that their right hands resembled his: the fourth had lost his left eye. Recognizing them, Covenant wanted to cry out against their intransigence. They should have obeyed the summons of their Dead ancestors.

But he did not. Instead he found solace in the company of the Ranyhyn and the Ramen—although he could not have explained in any mortal language why they comforted him. He knew only that they had never striven to reject the boundaries of themselves. And that the Ranyhyn had warned Linden as clearly as they could.

Like the Ramen, the horses appeared to study the *Haruchai* warily, as if the half-hand warriors posed a threat which Covenant could not recall.

The Stonedownor he identified more by the *orcrest* in his hand and the fate on his forehead than by his features or devotion. The young man had chosen his doom when he had first closed his fingers on the Sunstone. He could not alter his path now without ceasing to be who he was.

Everyone who had remained near Linden in this place, this transcendent violation, watched Covenant with shock or consternation or bitterness. However, he was not yet fully present among them. He was only conscious of them dimly, like figures standing at the fringes of a dream. His first frail instants of concrete awareness were focused on Linden.

The anguish on her face, loved and broken, held him. It kept him from losing his way among the cracks of his mind.

She stood defenseless a few paces in front of him. His ring and her Staff had fallen from her stricken fingers. In the silver glare of the *krill*, the traced stains on her jeans looked as black as accusations. The red flannel of her shirt was snagged and torn as though she had made her way to him through a wilderness of thorns. She seemed empty of resolve or hope, fundamentally beaten, as if he had betrayed her.

The sight of her, unconsoled and inconsolable, magnified the stresses which damaged him. But it also anchored him to his mortality. The fault of her plight was his. He had ignored too much of the Law which had bound and preserved him.

Moments or lifetimes ago, he had said, Oh, Linden. What have you done?—but not in horror. Rather she had filled him with awe. He had loved her across the entire span of the Arch of Time, and she had become capable of deciding the outcome of worlds.

Done, Timewarden? Infelice had answered. *She has roused the Worm of the World's End.* But he cared nothing for Infelice herself: only the fate of her people concerned him. —*every* Elohim *will be devoured.* Involuntarily he was remembering his own sins. They seemed more real than the people or beings around him.

Trust yourself, he had told Linden when he should not have spoken to her at all, not under any circumstance. He had said, *You need the Staff of Law*, and *Do something they don't expect*. He had even addressed her friends through Anele, although their names and exigencies were lost among the cracks of his sentience. And he had pleaded with her to find him—

Defying every necessity that sustained the Earth and the Land, he had pointed her toward the ineffable catastrophe of his resurrection.

Still he could not grasp what Linden's companions were doing. He had not known an illucid instant since his passing; but now people were in motion for reasons which bewildered him.

Shouting, "Desecrator!" one of the *Haruchai* rushed to strike her. A single blow of his fist would crush her skull. But another *Haruchai*, the man who had lost an eye, opposed her attacker; flung him away in a flurry of strikes and counters.

The two remaining *Haruchai* also charged at Linden. One stumbled under an onslaught of Ramen. Aided by the Stonedownor, the three Ramen kept that *Haruchai* from his target. And his kinsman was impeded by Ranyhyn. A roan stallion kicked the man in the chest; sent him sprawling backward.

"Yes!" Kevin Landwaster shouted. "*Slay* her! She merits death!"

But Berek Halfhand's great voice answered, "*Hold!* Restrain yourselves, *Haruchai*! Matters beyond your comprehension lie between the Timewarden and the Chosen. You have no part in them!"

"This night is sacred," added Damelon Giantfriend more quietly. "Your strife is unseemly. Beings mightier than you would not contend here."

Elena may have been weeping. Caer-Caveral stood apart from her, distancing himself from her distress.

Perhaps out of respect for the Lords, or perhaps for some reason of their own, the *Haruchai* ceased their struggles.

Covenant made no sense of it. He could more easily have explained why the Wraiths had not intervened. The *Haruchai* were simply too human and necessary to invoke the forces which defended Andelain. Still he said nothing. There was no room in his crippled apprehension for anything or anyone except Linden.

She was moving as well, as if she had been released by the quick violence of the *Haruchai*. Every line of her form was agony and protest as she strode toward him. Flagrant with pain, she seemed to rear over him as she raised her arm. When she struck him, he was too confused to duck his head or defend himself.

"God *damn* you!" she cried: a tortured wail. "Why didn't you *say* something? You could have *told* me—!"

Covenant gaped in wonder at the forgotten sensation of physical hurt as Linden fell to her knees in front of him. She covered her face with her hands; but she could not stop the sobs bursting from the bottom of her heart. Nearly shouting, she wept as if she were being torn out of herself by the roots.

He recognized her torment. But it was the rich sting of her blow that brought him into focus at last. For the first time since his death in agony, and his transfiguration, he tasted the crisp balm of Andelain's air, cooled and accentuated by the darkness that enclosed the Hills. It should have eased him, but it did not.

"Oh, Linden," he gasped softly. Fearing that she would repudiate his touch, he tried to put his arms around her nonetheless. His movements were awkward with disuse; weak; almost numb. Yet he clasped her to his chest. "I shouldn't have said any-thing at all. In your dreams. Through Anele. The risk was too great. But I was afraid you might lose hope. I couldn't—" He swallowed implications of ruin. "Couldn't just abandon you.

"You haven't done anything wrong. This is my fault. I was too weak."

He meant, I was too human. Even living in the Arch. I couldn't watch you suffer and let you think you were alone.

I would spare you the cost of what you've done if I knew how.

"Anything *wrong*?" snapped Infelice. "You rave, Timewarden. Your transformation is an immitigable evil. It has undone you. Do you not see that she has wrought the destruction of the Earth?"

Anger and Earthpower glittered around the *Elohim* as if she wore garments of disillusioned gems. Even in her wrath, she should have been lovely to behold. But everything that Thomas Covenant still possessed was concentrated on Linden: her sob-wracked body in his arms; her hair against the side of his face. Immersed in her distress, he ignored Infelice.

Loric Vilesilencer did not. "Be still, *Elohim*," he growled. "The fault of this—if it *is* fault—is yours as much as his or hers. You fear only for yourselves. You care nothing for the Earth. Yet there is much here that surpasses your self-regard."

"No!" protested Kevin urgently. "The *Elohim* speaks sooth. Have I suffered dam-nation and learned naught? She has performed a Desecration which exceeds com-prehension. The Humbled know it, if the Timewarden does not. The Chosen herself knows it."

"Enough, Loric-son," Berek said in a voice of commandment. "The fate of life belongs to those who know love and death. It is not our place to judge, or to condemn. And Time remains to us, as it does to the living. The making of worlds is not accom-plished in an instant. It cannot be instantly undone. Much must transpire before the deeds of the Chosen bear their last fruit."

Holding Linden's knotted grief and horror, Covenant tried to grapple with all that he had lost. He needed to retain as much as he could; but a numbness like lethargy hampered him. When Kevin spoke of damnation and Desecration, the bedrock plates of Covenant's mind shifted against each other. His concentration broke: he seemed to slip out of the present. He still held Linden; still saw that the *Haruchai* were barely able to contain their desire to deliver death; still felt the troubled emotions of the Dead High Lords. The Ramen and the Ranyhyn, the Stonedownor and one *Haruchai*, remained poised to defend Linden. At the same time, however, he found himself remembering—

The Stonedownor had come to stand behind Linden; place his hands softly on her shoulders. "Ah, Linden." His voice ached. "Do not weep so. I grasp little of what has occurred. But an august spirit has avowed that time remains to us. Can you not hear him? Surely the powers gathered here may accomplish much. And we have not yet attempted to redeem your son. In his name—"

The young man said more, but Covenant did not recognize it. He was remembering Kevin's confrontation with Lord Foul in Kiril Threndor, Heart of Thunder. Pieces of his mind witnessed the first moments of the Ritual of Desecration as if they were superimposed on Linden and Andelain.

There Kevin's despair was as vivid as the chiaroscuro glinting from Kiril Threndor's myriad-faceted stone: his self-loathing; his desire to punish himself. His ravaged love and failure exalted the carious illumination of Lord Foul's malice. If Covenant had been truly present in the chamber, he would have tried to stop Kevin. He would have had no choice: his own spirit would have been torn by the fangs of Lord Foul's eyes, clawed by the ragged nails of Kevin's desperation.

But he could not stay to watch the Ritual enacted. He had seen it before, and was unable to control the images which slid along the fault-lines within him. One thing led to another in the wrong direction. Instead of witnessing the culmination of Kevin's self-betrayal, he followed Lord Foul backward in time.

While Linden struggled to master herself in his embrace, and the Stonedownor attempted to soothe or rally her, Covenant visited the Despiser's brief decades masquerading among the Lords of the Council, accepted as a-Jeroth because none of the Lords could name their reasons for being reluctant to trust him. From there, Covenant's recollections involuntarily retreated to the many centuries when Lord Foul had inhabited the Lower Land, unknown to the Council, or to any of the peoples who preceded the Lords; unrecognized by anyone except the Forestals who preserved the truncated awareness of the One Forest. During that long age, the Despiser was hampered by the Colossus of the Fall, and by the fierce strength of the Forestals. Therefore he had hidden himself even from the Ravers, until the first waning of the Interdict freed them to do his bidding. Instead he bred other servants among the twisted denizens of Sarangrave Flat and the Great Swamp, and built Foul's Creche, and spawned his armies, and readied his powers—and quested unceasingly for the most useful of the banes buried deep under Mount Thunder.

But before that—

Covenant could not stop himself, even though Linden's wretchedness wrung his heart, and her companions waited as if they expected him to offer some salvific revelation.

Before that, the Despiser considered the Insequent, rejecting them because their theurgies were too dissociated to serve him. In regions of the Earth so distant that even the Giants had never visited them, he submerged himself among the Demimages of Vidik Amar, who wielded a contingent magic; but he found that when he had corrupted them to his purpose, they turned against each other, diminishing themselves in the name of Despite. Earlier, he nurtured his resentment within the eager energies of the Soulbiter, although they could not accomplish his purpose. Earlier still, he spent an age of failure with the cunning folk who would one day give birth to Kasreyn of the Gyre. And before that, he essayed an approach to the Worm of the World's End. But the Worm was not of his making. He could not rouse it directly: he could only disturb its slumber by damaging the One Tree. And the Guardian of the One Tree was proof against him.

Covenant remembered the sources of the Despiser's frustration, the roots of his accumulating, minatory fury. He recognized the Despiser's own secret despair, concealed even from himself, and enacted on the beings around him instead.

Roughly Linden pushed herself back from Covenant. He could not stop her, or try to understand her: he only saw and felt her through the veils of Lord Foul's past. Her face was a smear of tears, and her chest shook with the effort of stifling her sobs. Her torment was as acute as Kevin's, and as punitive. But her straits were more cruel than his. She had committed her Desecration—and she had survived it.

Clenching herself against spasms of renewed weeping, she fought to speak.

"All you had to do. *All* you had to do. Was tell me. How to find Jeremiah." For a moment, she knotted her fists, beat them against her face. "Then I wouldn't—"

Her features twisted as if she were about to howl.

The *Haruchai* with one eye had moved to stand beside her. "He could not, Chosen," he said flatly. "His silence was required. I endeavored to forewarn you. But you were unable to heed me. You do not forgive, and cannot harken to other counsel."

Like Covenant, Linden did not appear to hear him.

But Covenant remembered.

Spectres which may not be denied—

—will come to affirm the necessity of freedom.

Nevertheless the *Haruchai*'s words were too recent: they could not break the grip of Lord Foul's striving across hundreds or thousands of centuries.

Still Linden needed Covenant: some part of him felt that. She needed something from him that he could not give while he remained trapped among the fragments of the past. In spite of his own pain and bewilderment, he could not willingly ignore her.

Nor could he contain the pressure of remembrance which severed him from himself.

"Hit me," he panted thinly. His voice was so frayed and raw that he hardly heard it. "Hit me again."

A fire that might have been shock or shame or rage burned away Linden's tears; but she did not hesitate. Flinging her whole hurt into the blow, she struck his cheek as hard as she could.

Physical pain. The shock and sting of abused skin. The harsh jerk of his neck as his head snapped back. Air which should have healed him in his lungs.

He saw her clearly again, as if she had slapped away his confusion.

"I'm sorry," he said: the best answer he had. "I'm too full of time. I can't hold on to it. But pieces—"

Her open anguish stopped him. He was not saying what she needed to hear. The Stonedownor—Liand, his name was Liand—tried to comfort her, but his words and his gentle hands did not touch her distress. The *Haruchai* was called Stave. His single eye considered Covenant with ungiving severity.

Linden had been brought to this place—to the Dead, and to Loric's *krill*, and to the devastation of the world—by forces as great in their own way as the pressures which fractured Covenant.

"I couldn't tell you then," he said; groaned. "I couldn't say anything. None of us could." He meant the Dead around him. "The necessity of freedom—It's absolute. You have to make your own choices. Everything hinges on that. If I told you where to find your son—or warned you what might happen if you used the *krill* the way you did—I would have changed your decisions. I would have changed the nature of what you had to choose."

The nature of the risks that she had to take.

"That's what Lord Foul does. He changes your choices. He wasn't trying to stop you when you were attacked on your way here. His allies fought you because he wanted to make you more determined. So you would think you were doing the right thing."

"His servants have their own desires," Infelice told Linden. Her tone was acid, gemmed in gall. "Some among them do not believe that they serve him. In folly, they imagine that their aspirations exceed his, or that they act in their own names. But they cannot conceive the height and breadth of his intent. Like yours, all of their deeds conduce to his ends.

"Did we not caution you to beware the halfhand? Did we not speak to the peoples of the Land, seeking to ensure that you were forewarned?"

"Enough, *Elohim*," Berek's shade demanded. "Your plight is not forgotten. Permit the Timewarden to speak while he remains able to do so."

Covenant ignored Infelice; ignored Berek. "I couldn't treat you that way," he went on, imploring Linden to understand him. "No matter what happened. I couldn't tamper with anything you decided to do. I've already taken too many chances. If you need to blame someone, blame me.

"But if the Earth has any hope—any hope at all—it depends on you. It has ever since Joan brought you here. And it still does. Freedom isn't just a condition for using wild magic. It's a condition for *life*. Without it, everything eventually turns into Despite."

Abruptly Linden pushed herself to her feet; distanced herself from him. He saw a fresh storm of tears gather in her, but she closed herself against it. "*No*." Her protest was a rough scrape of sound, bloody and betrayed. "That isn't right. It doesn't work that way. *You're* the one who saves the world. I just want to save my son."

He ached for her through the clamor of his own dismay: the heavy labor of his pulse, needless for millennia; the gasp of air in his lungs; the burning of his face where she had struck him; the excruciation of Time as it bled away. She had every reason to feel betrayed. She had believed that he loved her—

He did love her. He had loved her during every instant that the Arch had ever contained. If he had not loved her, he would never have found the strength to sacrifice himself against the Despiser. But for that very reason, he shied away from the sight of her outrage and grief. Slipping again, he fell like debris into fissured memories where his mind and his volition could be ground to powder.

For reasons that eluded him, he found himself regarding the ornately clad figure of the Harrow.

The Insequent still sat his destrier as though he had no part to play in what transpired around him. But the deep voids of his eyes were fixed hungrily on the ring and the Staff that Linden had dropped as if in abandonment.

The Harrow had known the Vizard. Of course he had. And the Vizard had possessed knowledge which the Harrow lacked. Inspired by some leap of imagination, or by his own assiduous study, the Vizard had grasped the almost mystical significance, the potential use, of Jeremiah's talent for constructs. And he had craved that resource for himself. He had seen in it the possibility that he might one day hold sway over the entire race of the *Elohim*. By that means, he would show himself greater than any of his people.

But he had made a damning mistake: he had tried to eliminate the implied threat of the Harrow. By their very nature, the Harrow's intentions would obliquely thwart the Vizard's. If the Harrow attained his goal, Jeremiah would be freed from Lord Foul's possession—and then Jeremiah would surely pass beyond the Vizard's reach.

Therefore the Vizard had violated the most vital of the restrictions which the Insequent imposed upon themselves. Goaded by the scale of his own ambitions, he had opposed the Harrow's private designs. Thus the Vizard was lost to mind and name and life. The combined will of every Insequent had imposed his destruction. From Covenant's former place among the uncounted instants of the Arch, he had watched the Vizard fail and die.

It was the same fate that the Mahdoubt had suffered—

On some other level of his attention, Covenant understood that the Harrow would not attempt to snatch up the ring and the Staff: not while Infelice stood ready to resist him, and the Wraiths would come to preclude their conflict. But such concerns would not hinder the Harrow much longer.

Abruptly Stave stepped forward and slapped Covenant in Linden's stead. The *Haruchai* measured his blow precisely: it was not as hard as Linden's, although he could have snapped Covenant's neck with ease. But it was enough.

Renewed pain restored Covenant to the present.

At once, two of the other *Haruchai* sprang at Stave. They dragged him away roughly, ignoring the fact that he did not resist them. When the Ramen rushed to his aid—even the Manethrall whose lost eyes were bandaged—Stave stopped them with a word.

Facing the aggravated injury of Linden's gaze, Covenant tried again to answer her.

"I know. You've already changed the fate of the Earth, but you still don't believe you can do things like that. You just want to find your son.

"I can't tell you. I have no idea where he is. I used to know. But it's gone. It's just gone." He had already been reduced to a husk of his former self. With every breath, every heartbeat, the sum of his memories shrank. He imagined that he had once labored to protect Jeremiah's spirit from Lord Foul's taint. Yet he could no longer recall his efforts. "Everything I remember is broken. And I'm losing more all the time. There isn't enough of me to hold it."

He retained only the fragments that lay hidden among the cracks in his awareness. When he slipped into them, his mind lost its connection to his new flesh.

"Linden?" Liand asked softly, pleading with her. "What can be done? What remains to us? We cannot continue to strike him. If he is indeed unable to recollect—"

"No." Linden shook her head urgently; frantically. "No." She took a step backward. The avid brilliance of the *krill* limned her form, left her features in darkness. "This is wrong. It can't be this way.

"What did you want me to do? When you urged me to find you? What did you think I could accomplish?"

—hold it, Covenant thought. Hold them all. For a moment, the sight of Giantships tugged at him, pulling him down. He saw the wooden vessels of the Unhomed sunk by *turiya* Kinslaughterer while the Giants waited for death in their homes. The suction as the ships foundered tried to drag Covenant with them. None of them were left at sea: they had returned to The Grieve to be fitted with Gildenlode keels and rudders so that they might be able to find their way Home; end their long bereavement—

But Covenant struggled to remain present for Linden's sake.

Fumbling, unsure of his movements, he forced himself to stand and face her. "It isn't up to me." He was hardly able to feel his hands and feet. "I just didn't want—" His fingers twitched involuntarily, as if he were reaching for something. But he was unaware of them. They were as useless as the knowledge which had bled out of him. "That old man. The beggar. The Creator. He abandoned you before you ever came here. I didn't want you to think I'd abandoned you too."

"The Timewarden is diminished," Infelice told Linden. Her voice sounded raw, almost flayed. "Before he became less than he was, he conceived that you might discover some less fatal means to span the gulf between the living and the Dead. He dreamed that you might earn or coerce his vast awareness from him without dooming this Creation."

You would not be driven by mistaken love to bring about the end of all things!

Infelice may have been right. Or not. Covenant had lost those memories as well.

A short distance beyond the *krill*, two of the *Haruchai*—the Humbled—had released Stave. Covenant almost knew their names. Striding ahead of Stave, they joined their hand-maimed comrade among the Ramen and the Ranyhyn. But it was Stave who announced, "Then the burden falls to you, *Elohim*. Your knowledge is also vast. Where is the Chosen's son? How may Corruption and his servants be opposed? How may the Worm be returned to slumber?"

Adrift in his dismembered mind, Covenant finally identified Mahrtiir: the Manethrall. The man had been terribly wounded in the battle of First Woodhelven. And the girl and the man with him were— They were— Covenant clung to Linden's face with his grieving gaze. The Ramen with the Manethrall were his Cords. Pahni and Bhapa.

"Have I not spoken of this?" retorted Infelice. "Like the Wildwielder herself, her son—and the Timewarden's also, as well as his mate—are a shadow upon our hearts. Her son has been hidden from us. And the Worm cannot be returned to slumber. By the measure of mountains, it is a small thing, no more than a range of hills. An earthquake might swallow it. Yet its power surpasses comprehension. No upheaval or convulsion will hinder it. Against any obstruction, it will feed and grow mighty until it consumes the essence of the Earth. Then all life and Time will cease. Naught remains for us except extinction."

"All the more reason for vengeance," growled Kevin's shade. "Her crimes must be answered, as mine have been. The Humbled serve the Land falsely if they continue to permit her life."

Elena moaned as though she shared the Landwaster's ire—and loathed herself for doing so. Caer-Caveral regarded her with a bitter scowl, but said nothing.

"Have done, son of Loric," High Lord Berek ordered. "I will not caution you again. Your crimes have not yet been truly answered. Your fathers will speak of you ere this night is done. Until you have heard what is in our hearts, you will withhold your denunciations of the Chosen."

The Humbled appeared to heed Kevin rather than Berek. They bowed to the last of the Lord-Fatherer's line as if to acknowledge his despair; to honor his counsel. But they did not strike at Linden again. Instead they arrayed themselves between Covenant and the bedizened form of Infelice.

One of them said, "We require certainty, *Elohim*." Galt, that was his name. Beneath its inflectionless surface, his voice thrummed with intensity. "Do you avow that it is indeed Thomas Covenant, ur-Lord and Unbeliever, white gold wielder, who now stands before us, returned from death to flesh and life?"

Covenant's eyes felt as untrustworthy as his hands. Cold or numbness blurred his sight in spite of Andelain's clarity. Nevertheless he saw that the emotions and pressures of the beings around Linden did not console her. They could not. She hardly seemed to hear Kevin's acid recrimination, or Infelice's. Berek's oblique defense did not touch her.

"Self-doubt?" asked the Harrow, mocking the *Haruchai*. "You also have become less than you were. The truth must surely be plain to all who have witnessed the lady's theurgy. Naught but the Timewarden's absolute resurrection could so pierce the self-absorption of the *Elohim*."

The Humbled ignored the Insequent. As one, Galt and Branl and—Covenant clutched at the name—and Clyme turned to face the result of Linden's terrifying gamble.

Galt seemed to speak for every *Haruchai* except Stave as he said, "Then command us, Unbeliever, Timewarden. Reveal what must be done. We know the treachery of your false son, and the madness of the Chosen. We will serve you with our last strength."

Covenant tried to focus on Galt. But the *krill* plucked at his attention, luring him with images which had once been as familiar as Time. In shards and slivers, flaws, he caught glimpses of Loric's prolonged, arduous search for a stone which could be shaped into the gem that formed the nexus of the dagger: a search which had taken him deep under *Melenkurion* Skyweir, following the Black River inward from Garroting Deep until he found a fragment of crystal made perfect by eons of contact with the Blood of the Earth. Like peering through cracked glass, Covenant saw Loric forge the metal of the *krill*, striving to emulate white gold. He lacked the raw materials to fashion white gold itself. But from his inherited and acquired lore, he had gleaned a comprehension of alloys: he worked with ores that could be transmuted and commingled until they became strong enough to sustain the pristine possibilities of the gem. If Covenant allowed himself to drift, he would be able to watch as though he stood at Loric's side while the dour High Lord sweated over his incantations and fires—

But Linden needed something from Covenant, something that his lost memories could not supply. And he had already failed her too often. If he slipped away now, he might break the promise implied by speaking to her when he should have remained silent. *Trust yourself. Do something they don't expect.* Broken as he was, he could still see that she hung on the brink, the outermost edge, of Kevin's despair. Her sense of abandonment, of betrayal, might topple her. Any nudge—Infelice's flagrant terror and scorn, the Harrow's machinations, Kevin's condemnation, the repudiation of the Humbled—might send her plunging into an abyss from which she could not be retrieved.

Desperately Covenant clung to the present. Wavering on his feet, he struggled to meet the demand of the Humbled. He could not distinguish it from Linden's need.

"What will you do?" he countered. "If I don't command you? If I refuse to respect what you've done to yourselves?"

Fingers had been severed from their right hands in his name; but he did not want that honor.

Branl's eyes widened. Clyme almost appeared to wince. But Galt did not hesitate.

"Then I will ride to Revelstone," he announced inflexibly, "that I may warn the Masters of the Chosen's Desecration. Clyme and Branl will remain with her to prevent further evil. Your ring will be returned to you. If you do not claim the Staff of Law, it will be conveyed to Revelstone, where it may be preserved for the Land's last defense."

Liand opened his mouth to protest. Mahrtiir's glower promised defiance. The Ranyhyn tossed their heads restively. But Linden did not appear to hear the Humbled. She stared at Covenant as though he filled her with horror that had no end.

"Then listen," Covenant told Galt with as much force as he could find in his riven spirit. "And pay attention. I can only say this once.

"The Wraiths allowed her. They preserve Andelain, and they *allowed* her. Hellfire, doesn't that *mean* anything to you?"

Shedding memories like pieces of his soul, he met Linden's appalled stare.

"Linden." Nearly undone by weakness and rue—by the numbness in his fingers and the frailty of his mind—he strained to make himself heard. "I've said it before. I know this is hard. I know you think you've come to the end of what you can do. But you aren't done. And I trust you. Do you hear me? I *believe* in you. I'll do everything I can to help. If there's anything left—"

Linden flinched as though he had promised her the opposite of his intent. On her face, new hurts twisted against older shocks and chagrin. "Can you see it?" she asked Liand or Mahrtiir or Stave. Her voice throbbed like internal bleeding, as if she spoke with her heart's blood. "He's right. He can't hold on. Something inside him is collapsing. I brought him back, but I didn't do it right. He isn't whole.

"And he has leprosy."

To that, Covenant had no answer.

Already falling, he turned back to the Humbled.

"As for you. I command—" His voice frayed and failed: he could not command anyone. But because he loved Linden, he managed to find a few more words. They felt like the last words in the world. "She's more important than I am. If you have to choose, choose her. She's the only one who can do this."

He wanted to say more, but his wounds were too much for his mortal flesh. Within him, one age of the Earth bled into another, and he toppled to the grass as if he had been felled.

2 .

Unfinished Needs

Linden Avery stood, staring and paralyzed, as if she had finally learned the true meaning of horror. Nothing in her life had prepared her for the outcome of her granite desperation. Long ago, she had been forced to watch her father's suicide: in fear and pity, she had imposed her mother's death: she had seen Thomas Covenant stabbed to death in his former world—and later slain again by the Despiser. A Raver had taught her to dread her own capacity for evil. Under *Melenkurion* Skyweir, she had been forced to do battle against her chosen son. But such things had become trivial. They were too small and human to inure her now.

Her mind was empty of words. She could not respond to Liand's stricken empathy, or to the consternation and support of the Ramen, or to Stave's rigid loyalty. The antagonism of the Humbled meant nothing to her. Neither Infelice nor the Harrow held any import. But she was not stunned or numb. She was *not*. She had not expended her remorse with weeping, or her rage with blows, or her revulsion— Nor had she been silenced by Covenant's faltering attempts to explain himself, or by his inadequate affirmation. Instead she was crowded to bursting with dismay.

Dismay: not despair. Despair was darkness, the nailed lid of a coffin. Her dismay was a moral convulsion, the shock of seeing her whole reality distorted beyond recognition. She had left any ordinary loss of hope or faith behind as soon as she had realized that Covenant was not whole. Now she felt an appalled chagrin like the onset of concussion, simultaneously paralyzing and urgent. The cost of what she had done dwarfed thought. The only sentences remaining to her had been spoken by others; and they were tocsins.

She has roused the Worm of the World's End.

She loved the Land. She loved Thomas Covenant and Jeremiah. The Ramen and the Ranyhyn and the Giants. Liand and Stave and poor Anele. Yet she had doomed them all. Resurrecting Covenant, she had given Lord Foul his heart's desire.

Within her she holds the devastation of the Earth—

Through Anele, Sunder and Hollian had tried to warn her. *He did not know of your intent.* The Ranyhyn had tried: perhaps everyone had tried. *There is strength in ire, Chosen. But it may also become a snare.* Days ago, she had dreamed that she had become carrion: food for abhorrent things feasting on death. Confident and cruel, the Despiser himself had given her a vision of his intentions.

Nevertheless she had defied every caution. In fury at what had been done to her son, she had violated one of the essential Laws which made life possible, allowed the Earth to exist: the Laws which she should have served. In one flagrant act, she had broken every promise that she had ever made.

Good cannot be accomplished by evil means.

This was the result. Covenant sprawled facedown on the betrayed grass of Andelain. The old scar on his forehead, like the wound in his T-shirt, was hidden; but the strict silver of his hair was accusation enough. Long ago, Lord Foul's efforts to kill him had burned him clean of venom and dross. The transformation of his hair was only one outcome of that savage *caamora*. Now the stark light of the *krill* appeared to concentrate there—and on his halfhand, emphasizing his lost fingers. They seemed to reach toward her in spite of his collapse, as if he were still pleading with her even though she had set in motion the world's ruin.

He was only unconscious: the violence of what she had done to him had not burst his heart. She could be sure of that. Wielding catastrophic quantities of power, she had whetted her senses to an unbearable edge. Her nerves wailed with too much percipience. She saw clearly that Covenant had been felled by shock and strain, not by injury. Physically her extravagance had not harmed him.

But his mind— Oh, God, his *mind*. Webbed with cracks, it resembled a clay goblet in the instant before the vessel shattered. The imminent fragments of who he was remained individually intact. In some sense, they clung to each other. If time stopped here—if this instant did not move on to the next—the goblet might yet hold water. A cunning potter might have been able to make the clay whole again.

But Linden did not know how to stop time. She only knew how to destroy it.

Berek's spectre had said, *The making of worlds is not accomplished in an instant. It cannot be instantly undone.* Nevertheless Linden Avery, Chosen, Ringthane, and Wild-wielder, had made the end of all things inevitable.

In addition, Covenant was rife with renewed leprosy. His illness had deadened most of the nerves in his fingers and toes. There were insensate patches on the backs and palms of his hands, the soles of his feet. But that, at least, was not her doing. Rather it was an oblique effect of Kevin's Dirt. The bitter truncation which hampered health-sense and Law, blunted every expression of Earthpower, had diminished Covenant more profoundly. He had become an outcast of Time; a pariah to his own nature, and to his long service against Despite: an icon of the Land's immedicable peril.

In the life that she had lost, she could have treated his bodily illness, if not his riven mind. Her former world had discovered drugs to end the ravages of this disease. Here she felt helpless. She feared what might happen if she used Earthpower and Law to attempt healing either his illness or his consciousness without his consent.

She, too, had become an icon: an embodiment of loss and shame and unheeded warnings. She had made of her life a wasteland in which she did not know how to live.

And I trust you. I'll do everything I can to help.

In her dismay, Covenant's reassurances sounded like mockery.

At that moment, there was no part of her still capable of attending to the distress of her friends. Liand and Stave; Mahrtiir, Pahni, and Bhapa; the Ranyhyn: she had nothing left for them. If the Humbled or the Law-Breakers, Infelice or the Harrow, had spoken to her, she would not have been able to hear them.

Nevertheless there were powers abroad in the night that could reach her. When the great voice of Berek Halfhand announced, "The time has come to speak of the Ritual of Desecration," she staggered as though she had been struck.

She believed that he meant to excoriate her.

While she flinched, however, Loric Vilesilencer turned to the first High Lord. Grim and gaunt, the spectre of the *krill's* maker countered, "Is it not my place to do so?"

"It is," Berek acknowledged. Lambent with his own ghostly silver, he appeared to gain definition from the unresolved illumination of the *krill*. The gem's light still held a throb of eagerness and wild magic; but it did not pale his earned majesty. Instead it seemed to enhance his strength. "Yet you well know that there are words which cannot be heard by a son who deems that he has failed his father. The love which lies between them precludes heed."

Liand stared with open wonder. Stave watched warily. The Ramen held themselves ready, taut with innominate expectations. Gradually Linden understood that the attention of the Dead was not directed toward her. Though they spoke to each other, their emanations were concentrated, not on her, but on Kevin Landwaster, who stood appalled and ghastly in the east as if he had witnessed the fruition of his worst fears— and now expected to be punished for Linden's crimes as well as his own.

That recognition plucked at her; intruded on her dismay. Like her, Kevin had accomplished only evil by evil means. His anguish touched her when she had lost her ability to respond to anything else.

"Indeed, it is so," Damelon added. Like Berek, he addressed Loric. The tranquility of his earlier smile had become sadness and affection. "Though you are the son of my heart, and entirely beloved, do you not believe that I question your deeds and courage, as you do? Do you not suffer gall, judging that you have not matched the standard which I have set for you? And if I avow that you merit my pride in each and all of your endeavors, will you hear me? Will you not believe that my words are inspired by love rather than by worth?"

With an air of reluctance, High Lord Loric nodded.

"Thus it falls to me to speak," proclaimed Berek.

His steps did not mark the rich grass as he came slowly forward. "Kevin son of Loric, hear and give heed," he demanded in a tone that was both stern and gentle. "We share no bond apart from the heritage of lore and High Lordship. The inheritance of blood is too distant to constrain me. Thus I am able to state freely that your sires are grieved by the harm which you have wrought, but they are not shamed."

As he moved, he appeared to approach Linden and the *krill* and Covenant's fallen form. If he had so much as glanced at her, she would have flinched again. But his gaze was fixed solely on the Landwaster: his strides would take him past her to Loric's son.

At the same time, Damelon and Loric also moved, walking carefully toward Kevin as though they wished him to comprehend that he was not threatened.

Kevin stared wildly. A kind of terror poured from him, contradicting the benison of Andelain. He may have imagined that the words and attitudes of his ancestors were false; intended to exacerbate his torment. Or he may have feared that they would trivialize his sufferings, implying that his despair was devoid of significance to anyone but himself.

In his place, Linden would have felt those dreads.

Nevertheless Loric's son did not withdraw. Perhaps he could not: perhaps the same commandment which had brought him here precluded any word or deed that might have eased his pain.

In spite of her own plight, or because of it, Linden mourned for him.

At once stentorian and kindly, Berek continued, "Only the great of heart may despair greatly." His voice seemed to echo back from the lost stars. "You are loved and treasured, not for the outcome of your extremity, but rather for the open passion by which you were swayed to Desecration. That same quality warranted the Vow of the *Haruchai*. It was not false."

In moments, the first High Lord had passed Linden as he and his descendants gathered before Kevin. "Doubtless such passion may cause immeasurable pain. But it has not released the Despiser. It cannot. Mistaken though it may be, no act of love and horror—or indeed of self-repudiation—is potent to grant the Despiser his desires." Together, Berek, Damelon, and Loric drew near enough to touch the Land-waster. "He may be freed only by one who is compelled by rage, and contemptuous of consequence."

Fervid with apprehension, Kevin faced his progenitors. The *krill* glared argent in his eyes.

"High Lord Kevin son of Loric," concluded Berek. "Others may have fallen—or risen—to that extreme. You have not. You did not. None here can assert with certainty that they would not have done as you did in your place."

"That is sooth, my son," Loric murmured roughly, "a word of truth in this fate-ridden time. If I did not speak often or plainly enough of my own encounters with despair, or of the occasions on which I trembled at the very threshold of Desecration, then was I a poor father indeed, and your reproaches must be for me rather than for yourself."

When he heard his father, something within Kevin broke. Linden saw the chains which had bound his spirit snap as he opened himself to Loric's embrace.

At once, Loric threw his arms fiercely around his son. Kevin's eyes bled reflected silver like astonishment as Damelon and then Berek enclosed father and son with their acceptance. Hugged and held by his forebears, Kevin wept as relief found its way at last into his wracked soul.

And as he wept, he appeared to be transformed by the theurgy of the *krill*; or by Andelain. Briefly he became a glode amid the surrounding night, lucent and exalted. Then he faded until he was only an outline of wisps that evaporated into nothingness.

At the same time, Loric and Damelon also faded, accompanying the last of their line toward his rest. Soon only Berek remained.

His own knowledge of despair and striving shone from him as he turned toward Linden.

However, the moment when she might have winced or hidden her head had passed. Nor did she meet the first Halfhand's gaze. There was another spectre in the hollow as full of anguish as Kevin had been, and as sorely bereft. Berek should have directed the balm of his compassion elsewhere. Linden had no use for it.

But she was wrong about him: he did not mean to comfort her. His tone sharpened as he began to speak. His words seemed to fall on her like stones.

"Linden Avery, you are scantly known to me. Nonetheless I behold what you have become. You have exceeded the healer who once touched my heart, offering hope amid vast suffering and rue. Now you have made of yourself a Gallows Howe, its soil barren, drenched with fury and recrimination. Therefore you must exceed yourself yet again, while the world awaits its doom. If you do not, the woe of all who live will be both cruel and brief.

"Are you dismayed by the hurt of your deeds? Then make amends. Do not imagine that you have come to the end of service and healing. The woman who entered my camp to meet death and give battle would not have permitted herself that Desecration."

Linden heard him, but she did not listen. Gallows Howe held truths unknown to Berek and his descendants. Ire was only one aspect of what she had learned in Caerroil Wildwood's demesne—and in her ordeal under *Melenkurion* Skyweir. By their stature and potency, the ancient Lords had drawn her beyond herself. Now she felt called to the Law-Breakers.

To Elena, daughter of Lena and Covenant, who had pierced the Law of Death because she had trusted Kevin's pain—and who, like Linden, had failed to heed the warning of the Ranyhyn.

Linden herself had become a Law-Breaker. And she could not lay claim to the redemptive mystery which had impelled Caer-Caveral to breach the Law of Life so that Covenant's spirit would remain to ward the Arch of Time when his body had been slain—and so that Hollian and her unborn son could live again. The Dead Forestal of Andelain would not understand Linden.

Only Elena could comprehend her now that Linden also had ignored the Ranyhyn, and all of her choices had become calamities.

Moving around Covenant's sprawled helplessness and the *krill*'s compulsory light—leaving her Staff and Covenant's ring unregarded on the grass—Linden crossed the hollow to approach the last Forestal and the stricken High Lord.

On some level, she felt Berek's shade watching her. She sensed his efforts to gauge the condition of her soul—or the direction of her thoughts. But she had no attention to spare for him; and after a moment, he seemed to sigh. Unreassured, he faded as well, following his descendants as if she had dismissed him.

In the absence of those towering spirits—and of the Wraiths, fled from Linden's great wrong—her companions began to emerge from their entrancement and shock. Liand and the Ramen became restive, fretted by alarms. The Humbled and even Stave gazed after Linden as though they disapproved of her refusal to acknowledge or answer Berek Halfhand. The Harrow watched Linden avidly while Infelice shed distress like damaged jewels.

But Linden ignored them as well. A score of paces, or perhaps more, brought her face-to-face with the Law-Breakers, who had escorted Covenant out of Time to meet her uttermost need.

Elena seemed unable to meet her gaze. Regret and grief twisted the High Lord's features as she studied the grass at Linden's feet, the stains on Linden's jeans. Lit by the *krill*, torn hair framed Elena's galled face, her naked self-abhorrence.

At any other time, Linden might have been moved by empathy to remain silent. Elena was Covenant's daughter. In simple kindness, if for no other reason, Linden might have tried to show the spectre as much consideration as she had given Joan.

But Roger also was Covenant's child. Linden had no patience for Elena. She could not afford to treat Elena's failings more gently than her own. Linden had committed an absolute crime. Only absolute responses would suffice.

Berek was right about her: she had become a kind of Gallows Howe. The sorrow that she had felt for Kevin Landwaster was like Caerroil Wildwood's grief for his trees— and for his future. It remained with her; but its implied vulnerability had already bled away into soil made barren by death. Like the former Forestal of Garroting Deep, she was aghast at the scale of her own inadequacy. But she had none of his fury, and no one to blame. She was too full of dismay to consider Elena's frailty.

Perhaps Elena understood the gift which Berek, Damelon, and Loric had given Kevin. Her spirit as she avoided Linden's gaze seemed to yearn for some forgiving touch. In her, hope was commingled with a raw fear that she would be refused.

But Linden had gone too far beyond hope and despair to comfort Elena. Covenant's daughter needed *his* consolation, not Linden's.

In a low voice, taut and bitter, she demanded, "Stop feeling sorry for yourself." She was speaking to herself as much as to Elena's woe. "It doesn't accomplish anything. You've suffered enough. Tell me what to do now."

Tell me how to bear what I've done.

She needed an answer. But apparently she—like Elena herself—had misjudged the Dead. In a different form, Elena may once have aided Covenant: she had no aid to offer now. Instead an echo of Linden's dismay twisted her features. Raising her face to the doomed stars, she uttered a wail of desolation: the stark cry of a woman whose wracked heart had been denied.

Then she flared briefly in the *krill*'s light and vanished, following the distant ancestors of her High Lordship out of the vale; out of the night.

From the bottom of the hollow, Linden's friends gazed at her as if she had smitten their hearts. Infelice's distress matched the outrage of the Humbled.

"Elena!" Linden cried urgently. "Come back! I need you!" But her appeal died, forlorn, among the benighted trees, and found no reply.

Instead Caer-Caveral faced her with severity and indignation in every line of his spectral form.

"You judge harshly, Wildwielder. The Landwaster himself has been granted solace. Does your heart hold no compassion for Elena daughter of Lena, whose daring and folly compelled her to spend herself in service to the Despiser?"

"Damnit," Linden retorted without flinching, "that's not the point. Compassion isn't going to save any of us." There was nothing left to save except Jeremiah. "*Somebody* has to tell me what to do."

The Dead Forestal folded his arms across his chest, holding his scepter in the crook of his elbow; forbidding her. "Cease your protests." He had set aside every impulse or emotion that might have resembled mercy. "They are bootless. We have no counsel for you."

Linden beat her fists on her temples. She would have clutched at Caer-Caveral if he had been anything more than an eidolon. "Then tell me why you won't help me. When Covenant was here before, you gave him everything," advice and Vain as well as the location of the One Tree. The Forestal and Covenant's Dead had prepared every step of his path to death and triumph. "Why didn't you care about 'the necessity of freedom' *then*? He's Thomas Covenant. He would have found a way without you. I'm just lost.

"Why have you forsaken me?"

Caer-Caveral glowered at her, shedding reminders of his slain song. "Much has been altered since the Unbeliever last walked among the living. You are indeed forsaken, by the Dead as by the Earth's Creator. How could it be otherwise, when all of your deeds conduce to ruin?"

Then he said, "In pity, however," although his tone held no pity, "I will observe that the Unbeliever entered Andelain alone, for no companion dared to stand at his side. He had neither health-sense nor the Staff of Law. The Ranyhyn had not cautioned him. He knew only love and compassion. Thus his need was greater than yours. For that reason, he was given gifts.

"Yet the Dead shaped none of his choices. He did not come seeking guidance. Nor did he request aid. In sooth, he did not tread any path which he did not determine for himself—or which you did not determine on his behalf.

"You have companions, Chosen, who have not faltered in your service. If you must have counsel, require it of them. They have no knowledge which you do not share, but their hearts are not consumed by darkness."

Abruptly Caer-Caveral unclasped his arms; gripped his scepter in one fist. Whirling the gnarled wood about him as though he were invoking music, a melody which had been silent for millennia, he removed himself from the night, leaving Linden alone on the slope of the vale.

Beyond her, Andelain's trees looked chthonic in the light of the *krill*. Behind her stood the charred stump of the Forestal's former life, the *krill* itself, Thomas Covenant's sprawled unconsciousness. The conflicting concerns and passions of her companions tugged at her nerves like accusations or pleading. And among them on the grass lay the Staff of Law and Covenant's wild gold ring as if those instruments of power formed the pivot on which the fate of worlds turned.

For a moment, Linden yearned to simply walk away. She had done something like that once before in Andelain, when her fears for or of Covenant had raised a wall between them. She could stride into the darkness and try to lose herself among the kindly folds of the Hills. There copses and greenswards and beauty might appease her guilt with their lenitive beneficence; soothe her savaged heart. She could walk and walk until there was nothing left of her, and the burden of the Land's unanswerable needs fell to someone else.

But to do so would be to forsake Jeremiah, as she herself had been forsaken. And her friends deserved more from her. After what she had done to him, Covenant deserved more.

Days ago, Manethrall Mahrtiir had told her, *Therein lay Kevin Landwaster's error— aye, and great* Kelenbhrabanal's *also. When all hope was gone, they heeded the counsels of despair. Had they continued to strive, defying their doom, some unforeseen wonder might have occurred.*

Linden no longer believed in unforeseen wonders. They were Covenant's province— and she had crippled him. Nevertheless she turned her back on the surrounding darkness and walked slowly down to rejoin her friends and the Ranyhyn, the Humbled and Infelice and the Harrow.

None of them attended Covenant's unconsciousness, although the Humbled stood guard over him. They were chary of him; restrained by awe, or by the fear that they might harm him inadvertently. Nevertheless everyone watching Linden understood too much: she could see that. For those who cared about her, what she had done was an ictus in their hearts. Liand and the Ramen lacked the Harrow's provocative knowledge, Infelice's Earth-spanning consciousness, the shared memories of the *Haruchai*. None of her friends—or her antagonists—could match the strange and singular insight of the Ranyhyn. But they all were gifted with health-sense; percipience. The *Elohim*'s announcement that Linden had invoked the destruction of the Earth may have sounded abstract to Liand and the Ramen; even to the Humbled and Stave. Still they knew that they had witnessed an irreversible catastrophe; that she had vindicated every warning, fulfilled every dire prophecy—

When your deeds have come to doom, as they must—

You have it within you to perform horrors.

How had the Harrow and even the Viles known how badly she would fail her loves?

But Linden did not allow herself to hide her head as she approached the *krill* and Covenant's limp form. She did not intend to conceal her fatal heart behind a veil of shame. If she had indeed *roused the Worm of the World's End*, she meant to bear as much of the cost as her flesh could endure.

Bhapa and Pahni did not meet her eyes. Apparently they could not. Pahni clung to Liand, hiding her shock and terror against his shoulder. Bhapa studied the grass at his feet as though he feared that Linden's gaze would make him weep. But the bandage over Mahrtiir's face was too mundane to conceal the ferocity of his glower.

Stave had regained his impassivity. Perhaps he had never lost it. His stance was a query, not a repudiation. But the Humbled were not so restrained. Behind their familiar ready poise, they seemed to tremble with the force of their eagerness to strike her down.

Covenant had told them to choose her. They did not appear inclined to heed him.

Around the Humbled, the Ranyhyn remained watchful, wary; prepared to defend Linden again. As Linden drew near, Hyn nickered softly. The mare's call sounded sorrowful and resigned, as if she blamed herself. In spite of what Linden had done, the horses held fast to their fidelity. Perhaps they still trusted her. If they considered Infelice or the Harrow relevant to the fate of the Land—or to their own imperatives—they did not show it.

Of them all, however, all of Linden's friends, only Liand looked at her and spoke.

Every hint of the young dignity which he had displayed upon other occasions was gone. The stature of his Stonedownor heritage had deserted him. He had replaced his Sunstone in its pouch: he did not reach for it now. Linden had never seen him look so small, or so lorn. The raven wings of his eyebrows articulated his uncertainty.

She expected him to plead for an explanation; a justification. Hell, she half expected him to castigate her. He and everyone else had earned that right. But he did not.

Instead he asked, hoarse with empathy, "Will you not heal him?" Helplessly he indicated Covenant. "Linden, the pain of his incarnation wracks him. He cannot contain the greatness of his spirit. There is also an illness which I do not comprehend, though it appears paltry by the measure of his rent mind.

"The Staff of Law lies there." Liand pointed at the shaft of wood, iron-shod and ebony and runed. "Will you not grant him the benison of its flame? He has suffered beyond my power to imagine it." His tone held no accusation. "Will you not ease his plight?"

Linden shook her head. She was too full of dismay to falter. And the first shock of horror had passed. She was beginning to regain her ability to consider what she did.

"Don't you think," she asked Liand precisely, "that I've done enough harm already?"

Covenant was not warded by any power which might repulse her touch. But she could not affect the state of his mind—his spirit—without entering into him with her health-sense. Without *possessing* him. Long ago, she had done such things: she knew now that they were violations as profound as any rape. In addition, she could not foresee the effects of any change that she might make in Covenant's truncated transcendence. Years of experience had taught her that any sentience which did not heal itself might be forever flawed. And on this subject, the Ranyhyn had warned her clearly enough. They had shown her the likely outcome if she imposed her will on Covenant. Or on Jeremiah.

Some evils could not be twisted to serve any purpose but their own. Manipulating Covenant's condition for her own benefit would make her no better than the vile succubus that feasted on Jeremiah's neck. Perhaps some obdurate instinct for salvation would enable Covenant to find his way through the maze of his fissured consciousness. Linden would not.

Liand winced at her answer: at the words themselves, or at their acrid sound in the lush night. Pahni stifled a whimper against his shoulder. Mahrtiir's fierce silence conveyed the impression that he was mustering arguments to persuade her.

But Linden moved past them as though she had been indurated to any simple or direct form of compassion. She made no effort to retrieve her Staff or Covenant's ring. Jeremiah's ruined toy in her pocket was enough for her: the bullet hole and the small tears in her shirt were enough. Ignoring the grim enmity of the Humbled, she went to confront Infelice.

Now that the crisis of Linden's powers had passed, the echo of wild magic from Loric's *krill* did not outshine the *Elohim*'s refulgence. Infelice stood before Linden like a cynosure of loveliness and aghast hauteur. Wreathed about her limbs, her bedizened garment resembled weeping woven of gemstones and recrimination.

The Mahdoubt had told Linden that *There is hope in contradiction.* Long ago, Covenant had said the same thing. Before that, High Lord Mhoram had said it.

But the Mahdoubt had fallen into madness and death for Linden's sake; and Covenant lay shattered on the grass. Linden had never known Mhoram.

Without preamble, she said, "The Dead are gone." She did not doubt that Sunder and Hollian had already bid farewell to their immeasurably bereft son; that Grimmand Honninscrave had left the Swordmainnir to consider all that they had lost. "And Covenant can't help me. I've hurt him too badly." Nor could the Harrow's knowledge, the fruit of his long diligence and greed, be compared to the immortal awareness of the *Elohim*. "That only leaves you.

"Tell me how to find my son."

The Harrow had averred that Infelice would not or could not do so.

"Wildwielder," the *Elohim* retorted sharply: a reprimand. "You yourself have asked if the harm which you have wrought does not suffice. Will you compound ruin with delirancy? Your son is an abomination. His uses are abominable. Did not the first Half-hand say that you must exceed yourself yet again? He wished to convey that you must set aside this mad craving for your son."

Linden shook her head again. Infelice's words slipped past her like shadows, wasted and empty of affect. No objurgation could touch her while she remained deaf to despair.

And she did not choose to credit the *Elohim*'s interpretation of High Lord Berek's insistence—

"Then tell me," she said as though Infelice had not spoken, "how to stop the Worm."

"*Stop the Worm?*" The woman's voice nearly cracked. "Do you imagine that such a being may be hindered or halted in any manner? Your ignorance is as extreme as your transgressions."

Behind Linden, the Harrow chuckled softly; but she heard no humor in the sound.

"So explain it to me," she demanded. "Cure my ignorance. Why does such a being even exist? What's it *for*? What made the Creator think that the Worm of the World's End was a good idea? Did he want to kill his own creation? Was all of this," all of life and time, "just some cruel experiment to see how long it would take us to do every-thing wrong?"

"Fool!" retorted Infelice. Impatiently she dismissed the worth of Linden's question. "How otherwise might the Creator have devised a living world? You have named your-self a healer. How do you fail to grasp that life cannot exist without death?"

Her voice wove a skein of sorrow and repugnance among the trees. "From the smallest blade of grass to the most feral Sandgorgon or *skurj*, all that lives is able to do so only because it contains within itself the seeds of its own end. If living things did not decline and perish, they would soon crowd out all other life and time and hope. For this reason, every living thing ages and dies. And if its life is long, then its capacity for procreation is foreshortened."

While the *Elohim* spoke, Linden's friends came to stand at her back, leaving only Bhapa to watch over Covenant with the Humbled; but neither she nor Infelice regarded them.

"Without difficulty, the Creator could doubtless have placed as many earths and heavens as he desired within the Arch of Time. But he could not conceive a *living* world that did not contain the means of its own death."

Abruptly Infelice looked toward the Harrow; and her wrath mounted. "There this flagrant Insequent reveals the folly of his greed. With Earthpower and wild magic, he imagines that he will be empowered to unmake the Worm, thereby ensuring the continuance of the Earth. But the unmaking of the Worm will unmake all life. Such power cannot be countered without unleashing absolute havoc. While the Earth endures, the Worm is *needful*. The Harrow dreams of glory, but he will accomplish only extinction."

Now the Harrow laughed outright, rich and deep, and entirely devoid of mirth. "You mistake me, *Elohim*," he replied. "Such has been your custom toward the Insequent for many an age. I am not your Wildwielder, steeped in ignorance and mislove. I have other desires, intentions which will transcend your self-regard."

Linden had no interest in the hostility between the Insequent and the *Elohim*: it was of no use to her. Before she could intervene, however, Stave raised his voice to ask Infelice, "How, then, does it chance that the *Elohim* do not know death? Why have you been spared the hope and doom of all other life? I discern no merit in you to sanction your freedom from mortality."

"Puerile wight!" Infelice snapped at once. "Do you dare? The *Elohim* do not suffer affront from such as you."

Yet a glance at Linden caused Infelice to quell the chiming swirl of her wrath. Apparently Linden held a kind of sway over the suzerain *Elohim*; an influence or import which Linden did not understand.

With elaborate restraint, Infelice explained, "The *Elohim* do not participate in death because our purpose is deathless. We neither multiply nor change nor die because we were created to be the stewards of the Worm.

"Betimes we have intervened in perils which endanger life upon or within the Earth, but that is not our chief end. Rather our Würd requires of us that we preserve the Worm's slumber. Understand, Wildwielder, that we have no virtu to impose sleep. Instead it is our task to pacify and soothe. Thus by our very nature we serve all lesser manifestations of life.

"When we have countered wrongs such as the *skurj*, or the decimation of the One Forest, we have done so that the Worm may not be made restive by harm. And when we have permitted powers such as Forestals, or the Colossus of the Fall, to be fashioned from our essence, we have done so to refresh the corresponding vitality of the One Tree, that we may be left in peace." More and more as she spoke, her words seemed to weave the arching trees and the deep night and the light of the *krill* into an elegy, delicate as silver bells, and rich with grief. "Our *purpose* is peace, the means and outcome of our self-contemplation. The Forestals—and others—are our surrogates, just as we are the Creator's surrogates. They serve as the Creator's hold and bastion in our stead, preserving life which strives and dies while we preserve the Earth."

Then the elegy became a dirge throbbing with bitterness.

"Yet even such sacrifices are not the full tale of our worth to the Earth. I have named the One Tree. Setting aside the irenic reverie of ourselves, we have sought to deflect every threat which endangers the Tree, for it nurtures life just as the Worm enacts death. Thus the Earth began its true decline toward woe when an Insequent became the Guardian of the One Tree. The Theomach's cunning was great, but his vaunted knowledge did not suffice for such a burden. Still less has Brinn of the *Haruchai*'s prowess sufficed, though he achieved the Theomach's demise. By such deeds was the sanctity of the One Tree diminished, and the depth of the Worm's slumber was made less.

"Our tragedy is this, that the shadow upon our hearts has become an utter darkness. The harm has grown beyond our power to intervene. The Worm is roused and ravenous, and we cannot renew its slumber. By what this Insequent has rightly named mislove, Wildwielder, you have doomed us. Because of you, we will be the first to feed the hunger which you have called forth."

While Infelice answered Stave's challenge, Linden fretted. On some level, she recognized the pertinence of the *Elohim*'s revelations. But they did not shape or soften the extremity of her circumstances. *Your remorse will surpass your strength to bear it.* She needed facts, details; a concrete understanding of what she had released.

Earlier Berek Halfhand had said, *The making of worlds is not accomplished in an instant. It cannot be instantly undone. Much must transpire before the deeds of the Chosen find their last outcome.* Linden clung to that—and demanded more from Infelice.

"All right," she muttered grimly. "I get it.

"So what happens now? The Worm is awake. Somewhere. What will it do? How is it going to destroy the Earth? How much time have we got?"

The world's remaining days were her only concern. The Worm itself was Covenant's problem, not hers. He or no one would rise to that crisis. In either case, she had her own task to perform before the end.

—you aren't done. Covenant had recognized the truth. And he had professed that she might succeed. *She's the only one who can do this.* She chose to believe that he had referred to her one remaining responsibility.

"The Worm's slumbers have been long and long." Infelice spoke softly, but acid and bile twisted her mien. "Rousing, it is galled by hunger. As any living thing, it must feed. And as we are its stewards, so are we also its sustenance. Such is our Würd. The Worm must feed upon us. Only when it is sated with *Elohim* will it turn to the accomplishment of its greater purpose. If any of our kind remain unconsumed, we will endure solely to witness the end of all things, and so pass into the last dark."

—feed upon us. Perhaps Linden should have been shaken. Earlier Infelice had said that *every* Elohim *will be devoured*, but Linden had hardly heard her. Now Linden might have stopped to consider the cost of what she had done.

But Infelice had not given her what she needed. Linden tried again. "How long will it take? Hours? Days? Weeks?"

Like angry weeping, the *Elohim* replied, "We will seek to delay our passing because we must. We will flee and conceal ourselves at such distances as we are able to attain, requiring the Worm to scent us out singly, for we do not wish to perish. With sustenance, however, the Worm's might will grow. Ere a handful of days have passed, its puissance will discover and consume us. Then there will be no force in all the Earth great enough to delay the Worm."

Again the Harrow gave his humorless laugh; but no one heeded him.

"All right," Linden repeated. "A handful of days." But she was no longer looking at Infelice. Her attention had veered away. "That isn't much." Stave or the Humbled may have had further questions for the *Elohim*. Like Linden herself, the *Haruchai* did not forgive. There were many things of which they could have accused Infelice. And Mahrtiir may have wished to protest the implied fate of the Ranyhyn. Linden would have let them say whatever they wanted. She was not speaking to them as she muttered, "I need to face this. I can't put it off any longer."

She expected the Harrow to offer her a bargain. An exchange. Paralysis or urgency was the only choice left to her; and Jeremiah needed her.

Do it, she told herself. While you still can.

But when Linden turned away from Infelice, the Ramen and Liand joined her. A moment later, the Manethrall stepped in front of her, compelling her to consider his blinded visage.

"Ringthane," he began gruffly. "Chosen. There is much here which transcends us. We are Ramen, servants of the great Ranyhyn. For millennia, we have been content to be who we are. We do not participate in the outcome of worlds.

"But there is one matter of which I must speak."

Linden stared at him. Her face felt too stiff with emotion to hold any expression. She may have looked as ungiving as Stave's kindred. But Mahrtiir was her friend. He had lost his eyes, and with them some measure of his self-worth, in her aid. With an effort, she said, "I'm listening."

Carefully the Manethrall said, "Since we are assured that it must be so, I grant that the harm of the first Ringthane's resurrection is vast and terrible. But it is done. It cannot be undone. And his need remains. It is present and immediate. To heal him now will not redeem that which is past, but may do much to relieve that which is to come."

He was asking her to take a risk that she had already refused. For his sake, however, and for her other friends, she essayed an answer.

"I can't really explain it. If you haven't been possessed, you don't know what it's like to have someone else messing around inside you," heart and soul. "Just doing that to him would be bad enough. But this is worse. A broken mind isn't as simple as a cut, or a compound fracture, or an infection. Just one mistake—"

In the Verge of Wandering, she had tried to enter Anele in order to ease his madness, or his vulnerability. But she was grateful now that he had repulsed her. Her efforts would almost certainly have damaged him in some insidious fashion. She was neither wise nor unselfish enough to impose her wishes on him without transgressing his integrity.

She had spent years learning that lesson.

"If I interfere now, it won't be any different than resurrecting him. I'll take away his ability to make his own choices." To save or damn himself. "After what I've done, I owe him at least a little respect."

"Linden," Liand murmured, not in protest, but in chagrin and concern, "is it truly so *wrong* that you have restored a man whom you once loved? To some extent, I grasp the peril of—"

"You do not," Galt stated severely. "Had Linden Avery not roused the Worm of the World's End, still would her deed be a Desecration as vile as any Fall, and as fatal. In her own name, and for no purpose other than to ease her own heart, she has violated Laws upon which the continuance of life depends. The result is an unraveling of *necessity*, of act and consequence." His tone was pitiless. Through him, the Humbled passed judgment. "In the end, only evil can ensue.

"A woman who has committed such crimes will commit others. She must not be permitted to perform further atrocities."

Clearly the Humbled did not intend to let Linden intervene in Covenant's plight.

The Manethrall and his Cords stiffened. Mahrtiir twitched his garrote into his hands. But neither the *Haruchai* nor the Ranyhyn moved. Therefore the Ramen did not.

"Nevertheless," Stave remarked without inflection, "you will not raise your hand against her. The Unbeliever has instructed your forbearance. The Ranyhyn have declared their devoir against you. And I will not stand aside. No friend of the Chosen will stand aside. Mayhap even the Giants, who have named her Giantfriend, will abide by their allegiance. If you intend to impose your will upon the Chosen, you must oppose all who have gathered here in her name. And you must defy the given command of the ur-Lord, Thomas Covenant."

Linden ignored the denunciation of the Humbled. She did not listen to Stave's affirmation. She meant to confront the Harrow. She had nowhere else to turn. She had already done everything else wrong. Lord Foul's release had become inevitable. Nevertheless one task remained to her.

Did the Harrow covet her Staff and Covenant's ring? Let him. If he accepted her instruments of power, the result would not be what he appeared to expect.

Before she could speak, however, Liand's murmur and a shift in the attention of the Ramen caught her. Following their gaze, she saw the Giants emerge from the enfolding night. Spectral in the brightness of the *krill*, Rime Coldspray and her comrades strode into the vale, bringing Anele with them.

Anele, at least, seemed to be at peace. Linden saw at a glance that his protective madness remained. He was swaddled in incoherence. But he had found—or had been led to—a place of rest amid his private turmoil. She could almost believe that he had been given a sense of purpose by his parents; an insight into the needs which compelled his fractured striving.

When your deeds have come to doom, as they must, remember that he is the hope of the Land. Apparently Sunder and Hollian imagined that their son still had a vital role to play, despite the awakening of the Worm.

In contrast, the emanations of the Giants spoke of gritted teeth and grim resolve. The manner in which they advanced upon Linden and her companions, and the darkness of their scowling, announced that they knew what had transpired here. Drawing them away, the shade of Grimmand Honninscrave must have explained what their absence had permitted or prevented. Perhaps Honninscrave had told the Swordmainnir why the Dead had sought to ensure that the living did not participate in or disrupt Linden's choices.

Apparently, however, the former Master of Starfare's Gem had revealed other things as well. The Giants spared a moment of sorrow for Covenant's unconsciousness. They acknowledged Linden with ambivalent nods and grimaces, as if they had not made up their minds about her: they glowered ominously at the Harrow and the Humbled. But they did not pause for Stave or the Ramen or Liand. Instead they strode toward Infelice with demands in their eyes and anger in their stalwart arms.

Hardly aware of what she did, Linden turned to learn what impelled the Giants.

As they confronted Infelice, her expression became imperious. Bitterly she drifted into the air until her face was level with the combative glaring of the Swordmainnir. Her lambent form demanded an obeisance which the Giants did not deign to grant.

"In a distant age," Rime Coldspray said at once, "our ancestors were misled to accept a false bargain with the *Elohim*. That the bargain was false in all sooth has been made plain to us. And it has now been betrayed through no deed of ours. We require restitution."

A bargain? Linden wondered. What bargain?

Infelice lifted her chin haughtily. "And do you conceive that restitution is mine to grant?"

"How could it be otherwise?" retorted the Ironhand. "The bargain was made at your behest. The falseness is yours. With oblique misstatement and bland prevarication, you offered a true benefit to obtain a vile payment which no Giant who has ever lived would have proffered knowingly. Now you have claimed payment for that gift purchased with lies—and the guerdon has been withdrawn. Therefore our payment must be returned to us."

Dimly Linden remembered hearing the Giants of the Search mention a bargain. Ten years ago in her life. But something had reminded her of it recently.

The eyes of the *Elohim* flared like faceted fires. "You reason falsely, Giant. I concede that our bargain has been betrayed through no deed of yours. Indeed, I concede that your witless ancestors concealed from themselves the truth of their own profligate unwisdom. But we did not impose their misapprehension. We merely permitted it. Nor have we condoned the betrayal of our bargain. That the *mere*-son sees fit to serve mad Kastenessen does not occur by our choice, or with our consent. For both Kastenessen's malice and Esmer's treachery, we are blameless."

Yes. Linden nodded to herself. Esmer. That was it.

"Nevertheless," Coldspray insisted, "you have dealt falsely with Giants. The burden of restitution is yours."

"That is illusion," countered Infelice. "Of a certainty, I am able to restore your gift of tongues—a gift which the *mere*-son will revoke once more when I have fled, as I must. But I cannot release the *geas* which grips the kinsman whom you name Longwrath."

Linden winced when she heard that name; and Liand caught his breath. But Infelice did not pause.

"Such restitution"—she sneered the word—"is not mine to grant. The bargain which you name false was freely made, without coercion or constraint. In return for your gift of tongues, we sought the life of one then-unborn Giant at a time and in a circumstance of our choosing. If we did not say as much in language unmistakable to Giants, the fault lies in you. Whether by misapprehension or by self-delusion, the word of your kind was given. That deed is done. The *geas* which we required was set in motion then to seek its fulfillment now. It cannot be released, other than by the unmaking of its origin.

"We will not alter our past. Doing so will hasten the destruction of the Arch—and while we live we will cling to life."

"Yet it was a dishonest bargain, *Elohim*," protested Frostheart Grueburn. "Do you equate the granting of a tale with the surrender of a life?"

"A tale *is* a life," Infelice stated.

"Nonetheless," Grueburn continued, "you concealed from our ancestors that you craved a weapon potent to procure Linden Giantfriend's death. Had they known that you wished to claim the life of any Giant for any purpose, they would have turned their backs and departed in repugnance."

Infelice snorted her disdain. "There was no dishonesty. Our purposes are our own. We do not choose to reveal them. I acknowledge that your ancestors altogether misunderstood us. Still they accepted our bargain. If you find wrong in this, find it in your own kind, whose desire to comprehend the many tongues of the Earth outweighed their desire to comprehend the *Elohim*. We cannot be held accountable for their willingness to bind their descendants to a bargain which you now execrate."

God, Linden thought in wan surprise. The *Elohim* had planned for this. All those millennia ago. Longwrath's madness was not Earth-Sight: it was manipulation. *It was for this! To avert this present moment.* By misleading his ancestors, the *Elohim* had acquired the power to compel him against her, hoping that he would slay her before she entered Andelain with her Staff and Covenant's ring.

"That's unconscionable," she found herself saying, although she had not intended to speak. "Lord Foul would be proud of you. If you wanted me dead, you could have killed me yourselves. You've had plenty of chances. Tricking other people into doing your dirty work isn't just shortsighted. It's suicidal. You could have had allies. Now all you've got are people who won't be sorry to see you die first."

—are we not equal to all things?

We are the Elohim, *the heart of the Earth. We stand at the center of all that lives and moves and is. No other being or need may judge us—*

That, Esmer himself had proclaimed, that arrogance, that self-absorption, *is shadow enough to darken the heart of any being.*

"Well said, my lady!" The Harrow clapped his hands loudly. "I begin to believe that there is hope for the Earth, when every stratagem but mine has failed."

The entire company ignored him.

"You denounce yourself, Linden Avery," Galt asserted flatly. "The false dealings of the *Elohim* are yours as well."

Linden accepted the charge. She, too, was guilty of self-absorption. Yes, and perhaps even of arrogance. *I need you to doubt me.* She had no other excuse for her actions.

No excuse except her yearning for Thomas Covenant and her compulsory love for Jeremiah.

But Rime Coldspray and then the rest of the Giants turned away from Infelice. Perhaps they had not truly expected to win any form of concession. Moving to stand among the Ranyhyn and the Humbled, they towered against the night sky; the lost stars and the fathomless dark.

"It may be, *Haruchai*," the Ironhand replied to Galt, "that your certainty is apt. Yet Grimmand Honninscrave, whose valor and sacrifice were known to your ancestors, has assured us that the Dead do not pronounce judgment so readily. Mayhap Cail and others of your forefathers would have endeavored to sway you, had you consented to heed them.

"With honored Honninscrave, we have spoken of many things"—her tone was as hard as the stone of her glaive—"not neglecting the Worm of the World's End. He described the necessity of freedom in terms too eloquent to be ignored. He did not call us away from Linden Giantfriend's side so that we would be deprived of our own freedom of response, but rather so that we would not be provoked by events to determine our response in haste. And he said much concerning all that the Giants of the Search learned of Thomas Covenant and Linden Avery."

Linden listened almost involuntarily. She meant to turn her attention to the Harrow. But her new understanding of Longwrath's plight clung to her like Honninscrave's death in possession and defiance.

At Linden's side, Liand's eyes shone as though he had already guessed what the Ironhand would reveal.

"That they are mortal," the leader of the Swordmainnir went on, "and thus driven to error, cannot be denied. But the same must be said of Giants and *Haruchai*—and now also of *Elohim*. And Honninscrave reminded us of the First's deep love, and of Pitchwife's, and of his own, which both Thomas Covenant and Linden Avery earned by their courage and resolve, by their given friendship, and by their final refusal to honor the dictates of despair. If we doubt Linden Giantfriend, he acknowledged, we have just cause. But he also avowed that we have just cause to rely upon the lessons of past millennia, lessons of lealty and trust. Indeed, he assured us that his own dreads are preeminently *for* her rather than *of* her. Remain uncertain, as do the Dead, he urged us, and abide by the leanings of your hearts.

"*Haruchai*, our hearts incline to Linden Avery, and also to Thomas Covenant. The peril of his incarnation is plain, as is that of her obduracy and might. He has suffered great harm, and the darkness within her is vivid to all who gaze upon her. Yet he remains a man who has risen to the salvation of the Land. And she has repeatedly demonstrated her capacity for unforeseen healings.

"If you are compelled to pass judgment," the Ironhand concluded as if she were closing her fist, "do so among yourselves. We will not hear you. In spite of our uncertainty, we have elected to keep faith with our own past—and with hers."

Short days ago, Coldspray had declared, *After our children, tales are our greatest treasures. But there can be no story without hazard and daring, fortitude and uncertainty. And joy is in the ears that hear, not in the mouth that speaks.*

Galt held the Ironhand's gaze without blinking. Clyme and Branl did the same. However, they shared their thoughts in silence rather than aloud. To that extent, at least, they respected the attitude of the Giants. Only Stave heard his kindred; and he said nothing.

"Do you know—?" Linden tried to ask. But her throat closed as if she were still capable of weeping. Dismay filled her mouth like ashes or sand, and she had to swallow hard before she could find her voice. "Do you know what happened to Anele? Did Honninscrave," oh, God, Honninscrave, who had deliberately accepted a Raver so that Lord Foul's servant could be torn apart, "say anything about him?"

Coldspray shook her head, and her manner softened. "Of the old man, we know only what your eyes have beheld. We see that he has found solance among his Dead. But his state does not affect the heading of our choices. For that reason, I deem, Honninscrave did not speak of him."

"I suppose you're right," Linden murmured as if to herself. "His freedom is as necessary as anyone else's. If we knew what was going on inside him, we might interfere somehow."

Struggling against the Giants' effect on her, she prepared herself to turn toward the Harrow again. *You have companions, Chosen—* She had an abundance of friends: the Swordmainnir had made that obvious. *—who have not faltered in your service.* Only the Humbled and Infelice wished to oppose her. But that changed nothing. She had set in motion the end of the world. She could not alter it. There was only one thing left for her to do.

Surely she should retrieve her Staff and Covenant's ring? They remained on the grass, discarded as if they had betrayed her. They would have no value to her unless she claimed them again.

Perhaps, she thought, she should try to claim Loric's *krill* as well. Its brightness defended Andelain; but now Andelain was doomed. Loric's dagger may have been the highest achievement of the Old Lords—and it could not save the Hills. Nevertheless it might continue to draw power from Joan's wedding band when Covenant's was gone.

It might save Linden herself.

Or Jeremiah.

Briefly.

That was all she asked. She had gone too far, and done too much harm, to expect anything more.

Yet she hesitated without knowing why. The Staff of Law belonged to her. In some sense, Covenant had left his ring to her. But she had no claim on the *krill*. No right to it.

She wanted to ask the Harrow, Do you still believe that Infelice will stop you from taking me to Jeremiah? Even now?

But this decision was hers to make. It did not belong to either the *Elohim* or the Insequent.

Before she could make her last remaining choice, however, Manethrall Mahrtiir abruptly jerked up his head.

"*Aliantha!*" he barked as if he were astonished or ashamed that he had not thought of this earlier. "Cords, find *aliantha.*"

Bhapa and Pahni exchanged a baffled glance. In confusion, Pahni looked quickly at Liand. But they were Ramen: they obeyed their Manethrall at once. Dodging between the Ranyhyn, they sprinted up the slopes of the hollow until they passed beyond the reach of the *krill*'s argence.

"Manethrall?" asked Stave.

Perplexed, Coldspray, Grueburn, and their comrades frowned at Mahrtiir.

"The first Ringthane must have healing," he replied harshly. "There is much here that lies beyond my comprehension—aye, beyond even my desire for comprehension. Yet it is plain to me, though I have no sight, that some portion of his suffering is mere human frailty. He has been given flesh which is too weak and flawed to contain his spirit.

"No balm known to the Ramen will ease the ardor and constriction of his reborn pain. But *aliantha* will supply the most urgent needs of his flesh. Mayhap it will grant him the strength to awaken—and perhaps to speak."

Stave nodded; and some of the grimness lifted from the faces of the Giants. "Manethrall!" Liand exclaimed gladly. "The sight which you do not possess surpasses mine, which is whole. *Aliantha*, indeed! Why was this not our first thought rather than our last?"

Because, Linden answered to herself mordantly, you were distracted. As she had been. Like her companions, she had concentrated on other forms of healing.

Now she felt that she would never be able to meet Covenant's gaze again. She could hardly bear to look into the faces of her friends, whom she had misled and misused.

She meant to leave them all behind. She did not want to expose them to the hazards of the Harrow's dark intentions.

Covenant had professed his faith in her. *She's the only one who can do this.* Linden would have found his sick and shattered condition easier to endure if he had spurned her utterly.

The idea that he still trusted her felt like a cruel joke.

Among Andelain's wealth of gifts, the Cords did not have to search far for treasure-berries. Pahni had already re-entered the vale with a handful of the viridian fruit. And as she hastened fluidly down the slope, Bhapa caught the light at the rim of the hollow. At the same time, Mahrtiir walked around the Ranyhyn and the Giants and the *krill* to approach Covenant. Kneeling, the Manethrall gently, kindly, eased the Unbeliever around onto his back. Then Mahrtiir seated himself cross-legged at Covenant's head and lifted it onto the support of his shins.

Linden could not watch. Deliberately she turned away from the group around Covenant as she stooped to grasp the carved black wood of her Staff. For an instant, she feared that she had burned away its readiness for Earthpower and Law. At once, however, she found that the Staff was whole, unharmed. Its strict warmth steadied her hand as she picked up Covenant's ring, looped its chain over her head, and let the white gold dangle against her sternum.

Now, she commanded herself. Do it now.

Nevertheless she hesitated, gripped by a pang like a premonition of loss. Her own

intentions frightened her. Even more than her Staff, Covenant's wedding band symbolized the meaning of her life. When she surrendered such things, she would have
nothing left.

Nothing apart from Jeremiah.

His need compelled her. If she kept nothing for herself except her son, she would
find a way to be content.

Clutching the Staff until her knuckles ached, she crossed lush grass to bargain with
the Harrow.

As ornately clad as a courtier, the Insequent sat his huge destrier a dozen or more
paces away from everyone else. As Linden approached, the beast rolled its eyes in terror
or fury: the muscles of its flanks quivered. Yet it stood stiffly under the Harrow's steady
hand. The bottomless gulfs of his eyes regarded her hungrily, but did not attempt to
draw her into their depths. A smile like a smug obscenity twisted his mouth. In order
to face him, she had to remind herself grimly that his power was like his apparel,
acquired rather than innate. Behind his condescension and his greed and his complex
magicks, he was a more ordinary man than Liand of Mithil Stonedown, who had
inherited the ancient birthright of his people.

If Linden could have closed her senses to the company behind her, she would have
done so. But her nerves were still too raw; too exposed. Involuntarily she felt the Ranyhyn move until they formed a wide circle around Covenant and Mahrtiir and the
Cords, Liand and the Humbled. There the star-browed horses stood as if to bear witness. And among the Ranyhyn, the Giants assembled. Even the attention of the *Elohim*
was fixed on Covenant rather than on Linden and the Harrow.

Only Stave walked away from the Manethrall's efforts to care for the first Ringthane. Alone the outcast *Haruchai* came to stand with Linden.

She did not want to follow what Mahrtiir was doing, she did *not*. In spite of her
efforts to seal her senses, however, she felt his tension and concern as he accepted a
treasure-berry from Pahni and broke it open with his teeth to remove the seed. He
could not know what would happen when he fed *aliantha* to Covenant. He could only
remain true to himself—and put his trust in the Land's largesse.

Carefully he parted Covenant's lips to accept the fruit. Then he began to stroke
Covenant's throat, encouraging the unconscious man to swallow.

Linden glared into the Harrow's eyes as if she were impervious to his assumed
superiority. Hoarsely she rasped, "You said that you can take me to my son."

*There is a service which I am able to perform for you, and which you will not obtain
from any other living being.*

"Indeed." The Insequent's voice was deep and fertile; ripe with avarice. He met
her gaze like a man who yearned to devour her. "My knowledge encompasses both
his hiding place and the means by which he has remained hidden. And I am able to

move at will from one place to another in this time, as the foolish Mahdoubt has informed you."

For moments that felt long to Linden's unwilling nerves, Covenant did not respond to the *aliantha* on his tongue. But Mahrtiir was patient. And even if Covenant did not swallow, his mouth itself would absorb some of the berry's virtue.

"The Worm of the World's End is coming," she replied to the Harrow, speaking as distinctly as the quaver in her heart allowed. "There's nothing you can do about it. Does that make you re-think anything? Anything at all? Do you still want what I have?"

Did he still covet the responsibility implied by the Staff of Law and Covenant's ring?

Suspense gathered around Covenant and the Manethrall. The Giants and the Humbled, the Cords and Liand and even the Ranyhyn studied the fallen Timewarden for some sign that the fruit's rich juice or Mahrtiir's ministrations might unclose his throat.

Linden felt the collective sigh of the Swordmainnir as Covenant swallowed reflexively.

The Manethrall bowed his head over Covenant for a moment. Then he readied another treasure-berry.

"I do, lady," answered the Harrow avidly. "And I am not as ignorant of the Worm as Infelice chooses to imagine. The Earth's ruin need not transpire as she asserts that it must. With the powers that you will enable me to wield, and by means which the *Elohim* fear to contemplate, I will demonstrate that no doom is inevitable—apart from the destruction which falls upon those who dare to oppose me."

"All right." Linden took a moment to confirm that she was sure. But the possibility that Covenant might awaken did not affect her decision. She needed to take one more absolute risk. Nothing less would serve her now. And she knew the cost of trying to escape her burdens. "If you're that arrogant—or that blind—or that clever—tell me what you'll offer in exchange."

Without visible transition, Infelice stood in the air near Linden and the Harrow, floating so that she could face him directly with her gleaming indignation—or so that she could fling her distress down at Linden.

An instant later, the whole vale was transformed as a host of Wraiths came streaming into the hollow from every direction. Warmly they lit the dark. In spite of herself, Linden turned her head, expecting to see scores or hundreds of dancing eldritch candleflames rush toward her as if they had been summoned by the possibility of conflict between the *Elohim* and the Insequent.

But they did not appear to be aware of her; or of Infelice and the Harrow. Instead they gathered around Mahrtiir and Covenant.

Infelice demanded Linden's attention. "Linden Avery," she protested in anguish and ire, "Wildwielder, you must not. Does the harm of this night fail to content you? The Insequent speaks of forces which he cannot comprehend. He will hasten the reaving of the *Elohim* and accomplish no worthy purpose. He will merely gain for himself a scant, false glory while the world falls."

Stave ignored the *Elohim*. He did not glance at the Wraiths or Covenant. As if Infelice had not spoken, he said inflexibly, "Be wary, Chosen. I mislike the word of this Insequent. And the exchange which you contemplate is unequal in his favor. It may be greatly so. With wild magic and Law, perhaps wielded through High Lord Loric's *krill*, he will acquire an imponderable might—and you will receive only your son. He may prove powerless against the Worm, and still wreak untold havoc ere the end, leaving naught but despair to those who briefly retain their lives."

Linden hardly heard either of them. Held by surprise at the return of the Wraiths, she watched them bob and flicker over Covenant's unconsciousness. The precise yellow-and-orange of their fires countered the inhuman silver of the *krill*. Chiming like the highest bells of a distant carillon, nameless and ineffable, they alit in throngs on his arms and legs, his torso, his face. And each touch was an infusion of their arcane vitality. Together they wove health through him, repairing his over-burdened flesh.

In spite of their generosity, Linden discerned no indication that the Wraiths would or could affect the fissuring of his mind. Nor did they relieve his leprosy. It was inherent to him. It may have been necessary. Nevertheless they swarmed to expend themselves so that his body would be able to bear the strain of his incalculable spirit.

When each Wraith had given its gift, its answer to the animosity between the *Elohim* and the Insequent, it danced away so that its place could be taken by another small flame.

Reassured, Linden faced Infelice and the Harrow again. Fervently she replied to both Stave and the *Elohim*.

"I'm not worried about that. If he's wrong—if he can't stop the Worm—he'll die like the rest of us. But he may not be wrong. He didn't work so long and hard for this just so that he can enjoy a few days of empty superiority. And I am going to free my son. I can't do anything else, but I can try to do that. I'm going to stop his suffering. I'm going to hold him in my arms at least one more time before the Worm gets us. If he and I have to die, his last memory is going to be that I love him."

For the span of several heartbeats, Stave considered Linden. When he was confident of what he saw with his single eye, he said simply, "Then I am content."

"*I* am not!" shouted Infelice: a raw blare of passion that reminded Linden of Esmer's eerie power. "Wildwielder, you have become Desecration incarnate. Your folly is too vast to be called by any other name. Do you not grasp that the Harrow intends a fate far more malign than mere extinction for the *Elohim*?"

Before she could continue, the Harrow laughed contemptuously. "You are mistaken, *Elohim*, as is your wont. When I have gained that which I crave, you and your
kind will be spared, left free to nurture your surquedry in any form that pleases you. I
will either fail or succeed. If I fail, your plight remains unaltered. If I succeed, you will
be restored to your rightful place in the life of the Earth. Therefore silence your plaint.
It is naught but pettiness and self-pity."

"Do you conceive," countered Infelice, "that your word has worth in such matters?
It does not. This is some elaborate chicane to gain your desires. You are *mortal*, Insequent. Your human mind cannot contain the scale of your doomed intent."

Linden braced herself to tell Infelice and the Harrow to *shut up*. She had had enough
of their antagonism: it shed no light on the darkness of her decisions. But before she
could demand their silence, she heard Covenant.

The Wraiths had revived him. Still lying with his head propped on Mahrtiir's shins,
he spoke softly: a mere wisp of sound in the fretted night. Nevertheless his voice carried as though he had the authority to command the very air of the vale.

"Do any of you have a better idea?"

Linden wheeled toward him as if he had reached out and snatched at her arm; as if
she had no choice.

The gathering around him had parted: she could see him clearly. He had not risen
from the grass into the light of the *krill*. But Wraiths still danced about him, a penumbra of gentle fires. In spite of the distance between them, Linden saw him with
frightening clarity.

The pallor of his features displayed his weakness. Neither *aliantha* nor the Wraiths
had relieved his fundamental flaws or his illness. He still resembled an invalid, too
weak to stand; perhaps too weak to think. With her health-sense, Linden could almost
identify the fault-lines along which the bedrock of his mind had cracked.

Yet the galls of his face retained their compelling severity. He looked like a fallen
prophet, brought low before he could proclaim the Land's fate.

Beneath the shock of his white hair, the scar on his forehead gleamed like an accusation. See? it seemed to say. This is my mortality. My pain. It's your doing.

While Linden studied him, he turned his gaze on everyone around him. But none
of them answered him. Even the Humbled did not. Linden expected them to reiter-
ate their denunciations of her; yet Branl, Galt, and Clyme said nothing. Covenant's
authority held them in the same way that it ruled the atmosphere of the hollow.

"In that case"—he sounded sure in spite of his frailty—"I think we should do this
Linden's way. She can make this kind of decision. The rest of us can't." After a moment,
he found the strength to add, "Mhoram would approve."

At once, Infelice fled like a wail from the hollow. She disappeared as though

Covenant had banished her; as though her cause were lost without the Timewarden's support.

In the wake of her departure, the Harrow's air of smug triumph made Linden wish that she could strike him down.

3.

Bargaining with Fate

Hardly conscious of her own movements, Linden turned her back on the Harrow and hastened toward Covenant. With all of her senses, she examined her former lover. Was it possible that the Wraiths had healed his creviced mind? That she had misinterpreted the effects of the eldritch flames? Had they made him whole?

Did he even know what he was saying when he gave Linden his support? When he horrified Infelice so profoundly that the *Elohim* fled in despair?

Unregarded, Giants loomed in front of her. Then they stood behind her. She passed among Ranyhyn and *Haruchai* without noticing them. Liand and the Cords hovered around Covenant: Mahrtiir supported the Unbeliever's head. But she did not look at them. All of her attention was fixed on Thomas Covenant.

For the moment, at least, she had forgotten dismay and shame.

Braced by the Manethrall, Covenant now sat more upright, leaning against Mahrtiir's chest. He seemed unaware of Linden's approach. He may have been unaware that he had spoken. The scar on his forehead was turned away. While she held her breath and bit her lip, he concentrated on accepting treasure-berries one at a time from Pahni's hands, or from Bhapa's. In spite of his evident hunger, he ate with slow care. The seeds he gave to Liand, who scattered them gladly around the vale.

Peering into Covenant as intimately as she could without violating his spirit, Linden confirmed that the Wraiths had not mended the faults which fractured his thoughts. Nor had they ameliorated his leprosy. They could not: Kevin's Dirt hindered them in spite of the power that they drew from Loric's dagger. They had only repaired the physical violence of his return to life. They had not restored the man he had once been.

Linden had forced him too far beyond the bounds of Law. Now he appeared to exist outside any mundane definition of health. The profuse miracles of Andelain and the Land could nurture his flesh, but could not draw him back into the ambit of simple humanity.

Seeing him like this, alert and damned, and growing stronger in ways that would only enable him to endure more pain, Linden wanted to weep again. But she did not. Perhaps she could not. The consequences of her rage and folly and hope had left her siccant. Within herself, she resembled a wasteland.

She was only peripherally aware that the Wraiths had begun to drift away, chiming a lucent and inconsolable lament as they bobbed out of the hollow. Apparently they had done what they could. Now they went elsewhere as though they did not wish to witness what came next.

At the same time, the Ranyhyn turned aside. Alert and sure, they separated themselves from the company, heading south.

Linden hardly noticed their departure. Covenant, she tried to say. But she had no words for what she needed from him. They had been burned out of her by her own extravagance. Perhaps she could have suffered the awakening of the Worm if she had succeeded at reincarnating him as she remembered him. But her flagrant display of power had achieved something worse than failure. No mere expression of regret would exculpate her.

Nevertheless her distress caught the attention of her friends. Mahrtiir lifted his head. Pahni looked up at Linden: hope flared suddenly in the young Cord's eyes and then faded, extinguished by what she saw. Bhapa regarded Linden like a man who had lost faith and now sought to regain it.

The Humbled appeared to ignore her. Anele had stretched out on the thick grass near Covenant's feet. There he slept with one hand covering his mouth like a man who feared that he might babble in his dreams. But the Giants turned toward Linden expectantly.

Liand hesitated for only an instant. Then he moved to stand in front of Linden. The black augury of his eyebrows emphasized the questions thronging in his kind eyes. Yet he reached out and clasped her shoulders gently as if he meant to reassure her.

"Linden," he began in a tone of deliberate calm, "it is too much. Too much has transpired. Of these events, too many lie beyond my comprehension. We have been informed that the last crisis of the Earth now approaches, yet such avowals appear empty of meaning before the wonder and terror which you have wrought.

"Other needs press upon you. It is my intent to respect them, as I have respected you from the first, and will continue to the last. This, however, I must ask.

"I perceive that your understanding of what has occurred exceeds that of any Stone-downor or Raman. In one form, it surpasses even that of the Masters, whose memories span millennia. In another, it out-runs the wide learning of these Giants, though they have journeyed distances and met perils inconceivable to me. Nonetheless I ask this of you. Was it not impossible for you to have foreseen the outcome of your deeds here? Do you not share with each and all of your companions, Masters and Giants and Ramen alike, an inability to scry the future? And if you have no gift of prescience, are you not by that lack rendered blameless?

"Upon the rocks in Salva Gildenbourne, when we were beset by the *skurj*, I hazarded our lives by wielding both *orcrest* and the Staff of Law in an attempt to summon rain—an attempt which exceeded every gift of knowledge and skill and strength within me. That we evaded Kastenessen's snare is no tribute to my foresight. I was merely foolish, foolish and desperate. Yet my folly was transformed to hope, not by any deed of mine, but through the aid of the Demondim-spawn, and with your own far greater might.

"Linden—my friend—" Briefly Liand faltered, overcome by compassion. Then he regained a measure of dignity. "May the same not be said of you? Can any being or power aver with certainty that your folly will not be transformed to hope by the succor of some lore or theurgy"—he referred to Covenant with a glance—"which we cannot foresee?"

Linden shook her head. She heard his sincerity. She felt it in the grasp of his hands. Still she rejected it. She had been given too many warnings. The horserite visions of the Ranyhyn may have been difficult to interpret: the images with which Lord Foul had afflicted her during her translation to the Land were not.

"Not this time," she replied roughly. "I could have known. I just couldn't let anything stop me."

Under *Melenkurion* Skyweir, she had learned that she was nothing without Covenant. Her need to rescue Jeremiah demanded more of her than she contained.

And she did not forgive.

Her response hurt Liand. It may have pained the Ramen and the Swordmainnir—or vindicated the Humbled. But Covenant distracted them before anyone could protest.

Unsteadily he pulled away from Mahrtiir, struggled to his feet. Frowning, he considered everyone around him. When he looked at Linden, however, she discerned that his gaze did not entirely focus on her. Instead he gave the impression that he saw someone else in her place: another version of herself, perhaps, or a different woman altogether.

"Think of the Creator and the Despiser as brothers," he remarked in an abstract tone. "Or *doppelgangers* of each other. That isn't really true. The concepts are too big for words. But it's a way to try to understand. It's at least as true as saying the stars are the Creator's children. Or the Arch of Time is like a rainbow. You could say Creation and Despite are the same thing, but they take such radically different forms they might as well be mysteries to each other. It's all a paradox. It has to be."

In another, more consecutive state of mind, he might have said, *There is hope in contradiction.*

"Covenant?" Linden asked as though his name had been wrung from her against her will. Surging upright, the Manethrall inquired like an echo, "Ringthane?"

Covenant did not respond. He may not have heard them. Instead he turned to Liand.

"I like your *orcrest* analogy." He spoke as if he were continuing a casual conversation that he and the Stonedownor had begun earlier. "It doesn't really apply. You didn't risk anybody except yourself. Trying to bring rain didn't make the danger you were already in worse. Earthpower and Law can't stop the *skurj*. Not while Kevin's Dirt is still there. But you're still right. There are always surprises. And sometimes they help."

Around him, the Giants shuffled their feet. They had heard too many tales about the Unbeliever, the ur-Lord—and none of those stories matched the man who now occupied Covenant's body.

Linden tried again. "Covenant? Where are you? In your mind? What are you remembering?"

"Linden?" He cocked an eyebrow at her as if he were startled to find her near him; as if he had expected her to flee like Infelice. Still his manner remained abstract, almost nonchalant. "Do you remember Diassomer Mininderain?"

"No." Her reaction was far more personal than his. "I mean yes. I've only heard the name. Sunder told us about her," when he had led Covenant and her away from Mithil Stonedown into the ravages of the Sunbane millennia ago. "The Rede of the Clave mentioned her."

Covenant nodded. "That's right. It's almost true." As if he were quoting lines which he had heard only moments ago, he recited,

"Diassomer Mininderain,
The mate of might, and Master's wife,
All stars' and heavens' chatelaine,
With power over realm and strife,
Attended well, the story tells,
To a-Jeroth of the Seven Hells."

Linden remembered in spite of her confusion. *Oh, come, my love, and bed with me—*
Covenant had fallen into a private crevasse. Diassomer Mininderain had nothing to do with Linden, or with the dilemmas of her friends, or with the ending of the

Earth. That woman was only a myth promulgated by the Clave for Lord Foul's malign reasons.

"Covenant, please," Linden begged. "Make sense." She had done this to him. "We need you. I need you. Help us if you can."

A shudder ran through him. Briefly he grimaced as if she had twisted his heart. "I'm sorry." His hands made incomplete gestures like truncated supplications. "There are so many strands. I want to distinguish— But I don't know how."

Then his air of abstraction claimed him again. "If Creation and Despite have some kind of relevance to eternity—if they're part of what eternity means somehow—other things may be relevant as well. One might be Indifference. Another might be Love. They're all the same thing. But they're all different."

"Covenant!" Linden could not blunt the edge of desperation in her voice. "Please! We need you *here*."

I think we should do this Linden's way. Had he been referring to her intention to meet the Harrow's demands? *She can make this kind of decision. The rest of us can't.*

She had already done so much harm—

Liand's earnest face added his appeal to hers. Distinctly Rime Coldspray said, "Covenant Giantfriend," as if she hoped to remind him of who he was. "You redeemed the Dead of The Grieve from their long sorrow. Will you not now grant some boon or balm to our dolor and gall?"

But Covenant was trapped in his memories. He gave no sign that he had heard the Ironhand.

"Old stories—I mean the really old stories, like creation myths—are always true. Not literally, of course. Words aren't good enough. And people always change the stories to suit themselves. But the stories are still true. Like the Clave's version of what the Earth and Time are *for*. Or Diassomer Mininderain.

"None of this is her fault. She just can't forgive it."

Acute with blandishments and spells
Spoke a-Jeroth of the Seven Hells.

Linden found that she could not beseech him further. Helplessly she remembered: she had never been able to break the grip of her past, or of the Land's.

With a-Jeroth the lady ran;
Diassomer with fear and dread
Fled from the Master's ruling span.
On Earth she hides her trembling head,

While all about her laughter wells
From a-Jeroth of the Seven Hells.

"She was—or is—or has always been—an aspect of eternity. Maybe she was Love. The Lover. And maybe she fell when the Despiser did. That's possible. Despite isn't the opposite of Love. That's Indifference. Love has more in common with Despite and Creation than with Indifference."

"Forgive!" she cries with woe and pain;
Her treacher's laughter hurts her sore.
"His blandishments have been my bane.
I yearn my Master to adore."
For in her ears the spurning knells
Of a-Jeroth of the Seven Hells.

"But being trapped in Time is different for Love than it is for Despite." Covenant frowned again. "This is all just words." Then he resumed. "It outraged the Despiser, but it made Diassomer Mininderain insane. The Despiser tricked her. And the Creator can't free her without dismantling what he created. She's sort of like Joan, in a way. If words made any sense. If Joan weren't so human and frail."

Wrath is the Master—fire and rage.
Retribution fills his hands.
Attacking comes he, sword and gage,
'Gainst treachery in all the lands.

Mininderain he treats with rue;
No heaven-home for broken trust,
But children given to pursue
All treachery to death and dust.
Thus Earth became a gallow-fells
For a-Jeroth of the Seven Hells.

"The Despiser has to cause as much pain as he can while he tries to get free. It helps him fight off his own despair. Diassomer Mininderain feeds off anything that's still capable of love. She eats— But that's not all she does. She still *hates*. She had as much to do with making the *merewives* as Kastenessen's mortal lover did. And she's involved in Kevin's Dirt somehow."

Linden had lost her way. Covenant evoked a host of recollections and bafflements
and lost affection. He seemed to have reached the point of what he was trying to say,
but she could not guess what it might be. When he fell silent, gazing about him as
though he had made everything clear, she asked the first question that she could find
in her desiccated heart.

"So why didn't I see that old man? The one who told me that 'There is also love in
the world.' Why didn't he warn me?"

*You are indeed forsaken, by the Dead as by the Earth's Creator. How could it be other-
wise, when all of your deeds conduce to ruin?*

If he had accosted her—if she had caught so much as a glimpse of him—she would
have known what his presence meant. She might have been able to save Jeremiah.

Covenant's face tightened, drawing his features into lines like strictures. Suddenly,
for no reason that she could imagine, he was *present* in front of her, alert in every
sense. Sliding along a flaw or fissure, he had returned to Andelain and night and the
brilliance of the *krill*. The harsh compassion in his voice was so familiar that it made
her ache.

"Maybe he's given up. Maybe he knows there's nothing he can do."

Forget him in this ecstasy.

At once, several of the Giants protested, prompted by their instinctive passion for
life. "What, abandoned his Creation? The Earth entire?" But their incredulity bypassed
Linden, leaving her hollow. Of *course* the Creator had turned his back. He had looked
into her and seen what she was. Now he was done with her.

She was done with him as well. He had failed her. Ignoring the Giants, and the
chagrin among the Ramen, she tried by force of will to keep Covenant from slipping
away again.

"What about Jeremiah? You know everything that's happened since Lord Foul
killed you. Maybe you know everything that's ever happened. Lord Foul touched him
before I came here with you ten years ago. According to Roger, the Despiser owns him."

He's belonged *to Foul for years.* And the Mahdoubt had said, *a-Jeroth's mark was placed
upon the boy when he was yet a small child*— "Is that true?"

Had Jeremiah invited the *croyel* to possess him? Was there no hope for him at all?

For a moment, Covenant ducked his head as if Linden had shamed him. But he did
not fall. When he looked at her again, his mouth was twisted with anger, and his eyes
caught a combative gleam from the *krill*.

"I did what I could," he said as if the words were stones, heavy and undeniable,
"without risking the Arch. Maybe it was enough. If it wasn't, we'll *make* it enough.
That boy doesn't deserve what's happened to him. Hellfire, Linden, he was practically
a *toddler*. I refuse to believe he made choices then that can't be undone."

Briefly Covenant glanced away as if he were gazing into unfathomable distances.

"There are things the Despiser doesn't understand. He can't. No matter how clever he is. Like the Creator—like all of us—he has his blind side. Some things he just doesn't see."

Then his attention returned to Linden so fiercely that she seemed to feel his hands holding the sides of her face, compelling her, although he had not stepped toward her or raised his arms.

"Listen to me, Linden. None of the love you lavished on your son was wasted. That isn't even possible. Until we know more about what's happened to him, just trust yourself."

Abruptly Stave spoke. In a peremptory tone, as though he had missed an opportunity and meant to recapture it, he asked, "Ur-Lord, is it conceivable that the Creator has forsaken the Chosen and the Earth because he is no longer needed?"

A wince of surprise or regret twisted one side of Covenant's mouth. "Ah, hell," he sighed. "Why not? Anything is conceivable. At least until the Worm gets enough to eat."

"On that matter, Giantfriend," put in Rime Coldspray before Stave could continue, "have we been given sooth? Is the time remaining to us measured in days rather than in hours?"

Covenant nodded with a hint of his earlier abstraction. "Berek's right. Creating realities takes time. So does destroying them. I'm not part of the Arch anymore. I can't protect it. But that doesn't mean it's going to crumble while we stand here talking about it."

Stave did not waver. "Ur-Lord," he insisted, "is it conceivable that the Creator's abandonment benefits his creation?"

Covenant scowled at the outcast Master. "Think that if you want. Hell, believe it if you can. It's as good as any other explanation. I can't imagine what the benefit might be. But maybe that's just one of *my* blind spots." Harshly he concluded, "Anything is better than giving up."

With his lone eye and his impassive mien, Stave regarded Covenant as though the Unbeliever had made his point for him.

It is ever thus. Obliquely Linden remembered Mahrtiir's advice before she and her friends had left the wreckage of First Woodhelven. *Attempts must be made, even when there can be no hope. The alternative is despair. And betimes some wonder is wrought to redeem us.*

Apparently Stave shared the Manethrall's conviction.

There are always surprises. And sometimes they help.

Linden still had one last attempt to make. And Stave would support her. The Ramen would do the same. As would Liand.

She was less sure of the Giants; but she suspected that their love of children would sway them. As for the Humbled— They would argue against her, of course. But Covenant had already commanded them to *choose her*.

If she could, she meant to spare all of them the risk of her final gamble.

"In that case," she said, pleading for Covenant's permission; for a confirmation of his approval, "I should go finish talking to the Harrow."

She had more questions for Covenant; many more. But she lacked the courage to ask them. If she had simply allowed herself to think them in words—Do you really believe that I'm still capable of something good? or, Do you still love me?—she might have fallen to her knees. Any answer, any answer at all, would have been more than she could bear.

Before Covenant could respond, however—before she could turn away with or without his reassurance—Galt intervened.

"Unbeliever, you must not permit this." His voice was a blade sharpened by uncharacteristic passion. "To rouse the Worm was Desecration. To go now in search of her son, trusting to the word of this Insequent, is rank madness."

Covenant's emanations were vivid to Linden's percipience: he stood on the verge of another drop. An abyss yawned at the feet of his mind. She held her breath, expecting him to fall. But something in Galt's tone, or in Covenant's own determination, kept him from stumbling over the edge.

"It makes more sense than you think." His asperity dulled the edge of Galt's demand. "We aren't strong enough. I'm not all here. Kevin's Dirt limits what she can do with her Staff. And she doesn't really know how to use that ring. I wanted her to have it, but still— She isn't its rightful wielder.

"As matters stand, we don't have enough power." His halfhand displayed its emptiness. "Or the right kind of power. We can't stop the Worm. While we're trying to figure out how to save the Earth—if that's even possible—we might as well do something useful."

"Unbeliever," Galt protested. "Ur-Lord. Ringthane. You must hear me. Linden Avery's purpose is intolerable. She will surrender all hope and receive only her son— and that only if the word of this Insequent is worthy of trust. We have learned an unwonted esteem for the Mahdoubt, but the Insequent as a race are as contemptuous and cruel as the *Elohim*. They serve only themselves. And when the Harrow has gained white gold and the Staff of Law, he will possess less efficacy against the Worm than Linden Avery now holds, for he is the rightful wielder of neither.

"Surely there are other deeds within our strength which may serve to forestall the outcome of this Desecration. You must not permit—"

Covenant tried to hold—Linden saw that—but he failed. While she watched, he toppled into himself; slid down an inner slope. For reasons that no longer made sense, he waved her away, sending her toward the Harrow. Then he draped an arm over Galt's shoulders and turned the Master in the opposite direction.

"Listen," he said lightly, casually, as if he were gliding on oil, "did I ever tell you how the Theomach replaced the *Elohim* who guarded the One Tree? I can't remember what we've talked about. The whole world is stories. Maybe I haven't told them all.

"They didn't call him the Guardian. He was the Appointed. The *first* Appointed. He used a different form every time somebody approached the Tree. He used different names. But he always stood in the way. Until the Theomach out-did him."

In spite of his tone, Covenant's manner seemed disjointed, confused by falling, as he drew the three Humbled with him. Yet somehow he contrived to insist; or the Masters felt required to attend him.

Indirectly he spared Linden the contention of the Humbled as she forced herself to approach the Harrow.

At once, Stave and Liand took positions at her shoulders. Mahrtiir instructed his Cords to watch over Covenant with Galt, Clyme, and Branl: then the Manethrall followed her. After an instant of hesitation, the Ironhand sent a few of her Swordmainnir to hear whatever Covenant might reveal to the Humbled. With the rest of her comrades, Coldspray joined Mahrtiir.

The Harrow waited where Linden had left him, as sure of himself as a plinth of marble. His chlamys hung at a jaunty angle from his shoulders. In the glow of the *krill*, the umber beads of his doublet looked strangely moist, as though they oozed damp theurgies. His trim beard jutted avidly.

Tense with fright or ire, as if the beast knew what Linden's approach signified, the Harrow's destrier watched her askance. But he had trained his mount well: it stood its ground.

"Lady." The Insequent inclined his head with grave mockery. "On such a night, I am tolerant of interruption. Yet the hour is late, and the time has come for my long labors to bear their intended fruit. There can be no more apt occasion for my triumph than *Banas Nimoram* and the rousing of the Worm. The *Elohim* has fled, bearing her arrogance and self-woe to the distant reaches of the Earth. We must now speak of your son."

Linden remembered too well the deep sound of his voice; his fertile taunts. *There is a service which I am able to perform for you, and which you will not obtain from any other living being.* She ached to defy his scorn. But she had created a crisis for herself, and her friends, and Thomas Covenant—for the entire living world—to which she had no answer except the most extreme sacrifice. And she had already made her decision. She recognized the danger. But she did not know—

"That's right." She glared up at him as if she could still bargain with him as an equal, in spite of her dismay. "My son. Here's the problem. You want a lot, but you don't give anything. You claim that you know where he is. You claim that you can take me to him. But you haven't offered me even one reason to believe you. For all I know, this is just an elaborate charade. My God, Jeremiah is hidden from Esmer and the *Elohim*. As far as I know, Covenant can't locate him. How am I supposed to believe that you're the only one who knows where he is?

"How am I supposed to believe that you and no one else can help me get there?"

"You mistake me, lady." The Harrow chuckled softly. "I did not avow that no other being is able to discern his covert, though it is certain that the *mere*-son and the *Elohim* cannot. Nor have I claimed that no other being is able to convey you thither. I merely state absolutely that no other being can both discern his hiding place and transport you to him."

Before Linden could respond, Stave asked stiffly, "Other beings have knowledge of this covert? Name them, Insequent."

She expected the Harrow to refuse; but he did not. "The unnatural lore of the ur-viles and Waynhim is capable of much," he replied. "However, I will not translate their tongue for your edification. Nor will the *mere*-son, who fears them beyond measure. And he has deprived these Giants of the gift which once enabled them to comprehend the speech of such creatures.

"Lady," he added with a hint of glee, "you have no path except to accept my aid in exchange for those instruments of power which I covet."

"You're wrong," retorted Linden. "I can always refuse. In fact, that's my only sane path, since you still haven't given me a reason to believe you. Your whole attitude is inherently dishonest. Why should I just *trust* you?"

He smirked through his whiskers. "And must I therefore trust *you*? Must I convey you to your son in the fond hope that only then will you honor your own word? Lady, no. I have witnessed the extent of your folly. I will not assume that you are honorable merely because you wish me to do so."

His argument stopped Linden: she could not imagine a way to counter it. If she had been in his place, would she have trusted a person who had violated the essence of Law in order to drag Covenant out of his place in the Arch of Time? She wanted to believe that she would have found room in her heart for any parent who sought to save a child; that she would not have been as self-absorbed and uncaring as the Harrow. But she had already demonstrated that she was capable of defying every consequence in order to get what she wanted. She remained ready to take any risk for Jeremiah's sake; but she could not pretend that she was morally superior to the Harrow. His distrust was as valid as hers; as entirely justified.

Esmer had once said, *That which appears evil need not have been so from the beginning, and need not remain so until the end.* She wanted to say the same about herself, but she knew that the Harrow would only laugh.

"Then think of something," she murmured weakly. "We're at an impasse. Find a way out."

Surely she could not surrender Covenant's ring and her Staff without *some* assurance—?

"Lady," he answered without hesitation, "that I speak sooth is confirmed by who and what I am. The word of any Insequent is as precious as wealth. We do not speak falsehood. It demeans knowledge, which we revere. Condoning lies, I would cease to be who I am.

"I grant, however, that you do not know me. For you, my word cannot suffice. Therefore I will pledge my oath. You have cause to trust that such an oath will bind me. As I have previously forsworn my purpose against your mind and spirit and flesh, so will I swear now that I am certain of your son's covert, and that I am able to convey you to him. In exchange for your instruments of power, I will further avow that when I have effected your reunion with your child, I will return you wheresoever you desire. To reassure you, I once again adjure all of the Insequent to heed me. If I do not abide by this second oath, as I have honored the first, I pray that the vengeance of my people upon me will be both cruel and prolonged."

Linden did her best to meet the empty blackness of his gaze. "That's it?" Her voice was little more than a whisper of dried leaves gusting over barren ground. She had difficulty swallowing. "That's your oath?"

The radiance of the *krill* lit every line of his face, but could not touch the depths of his eyes.

"It is," he assented, "if we are in agreement." Mirth stirred beneath the surface of his tone. "Place into my hands the white gold ring and the Staff of Law, and I will abide by my vow precisely as I have pronounced it. Refuse, and I will be bound by no oath but that which the Mahdoubt wrested from me, at the cost of her mind and use and life."

According to the Theomach, the Insequent were *seldom petty* when their desires opposed those of the *Elohim*.

Sighing, Linden reached up to pull the chain of Covenant's ring over her head.

"Linden," murmured Liand anxiously, "this troubles me. In one matter, I concur with the Humbled. The Harrow cannot equal the puissance which you have won from both your Staff and the white ring. Is it not certain that the hope of the Land, dim though it may be, will dwindle if his wishes are granted?"

"Stonedownor—" Mahrtiir began gruffly.

Liand refused to be interrupted. "And is it not certain also that the fell creature which you have named the *croyel* retains possession of your son? How will you win his freedom if you wield neither Earthpower nor wild magic?"

"Liand," said the Manethrall more firmly, "desist. Every friend of the Ringthane shares your apprehensions. Yet this choice is hers, not ours. And there lives no parent among the Ramen who would not choose as she does. Only the opposition of the

Ranyhyn would suffice to deter us—and behold!" He gestured around the vale. "They have departed. By this token is their faith in the Ringthane confirmed."

The absence of the horses did not concern Linden. They would return when they were called; or when they were needed.

"She has followed her heart to our present straits," Mahrtiir concluded. "If she does not continue to do so, all that she has hazarded and lost will come to naught."

At the Manethrall's command, Liand subsided; and Rime Coldspray nodded her approval. If Stave agreed with either Liand or Mahrtiir, he did not say so. But he had sons among the Masters, sons who had participated in casting him out of their mental communion. Nevertheless he had said of them—and of all the children of the *Haruchai*—that *They are born to strength, and it is their birthright to remain who they are.*

Had Covenant not told Linden long ago that Lord Foul could not gain his ends through decisions like the one she made here?

She held Covenant's wedding band in her left hand as though she were testing the weight of her surrender. The fingers of her right gripped the Staff as they had under *Melenkurion* Skyweir; as if they were still cramped and sealed by pain and blood.

Extending her arms toward the Harrow cost her an effort so severe that she feared it might burst a vessel in her brain. His grin stretched into a shape that resembled madness or murder as he reached out to accept the instruments he craved.

A new voice stopped him: a voice that she had never heard before. Its pitch lay midway between the Theomach's light assurance and the Harrow's ripe bass, and it lisped slightly, giving each word a foppish timbre.

"For this I have come."

The Harrow jerked up his head, already glaring in surprise and indignation. Snatching at their weapons, the Giants and Mahrtiir whirled to face the newcomer. While Liand stared, Stave adjusted his protective posture at Linden's shoulder.

She dropped her arms as though her burdens had become too heavy for her. Then she turned.

Into the vale from the north rode a stranger. He was mounted on a mangy, shovel-headed horse so spavined that it should have been unable to support his improbable bulk. In spite of its gaunt ribs and sagging spine, however, the beast looked irascible enough to be a mule; and it bore its rider with an air of sideways malice, as if it had been waiting indefinitely for its chance to do him harm.

But Linden spared only a glance for the horse. Its rider compelled her attention.

Her first impression was one of grotesque corpulence; but then she saw that his apparent size was exaggerated by his apparel. He seemed to be clad entirely in ribbands: thousands of them in every conceivable hue and texture. Garish in the *krill*'s light, they fluttered and streamed from his head, his limbs, his torso, as if they were constantly unwinding themselves without ever quite flying loose. Independent of the night's stillness and his own movements, they flapped in all directions, surrounding him like a penumbra of wind-tugged cloth; a personal effluvium of cerise and incarnadine and carbuncle, ecru and ivory, turquoise and viridian and azure, blue as deep as velvet, yellows ranging from the fulvous and the sulphuric to the palest gold.

His hands were bare: they grappled with the reins of his mount as if he had never ridden before. And his face also was exposed, revealing eyes wide with perpetual astonishment, a nose like a luxuriant toadstool, and lips too plump for any explanation except gluttony. Wrapped in waving layers, several chins may have wobbled below his jaw, shaken by the lurching gait of his mount; but his garb muffled such details.

A cacophony of ribbands and colors, he approached the group around Linden and the Harrow until he was near enough to be struck down by one of the Swordmainnir. Then he hauled his recalcitrant horse to a halt.

"*You*," spat the Harrow in obvious recognition. "Was the Mahdoubt's doom insufficient to warn away your folly? Do you covet the decline of your beloved flesh to carrion?"

The newcomer ignored the Harrow. Facing Linden past Stave and two of the Giants, he twirled his arms and ribbands, apparently bowing. "Lady," he announced in a tone like his fat, "by good chance I am timely arrived." His lisp detracted from his attempt at dignity. "There are matters which must be considered ere your bargain with the Harrow is sealed."

While she stared at him, he continued, "With your gracious consent, I will make myself known to you." Holding up one finger as if to test the direction of a breeze which she could not feel—or perhaps to warn the Harrow against speaking—he said, "I am the Ardent. As you have doubtless surmised, I am of the Insequent. Indeed, I share some slight kinship with the Harrow. Unlike him, however, I am an acolyte—if such as the Insequent may be said to have acolytes—of the Mahdoubt. I lack both her kindliness and her arduous knowledge of Time. Also I lay no claim to her manifest valor. Yet I esteem her example highly. So great is my esteem, indeed, that I follow her as I would a guide, though even the most casual glance at my person will discern that I require no guidance."

His otiose self-confidence made him sound ludicrous.

"That, at least," grumbled the Harrow, "is a form of sooth. Prepare a feast within a hundred leagues of the Ardent, and you will find him at table ere the first course is presented."

In response, the Ardent waggled his finger, now clearly cautioning the Harrow to silence—and clearly expecting the Harrow to comply.

"Lady," he added, "you may regard me as a friend." Each word was a dollop of cream. "Doubtless there are those who deem that the Insequent know nothing of friendship. And doubtless they have cause for their conviction. You, however, will think otherwise.

You have known the discretion and regard of the Theomach, he whom the Harrow seeks to displace as the greatest of our kind. Also you have been served as both friend and ally by the Mahdoubt. You will grant me leave to demonstrate that my nature is as benignant as hers, though her wisdom and fortitude elude me."

Liand put his hand on Linden's arm, but did not ask for her attention. Rather he seemed to touch her to remind himself that he and she, at least, remained solid; that they had not wandered inadvertently into the illimitable possibilities of dreams—

"Here is a wonder indeed," exclaimed Rime Coldspray softly. "Had we any prospect of continued life, we would hear such tales gladly wheresoever we sailed—aye, and count ourselves fortunate to do so."

"Enough!" demanded the Harrow darkly. "Name your desires and depart, fatuous one. You cannot be madman enough to intend interference. Therefore your presence serves no purpose, and your words waste the hearing of them."

The Ardent did not deign to reply. Instead he flapped his upraised hand, and at once a long streamer extended itself from his habiliments toward the Harrow. The ribband had a niveous color as it fluttered away from the Ardent, but wafting it modulated to match the Harrow's dun-and-loam hues. Although it remained anchored among the rest of the Ardent's coverings, it lengthened quickly. And when it reached the Harrow, it began to wind around his head, floating nearer and nearer until it looked like it would soon cover and seal his face; his eyes or his mouth.

Reflexively Linden held her breath. Was it possible? Could the Ardent *suffocate* the Harrow? With a strip of *cloth*?

They were both men, as human as she was. Only their arcane studies gave them theurgy.

Liand's fingers dug into her arm. The Giants watched open-mouthed, as if they were torn between amusement and alarm.

For a moment, the Harrow slapped at the ribband furiously. But it evaded him, as illusive as a swarm of gnats. Abruptly he stopped swatting, dropped his hands to his doublet. His fingers began forming strange shapes on the ornaments of his garment.

"Paugh!" the Ardent snorted in plump disdain. "Rub not your beads at me. You deem yourself worthy to determine the fate of the Earth. Very well. I will speak to you while the lady strives to gather her wits."

Briefly his ribband twisted itself into a shape that mocked the Harrow. Then it withdrew to resume swaddling its wearer.

Assuming an air of lugubrious portent, the Ardent explained, "The Insequent are cognizant of your purpose. Also we perceive that the destruction of all things gathers against us. Indeed, some among us foretell that much depends upon the worth of your oath and the outcome of your desires. And many centuries of study have taught us that it is the nature of avarice to mislead. One who is driven by greed—as I acknowledge that I am—may speak sooth to disguise sooth. If you are permitted to do so, you may abide by your oath and yet betray the lady, for she cannot comprehend the omissions concealed within your words.

"Therefore I am come, bearing in my person the conjoined resolve of our kind. This in itself is of vast import, as I am. Heretofore no cause or exigency has lured the Insequent as a race from the solitary study and hunger which alone enables our multifarious accomplishments. Yet we crave life, as life itself craves continuance, and the utter termination of every desire and appetite has now been made imminent. If the Earth falls, no Insequent will remain to mourn its passing. For this reason, as we would for no lesser cause, we have set aside our solitude, that we may unite our intent in my person. I embody all that has made of our kind who we are.

"As sigil and emblem that I am the authorized emissary of the Insequent, I proffer this hint of my powers."

Around his head, ribbands twined and waved as if of their own volition, seeming to grow first longer and then shorter as they fluttered like the language of an obscure ritual. Limned in argence, they performed a florid masque. Then, before Linden—or the Harrow, apparently—could guess what this display might mean, the Harrow's destrier vanished between his legs.

Deprived of his mount, he fell heavily to the greensward; landed with an involuntary grunt and a bitter obscenity.

The laughter of the Giants stoked his anger as he sprang to his feet. Linden expected him to summon a counterattack of some kind. Instead of striking out, however, he merely adjusted his doublet, restored his chlamys to its insouciant angle across his shoulders. Although his aura fumed hotly, he seemed to see something in the Ardent's magicks that was invisible to Linden; something that compelled restraint.

Smiling down at his fellow Insequent, the Ardent stated, "We will in no way intrude upon your bargain with the lady, or upon your purposes thereafter. Indeed, I am instructed to assist them. The long strictures of our kind we will honor. Nevertheless I am come to impose this condition, that the lady herself must be the sole arbiter of the terms of your oath."

For an instant, the Harrow looked shocked. Then outrage darkened his features. He appeared to be mustering a curse as the Ardent insisted, "She alone will determine what is encompassed by your oath and what is not. Nor will we deem your oath fulfilled until she declares that she is content.

"Also," he proclaimed ostentatiously, "I will accompany you in the name of all those Insequent whom you have invoked. Doubtless you contemplate some escape from your oath, which I will prevent. And it may chance that you will require my aid."

Contradicting his florid manner, a haunted look darkened his gaze when he spoke of aid. But it was brief; gone almost as soon as Linden noticed it.

She blinked at the two men as if she were dazed. Too much had happened: she could not think clearly. —abide by your oath and yet betray— How was it possible that the Ardent's apprehensions made no sense to her? Her desire to redeem her son must have wider implications than she had realized. But she felt entirely unable to imagine what they were.

Abruptly Mahrtiir growled, "Have done, Insequent. The Ringthane has friends enough. Your pretense of concern conveys naught. Speak plainly or desist. Name the betrayal contemplated by the Harrow, that we may gauge the worth of your intent."

The Ardent inclined his head to acknowledge Mahrtiir. Unexpectedly grave, he replied, "Manethrall, I cannot. Think no ill of me when I observe that any effort to shape or guide the lady's deeds and choices will be seen—and seen rightly—as dire interference. My mission is to ensure the terms and fulfillment of the Harrow's oath, not to instruct the lady in their interpretation.

"Misliking the Harrow as I do, I would find no small joy in thwarting him. Have I not admitted that I, too, am prone to greed? But here I personify the united will of the Insequent. Any deviation from that resolve will breach the sacred prohibition which enables the Insequent to endure and prosper. Answering you, I will bring down my own destruction and accomplish only sorrow."

Linden had heard such reasoning before. Both the Theomach and the Mahdoubt, in their distinct fashions, had presented similar arguments.

When she understood that the Ardent was trying to walk a path as straight and strict as theirs—that his ambiguities were necessary to the singular ethics of the Insequent—she at last found her voice. Hardly knowing what she meant to say, she suggested unsteadily, "In that case, let's play fair. If the Harrow can't ride, you shouldn't sit there looking down on him."

Or on her.

The Harrow flashed her a glance that she could not read. The emptiness of his eyes swallowed the character of his reaction.

The Ardent surprised her again by emitting a loud guffaw. "Well said, lady. Doubtless you merit the Mahdoubt's regard, ill-considered though your many extravagances may appear to be. I am neither mightier nor less flawed than the Harrow. I have merely been elected to enact the will of the Insequent."

Laughing again, he sent out streamers of chartreuse and fuligin on all sides, bands interwoven with crimson and cerulean. They seemed to float independent of him, as though they might tug free at any moment. But he did not loose them—or they did not loose themselves. Instead, by some means that baffled Linden's senses, they caused his mount to disappear.

Unlike the Harrow, however, he did not fall. Cradled in ribbands, he drifted gently to the grass as if his bulk were as light as air.

Delighted by his display, the Giants laughed with him. Obviously pleased, the Ardent gazed up at them with the open wonder of a child. Flapping his arms, he caused his apparel to unfurl and cavort in a glad gambol.

Their momentary mirth did not touch Linden. But it gave her a chance to gather herself and think. While the Harrow ground his teeth, waiting in vexation for the laughter to subside, she tried to guess where the potential for betrayal might lie in his vow.

Peripherally she was aware of Covenant and his escort. Ignoring or avoiding her and the Insequent, he had walked the Humbled and their accompaniment of Giants and Ramen to the rim of the hollow. There, however, he turned and began to move slowly back toward the dead stump and Loric's *krill*. His manner still seemed disjointed, torn between understanding and bewilderment. He had not yet found his way back to the present.

Grasping at allusions, Linden asked Stave quietly, "What are they talking about?" With a nod, she indicated Covenant and the Masters. "Has Covenant explained the Theomach? Or the Insequent?"

Stave could still hear the mental communion of the *Haruchai*, although he had learned to close his own thoughts against them. In a low voice, he answered, "The ur-Lord does not speak of the Theomach. His offer to do so he appeared to forget when it had been uttered." He may have meant, When it had accomplished its purpose by distracting the Humbled. "Rather he rambles forward and back through the most ancient history of the *Haruchai*, relating tales which none have forgotten. The Giants appear gladdened to hear of unfamiliar events. Saying nothing, the Cords remain wary of the Humbled."

"Will they attack the Ardent?" asked Linden. "Galt and the others?"

Long days ago, they had assailed the Harrow without warning.

"Not while the Unbeliever holds their allegiance. They see no future for the Land which does not rest with Thomas Covenant."

Linden sighed to herself. She also saw no future— But that was not her concern. She had other needs to meet.

Once again, she faced the challenge of the Harrow.

—it is the nature of avarice to mislead. She could not guess what secret intentions might lie hidden beneath the surface of his oath. Nevertheless she was sure of one question that he had not answered.

"All right," she murmured when silence had fallen around her. Staring into the Harrow's blackness, she said, "I know what I've offered you. I know what you've sworn to do if I keep my end of the bargain. But I don't know why you still care. The Worm of the World's End is coming." How had he known that she would rouse the Worm? "What can you possibly gain with my Staff and Covenant's ring?" He had conceived his desires before the silence of Covenant's spectre had provoked her determination to attempt Covenant's resurrection. "You aren't crazy enough to think they can protect you when the Arch collapses. But you've avoided telling me what you think you can accomplish.

"You said that Infelice is wrong about 'the Earth's ruin.'" —*no doom is inevitable*— "I want you to explain what you're going to do once we've rescued Jeremiah."

"I will not," the Harrow retorted at once. "The Ardent's assertions are specious. My purposes are my own. I will not speak of them to those whose aid I do not require."

Before Linden could muster a response, the Ardent put in, "Doubtless you desire to say nothing of such matters. I must assure you, however, that you will not remain silent." He sounded supremely confident—and secretly fearful. "You cannot be blind to the might with which I have been entrusted. The lady, and only the lady, will interpret the terms of your vow. That benison has been vouchsafed to her, in answer to your greed. You will satisfy her, or you will quell your hunger for her instruments of power."

"If I do so," the Harrow protested hotly, "the Earth entire must perish."

"Perchance," admitted the Ardent. He seemed untroubled by the prospect. "Or perchance you are mistaken. My concern—and the forces which I am able to invoke—pertain chiefly to the lady's contentment in her dealings with you."

"I will *not*—" the Harrow tried to insist.

The Ardent interrupted him. With a troubled smile, the beribboned Insequent asked, "Must I demonstrate the puissance invested in me?"

Linden sensed a struggle between the two men, although no aspect of their contest was visible to ordinary sight. The Ardent continued smiling while the Harrow scowled. If they tested each other, they did so in a way that resembled the Mahdoubt's eerie battle with the Harrow. Linden half expected one or the other of them to flicker and fade—

Behind her, Covenant had reached the *krill*. Now he walked around it, studying it as he talked softly to the Humbled, the Swordmainnir, the Cords. As ever, Linden could not discern the emotions of the *Haruchai*; but she felt Bhapa's growing bafflement, Pahni's yearning to stand with Liand. The Giants listened with perplexed attention, as if Covenant spoke a foreign tongue.

Abruptly the Harrow shrugged. He betrayed no sign of strain as he shifted his attention from the Ardent to Linden.

Without preamble, he announced, "Infelice conceives that I crave your son's supernal gifts for my own use. In this her sight is clear."

In an instant, everything changed for Linden. Shock like a brush of flame burned her skin from head to foot: realities seemed to reel and veer: the bottom fell out of her heart, into the Harrow's eyes. Gasping for breath, she tried to cry out, You *bastard*, you son of a *bitch!* But she failed. *You want to use him? After everything that he's already suffered?*

The Ardent beamed at her as though the outcome of his insistence pleased him.

"Linden!" protested Liand. "Your *son?* Is this Insequent as heartless as he names the *Elohim?*"

Oh, God. With an effort, Linden forced herself to breathe; fought for steadiness. She had not yet surrendered her powers: she could still make choices.

She alone will determine what is encompassed by your oath and what is not.

The Ardent had implied that he would prevent the Harrow from doing anything to Jeremiah without her consent. She could afford to hear the rest of the Harrow's self-justification.

That thought or hope or blind wish enabled her to demand through her teeth, "Go on."

"Yet Infelice is ignorant," the Harrow explained, "of the precise use which I desire. She imagines—and dreads—that my intent resembles the Vizard's. This is the 'eternal loss' which she abhors. She deems that I desire a prison for the *Elohim*—and that I am witless enough to believe that the Worm will withdraw from harm if it is deprived of its natural repast.

"But I am not such a fool. The *Elohim* are little more than Earthpower made sapient. If the Worm cannot feed upon them, it will devour other sustenance until it attains the culmination of its hunger. In this, it resembles any beast. To imprison the *Elohim* will gratify my pride. It will gain naught else.

"Lady—" The Harrow hesitated briefly; glanced at the Ardent. Then he shrugged again. "It is my intent to wield both Law and wild magic in your son's service. With such forces at his command, he will possess might sufficient to devise a gaol into which the Worm must enter, and from which it will be unable to emerge. This you cannot accomplish in my stead. The reasons are many. I will cite two.

"First, you lack my knowledge of such theurgies. Regardless of your own desires and extremity, you do not comprehend the precise form of aid which your son will require. You cannot be guided by insights which you have not earned. Through your intervention, your son's failure will be assured.

"Second, he alone is not adequately lorewise to fashion the gaol I envision. He has not been granted centuries of study in which to perfect his gifts. Therefore I must rely upon the connivance of the *croyel.*"

Linden understood him immediately; involuntarily. The *croyel:* the dire succubus which she had last seen feeding on Jeremiah's neck, draining his life and mind while it gave him power. Swift as instinct, she grasped that the Harrow meant to leave *her son* under that vicious being's control. The dark Insequent needed more than Earthpower and wild magic and Jeremiah's talent for constructs: he needed the *croyel*'s specific powers and knowledge.

The mere idea filled her with fury. For Jeremiah's sake, she wanted to strike the Harrow down, stamp out his life. And for Jeremiah's sake, she restrained herself. She believed the Harrow's claim that he alone could take her to her son.

"Will you permit this?" Liand flung his own anger and dismay at the Ardent. "Is this the measure of your kind, that you are careless of a child's pain? Was the Mahdoubt alone in her compassion?"

The Ardent twisted his features into an expression of distress. His ribbands spun ambiguously about him, signaling emotions that meant nothing to Linden. But he did not answer.

She alone will determine—Nor will we deem your oath fulfilled—

"You still aren't telling the truth," she insisted. "You've wanted my power ever since we first met. You wanted Jeremiah and the *croyel*. But you didn't know that I was going to wake up the Worm. You couldn't. How am I supposed to trust you now?"

The Harrow gave her a glare like an abyss. "Lady, I repeat that the Insequent do not utter falsehood. The awakening of the Worm was not necessary to my desires. For one with the knowledge which I possess, and with the powers which I will hold, the Worm sleeping would have been as readily ensnared as the Worm roused. Indeed, it was my first intent to deprive the *Elohim* of all purpose and worth forever, as well as to preserve the Earth from ruin, by ensuring that the Worm *could not* be roused.

"That is no longer possible. Therefore I have adjusted my intent to accommodate the extravagance of your folly."

"All right." Linden did not waste herself arguing with him. "Go on," she repeated bitterly. "Finish this."

The Harrow sighed; but he did not refuse.

"The *croyel*'s noisome magicks and cunning are essential to the achievement of my aim. This you will not permit while you remain able to prevent it. Thus it is necessary to the salvation of the Earth that *I* possess your Staff and the white gold ring, and that *you* do not."

Linden looked to the Ardent. "And if that wasn't my original understanding of our agreement? What happens then?"

Bands of color wafted up and down the Ardent's form, signing certainty, masking alarm. "Then your will prevails, lady. The Harrow must abandon his purpose for your son, or he must set aside his craving for your instruments of power. The Insequent as a people will countenance no other outcome."

Stave glanced at the group around Covenant and the *krill*. Then he turned his gaze on the Harrow.

"There is another matter to consider also. If Infelice has spoken sooth in aught, we must recognize that life cannot endure without death. The Worm of the World's End is necessary to the Earth's continuance. If your vaunt succeeds, and the Worm is imprisoned, will not this habitation cease to sustain life? Will not the whole of this creation become barrenness?"

"Well said, *Haruchai*," muttered Mahrtiir. "The Harrow is derangement made flesh. His greed will hasten every destruction."

Linden heard Stave; but her attention was fixed on the Harrow. Her heart thudded in her chest as though it had reached the limit of its endurance. If he called her bluff by recanting his claims—if he mastered his cupidity—Jeremiah would be lost to her. He would die alone in torment when the Earth perished.

"I'm waiting." Her every word trembled. The Harrow had not acknowledged Stave's query. "What's it going to be?"

If he dared her to find Jeremiah without his help, she would surely crumble.

For a moment, he addressed the Ardent rather than Linden. "You demand much," he said: the deep snarl of a beast. "Three things I sought from the lady. One I have already eschewed. It was denied to me by the Mahdoubt's unconscionable obstruction. Do you truly dream that I will surrender still more of my desires?"

Then he replied to Linden. Harsh as acid, he said, "The conjoined resolve of the Insequent suffices to command me. Lady, I will honor your reading of my oath. My purpose for your son I set aside—for the present.

"Yet yours," he promised fiercely, "will be an empty triumph. You evade my intent to no avail. When we have retrieved your son, the only powers which offer hope to the Earth will remain in my possession. You will strive as you may to free your son from the *croyel*. In that endeavor, I did *not* vow my aid. And when you have failed, as you must—when you stand powerless before the world's doom—I will inquire if by chance you have reconsidered the terms of your 'contentment.'"

A moment later, he added with less anger, "The doom-saying of the *Elohim* does not merit credence. They care only for their own lives. If the Worm is imprisoned, they may indeed cease to exist. But the Earth and all other life continued while the Worm slumbered. If it is imprisoned, they will endure. I do not propose to *slay* it."

Linden might have asked the Ardent, Is that true? But she was trembling too hard to speak. Now, she told herself. Do it now. Before he changes his mind.

The time had come for absolute answers. She was going to give Covenant's wedding band and the Staff of Law to the Harrow. As soon as she could make her muscles obey her—

Infelice had told her, *Your remorse will surpass your strength to bear it*. She did not doubt the *Elohim*. Nevertheless she was prepared to bear any burden in order to save her son. Long ago, she had recognized that even the Land and Thomas Covenant did not mean as much to her as Jeremiah.

And Covenant had said, *I think we should do this Linden's way*. He may have understood the implications of his support.

"All right." She could not yet control her voice, but she did not let her weakness stop her. "I'm not ready to leave. There are still a few things that I have to do. But I want to make this bargain," bind the Harrow to his word, "while the Ardent is here to keep you honest."

Nothing relieved the darkness of the Harrow's gaze. Perhaps nothing could. But his attention sharpened suddenly: every line of his elegant form became vivid. His aura was a blaze of vindicated avarice.

"Linden?" Liand murmured in alarm. "Ringthane," asked the Manethrall, "are you certain?" But they were not trying to dissuade her. They were only cautioning her. In spite of everything, they believed in her—

Stave was *Haruchai*: she could not sense the character of his emotions. Nevertheless she trusted that he would not interfere—and that he would warn her if the Humbled came to stop her.

They must have been aware of her. Yet somehow Covenant's concentration on the *krill* held them back.

With unwonted anxiety, Rime Coldspray said, "I mislike this course. Linden Avery, I have named you Giantfriend. We will not oppose you. But I fear that you sail seas as hurtful and chartless as the Soulbiter, where every heading brings despair."

Linden ached for her friends. But there was nothing that she could say to reassure them. She feared as many things as they did, and with more reason. She knew her own inadequacy better than they could.

Deliberately she took a last step toward the Harrow.

Unable to quash the tremors that undermined her strength, she tried to lift both of her arms at the same time; tried and failed. Covenant's ring was closed in her left hand: from her fist dangled the chain which for ten years had carried her only reminder of his love. Her right gripped desperation around the Staff of Law. For one more moment, she hesitated, torn between self-imposed bereavements.

Mere days or entire lifetimes ago, she had refused the ring to Roger Covenant even though she had believed that he was his father. Now, shivering as if she were feverish, she offered Covenant's wedding band to the Harrow.

He snatched at the chain; took the ring from her like a man who feared that she would change her mind.

Releasing the Staff required a greater effort, not because Covenant's ring had less emotional weight, but because the Staff was *hers*. With it, she had effaced *caesures*; mended wounds; unmade the Sunbane. She had transformed the pure wood to blackness in battle. Caerroil Wildwood himself had given her his gift of runes.

In dreams, Covenant had told her that she needed her Staff.

Unclosing her fingers was a fundamental abnegation. She felt that she was selling her soul; defying the necessity of freedom. Voluntarily giving up her right to choose. She could not have abandoned so much of herself for any cause except Jeremiah.

That boy doesn't deserve what's happened to him.

Then she had to avert her eyes. The Harrow's glee as he grasped the Staff and held it high, brandishing it and Covenant's ring like trophies, was too savage to be borne.

"Behold, my people!" he shouted at the stars. "Witness and tremble! Soon I will show myself the greatest of all Insequent, the greatest who has ever lived!"

If she had watched him, she might have lost heart altogether.

Her companions seemed unable to speak. They had not shared her visions. To them, the idea that she had roused the Worm must have felt vaguely unreal; impossible to imagine. But even Liand, the least experienced and least informed of her friends, understood the magnitude of her surrender to the Harrow.

A short distance away, the Ardent's ribbands wavered aimlessly, as if he sought to conceal a private terror.

Perhaps the thought that without power she could no longer be held responsible for the world's doom should have allowed her a measure of relief; but it did not. Instead she felt fatally weakened, as if she had dealt herself a wound too grievous to survive.

4.

After Unwisdom

Linden Avery wanted to sit down on the benign grass and cover her face. She was full of shame, and had no right to it. In giving the Harrow what he wanted, if not in wrenching Thomas Covenant out of the Arch of Time, she had known what she was doing. She had made her choice deliberately. She could not excuse herself with blame.

Help me? she wanted to ask, although she hardly knew who might remain able or willing to aid her. Please?

You have companions, Chosen, who have not faltered in your service. If you must have counsel, require it of them.

Among them, only Liand retained any theurgy—and she had ignored his advice. She had not heeded any of her friends.

Too diminished to continue standing in front of the Harrow, Linden walked hesitantly toward Covenant. For the moment, at least, he had become a lesser pain, in spite of his uncontrollable lapses and his leprosy.

And he would be safe in Andelain—all of her companions would be safe—when the Harrow took her away. While Loric's *krill* reflected wild magic from Joan's ring, the Wraiths could refuse any evil. Even Kastenessen and the *skurj*, even Roger and Esmer, were precluded from bearing their malice among the Hills.

Nevertheless such things did not comfort her. The emptiness of her hands left her vulnerable in more ways than she could count. She was acutely conscious of the floundering dismay with which her friends followed her away from the Harrow. The bullet hole in her shirt had no significance now that the red flannel did not cover Covenant's wedding band. Instead the wound of her death, like the strip that she had torn from the fabric for the Mahdoubt's gown, and the small rents plucked by twigs and branches, merely made her look as tattered as her spirit.

In contrast, the grass stains on her jeans had never felt so fatal. They dragged at her steps like omens or arcane stigmata.

She had nothing to hold on to except Jeremiah's crumpled racecar deep in her pocket. It was her only defense. Her son needed her. She did not know another way to save him.

In the bottom of the hollow, Covenant still paced slowly around the radiance of the *krill*, studying it as if it had the capacity to anchor him somewhere in time, if only he could discover how to use it. As he moved, he spoke in a low voice; delivered a steady monologue that seemed to serve no purpose except to occupy his companions.

He may have been striving to retain as many of his splintered memories as he could.

The Humbled, Pahni and Bhapa, and three or four Giants stood in a loose circle that encompassed Covenant and the charred stump of Caer-Caveral's corpse. The attitudes of the Giants and the Cords conveyed the impression that they had given up trying to find a coherent—or pertinent—narrative in Covenant's musings. The blank stoicism of the Humbled concealed the character of their attention; but they appeared to be waiting for the ur-Lord, the Unbeliever, to become the man he had once been.

Belatedly Linden realized that the Humbled had no reason to assail her now. If they wished to prevent any further misuse of Earthpower and wild magic, they would have to battle the Harrow, who had already demonstrated that he was proof against them. And against Branl, Galt, and Clyme, the Ardent might side with his fellow Insequent. Linden could not imagine what use the Ardent might make of his ribbands, or his other magicks; but she did not doubt that it would be effective. In spite of his lisp

and his corpulence, he had convinced her that he did indeed wield enhanced powers, for good or ill. The Harrow would not have acceded to the Ardent's conditions
otherwise.

Yearning wordlessly for some further reassurance from the man whom she had
most harmed, Linden studied Covenant closely. She would need his attention soon,
before she exhausted the Harrow's patience—or the Ardent's. She wanted to believe
that she was still capable of a few undestructive decisions; that she could at least ensure
the immediate safety of her friends before she went with the Harrow to watch the
croyel swallow blood from Jeremiah's neck. But she feared that her bargain with the
Harrow had cost her the last of her credibility. Even Liand, Stave, and Mahrtiir might
not heed her now, if Covenant did not take her part.

He would not be able to help her if he could not find his way out of the faults that
riddled his mind. But he was still lost in the ramifications of time. He seemed to drift,
rudderless, through a Sargasso of memories which were of no use to him.

And his leprosy— Ah, God. His leprosy was growing worse, exacerbated by the pall
of Kevin's Dirt. Here in Andelain, the effects of that dire fug were muted. Perhaps the
Wraiths blunted the evil which Kastenessen, Esmer, and *moksha* Raver had inflicted
upon the Upper Land. Nevertheless Kevin's Dirt remained: Linden tasted it when
she peered up at the stars and the night sky. Already Covenant's hands and feet were
almost entirely numb. If his condition continued to deteriorate, it was only a matter of
time until his sight began to fail.

He moved awkwardly, as though he had lost or forgotten precise control over his
muscles. Yet he seemed unaware of his ailment. Instead his attention was focused on
the *krill*—or on the unpredictable slippage of his thoughts.

"Someone," he remarked as if this idea followed from what he had been saying. "I
forget who. I want to think it was Mhoram, but it may have been Berek. When he was
rallying the scraps of his army after he came back from Mount Thunder.

"He said—" Covenant paused; closed his eyes for a moment. Frowning at the effort
of coherent recall, he recited, "'There is no doom so black or deep that courage and
clear sight may not find another truth beyond it.'" Then he looked at Clyme, Galt, and
Branl in turn. "Does that make sense to you? It should. But if it doesn't—"

Stiffly he started walking again, pacing his circle around Loric's *krill* as if he sought
to circumscribe his own confusion; contain it somehow. "It's my fault, really. I asked
you to protect Revelstone, but I wasn't clear. No one can blame *you* if they don't
like how you kept your promise. I didn't tell you I wanted you to protect what Revelstone *means*."

He seemed to think that the Masters—like Linden—might crave his absolution.
Against every obstacle, he struggled to keep faith with the deeds and necessities which
had brought the Land to its last crisis.

While Covenant talked, Liand approached Mahrtiir. Softly the Stonedownor asked, "Manethrall, would it not be well to send Bhapa and Pahni in search of hurt-loam? Surely some may be found among Andelain's riches of health and wonder. I know not whether Thomas Covenant's mind may be healed—or whether, as Linden has averred, the attempt would be unwise. Yet the strange corruption which gnaws at his flesh—"

"No!" With an almost audible jolt, Covenant's awareness recovered its focus. Suddenly he was *present*, as vivid as a seer. Wheeling, he faced Liand and Mahrtiir. "No hurtloam," he said sharply. "I don't expect you to understand. But I *need* this." He brandished his hands. "I need to be numb. It doesn't just make me who I am. It makes me who I *can* be."

Before the Manethrall or the Stonedownor could respond, Covenant strode around the dead stump toward Liand. But he did not advance on her. As soon as he stood between her and the shining dagger, he stopped.

She, too, stopped—helplessly, as if he had commanded a distance between them. With Stave at her shoulder and the troubled bulk of the Giants at her back, she waited to hear what he would say. She did not know how to speak first; to ask for his succor. Her needs were a crowding throng, so many that she could hardly name them.

The light of the *krill* cast his features into shadow. She could not distinguish his expression. The scar on his forehead was a pale crease across his thoughts.

"Linden." Limned in argent, he spoke as if her name twisted his heart. "I'm sorry. I should have told you sooner." His tone accused himself. "If I could have held on to my mind."

There he appeared to slip, distracted by some errant recollection. "I did practically the same thing myself once. The Land needed me, and I turned my back. We've talked about that. I meant to remind you." His manner suggested that he was trying to say too many different things at once. Linden felt his struggle to organize his thoughts. "Mhoram urged me not to worry about it. He wanted me to know there are some motives that simply *can't* serve Lord Foul. No matter how the Despiser squirms, he can't twist them to give him what he wants."

Mistaken though it may be, no act of love and horror—or indeed of self-repudiation—is potent to grant the Despiser his desires. He may be freed only by one who is compelled by rage, and contemptuous of consequence.

Then Linden saw Covenant gather his resolve. Awkwardness made him brusque.

"But that's not what I want to say. I'm going to take the *krill*."

At once, everything around him intensified. Several of the Giants caught their breath. Rime Coldspray hissed a wordless objurgation. Anele stirred restlessly in his sleep, as if he had been disturbed by the sound of distant thunder. Liand's protests were stilled by Mahrtiir's sudden grasp on his arm. In fright, Pahni moved to stand with the

Stonedownor. Bhapa stared, wide-eyed, at the Unbeliever. Linden half expected the Wraiths to return in refusal.

At the same time, the Humbled seemed to take on substance and clarity as if they had been vindicated; as if their faith in the ur-Lord had been confirmed.

"I know," Covenant muttered. "That'll leave Andelain unprotected—which personally makes me want to puke. Without it, the Wraiths won't have the right kind of strength to guard the borders. They won't be able to prevent—"

"But one of us ought to have a weapon of some kind. Wherever we're going, we're likely to need it. As long as Joan is still alive—as long as she has her ring—that knife can cut through practically anything." For a moment, he faltered. "I hope that doesn't make me 'contemptuous of consequence.'"

While he appeared to search for words, Linden grasped her opportunity. Quickly she asked, "Where *are* we going?" She had no intention of taking Covenant—or anyone else—with her. "The Harrow doesn't want to tell me."

"Ah, hell, Linden," Covenant muttered in disgust. "If I knew—if I could remember—I would say so." With the heel of his halfhand, he thumped his forehead. "It's such a mess in here." Briefly a grin like a grimace distorted his face. "If you don't want to hit me again, threaten me with hurtloam. It's amazing how that helps me concentrate.

"But we're going to need a weapon," he resumed. "*That* I'm sure of. You shouldn't have to do everything yourself. And this is *my* problem. I've already done too many things wrong. Even when I was part of the Arch, I was too human—

"I got you into this." Earlier he had blamed himself for misleading her by speaking to her in her dreams, and through Anele. "I should at least try to help you save your son."

As if he were bracing himself for an ordeal, he turned to confront Loric's *krill*.

"Wait!" Linden said urgently. "Wait a minute. This isn't what I want." Mere moments ago, she had believed that she had surrendered everything. Now she saw that she had been mistaken. She also needed to prevent him from accompanying her; from taking any more risks for her sake. "You promised—"

Once, millennia ago in the Land, Thomas Covenant had avowed that he would never use power again.

"I know," he repeated over his shoulder. "I was trying to make myself innocent. Impotent or helpless. I couldn't think of any other way to stop Lord Foul.

"But you were right all along. Sometimes just being innocent or ignorant or even good isn't enough. Maybe that's always true. Maybe we're all like Esmer. If we want to do good, we have to take the risk of evil. The risk that we actually *are* evil."

In the background of Covenant's voice, Linden seemed to hear Dr. Berenford. *Guilt is power.* When the old physician had first asked for her help with Covenant ten years ago, he had described the theme of one of Covenant's novels. *Only the damned can be saved.*

Like Covenant, Linden was the prisoner of her memories.

"This won't be the first promise I've broken," he finished harshly. "Maybe it'll be the last."

She wanted to stop him. For Andelain's sake, she should have shouted objections to the heavens. But he had already reached for the ineffable puissance of the dagger.

Neither the Humbled nor Stave made any attempt to prevent him.

He would not be able to withdraw the *krill*. He was only human now, and the blade was deeply embedded. Over the centuries, the stump had become as hard as ironwood. In fact, he should not even have been able to touch the knife. Linden had felt its heat. Sunder had carried it wrapped in cloth so that it would not burn his skin. Nevertheless Covenant closed both hands around the weapon's haft. His shoulders hunched as he began to pull.

Silhouetted against the light, he seemed to loom larger—black and ominous—as he strained to draw the knife from its ancient sheath. Linden could not see his face, but she could feel his muscles tremble. And—

Oh, God!

—she could smell the nauseating sweetness as his flesh began to burn. The dagger was not merely hot: it was suddenly *too* hot. A new rush of power blazed like incandescence from the gem: *Joan's* power. A rightful white gold wielder— No ordinary fabric would have given Covenant enough protection. He would sear the skin from his bones before he moved the *krill*.

"Linden!" panted Liand. Pahni and Mahrtiir had to hold him back. "*Linden.*"

The halved clutch of Covenant's right hand slipped. Smoke curled from his grasp: the odor of cooked meat became more acute. But he did not admit defeat. Hooking the two fingers of his halfhand over the blade's guards, he continued to pull against the clasp of Caer-Caveral's death.

I *need* this. I need to be numb.

Now the *krill*'s gem burned directly into his palm. In another moment, his hands would catch flame: they would be permanently crippled. But he did not appear to feel the pain; gave no sign that he recognized the smell. His leprosy enabled him to keep his grip, but it also prevented him from knowing how badly he was damaging himself.

"Covenant Giantfriend!" Rime Coldspray towered over him; yet the stark extremity of his efforts made him seem her equal. "Stand aside! This is *caamora*, the province of Giants. Will you maim yourself and be made useless? Your flesh cannot endure such grief! You must permit me—"

Joan was doing this, *Joan.* Somehow she—or *turiya* Herem—recognized Covenant's grasp on the *krill*. The Raver surely guided her; but the wild magic was hers.

Still Covenant heaved with his whole strength. Strain tore a hoarse snarl between his teeth, but did not free the knife.

A cry rose like bile in Linden's throat. She swallowed it so that she would not vomit.

"Ironhand!" barked Stave. "Aid me!"

Swift as thought, the former Master sprang to Covenant's side; dropped to one knee. With both fists, he began punching at the stump as if he imagined that he could batter it apart.

The wood was too hard for him; too old and enduring. It could have resisted an axe as easily as it ignored his blows. But Galt, Branl, and Clyme followed his example: they were no more than a heartbeat behind him. Their pounding shook the dead trunk to its roots. The earth seemed to absorb the pain that should have made Covenant let go.

An instant later, Coldspray's massive fists hammered down onto the stump; struck with the force of bludgeons. The thunder that troubled Anele filled the hollow.

With the Ironhand's second blow, the wood splintered. Caer-Caveral's last legacy was shattered as if it had been blasted by lightning.

In that instant, Linden felt a tremor in the ground: a shudder so fundamental that she heard it in the marrow of her bones rather than with her ears. She sensed realities grinding against each other. Briefly the trees and even the grass of Andelain appeared to tremble as if in dread.

Violently released, Covenant staggered backward. If Frostheart Grueburn had not caught him, he would have fallen. Effort or realized agony ripped a howl from the depths of his chest. The *krill* spun from his grasp: he could not hold it. Shafts and flashes of silver cartwheeled through the branches of the nearby trees, etching every leaf as they passed. Small scraps of skin smoked and melted like wax on the gem as the dagger fell to the grass.

In shreds of illumination, Linden saw the flesh of Covenant's palms and fingers bubbling—

A tumult of shouts and consternation answered the sight. Ignoring Covenant's prohibition, the Manethrall commanded his Cords, "Hurtloam! *Now!*" As Pahni and Bhapa sped away, Liand rushed to help Grueburn support Covenant. With one hand, the Stonedownor snatched at his *orcrest* as if it were an instrument of healing. Giants protested the sight of Covenant's hands.

"*Haruchai!*" roared the Ironhand. "Swordmainnir! A foe extends evil into the heart of Andelain, regardless of the Wraiths. Watch and ward! An attack may follow!"

Like Linden, Coldspray had discerned Joan's fury. But the Ironhand did not know that it was *Joan's.*

Covenant held out his hands as if he were pleading. His breath came in huge excruciated gasps.

Hardly aware of what she did, Linden reached out for the power of the Staff. The Harrow held it, but it was hers: she could feel its ready possibilities. And once before, in the caves of the Waynhim, she had called Earthpower from the Staff when it was some distance away. She could still make use of it—

She could not. The Harrow's avid claim blocked her. The black wood was lambent with magic and Law; but neither fire nor healing answered her call.

"I am impatient, lady." The brown-clad Insequent's voice was deep loam. "Have done with these delays. Accompany me."

He tried to sound scornful, but Linden heard him clearly. He was not impatient: he was alarmed. Instinctively she guessed that he did not want Covenant to wield the *krill*.

She ignored him. If she had known how to do so, she would have summoned the Wraiths. The sight of Covenant's ruined hands nearly stopped her heart.

With waddling steps, the Ardent approached the cluster around Covenant. And as he drew near, his garish apparel expanded. Amid a cloud of floating colors, he advanced until he gained an unobstructed view of Covenant's hands. Then with a florid gesture he sent bright ribbands curling and probing toward the Unbeliever.

"Joan," Covenant panted, fighting to manage more pain than he could contain.

Crimson and opalescent strips found his hands. Two or three of the Swordmainnir started to swat the bands away, then stopped themselves.

Unregarded on the ground, the *krill*'s heat began to fade. It remained too hot for Linden, Liand, or the Ramen to touch safely; but the rush of force which had damaged Covenant dwindled away.

"She or *turiya* felt what I was doing."

Clutching his unused Sunstone, Liand watched as streamers of cloth began to wrap Covenant's hands, his heat-ravaged fingers.

"She tried to stop me."

Silken as caresses, the ribbands glided over his skin, twined around each other seamlessly as they formed bandages which were still part of the Ardent's raiment.

Their theurgy was invisible to Linden's senses. Nevertheless Covenant's relief was immediate. While her heart tried to beat, his pain sank away like water into parched sand. A moment of light-headedness nearly broke her balance.

"If that poor woman could concentrate," he said, sighing. By degrees, he began to breathe more easily. "If Foul hadn't hurt her so badly."

"That was well done," the Ardent announced with plumy satisfaction, "though I alone proclaim it so." Another gesture detached Covenant's bandages from the fluttering aura of his garments; sent them to secure themselves. "If you will abide by my counsel, Timewarden, you will not remove my bindings. The easing of pain is a less arduous magic than the mending of flesh. Also it cannot be doubted that you will find subsequent need for such protection. My gift will prove a greater benison if it is permitted to remain as it is."

Covenant did not appear to hear the Insequent. His voice grew stronger as he finished, "She wanted to kill me, but she's in too much pain herself. She'll probably try again later. For now, she's done as much as she can."

How he knew this, Linden could not imagine. Nonetheless she agreed with him. She had recognized Joan's ferocity herself. And she was familiar with the frailty of Joan's damaged mind.

Marveling, the Manethrall studied Covenant. But what he saw with his eyeless senses appeared to satisfy him. Lifting his face to the sky, he gave a whinnying cry to recall his Cords.

As the sound carried through the night, Linden found herself kneeling on the grass among Giants who seemed as tall as trees. She did not remember sagging to the ground: she simply had no strength to stand. Still she continued to watch Covenant as he stretched and flexed his wrapped fingers in evident wonder. She did not breathe normally until he stooped to grasp the *krill* again. As he lifted it, its radiance lit his hair like silver fire—but holding it did not hurt him.

With an air of self-congratulation, the Ardent withdrew to consider the company from the slope of the hollow. His manner—and Covenant's—confirmed that the danger had passed.

Sighing, Linden let herself fall back to sit with her knees hugged against her chest, and her face hidden. She had given in to the Harrow too readily. Now she was useless.

Projecting more confidence, the Harrow repeated, "I am impatient, lady. Do you seek to prolong your son's plight?"

No one paid any attention to him.

While Mahrtiir's call receded among the trees, the Giants began to relax. Cabledarm or Cirrus Kindwind murmured a low jest that Linden did not hear: two or three of the Ironhand's company chuckled in response. Perhaps to reassure him, Galesend gave Liand's shoulder a friendly shake that staggered him. Coldspray rolled her head to loosen a heavy burden of tension from her neck.

The Humbled gathered around Covenant as if to guard him from his companions. At the same time, Stave returned among the Giants to stand near Linden. Prostrate on the grass, Anele continued sleeping as though nothing had happened to disturb the respite which he had received from his parents.

There were things that Linden needed to do: she was sure of it. Questions to ask. Decisions to make—or insist upon. Actions to take. The Harrow was right. Surely the time had come to require him to keep his side of the bargain?

But her hands seemed to weigh more now than they did when she had carried the Staff. Without Covenant's ring on its chain around her neck, she did not know how to lift up her head. Soon, she told herself. Soon— But right now she felt too deprived and beaten to do anything except huddle into herself and try to slip sideways into some realm of memory or helplessness where she could not be held responsible.

Tried to stop me.

He did not know of your intent.

She'll probably try again later.

The night after the battle of First Woodhelven, Linden had dreamed that she had become carrion. Like Joan, she needed to gather the remnants of her strength—or her mind—and could not.

For a while, Covenant peered at the *krill* and his bandaged hands as if he had forgotten what they meant; as if he had stumbled into another crevasse and lost his place. But then he seemed to shake himself free from the tug of the past. Frowning, he asked the Humbled for something that he could use to wrap Loric's weapon. A little extra protection, he said, in case Joan renewed her attack unexpectedly.

Without hesitation, Galt tore off a hand's width of cloth from the hem of his tunic. Although the material resembled vellum, as tough as canvas in spite of its softness, he ripped it with no sign of strain. Characteristically expressionless, he offered the fabric to Covenant.

Nodding his approval, Covenant folded the ochre cloth around the *krill*; shrouded the light of the gem. In sudden darkness relieved only by the glittering of the stars, he tucked the bundle into the waist of his jeans. However, he did not thank Galt: apparently his approval had limits. Instead he turned to the Ironhand of the Swordmainnir. Linden felt his continued struggle to remain present as he said abruptly, "Your ancestors weren't exactly told the truth when they negotiated for your gift of tongues. The *Elohim* misused you, if they didn't outright lie."

In a distant age, our ancestors were misled—

Vaguely Linden wished for the elucidation of Wraiths; for some benevolent light to illumine *courage and clear sight*. But those instances of the Land's essential mystery did not come.

—to accept a false bargain with the Elohim.

She did not know why Covenant spoke of such things now.

"Is this needful, Covenant Timewarden?" Night shrouded Coldspray's voice as well as her face. "It alters naught."

"Sure," Covenant assented. "But it'll help us understand what's at stake. We'll be better off in the long run—assuming there *is* a long run—if we know why Longwrath matters so much. I'm wondering why you didn't take him to *Elemesnedene* and ask the *Elohim* to cure him. Did you know what was wrong with him all along? Did you know they wouldn't help?" He paused, grappling for a handhold on the rim of an inner flaw. Then he added, "The more you explain, the less I need to remember."

"The Staff of Law is yours," the Ardent remarked to the Harrow, "for the nonce. Will you not summon its flame to light these troubled hearts?"

"Their burdens are not mine," retorted the Harrow. "I desire only to depart."

Coldspray gazed at Covenant with her fists braced on her hips. Her stance suggested anger, bitterness. But beneath the surface lay a darker emotion.

"What say you, Giants?" she asked as if she were grinding her teeth. "Must I speak of our ancient fault *here*, in precious Andelain, while the Earth's last peril mounts against us?"

"Speak as you wish," put in the Harrow, "when the lady has allowed me to uphold our bargain. Only sway her to accompany me now. When I have forestalled the Worm, you will have leisure enough for any tale."

The company around Covenant ignored the Insequent. For a moment, Coldspray's comrades glanced at each other uncomfortably. Like the *Haruchai*, they seemed to see well enough without the benefit of fire or moonlight or wild magic. Then Frostheart Grueburn said softly, "In this fraught night, I find that I have no stomach for secrets or shame." Her voice was a low growl at the back of her throat. "Linden Giantfriend has set aside her concealments. She has declared her deepest intentions. Do we fear now to be humbled in her presence? You have claimed some measure of fault for Longwrath's madness, but the fault is neither yours nor ours. It belongs to the machinations of the *Elohim*, as honored Grimmand Honninscrave has made plain. Let us reveal our ancient folly and be done with it. Joy is in the ears that hear, not in the mouth that speaks."

Several of the Swordmainnir murmured agreement. Others may have nodded.

"*When* I have forestalled the Worm—" the Harrow tried to insist. But the Ardent interrupted him.

"The desires of the lady prevail here, impetuous one." The Ardent's lisp became more pronounced, as if he were mocking the Harrow. "She will accompany us when she deigns to do so, in her own fashion, and by her own means. Until that moment, be content to wait."

"I will not," said the Harrow hotly.

The Ardent hesitated. When he replied, he spoke in a low voice, almost whispering.

"Must I utter your true name to silence you?"

Anger clenched the Harrow's fists, knotted the muscles at the corners of his jaw. "You will not. That will be interference beyond question. You will forfeit your life."

Nevertheless he did not hazard further provocation.

Still no one heeded either of the Insequent. Squaring her shoulders, Rime Coldspray confronted Covenant's inquiry. As if she were ready to receive or deliver a blow, she said, "Very well, Thomas Covenant, Timewarden and Earthfriend. I will speak of the truth which has been revealed to us. I will explain that Giants are as prone to error and unwisdom as any people of the Earth."

Resting her forehead on her knees, Linden allowed the night to fill her as though she had become a vessel of darkness. She did not care why Covenant sought to probe the Giants. She cared only that he strove to remain present; that he might find a way to lift her out of her failures. A way to spare her—

You judge harshly, Wildwielder. She should have tried to ease Elena's long anguish. But there was nothing that Linden could do for Covenant's daughter until she discovered some form of mercy for herself.

That the bargain was false in all sooth has been made plain to us. Longwrath had tried to kill her because the *Elohim* wanted her dead.

"Your query," Coldspray began, "concerns the gift of tongues for which the Giants once bargained with the *Elohim.* In the many journeys of our kind, we have learned that the peoples of the Earth tell their tales to please or comfort or obscure themselves, suppressing aspects which they mislike and glorifying portions which give them pleasure. For uncounted millennia, we have held to a different creed. Believing that joy is in the ears that hear, not in the mouth that speaks, we have told our tales fully or not at all—and have taken pride in doing so.

"Now we must hear joy in the knowledge that our ancestors were blind to machination and distorted truth. More, we must honor them for a blindness which was in some degree voluntary. So delighted were they with the gift of tongues, and with themselves, that they did not closely examine the proffer of the *Elohim.*

"We must hear joy in the recognition that Longwrath was in part betrayed to suffering and madness by his own people."

Linden listened with only part of her attention. She remembered the deranged Giant's lust for her death more vividly than the account of this bargain that she had heard from Grimmand Honninscrave long ago. In a moment of imposed sanity, Anele had warned her, *All who live share the Land's plight. Its cost will be borne by all who live. This you cannot alter. In the attempt, you may achieve only ruin.* Nevertheless she was determined to leave her friends behind when she went with the Harrow. As soon as she gathered her strength— She already had too many victims. Jeremiah needed her. Other lives might have been better served if Longwrath had killed her.

Grimly the Ironhand explained, "You and Linden Avery, who was then the Sun-Sage, were informed that we received our gift in return for our tale of Bahgoon the Unbearable, and of Thelma Twofist, who tamed him. That is sooth—to the extent that our ancestors chose to believe it so. But we have learned that it is also falsehood. We perceive now that the *Elohim* found worth, not in the tale itself, but rather in one facet of it—and in our willingness to speak of that facet mirthfully. In their eyes, our mirth justified their intent.

"The tale itself I will not tell. Here I seek only to account for the feigned generosity of the *Elohim*. The pith of the matter is this. For the many deeds and attributes which caused him to be named Unbearable, Bahgoon was delivered involuntarily and forcibly into the un-tender care of Thelma Twofist.

"She was a Giant of enormous might, legendary belligerence, and indeed extreme ugliness. By her own choice, she lived apart from all others, for all who knew her feared her, and she felt only disdain for their alarm, which she deemed cowardice. Bahgoon she was given to be her servant, against his vehement protests and frantic opposition, because our ancestors could no longer endure his presence, because no other Giant could restrain his conduct—and because our ancestors considered his new place in Thelma's service a fit reward for his multitude of offenses."

Coldspray sighed. "That she found means to tame him, and that they discovered together an embattled and extravagant happiness, inspires our delight in their tale. However, the *Elohim* misheard the humor of the Giants—or elected to interpret it in another fashion. The aspect of the tale which intrigued them, and which swayed them to proffer their gift of tongues, was the coercion of Bahgoon, not its unforeseen outcome. They discerned clearly our eagerness—indeed our hunger—for friendship and knowledge throughout the Earth. And they assured themselves that we did not scruple to send our own to apparent woe when we saw no other course. They shared a similar trait, as the doom of each Appointed demonstrates. But they did not speak of such matters. Rather they expressed only their own delight. And they offered this bargain, the gift of tongues in exchange for the tale of Bahgoon and Thelma—and for all that the tale implied."

The Ironhand did not meet Covenant's gaze, or Linden's. Instead she studied the grass at the feet of the *Haruchai* like a woman who expected to be judged. Her manner said clearly that she and her comrades had already judged themselves.

"Because our ancestors had been dazzled by the splendor of the *Elohim*," she continued, "and because they were avid for the offered gift, they did not inquire into the perceived implications of the tale. Glad, and gladly blind, they accepted the bargain. Only now, when the harm cannot be recalled, have we heard the truth of the exchange. The eagerness of our ancestors to accept the terms, the *Elohim* interpreted as consent to the unwilling servitude of an unnamed Giant in a distant and uncertain future. Involuntarily misled," she stated harshly, "or perhaps voluntarily, our ancestors condoned the sacrifice of Lostson Longwrath's life to any use which the *Elohim* craved."

Finally she raised her eyes to Covenant's. With an air of troubled defiance, as though she meant to face any accusation squarely, she concluded, "This understanding Grimmand Honninscrave gave to us, or perhaps inflicted upon us, that we might better comprehend the choices required of Linden Giantfriend. Aye, and her deeds also. He strongly desired us to grasp that the errors, and indeed the faults, of the Giants are many and grievous. Long ago, we traded the life and pain of a kinsman for one mere gift of the *Elohim*. For that reason, we must be chary of finding faults and errors in others, and especially in Linden Giantfriend, whose folly may yet prove wisdom, just as the thoughtless delight of our ancestors has birthed only sorrow."

Lit by nothing more than starlight, only Covenant's silvered hair seemed to define him. Nevertheless Linden knew before he spoke that he would not castigate Rime Coldspray or any of her people. Rather his whole body seemed to yearn with empathy and resisted slippage as he said gruffly, "Thank you. That helps. Now I remember why I've always loved Giants so much. Saltheart Foamfollower was my friend at a time when I didn't even know what friendship was. And he found a better use for his life than anything I could have imagined."

A moment later, he added, "In any case, Longwrath didn't succeed. If we can keep Linden alive long enough, the *Elohim* won't have any reason to care what he does. Maybe then they'll let him go, and he can find a little peace."

Linden hoped that Coldspray would laugh now. A little peace. Before the world ended. Surely the Giants would appreciate the joke? She wanted one more chance to hear their open-hearted mirth before she left them behind. But neither the Ironhand nor any of the other Giants appeared to hear joy in Covenant's response.

Instead Coldspray said like a promise, "By that measure, Saltheart Foamfollower was among the greatest of Giants. We honor him as we do Grimmand Honninscrave and Cable Seadreamer. If the days which remain to us are kind, we will be granted opportunity to make amends, as they did, for the unwisdom of our forebears."

Before Covenant could reply, Mahrtiir stepped forward. "Your words are sorrow in my ears, Giant." He sounded reluctant, hampered by emotions which he did not wish to express. Nonetheless he said, "All who live fall prey to unwisdom. It is not otherwise with the Ramen. Had we not guided the Ranyhyn to remain apart from the Land after the bale of the Sunbane had passed, much that has transpired in this age might have been averted. Their presence would surely have tempered the thoughts and purposes of the Masters.

"If your striving to ease Longwrath's plight does not suffice as vindication, your bravery and bereavement against the *skurj* must. No single act of folly may outweigh a thousand—no, a thousand thousand—deeds of valor and generosity.

"It is to your ancestors' credit, I deem, that the *Elohim* could not win their desires without prevarication."

Linden nodded, assenting vaguely. She remembered hearing Mahrtiir admit, *I seek a tale which will remain in the memories of the Ramen when my life has ended.* He may have yearned to make amends for the long absence of his people and the Ranyhyn.

He had called his people *too cautious to be remembered.*

In response, Coldspray bowed. "For your courtesy, Manethrall of the Ramen, I thank you. Our remorse—aye, and our ire—are our own. We do not lightly set them aside. Yet your kindness and counsel hold great merit in our hearts. We will treasure them."

Abruptly the Harrow snapped, "Have done with these petty considerations. Even now, the Worm bestirs itself. As Infelice has informed you, its size is not vast. Yet its puissance will outrun its mere bulk. If we do not act, and act soon, none of you will survive to bemoan your faults and errors."

His voice hurt the night: it tarnished Mahrtiir's compassion as well as Coldspray's troubled honesty. Linden was on her feet before she realized that she had surged up from the grass; before she recognized her own anger.

Across the distance between them, she demanded, "*Stop* this. You haven't earned the right to sneer at any of us. You've been just about as honest as the *Elohim*, and that's not saying much, so *shut up* already."

Apparently the lessons of Gallows Howe continued to guide her past the boundaries of her weakness; her fathomless chagrin.

"Yet, lady," retorted the Harrow, "it is I who hold white gold and the Staff of Law, and you who are powerless." Darkness shrouded his features, but his gaze felt like a threat, black and bottomless. "Scorn me now, if that is your wish. The day will come when you will implore me to make any use of your son that chances to please me. On that day, you will learn that you have cause to repent your vexation and delay, for much will be lost that might have been saved."

"Doubtless that is your belief," the Ardent put in. Something had changed for him. His tumid assurance was gone, replaced by an air of worry. Perhaps he had frightened himself by threatening to reveal the Harrow's true name. "Certain of the Insequent have delved deeply into matters of augury, prescience, and consequence, seeking an awareness of Time to compare with the Theomach's. Among those adepts, however, some foresee one outcome, and some another. Deprived of the Timewarden, the Arch is weakened. Possibilities multiply at every word and deed. You would do well to consider that your haste may promote events and choices which do not please you."

The ferocity of the Harrow's glower bit at Linden's senses: she could hear the way he ground his teeth, feel his fingertips drumming on his beads. Nevertheless he contained himself.

If the Ardent spoke the Harrow's true name, that would constitute *interference* by any definition that Linden understood. It would doom the Ardent. But it would also give her power over the Harrow.

She was fed up with both of them. In disgust, she turned back to Covenant and her other companions. Unexpected anger had roused her from her emptiness. She was ready now; as ready as she would ever be.

—much will be lost that might have been saved.

When she looked at Covenant, she saw that he had fallen out of the present again. His mind wandered a trackless wilderness as fractured as the rubble where Joan exerted her madness, flinging out anguish to destroy discrete instances of time. For the moment, at least, he was lost; unreachable.

In contrast, Anele had finally awakened. Rising to his feet, he gazed about him as if he sought a direction or destination imperceptible to any sight but his blindness. Eased, perhaps, by the benignant air and grass of Andelain, or by the intercession of Sunder and Hollian, he seemed almost sane as he murmured, "The time has come. Anele must have stone. He remembers both his father and his mother. He must have stone."

Then he scented the air, apparently attracted to the smell of the *aliantha* that Pahni still held.

Covenant jerked up his head. "What's that?" he asked. "What's that? Did you say stone?" He sounded confused, trapped amid conflicting recognitions. "I remember your father and mother too. Why do you need stone?"

If Anele heard Covenant, he did not show it. Instead the old man approached Pahni, mutely holding out his hands. When she gave him her treasure-berries, he began to eat as if he had been fasting for days.

Linden sighed. In what seemed like a previous life, Anele had urged her to *Seek deep rock. The oldest stone. Only there the memory remains.*

The last days of the Land are counted. Without forbidding, there is too little time.

In retrospect, he seemed prescient. Still she had no idea what he meant.

"Covenant." Deliberately she tried to make her voice sound like a slap, hoping to bring him back from his inner maze. "Do you understand what Anele is talking about?"

Covenant gazed at her without any expression that she could interpret. "Sunder had *orcrest*," he muttered. "Hollian had *lianar*. They weren't Lords, but they were full of Earthpower. It's all about wood and stone." Without warning, he raised his fists, punched himself on both temples simultaneously. "If I could just damn *remember*—!"

Linden flinched at his sudden vehemence. Pahni did the same. "Thomas Covenant," protested Coldspray softly. "Giantfriend." Branl, Galt, and Clyme moved to protect Covenant from himself.

Straining, Covenant panted through his teeth, "The Harrow knows. The *Elohim* aren't the only food. The Worm can always get what it needs. But they're the *right* food. As long as it can find them, the Worm won't want to feed on anything else. The better they hide, the more time we have.

"But when it's eaten *enough*—"

He tried to finish the sentence. In spite of his efforts, however, he seemed to gag on what he wanted to say; or his mind skidded out from under him as if he stood on a surface as slick as the tunnel leading to the EarthBlood.

Linden understood him no better than she did Anele. Nonetheless he had given her an idea. Obliquely he had supplied her with an argument; a lever.

Now, she told herself. Now or never. Jeremiah needed her; or she needed him. More delays would only increase her doubts. They might cost her her ability to take any action at all.

As if she were speaking to the darkness, she asked, "Liand, will you give us some light?"

Andelain lacked none of its numinous mystery in the absence of the *krill*'s brilliance. The Hills seemed complete as they were. Doubtless the young Stonedownor had not felt the need to see more brightly than his health-sense allowed. No one except Linden felt that need. Yet he complied without hesitation. Taking his piece of Sunstone from the pouch at his waist, he held it up in the palm of his hand and invoked his heritage.

From the *orcrest* came a glow so pure that it appeared to have been washed clean. Steadily the shining expanded into the vale. And as it did so, it revealed Linden's companions as if it had reified them. Lit white, they looked ghostly for a moment, as spectral as the Dead: a small throng like omens or supplicants around Covenant and Linden. Then they resumed their substance.

To Liand, Linden said like Covenant, "Thank you. That helps."

She wanted everyone with her to see that she had made her decision and would not be dissuaded.

For a moment, she met Stave's single gaze, the flat stares of the Humbled, Rime Coldspray's troubled frown, the anxieties of the Cords. One by one, she scanned the Ironhand's comrades, and Mahrtiir, and Covenant. To Anele she nodded, although she had no reason to think that he was aware of her. In her living room, Jeremiah had once built a construct of Mount Thunder. He had given her a hint—

Seek deep rock.

Leaving everyone else behind, she could still take Anele with her.

Finally she fixed her attention on Liand as if he were the spokesman for all of her friends and uncertainties; as if he were the only one who needed to be convinced. While Covenant wandered in the world's past, he could not countermand her.

"It's time," she said carefully; almost steadily. "Anele and I are going with the Harrow." And with the Ardent, presumably. "But we're going alone."

She felt reactions as quick as heartbeats around her; but she kept her gaze on Liand. If she could persuade him—

Ah, Liand. *I wish I could spare you. Hell, I wish any of us could spare you.*

—the others might follow his example.

His stark eyebrows arched in surprise. Objections crowded into his mouth so swiftly that for the moment he could not articulate any of them. The light of his *orcrest* faltered briefly. In that instant of wavering, he looked somehow younger and more vulnerable, as though he had been personally spurned.

Tightening her grip on herself, Linden said, "The rest of you have more important things to do. You're going to stay here." Where Andelain would preserve them for a while. "Jeremiah is my son. I can't abandon him. I've already made that bargain. But I won't risk you for him.

"And the Land still needs defenders," she went on, hurrying to forestall Liand's expostulations. "It needs you and your Sunstone. It needs Covenant and the *krill*. It needs Giants and *Haruchai* and Ramen and Ranyhyn. Even if we didn't have so many enemies and monsters to worry about, someone has to do *some*thing about the Worm. Someone has to preserve the *Elohim*, as many as possible," to slow or weaken the Worm, "and that someone isn't me. I don't have any power now." No power—and no idea how she might reclaim her son from the *croyel*. "I'm not the one who saves worlds.

"I can't actually imagine what hope is anymore," she finished, bracing herself for a storm of protests. She had staked her whole heart on Covenant—and she had failed him. "But if there *is* such a thing—if it still exists—it depends on you. I have to go to Jeremiah. I can't do anything else. You have to stay here."

Her particular intensity seemed to seal Liand's throat. His mouth opened and closed on stillborn arguments. She saw in his eyes that her assertion had shocked him more profoundly, or more intimately, than Covenant's resurrection.

The impassivity of the Masters may have expressed approval: Stave's did not. Like Liand, Mahrtiir was silent. Behind his bandage, he appeared to weigh Linden's needs against the Land's; her desires against his own. Pahni made no attempt to conceal her visceral eagerness, her hope that Liand would be spared. Anxious and torn, Bhapa studied Linden for signs that she might waver.

But the Giants—

Rime Coldspray was the first to burst out laughing. Almost immediately, however, her comrades joined her. Stentorian and unconstrained, their loud humor filled the night: it seemed to cast back every darkness. Together they laughed until tears streamed down their faces; laughed as if laughter were another form of *caamora*, able to purge and cleanse until only wholeness remained. Under the stars, the vale rang with Giantish peals.

Earlier Linden had ached to hear the Swordmainnir laugh. Now their mirth daunted her: it seemed to defeat her. Once she had been stone. Now she had become as breakable as unfired clay. How could she hold up her head, or insist on protecting her friends, when the Giants found such glee in her arguments; her pleading?

"Ah, Linden Giantfriend," the Ironhand chuckled as she subsided. "You are a wonderment in all sooth. Your words resemble a tale of woe, but they are not. They are a flight of fancy. Do you conceive that any Giant would turn aside from such a quest as yours? Ha! The lure of extravagant hazards is too great. And we can do naught to preserve the *Elohim*. We have no virtue to discover their many coverts—and no wish to do so. Both the World's End and the Land's many other perils will await our return from your son's imprisonment. If they do not, they are too immense to be opposed by any force within our compass.

"We will accompany you, Linden Giantfriend, with your consent or without it. We cannot do otherwise, lest we lose the gift of joy entirely."

The other women chortled their assent as if it were delight.

Hearing them, Liand's face cleared. Their laughter banished his dismay. And for Mahrtiir also, the tension of an inner conflict eased. He was palpably relieved to turn away from responsibilities which exceeded his image of himself; and his devotion to Linden was strong. Bhapa's reaction resembled Mahrtiir's. As for Pahni, she was a Ramen Cord: she would follow where her Manethrall led, in spite of her fear for Liand.

Groaning to herself, Linden saw the four of them side with the Giants. She would not be able to dissuade them now. She could only compel them to remain behind by telling the Harrow that her interpretation of his bargain required him to exclude them.

If she did so, the Ardent would support her. She could draw on his magicks when she had none of her own.

Yet the Giants had moved her: she felt fundamentally shaken. Their laughter seemed as irrefusable as Jeremiah's plight.

Dourly the Humbled nodded. "In this circumstance," Galt said, "we will regret your departure. It is madness compounded with madness. Beyond question, some better use for your lives and efforts might be found. Understand, then, that neither we nor the ur-Lord will join your folly. Here he and the Wraiths of Andelain and High Lord Loric's *krill* may yet provide a bastion against havoc. Mayhap new counsels may now be gained among the Dead. And we do not fear to place our faith in the Unbeliever, though he has been severed from himself, making him less than he was.

"While the Earth endures, the Masters stand with Thomas Covenant. But we will do so *here* rather than under the thrall of any Insequent."

As Galt spoke, Linden's heart twisted. Surely this was what she wanted? To keep Covenant safe in Andelain? She owed him at least that much after everything that she had done to damage and misuse him. And yet she did not want to part from him. She did *not*. Even Jeremiah would not fill Covenant's place in her heart.

Like him, she was caught in a flaw within herself. But hers was an emotional fissure, not a broken memory. She wanted—and did not want—and could not choose.

For his part, the Harrow did not hesitate. In a loud voice, he proclaimed, "Your debates are empty breath, wasted while time crowds against us. You seek to persuade the lady, but *I* do not heed you. My oath I have given to her alone. I will not accept the burden of her companions."

"Aye," the Ardent interjected, "if that is her interpretation." Like his assurance, his lisp was fading. "Should she wish to seek her son without accompaniment, her desires will be enforced. But should she find herself loath to proceed both friendless and bereft—" His voice trailed away like the fluttering of his ribbands.

As if by incantation, Linden's indecisions were dispelled. The Harrow's tone enabled her to stand on ground as solid as it was unexpected. In an instant, she discarded her previous resolve. He wished to leave her companions behind—and she did not trust him. His hungers were too extreme: he *needed* her helplessness. Without it, he could not be confident that she would eventually surrender Jeremiah to his designs.

The Giants and the Ramen, Liand and Stave: they might be able to aid her son in ways that she could not yet imagine. She believed that Anele would be granted *deep rock*. And while Covenant remained in Andelain with the Humbled and the *krill*, she could feel sure that the Land had not been utterly forsaken.

She could bear to leave Covenant behind if it meant preserving some manner of hope for the Land.

Turning to the Harrow, she surrendered again; but not to him. Not to him.

"In that case," she said distinctly, "I've changed my mind. I want my friends with me." *All who live share the Land's plight.*

"And I have said," the Harrow retorted in fury, "that I do not *heed* you. This purpose is *mine*. The knowledge necessary to accomplish it is *mine*. I will not countenance the corruption of all that I have craved and sought."

The Ardent flinched. His eyes rolled. For a moment, he looked like he might turn his back and flee. But then some form of courage or coercion came to his aid. Thickly he intoned, "Lady, it is both my pleasure and my task by the will of the Insequent to inform you that the Harrow's true name is—"

The Harrow wheeled on his ribboned opponent. "*Silence*, fool!" he roared. "If you betray me in this fashion, you betray yourself as well. Revealing my name, you will empower the lady to command me. Thus you will destroy my intent—and you will perish, damned by your own deed.

"But I will not permit it. Rather than suffer ruin at your hand, I will forsake my design utterly.

"What then, fat one, fool, meddler? Will you drive me to depart, abandoning the Earth to its end, merely to gratify your gangrel corpulence? Must I leave the lady to grieve for her son while she may? Are you blind to the truth that neither you nor the combined will of the Insequent suffice to alter the world's doom? You cannot discover the prison of the lady's son. Without him, you are lost. *All* is lost."

Wreathed in bands of color like anxiety, the Ardent replied, "This outcome some among the Insequent have foreseen. Others disagree. One matter on which all concur, however, is that of the lady's import. To an extent which you fear to acknowledge, the fate of life rests with her as much as with her son.

"Yet that is not the substance of our contention. Its crux is this. Do my pronouncements, or the lady's desires, suffice to daunt you? Is your purpose, or your pride, so fragile that you cannot suffer obstruction? If not, you must concede that your avarice forbids you to turn from your chosen path."

"*My* avarice?" barked the Harrow scornfully. His fingers twitched, eager for the magic of his beads and fringes. "*I* am not a living embodiment of gluttony. There can be no comparison between us. Where I have hazarded my life assiduously for centuries, you have merely feasted. You cannot out-face me. You prize your gross flesh too highly."

Feigning confidence, the Ardent answered, "Thus you display ignorance rather than knowledge. Truly I prize my flesh, as I do all sustenance. But I do not fear death when I am able to spend the last of my days feasting. I will happily perish in surfeit and satiation while the Worm devours the Earth."

Then his manner changed. Between one word and the next, sharpness emerged like a knife from the concealment of his garb.

"However, I also do not scruple to betray you. I fear, but I do not scruple. If I must, I will ensure that you cannot abandon your purpose. Depart if you wish. Forsake your intent. You will gain naught. I need only speak your true name, and the lady will receive from you all that she requires."

"And when you have uttered my true name," countered the Harrow viciously, "I will reveal yours." He seemed barely able to contain his rage: it congested his voice like alluvial mud.

But his antagonist did not falter. "Thus the lady will be empowered to compel us both equally. For me, nothing will be lost. As you have observed, I will be damned by my own deed. For you, however, all that you have ever craved will fray and fade."

The Ardent may have been bluffing: Linden could not tell. Beneath his flamboyant magicks, he was as mundane as she was; as legible as Liand or the Ramen. But the acquired power of his ribbands obscured aspects of his aura, distracted her senses.

Nevertheless she was already sure of the outcome. The Harrow would acquiesce. His hungers were as bottomless as his eyes. They ruled him.

Turning her back on both of the Insequent, she forced herself to face Covenant again. She wanted to find some way to say goodbye, if not to him then to the love that they had once shared.

Long ago, she had heard Pitchwife singing,

I know not how to say Farewell,
  When Farewell is the word

That stays alone for me to say
   Or will be heard.

She hoped that she would return to Andelain with Jeremiah. But she no longer had any power to impose her will on events: no power apart from the Ardent's support. Anything might happen after the Harrow fulfilled his part of their bargain.

Covenant's attention still wandered the maze of his memories, dissociated and lost. He might not hear her. Nevertheless she had to try. She could too easily imagine that this would be her last chance—

Hoarse with strain, she began, "Covenant"—oh, Covenant!—"I'm sorry. I've done everything wrong," ever since the Mahdoubt had returned her to her proper time. "I should have trusted you." She should have at least *tried* to understand the silence of the Dead. "Now it's come to this."

Her friends hovered around her. Behind them, the Harrow and the Ardent had fallen silent. Bitterly the Harrow chafed at this new delay. In his own fashion, he, too, had surrendered— But Linden had no attention to spare for anyone except Covenant.

"The only thing that doesn't scare me is leaving you here. You're struggling now, but you'll find your way out of it." She made a ragged effort to smile. "By the time I get back, you'll probably know how to save the Land." The Harrow's plans she distrusted: intuitively she suspected that he would not be allowed to carry them out. The Land had too many powerful foes. "That wouldn't surprise me. If you can't do it, no one can."

With a suddenness that startled her, nearly made her flinch, Covenant's eyes sprang into focus. His chin came up, emphasizing the severity of his features, the exigency of his grey gaze. Before she could react, he answered like a growl, "Oh, *hell*, no."

She seemed to hear gruff affection in his voice.

"After all the trouble of resurrecting me," he announced, "the least you can do is take me with you. I may not look like much, but you need me. And God knows I need you. Right now, I'm not coherent enough to do anything on my own. You're about the only power there is that can actually hold me together. For a few minutes, anyway. And we've got time—"

The response of the Masters was swift. Galt stepped between Linden and Covenant as if to deny her claim on the Unbeliever. One on each side, Branl and Clyme gripped Covenant's arms.

"Ur-Lord, no." An almost subliminal tremor of vehemence marred Galt's inflexibility. "This we will not permit. We cannot. The Land's plight precludes it."

Tension ran through the Ramen. Protests crowded Liand's heart. Several of the Swordmainnir clenched their fists. But none of them moved or spoke. Stave did not interfere, although he must have known what the Humbled would do. The rest of Linden's companions may have been waiting for some sign from him, or from Linden—or from Covenant.

—you need me. Linden's pulse thudded in her throat. —I need you. Covenant's words released a cascade of emotions that threatened to sweep aside her defenses. With equal fervor, she wanted him to accompany her and to remain behind. Please, she tried to say. You don't have to do this. But her old ache for his presence and his irrefusable courage stopped her.

"You're wrong," Covenant informed Galt. "Weren't you listening? I told you. If you have to choose, choose her." He did not struggle; but now his tone held no hint of affection. He sounded raw, rubbed sore by the difficulty of controlling his frangible thoughts. "I know you don't trust the Insequent. You shouldn't. But you think you can avoid compromising any more of your commitments if the four of us stay here. Well, I'm sorry. That isn't possible. Everything is just going to get messier from now on. If you want to have any say in what happens anywhere, you'll have to get your hands dirty.

"Can't you see that I'm broken?" he asked: a sigh of exasperation. "We're all broken, one way or another. Broken or maimed. Bereft to the marrow of our bones. We can't heal anything, or stop anything, if we stay here."

Galt did not step aside. Clyme and Branl did not release Covenant. But when Galt began to say, "The Masters—" an uncharacteristic hitch in his voice forced him to pause and swallow. "The Masters," he repeated, "elected to withhold judgment concerning Linden Avery. While they remained uncertain, it became the task of the Humbled to forestall Desecration. In this we have failed. When our kinsmen are apprised of what has transpired here, they will surely judge us as we judge ourselves. Now we will bear the cost of our failure, as we must.

"If that cost includes opposition to your will, Unbeliever—" Again his voice seemed to catch in his chest. "If it requires us to act upon our certainty that Linden Avery now serves Corruption, we will do what we must to prevent further Desecration."

Uncounted days ago, Lord Foul had assured Linden that *the* Haruchai *serve me, albeit unwittingly.*

"Hellfire, Galt!" Covenant retorted without hesitation. "You should have gone with Cail. You should have let him talk to you.

"Have you never bothered to wonder *why* Lord Foul and Kastenessen and the damn Harrow and even my lost son want Jeremiah so badly? Have you never considered the idea that he must be crucial? Hasn't it occurred to you yet that if he can be hidden from the actual *Elohim*, there must be powers at work here you don't understand? Powers you weren't aware of when you took on the job of being Masters?

"Hell and blood! You make your commitments, and you stand by them. I respect that. But even the bedrock of the world shifts when it has to. If ordinary stone didn't have enough wisdom to change, there wouldn't be anything here for you to stand *on*."

Linden held her breath, hoping or praying or simply wishing that Covenant would be able to persuade the Humbled. Oh, she could have determined the outcome for him. If she told the Ardent that her interpretation of the Harrow's bargain included Covenant, the two Insequent would have no difficulty separating him from the Masters. Nevertheless she said nothing. She had already imposed her desires on him in ways that now seemed unjustifiable. She still believed that the Land needed the rigid loyalty of the *Haruchai*. And her years among the mentally and emotionally crippled in her former life had taught her that Covenant's insistence on what he wanted now might conduce to the healing of his mind; his memories. The longer he remained engaged with his actual circumstances and companions, the stronger his grip on himself might become.

That was a form of hope which she had not expected; and she clung to it.

Still she saw nothing that resembled compromise or acceptance in the lines of Galt's back. Lit by the Sunstone, Clyme and Branl looked as blank as ancient carvings, their expressions worn away by ages of intransigence.

"Yet we remain *Haruchai* rather than stone," replied Galt. To the extent that his nature permitted supplication, he may have been pleading with Covenant. "Stone does not choose, ur-Lord. It merely submits to forces which it cannot withstand. Choice and battle are our birthright. We are the Masters of the Land because we elected to honor the promise of our ancestors to its fullest extent. And we"—he indicated Branl, Clyme, and himself—"are the Humbled because we earned our place by long combat. We are the avatars of the ancient failure of the Bloodguard, and must not continue to fail. You cannot ask it of us to countenance your departure in the Harrow's company, and in Linden Avery's. To do so is to ask that we become other than we are."

Covenant shook his head. "That's exactly why you're going to let me go. And why you're going to come with us. In your whole history, no *Haruchai* has ever been given a chance to undo a Desecration. Or to help transform it. A chance to find out what's on the other side of failure. And you have *never* had a chance to recover from what the Vizard did to you. Cail would have told you that, if you were willing to listen."

Perhaps it was only adrenaline that held the shards of his mind together. Or perhaps he truly did not want to be separated from Linden. He may even have cared about Jeremiah's straits; cared deeply. He was capable of such compassion.

Beyond question he cared about the fate of the Humbled.

"Besides," he added like a shrug, "what's the alternative? Staying behind won't accomplish anything. The Worm isn't here. Neither is Lord Foul. If we want to stop them, we'll have to go where they are. That means we'll have to face Kastenessen and the *skurj* and Roger and *caesures* and Ravers and even Joan. If you think we can do all that alone—if you think we don't need as many friends and allies as we can get—you're out of your minds."

Hardly aware of what she did, Linden raised her hand to touch Covenant's ring through the plucked flannel of her shirt; to anchor herself on its cold comfort as she had done for years. But it was gone. And her hands were empty without the Staff.

Liand gripped his *orcrest* so tightly that its light shook, casting ambiguous shadows over the figures grouped around Covenant.

Finally Stave intervened. From his place at Linden's side, he said, "The Unbeliever has spoken. You will acquiesce. How otherwise will the Humbled redeem themselves in my sight?"

Galt glanced at Clyme; at Branl. "Is there no other recourse?" he asked aloud when he could have addressed them mind to mind.

They shook their heads slightly: so slightly that Linden almost missed the glint of resignation or remorse in their eyes.

"Then," Galt pronounced, "we redeem ourselves thus."

Wheeling so swiftly that Linden did not see him move, he flung a killing blow at her face.

Her death would cancel her bargain with the Harrow. He would take Covenant's ring and her Staff, and retrieve Jeremiah for his own use. By the inhumane standards of the Masters, that would put an end to her many Desecrations.

Yet Galt's blow did not touch her. Stave reached out and caught Galt's fist easily, as if he had seen or heard the attack coming before Galt moved. The smack of knuckles against flesh made Linden flinch, but did not harm her.

Liand yelped. Too late, the Ramen snatched at their garrotes. Coldspray and two other Giants surged forward with their heavy fists cocked.

But Galt did not strike again, or resist Stave's grasp. Instead he nodded once and stepped back. At the same time, Clyme and Branl released Covenant and held out their hands, open and empty, as if to show that they, too, had surrendered.

"It appears," the Ardent remarked to the Harrow, "that the scale of your entourage has been increased yet again." He sounded smug once more. "Doubtless you will welcome these added witnesses to the grand culmination of your designs."

The Harrow muttered a curse under his breath; but Linden could not hear what it was.

She did not move. She hardly dared to breathe. She was afraid that anything she might say or do would shatter the spell, the mystery, of what had just occurred.

Somehow Stave the outcast and Thomas Covenant the Unbeliever had swayed the Humbled.

5.

Preparations

Linden hardly knew how to feel. She was awash in so many conflicting emotions that she could not steer her way through them. Dismay still filled the bottom of her heart like shoals. But over those unanswerable rocks, strong currents and eddies seemed to run in every direction.

She had resurrected Covenant at a terrible cost. She had purchased the means to reach her son by making herself powerless to aid him. Yet Covenant had reaffirmed his belief in her, his unmerited support. Indeed, he had backed her with such certainty that even the Humbled—the *Humbled*—had been moved.

She was desperately grateful for everything that he had said and done; for anything that hinted that his love might be great enough to cover even her vast crime. Nevertheless his attitude weakened her. Like Liand's overt compassion in Revelstone days ago, Covenant's reasoning eroded her grip on herself. According to the contradictory logic of her emotions, he diminished her by denying that her every deed was wrong. If everything that she had done deserved repudiation, at least she knew where she stood. Blame told her who she was. It gave her meaning. Without it, she was less than powerless: she was insignificant.

In that way, her gratitude implied both hope and despair.

Perhaps this was what it meant to have friends and the possibility of love: to become smaller, too inadequate and fallible for words—and thereby to find herself no longer alone. No longer either solely culpable or solely necessary.

If so, her position now was the opposite of Stave's. Being cast out had given him the strength to stand alone, entirely isolated from his people. And that in turn had made it possible for him to be her friend in ways that no other *Haruchai* could comprehend, by solitary choice rather than by communal necessity.

Long ago, Covenant's circumstances had resembled Stave's. Being a pariah on Haven Farm had taught him the courage and fortitude to care for Joan unaided.

Linden, too, had once been alone. Alone and strong. Now the poles of her dilemma had been reversed. She had been weakened by acceptance and affirmation and trust. Together the Giants and the Ramen, Liand and Stave, Covenant and even the Humbled: they had brought her to the end of her choices.

She was not sure that she could bear it.

She was sitting on the grass again with her knees gripped to her chest; hiding her face. She needed time to recover from the joy and terror of Covenant's declarations.

Have you never bothered to wonder why *Lord Foul and Kastenessen and the damn Harrow and even my lost son want Jeremiah so badly?*

Roger and the *croyel* dreamed of becoming *gods*.

Apparently Covenant believed that Jeremiah's plight and the Land's could not be distinguished from each other.

Around her, Linden's friends also seemed to need time. Stave and the Masters regarded each other impassively; but Pahni and Bhapa stared openly at Clyme, Galt, and Branl as though they had never seen such men before. Through his bandage, Mahrtiir appeared to study the Humbled with a comparable surprise. He may have been wondering to what extent this unforeseen alteration in the posture of the Masters could be trusted.

Liand's features displayed mingled awe and vindication. He had known the intransigence of the Masters all his life: clearly he considered Covenant's accomplishment a great feat. And Covenant had validated Liand's instinctive commitments. The Stonedownor held up the light of his *orcrest* as if he were proud to offer illumination to the Unbeliever.

The Swordmainnir conferred cautiously with each other. The tension of their impulse to defend Linden was slow to dissipate. Cirrus Kindwind and Cabledarm muttered together, sharing their uncertainty about the Humbled. Bluntfist, Latebirth, and Onyx Stonemage reminded each other—no doubt unnecessarily—of various Giantish tales concerning Thomas Covenant. With Frostheart Grueburn and Stormpast Galesend, Rime Coldspray discussed the innominate contingencies of a journey with the Harrow and the Ardent. They did not know where they were going, or what they would encounter when they arrived. Nevertheless they envisioned potential dangers as best they could, and considered possible responses. At the same time, the Ironhand apportioned simpler tasks. As before, she asked Grueburn to watch over Linden and Galesend to care for Anele. Stonemage and Latebirth would guard Liand and the Manethrall respectively: Cabledarm and Halewhole Bluntfist, Pahni and Bhapa. Covenant she left to the Humbled.

Meanwhile Anele fretted inchoately, as if he alone felt any need for haste.

But Covenant had slipped again. In a weary murmur, as if his tenuous clarity had drained him, he talked about the birth of Sandgorgons in the Great Desert, describing to himself the mindless confluence of Earthpower and storms and barren sand which had manifested itself in those feral monsters. His knotted frown and the hunch of his shoulders gave the impression that he feared his memories—or feared his inability to identify their importance. His wrapped hands made gestures that went nowhere.

Standing on the slope behind Linden, the Harrow ground his teeth in palpable frustration while the Ardent played restlessly with his ribbands.

Liand—of course—was the first to step aside from his own concerns. Still holding his Sunstone so that everyone could see, he crossed the greensward to kneel in front of Linden. With her face covered, she did not look at him. Nonetheless her health-sense was as precise as vision. His concern added itself to the emotional tides and eddies that swirled through her as if she had been reduced to flotsam.

"Linden," he breathed, addressing himself only to her. "Linden Avery. I see the distress which feeds upon your heart. None here do not. Even Anele is disturbed by it, and I do not doubt that the Unbeliever would seek to console you, were he able to escape his wounded mind.

"Will you not take comfort from the desire of your friends to accompany you in all things?

"I do not speak of the *Haruchai*. They do as they must. Even Stave does so. Nor do I speak of the Giants, who delight in extremity and hazard. No, Linden. I speak of your lesser companions, we who have stood at your side from the first.

"Manethrall Mahrtiir, Bhapa, Pahni, and I lack the heritage of Earthpower which exalts of the *Haruchai* and the Giants. Even Anele is a being of power where we are not. Yet we have confronted monsters and mysteries in your name. We have dared Demondim and *skurj*, *kresh* and Cavewights. And we have twice endured *caesures*. Within the second, I have participated in your thoughts, sharing the pain and force and darkness and yearning of your spirit.

"Will you not consider that we choose to remain at your side, knowing that you have dared the Earth's doom? Will you not permit our trust to ease you?"

Linden could not face him. Nor could she explain herself: her emotions ran in too many directions to be named. Instead, muffled against her knees, she said, "I had a chance to take pity on Elena," Covenant's endlessly suffering daughter, "and I couldn't do it." She had not merely Desecrated Law to resurrect Covenant: she had failed to resurrect him whole. "I'm glad you're coming with me. I'm glad you're all coming. But I'm as broken as Covenant is. I've fallen—somewhere—and I don't know how to climb out."

She felt Liand stiffen as she replied. At first, she thought that she had hurt him. But then she read him more clearly. He did not feel rejected. Instead he was drawing on the dignity with which he had often answered her efforts to spare him.

"Then," he told her sternly, "there is no other path for you. You must walk it or perish. Arise now and allow the Harrow to fulfill the terms of your exchange. Every delay heightens your own peril as much as your son's."

Lost in her confusion, Linden was surprised to find that Liand of Mithil Stonedown the authority to command her. He diminished her: truly he did. At the same time, however, he bestowed new reasons for gratitude.

"All right," she answered indistinctly, although she did not move. "I understand. Just give me a minute. Tell everyone to get ready. We'll leave soon."

When Liand rose to his feet and turned away, he seemed to take some of her tossed and eddying emotional currents with him.

"Cords," she heard Mahrtiir say, "this company requires water and sustenance. We have endured much without rest or aliment. *Aliantha* we must have, and also a stream to quench our thirst."

At once, Bhapa moved to obey his Manethrall. Pahni lingered long enough to turn a glance of yearning and veiled alarm on Liand. Then she, too, obeyed Mahrtiir.

"Aye, Manethrall," assented the Ironhand. "The Ramen are provident as well as courteous. For many reasons, we grieve those Giants whom the Land names the Unhomed. Among our sorrows is this, that their fate precluded us from hearing their tales of both the Ranyhyn and the Ramen."

As the Cords jogged away in opposite directions, Mahrtiir replied to Coldspray, "Already the benisons of your presence have been many and inestimable. I do not doubt that they will continue. But the Ramen are a short-spoken people. And even among my kind, I am considered curt. I lack the gifts of speech to offer sufficient honor. Know, however, that where my mouth is empty my heart is full."

The Ironhand and several of her comrades laughed in response. Chuckling, Kindwind replied, "You measure yourself unjustly, Manethrall. Were we uncertain that our path lies with Linden Giantfriend—which we are not—still would we gladly follow where a man who speaks as you do leads."

All right, Linden told herself. You can do this. It's the last thing you have to do. You might as well face it.

Sighing under the weight of her remaining burden, she raised her head and climbed slowly to her feet.

Covenant had closed his eyes. He gave the impression that he was asleep on his feet. However, Linden could still sense the turmoil in his mind. Tucked into the waist of his jeans, the *krill* throbbed intermittently with new heat. Guided by *turiya*, Joan may have been testing his vulnerability. Doubtless she and the Raver had become stronger when Linden had torn Covenant out of the Arch of Time. They would hurt or kill him if they were given the opportunity. For the present, however, they were content to probe and wait.

Linden wanted to ask Covenant what would happen to Andelain and the Wraiths when the mystic force of Loric's *krill* was taken elsewhere. But she could guess well enough. Roger and his Cavewights had neither the desire nor the sheer numbers to expend their energies against Andelain. And she still believed that Kastenessen's pain-driven fury was too single-minded to encompass the Hills. His rage was directed primarily at his fellow *Elohim*: he did not care about mere grass and trees and health and loveliness. The *skurj*, on the other hand— Their voracity might be drawn to the wealth of Earthpower here. And even if Kastenessen sent his monsters elsewhere for some purpose which Linden could not imagine, the Sandgorgons might come. Through Stave, she had offered them distractions enough to occupy them until they were overtaken by the world's end. But among them they retained remnants, scraps, of *samadhi* Sheol's malign spirit; and the Raver's loathing of trees was as enduring and insatiable as the Ravers themselves. Like Salva Gildenbourne, Andelain might present a feast which the Sandgorgons could not ignore.

Linden agreed with the Humbled: she had given up too much when she had accepted the Harrow's terms. The fact that she could not have made any other choice did not console her.

Waiting for the Cords, she confirmed that Jeremiah's crumpled racecar remained deep in one of her pockets. The ruined toy was all that she retained of her son. If her friends and Covenant could not rid Jeremiah of the *croyel*, the one thing that he had taken from his former life might be all that she would ever have.

After a moment, Liand said carefully, "Linden." He stood to the side so that his *orcrest* lit both Linden and Covenant. "One question remains. What must be done to preserve Anele? We know nothing of where we will be conveyed, and we have lost all that we bore from Revelstone. Only the armor of the Giants remains to ward him, and I fear that they will have need of it."

Anele, Linden thought. Ah, God. *When your deeds have come to doom, as they must, remember that he is the hope of the Land.* To her, the old man appeared to be both the most and the least helpless of her companions. He may also have been the most or the least necessary.

But on the day of Jeremiah's abduction by Roger, her son had devised two astonishing constructs in her living room. Out of bright plastic bits like tiny bricks, he had formed large structures which she could not fail to recognize: one of Revelstone; the other of Mount Thunder, ancient Gravin Threndor. Among the Wightwarrens deep in the chest of the mountain ten years and several millennia ago, she and Covenant had gone to the chamber of Kiril Threndor to confront Lord Foul.

Since her translation to the Land in Jeremiah's wake, she had learned to think of his last voluntary creations as guides or instructions—or as warnings. Certainly she would not have traveled to Andelain to resurrect Covenant if she had not first found the Staff of Law and been taken to Revelstone, where she had fallen victim to Roger's insidious glamour.

She believed now that she knew where the Harrow would take her, for good or ill.

Unfortunately she could not close her mind to an alternative interpretation of her son's constructs. If Lord Foul had indeed claimed Jeremiah years ago, those images of

Revelstone and Mount Thunder may not have been voluntary. They may have been manipulations; ploys designed to make her serve the Despiser.

Yet in the Hall of Gifts, Stave had spoken of children among his people. —*it is their birthright to remain who they are.* And he had asked, *Are you certain that the same may not be said of your son?*

Linden wanted to say the same of Jeremiah so badly that she feared to do so. *I refuse to believe he made choices then that can't be undone.* Nevertheless the nature of the intent which had inspired his constructs in her living room did not affect her answer to Liand's question.

"I don't think that we need to worry about Anele. If I'm right, we're going underground. It'll all be stone. Old stone. The kind that he understands."

"You were there," she said, remembering. "In Salva Gildenbourne. Before that first *skurj* attacked us, and we met the Giants. He read or heard something in the sand," the residue of rocks which must have been old long before Covenant's first appearance in the Land.

There Anele had spoken of *the necessary forbidding of evils*—a forbidding like the repulsion which the Colossus of the Fall had once wielded. But that strength was long gone. It had failed with the passing of the One Forest and the Forestals.

Without forbidding, there is too little time.

"Aye," Liand acknowledged. "At that time, he instructed you to 'Seek deep rock. The oldest stone. Only there the memory remains.' But how do you conclude that your son is imprisoned beneath the earth?"

Anele had also said, *Forget understanding. Forget purpose. Forget the* Elohim. *They, too, are imperiled.*

Like so many of the old man's utterances, that one had been as urgent as prophecy, and as cryptic. Now, too late, Linden knew what it meant.

And she knew something else as well. When he stood on rock—or on the remnants of rocks—Anele's pronouncements held truth. Whether or not she grasped their significance, she needed to hear and heed them.

Become as trees, the roots of trees. Seek deep rock.

She shrugged. "I can't be sure. But Lord Foul likes to hide his secrets in stone. Nothing else is strong enough to hold them."

"That I must believe," admitted the young man. "Nonetheless I fear for Anele. The purpose which lies in wait beneath his madness—" Liand shook himself to loosen the trepidation that tightened his shoulders. "Linden, I do not merely fear for him. For causes which I cannot name, I fear Anele himself, though unpossessed he offers harm to none."

Briefly Linden met the Stonedownor's troubled gaze. Then she looked away. "You should probably trust your instincts. But I don't feel what you do. To me, he looks more dangerous to himself than to anyone else." After a moment, she added, "I just wish that I knew what Sunder and Hollian said to him. Or what they did for him. I wish I knew what they know about him."

But she had nowhere to turn for answers. Unless Covenant chanced upon a relevant memory, and was able to explain it, she could only wait for events to reveal the exigencies that ruled Anele. She was responsible for most of the delays which had prevented her departure with the Harrow; yet now she felt helpless to do anything except wait.

ॐ

E ventually the Cords returned to the vale. Both Bhapa and Pahni bore handfuls of treasure-berries; and Bhapa announced that he had found a brook perhaps a hundred paces beyond the eastern rim of the hollow.

Trusting the *Haruchai* and the Ramen to stand guard, Rime Coldspray and her Swordmainnir strode away in various directions, some to forage for more *aliantha*, others heading toward water. While Bhapa and Pahni offered the viridian fruit to Linden and Liand, Anele and Stave, Branl tried to get the Unbeliever's attention. But Covenant did not emerge from his recollections. Perhaps he had already eaten enough to satisfy his new mortality.

Linden accepted a few of the berries after Anele had taken as much as his hands could hold. She would need more: she knew that. And she, too, would have to visit the brook. For the moment, however, she was content to send Liand off with Pahni to search and drink. Bhapa also she encouraged to fend for himself. She wanted a chance to talk to the Ardent.

Accompanied only by Stave and Mahrtiir, she ascended the shallow slope toward the garish Insequent. The Harrow studied her suspiciously as she approached, but said nothing. Covenant's ring he clenched in one fist as if he sought to squeeze wild magic from it by sheer force. The Staff of Law he hugged to his chest like a shield.

"Lady." The Ardent bowed in a fanfare of ribbands. "Doubtless the moment draws nigh when we will depart this vale of rue. And doubtless we are one and all devout in our hope that occasions more pleasurable lie before us. It is apparent, however, that uncertainties remain to disturb you. I will endeavor to ease you, if I may do so without interference in the Harrow's designs."

"Without *more* interference," muttered the Harrow darkly. Then he clamped his jaws shut.

Linden hardly knew how much to trust the Ardent, but she answered his bow with a nod. "I appreciate what you've already done." Her gratitude seemed to float on a vast sea of dread, but she did not mean to speak of her fears. "Unfortunately I can't think of any questions about the Harrow that you might be free to answer. I wanted to ask you something else.

"The Harrow seems to believe that all you care about is gluttony. But I'm not convinced. What you want isn't that simple. If it's fair to say that all of the Insequent are ruled by greed," for knowledge, or for personal glory, or for service, "what are *you* greedy for? Why did your people pick you? What are you trying to get for yourself?"

Decorating himself with flutters, the Ardent beamed at her. "You are insightful, lady—and mayhap wise as well—in spite of your manifold follies. Doubtless others have observed these qualities in you."

The Theomach had called her *clever* as well as *wise*. Surely she had made enough mistakes to prove him wrong?

"It is not without cause," continued the Ardent without pausing, "that the Harrow regards me with disdain." Every sentence emphasized his lisp. "Yet his scorn misleads him. Gluttony I affirm. However, feasting and the adoration of viands are but one manifestation of my distinctive hunger, the unsated quest which you have named greed. My appetites are not limited to the delights of the flesh.

"Lady, my true hunger is for that which is utterly singular, entirely unique. I crave the experience of that which lacks all precedent and cannot be repeated. I have not attained my happy bulk by repetition, or indeed by quantity, but rather by seeking out and enjoying every form of sustenance which the wide Earth proffers. And I desire other uniquenesses as well. I wish to taste and see and hear and feel and do all things that are new to me, or to the world, or that are too fleeting to recur. And I wish to savor sensations in which no other being ever can or ever will participate. For this quality, and because I am an acolyte of the Mahdoubt, I was chosen. The Insequent perceive that I cannot fail their trust without betraying my own greed.

"I have witnessed the mating of *Nicor* merely because no other Insequent, or any self-aware creature, has done so. For the same reason, I have stood upon the mightiest peaks of the Earth, not excluding great *Melenkurion* Skyweir. Yet those are lesser joys because the day may come when others also experience them.

"*This*"—he expanded his ribbands until they seemed to include the whole hollow and all that had occurred within it—"is truly unprecedented. Nor will it ever recur. And my presence within it is unprecedented, unrepeatable, ecstatically unique. *I speak for the Insequent as a people.* Those powers which they are able to invest in me, I possess. Ere now, such a confluence has never transpired. Come what may, it will never transpire again. And no other living being will ever know its fraught joys.

"Behold me, lady, at the crown and culmination of my greed." Bright bands of color wove around him as if he and they formed a tapestry of exaltation. "Never will I be deemed the greatest of the Insequent. Nor will my deeds determine the outcome of the Earth. Yet I do not scruple to proclaim that no Insequent has achieved the fruition which I attain here. No other Insequent will attain it. Even the Harrow in his vainglory will not."

Linden stared at him, trying to grasp the implications of his peroration. Although his human aura remained partially concealed by his raiment, she discerned that he was telling the truth. But how would such a man react in a crisis? A crisis was certain: she knew the Despiser too well to believe otherwise. What would a man who prized unique sensations above all else do when he faced butchery and was threatened with death?

He had threatened to reveal the Harrow's true name—the most fatal act an Insequent could commit—but he may have been bluffing.

While she pondered that question, looking for ways to examine the Ardent further, the Harrow said to him in a black voice, "Yet you know naught of the deep places of the Earth."

The plump Insequent raised his eyebrows as though the Harrow's statement touched a sore place in him. "That is sooth," he conceded in a more subdued manner. "I fear them. They are hazardous beyond estimation. Indeed, some few among the Insequent have perished in their search for knowledge of those depths. I need only name the Auriference.

"In a distant age," he explained to Linden, "a time that far preceded that of the Theomach, she delved deeply, seeking a knowledge both ancient and immeasurable. Desiring as did the Theomach to be named the greatest of the Insequent, she found only the loss of use and mind and life. Yet her end was by no act of the Insequent. Rather she was unmade by evils too vicious to be contemplated. For that reason, our kind has largely eschewed the Land, deeming that its perils exceed its grandeur and mystery. The exceptions are infrequent and secret—though it is surely plain to all that the Harrow stands among them.

"By my own deeds," he concluded, "my doom is bound to yours, and to the Harrow's. I do not aspire to end my days in terror."

Linden expected some mordant retort from the Harrow. But he only grinned fiercely through his beard and said nothing.

After a moment, Stave announced quietly, "Chosen, the Swordmainnir return. The Cords and the Stonedownor are refreshed, and Anele's hunger has been satisfied. You and the Manethrall must now seek out the brook. To preserve your strength, you must have water."

He was right: Linden knew that. But she was reluctant to stop probing the Insequent. Indirectly the Harrow had confirmed that Jeremiah had been hidden underground. And the Ardent's fulsome account of himself did not reassure her. If he already feared what might happen to him—

However, she suspected that more questions would not bring more answers. And Jeremiah had been left too long at the *croyel*'s mercy.

Please, she wanted to say to the Ardent. Don't abandon us. Not while that monster has my son. But she lacked the eloquence to move him.

Surely he understood the danger—?

Nodding once more to the Ardent, if in supplication rather than in gratitude, she let Stave and Mahrtiir lead her away.

ᘏᘏᘏ

W hen she and the Manethrall had quenched their thirst, eaten *aliantha*, and rejoined the rest of her companions, Linden saw that they were ready; as ready as they would ever be. Liand's mastery of his *orcrest* seemed steady enough. But Covenant's ability to make use of Loric's *krill* was unpredictable at best. It might do him more harm than good, if Joan and *turiya* chose some crucial moment to assail him. The company would have to rely upon the weight and weapons and skill of the Giants, and the resolute prowess of the *Haruchai*. In *the deep places of the Earth*, the abilities of the Ramen might be of little use.

Linden herself had nothing to contribute.

Yet Mahrtiir emanated a grim eagerness in spite of his blindness and his Ramen fear of enclosure. In darkness, the loss of his eyes might have the effect of an advantage. And his fierce desire to participate in a tale worth remembering had not waned.

Bhapa doubted himself too much to share his Manethrall's anticipation. Clearly, however, he found reassurance in Mahrtiir's attitude. But Pahni's fears for Liand were growing. She stood at his shoulder as though she ached to cast off her reserve and cling to him openly. Because she was Ramen and followed her Manethrall, she would face any hazard and fight to the end of her life. Still her concern for Liand outweighed any other apprehension.

I wish I could spare you. Hell, I wish any of us could spare you. But I can't see any way around it.

For himself, Liand did not share Pahni's alarm. When Linden had allowed him to accompany her away from his life in Mithil Stonedown, she had opened the way for a discovery of both the Land and himself: a discovery that still thrilled him. Inadvertently she had cast a glamour over him which she distrusted and he did not. It had made him the first true Stonedownor since before the time of the Sunbane.

And he had new strengths now; strengths that might sustain him if or when Linden failed to justify his faith in her.

Beyond her more human friends, the Giants shared a measure of Mahrtiir's grimness and excitement. Knowing the Earth as they did, they could probably imagine the dangers better than any Raman. Yet they treasured the tales that resulted from hazard and daring. And they loved stone: they did not fear to seek Jeremiah, or any fate, underground. Linden saw possibilities for joy in them that the Manethrall lacked.

Like the Humbled, Stave remained entirely himself: unreadable in his dedication to the absolute in any situation; his apparent rejection of all sorrow. But Anele grew increasingly impatient. Linden could not guess what prompted his restiveness, but it was evident in his tense shoulders and twitching fingers; in the way he jerked his head from side to side as if he were hearing a multitude of voices. His gaze, milky and sightless, darted from place to place as though he expected horrors to emerge from the sumptuous grass.

And Covenant, the man whom Linden had loved and lost, as she had loved and lost her son: he remained as alone as Jeremiah in spite of his physical presence. Indeed, he seemed immured under a mountain of mental or spiritual rubble. His efforts to extricate himself were palpable, so plain that Linden could almost follow their progress.

Huddling into himself, he talked inexplicably of a time when he and Lord Mhoram had stood looking down into Treacher's Gorge while an army of Cavewights marched forth.

"So many of them," he muttered. "Too many to count. Lord Foul used them whenever he wanted fodder for one of his wars. He spent thousands of them fighting Hile Troy. And thousands more against Revelstone. They're intelligent enough to be used. They're just not smart enough to recognize lies. They're so good at killing, it's easy to forget how badly they've been misled.

"Hell, they don't *need* wars. The Wightwarrens have everything they want. They didn't ask to be shock troops. Even poor Drool— His only real mistake was listening to Lord Foul. Everything after that was the Despiser's doing."

Covenant's eyebrows were an arch of strain across his forehead. From time to time, he punched his bound fists against each other if he hoped that the pain would jolt him back into coherence. Dampness in his eyes suggested that he might weep. To Linden, he seemed altogether pitiable.

That was her doing. Hers.

And yet, somehow, he remained Thomas Covenant, the man who had twice defeated Lord Foul. The cut lines of his visage and the gauntness of his frame, even the potential tears in his eyes, did not imply frailty. Rather they conveyed an austere authority. He resembled a sovereign brought low, accustomed to command in spite of his ragged state. In the light of Liand's Sunstone, his silver hair shone like an oriflamme, and the pale scar on his forehead gleamed like an anointment.

The bandages on his hands—cerise and incarnadine, opalescent and viridian—were grotesqueries that only emphasized his stature.

Linden's eyes burned at the sight of him; at his suffering and his unextinguished spirit. Oh, he diminished her. That was his nature—or hers. Nonetheless his effect on her had shifted. His support against the Humbled made her ache to prove worthy of him. To win back whatever love she had lost during his immeasurable absence with the Arch of Time.

She trusted that he would respond when she needed him.

She was less confident of the Humbled. They had changed their minds once. They might do so again. But when she finally said to Stave, "Let's go. I've kept us all waiting too long," the three Masters began urging Covenant toward the Harrow.

Stoically Galt, Branl, and Clyme clung to their right to believe in themselves. *How otherwise will the Humbled redeem themselves in my sight?* Beyond question, they feared grief more than any peril. The Vizard had taught them too well. Being *Haruchai*, they did not know how to distinguish between sorrow and humiliation.

Summoning her resolve, Linden led her companions to dare the outcome of her last gamble.

"Are you done with hesitation, lady?" asked the Harrow acidly. "Even now, the Worm feeds. Ere long, its hunger will become a convulsion in the fundament of the Earth. Will you at last permit me to uphold our bargain?"

Linden stared into the black emptiness of his eyes as if she had become fearless. "Let's be clear." Her voice felt stiff in her throat, brittle and unwieldy. But it did not tremble. "You've already got what you wanted from me. Now you're going to take us to my son. All of us. And you're going to bring us all back when we've rescued him. You're going to bring him with us."

"I have said so," the Harrow retorted. "I have vowed it. I will fulfill my oath."

The Ardent nodded. "Allay your doubts, lady." His anxiety had reclaimed him, quashing his complacent lisp. "The word of any Insequent is as necessary as breath. Knowledge is a strict treasure. It does not suffer falsehood. Should the Harrow fail to perform all that you have asked, all that he has gained will be reft from him. And"— the Ardent's ribbands twisted like flinching—"I am present to aid the completion of his bargain."

"All right." Thoughts of Jeremiah compelled Linden. "Tell us what you need us to do."

Immediately, vehement with eagerness, the Harrow commanded, "Stand near together. It will ease our passage if the Giants bear those who consent. The Ardent and I will combine our theurgies to preclude any misstep arising from your excess of companions."

Linden glanced around at the Ramen and Liand. When she saw that they agreed, she looked to the Ironhand.

Mutely Coldspray gestured at her comrades. At once, Latebirth, Cabledarm, and

Bluntfist lifted the Ramen into their arms. Stonemage picked up Liand and seated him on one of her massive forearms. While Galesend did the same for Anele, Frostheart Grueburn took Linden. Only Cirrus Kindwind, who had lost an arm against the *skurj*, and Coldspray herself were unencumbered as the Swordmainnir crowded into a cluster.

Stave stood beside Grueburn. The Humbled formed a knot around Covenant close to the Ironhand.

Linden felt wariness on all sides. In this formation, the Giants could not draw their weapons. Only the *Haruchai* would be able to react swiftly to a sudden threat. Nevertheless no one resisted the Harrow's instructions.

He and the Ardent positioned themselves on opposite sides of the company. While the Harrow began to rub his beads in an elaborate pattern, muttering as his fingers skittered from place to place, the Ardent sent out bright streamers to enclose Linden and her companions. His ribbands spread far enough to touch the Harrow's shoulders; but the Harrow ignored them.

Still muttering, he demanded, "Douse your magic, youth. It intrudes."

Linden understood. The Sunstone was an instrument of Earthpower: it expressed Liand's strength according to the strictures of Law. Clearly the Harrow intended to step outside such boundaries, as he did whenever he translated himself from one location to another.

For a moment, Liand considered the Harrow's order. Then he shrugged and eased his grip on the *orcrest*, allowing its illumination to fade until the stone lay inert in his hand. But he did not return it to its pouch at his waist.

Lit only by the pinprick glittering of the stars, Linden and her companions waited, dark as shadows, for the Harrow to complete his preparations.

Linden held her breath. She was going to Jeremiah: she repeated that to herself again and again. Going to Jeremiah. After all this time: after so much struggle and inadequacy, so much bitter victory and expensive failure. Soon she would need to find the courage for what she would see, the *croyel* clinging to her son's helpless back, chewing viciously on the side of his neck; filling her vacant boy with feral hate.

And she had to pray that at least one of her companions possessed the force necessary to make the monster *let go*—

Of its own will, the *croyel* would never allow her to hold Jeremiah in her arms. Never.

Leaning against Grueburn's stone cataphract, Linden waited; tried to hope. She felt no power gather around her. Nothing more eldritch than Andelain itself seemed to inhabit the night. But she had never been able to sense the peculiar magicks of the Insequent. Like the Theomach's and the Mahdoubt's, the Harrow's form of wizardry articulated itself in a dimension of reality or time which lay outside the reach of her perceptions.

She did not know that anything had happened until the stars, and the deeper night beneath the surrounding trees, and the Hills themselves vanished into utter darkness. Then heavy stone and cold closed over her—over all of her company—like the sealing of a tomb.

6.

Seek Deep Stone

Tightly guarded by the Humbled, Thomas Covenant was snatched out of recollections of Cavewights to find himself standing on the wrought span, long and narrow, that bridged the abyss between the imponderable gutrock of Mount Thunder and the portal of the Lost Deep.

The magicks of the Insequent and his fear for Linden had wrenched him out of his memories. It was possible that no one else understood how badly she could be hurt here.

He saw nothing. The darkness was absolute, encased by leagues of complex stone. He was probably days of tortuous ascents below the nearest caves and tunnels of the Wightwarrens. Nonetheless he had no impression of the terrible chasm that stretched beneath his feet: he could hardly taste the ancient dust in the stagnant, dying air. The cold had not reached him yet. He was numb with leprosy, and had no health-sense to identify his circumstances.

Nevertheless the pervasive brume of Kevin's Dirt was stifling. He was dangerously close to its source; to the living bane that Kastenessen and Esmer and *moksha* Raver had tapped or harnessed in order to generate the fug which hampered the Staff of Law.

So near that unanswerable evil, Linden and Liand and the Ramen were surely as truncated, as blind and nearly insensate, as he was. Anele's heritage of Earthpower might preserve him; but even the percipience of the *Haruchai* and the Giants was likely to fail. In moments, every one of Linden's companions would be effectively as eyeless as Mahrtiir, as deaf as seas, as unresponsive to touch as bluff rock.

Unaware of the danger—

The absence of light was so complete that the stubborn granite in every direction could no longer recall illumination.

Yet Covenant knew exactly where he was. Of course he did. From the perspective of the Arch, his spirit had visited this place too often to be mistaken. Scant hours ago, he had been painfully familiar with the Lost Deep—and with the fragile reach of stone which provided its only access to or from the outer world. Remembering it now, he remembered also that even the Harrow in his avarice had never passed beyond this span. The Insequent's claim that he knew where to find Linden's son was based, not on direct observation, but on other forms of knowledge.

By increments, a dull ache invaded Covenant's chest. The sensation inspired a kind of panic. Perhaps the source of Kevin's Dirt had already noticed the intrusion of the Staff of Law and white gold, of *orcrest* and Loric's *krill*, if not the presence of Giants and *Haruchai* and ordinary humans. But he was human himself now. After a moment, he realized that what he felt was oxygen deprivation, not the dire approach of hate. The icy air was too old to sustain him: he was beginning to suffocate.

No one spoke. No one had spoken. The entire company seemed paralyzed, held motionless by shock or terror. By darkness or cold or anoxia. But then Anele began coughing—and the Giants shifted slightly, making room for the Humbled—and a far more immediate alarm seized Covenant.

"Don't move!" he wheezed urgently. "Don't anyone move."

He wanted to say more. Hellfire! Don't you know where we *are*? But a spasm of coughing closed his throat. Every effort to breathe filled his lungs with dust.

The span was narrow. Anyone who fell would plunge long enough to wish for death before the end.

Linden? he tried to call out; tried and could not. He had not coughed for millennia. Freed from the necessities of muscles and irritated tissues, he had forgotten how to manage them. Coughing wracked him until his mind spun as if he had been stricken with vertigo.

Then he heard Linden's voice. "Liand," she gasped: a severe effort. "*Orcrest.*"

For a time that felt interminable, nothing happened. Liand must have been over-whelmed by the suddenness with which he had lost his health-sense; or by simple darkness and alarm. And no one aided him. Blinded, they did not know how.

The Harrow should have taken action. This was *his* doing. But perhaps he was content to let his companions—his victims—fall. He had not vowed to defend them from the dangers of this journey. Under the circumstances, the prospect of being rid of Linden and her friends probably pleased him.

He had no experience with Linden's Staff.

In that case, the Ardent—

Damnation, it was cold. Covenant felt a kind of astonished fury at his inability to stop coughing; to open his throat and draw breath and speak. What was the good of his resurrection if he could not control his own body?

The Ardent feared *the deep places of the Earth*. With ample reason.

One or more of the Ramen retched for air. The Giants moved cautiously away from each other in spite of Covenant's warning. They did not fear cold or darkness or old stone: they may have wanted a little space in which to clear their lungs. Or perhaps they sought room to protect the people they carried.

"Heed the Unbeliever," Stave said as if mere suffocation and sightlessness and chill could not impinge upon him. "Stonedownor, heed the Chosen."

The Giants stopped. Liand made a hoarse sound. Somewhere in the darkness, he struggled to regain his concentration.

Gradually light began to emerge from the young man's right fist.

By slow degrees at first, the glow swelled. Benighted and heavy, the bulk of the Swordmainnir took shape. The Humbled appeared around Covenant as though they had condensed from the thinner substance of shadows. Linden leaned, panting, on Grueburn's breastplate. Held by Galesend, Anele had covered his face with his hands in terror.

Then Liand grew stronger. The ramifications of exerted Earthpower purified the air around him, enabling him to breathe more easily.

In a rush, radiance burst out to contradict the dark.

A strangled cry came from Liand. The Ironhand barked, "Stone and Sea!" Her comrades hissed imprecations and oaths. "Oh, God," Linden repeated like a wail, "oh, God," but softly, softly, as if she feared the sound of her own voice.

Cold echoes mocked every word.

Like Liand, the rest of the company began to inhale better air. They grew stronger; strong enough to recognize the extremity of their situation.

Covenant and four *Haruchai* and eight Giants stood near the apex of the bridge, facing their destination. Ahead of them, the Harrow still muttered incantations or invocations. At the rear of the company, the Ardent gagged on protests that choked him. He had withdrawn his ribbands; wrapped them like a form of armor around his corpulence.

Beneath their feet, the smooth span of the bridge traced a shallow arc upward and then down toward the portal of the Lost Deep: a high, arched entryway with nothing beyond it except an impermeable black, a darkness which the Sunstone could not pierce. A host could have entered there, or issued forth; but here the stone was no more than two Giants' paces wide. It looked too fragile to hold so much weight.

Across this stone, the Viles had left their elaborate demesne in order to measure their lore against the wider world; and so they had learned doubt and then loathing and then doom.

They had not been burdened by flesh. Their makings, the Demondim, had seldom troubled to inhabit bodies. And with the exception of their loremasters, the ur-viles that had once labored in the loreworks were hands shorter than Covenant; more slight than even Pahni. The Waynhim were smaller still. None of them had needed a sturdy bridge.

But the white shining of Liand's Sunstone reached farther. In spite of his dismay, he extended light into a vast space that made the figures on the bridge seem tiny by comparison.

Overhead a crude dome formed the ceiling of an immense cavern. From the gutrock depended a number of tapering stalactites massive as towers, knaggy as gnarled wood. They glistened with moisture. Among them, spangles of quartz and other crystals cast giddy reflections, as elusive as wheeling stars. None of the stalactites hung directly over the bridge. Yet they looked so ponderous that the mere wind of their passing if they fell might crack the span.

From their tips, streams of water trickled downward, pulling Covenant's gaze with them.

Downward.

Downward.

Into an abyss that seemed to have no bottom. If those delicate rivulets struck rock somewhere far below the bridge, their plash was too distant to be audible.

The depths called to Covenant. Dizziness clutched at his stomach; his head. Involuntarily he stumbled. Galt's hands gripped his arms like iron bands, but he did not feel them. Everyone around him seemed to recede until they were beyond reach; unable to aid him. Coldspray rasped questions that had no meaning. His mind whirled, sucking away its own substance.

His spirit had forgotten vertigo: his flesh had not. It urged him to pitch himself into the chasm; to satisfy this whirlpool of nausea by falling and falling like the water, endlessly, until his body redeemed itself in the depths.

If Galt had given him a chance—

"No," the Ardent wheezed, straining for air. "I cannot. The Harrow has misled himself." Fright ached in his voice. "The span is warded. *We must not fall!*"

Like a mirage of himself, the Insequent fled toward the safer rock of Mount Thunder's roots, away from the portal.

"Withdraw," Coldspray commanded through her teeth. "Follow the Ardent. Now. With care. This stone is seamed with age, ancient beyond reckoning. Our weight may surpass its endurance."

The sound of her voice seemed to spread cracks through the rock, flaws like the fissures that riddled Covenant's thoughts. He imagined bits of granite breaking off from the edges of the span, following threads of moisture down to their eternal end. The bridge had begun to fail. Or it would fail. Vertigo reduced his friable balance, his human awareness, to rubble.

"No," countered Clyme. "The Harrow will forsake us, as the Ardent has done. This mad endeavor will accomplish only ruin if we permit the holder of Staff and ring to precede us."

"He won't," Linden groaned urgently. "He promised. He's going to take us to Jeremiah. And bring us back. If he doesn't, he'll destroy himself."

Her voice created an eyot of sanity in Covenant's reeling mind. Uncounted millennia ago, he had been familiar with vertigo. Occasionally he had been able to manage it. And Linden was right, of course she was. In addition, the Harrow— Like another piece of sanity, Covenant remembered that the Harrow had never opened the portal. Perhaps he did not know how.

Or how to use the Staff of Law.

He did not care about Linden's pain.

The bridge was a way in; but it was also a snare. A defense. Protected. If the Harrow erred, he would shatter the span.

"*Now*," insisted Rime Coldspray. "We will consider other choices when we have attained more trustworthy rock."

Without waiting for the assent of the Humbled, she began to descend the bridge, stepping as gently as her size permitted.

At once, Frostheart Grueburn followed with Linden.

"Bring Covenant!" Linden ordered; pleaded. She must have been speaking to the Humbled. The rest of the Swordmainnir had already shifted their feet, readying themselves to obey Coldspray one at a time.

Chunks of stone still crumbled and fell from the rims of the span; but now Covenant understood that he was imagining them.

"Faugh!" spat the Harrow. "The Ardent's alarm does not surprise me. Selecting him, the Insequent have betrayed themselves. But I did not foresee cowardice in those who name themselves the lady's friends. I will summon you when I have secured the safety of your passage."

Muttering again, he crossed the crest of the span like a man who had come too far to remember fear.

Past the edges of the stone, the abyss called to Covenant; sang to him like the siren lure of the *merewives*. But Galt did not release him. Branl and Clyme stood on either side as if to prevent him from breaking away; as if he had ever been strong enough to resist the *Haruchai*.

He continued to resist the whirl in his head. Arduously he gathered scraps of sanity from the inadequate air, accreting them like shards of iron to a magnet. Liand's blazing Sunstone cleansed the atmosphere to some extent, dispelling increments of depletion and staleness; but it was not enough. Covenant's dizziness was old and obdurate—and he had not re-learned the limitations of his carnal life. He had to fight for every shred of self-mastery.

His plight recalled the descent from Kevin's Watch. Foamfollower had carried him once; but twice he had accomplished that feat by force of will. And the Harrow had never opened the portal to the Lost Deep. Wild magic would betray him there. He would need the Staff of Law. And cunning. And subtlety. Even though he had not had time to learn the Staff's uses.

The portal was the reason. It explained why the Harrow had transported everyone *here*, instead of directly to Jeremiah. The defenses which the Viles had woven for their demesne were complex and duplicitous. If he did not enter the Lost Deep correctly, the entire subterranean realm might collapse. Or he and everyone with him might be slain in some more oblique and cruel fashion.

That Covenant understood. Memories might aid him—or they might bring madness. Understanding was sanity. And sanity made an island in the gyre of his flawed consciousness; a clear space in which he could remain himself.

By degrees, he recognized the import of Galt's grip on his arms; recognized it and was grateful.

In one direction, the Harrow neared the culmination of the bridge. In the other, Giants moved cautiously toward the nearer wall of the cavern. They went in single file ahead of the Humbled and Covenant, carefully removing the stress of their weight from the span. The Ironhand and Grueburn had already reached the foot of the arc. Ignoring Linden's protests, Stave had accompanied them. Latebirth and Mahrtiir would join them in three or four more strides, followed by Onyx Stonemage and Liand.

Covenant began to recover a measure of stability. Maybe, he thought, refusing his desire to fall: maybe he should ask the Humbled to take him to the Harrow. Like the Insequent, he had never wielded the Staff of Law. And his bandaged hands were almost entirely numb. He did not know how well or thoroughly they had been healed. But he might remember something. Somewhere among the remains of his fading recall, he might find knowledge that the Harrow needed—

He did not want to remember what lived in the abyss below him. Nonetheless his need to rescue Jeremiah was as great as Linden's, although he no longer knew why.

Yet he feared the Lost Deep instinctively. It was rife with reminders of events and powers so inhuman and old that they might drag him dozens of millennia away from his present; from any possibility of helping Linden. He was not confident that he would be able to stand against his memories: not while the consequences of his resurrection threatened to betray him at every step.

Perhaps the Harrow already knew how to open the portal without precipitating a catastrophe.

Fuming to himself, he urged his guardians to follow the Swordmainnir.

Cirrus Kindwind was the last: she eased her way down the arc after Bluntfist and Bhapa. Trying to secure his tenuous poise, Covenant fixed his gaze straight ahead, past Kindwind's shoulders toward the ragged stone of the cavern wall. The chasm tugged at his attention, but he refused to glance aside.

In another step, Stormpast Galesend would leave the bridge. Then the weight of five Giants would be gone: Linden, Mahrtiir, Liand, and Anele would safe. And Grueburn and Stonemage had already set down their burdens. With Coldspray, they braced themselves at the edge of the abyss, ready to catch anyone who might be forced to jump.

Their breath steamed in great gusts like intimations of dread.

Beyond them, a crude tunnel twisted away into the sealed midnight of Mount Thunder's roots. In the light of the Sunstone, Covenant saw that the roof of the tunnel was scarcely high enough to let the Giants stand upright. Before it writhed out of sight, the passage narrowed sharply. Where it debouched into the cavern, however, it opened like a fan formed of relatively level obsidian veined with malachite. The white purity of the *orcrest*'s illumination accentuated the green hue of the malachite. The branching of the veins through the obsidian gave them an eerie resemblance to the grass stains on Linden's jeans.

Galesend and then Latebirth gained the mouth of the tunnel. Holding Covenant between them like a prisoner or an invalid, the Humbled matched Kindwind's pace as she moved down the span.

Now Covenant could believe that the bridge would hold; and his balance improved. With each step, he found it easier to shut out the insistence of the gulf.

Presumably to ensure that Anele would not wander too near the abyss, Galesend put the old man on his feet within the mouth of the tunnel, near the area where the obsidian tapered to an end. Then she turned back to welcome Latebirth.

For reasons that had slumped from Covenant's shoulders like a garment which he had become too small to wear, he felt a twist of anxiety on Anele's behalf. Dooms hinged on him, as they did on the Harrow. —*remember that he is the hope of the Land.* Someone had said that: someone Covenant trusted. *When your deeds have come to doom*— His memories seemed random, involuntary; impossible to control. Cracks and crevices hemmed him on all sides, cutting him off from ordinary humanity. —*as they must*— In his own eyes, he would not have been more obviously a leper if the scar on his forehead had been a brand. Yet Linden's gaze clung to his with the desperation of a woman who believed that he clasped her fate in his insensible hands.

Hell and blood, she must have been freezing— He may have been shivering himself:

he was not sure. But the small tears in her shirt were as vivid to him as the bullet hole over her heart. Cold would leak through the red flannel like water. Whenever she exhaled, steam rose like frailty from her lungs.

She had given up so much, and had lost more. Too much.

Holding her gaze, Covenant became stronger for her sake. Every moment that he retained his grip on the present cost him more of his memories; deprived him ineluctably of the ineffable knowledge which had inspired him to speak to her from the Arch of Time. Already his awareness of what he needed to do, and why, had dwindled to indeterminate and unpredictable debris. But Linden needed him. In some fashion that he could no longer define, the Earth and the Land and Jeremiah needed him as much as they needed her. Grimly he increased his pace, drawing the Humbled with him as he crowded closer to Cirrus Kindwind's back.

At irregular intervals, the *krill* throbbed ominously against his abdomen; but he ignored it.

As Halewhole Bluntfist carried Bhapa off the bridge, Coldspray, Grueburn, and Stonemage began to relax. Now Kindwind, Covenant, and the Humbled were close to safety.

Lacking percipience, Covenant could not sense the Harrow. Too many of his nerves were dead. He did not doubt that the Insequent had reached the far end of the span. But he had no idea what that avid man might do there, or how his efforts would fare. Nevertheless Covenant did not risk turning his head to look. His balance was still precarious. If he let it, the abyss would renew its grip in an instant.

Like Linden, he had lost and given up too much.

He hoped that her health-sense had not been entirely stifled, despite her proximity to the fierce source of Kevin's Dirt. If Liand's exertion of Earthpower could impose a partial cleanliness on the air, it might also preserve a measure of her discernment. And if she could still *see*, then surely the senses of the Giants and the *Haruchai* would retain their native vitality. The Ramen, and even Liand himself, might feel as numb as Covenant, but their perceptions would not be entirely superficial.

Yet no effect of *orcrest* could relieve Covenant's leprosy, or ease his particular vulnerabilities. As he left the bridge to stand on obsidian and malachite, he felt more useless than he had when Linden had first reclaimed him. He had no idea what to say to her, or to any of her companions. Her relief was unmistakable. The Ramen and even the Giants appeared to breathe more easily now that everyone was safe, at least for the moment. But it was only a matter of time before one of them studied what the Harrow was doing, or not doing, and asked, Now what? And Covenant could not remember what they all needed to know.

It was also only a matter of time before the Earth's deepest lamentation noticed the intrusion of theurgy in Her dominions. Loric's *krill* and Liand's *orcrest* would attract attention. Long ages of stupor might continue to hold Her for a while, but then She would respond.

And if or when Linden reached Jeremiah, Kastenessen and Esmer and the *Elohim* and even the buried bane would know where to look—

Whether Covenant's companions realized it or not, they had no one to turn to for answers except the Ardent.

The beribboned Insequent stood in the mouth of the tunnel near Anele. He kept his back to the abyss; did not look at anyone. If he had received any benefit from Liand's exertion of Earthpower, he did not show it. Instead he continued to breathe heavily, as if he had carried his fat and fear for leagues under the mountain. The multitudinous strips of his apparel remained clenched around him as tightly as a fist.

Had the will and power of his people deserted him? He seemed overwhelmed; too daunted to carry out their wishes. As useless as Covenant—

Covenant found everyone except the Ardent and Anele looking at him. Even Linden's closest friends watched his every movement as though they expected him to perform a miracle of some kind. Take command of the situation. Tell them what to do.

Clearly they retained enough health-sense to see that his mind was present. As he had hoped, the *orcrest*'s Earthpower resisted the worst effects of Kevin's Dirt. Linden's eyes clung to him. She was unutterably precious to him, and wounded past bearing. In some other life—the life that she deserved—he would have wrapped his arms around her and held her until her loneliness eased.

But he had no value to her here: not as he was.

"Hellfire," he muttered simply to break the silence. "That was fun." Trying to rub sensations of futility from his face with his bound hands, he asked, "Can any of you see what the Harrow is doing? I'm afraid to look."

No one glanced away. Even the Humbled regarded him stolidly.

Softly, as if she were reluctant to awaken echoes, Rime Coldspray replied, "The Harrow has gained the archway or portal at the foot of the span. Now he bows on one knee at the verge of an extreme dark which the Stonedownor's legacy cannot penetrate. Perhaps he prepares incantations. Perhaps not. The white gold ring he holds to his forehead in one fist. The Staff of Law he grips upright before him. To my diminished sight, however, he appears to wield no magicks. Rather he remains merely bowed as in contemplation."

The rim of the precipice was too near. Trickles and streams of water fell from the tips of the stalactites as if they were draining the life-blood out of the world's veins drop by drop. The web of malachite that defined or defied the obsidian under Covenant's boots created the illusion that its strands flowed ceaselessly toward the abysm.

"He's trying to find the way in." Covenant was hardly aware of his own voice. The Ardent's alarm was contagious. It bred vertigo. "Past that blank place is the Lost Deep.

The home of the Viles, back when the Viles still existed. That's where they did their breeding—and the Demondim did—and the ur-viles. But it's protected. If the Harrow can't open it, we won't get in.

"That's why we're here. Why we aren't already with Jeremiah. No one can get in if that portal isn't opened first."

The Masters and Stave regarded him as though nothing that he might say could surprise them. The Giants only frowned in concentration, absorbing new information. But Linden stared at Covenant with darkness in her eyes. Her cheeks were pale, drained of blood. And the Ramen and Liand appeared to take their cue from her—or from the Ardent's labored breathing. Innominate uncertainties and dreads marked their faces like fretwork. Cowed by the mass of immeasurable stone above him, even the Manethrall gave the impression that he could be intimidated.

While he was still able to hold them, Covenant scrambled to articulate his memories. "This chasm. It's how the Viles guarded themselves. Isolated themselves. It isn't *just* a chasm. A terrible power lives here.

"Hell and blood," he panted through his teeth. "This is hard. I can't think—" Every word was as dangerous as falling. He spoke in puffs of vapor that became nothing. He could not help Linden. "When the Viles formed that bridge, they called it the Hazard. But translation doesn't do it justice. When they said 'Hazard,' they didn't just mean that terrible power. And they didn't just mean they covered the bridge with wards so it would shatter if someone tried to enter the Lost Deep without knowing how. It was *their* hazard, too.

"Making it, they risked everything. Who they were. What they meant to themselves. It was their only link to the rest of the Land. The rest of the Earth. When they crossed out of the Lost Deep, everything they'd ever done or cared about might be destroyed. While they kept themselves isolated, they could imagine they were perfect. But they were smart enough to know the world is a big place. Even the Land is a big place. They might meet beings and forces that would make them look paltry.

"They created the Hazard because they were too intelligent to be content with ideas of perfection that hadn't been tested. Compared. Measured."

The *Haruchai* would understand that better than anyone.

Behind him, he heard Anele muttering: a babble of agitation. But Linden's stare held him. He did not want to drop her gaze, even for a moment. If he had been able to look into her eyes—into her heart—during his long participation in the Arch, he might have been content to remain there until all things ended.

"Does the Harrow know how to open the door?"

Linden's question cut at Covenant: he had no numbness to cover that hurt. His scant memories became more useless whenever he needed them. All that time spent among the millennia, wasted—

Thickly he admitted, "You'll have to ask the Ardent. I've forgotten. If I ever knew."

He had no idea how to open the portal himself. He recalled only that wild magic would shatter the Hazard. For this task, the Harrow had to depend on the Staff of Law.

It belonged to Linden.

Briefly she searched him as if she thought that the sheer force of her yearning would compel remembrance. But the pressure accumulating within her demanded release: he could see that without percipience. While his pulse labored helplessly in his chest, and the cold tightened its grip, she turned away, drawing his attention with her.

Her lips were pallid and chilled as she repeated her question to the Insequent. Covenant drew inferences of shivering from the sound of her voice.

Why else had the Ardent insisted on accompanying Linden and her companions?

The fat man did not reply directly. He did not face her. Perhaps he could not. Instead he released a few of his ribbands in a flutter that suggested negation.

"I cannot aid him here." His voice was a taut wheeze. "This has been his life's quest. It is not mine. Nor has it been any other living Insequent's. I possess no knowledge, either earned or given, to ease his dilemma."

Hurt by Linden's desperation, Covenant demanded, "Then why exactly *are* you here? Your people didn't pick you just because you happen to like new experiences. They must have had something more constructive in mind. Otherwise what was the point?"

The Ardent flinched as if a lash had licked across his back. His raiment expanded and contracted with every hoarse breath. Nevertheless Covenant's challenge seemed to strike a spark of indignation or resolve within him. Summoning fortitude as though he had found it hidden within his garish apparel, he lifted his head, straightened his back. Slowly he turned. Strips of cerise and azure wiped the sweat from his forehead and his plump cheeks. They appeared to do so of their own volition.

"It is my task to ensure that the Harrow abides by his oath. That mission I have begun. I will continue it. I will assist him when I am able to do so. For the nonce, however, Timewarden, I have another purpose, one which the conjoined will of the Insequent has urged. I have drawn you hither, to my side rather than to the Harrow's. Him you cannot succor. Here knowledge which you have forgotten may be restored.

"Among those who assiduously seek out auguries and prescience, there is disagreement concerning the outcome of our present quest. Yet all concur that we must stand in this place at this time. Here we are vouchsafed an opportunity which will not recur, and which is greatly to be desired."

"What opportunity?" Linden's voice shook on the verge of hysteria. "How does this help us find my son?"

"It does not—" began the Insequent.

Before he could continue, Rime Coldspray put in, "Stonedownor, this illumination is a great boon." She sounded studiously nonchalant, casual, like a woman trying to ease the tension of her companions. "Can it be extended to supply warmth as well? Clearly the Ramen are hardy, inured to extremes. The same may be said of Giants and *Haruchai*. But Linden Giantfriend suffers here, as you also suffer. And it appears that the Timewarden is shielded only by his illness."

Covenant nodded reflexively. The state of his hands and feet gave him no protection. Fingers of ice had found their way through his clothes into his unfamiliar flesh. He trembled to the rhythm of Linden's shivering. But he did not care about himself. Even wrapped in vellum, the *krill*'s heat defended his physical core. And whenever Joan probed the gem, he gained more warmth. Inadvertently she did him good.

Linden was more at risk.

"It does not," repeated the Ardent. "Nonetheless it is needful."

Studying Linden, Liand replied to the Ironhand, "I have not made the attempt." His concern was evident. "Yet at every turn the virtues of *orcrest* have surpassed my imagination. If it gives light, banishes the effects of Kevin's Dirt, and cleanses this foul air, perhaps it may also emit heat. I will endeavor—"

"Needful how?" insisted Linden.

"Chosen," Stave said flatly: a veiled command. "Attend to Anele."

Linden hardly appeared to hear the former Master. Her attention clung to the Ardent. But Covenant forced himself to glance toward the old man.

How could he not remember this? Surely it was the task for which he had been resurrected? To remember—and give warning?

The marks on Linden's jeans should have reminded him—

Pahni drew a sharp breath as she followed Covenant's gaze. Baffled in his efforts to concentrate on the Sunstone, Liand looked momentarily flustered. Then his black brows arched in surprise. Blindly Mahrtiir faced Linden's first companion.

"Is this possession?" Stormpast Galesend asked, anxious for the man she had been charged to carry. "Is it some new manifestation of his madness? Stone and Sea! The diminishment of my sight vexes me."

Wincing, Linden wheeled away from the Ardent.

Anele lay facedown on the uneven obsidian with his arms and legs outstretched as if in deliberate prostration. Beneath his scrawny frame, veins of green radiated outward as though they depicted rays of light. Somehow the malachite conveyed the impression that it throbbed to the beat of his pulse.

Those veins resembled the stains which Covenant had once worn after passing through Morinmoss.

To Covenant, Anele looked only frail and beaten, as if he had been felled. But Liand murmured in wonder, "*See* him, Linden." And one of the Swordmainnir added, "Aye, behold."

Covenant wanted to ask, See what? Almost at once, however, Linden breathed, "That's not possession. It's Earthpower. He's on fire with it. His birthright— I've never seen it so strong. Or so close to the surface."

With an air of respect, even of reverence, the Ardent backed away from Anele; cleared a space around the old man.

In a voice like stone and apprehension and sorrow crushed together until they were in danger of crumbling, the old man said distinctly, "It is here."

The words themselves, or the tone in which Anele spoke them, ignited memories in Covenant—

Seek deep rock.

—memories so recent and explicit that they should have been impossible to forget.

The Harrow had brought Linden's company to stone so deep that no human capable of interpreting it had ever touched it before.

In Salva Gildenbourne, Anele had tried to explain something to Linden. Who else had heard him? Who else, apart from Covenant before his reincarnation? Stave? Liand?

"Here, Anele?" Linden asked in steam and cold. "What's here? What is the stone telling you?"

What had awakened the old man's inherited strength?

"The wood of the world has forgotten." Anele sounded as harsh as the rock beneath him. "It cannot reclaim itself. It requires aid. Yet this stone remembers."

Covenant remembered other things instead. A different time. A distant place.

Wood is too brief. All vastness is forgotten.

He expected to see Anele's limbs straining, fingers clawing at the obsidian. But there was no effort in Anele's splayed fingers. His whole body looked limp, as if he were slowly melting into the gutrock. Only his voice was tight; wakeful.

"There must be forbidding."

Without forbidding, there is too little time.

The Giants gathered around Linden and Stave, Liand and the old man. Instinctively they formed a protective cordon, although there was nothing that they could do to ease or aid him. Linden knelt at Anele's side. Liand held his *orcrest* high. Its light cast grotesque shadows of the Swordmainnir on the crude walls of the passage. The vapor of their breathing spread out and vanished, inhaled by the surrounding dark.

The Humbled remained close to Covenant. Their halfhands seemed to mock him at the edges of his vision. He suspected that they would stop him if he tried to approach Anele. They had never trusted Anele's legacy—or any use of Earthpower.

"Anele," Linden whispered. "Tell me."

"Even here it is felt," the old man said as if he were answering her. "Written. Lamented." But the words were not a reply. Anele's fixation on the lines of malachite within the obsidian was complete. He responded to the world's oldest secrets, not to her. "The rousing of the Worm. It devours the magic of the Earth. The life. But its hunger is too great. When it has depleted lesser sustenance, it must come to the Land."

Lesser sustenance? He must have meant the *Elohim*. But Covenant could not be sure. His own memories were too fresh.

There is too much. Power and peril. Malevolence. Ruin. And too little time. The last days of the Land are counted.

On some level, however, he knew that Anele was right. The Worm was eating the magic out of the world. But it needed more than it could obtain from any *Elohim*—or from all of the *Elohim*.

By its very nature, the Worm would give Lord Foul what the Despiser had always craved.

Covenant did not know how Linden would be able to bear that responsibility.

"Heed him well," the Ardent advised in a hushed murmur. "This has been foreseen. It is knowledge which has been hidden since the rising of the first dawn within the Arch, shared by none but the *Elohim*. He must be heeded."

"We heed him very well," returned Rime Coldspray in a low growl. She may have wanted to silence the Insequent.

"The Worm will come." Gradually Anele's voice took on a ritual cadence, a sound of litany, as if he recited a sacral truth. "It must. Bringing with it the last crisis of the Earth, it will come. Here it will discover its final nourishment."

Become as trees, the roots of trees. Seek deep rock.

Liand's upraised arm trembled with cold and effort. The Sunstone shook, stirring shadows like shaken leaves. Stave's lone eye caught the radiance in a flicker of gleams as if he were gazing into the fiery face of apocalypse.

"Here?" Linden asked, still whispering. Bereft or abandoned: Covenant could not tell the difference. "In the Lost Deep? In that chasm? What nourishment?"

Surely she knew that Anele did not hear her?

—the necessary forbidding of evils—

If the Earth had no hope, there was none for Jeremiah—or for any love.

"If it is not forbidden, it will have Earthpower," Anele said in tones of rock and woe. "If it is not opposed by the forgotten truths of stone and wood, *orcrest* and refusal, it will have life. The very blood of life from the most potent and private recesses of the Earth's heart. When the Worm of the World's End drinks the Blood of the Earth, its puissance will consume the Arch of Time."

"Anele!" Linden cried softly. "Are you sure? Anele? What forgotten truths?"

Beyond question the old man did not hear her. He said nothing further. He may have fallen asleep, exhausted by prophecy.

To *Melenkurion* Skyweir, Covenant thought dumbly. Of course. Not here. Not to the Lost Deep, or to any place within Mount Thunder. The Despiser had buried too much evil in these depths. The Worm needed Earthpower concentrated and pure, the world's essential chrism.

As pure as *orcrest*. As pure as the wrath of Forestals, who had possessed the power to refuse—

"It is done," the Ardent announced with quiet satisfaction. "As it was foreseen, so it has transpired. And I alone among the Insequent bear witness. The Harrow himself has heard no single word. He cares naught for the joy of such epiphanies."

Some of the Giants closed their fists, glared at the Ardent. Others ignored the Insequent. The Humbled watched impassively as Linden bowed her head over Anele. In Liand's unsteady light, the Ramen seemed to shrink as though they were being made smaller by the loss of open skies and plains, of sunshine and Ranyhyn.

But Covenant shared none of their reactions. He was slipping again, skidding down a scree of moments into the Land's past. Losing the present. There was evil in the chasm. It was going to wake up. He could not stop himself.

—*the necessary forbidding*—

He did not understand how he could have failed to remember.

7.

Crossing the Hazard

Linden was pulled in too many directions at once. She had no time to comprehend what she heard or sensed or needed. Kneeling at Anele's side in the distressed light of Liand's *orcrest*, she felt Covenant's mind lose its grip on the present; felt him fall into himself. But there was nothing she could do about that, nothing. His dilemmas were beyond her. Without her Staff and his ring, she had no purpose of any kind except to reach her son.

That, too, might be impossible now. She and her companions had gathered on the wrong side of a bottomless chasm. *A terrible power lives here.* The cold was already terrible.

That the Harrow had bound himself with oaths did not comfort her. *No one can get in if that portal isn't opened first.* The shock of being in this immured cavern, without full percipience or clean air, was not as great as her fear that he did not know how to unseal the way into the Lost Deep.

The Worm of the World's End was coming to the Land.

Like an echo of the paresthesia that had afflicted her among the Viles millennia ago, she seemed to smell the hard respiration of the Giants, taste the vapor they exhaled. Their confusion as they scrambled to absorb Anele's revelations stung her nerves.

Here it will discover its final nourishment. The very blood of life from the most potent and private recesses of the Earth's heart.

The old man was unconscious now, exhausted by his encounter with the world's oldest secrets.

Without forbidding, there is too little time.

Linden could not imagine where anyone would find or wield enough power to *forbid* the Worm of the World's End. Covenant and wild magic might conceivably have done so. But his mind was broken, and Linden had given his ring to the Harrow.

She did not believe that the Harrow would be able to *keep* Covenant's ring. She hardly considered it likely that he would retain her Staff. He was counting too heavily on the inability of beings like the *Elohim* and Esmer to locate Jeremiah. And there were other enemies—

She had surrendered to the Harrow in part because she suspected that forces greater than her human desperation would oppose his intentions for her son.

But first the portal had to be opened. With one mistake, *any* mistake, the Harrow would break the fragile span of stone; doom Jeremiah. The Staff of Law and Covenant's ring would be lost.

And *A terrible power lives here*: another warning that Linden could not afford to heed.

Outwardly she seemed steady enough. Her hands did not shake. The steam of her breathing did not blind her. Nevertheless her heart shivered as if she were too cold to move—

—as cold as she had felt in the winter of the Land's past, where Roger Covenant and the *croyel* had betrayed her.

After a moment, however, Rime Coldspray spoke. "Doubtless we have been granted a precious insight." She sounded like a clenched fist. "In this, the Ardent has spoken sooth. Here we have gained knowledge of the world's plight which we could not have obtained by other means. Yet it is of no present import. It will serve no purpose if we do not both retrieve Linden Giantfriend's son and evade the perils of this demesne."

No present import. Yes. Coldspray's voice seemed to draw the Ironhand and all of the Giants out of the shadows cast by Liand's wavering light. Her tone restored their normal solidity. Linden's impression that she could hear or feel the echoes of extinct Viles receded.

—if we do not both—

Repulsed by the taste of the stale air, she took a flinching breath. The Sunstone made respiration possible; but the atmosphere of the cavern was too stagnant to be refreshed by mere *orcrest*. —if we do not— Coldspray had broken the trance of Anele's utterances. Now it was Linden's turn.

But she had too many concerns. She wanted to help or caution the Harrow, and understand Anele, and catch hold of Covenant as he fell like water dripping from the stalactites. She believed that she would be content if she could find Jeremiah; if she could close her arms around him one last time. She tried to believe that. But it was not the truth. She needed to see him freed from the *croyel*. And she would never be content without Covenant.

For her own sake, she wanted Covenant to be whole. Then she might be able to forgive herself. But he was essential for less selfish reasons as well.

If she could not think clearly in this fug of stagnation and impercipience, she should at least move. Rise to her feet. Do something. But she was too weak. Shivering spread outward from her heart. The small effort of lifting her head was beyond her.

After a moment, Manethrall Mahrtiir asked tentatively, "Is it conceivable that the Harrow also has spoken sooth?" He sounded unsure of himself, almost timid; daunted by ancientness and immeasurable stone and intimations of evil. Truly blinded. "Will his intent for white gold and the Staff of Law and the Ringthane's son serve to forbid the Worm? Will his ploys suffice to preclude the Worm from the Blood of the Earth?"

Flatly Stave replied, "Anele's words suggest otherwise. To his ears, or in his sight, the requisite knowledge is remembered only here. The Harrow does not truly comprehend the Worm."

"Then," stated Galt, "the burden falls to the Unbeliever. The promises of the Harrow are false."

"Not so," the Ardent objected, swirling his raiment in repudiation. He spoke loudly; yet the anxiety in his eyes, and the hectic flush of his round cheeks, belied his tone. In spite of the chill, his face was damp with sweat and apprehension. "Doubtless he does not foresee all things to their ends. And perchance his intent is flawed by arrogance or ignorance. Nonetheless he must hold fast to his given oath. If he does not, he will perish in madness.

"The Insequent who have charged me to constrain and aid him foretell one thing and also another. Some scry wisdom and vindication where others find only auguries of failure. It is conceivable that both are equally prescient, alike inspired and fallible.

Therefore they conclude that the fate of the Earth is too conflicted to be known with any assurance. For that reason, I am sent to arbitrate uncertain outcomes.

"Perhaps a-Jeroth of the Seven Hells believes that his sight is sure. If he does so, the Insequent trust that he errs."

"You're probably right," Covenant said abruptly; harshly. "But what's the point?"

His voice snatched Linden out of her immobility. She found herself on her feet without realizing that she had arisen.

From a safe distance, and secured by the Humbled, he stood peering into the abyss. Linden retained enough health-sense to recognize that he had not returned to the present. He was a prophet of the past, and he spoke to ghosts. Wandering among his memories, he replied to questions that had not been asked by anyone living.

"You can't *kill* her," he snorted as if his answer disgusted him. "If she isn't as old as Lord Foul, she might as well be. And she's become just as dangerous. The only difference is, she doesn't *think*. She *feels*. He has ambitions she can't imagine—and he's way more patient. Most of the time, she sleeps because she doesn't know any other way to endure her frustration."

Then Covenant apparently slipped into another fissure. He fell silent. His bandaged hands twitched as if they were groping for something tangible; some bedrock fact or perception to which he could cling. But he did not find one.

Liand cleared his throat. "Linden." He made a palpable effort to sound less intimidated than Mahrtiir. "The Harrow does not act. If he attempts some incantation, he does so in silence, motionless. Should his knowledge prove insufficient—"

The Stonedownor's voice faded into a sigh of doubt.

"The Insequent," Clyme pronounced severely, "esteem their prowess too highly. Their arts demean the unwary, but they cannot redeem themselves."

The Ardent appeared to consider a retort, then swallow it.

For a moment, Linden stood like Covenant, as if she, too, had fallen into a memory from which she could not escape. But she was not trapped there. She was choosing necessary recollections.

First, the Harrow had once said to her, *I desire this curious stick to which you cling as though it possessed the virtue to ward you.*

The Staff of Law, *her* Staff. With wild magic and bereavement and love, she had fused the living powers of Vain and Findail into an instrument of Law. Under *Melenkurion Skyweir*, her Staff had been transformed to blackness in battle. Ten thousand years ago, Caerroil Wildwood had defined it with runes. His lore had contributed to Covenant's resurrection.

Second, I crave the circle of white gold which lies hidden by your raiment.

Wild magic. The crux and keystone of the Arch of Time. It was the essence of

Thomas Covenant's spirit reified in a fundamentally flawed and flawless alloy: his wedding band, the symbol and manifestation of his transcendent humanity.

And last, I covet the unfettered wrath at the center of your heart. It will nourish me as the Demondim did not.

Linden had not understood him then: she did now. He was referring to the legacy of Gallows Howe. He wanted her granite ire, her emotional extravagance, to help him impose his will on Jeremiah and the *croyel*. But the Mahdoubt had prevented him from claiming Linden. Finally she knew why. She knew, as the Harrow did not, that there was more to Gallows Howe than rage and slaughter, death and retribution.

Why else had the Forestal of Garroting Deep asked her a question that she did not know how to answer?

Because of the Mahdoubt's sacrifice, Linden could offer herself to the Harrow without fearing his power to consume her. When he had guided her to Jeremiah and the *croyel*, she would still be able to fight for her son.

Somehow.

Nodding in the direction of the Harrow, she tried to answer the expectant silence of her companions.

"I should go." To herself, she sounded vague and faint, as tenuous as a figure in a dream. "Opening that portal takes something more than Earthpower and Law. That's why the Harrow didn't just want my Staff and Covenant's ring. He wanted *me*.

"The ur-viles and Waynhim could help us, but they aren't here. They couldn't have brought us here. The Ardent says that there's nothing he can do. And I've at least *met* the Viles." *You serve a purpose not your own, and have no purpose.* "That's more than the Harrow can say. They were long gone before he started to study them. Everything he knows is based on inferences.

"I should try to help him before he makes a mistake and kills us."

She was still watching Covenant, hoping that he would hear her and respond. After a moment, however, she forced herself to look around at her friends. Facing Liand, and then Mahrtiir and his Cords, and then the Giants, she added, "Unless you have a better idea."

Liand could not conceal his anxiety, and did not try. Holding up the light of the *orcrest* seemed to take most of his strength. The Manethrall bowed his head as if he sought to veil his consternation; his weakness. Pahni clung to Liand's free arm, hid her face against his shoulder for comfort. Bhapa swallowed several times, opened and closed his mouth, apparently trying to find words for his chagrin. Then he glanced helplessly around him and gave up.

Towering above the rest of the company, the Giants met Linden's gaze squarely. Some of them looked abashed, perhaps reluctant to admit their alarm and uncertainty.

Grueburn and Cabledarm studied Linden as if they were trying to gauge her capacity to surprise them. But Rime Coldspray grinned like the blade of a scimitar, coldly, and with a keen edge.

"Linden Giantfriend, we displayed true Giantish folly when we elected to accompany the Harrow. To recant our unwisdom now would shame all who hear our tale." The Ironhand gave an exaggerated shrug. More seriously, she continued, "To remain as we are achieves naught. Covenant Timewarden has given us warning, and must be heeded. If you deem that your acquaintance with the Viles, or your familiarity with the Staff of Law, may be of aid to the Harrow, I pray only that he will permit your efforts."

The other Swordmainnir nodded with varying degrees of confidence. But Galt and Branl shook their heads; and Clyme asked inflexibly, "What magic do you possess, Linden Avery, that will meet our need? Are you not self-bereft of every vital resource?"

Before Linden could reply, Mahrtiir jerked up his head, took a step forward. "What concern is this of yours, sleepless one?" His old animosity toward the Masters countered the weight of his intimidation. "You have made plain that your devoir is to the Timewarden. Why then do you oppose the Ringthane in any attempt which may succor him as it does us?"

"Subsequent events—" began Clyme.

"—are not foreknown to you, *Haruchai*," put in the Ardent unexpectedly. "The lady seeks the recovery of her son. What further justification of her deeds do you require?"

"Subsequent events," Clyme repeated, "may reveal that the lady, as you name her, is not done with Desecration. Did not the Mahdoubt give battle and so perish to prevent the surrender which Linden Avery now contemplates?"

"Oh, stop." Linden wrapped her arms around her to contain her shivering. "I'm not going to *surrender*. If I do that, I'll never see Jeremiah again. There won't be anything left of me."

She had already given up everything else.

"Silence your pride," Stave advised the Humbled. He sounded distant; uninterested. But the play of reflections in his eye gave the impression that he was laughing to himself. "No deed or dare of the Chosen's will lessen the import of the Unbeliever's presence, or of your service to him. Come good or ill, boon or bane, he remains the Unbeliever, ur-Lord Thomas Covenant. And has he not urged you to accept her path? When you have no other guidance, it is poor fidelity to speak against his wishes."

If the Humbled debated Stave's counsel, or their own commitments, they did so in silence. None of them voiced any further objection.

"All right." Linden gave herself no chance to hesitate. She did not share Covenant's vertigo; but the depths of the cavern were crowded with terrors nonetheless. If she paused to think about them— "Stay here," she told her friends. "Don't try to cross until you can see that I've succeeded—or the Harrow has. There's no sense in risking yourselves yet. And I don't think that *orcrest* or the *krill* is likely to be of much use."

"Do not fear for us," Coldspray replied, still grinning sharply. "We have no wish to meet our deaths in this dire chasm."

"Good." More to encourage herself than to express approval, Linden nodded. "As long as Liand can hold off the worst of Kevin's Dirt, you'll probably know what happens as soon as I do."

While her companions watched and waited, Linden gripped herself tightly and started toward the span. When Stave moved to join her, she did not refuse his company.

From her perspective of trepidation, the bridge—the Hazard—looked more delicate and fragile than it had seemed earlier. *Making it, they risked everything. Who they were. What they meant to themselves.* As she did. And the ceiling of the immense cavern loomed, louring like thunderheads. Hints of chiaroscuro reflected back and forth among the stalactites, implying lightning. Any one of those wet and straining shapes was heavy enough to break the span if it fell.

Stave walked at her side, so close that his shoulder brushed hers. In spite of her fears for him—for all of her companions—she welcomed the support of his inhuman strength, his argute senses. His dedication might serve as valor if or when her dreads threatened to paralyze her.

Together, Linden Avery and the former Master left safer rock and began to ascend the shallow arc of the Hazard.

Really, she insisted to herself, this ought to be easy. It was a short walk, perhaps two hundred paces. If she kept her gaze fixed on the far wall, did not look down— Yet the black abyss seemed to reach up as though it meant to snatch her off the bridge. The darkness itself may have been alive.

Covenant gave no sign that he had noticed what she was doing.

She could still feel the taut attention of her friends behind her. But every step took her farther from Liand and light. As the radiance of the Sunstone dimmed, her health-sense faded with it. Soon she would not be able to discern her companions at all. Unless she turned to look—

Feeling like a coward, she murmured to Stave, "Don't let me fall. That chasm—" She shuddered. "It pulls at me."

Stave touched his solid shoulder to hers. "Even here, Chosen, the sight of the *Haruchai* is merely diminished. It has not failed. This stone is sure. The weight of the Giants together may endanger it. We do not."

He considered for a moment, then added, "Yet we must not tarry. There is evil here. Its malice lacks the distinct malevolence of Corruption, but it is malice nonetheless."

Linden believed him. She felt only the seduction of the plunge below her; but she trusted his perceptions.

The light continued to weaken as the span rose. The dead air became an ache in her lungs. With every step, she moved deeper into memories of winter; of killing cold fraught with manipulation and treachery, and full of Jeremiah's enslavement.

As her percipience waned, she lost her ability to locate the Harrow. His dun raiment had become indistinguishable from the dark portal. If he had found his way inward and gone ahead without her, she would not have known the difference. But Stave would have told her— And the Insequent had given his oath. The same strictures which had doomed the Mahdoubt ruled him as well.

On both sides of the Hazard, water trickled incessantly down the sides of the stalactites and fell like omens; promises of plummeting.

Then she and Stave passed the crest of the bridge and descended into shadow.

She was effectively blinded. An irrational certainty that she had begun to drift toward the unguarded rim of the span clutched at her. Fingers of ice reached through her clothes to torment her flesh. A whimper that she was barely able to contain clogged her throat.

But Stave took hold of her arm to steady her. "Calm your heart, Chosen," he said as though he feared neither echoes nor banes. "The Harrow awaits you. It appears that he has ceased his own efforts, whatever they may have been. Now he regards you with suspicion and hope. I deem that he dreads the consequences of error, and that his dread has defeated him. He will accept your aid, for his alternative is humiliation and death."

Linden trusted his reading of the Harrow. She had no choice. His firm grasp was all that kept her from hastening toward the relative sanctuary of broad granite at the foot of the bridge. She wanted to *get off* the Hazard. As her steps descended from darkness to darkness, her visceral conviction that the span would crack and collapse increased until it affected her more than bad air or cold or stifled percipience.

Through the drumming of her pulse, she hardly heard Stave announce, "The Chosen comes to proffer her assistance, Insequent. A courteous man would welcome her with light to ease her way."

"And do you now consider yourself an arbiter of courtesies, *Haruchai?*" the deep loam of the Harrow's voice replied. "You who only give battle or show disdain, disregarding the stature of those whom you encounter?

"My knowledge of courtesy exceeds yours, as does my prowess. Thus!"

Directly ahead of Linden, and no more than a dozen paces away, an umber illumination appeared as all of the beads on the Harrow's doublet began to glow simultaneously.

They cast a dull light that revealed little more than the Insequent and his immediate surroundings. But that was enough to let Linden see where she placed her feet.

The bridge ended in a buttressed shelf of gutrock just outside the high archway of the entrance to the Lost Deep. The Harrow's brown lumination did not extend beyond the plane of the portal: there it met sheer blackness as blunt and impermeable as burnished ebony. But Linden could see him and the foot of the span clearly enough.

Through the dusk crouching above her, she saw that the curve of the door was marked with strange symbols which she did not recognize.

The shelf extended for several long strides on either side of the sealed entrance. It was wide enough to accommodate the Giants. And in the center of the unobstructed stone, the Insequent still knelt as Rime Coldspray had described him: bent on one knee; gripping Covenant's ring near his forehead; holding Linden's Staff planted squarely on the stone. The chain on which she had worn the ring dangled from his fingers, swaying slightly. His posture suggested that her approach had interrupted his concentration. His fathomless eyes regarded her like smaller instances of the cavern's depths: more human than the abyss, but no less fatal.

"The *Haruchai* speaks of assistance, lady," the Harrow remarked, affecting scorn. But his contempt sounded hollow. "Do you conceive that I require any aid of yours?"

"Of course you do." An inward rush carried Linden off the bridge. Then she stopped, shivering with relief. In spite of the cold, the enduring granite under her boots affected her like certainty. "You knew that when we first met. You've been trying to open that door on your own, but you can't. And you can't afford to make a mistake."

When Stave released her arm, she grasped his to anchor her. "Those symbols," she asked the Insequent, glancing upward. "Can you read them? What do they say?"

The Harrow studied her, loathing the oath which the Mahdoubt had wrested from him. "Their import is no mystery. They proclaim merely that beyond this portal lies the demesne and habitation of the sovereign Viles, monarchs of this realm, great in lore and peril, and unforgiving of intrusion. Further, the symbols counsel all with the wit to read them to turn aside. Here any who enter unwelcomed will discover only doom."

Then he shrugged. "Sovereign or no, the Viles are long extinguished. Of their spawn, only those few ur-viles and Waynhim which betimes endeavor to serve you endure. I do not fear the doom of this place. When I have unbound its restrictions, no harm will remain to daunt me."

"In other words," Linden retorted, "you still don't have a clue." Her scorn was as hollow as his: she was too cold and truncated to feel disdain; had to fight too hard for breath. "I think that I can help you. If you let me."

"'Let you, lady?'" mused the Harrow as though the idea held little interest. "I do not oppose you. In what form do you crave my permit?"

Gallows Howe, she might have answered. Rage. Slaughter. That's what you think the Viles were like. You think that's how they would have answered intrusion. You think that I can unlock blackness with blackness.

But she did not waste her flagging energy on a useless attempt to correct his misap-prehensions. Already she was light-headed with hypoxia. The glow of the Harrow's beads did nothing to cleanse the air. Soon she would be too weak to stand.

Panting, she explained, "If you let me use my Staff." Before he could object, she added, "I'm not asking you to give it back. But somehow your hold on it blocks me." Once she could have drawn Earthpower from it without grasping it; but he had erected a barrier against her. "Just let me touch it." Let me be myself again, at least for a little while. "Let me borrow what it can do. Then I may be able to feel my way through the wards. If I *see* them, maybe I can open the door."

While the Harrow considered her, perhaps searching for some indication of trick-ery, Stave asked flatly, "Is this hesitation, Insequent? If the doom of the Lost Deep does not inspire dread, how does it chance that you fear the Chosen's aid?"

The Harrow scowled darkly, but did not respond to Stave's challenge. Instead he continued to scrutinize Linden until he found something that satisfied him. Then he nodded.

Swinging the chain of Covenant's ring as if that small movement were an arcane gesture, he said brusquely, "Make the attempt, lady."

In simple weakness, Linden wanted to lie down. Prone, she could take hold of her Staff by its end: all she needed was its touch. But pride or stubbornness kept her on her feet as she moved to stand, trembling, in front of the Insequent. Striving for steadiness, she reached out with both hands and closed her fingers around the Staff of Law.

Contact with the warm wood was like a rebirth.

She had no measure for the extent to which Kevin's Dirt had diminished her until her nerves felt the healing current of Earthpower and Law, the precise elucidation of Caerroil Wildwood's runes. Then she became able to recognize how wan and super-ficial her sight had been without percipience. God, how had she borne it? How did the people of the Land who had never known health-sense endure their lives? Her existence in her natural world, the world which she had lost, had been fundamen-tally transformed by her previous hours or months with Covenant. During that time, she had grown familiar with seeing and hearing and touching and tasting the spiri-tual essence of all things: the underlying life-pulse of vitality and wonder. She did not know who she would have been if she had never experienced the Land; but she believed that she would have remained emotionally crippled, as damaged and despair-ing as her parents. The legacy of her father's suicide and her mother's death would have continued to define her.

Now everything around her seemed to unfold, to blossom, as though she had stepped into a new dimension of reality. She felt the obdurate antiquity of the rock under her; the sheer age and indifference of the air; the specific stability and limitations of the Hazard; the ponderous downward yearning of the stalactites; the commingled

eagerness and submission of water as it gathered and trickled down the gnarled surfaces of the stalactites to fall like streams of time into the extinction of the abyss. She
perceived the Harrow's anxieties and hungers, and Stave's stubborn strength, as if they
impinged directly on her skin. She became aware of her own body—of its inherent
inadequacies, and of its bedrock desire to live—as if her veins and nerves, muscles and
sinews, were limned in light. And in the distance far below her, she sensed the restless
lurk of something evil—

But those were the Staff's passive effects. As soon as she began to draw on its power,
the stagnation was banished from her lungs: she could breathe cleanly again. New
energy ran like the effects of hurtloam through her veins. She recognized Liand's
brave and tiring efforts to keep his *orcrest* alight; identified each of the Giants and the
Ramen, each of the Humbled. She felt Anele's slumber and Covenant's trackless wandering. She could have pointed to the exact spot where Loric's *krill*, wrapped in vellum
and lambent with possibilities, was tucked into the waist of Covenant's jeans.

Nevertheless more immediate sensations demanded her attention. While the Harrow regarded her avidly, and Stave watched as if nothing had changed, she tasted the
presence of complex theurgies.

The blackness that filled the portal of the Lost Deep was not blank: it was a seething
mass of magicks, twisted and insidiously recursive. And its implications were not contained within the archway. Instead they extended in long looping tendrils, and in clusters like knot work, to form a web or skein of utter fuligin around the entire length of
the Hazard. In some respects, the portal's dark strands resembled Jeremiah's racetrack
construct: if she tried to follow their flow from one place to another, she would find
herself in a maze from which there was no egress. But Jeremiah's construct had been a
door: one through which only he could pass, but a door nonetheless. The tangle that
enclosed the bridge was formed for destruction. If even one of its strings were plucked,
it would convulse, taking the granite substance of the span with it. In an instant, the
bridge would become rubble falling endlessly into the depths.

In the initial wash of Earthpower, Linden saw that the wards defending the Hazard
were like the Demondim. *Having no tangible forms, they would be lost to will and deed
without some containing ensorcelment to preserve them from dissolution. Imagine that
they were bound to themselves by threads of lore and purpose.* And the Harrow had told
her that he had *learned the trick of unbinding them.* But apparently his knowledge did
not extend to undoing the magicks here—or he was unable to discern the similarity
between the way in which the Viles had given shape to the Demondim and the manner
in which they had guarded their hidden realm.

He did not know how to use the Staff—

To an extent, however, the web threatening the bridge was chaff; distraction. Anyone who did not try to enter the Lost Deep could cross the span repeatedly without

harm. The real danger, the crucial tangle, was *here*, concealed inside the portal's cryptic moiling. One touch to the wrong strand would release ruin. But plucking the correct thread would open the Lost Deep. Severing that thread would unravel the wards completely, erasing their power from the span.

Sighing to herself, Linden thought, Well, sure. If only it were that easy. Tugging or cutting the proper strand with Law and Earthpower might not be difficult. However, *identifying* that tendril within the sensory confusion of the Viles' lore would be as arduous as finding the *caesure* through which the Demondim horde had invoked the Illearth Stone. And here she did not have the horde's evanescent hints of emerald and migraine to guide her. She did not have the ichor of the ur-viles and Waynhim to augment her health-sense.

But that was not her only problem.

As she extended her discernment, the sensations of a malignant presence seething in the chasm suddenly increased. For a moment, a swift flurry of frightened heartbeats, she thought that the evil was rising—

It was not. Now Linden saw the truth. The bane only appeared to surge upward because it, or she, was so enormous; so potent. Worse, she was *sentient*— Oh, God in Heaven, the malevolence was not merely alive: it was a conscious being. Asleep, yes— Linden could feel that—but restive, and capable of intention. In its—her—virulence, she exceeded the Illearth Stone as a sea exceeded a lake. She did less harm only because she was so much more deeply entombed. Nonetheless to Linden she looked more terrible than a host of *skurj* and Sandgorgons.

Only wild magic could oppose such a being. The Staff of Law would be useless against her. Staring downward, Linden realized with horror that this evil was the source of Kevin's Dirt. Unconsciously, perhaps, but unmistakably, the bane supplied the raw force which Kastenessen and Esmer and *moksha* Raver had shaped to form their heinous brume.

If Linden's company failed to rescue Jeremiah and escape before that entity came fully awake—

A cry for Covenant's help caught in Linden's throat. Surely it was for this that she had compelled him to resume his life? So that he would spare her the burden of confronting abominations? She lacked his instinct for impossible solutions. Without him, she and Jeremiah and all of her friends were lost.

But he also was lost.

While she floundered, the Harrow commanded abruptly, "Speak, lady." He made a palpable attempt to sound severe, but flashes of alarm marred his tone. "How fare your efforts to demonstrate that I must have your aid?" In a smaller voice, he added, "We dare not linger here."

He was lorewise enough to recognize the peril dozing restlessly in the depths.

Stung by her own fears, Linden jerked her head to face him. Still gripping the Staff with both hands, she snapped, "You don't *know*, do you. You talk and talk, you like to tell us how you're going to save the world, but you have no idea what to do if that thing *wakes up*."

The Insequent flinched. Something in the gulfs of his eyes suggested fear. Yet he did not unclose his fingers from either the Staff of Law or the white gold ring. In his dreams of glory, he had found *the trick of unbinding* the wards before his presence disturbed the cavern's bane.

"Then I will concede, lady," he whispered softly, fiercely, "that in all sooth I require your assistance. The secret of unmaking the Demondim does not avail here. For that reason, I craved the wordless knowledge within the blackness of your heart. Your encounter with the ancient theurgy of Garroting Deep—the theurgy which scripted these runes—unveiled a mystery to you, though its meaning is beyond your comprehension. *I* would have known its use, but the Mahdoubt precluded me from acquiring it. Therefore the task is yours. Lady, we will perish here one and all if you do not immerse yourself in your darkest and most insatiable rage. You must become hate and vengeance or die."

Linden glared back as though all of her darkest passions were directed at him.

"This bane is unknown to the *Haruchai*," Stave observed, "and too distant for true discernment. Yet we perceive that it slumbers still. Mayhap there is no imminent need for haste."

The former Master was wrong. Linden had to get away from the cavern and the Hazard before the proximity of so much malevolence shredded her nerves.

She would never reach Jeremiah if she did not find and cut exactly the right strand of magic. The tendrils of the Viles did not only extend along the span: they also reached inward. Havoc would be wrought in the Lost Deep if she made any mistake. The damage might isolate Jeremiah permanently. It might kill him.

"Then give me my Staff," she demanded in a voice as low and grim as the Harrow's. "Let it go. I'll return it when I've found the way in. If I don't keep my promises, you don't have to keep yours. I'm not likely to forget that. But I can't face you *and* those wards while that monstrosity might wake up."

The Insequent bared his teeth in a feral grimace, wild and threatened. For a moment, Linden thought that he would refuse; that he might take the fatal risk of trying to open the portal himself. His greed—

But behind his mask of superiority, his fear was as strong as hers, and growing stronger. He needed her as badly as she needed her Staff. After a moment, he made an effort to swallow his pride. Without a word, he relinquished the written wood.

"Chosen," Stave said like an affirmation. "Linden."

At once, Linden accepted the Staff of Law, *her* Staff, and moved closer to the black seethe of magicks which blocked her from Jeremiah.

With the intensity of an absolute need, she ached for Covenant's presence. Even if he could not help or guide her, he would at least understand that the Harrow was wrong. Thomas Covenant had known the ancient inhabitants of this place from the perspective of the Arch of Time. He had witnessed every manifestation of their dangerous lore; seen into the heart of their most abstruse secrets. He would comprehend that the Harrow had been misled by his avarice.

The Harrow's knowledge of the Viles was too recent: he had gleaned it millennia after their self-loathing had faded from the Land. But Linden had faced them while they were poised on the cusp of Despite. And Covenant had known them when they had been justly considered *lofty and admirable.* According to Esmer, they had lived in *caverns as ornate and majestic as castles. There they devoted their vast power and knowledge to the making of beauty and wonder, and all of their works were filled with loveliness. For an age of the Earth, they spurned the heinous evils buried among the roots of Gravin Threndor—*

Covenant would understand. He had turned his back on scorn and punishment long before Lord Foul had slain him. The defenses of the Viles could not be opened by any power inspired by wrath and the hunger for retribution. Beings that had *risked everything* by forming the Hazard would not have done so out of rage. They would have been unacquainted with the desire for revenge.

Unless—,Linden thought suddenly. Unless the Viles had shaped their wards *after* the Ravers had taught them to loathe themselves. In that case, she rather than the Harrow might be wrong; and she was about to make her final mistake.

Far below her, one of the *heinous evils* stirred. Its sleep was troubled. Soon, inevitably, it would awaken.

Its emanations clawed at Linden until her assurance hung in tatters.

While she hesitated, caught by her old paralysis, Stave came closer. Apparently he could sense her turmoil. With one hand, he rested his strength firmly on her trembling shoulder.

"In your company," he remarked, "and not without difficulty, I have learned that there is merit in doubt." He sounded uncharacteristically casual, as if he were making a conscious effort to dispel trepidation. "Yet it is the nature of evil to feast upon fear, breeding distrust and inaction from doubt. And even in sleep, evil seduces. Chosen, you must close your heart to its lure. If the tales of the Lords are sooth, the Viles did not do so. Thus they persuaded themselves to their doom."

Linden had no choice: she had to trust her first impressions; trust that the convoluted, self-complicating blackness of the wards expressed the caution of majesty rather than the louring bitterness of disdain. If she did not, she would remain frozen in indecision.

With an effort, she straightened her back, squared her shoulders. Deliberately she unclosed one hand from the Staff to comb her hair back from her face. Then she touched Stave's fingers briefly—a small gesture of thanks—and resumed her grip on the graven ebony of the wood.

—close your heart—

Easily said. Deafening her senses to the somnolent ferocity of the bane was hard. But she had been an emergency room surgeon, trained to regard only the wound directly in front of her. With a kind of concentration that allowed no intrusion, she had once cut into Jeremiah's burned hand. Thinking of nothing else, she had amputated two of his fingers—and had saved the others as well as the thumb. Because of what she had done, he could use his remaining digits as deftly as a wizard.

Gradually the bane's aura lost its power to rend and shred. One strand and implication at a time, Linden tuned her percipience to the squirming moil of the entrance to the Lost Deep.

It was there, she was sure of it. The crucial tangle which formed the crux or keystone of the Viles' wards lay among the entwined permutations of the portal, not elsewhere. Otherwise the creatures could not have left or re-entered their realm. Somewhere within that midnight mass writhing like a nest of snakes—dark as vipers, swift as adders—was the one thread of theurgy which could render all the rest harmless.

As a perceptual challenge, Linden's task daunted her. It seemed impossible. Apart from the barrier's seething, it betrayed no features of any kind: no definitions or demarcations; no shapes apart from the tendrils themselves in constant motion. All of its implications led to confusion.

When she had detached herself from her fears, however, she found that she did not lack resources. Her encounter with the Viles informed her health-sense. She had experienced their eldritch paresthesia. She could not see the meaning of the strands; but she could hear that they *had* meaning. She could smell the austere suzerainty which had suffused their creation. As she opened her senses, she could almost taste the negligent skill with which the Viles had fashioned defenses that they considered a trivial and largely unnecessary precaution.

Now at last she could be certain that the Harrow was wrong. The scent and taste of the barrier expressed no ire, no desire for harm. The Viles had formed it out of wariness, not from fear or hatred.

Slowly, using the Staff only to whet her percipience, Linden reached out with one hand and brushed it lightly over the surface of the blackness. By touch, she listened to the lore which had written the wards.

It spoke no language that she knew. She would never grasp the ineffable knowledge of the Viles. Nevertheless it was as precise and sequacious as Caerroil Wildwood's runes. Although she could not decipher its meaning, the simple fact that it had meaning guided her. Its logic flowed past her fingers with both direction and purpose.

In one shape or another, every strand and implication, every uninterpretable sound and scent, ran toward or away from the essential conundrum of the Viles' intentions.

At its core, therefore, her task was one of comprehension: not of the wards, but of the Viles themselves. The tangle of their defenses was a manifestation of their skeined hearts. Millennia in the Land's past, she had heard and felt and tasted their insistent self-referential debates, their multifarious conflicted questing for the significance of who and what they were. And long days ago, Esmer had done what he could to explain *the sovereign and isolate Viles.*

For an age of the Earth, they had resembled the *Elohim*: hermetic and uninvolved, uninterested in anything that did not impinge upon their secret existence. But where the *Elohim* had cared for little except the contemplation of their own inherent beauties, the Viles had been makers of loveliness, glorying in the articulation of their powers; instinctively creative in spite of the sterility of their lives. And by that creativity, that impulse to reach beyond themselves, they had been wooed to consider the possibilities of a world which might surpass them.

Unlike the *Elohim*, they were able to imagine such things.

That their reaching outward had eventually exposed the Viles to the snare of self-loathing grieved Linden. But their tragedy was not germane to her present efforts. The Viles had devised their defenses at the outset of their search for significance; for a context in which to clarify their definition of themselves. Their magicks articulated the spirit in which they had begun their quest, not the outcome of that quest in wrath and ruin.

Immersed among tendrils, she found no trace of any ill. In the barricade, she descried only yearning.

And the implications of the snarled magicks culminated *there*: in that exact spot and specific strand within the general turmoil. She could not see it, hear it, feel it. Nevertheless she was familiar with the sensory entanglement of the Viles. Her own disorientation guided her.

After that, she forgot lurking evil; forgot the Harrow. Her companions on the far side of the Hazard did not affect her. She only needed to remember Stave's steady hand on her shoulder, and she was ready. Secured by his unyielding fidelity, she unwound a fine thread of Earthpower from the Staff. Trusting the taste of sounds, the scent of blackness, the tactile seethe of meaning, she inserted her thread delicately among the tendrils.

Amid such ebony, her power resembled a shout of gold, a vivid ache of flame and violation. But she was careful: oh, she was careful. Her thread was little more than a wisp, a spun wish. She did not impose it on the flowing wards. Instead she insinuated it into the current and let the disguised structure of the barrier carry Earthpower into its heart. And when fine gold reached the vital nexus of the theurgy, she was more careful still. Hardly breathing—hardly daring to think—she wrapped her thread around the essential strand.

As she tightened Earthpower on that strand, she smelled the Harrow's warnings, tasted the grip of Stave's hand. Ominous hues thrummed in the stone where she stood. About her head like ravens flew glints of incarnadine and sulphur from the bridge, the stalactites, the cavern walls. But she ignored them. Here, at least, she was done with doubt.

Now or never. Dare or die. Jeremiah needed her.

Shod wood on granite, a quick stamp of the Staff tightened her thread. Her delicate effort of Earthpower became as clenched as crimson: it smelled as rigid as iron.

With it, she snapped the necessary tendril.

For one wild jolt of time, an instant of impact, illusions of blackness whipped around her like released hawsers; harried her like furies. Ruinous serpents fled, squirming, in all directions.

Then the portal stood open, and nacre radiance shone forth from the Lost Deep like a welcome, and Linden would have fallen if Stave had not caught her. She needed his strength to drag her confused senses back from the brink of chaos.

Briefly the light fumed like her strained breathing. She smelled its pastel hues shift and waver as though they were the scents of a distant feast. Then her perceptions relapsed to their ordinary dimensions. When the Harrow spoke, he had become human and explicable.

"That, lady—" He appeared to choke on surprise and wonder. When he continued, he sounded hoarse. "In plain justice, I acknowledge it. That was well done."

But then he swallowed her effect on him: the effect of her ability to exceed him. More strongly, he stated, "Now I will have my Staff."

Light rich with iridescence and shifting colors spangled among the stalactites, filling the high space above the Hazard with suggestions of glory.

Linden may have nodded. Or not: she was unsure. As soon as the Staff left her hand, she felt Kevin's Dirt reassert itself. Almost immediately, it closed down on her like a lid; seeped into her like poison. Her sense of loss was so acute that she whimpered as if she had been beaten.

She had come to the end. There was nothing more that she could do.

Somewhere in the distance, Rime Coldspray announced, "Now, Swordmainnir. Linden Giantfriend has secured our passage. In caution and haste, we must bear our companions singly over the Hazard. The Masters will do what they must with Covenant Timewarden. The Ardent we leave to fend for himself. But the others we will convey safely."

"Be comforted, Chosen," Stave urged quietly. "You have succeeded where the Harrow failed. You have gained admittance to your son's imprisonment. Soon we will seek him out. And when you have reclaimed him, the Harrow will translate us hence. Then the cruelty of Kevin's Dirt will ease, restoring you to yourself."

"Assuredly," the Harrow pronounced, "I do not desire to linger." He sneered the words, but his scorn was hollow. Linden had humbled him. "Already the caution of your companions heightens our peril. Only my oath precludes me from hastening while your sycophants dally."

As Linden tried to gather herself, she found that her physical distress was waning. The illumination from the portal counteracted both stagnation and cold. There remained a chill in the air; an ache in her lungs. But she could breathe without shivering—and without the sensation that she was about to suffocate. Somehow the residual theurgy of the Lost Deep restored life to the atmosphere surrounding the Hazard.

And her sensitivity to the evil in the depths of the abyss was gone: an ambiguous boon. Numb to the bane's state, she feared reflexively that it had already begun to rise. But perceptions of its malice no longer eroded her resolve.

She had surrendered her Staff for a second time, and wanted to weep. But sorrow, like regret, was a luxury that she could not afford: not here. When she had accepted the burden of herself from Stave, she turned to watch her friends cross the span.

Coldspray had nearly reached the foot of the bridge, and Onyx Stonemage had already passed the top of the arc with Liand in her arms. Behind them came the three Humbled holding Covenant securely among them. At the far end of the Hazard, the other Giants waited to carry Manethrall Mahrtiir, Pahni, Bhapa, and Anele into the light.

Liand had quenched his Sunstone, returned the *orcrest* to its pouch at his waist. His posture leaning against Stonemage's cataphract implied weariness. Covenant appeared to be explaining something earnestly to Branl, Clyme, and Galt; but now the condition of his mind was hidden. The magicks of the Lost Deep did nothing to diminish Kevin's Dirt. The demeaning smog was too recent to be affected by the abandoned lore of the Viles.

When Coldspray reached Linden, Stave, and the Harrow, she bestowed a grin like a laugh of pride and pleasure on Linden. Then she studied the progress of the rest of the company.

Now Latebirth and Mahrtiir were on the bridge. Behind the remaining Giants, near the back of the veined fan of obsidian, the Ardent had wrapped his ribbands around him as if he were curling into a ball. Cowering—

As soon as Stonemage set Liand on his feet, he hurried toward Linden; clasped her strongly. Then, frowning his concern, he stepped back to scrutinize her.

"Linden—" he began. "This blindness maddens me. I cannot perceive—Have your efforts or the wards harmed you?"

Frostheart Grueburn followed Latebirth, with Stormpast Galesend carrying Anele a safe distance behind her.

Linden shook her head. She had no other answer.

The Harrow chewed his lips and twitched his fingers, fretting impatiently. But he did not voice his frustration.

Cabledarm with Pahni. Halewhole Bluntfist with Bhapa.

Latebirth reached the shelf of the portal; but when her feet found secure stone, she did not release Mahrtiir—and he did not ask it of her. Without percipience, he was entirely blind; more helpless than Anele, who still slept cradled against Galesend's armor. Behind his bandage, the Manethrall was more profoundly maimed than Cirrus Kindwind, the last of the Giants to essay the span. She had lost only a hand and forearm—

Still the Ardent remained wrapped around himself. In moments, Cabledarm and then Bluntfist rejoined their comrades; Kindwind passed the crest of the bridge—and the Ardent stood motionless, a parti-colored lump barely visible in the throat of the passage beyond him.

"Coward," growled the Harrow distinctly. "Impediment. Fop. The will of the Insequent in all sooth. For this I have countenanced interference in my designs."

Come on, Linden thought faintly. She felt as intangible as the Viles; as empty of effect as the Demondim against the Harrow. We have to rescue Jeremiah. *A terrible power lives here.*

Earlier the Ardent had appeared able to master his alarms, whatever they might be. Yet now he seemed unequal to them, even though Linden had removed the immediate danger. What did he really fear? His reluctance made her think that he had not told the truth about himself—or the whole truth.

As Kindwind put the Hazard behind her, however, and nodded to acknowledge her comrades, the fat Insequent stirred. Obscured by the shadow of the bridge, he began unwrapping strips of fabric from his apparel. Dim in the distance, he expanded as ribbands and hues were loosened until they formed a wide aura around him.

The flutter of his raiment resembled trembling, as timorous and uncertain as vapor.

Nevertheless he had found the reins that ruled his fears; or some other force compelled him. Abruptly he began to rise from the stone, lifted on swirling bands of cloth. And when he gained the air, colors as potent as incantations carried him forward. Floating within a cloud of ribbands, he moved onto the span.

Higher he rose, gaining momentum with very flourish of his raiment. At once lugubrious and majestic, he sailed upward until his head found the light. Some of the cloths supported him by pressing down on the bridge. Others anchored themselves among the stalactites. As he moved, they shifted to hold him aloft.

Perhaps he believed that by transporting himself in this manner he would avoid attracting the attention of the bane.

The Harrow barked a humorless laugh. "Truly the Ardent has been entrusted with the wishes and powers of the Insequent. His timidity and arrogance encompass every facet of our kind. Thus the folly of their presumption is revealed. The Earth would have been better served if they had not heeded their seers and augurs.

"Come!" he commanded Linden's company imperiously. "This delay is mindless. It will not become wisdom by protraction."

With a snort of contempt, he headed into the radiance of the Lost Deep.

No one followed him.

Jeremiah's plight nagged at Linden like an untreated wound. She should have rushed past the Harrow; should have fled from interminable days of anguish and inadequacy toward her son. But she had spent too much of her frayed spirit against the wards: she felt unable to go on without Covenant and her friends; and none of them moved. Even Liand and Stave did not. Instead they all stood as if in attendance, watching the Ardent's approach: the Swordmainnir with laughter in their eyes, the Masters impassively, Bhapa and Pahni in daunted wonder.

Only Covenant, Anele, and Mahrtiir did not regard the heavy Insequent in the air. And only Covenant spoke.

Peering past the rim of the abyss, he muttered, "She's going to get bigger. Every time She eats. Every time somebody who doesn't know or care how dangerous She is comes down here."

He showed no sign of vertigo. He must have been reliving a conversation which had taken place long ago.

Limned in pink and ecru and subtle viridian, the Harrow paused to wait again, cursing.

Past the Hazard's apex, the Ardent began his descent. And as he drifted forward, he gradually contracted his apparel so that he sank toward the bridge. Nearing the span's base, his bound feet were a mere arm's length from its surface. Softly as a bubble, he touched down as he reached the ledge.

His round face was flushed as though he had outrun the limits of his stamina. Sweat streamed from his forehead and cheeks, staining the neckbands of his garments. His eyes glared starkly, reflecting the pale illumination.

With his feet on the stone, he took two unsteady steps toward Linden. Then he stopped. Though he faced her, his gaze avoided hers.

"The will of the Insequent is a *geas*," he panted. "I cannot refuse it, though it appalls my heart." He may have been offering her an apology. "I must overcome myself. If I do not, I will fail you and my people as well as the living Earth."

The Ironhand nodded. "*Geas* or bravery," she replied, "it has sufficed. And perchance you will not be asked to dare such perils again. The way has been opened. When we have accomplished our purpose, you and the Harrow will be able remove us from these depths without confronting a second passage over that dire chasm."

To Linden, she added, "Shall we go now in search of your son? Remaining here, we achieve naught."

Linden did not respond. She felt hypnotized by the sweat on the Ardent's face, the raw fright in his eyes. The sensation that she had come to the end clung to her. Some stunned part of her was still immersed in the toils of the wards. She did not know how to shake free of them.

But Stave took her by the arm. With Liand at her other shoulder, the former Master turned her toward the portal.

Seeing the Harrow outlined against the moonstone glow, with her Staff and Covenant's ring clenched in his fists, Linden roused herself as if from a stupor. Though she felt emptied, like a broken cistern that could no longer hold water, she had surrendered too much to stop now. Not when the brown-clad Insequent was impatient to fulfill his promises.

Urged by the Giants, Stave and Liand encouraged her into the Lost Deep.

8.

Caverns Ornate and Majestic

At once, Coldspray and several of the Swordmainnir arrayed themselves around Linden, Stave, Liand, and the Cords. Their eagerness for adventure was bright on their faces, and they held their heads high. Behind them, Galesend and Latebirth carried Anele and Mahrtiir. And at the rear of the company, the Humbled escorted Covenant to meet the outcome of Linden's long quest.

The Harrow was too sure that he had beaten his enemies: the only foes that mattered. He would not be ready—

Linden was counting on that.

With her companions assembled around her like a cortege, Linden Avery the Chosen entered the abandoned habitation and loreworks of the Viles.

At first, she concentrated her ragged attention on the figure of the Harrow. Clad like the Mahdoubt, and the Ardent, and presumably even the Theomach, in the means and symbols of his arcane knowledge, he still waited for her. Even now, his oaths bound him. In frustration, he tapped one iron heel of the Staff on the polished floor within the portal. But the slight impact of metal on stone made no sound that she could hear. Instead his tapping gave off evanescent puffs of moonshine and pearl like wisps of incandescence.

When she drew near enough to release him from his impatience, he turned to lead the way again.

Focusing on him, she did not notice her surroundings until she heard or felt Liand's sharp intake of breath, sensed the whispered exclamations of the Giants. Involuntarily, as if she had no will or strength that was not provided by her companions, she lifted her head to look at the high chamber which formed the entrance hall to the Lost Deep.

The sight shocked her like a tectonic shift; a grinding of the Earth's bones so deeply buried that its tremors might take hours or even days to be felt on the surface.

She could not think of the chamber as a cavern, although it seemed as huge as the enclosure of the Banefire in Revelstone long ago. It stretched past the limits of her senses ahead and above her. And every handspan of its walls and vaulted ceiling and floor had been burnished to a lambent sheen, flawless and glowing. Indeed, the shaped rock was the source of the Deep's illumination. Every line and curve, plane and arc of the chamber emitted an eerie lucence composed of commingled and constantly shifting hues. With each beat of her heart, Linden encountered a different blend of the most pastel vermillion, the palest azure; the merest suggestions of charlock and viridian and lime.

In itself, the chamber was immense and wondrous. Yet it did not cause her sense of shock.

Apparently the entire space had been shaped for no other purpose than to house something that must have been a work of art; *the making of beauty and wonder*— Beyond question, the chamber was *filled with loveliness*.

Entering here, Linden and her companions had already walked partway into the ramified outlines of an elaborate castle rich in beauty and imaginative largesse. The structure was not solid. Instead it was composed only of outlines like strokes drawn on blank air; sweeps and delineations of—of bone? opaque crystal? smooth travertine shafts? If it had not looked entirely complete as it was, it might have been a model for an edifice which the Viles had once intended to build; a sketch done in three dimensions and mother-of-pearl. Yet no detail had been neglected. Flying buttresses radiated outward from the shape of a central keep, linking the keep to an elegant circle of turrets. Balconies and ramparts articulated what would have been the rounded walls of the keep, the supernal circles of the turrets. Bartizans and crenellations expressed the crowns of the turrets. Low walls explained the ramparts and balconies, the airy buttresses. In the base of the keep, a lowered drawbridge implied an entrance into a space filled with rooms and curving stairways: a faery dwelling without walls, barriers, substance.

And it was *familiar*. Linden had seen it before. During the last days of her former life, its exact duplicate had occupied the hallway inside the front door of her home: hers and Jeremiah's. Amid the mundane surroundings of the house, it had seemed so magical and dream-like that she had not asked him to take it down. She had loved it, and him, too much to wish it dismantled.

Nevertheless it had endured only until Roger Covenant had crashed through it like a wrecking ball, seeking her son—and his father's ring.

Now she understood that Jeremiah had seen this place. He had *seen* it. He had not drawn his castle from the raw stuff of his sealed imagination: he had copied it from *this*.

It told her that she was on the right path.

And it was further evidence that Jeremiah's spirit had indeed visited the Land years before Roger had stolen him from her. His racetrack construct in his bedroom had been a door. Roger and the *croyel* had told her the truth about that, if about little else.

Instinctively she stopped, halted by wonder and memory and nameless apprehensions. She did not recollect herself until Liand urged softly, "Linden! Your son is surely nigh. And the Harrow's impatience mounts. We must not linger."

With an effort, she looked at the Stonedownor as though she no longer knew who he was.

"Lady!" snapped the Harrow. "Despite his many follies, the youth speaks sooth. The Lost Deep matches the scope of its makers' dreams. The halls and loreworks are vast, extending for leagues. We need not lose our path among them, but our efforts will prove bootless if you cannot contain your wonder. This realm remains hazardous, as does the bane of the abyss."

His voice expanded to a shout. "We must have haste!"

You're right, Linden thought. You're. Right. But still she did not move. Scattered and broken Tinkertoys held her: the ruin of Roger's passage as he violated her home. She saw omens in the castle. Every line of the ramparts prefigured bereavement.

"Cease your reproaches, Insequent." The Ironhand sounded bemused by delight.

"If you require haste, it will be vouchsafed to you. But briefly, briefly, we must honor our astonishment." She gazed around as if the sheer size of her pleasure amazed her. "We are Giants, lovers of stone in every guise, yet never have we beheld such glory. This untrammeled perfection—" She stretched out her arms as if she wished to embrace the whole castle. "It is immaculate to the point of melody. In sooth, Insequent, its song is almost audible—"

Some of the Swordmainnir nodded. Others simply stared, entranced and mute.

"We will hasten to your heart's content," Rime Coldspray finished: a sigh of reverence or reverie. "But in a moment. In a moment—"

Her voice faded as she studied the lofty edifice.

"*Linden*," Liand insisted. "Linden, *hear* me. This place is indeed perilous, though I cannot name our jeopardy." He was a Stonedownor: he should have felt as enthralled as the Giants. "I know only that foreboding fills my heart. We must heed the Harrow or fail."

Oh, my son.

Deliberately Linden remembered the *croyel* clinging like a malnourished infant on Jeremiah's back; the claws and toes gouged into his flesh; the fangs chewing on the side of his neck to drink his blood. Then she was moving again. Liand and Stave held her arms while the Harrow strode ahead of her.

As if he were fearless, the man led her straight into the heart of the outlined keep.

Somewhere behind her, the Ardent murmured, "Fear nothing. Here the Harrow's knowledge is sure." Anxiety filled his voice with hues like moaning. "No wards threaten us while we abide his guidance. Doubtless I will revel in memories of this demesne's manifold wonders when—" He faltered and fell silent.

For a moment, Linden feared that only she, Stave, and Liand trailed after the Harrow. Glancing over her shoulder, however, she saw the Humbled behind her, escorting Covenant among them. Covenant's attention was everywhere at once, as though he strove to encompass every ageless memory implied by the castle and the cavern; but he took no notice of Linden.

Briefly she caught a whiff of Mahrtiir's voice. "Have our companions departed? Why do you not guard the Ringthane?" The words smelled querulous; vexed by helplessness.

Straining her neck, Linden finally felt the Giants shake off their enchantment and start forward. Latebirth still carried the Manethrall: Galesend cradled Anele. At the rear, Cirrus Kindwind herded the Cords ahead of her.

The Harrow passed through the central keep as though it did not exist; but Linden was loath to leave it. Here in some metaphysical fashion, Jeremiah had found an image of his secret heart. She wanted to pore over every line of the castle until she understood what had been hidden from her; until she knew how to reach past Jeremiah's torment and lift him free. An impossible hope. Like the stains on her jeans, the text of the castle was indecipherable. She might examine it for years, and it would tell her nothing.

She did not have years. The time left to her could be measured in days at most.

Grimly she tried to quicken her pace.

Now that they were in motion, the Giants caught up with her easily, drawing the Ardent after them. With her companions, she passed among the outer turrets toward the far wall of the chamber.

A number of openings awaited her, all filled with modulating radiance. Some were narrow corridors that soon curved out of sight. Others were almost as high as the forehall of Revelstone, and seemed to extend indefinitely through the lucent rock. But the Harrow selected a passage without hesitation. Eagerly, urgently, he led the way into one of the narrower tunnels.

At every step, the Staff of Law touched the stone, invoking momentary exhalations of vapor. Linden felt rather than heard her friends' respiration. They breathed scents and colors instead of air.

Beyond the passage, they entered another chamber, smaller than the first, but still wide and round enough to accommodate a copse of wattle or a stand of jacaranda—and high enough to accept cedars. Indeed, the space dwarfed the jut of crude dark rock in its center. Supported by a low mound of unfinished basalt, bitter rock reared upward, gnarled and somehow grisly. It formed two sides that resembled jaws filled with ragged teeth. And between the jaws, there appeared to be a seat: the entire out-cropping may have been a throne.

Within the perfection of the chamber's walls, the upraised stone was a maimed thing, deformed by malice or indifference.

Linden could not imagine why the Viles had chosen to create such a shape. But she did not ask the Harrow to explain it. She felt repulsed by it. It seemed to emit an odor like ordure. If it were a sculpture, it was an exercise in derision.

Fortunately the Harrow strode past the jaws and the seat without glancing at them. Still certain, he selected a hallway beyond the throne and entered it swiftly, as if he wished to distance himself from the dire rock.

Trembling for no reason that she could name, and glad that Stave and Liand still held her arms, Linden followed the Insequent with the rest of her company close around her.

This hall was straight, featureless, and long: long enough for Linden to realize that her perceptions were suffering a kind of delinition. The glow of the stone became less a matter of sight and more a flowing series of sensations on her skin: brief caresses as loving as kisses; small scrapes that caused no pain; the tickling of feathers; warm breaths. The colors were the multitudinous susurrus of her companions. Like the

Harrow's, her steps were little clouds, and every touch of the Staff on the stone trailed streamers like rills of mist.

She was falling into paresthesia again, the neural confusion caused by the intangible essence of the Viles. Remnants of their lore lingered where they had once flourished. Soon she would have to follow the Harrow by smell and taste as much as by small pennons of illumined fog. Insidiously she was being led astray, guided out of contact with mundane existence.

Without percipience, she could not gauge how the residual theurgy of the Viles affected her companions. She had told them little about her arranged confrontation with the makers of the Demondim: words were impotent to convey the disorientation that the Viles engendered. Yet the pitch and timbre of Stave's hand, and of Liand's, held steady. Somehow they contrived to manage their delirant senses.

If the Giants or Linden's other companions felt any distress, she did not discern it. The shades of their breathing baffled interpretation.

She had experienced similar dislocations before. Nevertheless she was not ready when the hall opened.

As though she had crossed a threshold into an altogether different definition of reality, she entered a space as open, ornate, and majestic as a palace.

Here her perceptions resumed their normal dimensions; or they seemed to do so. In this place, the complex puissance of the Viles was gone, utterly banished—or else their lore had devised an illusion more oblique and bewildering than paresthesia. Only a vague squirming, an almost subliminal discomfort, warned Linden that her senses were confused; that the substance of what she saw had been fundamentally altered.

To all appearances, she stood in the ballroom of a vast palace or mansion, the dwelling of some supreme sovereign surrounded by incarnate wealth. On a burnished marmoreal floor, rugs overlapped each other in every direction. They were as sumptuous as cushions, and as richly woven as tapestries; yet they were also transparent, as clear as light; simultaneously solid and impalpable. Against the far walls, wide stairways with treads and banisters of flawless crystal arced upward like wings. At precise intervals among the rugs, shafts of glass spun in delicate filigree rose to five or six times the height of the Giants; and from elaborate arms atop the shafts hung chandeliers in profusion, each bedizened with scores or hundreds of lights as pure and white as stars, and as clinquant as precious metals. Along the walls, golden braziers gave off flames that suffused the air with tranquility. And in the center of the space, a fountain of ice—translucent and perfectly frozen—spouted toward the distant ceiling. It reached as high as the chandeliers, where it spread outward in a ceaseless spray, droplets as fine and faceted as jewels. Yet no current flowed. No bead fell. The ice was so motionless that it seemed sealed in time rather than in cold.

Above it, on the ceiling itself, mosaics as magnificent as choirs displayed their voices from wall to wall. The magic of their creation made them simultaneously as articulate as glory and as colorless as water.

Helpless to resist her amazement, Linden gazed around the palace like a woman bespelled. As she did so, some indistinct part of her observed that her companions appeared to feel the same dazzlement. Even the Humbled and Stave were lost in wonder. They wandered away from her, away from Covenant, in a kind of rapture, studying avidly every gleaming crystalline miracle. Liand drifted apart. The Giants separated to peer in awe and delight at the filigree shafts, or at the fountain held ineffably in abeyance. Some of them stooped to trail their fingers along the patterns that elaborated the rugs. Like the ecstatic figures in dreams, the Cords and Liand craned their necks to watch the dance of the chandeliers, hear the music of the mosaics. In spite of his blindness, Manethrall Mahrtiir was dazed by munificence.

Anele had awakened. Squirming in Galesend's arms, he asked her to put him down. When he stood on the glowing floor, however, he did not move. Instead he remained where Galesend had placed him, jerking his head from side to side with an air of rapt attention, saying nothing.

For some reason, the Ardent had wrapped his raiment tightly around himself again. Then he sank to the floor in a mound of garish and incondign hues. There he rocked himself from side to side like a child in need of comfort.

And Covenant— He, too, had drifted away. Standing before one of the braziers, he stared into the evanescent mansuetude of the flames as if they had ravished him.

In her tranced state, Linden saw no sign of the Harrow. But she did not care what had become of him. She could not: the palace ruled her as though her mind or her spirit had been consumed by astonishment.

Here she might find it possible to know and feel nothing except glad peace until she became as translucent as the fountain and the stairs, the rugs and the chandeliers.

Some time seemed to pass before she found the heart of her amazement and recognized the truth, the defining mystery of what the Viles had accomplished in the prime of their power. Inspired by her previous encounter with their theurgy, she saw that the entire palace and everything in it, the walls and rugs, the shafts of glass, the frozen fountain, the hanging anadems of the chandeliers, the voiced and melodious mosaics, even the golden luxury of the braziers and flames: all of it was made of water. Of *water*, pure and irreproachable. The magic enchanting her was the magic that had formed the edifice; the magic that sustained it millennia after its makers had perished from the Earth. Somehow the Viles had woven water into these multifarious shapes, these myriad details, and then had caused the water to remain—

The palace was a sculpture, a work of the most sublime art: an eldritch and enduring triumph of ability and will over the fluid inconstancy of time.

Esmer had hardly done the Viles justice when he had called them *lofty and admirable*. Their lore was indeed *terrible and matchless. —and all of their works were filled with loveliness.*

That such creatures had been lured into self-loathing was an abomination.

One of many. The history of the Land, and of the Earth, was littered with the rubble of atrocities for which Lord Foul deserved to be held accountable.

Yet Linden felt no umbrage, no desire to take action. Only the subtle nagging of discomfort along the length of her nerves marred her tranquility. In this place, this supernal masterpiece, the Despiser's many hurts warranted no concern. She could relax into a measureless contentment that explained more eloquently than any language why the Viles had taken so long to venture out of the Lost Deep. They, too, had been eased by their dreams and their labors; their transcendental achievements. Like them, she would have been reluctant to risk the meaning of her life elsewhere.

Now that she knew the secret of the palace, she saw it displayed everywhere. Tumbling freshets had supplied the substance of the shafts which upheld the chandeliers. Lakes as calm as Glimmermere had made the walls. Brooks giggling over their rocks in springtime had become the rugs; the vociferous mosaics. The fountain was a captured geyser.

A hint of anxiety still twisted in the private channels of her body, but she had forgotten what it meant. If Anele had not placed himself directly in front of her, interrupting her contemplation of miracles, she might not have noticed that he had set aside his passivity.

"Anele," he said with exaggerated precision, as if he found words difficult to utter. "Hears bells. Chiming. They disturb—He craves. Needs. Seeks." For a moment, he appeared to lose track of his thoughts. Then he gathered up their broken strands and offered them to Linden. "Redemption."

His hands trembled as he reached out to clasp her shoulders.

His touch was insistent, but gentle; so soft that she barely felt it. Nevertheless a small jolt ran through her as though he had reached past the obstacles of her shirt and her eased spirit to awaken her flesh with Earthpower.

Water, she thought indirectly. That was the secret. Its snared fluidity expressed to perfection the flowing bafflement that the Viles imposed on ordinary forms of discernment; mortal modes of understanding. In the Land's past, she had experienced a trammeled manifestation of that confusion. Here she would have seen smells, felt colors, tasted voices—if the Viles had not frozen water and theurgy into permanence.

While Anele held her shoulders, she found that she, too, heard a muffled ringing.

Before he could release her, she grasped one of his hands in both of hers, held it to her heart. Then she looked around, trying to locate the source of the sounds.

She found it between Liand and one of the spun shafts. While the Stonedownor studied the glitter of the chandelier in calm and enraptured delirium, the Harrow struck one heel of the Staff repeatedly on the rug where he stood. From that soft impact arose a silvery tintinnabulation like the urging of distant chimes.

Without Anele's hand clutched in hers, Linden might have lost sight of the Insequent again; or forgotten him. But the effect of the old man's skin against hers, the almost impalpable emanations of his inherited strength, elucidated her perceptions. Earthpower explained the Harrow. He was striving to invoke the fire of the Staff so that he could break free of the palace's ensorcelment.

Linden watched him with nothing more than the surface of her mind; felt only a detached curiosity. After a few moments, she might have lost interest and looked away, in spite of Anele's indirect adjuration. But as she considered the Harrow, he appeared to burst into flame. He and the Staff and his determination to claim Jeremiah became a pillar of conflagration as he began to move, striding toward an ornate stairway beyond the fountain.

Bewildered by magicks, he had forgotten his oath to take Linden with him; or perhaps his need to escape the seductions of water compelled him to neglect her.

As he left her behind, something buried within Linden stirred. Still clinging to Anele's hand, she also began to move.

Earthpower. That was it. She needed Earthpower: more than she could glean from the old man. His legacy was too deeply hidden within him, defended by layers of madness. She required a more direct source—

She needed her health-sense.

Walking as Anele had spoken, as if each step demanded an arduous and precise effort, she stepped toward Liand, drawing the old man with her.

None of her companions gave any sign that they could see her; that they knew who she was. No one else could help her.

In the same way that Anele had confronted her, she intruded on the Stonedownor's gaze.

He was her first real friend since she had lost her son. He had enabled her flight from Mithil Stonedown and the Masters with Anele when she had no other aid or guide. He trusted her in spite of all that she had done: he believed in her. Surely he would recognize her now? Surely he would hear her and respond?

He greeted her with a brief frown. Then he stared past or through her as though she had grown too spectral to disturb him.

"Liand." Only her grip on Anele's hand enabled her to speak. "Listen." The Harrow was ascending the stairs. He rose as if he were borne by flame. "I need *orcrest*."

The young man did not react. The palace held him in thrall. His slight awareness of her presence had faded.

Linden wanted to slap him, and could not. She wanted to reach into the pouch at his waist and take his Sunstone; but she lacked the strength, or the will. She had surrendered too much, and knew the cost. He did not deserve to have his heritage taken from him.

Fighting her own entrancement, her own weakness, she tugged Anele closer to Liand. Then, interlacing her fingers with Anele's so that the old man would not pull free, she guided his free hand to Liand's shoulder. Mutely she willed Anele to jolt the Stonedownor as he had jolted her.

Through his madness, Anele must have understood what she was doing; or he had his own reasons for desperation, his own fragmented needs. Still trembling, he stroked Liand's shoulder—

—and Liand twitched. His black eyebrows arched. His eyes veered into focus on Linden. He peered at her as if she were veiled by water.

At the top of the stair, the Harrow passed between hanging curtains and disappeared.

"Liand," Linden said again, "listen."

"Li—" Liand tried to say her name. "Lin—"

"Listen to me," she urged: a small sound, too distant and uncertain to compel attention. "I can't explain. I don't understand. But we need Earthpower. To remember who we are.

"We need *orcrest*."

Even the Giants: even the *Haruchai* were beyond her. The palace had turned their inherent strengths against them. And none of them carried any instruments of power. Covenant retained Loric's *krill*; but he had stumbled into his past before Linden's company had crossed the Hazard. Nothing that she could say or do would pierce his memories.

She had to follow the Harrow. If Liand did not rouse himself a little more; just a little—

Anele tightened his grip.

This time Liand succeeded at saying her name. "Linden?"

"*Orcrest*," she repeated. Her voice shook like Anele's arms. The old man had saved her more than once. He had drawn her out of her paralysis when she had first entered a *caesure*, seeking the Staff of Law. "We need it."

For a moment, Liand turned his bewilderment toward Anele. Then he appeared to shudder. "*Orcrest?*" he murmured distantly. "I had forgotten—"

Fumbling as if Anele had touched him with age and caducity as well as Earthpower, the Stonedownor opened his pouch and brought out the Sunstone.

For a time that seemed long to Linden, Liand frowned at the rock in his palm. He was relapsing into the magic of the palace; or she was. Dully she thought that his *orcrest* was not a stone at all. It was water impossibly piled onto itself when it should have poured away between his fingers. Soon he would hold nothing more than a few pellucid drops.

In spite of Anele's clasp, Linden was drifting. Like Liand, she would dissolve into wonder and forget that she was lost.

But Liand did not dissolve. Instead he closed his hand on the *orcrest*; and Linden remembered that the Harrow was gone.

At first, the Sunstone only glowed like the lambence of the Lost Deep, nacreous and commingled, indistinguishable from the illumination of the Viles. Yet even that distortion of the Sunstone's nature must have given Liand strength. He gripped the *orcrest* more firmly. By gentle increments, its radiance regained its more familiar white purity.

At the same time, Linden's sense of herself came back into focus. The Harrow, she thought distinctly. Jeremiah!

The Ardent lay swaddled as if he clad himself for burial. No one remained to insist on the sanctity of the Harrow's oath.

Liand brought forth brighter Earthpower. Linden's heart pounded as if she were suffocating; drowning—

"All right," she gasped. "Keep doing that." Echoes scattered from the chandeliers like cascades of gemstones. "Don't let go of Anele. We have to catch up with the Harrow."

Liand shook his head, struggled to clear his thoughts. "What of the Giants?" The muscles of his neck corded. "Pahni and the Ramen? Stave? If we forsake them—"

Linden started toward the stair, pulling Anele after her; hoping that Anele would pull Liand. "We don't have time." Water seemed to fill her lungs. "We'll come back when we know what the Harrow is doing." She was becoming water. "We have to find Jeremiah."

She was already ashamed that she had forgotten her son.

Anele tightened his grasp. Mad or sane, he followed her willingly. And he did not release Liand. After a moment, the Stonedownor set aside his reluctance. Together Linden and Anele encouraged Liand toward the wide arc of the stairway.

Strength enabled strength. Every increment of Earthpower that Liand summoned from the *orcrest* inspired him to summon more.

Following the Harrow, Linden climbed the stairs like a cresting wave.

If we forsake them— She was abandoning her other friends; abandoning Covenant. If she had heard the dangers of the palace described, she might have assumed that the intransigence of the *Haruchai* would protect them. The Giants and the Ramen were open to awe and joy: they had no defense. But Stave and the Humbled—

Yet the *Haruchai* also had no defense. They, too, were vulnerable to wonder and generosity, in spite of their wonted stoicism. How else had High Lord Kevin and the Council of Lords and Giants and Ranyhyn inspired the Vow of the Bloodguard?

How else had the Vizard humiliated them, if not by mocking the depth of their passions?

When Stave and the Masters regained themselves, they, too, would feel shame. Clyme and Branl and Galt and even Stave would judge themselves harshly. *Haruchai* did not forgive—

Nevertheless Linden did not turn back. Jeremiah came first. She would return for the rest of her companions when she no longer feared what the Harrow might do.

At the top of the staircase, heavy curtains hung like waterfalls over an arched opening in the wall: a way out of the chamber behind her; perhaps a way out of the palace itself. Thwarted by the magicks of the place, she detected no hint of the Harrow's passage. But she had seen him part the curtains and vanish.

Facing water in an opaque brocade of gold and silver and refined tourmaline, she paused for an instant to secure her clasp on Anele, her connection to Liand. Then she led them through the liquid fabric.

Beyond that barrier, she found that she had indeed left the ambit of the palace. At once, the sensation that she was immersed in water and theurgy left her, and her nerves extended their percipient reach. A narrow corridor pierced the gutrock crookedly ahead of her. Like all of the Lost Deep's stone, it had been refined to a lambent sheen: the passage was filled with light like an invitation. Here, however, the illumination did not mask the lingering scent of force and flame from the Staff of Law, or the faint emanations left behind by the Harrow's own sortilege.

Almost running, Linden headed into the corridor with Anele and Liand.

The hall curved and twisted, insidious as a serpent. Other passages or chambers branched out on both sides, but she ignored them. Sensing the Harrow, she was certain of her way. Liand breathed raggedly, worn down by his earlier efforts beyond the Hazard; but his strides were steady. Anele displayed his familiar, unlikely stamina. And Linden was sustained by images of Jeremiah. She believed that her son was near. If the Insequent did not forswear his oath—

One sweep and angle and opening after another, the way created the illusion of a maze; a place in which lives and intentions were lost. Yet Linden felt no secrets hidden in the walls, no concealed intersections, no disguising glamours. If the Viles, or Roger and the *croyel*, or *moksha* Raver had left snares to baffle her, she could not perceive them.

And the aura and inferences of the Harrow's passing remained steady.

Then Linden, Anele, and Liand rounded a corner. Abruptly the corridor emptied them into a round chamber shaped like a dome, a sphere cut in half by its pristine floor.

Here again, she could not think of the space as a cavern or cave. Its dimensions were too perfectly symmetrical to be a natural formation. Like the floor, the walls as they curved upward to meet over the precise center of the space were nitid with the Lost Deep's characteristic moonstone glow. The chamber was not as large as the other halls which she had entered and departed: it seemed almost intimate by comparison, although it could easily have held the Swordmainnir and several score of their comrades. Still it made Linden feel small to herself.

Its effect on her was not diminished by the fact that it had been flawed by time or theurgy.

The floor itself, like the four gaps in the walls, betrayed no sign of damage or alteration. The opening through which she and her companions had arrived was mirrored by one directly opposite her. Two others stood equidistant around the walls. Fashioned with the accustomed exactitude of the Viles, these corridors may have indicated the points of an arcane compass.

But in the center of the ceiling hung a raw lump or knob of rock that resembled travertine, crude and unreflective; porous; dark as a stain against the lit stone. And from that misshapen clot, eight arms or ridges of the same stigma ran down the walls as though they had been deposited by eons of dripping water.

The air was warmer than it had been elsewhere in the Deep. It suggested hot springs thick with minerals.

Yet time and water could not have caused those formations. Four of them reached straight toward the openings in the walls, where they branched like arches to delineate or emphasize the corridors. The other four clung to the walls at exact intervals between the openings. And when the darkness of each ridge or branch touched the floor, it merged into the smooth surface and stopped as if it had been cut off. As if it were no longer needed.

Natural forces would have left residue splayed across the floor. And the increased warmth: that, too, was not natural.

Linden recognized the source of the heat. She knew it well.

The increasing accuracy of her health-sense assured her that the knob and arms of calcareous rock were more recent than the chamber which they marred: far more recent. They must have been deposited within the past year, probably within the past season.

They looked fragile—so porous that she might have crumbled them with her fingers—but she already knew that they were strong enough for their purpose. She had expected to find something like them here, although she could not have imagined what form they would take.

Then free my son, she had demanded of Infelice. *Give him back to me.*

They will not, the Harrow had answered her. *They can not.*

The travertine was the construct that masked Jeremiah's presence from the *Elohim*: from Infelice and Kastenessen as well as from Esmer. The use that Roger and the *croyel* had made of Jeremiah's talents protected her son from every eldritch perception except the Harrow's more oblique and mortal knowledge—and perhaps from the strange lore of the ur-viles and Waynhim.

The Demondim-spawn could not have brought her here. They traveled in ways that she could not emulate. Perhaps they had tried to tell her where to look; but Esmer had refused to translate their speech.

Near the center of the chamber stood the Insequent. He held the Staff of Law braced on the stone near his feet and Covenant's ring raised over his head. But he made no attempt to wield those powers: not yet. Instead he glared into the acrid yellow gaze of the *croyel*, plainly trying to swallow the deformed creature's will and power with his bottomless eyes.

The creature still clung to Jeremiah's back: a hairless monster the size of a child, scrawny and insatiable. Its fingers gripped his shoulders while its toes dug into his ribs, rending his flesh like claws. Avidly its fangs chewed the side of his neck to drink his blood, devour his mind. Its virulent eyes implied howling and shrieks. But it did not exert its strength against the Harrow. Instead it appeared to revel in defying him.

Between those antagonists, Jeremiah stood slumped as if he were nothing more than the *croyel*'s puppet: a means to define and transport the creature's malice. His muddy, disfocused gaze regarded the floor with the blank stare of a youth who had lost hope long ago. From his slack slips, a small dribble of saliva ran into the nascent stubble on his chin. His arms hung, useless, at his sides. His fingers dangled as though they were empty of import; as though they had never held anything as ordinary and human as a red racecar.

He was an abused boy whose only escape from the prison of his maimed mind was through the *croyel*'s ferocity.

But he was alive.

9.

Hastening Doom

 In time you will behold the fruit of my endeavors.

Linden could hear Lord Foul as if he stood beside her, laughing like a scourge.

If your son serves me, he will do so in your presence. Jeremiah had done so under *Melenkurion* Skyweir. He did so now. Or the *croyel* used his unresisting body and trapped mind as a conveyance for its harsh appetites. Confident of its dominion, the creature faced the Harrow with mockery in its cruel eyes.

If I slaughter him, I will do so before you. Think on that when you seek to retrieve him from me.

Dull-eyed and vacant, Jeremiah remained on his feet only because the *croyel* compelled him. The false or transmuted alertness and excitement that Linden had seen in her son's face before she had exposed the succubus was absent. Every sign that he might be capable of outward consciousness was gone.

If you discover him, you will only hasten his doom.

While the Harrow strove to master the *croyel*, and received only contempt, Linden stood helpless, transfixed by dismay.

—this I vow.

Indirectly, indirectly, the Despiser had urged her to awaken the Worm of the World's End by resurrecting Covenant. Lord Foul had provided the circumstances and the impetus that goaded her damaged heart. By dismay and desperation, he had encouraged her to surrender her powers so that she would be brought here; so that she would be forced to bear witness and do nothing. So that her futility in the face of Jeremiah's need would break her at last.

The Despiser had underestimated her. Again. He had failed to grasp the scale of her willingness to suffer for her son's sake, or the acuity of her flayed perceptions. He did not know that she could hear vast pain masked by Lord Foul's exaltation.

"Linden?" Liand panted. "Is *this* your son's plight? You have described it, but words—" He strained for language. "Linden, that creature—that monster—! What it does to your son is an abomination."

As if she were clenching her own fist, Linden felt his hand tighten on the *orcrest*.

Fierce with ire, he began to draw forth more Earthpower, and still more. If the white purity of the Sunstone could be used as a weapon, he intended to assail the *croyel*. His desire to strike was as vivid as a shout.

His spirit was too clean to countenance atrocities: a handicap which she did not share.

She meant to stop him. She needed only the health-sense that his efforts supplied. She did not intend to let him sacrifice himself.

Before she could forestall the Stonedownor, however, the *croyel* raised Jeremiah's maimed hand. Undisturbed by the avid depths of the Harrow's eyes, the creature caused Jeremiah to gesture negligently in Liand's direction.

Warm as breath, a sudden wave of magic crashed into the young man.

It swatted him away; flung him hard against one of the dark ridges of travertine. The impact nearly shattered Linden's concentration: it may have shattered his bones. Blood red as an arterial hemorrhage burst from his mouth, splashed incrimination onto the luminous floor. Flopping like a doll stuffed with cloth and cotton, he sprawled face-first to the stone.

Apparently the *croyel* perceived a greater threat in Liand—or in *orcrest*—than in the Harrow. Or in Linden.

Instantly inert, the Sunstone fell from Liand's grasp; rolled away. A stride or two beyond his fingers, it came to rest.

At once, Linden's health-sense evaporated, denatured by her proximity to the source of Kevin's Dirt. Without transition, she was blinded to the truth of Jeremiah's anguish and Liand's injuries and the *croyel*'s evil.

At the same time, Anele wrenched free of her. His mouth stretched in a soundless wail as he turned; fled back into the corridor toward the palace.

Linden let him go. He could not aid her now. Perhaps his reappearance among the rest of her companions would serve to disenchant them.

They would take too long—

Part of her yearned to rush to Liand's side; gauge the extent of his wounds; help him as much as she was able. Part of her burned to leap past him and snatch up the Sunstone, hoping that its touch would restore some measure of her percipience. But she compelled herself to remain motionless. The *croyel* could crush her as easily as it had broken Liand. She had no defense.

She knew what to do. She had already made her decision. But she had to wait for the right moment.

The moment when both the Harrow and the creature would be distracted.

Where was Roger? Surely Thomas Covenant's son would not have left the *croyel* and Jeremiah unguarded? Linden was counting on that. Alone, the power of Kastenessen's hand was not enough for Roger. Nor were the complex magicks of the *croyel*. Like the creature, Roger required Jeremiah's supernal talents. Without them, Roger and the *croyel* would not survive the destruction of the Arch of Time to *become gods*.

Gradually the contest between the Harrow and the *croyel* eased or shifted. Linden saw the change in the loosening of the Insequent's shoulders, the adjustment of his posture. He must have decided to try different tactics.

"Do you dare me?" His voice held only triumph despite the scorn gleaming in the *croyel*'s eyes. Beside Jeremiah's vacancy, he was a figure of sculpted muscle, graceful garb, and dominance. "You see that my flesh and bone are no greater than those of the youth whom you possess. Therefore you conclude that I am a lesser being than yourself. Yet you are sorely mistaken. To your cost, you refuse the consummation of my gaze. Do you not perceive that I have learned the uses of the Staff of Law? And soon I will wield the incomparable forces of white gold. At that moment, my knowledge and magicks will become *perfection*.

"Doubtless your strengths are ancient and potent. Nonetheless you cannot stand against me."

Briefly the creature lifted its fangs from Jeremiah's neck to grin at the Harrow. Then it resumed its dire feeding.

"Nor can you hope for aid here," the Insequent continued. "The defense which you have devised blocks foe and friend alike. Even the halfhand who has been your companion and ally cannot broach this warded chamber."

Cannot—? Linden's chest tightened. The Harrow may have been telling the truth. Before the battle of First Woodhelven, he had pierced the glamour with which Roger had veiled himself and his Cavewights. Surely the Harrow would have recognized the danger if Roger had been present?

But when Roger had arrived to attack the Harrow and Esmer and Linden, he had left the *croyel* behind. He had approached and struck without the *croyel*'s support, the *croyel*'s theurgy.

Nevertheless the deep soil of the Harrow's disdain matched the creature's malign gaze.

"Oh, I do not question that he is aware of your location, as the *Elohim* are not. Indeed, I am certain that he participated in your choice to conceal yourself here, and that he assisted your passage hither. Yet when you erected the barrier which prevents the perception of the *Elohim*, you excluded him as well. Kastenessen's hand has grown into him. It has become native to his blood. And Kastenessen is *Elohim*. Thus your own cleverness delivers you to me.

"No other power will redeem you. You are *mine*."

With a flourish of the Staff, the Harrow sent sunshine flame blossoming into the dome.

Unintentionally he renewed a portion of Linden's health-sense.

Roger had told Linden that Kastenessen craved only the destruction of his people. She believed that. Kastenessen's pain ruled him. He had no other desires. Through Esmer, he had opposed the Harrow before. He would do so again, if he could—but only because he sought to prevent the Harrow from saving the *Elohim*. He did not want Jeremiah's gifts for his own use.

Roger and the *croyel* had other ambitions.

Mimicking the Harrow's display in its own fashion, the creature gestured with Jeremiah's halfhand again.

Linden flinched. She expected an invisible blow which would deprive her of use and name and life. But the *croyel*'s might was not directed at her. She felt none of its energy in the chamber at all.

Instead she sensed a summons.

Immediately children like incarnations of acid began to emerge from the other openings in the wall.

She knew them too well. They were *skest*: creatures of living vitriol, deformed and corrosive; deadly despite their small stature. Lit from within by a gangrenous green radiance, as if they were the impossible offspring of the Illearth Stone, they destroyed their foes by dissolving mortal flesh, reducing bones and sinews to macerated puddles. At one time, they had served the lurker of the Sarangrave. But more recently, Linden had seen them tending Joan. Trapped in freezing and hornets and madness within a *caesure*, Linden had watched acid-children care for Joan's physical needs while *turiya* Raver toyed with the frail woman's derangement. Linden had not expected to encounter them here.

Now she guessed that the *skest* performed a similar service for Jeremiah, nourishing the *croyel* through her son's possessed body. In effect, they kept Jeremiah alive for the creature's sake—and for Lord Foul's.

But the *skest* were also the *croyel*'s defenders. They issued from their corridors in numbers that seemed great enough to overwhelm the Harrow.

Studying him as closely as she could, Linden believed that he had not yet found a way to evoke wild magic from Covenant's ring. But with the Staff, the Insequent could wield a flail of burning Earthpower. He would fight to protect himself.

If one of the *skest* touched him, just one—Would the magicks which had preserved him from the Humbled and Stave suffice here? Linden did not think so. He was mortal: as human as Linden and Jeremiah. His power to ward off plain blows might not guard him against the more fatal touch of emerald corrosion. And *skest* were not Demondim— or Demondim-spawn. He could not simply unbind them from themselves.

And while he defended himself from them, the *croyel* could strike whenever it wished.

Clearly the Insequent recognized his peril. He retreated a few steps from Jeremiah and the *croyel*; surrounded himself with flames. His jaws chewed curses as he clenched Covenant's ring. Linden felt his extremity as he strove to bring forth argence.

But he was not its rightful wielder.

Neither was she. Yet Covenant's ring belonged to her far more than it did to the Harrow. Otherwise she could not have saved herself and Anele from the collapse of Kevin's Watch.

There were scores of *skest* in the chamber. More came behind them. Some of them burned like kindling when the Staff's fire caught them: they slumped into acrid pools that frothed and spat, gnawing chunks out of the granite floor. But they were many, and they kept coming. Soon they would be enough to encircle the Harrow's defenses.

Enough to threaten Linden: enough to kill her where she stood; or to drive her away from her son.

Liand would die in quick agony.

Now, she thought. The time was now.

At last, she moved.

She could not afford to fail.

She had regained only a fraction of her health-sense; but it sufficed to guide her. The *croyel* had struck Liand with terrible force. He had hit one of the calcified arms of the warding construct: hit it hard. When she scanned the ridge, she saw that the impact had weakened it.

She dashed to that spot, hoping that the *skest* would ignore her.

The travertine was porous and fragile: she was certain of it. And in that one place, it had been damaged. Nonetheless it was stone. It did not crumble easily. Stooping, she gripped the rimose deposit; dug her fingers in among its bulges and knags until her nails tore and her skin bled; pulled at the ridge until the flesh of her palms was shredded.

The stone held.

Behind her, the Harrow roared curses and invocations in alien tongues. *Skest* burned like pitch, eating away the perfection of the floor. Again the *croyel* raised his mouth from Jeremiah's neck to bare its teeth at the Insequent. The creature's glee stung the back of Linden's neck like the first caress of acid.

Her hands were not strong enough.

Part of her wept at her weakness. But that part belonged to the Linden Avery whom she had left behind under *Melenkurion* Skyweir. The Linden Avery who had stood with Caerroil Wildwood and the Mahdoubt on Gallows Howe did not hesitate.

Surging erect, she kicked furiously at the marred section of the gnarled arm; stomped with the heel of her boot.

Her blow skidded aside. Her own momentum flung her forward. When one kneecap hit the travertine, she felt the bone crack.

Enlivened by Earthpower, her nerves sensed the first flicker of wild magic as the Harrow began to invoke Covenant's ring. The bastard was going to *win*—

In spite of her pain, Linden kicked again. Hardly aware of what she did, she started screaming the Seven Words.

"*Melenkurion abatha!*"

Her second blow struck squarely.

"*Duroc minas mill!*"

Her third broke a chunk as large as her fist out of Jeremiah's construct.

"*Harad khabaal!*"

At once, the inherent power of the construct failed. The ridges lost their darkness. Swiftly the travertine lapsed to a more natural grey.

Staggering, Linden faced a throng of *skest*.

She barely had time to draw breath, blink tears from her vision, gasp at the agony in her knee. Then Roger Covenant arrived, shedding his glamour directly behind the Harrow.

Ecstatic with triumph, Roger shouted, "SUCK-er!"

Magma blared from his right fist as he punched fury straight through the center of the Harrow's back.

For an instant, the Harrow gaped at Kastenessen's hand; at the charred wound where Roger's fist emerged from his chest. He seemed unable to comprehend what had become of him. Then Roger snatched back his arm; and the Insequent fell dead.

The Staff and Covenant's ring dropped from his hands.

Chittering incomprehensibly, the *skest* drew back. Commanded by Roger or the *croyel*, they cleared a space around Roger, Jeremiah, the Harrow's corpse. If more of them waited in the corridors, they did not press into the chamber.

Linden's health-sense had evaporated again, but she was in too much pain to notice the difference. Roger was *here*. All he had to do now was bend down and pick up his father's ring. The *skest* had given him room. He could claim the Staff of Law at the same time, if he wanted it.

His victory would be complete.

Linden had done what she could—and it was too little. She had broken the spell of Jeremiah's construct. Surely now the *Elohim* were able to discern his location? Roger she had expected in some fashion. But she had also believed that at least one of the scattered *Elohim* would care enough to intervene. Or if none of Infelice's people responded, Kastenessen would—or Esmer—

Here Roger and the *croyel* could combine their powers. They could escape through time and distance, as they had done before.

Yet no *Elohim* came. Esmer did not.

And the Ardent had failed the will of the Insequent. Liand was severely injured: he may have been dying. Anele had fled. The rest of Linden's companions were held in thrall by the astonishment of the palace.

Sobbing at the scream in her knee, she dove headlong toward Liand's *orcrest*.

If the Sunstone reawakened even a few tiny glints of her percipience, she would be able to reach out for Earthpower and Law. She did not need to hold the Staff in order to use it: not now. She needed only a small spattering of health-sense—

A body hurtled past her into the chamber. She had no idea who or what it was. Pain and desperation blinded her to everything except *orcrest*. She hardly heard Roger's eager roar of defiance.

When her straining fingers closed on the Sunstone, she felt nothing. Nothing at all. The *orcrest* was only a lump of rock. She could not *see* it; could not touch its true vitality.

A surge of absolute despair broke over her: a crashing wave. Then it receded. She was too frantic to drown in it, or to be swept away.

Wrenching herself into a sitting position, she cocked her arm to hurl the Sunstone at Roger's head: the last throw of a woman whose fate was written in water.

Covenant's ring still lay amid a tumble of chain near Jeremiah's bare feet. The runed ebony length of the Staff rested an arm's length away. Roger had not claimed either instrument.

He had not had time.

Through a blaze of argent, Linden saw Thomas Covenant.

Somehow he had emerged from his memories; had shrugged off the enchantment of the palace. He must have sensed Roger's power, or the *croyel*'s; must have realized that Linden needed him.

Braced in the act of trying to slash downward with Loric's *krill*, Covenant confronted his son. He gripped the dagger in both fists, apparently striving to cripple or sever Kastenessen's hand. But Roger had blocked his father's cut with a blast of heat and scoria. Straining to strike, Covenant stood with his blade embedded in the furnace of Roger's power.

They had not touched each other physically: their blows met in the air between them. Roger's pyrotic theurgy held Covenant's blade in a grip of crimson and sulphur, as fluid and fatal as lava. Covenant answered with the salvific possibilities of wild magic channeled and focused by High Lord Loric's mighty lore. The *krill*'s pure gem was an expanding cynosure of incandescence.

Too *much* incandescence. Linden did not need health-sense to guess that Joan was pouring out her madness, trying to hurt the man who had been her husband. Somehow Joan—or *turiya* Herem—had recognized Covenant's grip on the *krill*, Covenant's intention. While he struggled against their son, she wielded her own ring in an effort to incinerate him.

She could not attack him directly. She was not present; and her own plight hampered her. But if she unleashed enough wild magic through the gem, she might make the *krill* so hot that it burned the flesh from his bones.

And Roger's power was the essence of the *skurj* multiplied by Kastenessen's immense might. Even a Giant could not have endured such heat.

Leprosy aggravated the numbness in Covenant's fingers. The Ardent had bandaged his hands in garish strips of magic and knowledge. The handle of the *krill* was wrapped in vellum. Yet the vehemence directed at him was too great. Linden watched in horror as the vellum charred and curled, cracking into flickers of flame. For a moment, the Ardent's bandages resisted. Then they, too, began to smolder.

Wailing, the *skest* crowded back against the walls. The *croyel* appeared to be searching for an opportunity to attack.

"Hell and *blood*, Roger!" Covenant shouted: a cry thick with excruciation. "You don't have to *do* this! There are better answers!"

"What makes you think I *want* your answers?" Roger retorted, fierce as scoria. "You're done being the hero, *Dad*!" He made "Dad" sound like a vile obscenity. "It's time somebody put you in your place! I'm just glad that somebody is going to be *me*!"

The *krill's* brilliance nearly blinded Linden. Its echo of wild magic was too bright to be borne. God! she thought, oh, God, there must be *caesures* all across the Land, Joan is trying to bring down the Arch by herself— Sudden flames undid the bandages from Covenant's hands. Soon he would be too badly hurt to hold the *krill*.

In an argent blur cruelly tainted with crimson and malice, Linden saw another figure sprint into the chamber. Indistinct amid the squall of magicks, Stave leapt as if he meant to join Covenant's battle. But he did not. Instead he stretched out in the air, landed full-length on the stone. His momentum carried him, skidding, beneath the conflagration of Kastenessen's hand and Joan's ring and Loric's *krill*.

Covenant withstood Roger's assault because Joan's efforts increased the *krill's* puissance. Nevertheless Covenant's flesh was dying. His protections were gone: flames ate at his fingers. Only the reek of Roger's magma masked the odor of burning meat.

Roger's concentration was fixed on his father: the *croyel's* was not. The creature's gaze resembled howling as it raised Jeremiah's arm to hurl hate like boulders down on Stave.

Yet Stave had taken the *croyel* by surprise. Before it could unleash its blast, he collided with the Harrow's body. A thrust of Stave's arms shoved the dead Insequent at Jeremiah.

The unexpected impact swept Jeremiah's feet out from under him. He fell awkwardly atop the Harrow, disrupting the *croyel's* magicks.

Through Jeremiah, the *croyel* clutched at Stave; failed to catch him. Stave was too swift. Snatching up Covenant's ring, he rolled aside, evading Jeremiah's hands—

—rolled onto and over the Staff of Law.

Then Linden thought that she heard Stave shout her name. From the core of the clashing theurgies, she seemed to see a black shaft like a spear arc through the air toward her as though it had been aimed at her chest.

She dropped the Sunstone. Pure reflex enabled her to reach out and catch the Staff.

In that instant, she was transformed.

Stave. Of course. When she needed him most.

Of the *Haruchai*, he alone knew how to silence his thoughts. Perhaps that skill—or the discipline to attain it—lessened the entrancement of the palace. He must have felt her absence and broken free when none of her other companions could do so. If he had been bestirred by Anele's return, he had not paused to rouse anyone else.

The touch of the Staff restored Linden's health-sense. Earthpower lifted her to her feet. The torn flesh of her fingers and palms seemed to heal itself. Stave had renewed her true heritage, the birthright that she had wrested from her parents' legacy of despair.

Jeremiah had already clambered upright. The *croyel* was summoning enough wrath to crush every bone in Stave's body.

Without a heartbeat's hesitation, Linden flung flame and Law into the fight.

She wanted to hurl her fire everywhere at once. Liand needed her. Covenant needed her urgently. Stave had no defense: not against the *croyel*'s theurgies. The *skest* might advance at any moment, rallied by Roger or the *croyel*. Surely one or both of them would turn their powers against her? If they were given an opportunity, they could transport themselves out of danger.

But she was limited by her mortality. She could not focus on so many perils simultaneously.

Trusting that Stave could fend for himself—that Roger and the *croyel* were done with Liand—that the *skest* were too frightened to advance—Linden threw her desperation at Covenant's son.

If Covenant's hands were crippled or burned away, no power known to her would repair them. Like Mahrtiir's eyes, like Stave's eye, they would be permanently lost. Covenant would not be able to hold Loric's *krill*. And he would be in too much pain to call up wild magic from his ring.

Linden wept for her son; but she fought for her former lover.

She had defeated Roger once before. She had faced his ferocity and *croyel*'s together, and had prevailed. But here she was hampered by Kevin's Dirt. And she could not draw on the supreme energies of the EarthBlood. As soon as Covenant failed—as soon as

Roger and the *croyel* joined their strengths against her—she would die. Magma and malevolence would extinguish her.

Yet somehow Covenant endured his agony; his scorched and melting skin. Roger could not aim Kastenessen's fist at Linden because he was forced to defend himself from his father.

Before the *croyel* could strike at Stave, the *Haruchai* bounded up from the floor. Imponderably swift, he whirled a flying kick at Jeremiah's head. The creature could not evade him.

But its backward flinch diminished the impact of the kick. Jeremiah's head snapped sideways: blood and saliva sprayed from his lips: he staggered. Wailing, *skest* scattered to avoid contact with their master. Yet Jeremiah did not go down.

Stave rushed after him. As Jeremiah hit the wall, Stave was poised to deliver a second blow.

A thin stream of blood dribbled from Jeremiah's mouth. Nonetheless the *croyel* was unharmed. Perhaps no merely physical assault could harm it. Spite and eagerness frothed in its eyes as its fangs bit down harder on Jeremiah's neck.

Involuntarily Jeremiah jerked up his halfhand—and Stave fell back as though he had crashed into an invisible wall.

He could not hope to defeat the *croyel*. In moments, he would be dead. Briefly, however, he had prevented the creature from aiding Roger against Covenant and Linden.

While she could, Linden poured Staff-fire straight at Roger's face; at his bitter mockery of his father's features.

Exalted by runes and blackness, weeping and frenzy, she compelled Roger to turn away from Covenant.

Covenant plunged, helpless, to his knees. Smoke rose from his twisted fingers. But he did not release the *krill*. As if his flesh had melted onto the dagger—had become one with it—he clutched it while he struggled to regain his feet.

Argent still blazed from the *krill*'s gem. But now its incandescence began to falter. Joan's awareness of him was fading. She was too weak to support *turiya*'s demands on her.

A quick glance told Linden that Covenant's hands would never be whole again. Given time and peace, she might be able to unclose his fingers from the *krill* without peeling away too much skin. She might be able to straighten them; heal them enough to let them flex. But with her best efforts she would never make them more useful than blunt stumps—

Distracted, she let a blast of Roger's rage brush her cheek. He may have burned her badly, perhaps disfigured her; yet she felt no pain. Her cracked kneecap did not trouble her. She had not forgotten Jeremiah and the *croyel*, or the waiting threat of the *skest*:

she had not forgotten Stave or Liand. For the moment, however, she fought as though nothing mattered except what had been done to Covenant's hands.

Goading herself with the Seven Words, she forced Roger to retreat from his father.

Somehow Covenant regained his feet. Every movement was shrill with pain; but he did not retreat. Instead he advanced on Roger, still aiming the *krill* at Kastenessen's hand.

Together, he and Linden might be able to beat Roger. She knew that Roger feared death. And she did not believe that he would allow harm to his grafted power; his halfhand. If Covenant could endure his suffering a little longer, he and Linden might succeed at driving Roger from the chamber.

Inadvertently Stave broke her concentration. Thwarted in his attack on the *croyel*, Stave countered by tossing Covenant's ring toward the ceiling.

Surprise and avarice drew the *croyel*'s gaze to follow the rise and fall of white gold. Avid for wild magic, the creature dropped its defenses; tried to claw the ring out of the air.

With all of his *Haruchai* muscle and speed, Stave punched the *croyel* between its gleaming eyes.

The creature's head jolted back, ripping its fangs out of Jeremiah's neck. Quickly, however, the deformed head whipped forward again. Its eyes focused fury on Stave.

As Stave caught the ring, closed it in his fist, Jeremiah's arm swept upward. Stave was flung into the air; hurled toward the waiting *skest*.

Stave—! Even his extraordinary reflexes could not save him now. He would land on living acid. His heart, or Linden's, might have time to beat as much as twice before the corrosion of the *skest* scoured the skin from his bones. He would die hideously, in swift torment.

Helpless to do otherwise, Linden wheeled away from Roger. With the Staff blazing in both hands, she swept all of her power like a scythe among the *skest*, trying frantically to cut them down, burn them to ash; clear a space for Stave.

She almost succeeded. Creatures by the score burst into flame and fell apart, spilling viscid conflagration across the floor. Vitriol ate at the Harrow's corpse. Twisting to right himself, Stave came down on his feet in a pool of fiery fluid.

He tried to leap away. But acid splashed his feet and calves; bit into his legs. Nearly crippled, he managed to sprawl beyond the edge of the vitriol. Then he tried to stand, and could not. Corrosion had eaten too deeply into his muscles. It was still burning.

Linden took a moment that she could not afford to slap her own fire at Stave's legs. Expecting death, she stopped the damage with Earthpower. Then she abandoned Stave to his injuries; spun away to face Roger's assault, and the *croyel*'s, and doom.

As she turned, however, she saw that Roger had not used her distraction to muster a killing blast. The *croyel* had not followed its attack on Stave. They had not joined together against Covenant.

Instead they had hastened toward each other. Already they had raised their arms, extending their magicks to form a portal. They were about to disappear—

Their powers would translate them to a time or a place where she could not hope to discover them again.

Covenant had seen what they were doing: he must have understood it. He stumbled toward them, aiming to thrust the *krill* between them before they could complete their sorcery. But he was too late. Linden felt their might gather while he was still too far away.

And he was directly between her and them. She could not fling fire at Roger and the *croyel* without scathing Covenant.

Stave may have been shouting at her, urging her to strike. He may have believed that Covenant would forgive her.

Nonetheless she froze for a moment.

In that small space of time, a concussion like a burst of thunder shook the chamber.

The floor split in a dozen places. Stone like geysers of rubble or scree spouted upward. The whole chamber lurched as though it had cracked free of its moorings.

Riding a jolt of theurgy, Esmer appeared between Roger and Jeremiah. "*No!*" Cail's son roared in a voice of horns and storm. "*This I will not permit!*"

The blast of his arrival knocked Roger and Jeremiah apart. Fuming, acid leaked away into fissures and upheavals.

Linden had no chance to notice the sudden bile in her throat, the nausea in her guts. Sick with shock, she saw that Esmer's condition had worsened since his last appearance. Clearly he was unable to treat the wounds inflicted on him during the battle of First Woodhelven. The grime and blood that fouled his rent cymar were unchanged; but now the festering burns and tears in his flesh wept rank fluids. The purulent reek of his hurts was both more human and more painful than the stench of Roger's halfhand.

He had told Linden that Kastenessen wanted him to suffer for aiding her. *His wrath is boundless.* But he retained his strength in spite of his bodily distress. He could be as devastating as a hurricane.

"Fool!" he raged at Linden. Spume boiled in the dark seas of his eyes. "You have revealed your discovery of your son to Kastenessen!"

Falling stone hit Linden's head and shoulders; battered Covenant, Stave, and Liand. Belatedly she raised Earthpower to fend off the detritus of Esmer's might. As she had during the earthquake under *Melenkurion* Skyweir, she protected herself: she shielded her companions. As then, she was hardly aware of what she did.

"So what?" she shouted back at Esmer. "You're already here!" Aid and betrayal. "You'll do whatever he wants!"

A hail of rock ruptured more of the *skest*, spilling their substance across the rent floor. The creatures that survived fled into their tunnels.

"In this," retorted Esmer, "*I do not serve him!* The *skurj* will do so! She Who Must Not Be Named will do so!"

Shattered rock continued to erupt, tossing Roger and Jeremiah from side to side, coercing them to defend themselves; holding them at bay. With the Staff, Linden deflected granite rain.

Where—? She expected ur-viles and Waynhim to swarm around her. *They keep watch against me.* Whenever Esmer had helped or endangered her, the creatures had appeared. They had been profligate with their own lives in her defense.

This time, however, they did not come. Esmer had been too swift for them, or too sudden—

While she warded herself and her friends with flame, Esmer surged like a running wave at Roger; crashed like a breaker over Covenant's son.

At once, the two of them vanished. For his own reasons, or Kastenessen's, or Lord Foul's, Esmer carried Roger away.

The fall of rock ceased as abruptly as it had begun.

The *croyel*'s dismay drew a yelp from Jeremiah. Frantically the boy brandished his arms. With one hand, he hailed or harried *skest* back into the chamber. With the other, he slapped Covenant aside as though Covenant's opposition and anguish were trivial. Then he hurled frenzy like a battering ram at Linden.

She met the burst with Earthpower; blocked it. But it hit her barrier so fiercely that the Staff bucked in her grasp. The creature's fury shoved her backward.

Its desperation matched hers.

Skest rushed to attack. Covenant tumbled away. His hands seemed fused to the *krill*.

By sheer force of will, Stave wrenched himself to his feet. He still clenched Covenant's ring. Its chain swung between his fingers. Limping on savaged legs, he struggled toward Liand.

"Defend yourself, Chosen," he panted hoarsely. "Preserve your son. I cannot combat the *skest*. I will aid Liand."

It was too much. There were too many *skest*. The *croyel* was too strong. And Linden could not call on the EarthBlood to make her greater than she was.

Nevertheless she flung herself forward, driven by love and need—and by a new surge of despair. Covenant and Liand and Stave were about to die; and she could not bear to abandon Jeremiah to the *croyel*'s cruelty.

But her plight required her to strike at her son. In abhorrence, she wielded Earth-power as if she were screaming.

Esmer had aided her. Where was the betrayal required by his conflicted nature? *I am made to be what I am.* Was it this, that she could only save Jeremiah by attacking him? By *killing* him? If so, her horror would delight the Despiser.

But she did not believe it. Lord Foul did not desire Jeremiah's death. Esmer had told her, *Your son is beyond price.* No matter how keenly Lord Foul relished her distress, he did not wish her to kill Jeremiah. He still had a use for her son—

—of my deeper purpose I will not speak.

No, this fight did not serve the Despiser's purposes, or Kastenessen's: not now that the *croyel* had been prevented from escaping with Jeremiah. Esmer had not yet revealed his treachery; or he had masked it too cunningly for Linden to see it.

Howling fire, she tried to divide her focus between the *croyel* and the *skest*, and could not. The creature feeding on Jeremiah was too strong. And it appeared able to summon an endless number of misshapen children, glowing and fatal.

Stave had wrestled Liand into his arms, but the damage to his legs crippled his efforts to escape. Rife with hurts, Covenant had climbed back to his feet, bracing himself against the wall where Jeremiah had thrown him. In his ruined hands, the light of the *krill* wavered and pulsed as though it were unsure of its use. For the moment, at least, he was spared Joan's virulence. In that brief reprieve, he staggered arduously toward the lost boy. Like Stave, however, he had been too badly hurt to move quickly. Agony galled his face. Only stubbornness kept him upright.

Frantic and failing, Linden alternated her attacks. She hit the *croyel*'s defenses as hard as she could. Then she swept flame through the *skest* until they ruptured and burned. As soon as she had beaten them back, she scrambled to assail the *croyel* again.

If she did not flail Earthpower from place to place fast enough, the monster would have time to muster a lethal blast—or one of the *skest* would touch her companions—or—

It was altogether too much. When Covenant stumbled and fell, she could do nothing to save him.

Galt caught Covenant before his knees struck the floor again. A flicker of an instant later, Clyme also reached the Unbeliever. At the same time, Branl committed his whole body to a blow at Jeremiah's head.

Flinching, the *croyel* punched Branl with a fist of theurgy. The Humbled was knocked backward: he collided with the far wall hard enough to shatter bones. Only his preternatural *Haruchai* toughness spared him from injuries worse than Stave's.

Before the *croyel* could attack again, Rime Coldspray charged into the chamber with Grueburn and Cabledarm roaring at her back. From the passage leading to the palace, ribbands like lurid snakes squirmed outward. They coiled around Stave and

Liand, snatched the *Haruchai* and the Stonedownor back from the *skest*. Another strip of cloth retrieved Liand's *orcrest*.

As soon as their path was clear, more Giants rushed to join the fray.

They used their swords, iron and stone, instead of their feet. Their native immunity to fire did not shield them from living acid, although it gave them a measure of protection from the spilth and spray of slain *skest*. They were not burned as badly as Stave had been. The *croyel* tried to blast them from their feet, but the Swordmainnir were too many and too strong. And when Jeremiah's possessor strove to concentrate its force on any single foe, ribbands slapped at its face, flicked at its eyes.

Bluntfist and then Stonemage unclosed their cataphracts, shrugged the stone from their shoulders. Using their armor like spades or bludgeons, they crushed *skest*; deflected the spatter of green corrosion. In moments, they cleared a space around Covenant, Galt, and Clyme. The whole floor steamed as acid consumed itself on rock. Together, the Giants guarded Linden.

Feverishly the *croyel* struggled to fling its powers everywhere; but its blows had less and less effect. Galvanized by the arrival of her friends, Linden lashed the creature with Earthpower. While fumes bit into her lungs, she intercepted the creature's magicks, deflected them, turned them against the *skest*. From the comparative safety of the corridor, the Ardent extended his raiment to harass the *croyel*. Bands of color harried the creature as if they were alive.

Dying, the *skest* filled the chamber with their liquid wails. Chunks of the broken floor boiled and melted, but the lore-hardened stone and iron of the Giants withstood the acid.

Abruptly the *croyel* stopped striking out. In a chorus of frayed screams, the surviving *skest* turned and ran, abandoning their master. The Giants seemed to freeze in place. Twisting around each other, bands of viridian and garnet and azure withdrew into the passage.

Instinctively Linden quenched her fire.

Covenant stood behind Jeremiah. At Covenant's back, Galt supported the Unbeliever. Clyme gripped Jeremiah's shoulders so that the boy could not pull away.

With both marred fists, Covenant had slipped the *krill* between Jeremiah's neck and the *croyel*'s throat. The lore-forged keenness of the dagger had already drawn a thin line of rank blood across the creature's skin.

"Listen!" Covenant panted in the *croyel*'s ear. "Pay attention." Every word was a rasp of pain. "You know I can't kill you without killing Jeremiah. I don't have the right kind of power to keep him alive while I cut your throat. You know that. I know that. But you don't know *me*. You don't know how far I'm willing to go. If *you* had this knife, you would kill me in a heartbeat. So don't try me." Through his teeth, he repeated, "*Don't try me.*"

Linden saw terror bubbling like a witch's brew in the background of the creature's stare.

As Covenant spoke, the gem of the *krill* began to shine more brightly. Soon its blaze seemed to efface the creature's terrified eyes, its ready fangs, its malice. Exposed by incandescence, Jeremiah's bones became visible through his vulnerable flesh. The heat flooding into Covenant stretched his face in a scream which he refused to utter.

Scowling as if they, too, were in agony, Galt and Clyme kept Covenant from falling; kept the *croyel* from pulling away.

Finally Linden's cracked knee failed. If Bhapa and Pahni had not caught her arms, she would have prostrated herself on the wreckage of the floor.

She only knew that Esmer had returned amid a swarm of ur-viles and Waynhim because she felt like vomiting.

10.

By Evil Means

Kept upright only by the Cords, Linden stood like a ruin of herself; a crumbling edifice overgrown with consequences. The possibilities that she had surrendered to the Harrow had been restored. The warmth of the Staff lingered in her hands. While he lived, Stave would return Covenant's ring to no one but her. But she had no idea what to do with such powers now. The cost—

The cost was of her own making, and it was too high.

She had exposed all of her friends to the source of Kevin's Dirt. She had allowed Liand to be broken, perhaps killed. She had seen Stave nearly crippled by acid; had witnessed the Harrow's murder. Helpless to stop either of them, she had watched Esmer transport Roger to safety or destruction. She had fought and fought, battling forces which surpassed her.

Because of her, Covenant's hands—

This was the result. The Harrow's remains lay, acid-bitten and melting, among the cracks and rubble of the floor. And Esmer had returned. She had no defense against him. The fact that the last ur-viles and Waynhim had arrived in his wake did not comfort her at all.

She had not slept since her first night in Andelain; had eaten nothing since her last meal of treasure-berries. Her emotional condition resembled her shirt: ripped along one hem to patch the Mahdoubt's gown; plucked and snagged in headlong flight through Salva Gildenbourne; pierced by lead and death. The stains on her jeans mapped her fate: —*written in water*, the green sap of grass. Unexpressed tears filled her heart.

Leaning on one leg to spare her damaged knee, she could still feel the tremors of Esmer's power in the marred stone.

On either side, Bhapa and Pahni supported her. Unlike Mahrtiir, the older Cord did not appear to feel diminished by crushing leagues of gutrock, beyond any prospect of open skies and plains and Ranyhyn. Accustomed to self-doubt, his concern was for his Manethrall and his companions, not himself. But Pahni was not merely daunted by powers and perils which other Ramen had never experienced. She was also terrified for Liand.

"Ringthane," she breathed urgently. "Ringthane, heed me. Liand is grievously hurt. He nears death. Ringthane—Linden Avery—I love him. I implore your healing."

Linden understood. Liand needed her. As did Stave. And perhaps Branl as well, although the Master would refuse her aid. The burns of the Giants tugged at her attention. But her heart wept for Jeremiah, who stood like a limp manikin in the *croyel*'s grasp. His bones shone as if they were on fire. She regarded the keen edge of the *krill* at the creature's throat, and the killing brilliance of the gem, and Covenant's unbearable courage, and could not move.

Covenant alone gave her any hope. With Loric's blade, he had found a way to control the *croyel*. But he was failing. Joan's power had done him irremediable harm, and it burned brighter with every passing moment—

God, Joan must hate him! Or perhaps he represented everything that she loathed in herself. Even *turiya* Herem's possession hardly sufficed to account for her focused vehemence now. The Raver could only keep her alive, and fan the fires of her rage, and blaze with delight. He had not caused her long years of self-inflicted anguish.

Linden did not know why Covenant had not already screamed and fallen. To some extent, his leprosy shielded him. His proximity to the source of Kevin's Dirt accentuated his affliction. The essential pathways of agony had been killed or cauterized. But still—

Was that his secret? The keystone of his impossible valor? Had alienation and numbness somehow made him more than human?

Around Linden, the rest of her companions gathered. Galesend bore Anele, who had fallen asleep again. Latebirth still carried Mahrtiir, while Onyx Stonemage cradled

Liand's unconscious form. Limping on gnawed legs, in feral pain which he refused to acknowledge, Stave preceded the Ardent. Wreathed in ribbands, the Insequent approached unsteadily. Stifling his confessed fears, he forced himself to join Linden's friends. In a knot of cloth, he gripped Liand's *orcrest*.

Among the Giants, ur-viles and Waynhim stood upright, or braced themselves on all fours, barking quietly: a low clamor of objurgation or alarm. The Ironhand gripped her stone glaive, poised to cut, against Esmer's neck. But Esmer ignored her as if her great size and strength were trivial; meaningless. Distress seethed in his gaze: he seemed to weep like Linden's heart.

He did not move—and Rime Coldspray did not. Her eyes were fixed on Jeremiah and Covenant and the *krill*.

Hoarsely Mahrtiir asked, "Do we confront the *croyel*?" Apparently the Staff in Linden's hands had restored a portion of his health-sense. "Does this malice possess the Ringthane's son?"

No one answered him. Like Pahni, Esmer studied Linden. The Ardent watched Cail's son fearfully. Everyone else seemed transfixed by Covenant's struggle to withstand Joan.

His hands would never be healed.

His scar reflected argent like a scream cut into the flesh of his forehead. His silver hair resembled flames of wild magic: his mind may have been on fire. In spite of his illness, he was wracked by so much pain—

As if he did not expect anyone to hear him, he gasped, "Joan knows what I'm doing." His voice implied a wailing defeat. "Or *turiya* does. She's stronger now. I'm not protecting the Arch. I can't hold on."

Linden would have been willing to maim herself for his sake; but she did not know how to block Joan's madness. She had never known.

Covenant held the *croyel*. Clyme held Jeremiah.

Clarion and commanding, Stave demanded, "Branl! Galt!"

The Humbled must have heard Stave's thoughts, understood his instructions. Striding forward quickly, Branl wrenched a wide band of ochre cloth from the hem of his tunic. Then he took Galt's place supporting Covenant, gave the fabric to Galt.

At once, Galt folded the cloth over his right hand and reached to remove the *krill* from Covenant's grasp; to assume Covenant's threat against the *croyel*.

Linden caught her breath, bit her lip. She feared that Covenant's hands were too badly burned to open. She expected his flesh to peel off the bones when he tried to unclose his fingers—or when Galt pried them loose. Unaware that she had moved, she stood at Covenant's shoulder with the kind fire of Earthpower flowering from the Staff. While Galt extended his hand to replace Covenant's, she sent rich flames to curl around Covenant's forearms, fill his veins, save his fingers.

For the moment, she ignored the horror of her son's straits. Instead she concentrated utterly and solely on the challenge of preserving Covenant's hands so that he would be able to let go.

The effort tore a cry past Covenant's restraint: a shocking howl. But Galt nudged gently at his fingers while Linden laved his suffering with Earthpower. One joint at a time, he released his grasp.

Immediately Branl pulled Covenant aside while Galt claimed High Lord Loric's *krill*; accepted the task of restraining the *croyel*. With his left hand, Galt gripped Jeremiah's shoulder so that Clyme could step away.

As soon as Covenant's touch was withdrawn, Joan's savagery faltered. She or *turiya* Raver must have sensed his absence: her efforts were useless now. Flickering, the gem faded to its more ordinary radiance. The *krill*'s heat remained, but it did not wound Galt's wrapped hand.

Through the silence of the company, and the raw residue of acid in the air, Stave said flatly, "Well done."

The Humbled appeared to ignore his approval.

Branl kept Covenant on his feet; but Linden closed her arms around him nonetheless, enfolding him in Earthpower and gratitude. How had he known that she needed him? That his own son had come to preserve Jeremiah's victimization? She could not imagine how or why Covenant had responded. Yet somehow he had found his way through the maze of his memories as well as the bewildering wonders of the arcane palace for her sake, or for Jeremiah's.

"Linden." Covenant's voice was a mere husk of sound. His pain ached in her arms. "Help Liand. We need him." He was too weak and damaged to move. Nevertheless he seemed to push her away from him. "We need him."

I wish I could spare you. But I can't see any way around it.

Pahni tugged as firmly as she dared at Linden. "Ringthane, I beseech you." She may have been weeping. "If you will not heed me, harken to the Timewarden. Liand must have healing."

Mahrtiir said something to Pahni—a reprimand? an admonition?—but Linden could not hear him. He was too far away; or her senses were deafened by Covenant's extremity and the *croyel*'s thwarted ferocity and Jeremiah's helplessness.

Abruptly Esmer blared, "Wildwielder, this is madness! Is it nothing to you that I have come, or that these Demondim-spawn have pursued me to their doom in your name? Will you waste the remnants of your life thus, accepting the ruin which my betrayals prepare for you? Is this death your heart's true desire?"

The Ironhand pressed her sword against the side of Esmer's neck. "Be still, *mere*-son," she rasped through her teeth. "Some respite Linden Giantfriend must have. Many of us who name ourselves her friends have failed her. We will grant her this brief pause.

"I do not doubt that you are proof against my blade. But if I cannot have your life, I will have your silence."

Esmer did not grant Coldspray the courtesy of a glance. "By my hand and your own folly," he told Linden, "the slaughter of all whom you hold dear is imminent. Soon none of this company will remain to lament the ravage of the Earth. Will you condone this outcome merely because I propagate futility? Are you now content that all love and life must perish?"

Cursing, the Ironhand lowered her sword and raised her fist. With all of her bulk and muscle, she punched Esmer in the face.

She was a warrior: she had a warrior's instincts.

Linden heard the sodden smack of knuckles on bone. Esmer's head jerked back; snapped forward again. Blood oozed from a deep contusion on his cheek. The muscles at the corners of his jaw bunched and released, bunched and released, as if he were withholding a thunderstorm. But he did not acknowledge Rime Coldspray with so much as a flick of his eyes.

Nevertheless he fell silent.

Linden sagged as if she had suffered a new defeat. —*see any way around it.* The thought of leaving Covenant's wounds without further care rent her. She had only begun—Still she compelled herself to step away.

Now she did not look at Jeremiah and Galt, the *croyel* and the *krill*. Help Liand. We need him. She wanted to hold Jeremiah in her arms before the world ended. She had come for that when she had failed or sacrificed every other purpose. But she could not touch him: not while the *croyel* ruled him. In this one respect, her health-sense was a weakness. The creature's evil was too intimate: it would sicken her. And the *croyel* might extend its mastery into her if she embraced her son.

He may be freed only by one who is compelled by rage, and contemptuous of consequence. Berek's pronouncement seemed to refer to Jeremiah as much as to Lord Foul.

Will you condone this outcome—

Flagellating herself with dread and woe, she passed among the muttering ur-viles and Waynhim toward Onyx Stonemage. The Harrow's corpse she ignored. Accompanied by Pahni's anxiety, she approached Liand.

—merely because I propagate futility?

She would never forgive the old man in the ochre robe, the prophetic figure who should have warned her that she and Jeremiah were in danger. By his abandonment, he had betrayed her. If he had warned her, she would have fled, taking Jeremiah to a place where Roger could not find him. Every atrocity that had occurred since then—every abomination that Jeremiah and the Land had suffered, every crime that she herself had committed—would have been forestalled.

With each step, the pain in her knee increased. Her burned cheek seeped fluids. The nausea of Esmer's presence galled her. She had to be stronger than this. Because she was needed, she used her Staff to soothe her stomach, relieve the burn on her cheek, seal her cracked kneecap. Then she forgot her own condition in order to focus on Liand.

He hung limp in Stonemage's arms. Blood still pulsed from the corner of his mouth: a dwindling stream. His impact with Jeremiah's construct may have broken his back. Certainly he had shattered ribs, ruptured his pleural membrane—and perhaps his lungs. And his head had hit the wall hard. Linden imagined cerebral hemorrhage and edema in addition to his other traumas. Brain damage. Coma.

"Liand." Pahni murmured his name over and over again, beseeching him to live. "Liand."

Stonemage offered to set him down. Linden shook her head. If any residue of the slain *skest* touched him—

I wish I could spare you.

Her anger at herself she misdirected at the Ardent. "Give him his Sunstone. It doesn't belong to you."

With *orcrest*, Liand had become the first true Stonedownor in uncounted centuries. The Sunstone was his birthright.

"In all sooth," the fat Insequent murmured, "it does not." He sounded chastened; shamed. "Gladly I restore it."

Strips of his apparel stretched out. Deft as fingers, they slipped the Sunstone into the pouch at Liand's waist.

As the ribbands withdrew, Linden dismissed the Ardent from her mind. Studying her stricken friend, she felt beaten before she began. He was too badly hurt—and she was utterly drained. Even the Staff could not fill the dry reservoirs of her spirit.

She needed to weep. If she did not, she would go mad with fury. The former granite of her heart had broken in Andelain, when she had seen and understood the outcome of Covenant's reincarnation. The clenched igneous amalgam of extravagance and restraint which had carried her from the Land's past to her meeting with the Dead was changed. It had become something uncontainable and careless. If it claimed her now, she would indeed be *compelled by rage, and contemptuous of consequence.*

But she was a surgeon, trained for emergencies; and her training ran deep. She could not refuse to treat the patient in front of her. Even if Liand had not been who he was—

"Why him?" Ire made her voice shake. "I was here. The Harrow was here. Covenant and Stave were already coming." They must have been. Otherwise they would not have arrived in time to save her. "But that monster ignored us. It only hurt Liand."

No one answered her. She did not expect an answer. Nevertheless she needed the question. It might help her regain a measure of her professional detachment, the ability to look at wounds as problems to be solved rather than as accusations.

There had to be a reason. No doubt the *croyel* had seen that she was powerless. And it had proven itself a match for the Harrow. But still—Liand was only Liand. And *orcrest* was only *orcrest*, a small thing compared to white gold and the Staff of Law. Facing such powers in the Harrow's hands, why had the creature bothered to strike at Liand?

Why had it feared him?

Over and over again, he had demonstrated that he could use his Sunstone to counter the effects of Kevin's Dirt. It had some kind of virtue against *wrongness*: a potential for spiritual restoration that she did not know how to gauge or define.

Covenant was right. If the *croyel* wanted Liand dead, Linden had to save him. He would be needed. Somehow.

If that thought did not count as detachment or clarity, it sufficed nonetheless. Will you waste the remnants of your life thus—? No. She would not.

Lifting flame into the air, she swept away the caustic fumes of corroded stone and burned flesh. Then she stepped closer to Stonemage and enveloped Liand in fire. Carefully, fearfully, she reached into him with her senses, seeking to identify the nature and scale of his wounds.

"Madness," Esmer repeated. His exasperation sounded like a growl of distant thunder. "Delay hastens your deaths, yet you linger as though you conceive yourselves equal to every bane and betrayal. Does the Stonedownor's life merit your destruction?"

"*Mere*-son—" began the Ironhand, warning him again.

Manethrall Mahrtiir interrupted Coldspray. "Attend, Swordmainnir. The Ringthane's exertion of the Staff renews health-sense. Now I discern the vileness which rules yon vacant boy, who is surely Linden Avery's son. And I perceive the *krill* in the hand of a Master. Why has that"—outrage mounted in his voice—"that *horror* not been slain? Do you not descry that the youth is in torment?"

His own uselessness seemed to infuriate Mahrtiir. Twisting in Latebirth's arms, he demanded, "Grant the *krill* to me. I will act where your resolve falters."

While Latebirth hesitated, Covenant panted hoarsely, "No. Mahrtiir, listen to me. You can't kill the *croyel* that way." Pain throbbed in every word. "I mean, you *can*, but you'll kill Jeremiah at the same time. Even the *Elohim* don't know how to kill one of the *croyel* without killing its host. It's too deep inside him. We can't cut it out.

"He's important. We can't risk him. As long as we can control the *croyel*, that's enough."

"And what is the boy's import?" countered Mahrtiir. "I inquire with respect, ur-Lord." The Manethrall did not sound respectful. "Do you speak of his worth to the Ringthane, or to the fate of the Earth? How may he be redeemed, if his life and this monster's are one?"

"Be eased, Manethrall," Latebirth put in to spare Covenant. "Your discernment returns. Therefore gaze closely. Behold the creature's terror. In all sooth, its vileness surpasses description. Yet it recognizes—" The Giant spoke to Mahrtiir, but she appeared to be cautioning the *croyel*. "It perceives that any struggle to free itself, or to strike against us, may result in the cutting of its throat. The *mere*-son asserts that we hasten our own deaths. We need not also speed the death of Linden Giantfriend's son."

Mahrtiir wrestled with his frustration, snarled Ramen obscenities under his breath. But he did not argue, or insist that Latebirth release him.

Linden ignored them. Liand's straits were too extreme. The human body was so fragile— Fragile and precious. One blow could stop its life as easily as snuffing a candle. The Stonedownor required the intervention of Earthpower. He required it *now*. Only his youth and strength had kept him alive this long.

Briefly she glanced up at the severity of Stonemage's mien, the hard glitter of her eyes, the embattled lines of her countenance. Then Linden Avery the Chosen tried to remember that she had once been a healer.

Keeping Liand wrapped in gentle fire, she began at his mouth and followed his bleeding inward because that was her easiest path. Blood would lead her to the center of his hurts. There she would be able to identify their ramifications.

As she sent her health-sense inward, she felt Stave drop the chain that supported Covenant's ring around her neck. Its slight weight seemed to steady her in spite of Esmer's strange ability to block wild magic.

Shaking her head, Frostheart Grueburn muttered, "The harsh clangor of these Demondim-spawn maddens me. I am a Giant, accustomed to comprehension. Yet I cannot grasp their speech."

"Ha!" exclaimed Coldspray. "Here is your occasion, Esmer *mere*-son. You wish to speak. And it is by your doing that we are denied our gift of tongues. Speak, then. Reveal what these creatures wish to make known."

"Fools," Esmer retorted sourly. "They say nothing that I would not freely convey, should you condescend to hear me."

"A moment," Latebirth interjected. "A moment, if you will grant it, Ironhand." Her blunt features and misted eyes were full of chagrin. "There is too much of which we know nothing. If he is able, let Stave speak of events that transpired here before the Ardent freed us from our sopor. When we grasp what has occurred, mayhap we will be better able to cede the *mere*-son our heed."

Fluttering his clothes to attract the attention of the company, the Ardent said meekly, "Permit me. Though he denies his hurt, this *Haruchai* is gravely wounded. The substance of the *skest* has not lost its virulence. It burrows inward still. And my knowledge does not extend to the amelioration of such hurts. Indeed, it is no longer sufficient to ease the Timewarden. Both in their turn will have need of the lady's gifts."

"Oh, surely," Esmer muttered, sneering. "Permit all who would do so to speak.

What need has this wise and mighty company for an awareness of its jeopardy, or for the scant counsels of the Demondim-spawn?"

"Unlike this *Haruchai*," continued the Ardent, addressing Rime Coldspray in spite of Esmer's protest, "his kinsmen have indeed been humbled. He contrived to free himself from the ensorcelment of the Viles. They could not. Yet none have fallen low as I. I have prided myself on the trust which the Insequent have placed in me—and I have learned that their trust was folly. My doom I have ensured. Permit me to make what amends I may."

"To be humbled," Stave replied, "comes in many guises, Insequent, as does to be humiliated." His raw tone betrayed his pain. "Yet you persist in striving. Perhaps my kinsmen will profit from your example."

Apparently he wished to remind the Humbled that the *Haruchai* had a long history of abandoning their commitments when they judged that they had failed.

Following blood, Linden found the ribs which had pierced Liand's lungs. Those bones led her to the places where they had splintered. As clearly as signposts, they pointed her toward crushed vertebrae and mangled nerves.

In her former life, she could have done enough to save his life. But even a team of neurosurgeons might have left him permanently crippled. Here, however, her powers surpassed scalpels and sutures, clamps and swabs. Her percipience was as precise as the most delicate of his veins, the smallest of his torn nerves. And with the Staff, she could—

If she took her time, and her frayed strength held, she could do everything that Liand's abused body begged of her.

But there were other demands—

Though he denies his hurt, this *Haruchai* is gravely wounded.

What need has this wise and mighty company for an awareness of its jeopardy—?

Covenant hands seemed to cry out for her care.

Grimly she concentrated on Liand and tried to let everything else go.

"Speak, then," Coldspray told the Insequent. "Relate your tale. But tell it briefly. I do not doubt the *mere*-son's warnings. We must soon hear him."

"Briefly." The Ardent nodded. Settling his bulk more comfortably on his legs, he explained, "It was the unfamiliar entrancements of the Viles which bemused us in their edifice of water and lore. For a time, I reveled in experiences beyond my ken. I was cognizant of the lady's doings, and the Timewarden's, as well as the Harrow's, but I was not inclined to regard them. The fabric of my resolve—I acknowledge it—was too loosely woven to shed the wonders of the palace.

"However, I was bestirred by the Harrow's passing. His death awakened the will of the Insequent within me. It was not their intent that I should cause or permit his ruin. He required my aid, and I did not provide it. By my inattention, therefore, I have caused their involvement in his designs to become true interference.

"My own fate is now assured. For a time, however, the *geas* of my people sustains me. I must attempt the fulfillment of the Harrow's oath. Compelled, I roused those who had not pursued him. Your subsequent tale you know.

"But the events which took place ere we entered this chamber were these."

Concisely the Ardent described what had transpired. Then he added, "Doubtless the appearance of the Demondim-spawn now rather than earlier has meaning. Perchance their lore revealed that his first efforts would deliver the lady's son to the *krill*. Or perchance his swiftness outpaced theirs. In either instance, they did not or could not oppose him. Yet now they have come. I must conclude that they hope to counter some new act of malice."

"Indeed," snorted Esmer. "I marvel at the insights of the Insequent, which are exceeded only by their ignorance."

While Linden worked, moving from the more fatal injuries to Liand's lungs toward the more maiming damage to his spine, she heard Bhapa whispering to Mahrtiir. Abruptly the Manethrall announced, "Cord Bhapa's sight is clear. Though the Ring-thane labors for Liand, her theurgy expands beyond his wounds. Bhapa has perceived how Stave may be succored."

Coldspray swore under her breath. "He descries sooth. Giants, we have been blinded by distraction.

"Stonemage?" she asked or commanded. "Cabledarm?"

Holding Liand for Linden, Stonemage nodded. Without pausing for Stave's permission, Cabledarm lifted the *Haruchai* high and set him down on Stonemage's shoulders, straddling her neck so that his ravaged legs dangled near Linden. There they were washed from sole to knee in the overflow of Linden's fire.

Indirectly Linden gave Stave a measure of relief while she focused on Liand.

At the same time, she felt Branl and Clyme draw Covenant to stand at her back. Apparently they sought to follow Cabledarm's example. Linden sensed his reluctance, but it was overcome by his burns. He did not resist as Branl and Clyme lifted his arms to rest his heat-mangled hands on Linden's shoulders.

If the Humbled believed that they had failed, as the Ardent had suggested, they might eventually withdraw their service; but they had not done so yet.

Still Linden heeded only Liand's injuries. Her attempts to discern and heal his hurts demanded all of her attention. Peripherally, however, she knew that the ambit of her flames contained Covenant's hands as well as Stave's legs. Like the restoration of Covenant's ring, that recognition anchored her. Now she did not need to fear that Covenant and Stave would suffer while she attended to Liand.

Calling upon more Earthpower, she did what she could.

"Still you delay." Hints of desperation marred Esmer's sarcasm. "Is there no end to your desire for death, or for the havoc of the world?"

The Ironhand sighed. "Cease your scorn, *mere*-son. It is bootless. We are who we are, and must act as we do. Neither your protests nor your desire to inflict dismay alter us."

"Mayhap, *mere*-son," the Ardent suggested, "you will begin your litany of hazards by accounting for the absence of any *Elohim*. Are they not 'equal to all things,' as they have proclaimed? Has the lady not unveiled this covert to their sight? And do they not fear her son? Why, then, do they not intervene for their own salvation?"

"They do not *intervene*," Esmer snapped harshly, "because they discern no need. By my deeds, as by my presence, I have ensured that the Wildwielder's son will perish. What remains to interrupt their terror of the Worm? While the boy cannot threaten them, they need dread only the Worm's hunger."

"Then tell us," Coldspray said like her glaive, "how you have ensured our doom. Since you chafe to do so, reveal the import of your deeds and presence."

After the simpler challenge of healing Liand's lungs and ribs, the task of repairing his spine stretched Linden's depleted stamina to its limits. There the damage was unspeakably complex. But she was immersed in her work now; and the strict vitality of the Staff aided her.

With percipience and Earthpower, she found the shards of vertebrae that pressed on his spinal cord. Those fragments she nudged aside so that she could mend the cord. Then she puzzled them back into their proper alignment. When they were all in place, she made split and shredded bones whole until she had reincarnated the structural integrity of Liand's back.

At the same time, obliquely, she soothed Stave's legs and Covenant's hands. Given time, Stave's hurts would now be able to heal. Covenant's fingers and palms would not.

"By the display of powers here," Esmer continued, "She Who Must Not Be Named has been fully roused." As he spoke, chagrin and anger scudded through his voice like squalls. "Even now, She rises to ravage your souls. Against Her ire, only white gold may hope for efficacy. But there can be no wild magic while I remain nigh the ring.

"Yet that is not the sum of your perils, or of my treachery." Fiercely Esmer accused himself. "I removed the Timewarden's son from this chamber. Doing so, I prevented the Wildwielder's child from flight. But I did not remove Kastenessen's halfhand to his death. Rather I restored him to the Wightwarrens.

"In his greed for eternity, he fears that the Wildwielder's son will be forever lost to him. Even now, he summons an army of Cavewights to join his efforts to reclaim the boy—and to confirm that no impossible twist of fate may retrieve you from ruin."

Surprised, the Ardent sent out a flurry of ribbands to press themselves against the unmarked stone of the walls and ceiling. His eyes rolled back until only the whites reflected the nacre of the Viles, the silver of the *krill*'s gem, the yellow fire of Law. In a tranced croon, he murmured, "It is so. Perhaps two leagues above us lie the Wight-warrens. There gather Cavewights in their thousands. They answer the halfhand's call to war.

"Millennia have passed since Drool Rockworm's resurrection was denied to them, but they have not forgotten their fury."

Deflected by memories, Linden faltered. Her senses stood at the threshold of the trauma to Liand's skull, Liand's brain; but she did not enter. —resurrection was denied— Long ago, the Cavewights had endeavored to restore their long-dead sovereign. Pitchwife and the First of the Search had interrupted their ritual, saving Linden and Covenant in the process. Later Covenant himself had turned that ritual against the creatures so that the Giants could reach Linden and the Staff of Law in Kiril Threndor.

She did not doubt that the wrath of the Cavewights had endured across the centuries. And she was no brain surgeon. The myriad implications of every neuron daunted her. With Earthpower and one mistake, she might erase Liand's mind altogether.

But one memory of her struggles in Mount Thunder brought others. Wielding the Staff, she had quenched the Sunbane, not by overpowering it, but rather by accepting it into herself; by denaturing its virulence with her love for Covenant and the Land.

And earlier, she had brought Covenant back from an imposed stasis by making his plight her own.

She might do the same for Liand. If she erred, she rather than the Stonedownor would bear the cost.

At her side, Pahni emanated supplications which Linden Avery the Chosen could not refuse.

"In addition," Esmer said like the knelling of storms, "*samadhi* Sheol has turned the Sandgorgons. Already they have begun the slaughter of Salva Gildenbourne. Soon, however, the Raver will direct them to more fatal deeds. And Kastenessen is now conscious of your presence here. In rage, he musters the *skurj*. Though She Who Must Not Be Named cannot fail, he covets your doom for himself. He fears the imprisonment which the Wildwielder's son may devise for him. And he intends also to defend the source of Kevin's Dirt."

As Esmer recited threats, the Ardent appeared to grow unaccountably stronger; more sure of himself. His expression suggested knowledge or abilities that Esmer lacked. But he did not interrupt.

Like the Harrow, he knew how to transport the company out of the mountain's depths. Out of danger.

"These creatures"—Cail's son indicated the Waynhim and ur-viles dismissively—"have already informed you that they cannot oppose the *skurj*. They offer guidance, but they cannot save you. Apart from white gold, no living power may oppose She

Who Must Not Be Named. Yet even this tally does not content a-Jeroth of the Seven Hells. At *moksha* Jehannum's urging, Kastenessen commands further betrayals."

Flinching as if his own treachery galled his many wounds, Esmer fell silent. Around him, the ur-viles and Waynhim muttered growls which the company could not interpret.

"Name them," Coldspray demanded when Esmer did not continue. "Tell the tale of your evils in full."

Conflicts seethed in Esmer's gaze. "I will not. They will be revealed when they are needed. For that reason, I must have the Wildwielder's heed. To her, I must repay the accumulating debt of my crimes."

"It may be," offered the Ardent with a hint of his complacent lisp, "that you are mistaken. Perchance it is her healing rather than her heed that you require. The poisons of your hurts corrupt your thoughts. You esteem your betrayals too highly."

Esmer's jaws clenched as if he wanted to shout lightning and thunder at the Insequent; but he made no retort.

Linden ignored them. The damage to Liand's head was both less and more than she had feared. His skull was merely cracked: no splinters of bone pierced the delicate channels and membranes of his brain. But the bruising caused by his impact with the wall was severe. Edema exerted more and more pressure on his brain, constricting the flow of necessary fluids, causing neurons to misfire. Soon the effects of the swelling might kill him.

Hurtloam would have healed him. Linden was too drained and uncertain to do so. She dreaded what would happen when she took Liand's hurt into herself. She had so many other dilemmas to confront, and her store of courage was already inadequate.

But fear had no place in the work that she had chosen when she had formed the Staff. And Liand's pain was not the Sunbane. Like her, it was only human.

At last, she surrendered to her task. Groaning, she extended herself and fire into him in order to relieve his last injury.

Abruptly Galt announced to Esmer, "This is the havoc with which you charged Stave." Galt remained behind Jeremiah and the *croyel*, controlling the monster with Loric's blade. "Because you are Cail's son, born of the *Haruchai*, you hold his race accountable for your divided nature. Nonetheless your deeds are your own. They spawn ruin because you choose that they should do so. If you perform treachery, the blame lies with you. It belongs neither to Cail nor to the *Haruchai*."

"Indeed," Esmer countered harshly. "What of it? Can you not discern my dearest wish, which is that I did not exist? Whom then shall I fault for the abomination of my birth? You avow that I choose. Cail also chose. The *merewives* did not. They do not. They are forces of seduction and revenge, nothing more. In their fashion, they are as mindless as storm and calm. Therefore they cannot be accused.

"If my powers sufficed to bring about my death, I would perish gladly. But they do not. For that reason also, *I must have the Wildwielder's heed*."

The stabbing of Liand's pain as it became Linden's blinded her. A blow like the jolt of a bludgeon nearly toppled her. She was no longer able to stand on her own: she could barely keep her grip on the Staff.

Fortunately she needed only a moment to draw his swelling into herself. Then her resolve failed, and she sagged with knives twisting in the back of her brain. Without the support of the Cords, she would have fallen. The Staff slipped from her fingers.

"Ringthane!" gasped Pahni. For a moment, her shock at Linden's collapse matched her concern for Liand. Neither she nor Bhapa caught the Staff. As it clattered to the stone, Earthpower vanished from the chamber.

Mahrtiir barked a curse: he could not restrain himself. Once again, he was truly blind.

"Permit me." With his apparel, the Ardent reached out to take Linden from Pahni and Bhapa. "Though I have entirely failed to demonstrate my worth, the time draws nigh when I will do so." Carefully he bore her to the wall and set her down to rest against the nitid rock. "Her distress is extreme, but it will pass. It is the Stonedownor's pain which wracks her. She has suffered no tangible wound."

When he had settled Linden, he commanded, "Restore the Staff of Law to her arms. Mayhap its touch will ease her."

Bhapa obeyed without hesitation. Soon Linden felt the warm wood against her chest. But she was immersed in agony and could not call upon the Staff's benign theurgy.

Moaning, Liand began to stir in Stonemage's arms. Pahni cried his name softly as he tried to lift his head.

"My hands." Covenant's voice cracked in dismay. "I need my hands. Hell and blood. I have to be able to hold the *krill*."

Then he groaned, "Oh, *Linden*. What have you done to yourself? You shouldn't—I was trying to help. I didn't want this to happen."

I must have the Wildwielder's heed.

Linden heard nothing, saw nothing. The glow of the walls had been effaced. Darkness filled the world: darkness and defeat. They fulfilled all of Esmer's predictions.

How had Liand borne this? Unconsciousness had been his only solace, but it was denied to her. She had no defense except the dark, and it was not enough.

Then a voice pierced her hurt. At her ear, someone who may have been Stave said firmly, "Drink, Chosen." She felt cold iron press against her lips. Somewhere in the darkness, she smelled *vitrim*. "The Waynhim offer succor. Already the ur-viles tend to the Unbeliever's hands. If they cannot restore his flesh, they will ease his suffering. And I also will accept their balm, though you have diminished my need. You must drink."

Like the barking of ghouls, Jeremiah began to laugh.

The sound transformed the blades in Linden's head. Without transition, they became an altogether different kind of wound.

Her son could not laugh. He could not. She knew that. With the Power of Command, she had exposed the truth of his possession. The *croyel* was laughing through him; using her son's lungs and throat and mouth to express its malice.

"So here you are, Mom." Contempt and fear throbbed in his voice. They cut at her like the daggers of Liand's transferred trauma. "Do you like what you've accomplished so far? You won't be able to keep me long. That bane's going to eat you alive, but she won't touch me. She won't like the taste. And Roger will come for me soon.

"But you know the best part?" He seemed to strive for a tone of superiority that eluded him. "You're wrong about me. The Mahdoubt saw the truth, but she talked herself out of it. I belong to the Despiser. I *do*. I've been his ever since I put my hand in that bonfire ten years ago. I even learned to enjoy it.

"You kept trying to reach me, you kept *trying*, and you're so earnest about it, I just had to laugh."

Jeremiah—He or the *croyel* made Linden want to scream. She ached for the fused rage which had sustained her on Gallows Howe; but she had lost that granite. She was too weak and blind and beaten to find it in herself again.

"You have no idea," her son continued, mocking her, "how much fun I had steering you here. With *Legos!* At first, you had me worried. You're so slow on the uptake. But once you got to Revelstone, you thought you figured it out. After that, all I had to do was wait."

"Oh, stop," Covenant rasped as though he had the authority to command the *croyel*. "You aren't fooling anybody. You didn't want *this*. If you did, you wouldn't be so scared now."

He sounded stronger than he should have been. With lore and *vitrim*, the ur-viles had done more for him than Linden could.

"You wanted us to come here," Covenant continued. "I believe *that*. Once the Worm woke up, Lord Foul could relax. He's sure he's going to escape the Arch. So now he's just looking for entertainment. Trying to cause as much despair as he can while he waits. You all are, you and the Ravers and Lord Foul and my son.

"But you didn't want *this*. It never occurred to you, any of you, that we might actually get here and trap you. You weren't counting on *her*." He must have meant She Who Must Not Be Named. "She doesn't care what you taste like. She'll take anything. You were counting on Roger. Now you're in as much trouble as the rest of us, and you're scared out of your mind.

"So stop sneering," Covenant ordered sternly. "If I tell him to do it, Galt will be glad to make a few cuts in your throat, just to remind you you're *vulnerable*."

Jeremiah did not reply. Apparently the *croyel* feared the *krill* too much to test Covenant's threat.

With Liand's edema compressing her brain, Linden would not have believed that she could feel more pain. Surely any increase would have driven her into a coma? *I belong to the Despiser.* But her son's tormentor had shown her that she was wrong.

Compelled by intolerable hurt and blindness, she gulped at the *vitrim* that Stave held to her lips.

The dank fluid of the Demondim-spawn tasted old and musty, thick with age or mold. Nevertheless she swallowed it greedily. It lacked the healing vitality of hurtloam; but it was full of strength. In its own way, it was as rich and vital as ichor. As she drank, its gifts helped her absorb the shock of Liand's wound.

Flashes of sight shot through her darkness, sharp brief gleams as though a shutter were being snapped open and shut. Like illusions woven of phosphenes and sensory confusion, she caught glimpses of Covenant confronting Jeremiah; of Stave crouched beside her; of Bhapa hovering while Pahni hugged Liand. In quick flickers, she seemed to see one of the Waynhim poised near her.

She was still too weak to do more than twitch her fingers. But now she did not need to grip the Staff in order to feel its potential fire; its readiness for use. Shutting her eyes against flashes that resembled reflections from polished blades, she reached out for Earthpower.

Slowly flame and Law eased her. After a while, she was able to close her fingers on the Staff. Then she struggled to her feet. Her head still throbbed, sending raw jabs down her spine, through her chest, along her limbs. But the scale of her pain shrank with every beat of her heart. Soon she would be able to think, and speak, and give heed.

As her health-sense burgeoned, however, the nature of her distress shifted: it was being transformed. By the theurgy of percipience, her physical hurt acquired an edged sensation of *wrongness*. On an almost subcutaneous level, she felt or heard the pulse of something rising; something hungry and wicked.

Its beat was as deep as a tectonic shift, the gathering violence of an earthquake.

She Who Must Not Be Named has been fully roused.

She's going to get bigger.

Swallowing instinctive terror, Linden looked at her companions.

Will you waste the remnants of your life thus—?

The Ironhand no longer held her glaive at Esmer's neck. Instead she and two of her Swordmainnir stood in a tight cordon around him, guarding against powers which they could not oppose. Latebirth and Galesend still carried Mahrtiir and Anele. Cabledarm watched over Stonemage and Liand while Bluntfist stood ready to help Galt if he needed aid.

Among them, the remaining ur-viles crouched on all fours, apparently waiting for some signal or command. *They offer guidance*—But their loremaster stood before Covenant. While Covenant swore through his teeth, muttering curses as familiar as endearments, the black creature used a knife of ruddy iron, lambent and steaming, to cut the palm of its other hand. Its acrid blood dripped onto Covenant's burns.

The state of his hands pierced Linden like another self-inflicted wound. The loremaster's blood ate into them like vitriol, but its effects were benignant. Drop by drop, the creature shed its own life to peel away strips of charred skin, comfort exposed flesh. Yet there was only so much that the loremaster's unnatural gifts could accomplish. His fingers and thumbs were swollen and maimed: their last phalanges were already dead. When Linden could add Earthpower to the ur-vile's magicks, his hands might regain a degree of use. To some extent, he might be able to grip weakly and touch—

But she would have to amputate the end of each finger and thumb at the knuckle to prevent their necrosis from spreading. And he would feel nothing: leprosy and the *krill*'s vehemence had destroyed those nerves completely.

As for his palms—The loremaster had done much to preserve them. They would be horribly scarred, but they were functionally intact. Nevertheless they, too, would never feel anything again.

In other ways, Linden's companions were comparatively whole. The native toughness of the Giants had sloughed away the worst effects of the *skest*. Stave's legs still bore corrosive wounds like teeth-marks, but he stood beside Linden without obvious discomfort. Branl gave no sign that his bruises and contusions troubled him. Held by Stonemage, and tended anxiously by Pahni, Liand was recovering, although he remained weak. The agility of the Cords had enabled them both to avoid acid and injury. Anele squirmed aimlessly in Galesend's arms, disturbed by impending calamities that he could not name. The Manethrall studied every detail around him with his restored health-sense, apparently seeking to imprint it on his memory.

By turns, the Waynhim offered *vitrim* to the rest of the company, ignoring only Esmer, the Ardent, and Jeremiah. Branl held a cup for Covenant to drink, but none of the Humbled accepted anything for themselves.

Earlier the Ardent had said that his doom was assured. Now, however, he did not comport himself like a man who felt doomed. Instead his manner suggested some of the smugness which he had displayed in Andelain. Perhaps he had regained his confidence in the powers which his people had entrusted to him.

In contrast, Esmer seemed to give off frustration like spume. His eyes were the color of wind-lashed seas. Among the tatters of his cymar, his festering wounds leaked pus and distress. On his cheek, the hurt of Coldspray's blow still bled.

His desire for Linden's attention was as clear as a cry.

She recognized the urgency of his appeal. *Will you condone this outcome*—? Through her own sensations, she felt the thudding of a subterranean pulse. It beat against her nerves like the harsh and riven labor of Mount Thunder's heart.

—She Who Must Not Be Named has been fully roused.

But neither Cail's son nor the approaching bane had brought Linden back from her immersion in Liand's wounds. She had been retrieved by the *croyel*'s mockery—and by Covenant's response.

I belong to the Despiser.

Esmer could wait. And the loremaster did not interrupt its efforts to preserve Covenant's hands. They, too, could wait a little longer.

More than anything else at that moment, Linden wanted to ensure that she would never hear Jeremiah's tormentor speak again.

I even learned to enjoy it.

Covenant had said, *Even the* Elohim *don't know how to kill one of the* croyel *without killing its host*; but Linden intended to discover the truth for herself.

Uncoiling flames like the thongs of a scourge, she extended her power to quench the *croyel*'s life.

Covenant's strangled protest she ignored. Law and Earthpower had renewed some of her percipience, in spite of her proximity to the source of Kevin's Dirt. If indeed the monster could not be slain without killing Jeremiah as well, she would be able to discern their symbiosis before she unleashed her full force.

Facing the creature's fright, the loose features of her son, Galt's stoic countenance, and the clear argence of the *krill*'s gem, Linden thrust her senses into the cesspit of the *croyel*'s yellow gaze—

—into a ravening as absolute as *caesures* or the Sunbane, but far more thetic—

—and found herself gazing outward through Jeremiah's vacant eyes. With his disfocused sight, she saw her own stricken expression as she struggled to understand what had become of him.

If he had any thoughts of his own, she could not find them. His mind had become a bubbling moil of fright and malevolence: his possessor's passions filled him completely. The voice of his own identity, if he still had one, was too small to be heard amid the clamor of the *croyel*'s yearning for escape and murder.

They have done this to my son!

In a brief blaze of thwarted love and chagrin, she flung flame like a howl at the ceiling. Covenant was right. The *croyel* was *too deep inside him.* It occupied Jeremiah's trapped self too intimately to be disentangled: not while Kevin's Dirt hampered her. If she tried to distinguish one life from the other, she would certainly destroy her son.

Sick with failure and bitterness, she felt that she was committing an act of cruelty as she turned away from Jeremiah.

Her companions stared at her as if she had stepped back from the precipice of another misjudgment as fatal as Covenant's resurrection. Liand tried to say her name. And Covenant sighed, "Linden." His tone was laden with mourning. "I'm so sorry. I tried to warn you."

But his empathy could not ease her now. She did not need solace: she needed an outlet for her ire and shame. Fierce as a Sandgorgon, or as one of the *skurj*, she moved to confront Esmer.

"All right," she said heavily. "You wanted my *heed*. You've got it." Dangers thronged in her voice. "But tell me something first. Show me that you're worth hearing.

"When we talked near Glimmermere, how did you know that I was going to meet the Viles? How did you know that I needed to understand some of their history?"

From her perspective, none of her experiences in the past had happened yet when Cail's son had spoken to her. If his own life were as consecutive as hers—

"I did not," Esmer replied as though her question were an affront. "I sought merely to account for the presence and purpose of the ur-viles. As I have done repeatedly."

Linden bit her lip; swallowed curses. "Then say what you have to say. Get it over with." The residue of Liand's trauma throbbed in her skull. "You've already betrayed us. You're betraying us right now," blocking her access to Covenant's ring. "You're going to betray us again soon." She did not doubt that he would make the attempt. "I can't even imagine what you think you can do to counterbalance that much harm."

He tried to face her; but his gaze shied away. Truths and falsehoods fought each other in his mien. "I do not offer words." He spoke as if his divided nature forced him to utter thorns. "I speak only to request the marred metal which you reclaimed from your son under *Melenkurion* Skyweir."

Like a man who expected to be struck, he winced.

"*What?*" While her friends gaped in surprise and confusion, Linden thrust a hand into her pocket to touch Jeremiah's crumpled racecar. "You want me to give you a *toy?*" The only thing that she had left of the boy whom she had loved for so many years? "Are you out of your mind? I won't—"

"Wildwielder!" Esmer cried as if she had dealt him a mortal blow. At once, however, he restrained himself. More quietly, he stated, "I will return it." His eyes oozed like his wounds. "Nevertheless I must have it. I must hold it."

Then his dismay broke loose. "Are you blind to my anguish? Do you not hear that my woe transcends endurance? Wildwielder, I beseech you. Grant me this small recompense for the abominations which I have wrought against you."

"Linden," murmured Liand. "Perhaps it would be wise—"

"Ringthane," Mahrtiir put in sternly. "This tortured wight strives ever to provide both aid and betrayal. His struggles we have witnessed to our cost—and also to our benefit. And I do not forget that he received his wounds in defense of the Demondim-spawn, whose fidelity is beyond question. I do not comprehend him. Yet is it not conceivable that he seeks now to ameliorate his wrongs in some fashion?"

Linden glared at Esmer. With her fingers, she measured the damage that the *croyel* had done to Jeremiah's racecar. He had brought the toy with him when Roger had abducted him: his last act of initiative or volition—and the only one which did not involve a construct. Had he picked up the car because Lord Foul had told him to do so? Because he belonged to the Despiser? Or did the toy represent something else? Had some private, unreachable part of him claimed the car because he needed it? Because it comforted him? Because it reminded him of her?

Because he was trying to tell her something—?

In the Hall of Gifts, Stave had spoken of the children of the *Haruchai*—and of his own sons. *They are born to strength, and it is their birthright to remain who they are.*

Then he had asked, *Are you certain that the same may not be said of your son?*

There, in the safety of Revelstone, she had replied like a promise, *I'm going to believe that he has the right to be himself.*

Since then, nothing fundamental had changed. The *croyel* still possessed Jeremiah—and it was still a liar. While he stood near her, the husk of a living boy, she had more difficulty trusting that some essential part of his nature held true to itself. Nevertheless nothing had changed. Not really.

In Andelain, Covenant had asserted, *I refuse to believe he made choices then that can't be undone.*

She had to put her faith in *some*thing.

That which appears evil need not have been so from the beginning, and need not remain so until the end.

Perhaps the same could be said of Esmer.

"All right." Trembling, she drew the racecar from her pocket. Shards of pain cut her heart with every beat. "But I want it back."

Esmer did not move. Like Caerroil Wildwood with the Staff of Law on Gallows Howe, he caused the mangled wreckage of the toy to rise from her grasp and float toward him. When he plucked the metal from the air, he folded it in both hands; enclosed it gently, as if he had captured a butterfly or some other fragile creature. For a moment, energies gathered around his head like storm clouds. The flesh of his fingers appeared to blur and melt. Then he tossed the red car upward as though he expected it to flap and flutter like a winged thing.

Instinctively Linden stepped forward, caught the racecar as it fell.

It was whole. Esmer had restored it perfectly. She could not see that it had ever been damaged. If some force had held it to its track, it could have followed the recursions of Jeremiah's raceway construct endlessly.

Needing witnesses, she held it up for her companions to see; but she was deaf to their reactions. Deliberately she showed it to Jeremiah and the *croyel*, hoping that the toy would look like an augury of hope to her son—and a threat to the monster. Then she inclined her head to Esmer: a show of thanks. She had no words for her gratitude; or for her sharp shame.

The racecar's renewed perfection filled her with weeping. At the same time, however, she saw it as a reproach, as mordant as recrimination: a reminder of the extent to which she had failed Jeremiah. Even Esmer, who intended treachery, had done more for her son than she could.

And Esmer's gift did not rectify any of his crimes.

But she kept what she felt to herself. There was nothing that she could have said without bursting into tears. When everyone around her had beheld the racecar, she shoved it back into her pocket. Then she turned to Covenant, although she spoke indirectly to the Ardent.

"It's time." Somehow she faced the strict compassion in Covenant's eyes. The loremaster had done what it could for his hands. She had done nothing. "That thing—whatever She is—She's coming." Because he was who he was, she made no attempt to conceal her weakness; her accumulating defeats. "We have to go."

In spite of his pain, Covenant seemed to peer into her heart. She saw understanding and sorrow in every flensed line of his visage, every inflection of his gaze. He had urged her to find him—and had faulted himself for doing so. His whole face proclaimed that he blamed her for none of her actions; none of their consequences.

Like her, however, he did not speak of what he felt. Instead he put his hands behind him as if he did not want her to feel responsible for them. "You're right." He made a visible effort to muffle the hurt of his burns, but it ached in his tone nonetheless. "She's getting close." Then he looked past her at the Ardent. "If you can do this without the Harrow—?"

The Ardent nodded without hesitation. "Assuredly. Here I do not fear that I will fail the intent of my people. Their powers will suffice.

"However"—he glanced around the company—"my task will be eased if we are less widely scattered. Giants, will you consent to bear the lady and her companions, as you have done before?"

"Aye," the Ironhand assented promptly. "To escape this snare, we would carry even the Demondim-spawn on our backs."

At once, Frostheart Grueburn approached Linden. Cabledarm drew Pahni away from Liand while Bluntfist scooped Bhapa into her arms.

"And you, Masters," the Ardent continued. "Will you allow a Giant to bear the Timewarden?"

Branl and Clyme nodded. With their permission, Cirrus Kindwind claimed

Covenant. Although she had lost a forearm and hand to the *skurj*, she did not need them to support him against the chest of her armor.

"Then gather about me," the Insequent instructed. To Galt, he said, "Bring the lady's son as nigh as you dare."

Stolidly Galt used the *krill* and his hold on Jeremiah's shoulder to press the boy closer to the Ardent.

Lifted from the floor, Linden settled into her familiar position sitting on Grueburn's arms. Quickly she confirmed that she still had Covenant's ring on its chain around her neck. Then she gripped her Staff hard in both hands.

At the same time, the Ardent unfurled wreaths and streamers of bright cloth and sent them wafting around the company. Soon a fluttering ribband had settled on Linden's shoulder and Grueburn's arm; on one shoulder or arm of each of her companions. Threatened by the *krill*, the *croyel* did not resist as a fulvous band rested on its deformed head. Within moments, the Ardent had placed his fabric touch on everyone except Esmer and the Demondim-spawn.

Abruptly the ur-viles and Waynhim resumed their barking. Their harsh clamor conveyed an urgency that Esmer did not deign to translate. The Waynhim scattered into the passage that led to the palace of enchanted water. The ur-viles made gestures that could have meant anything.

They offer guidance—

They may not have grasped the extent of the Ardent's powers.

—but they cannot save you.

The pulse of the bane's approach was growing stronger.

Across the small gap between Stonemage and Cabledarm, Liand and Pahni held hands. Squirming against Kindwind's cataphract, Covenant tried to find a position that did not gall his burns. Then he gave up. With his teeth clenched, he hugged his hands against his chest.

"No," Anele moaned, "no. Better the Worm. It merely feeds. It does not hate." His broken mind was trapped among images that appalled him.

The Ardent adjusted his plump features into lines of resolve. "Farewell, *mere*-son," he lisped to Esmer. "I wish you joy of your many betrayals. We will not abide to witness their outcome."

Tightening the touch of his ribbands, he began to whisper incantations in a language as incomprehensible as the guttural speech of the Demondim-spawn.

The insistence of the ur-viles became a feral snarling.

Esmer did not move to intervene. Instead he gave the Insequent a look of such scorn that Linden winced.

Esmer knew something that the Ardent did not. The ur-viles and Waynhim knew it.

The Ardent closed his eyes, apparently seeking to shut out distractions. He chanted more loudly. The strips of his apparel clenched and loosened to the rhythm of his spell. Other bands—garish garnet, stark fuligin, an azure as luminous as open skies—flurried around him as though he sought to silence the urgency of the ur-viles.

Esmer said nothing.

The Ardent's voice rose. His chanting began to vacillate between commanding tones and febrile supplications. Fresh sweat beaded on his forehead, his cheeks. He spat words like gibberish in a spray of saliva and imprecation.

"Here it comes," Covenant rasped softly.

The subliminal thud of malice drew closer. It punctuated the Ardent's rising desperation.

Then his eyes burst open. An expression of utter chagrin stretched his countenance. "*You!*" he gasped at Esmer.

Cail's son lifted his shoulders: a shrug of disdain. "The conjoined powers of the Insequent have made you mighty, but they have not altered the nature of your knowledge. The theurgies by which you bypass distances are a wan mimicry of wild magic." His scorn sounded like despair. "They are impotent in my presence."

He had promised more betrayals. *They will be revealed when they are needed.*

Roger had said of him, *He changes his mind too often. There's always a flaw somewhere.* This time, there was none.

Because of him, Linden's company was caught in the Lost Deep.

11.

Private Carrion

Here it comes.

Stupefied by shock, Linden gaped at Covenant. *They are impotent in my presence.* Her companions stared at Esmer in dismay. The consternation of the Giants was too great for protests or curses. Mahrtiir ground his teeth helplessly. Tears started in Pahni's eyes as she clutched Liand's urgent hand. In the nacre glow of the walls,

Bhapa looked pallid and stricken, as if he were about to faint. But the eyes of the Humbled held vindication. From the first, they had opposed the decisions which had brought the company here.

Despite the threat of the *krill*, the *croyel* grinned with all its teeth. Entirely possessed, Jeremiah looked as vacant as Covenant's home on Haven Farm. His slackness seemed to imply bonfires; conflagrations.

She Who Must Not Be Named was rising from the abyss. Linden had sensed that dire evil. *Against Her ire, only white gold may hope for efficacy.* Nevertheless her attention was fixed on Covenant. She could not look away.

Here it comes—?

In the appalled silence, she asked, "Did you know about this?" Her voice was little more than a hoarse whisper. "Why didn't you warn us?"

Covenant shook his head. "I guessed." Residual excruciation sawed in his tone. His eyes searched the walls as though they were all that remained of his memories; as though he sought salvation in recollections which eluded him. "He promised more treachery. I assumed he was hiding something."

"If you desire to flee your doom," said Esmer sternly, "you must cross the Hazard and discover some passage upward. Here you must perish. There is no escape from the Lost Deep."

"Behold!" He indicated the ur-viles with a dismissive flip of his hand. "Even now, they implore you to follow them."

"The *mere*-son speaks sooth." The Ardent trembled, anticipating terror. "I am defeated, blocked from use and name and life. This, too, is added to the sum of my failures. The knowledge and purposes of the Insequent are made naught by the *mere*-son's presence. I am an empty vessel awaiting only the fulfillment of death."

"Linden Giantfriend!" Coldspray demanded. Her fists clenched combatively. "What is your will?"

"Chosen," Stave urged before Linden could find her voice. "We must make the attempt. If we do not, we grant to Corruption a triumph which he has not yet won."

With an effort of will that seemed to tear her heart, Linden wrenched her gaze away from Covenant. Instinctively, however, she avoided Stave's steady stare and Coldspray's tension. Instead she looked at Mahrtiir as if only his blindness could counsel her.

Attempts must be made, even when there can be no hope. The Manethrall had told her that. *And betimes some wonder is wrought to redeem us.*

Even the loss of his eyes had not destroyed his spirit.

Against innumerable obstacles, Linden had found her son. Now she needed to save him. Somehow.

She was breaking; drowning in defeats. She felt it. But she also knew that Mahrtiir was right. Long ago, Covenant had taught her the same lesson.

Braced in Frostheart Grueburn's arms, she drew more light and health-sense from the Staff. Then she forced herself to meet the Ironhand's gaze.

"Run," she breathed. "I trust the ur-viles. I trust the Waynhim. They want to lead us. Let's go."

Her company had to get past the Hazard before She Who Must Not Be Named rose high enough to strike—and the portal of the Lost Deep was a considerable distance away.

Without hesitation, Rime Coldspray shouted, "Swordmainnir!" and at once, Latebirth wheeled to carry Mahrtiir into the passage taken by the Waynhim. Onyx Stonemage followed immediately with Liand. Goaded by dread, the Ardent went next, supporting himself in a flurry of cloth that filled the corridor because he could not run fast enough. Grueburn crowded close behind the Insequent: Stave trotted at Linden's side. Carrying Covenant, Cirrus Kindwind hurried after Grueburn, guarded by Clyme and Branl. As Linden was rushed into the tunnel, she felt the other Giants gather with their burdens. At the rear of the company, Galt pushed Jeremiah and the *croyel* into motion. Coldspray stayed with them to ensure that they did not lag—and that Galt did not lose control of Jeremiah's possessor.

Among them all dashed the ur-viles, barking encouragement or warnings. Without apparent effort, Esmer kept pace with the Ardent and Grueburn.

Linden wanted her son near her; but she understood why Galt and Coldspray came last. The *croyel* was not powerless: it was only afraid. If it decided to risk an attack, its place at the rear would limit its ability to hurt the rest of the company.

The Giants ran with giddy speed. The flawless passage was a moonstone blur. Staring forward, Linden concentrated on the Staff and percipience; extended Earthpower like sunlight to enclose all of her companions. They needed health-sense as badly as she did.

The ur-viles flinched at the Staff's strength. A few raced ahead: others dropped back. Law was inherently inimical to them. But they had demonstrated time and again that they could withstand its effects, at least briefly. Linden counted on that. She was not confident that she or any of her friends would be able to resist the seductions of the palace without fire and Law.

The bane's advance had become a visceral pounding. Its pulse thudded in Linden's bones. She half expected to feel the walls of the passage shake. But the roused evil's force was not physical: not yet. It was a drumbeat in the spirit rather than the substance of the stone. Without percipience, she might not have sensed it at all.

As if from a great distance, she heard Covenant mutter, "Hellfire! This is going to be close. We have to *hurry*."

The Giants were already running hard. The harsh strain of Grueburn's breathing rasped in Linden's ears. She could not imagine how Stave kept up with her. Galt and the Ironhand were falling behind with Jeremiah and the *croyel*. Yet Esmer matched the haste of the Swordmainnir easily.

Ahead of Linden, Latebirth and then Stonemage burst through curtains of ensor-celled water into the intricate wonders of the palace. On one of the crystal stairways, the two Giants were joined by the Waynhim, less than a dozen of the grey creatures: all that survived of their kind. As the Ardent and a number of the ur-viles entered the chamber, the Waynhim scampered downward, urging Linden's companions to follow.

An instant later, Grueburn rushed past the curtains; and Linden felt a jolt along her nerves, as if she had been plunged into the frigid waters of Glimmermere. She was exerting far more Earthpower than Liand had summoned earlier: her fire should have sufficed to shed any confusion. But the magicks which sustained the palace were obdurate and enduring. For a moment, her concentration faltered, and the effects of the Viles' eerie lore nearly caught her. Rugs as sumptuous as tapestries. Immaculate marble. The fountain and chandeliers—the mosaics—Then she tightened her grip on herself; on the Staff. While Grueburn took the stairs four at a time, Linden strove against achievements that surpassed her comprehension.

Kindwind descended the stairs almost on Grueburn's heels. Ahead of Linden, Late-birth was halfway to the egress from the palace. Behind Kindwind, Branl, and Clyme, Giants and ur-viles ran downward in a clamor of heavy feet and a scatter of lighter bodies. Lit by braziers of water and flame, Halewhole Bluntfist bore Bhapa between the curtains. They appeared to be the last—

The Ironhand, Jeremiah, and Galt had dropped so far back that Linden could barely descry them.

"Wait," she panted to Grueburn. "Wait. We're too far ahead. I can't protect them."

If Galt and Coldspray lost their way, the *croyel* might break free. The *krill*'s force was not Earthpower: it would not anchor the senses of the Master and the Ironhand. The *croyel* was strong enough to kill them both if Galt's threat slipped.

In response, a few ur-viles turned back, yelling as they raced up the stairs.

"Be reassured, Wildwielder." Esmer visibly loathed the contradiction which required him to translate for the Demondim-spawn. "The ur-viles will ward the *Haruchai* and your son, and also the Giant. The *croyel* will not elude the *krill*."

"Let them take care of it, Linden," urged Covenant. "We'll all be safer when we get past this place. You won't have to work so hard to keep us from drifting."

Linden had said that she trusted the ur-viles—Surely those creatures knew how to counter the theurgies of their makers' makers? Surely they retained enough of that imponderable lore? Biting her lip, she forced herself to leave Jeremiah's fate in the hands of the Demondim-spawn.

Grueburn and Kindwind ran after the Ardent, Latebirth, and Stonemage as if they were still pursuing Longwrath.

They seemed to cross the rich floor in an undifferentiated swirl of glances and imagery. Lights and jewels wheeled like a catastrophe of stars. The palace had appeared vast when Linden had wandered among its amazements earlier; but the speed of the Swordmainnir made it as transient as a mirage. Half obscured by the Ardent's apparel, Latebirth and Onyx Stonemage disappeared into the corridor ahead. Bluntfist pounded down the last stairs to the beat of the bane's hunger. Gradually Linden lost her awareness of Jeremiah altogether. She could not discern the ur-viles that had hastened to preserve him.

A moment later, Grueburn carried her into the next passage. Marble and mosaics disappeared suddenly, completely, as if they had been cut out of existence with a knife.

A storm of incipient hysteria pressed against Linden's self-command; her concentration on Earthpower. *She was leaving her son behind*—She did not trust anyone or anything enough to relieve her instinctive alarm.

Ahead of her, the Manethrall sat, watchful and ready, on Latebirth's arms as the Swordmain followed the Waynhim. Energized by the vitality of the Staff, Liand grew palpably stronger, shedding the aftereffects of his wounds while Stonemage ran. The Ardent deployed his ribbands in a frenzy like the fever of his timorous heart. Covenant seemed to be failing. Bit by bit, the hurt of his burns gnawed at his self-command. Nevertheless he clung grimly to his present.

Like Stave, Clyme and Branl looked impervious to any doom. At Linden's side, Esmer radiated a chaos of conflicting passions: anger and disdain, anticipation and abhorrence; a chagrin as immedicable as his wounds.

Behind them, Anele's head jerked anxiously from side to side. His whole body emitted a sharp gibber of fright. But he did nothing to hinder Galesend's steps.

Pahni's aura was a vivid ache of concern for Liand. Yet her Ramen discipline held. And Bhapa had regained his determination to face any peril for Linden's sake, and for Mahrtiir's. In spite of his naked apprehension, he sat leaning forward on Bluntfist's forearms as if he were prepared to fling himself bodily into the chasm of the Hazard; the maw of the bane.

For Linden, this tunnel passed like the previous one: a torrent of pearlescence and panic and Earthpower; curses and dread. By the simple lore of long strides and haste, the Giants foreshortened the distance.

Grueburn carried Linden into the next chamber before Linden realized that Latebirth, Stonemage, and the Ardent had reached the immaculate hall which contained the jut of rock like a misshapen throne.

In the center of the floor, jagged stone gaped like fangs at the ceiling. Even now, the maimed seat seemed indefinably abominable, as if here the Viles had sculpted an image or replica of something far more bitter and brutal.

Linden had reached the limit of her endurance: she could not abide her separation from her son; her bone-deep conviction that she was abandoning him. "Stop!" she called to the Giants. "I can't go on like this. I need to wait for Jeremiah!"

Already Cirrus Kindwind had brought Covenant into the chamber. Galesend, Cabledarm, and Bluntfist were close behind her. But Jeremiah remained beyond the reach of Linden's senses.

"Lady, we must have haste!" Words frothed on the Ardent's lips. "If any hope remains to us, it lies beyond the Hazard. Within the Lost Deep, we may be hunted and devoured at leisure. We must pass the abysm!"

Ur-viles and Waynhim shouted like dogs or crows; but Linden did not know how to heed them.

"And if She rises between us?" she retorted. "If we're on one side of the Hazard, and Jeremiah is on the other? I won't do it! We have to stay together. Everything we've done is wasted if we don't stay together."

Before the Ardent could protest, Mahrtiir put in, "I stand with the Ringthane, Giants, as I have done from the first. Also we have cause to consider that there may be no salvation for the Land if we do not redeem her son."

"If you fear to remain among us, Insequent," Stave added without inflection, "depart. I stand with the Chosen as well. And I deem that the Swordmainnir will not consent to abandon any member of their company."

"Aye," Frostheart Grueburn panted. "We are Giants, are we not? Having joined our fate to that of our companions, we will endure or perish with them. Also," she added, "children are precious to us. We cannot gainsay Linden Giantfriend in this."

The other Swordmainnir nodded; but Clyme stated flatly, "We concur with the Ardent. To delay here invites calamity. If the Land can be redeemed, its salvation lies with the Unbeliever, not with Linden Avery's boy.

"In addition"—his tone sharpened—"we question whether Esmer's presence is potent to quench wild magic when white gold is held by its rightful wielder. Linden Avery," he commanded, "release the ring to the ur-Lord. Let us discover whether he is as powerless as this scion of *merewives* wishes us to believe."

Oh, God. Clyme's order stung Linden to the heart. He might be right. The ring—*In the wrong hands, it's still pretty strong. But it doesn't really come alive until the person it belongs to chooses to use it.* Esmer's influence might not suffice to block the true white gold wielder.

Twisting in Grueburn's arms, Linden turned to Covenant. Days ago, unaware of Roger's glamour, she had declined to surrender the ring. In Andelain, struggling, she had sacrificed it to the Harrow. Now she did not hesitate. With one hand, she swept the chain over her head, extended Covenant's wedding band toward him.

"Here," she demanded; pleaded. "Take it. It's too dangerous for me. Even if Esmer weren't here, I couldn't save us."

Not from She Who Must Not Be Named.

Until that moment, Covenant had seemed preoccupied with pain, too hurt to react. Yet he heard her appeal. Meeting her gaze, he gave her a look of anguish, stricken and faltering, as if she had asked him to betray himself—or her. His hair resembled a silver conflagration, as if his thoughts burned with dismay.

Nevertheless he did not refuse. He may have believed that he was responsible for her plight; and he was not a man who shirked. Trembling, he reached out with his charred hands.

He would not be able to grip his ring, but he could cup it in his palms. Branl or Clyme would loop the chain around his neck.

Spitting spume like nausea, Esmer said, "You regard my treacheries too lightly." So swiftly that Linden hardly saw him move, he swept toward Covenant.

Branl and Clyme snatched at Esmer: Stave tried to catch him. They were too late. Unhindered, Cail's son tapped the scar in the center of Covenant's forehead with one finger. Then he let the Humbled and Stave drag him back.

Instantly Covenant's eyes drifted out of focus. As though he had been caught by a question that no one else could hear, he frowned. His arms dropped.

Esmer had not harmed him physically: Linden could see that. Covenant's scar glared whitely for a moment, stark as an incision. Then it faded, leaving no sign of any new injury.

Still Esmer had done enough. Swallowing gall, Linden fought her need to vomit.

Covenant's eyes rolled back, and his head lolled against Kindwind's armor, as he toppled into the maze of his fissured memories. Oh, he was not hurt: even his mind was not. Nonetheless he was gone. He had lost his grasp on the present. Instead of regarding Esmer or the *Haruchai* or even Linden, he wandered among the depths of Time.

While the Giants gathered protectively around Linden and Covenant, Esmer announced, "Now is the toll of my crimes complete." Mourning frayed his tone. "I need only remain among you to satisfy Kastenessen's malice and the *merewives'* loathing. She Who Must Not Be Named cares naught for any deed of mine, but other powers will exult in your ruin."

A scream rose in Linden's throat: enough Earthpower to shatter the ceiling; rain down rubble.

Before she could release it, however, Liand shouted her name; and the simple humanity of his cry stopped her. It reminded her that the danger was too great. She could not afford overt despair. Not now: not while the *croyel* still ruled Jeremiah.

Yet she required some form of release for her dismay, her baulked love. They were too extreme to be contained. Covenant was gone. He was gone *again*. Reflexively she dropped his chained ring. She did not see Stave catch it before it struck the floor. Between one instant and the next, she transformed her force.

Instead of wasting her strength on screams, she aimed her fire at Covenant's hands; tuned it to the pitch of healing. With a supreme effort of percipience and will, she set everything else aside in order to finish the necessary—and necessarily partial— restoration which the loremaster had begun.

If only for a moment, the chamber and the throne and her friends and even Esmer seemed to vanish. She forgot Jeremiah and the *croyel*. Every aspect of herself, every attainable resource, every baffled passion, she concentrated on Covenant.

The ur-vile had made a good start: it had secured the underlying integrity of his bones; preserved shreds of muscle and sinew; kept mutilated scraps of skin alive; sealed his palms. But the worst effects of his burns remained. Necrosis had already corrupted the ends of his fingers and thumbs. Soon that mortification would spread inward, rotting his tissues, poisoning his blood. If it went far enough, it would send sepsis throughout his body. Given time, it would kill him.

Lost in recollections and leprosy, he could neither protest nor grieve as Linden used her Staff to excise the ends of each finger and thumb, one after another, cutting them off at the knuckles. When she was done, he would still have digits. He would still be able to use them. Because his nerves were dead, he would not feel the ache of amputation. If he did not look at himself, he might forget that she had made him more of a halfhand than he had been before.

During moments that stretched for her, although they must have been brief, she labored over Covenant as she had once worked on her son. She cauterized exposed blood vessels, cleaned away potential infections, urged circulation back into his fingers. Separated dead flesh from living. Encouraged the formation of scabs. Gently she filled his veins with flame that mimicked hurtloam.

Everything was irrevocable. He would never regain what he had lost. But she did what she could. For a short time, she became a physician again, and did not count the cost.

But then she heard Liand repeat her name; and the part of her that had not forgotten Jeremiah reasserted itself.

In a burst of barking from the ur-viles and Waynhim, Rime Coldspray and Galt of the Humbled entered the chamber of the throne with Jeremiah and the *croyel*.

Galt appeared to concentrate exclusively on controlling his prisoner. But the Ironhand scanned the rest of the company; and as she did so, her expression asked them why they had stopped. Then she noticed Covenant, and her shoulders sagged.

"The Timewarden is lost to us again."

Fiercely Cirrus Kindwind answered, "This is the *mere*-son's doing. He avers now that the tale of his treacheries is complete. I hear no falsehood in him. Nonetheless I will credit no promise of his."

Esmer flinched as if Kindwind had hit him harder than any tangible blow. His eyes were the color of drizzling rains. But he did not protest.

The clamor of the Demondim-spawn mounted, incomprehensible as gibbering. Then it subsided to a low mutter.

Linden studied Jeremiah; searched him for signs that he had suffered during their separation. But he seemed unchanged. The *krill* kept the *croyel*'s teeth away from his neck. That small reprieve, at least, he had been granted. The creature no longer drank his blood. Nonetheless its claws still dug into his flesh: its power still possessed him.

As she regarded the *croyel*, it turned its head to gaze at the malformed throne with malignant rapture. A grin bared its fangs.

Involuntarily, as if the monster's attitude compelled her, Linden asked, "That thing." Her voice shook. "That throne. Do any of you recognize it? Do you know what it represents?"

She did not expect a reply from Esmer, although she felt sure that he or the Demondim-spawn could have answered her. But perhaps the Ardent—

The Insequent shook his head with an air of misery, as if he could sense dangers worse than jaws crowding toward him. Flatly Branl said, "The *Haruchai* have seen or heard nothing to account for it, or for any secret hidden within the Lost Deep."

Abruptly Jeremiah raised his head. Grinning like the *croyel*, he said, "It's a copy of a-Jeroth's throne in Ridjeck Thome. An exact copy. It might as well be the place where Lord Foul sat while he still thought he could get what he wants with armies and war. The Viles made it after they stopped worshipping themselves and started trying to do something useful with all that power.

"It's homage."

The *croyel*'s grin was as feral as its desire for Jeremiah's blood.

Instinctively Linden shied away from the sight. It hurt her more than Covenant's fragmented absence.

Homage? she thought bitterly. No. Jeremiah's possessor was lying again—or distorting the truth. The Demondim had been used by Lord Foul. The ur-viles had served him for centuries or millennia. But she had met Viles: she did not believe that they had ever bowed down to the Despiser.

Above Glimmermere, Esmer had asserted as much.

"Linden Giantfriend," insisted the Ironhand. "I fear that the Ardent's alarm augurs ill for us. We must attempt to cross the Hazard ere She Who Must Not Be Named rises.

"And"—she turned to Galt—"we must not be slowed by the boy. Master, I acknowledge your devoir. I honor it. But it impedes us. If you will permit me, I will hold the *krill* in your stead, bearing Linden Giantfriend's son as I do so. Doubtless there is evil in any contact with the *croyel*, but I am armored against it." She tapped her cataphract. "And we will no longer lag behind our companions."

Like Covenant, if in a different fashion, Linden was losing her grip on the present. She had struggled for too long; had depleted herself over and over again— Remembering the Viles, who had once been worthy of admiration, she also remembered her parents, from whom she learned her deepest nightmares. She did not know how to endure the *croyel*'s rapt avarice.

Briefly Galt appeared to hesitate. Presumably he, Branl, and Clyme were debating the implications of Coldspray's suggestion. Then the Humbled reached a decision.

Nodding to the Ironhand, Galt shifted to make room for her.

Quickly she stepped behind Galt. Reaching past him, she placed her hand over his where he gripped the *krill*. Her hand dwarfed his: when she took the dagger's guards between her thumb and forefinger, he was able to release his grasp without removing the protective cloth. Then he dropped his other hand to Jeremiah's arm so that the boy—or the *croyel*—could not twist away before Coldspray secured her clasp.

A moment later, Coldspray stooped to wrap her free arm around Jeremiah. Hugging the *croyel* against her armor, between her and the boy, and holding the edge of the *krill* steady at the creature's throat, she lifted her prisoners from the floor.

The *croyel* continued grinning as though it had seen a promise of rescue in the jagged throne.

After a glance at Linden, the Ironhand addressed her comrades. "Now, Swordmainnir, we must run indeed. If we do not cross from the Lost Deep before the chasm's bane assails us, we will not behold sunlight or open skies or hope again. We will not live to witness the outcome of the Earth."

"Aye," growled Grueburn past Linden's head. "No being who survives to hear our tale will say that we did not run."

Without a word, Stave raised Covenant's ring, urging Linden to reclaim it. But she shook her head. It belonged to Covenant: in Esmer's presence, it was useless to her. And it would be safer with Stave.

He would give it to her if or when she could use it.

The Waynhim sprinted ahead with the Ardent sailing close behind them. At once, the Giants followed, but in a new formation. Frostheart Grueburn went first, with Stave at her side and Rime Coldspray at her back. Then came Cirrus Kindwind and Covenant, with the Humbled arrayed around them, and Esmer gliding nearby. Next ran Stormpast Galesend and Onyx Stonemage carrying Anele and Liand. Behind them, at Mahrtiir's request, were Pahni and Bhapa, Cabledarm and Halewhole Bluntfist. The Manethrall and Latebirth brought up the rear. Clearly he considered the Ramen the most expendable members of the company—and himself the least valuable of the Ramen.

Among them all sped the ur-viles as if they were herding the Giants and the Humbled. But the black creatures kept a little distance between themselves and Linden's shining Staff.

By degrees, Linden absorbed new urgency from the rushing Giants. Her heart pounded to the subterranean rhythms of She Who Must Not Be Named. Sweat gathered on her palms. Behind her, the *krill*'s radiance cast dim shadows through the glow of the immaculate stone and her own illumination. Ahead, the Ardent's fright felt more and more like a wail. But it was not loud enough to muffle the growing ferocity of the bane's emanations. Linden could not seal her nerves against that massive pulse.

The Swordmainnir ran as though they intended to fling themselves down the throat of a volcano. Linden should have been preparing herself for She Who Must Not Be Named, sharpening her percipience to the exact hue and timbre of the bane. How else could she fight? But she already knew that she was too small to combat such forces. And Esmer had assured her that *Against Her ire, only white gold may hope for efficacy*.

Instead of bracing herself for battle, she tried to think of some way to sway Cail's son.

If Esmer departed, the Ardent would be able to convey the company to safety. Or Covenant might rediscover his connection to the present. With wild magic, he might be able to accomplish what Linden could not.

Sensations of immanent malice confirmed that Coldspray was right. —we will not behold sunlight or open skies or hope again. The entire company would die if Linden could not think of an argument persuasive or insidious or hurtful enough to change Esmer's mind.

☙❦❧

Harried by barking and desperation, the Giants ran, flashing through tunnels like hallucinations. They reached the cavern of the outlined castle and passed through it as though the elegant faery edifice were trivial. As they raced toward the portal of the Lost Deep, they did not slow their strides.

The Ardent's febrile haste blocked Linden's view ahead. Nevertheless she knew that the portal was near. She felt the shape of the stone, the vast spaces and stalactites; the inexorable ascent of the bane. Dark hungers became a roar that swelled as though some innominate hand swung wide a huge door.

Moments now: only moments. The hourglass of the company's fate was almost empty.

Then an impression of openness flared across Linden's senses. Riding his raiment, the Ardent followed the Waynhim onto the broad shelf that footed the slender span of the Hazard.

The Waynhim dashed up the bridge. Floating higher to distance himself from the depths, the Insequent pursued them. But Linden panted to Grueburn, "Stop. Stop."

As Grueburn cleared the entrance to the Lost Deep, she wrenched herself to a halt near the rim of the abyss to await Linden's instructions and the rest of her comrades.

Far below her, Linden saw the bane rising like an eruption of fire.

At first, its force was so great that she could not discern it clearly. It resembled a shapeless maw of flame so wide that it filled the chasm from wall to wall. But as she forced herself to concentrate, she realized that She Who Must Not Be Named was neither a maw nor shapeless. The monstrous being was not even flame: She resembled fire only because Her power was so extreme. And She had faces—

Oh, God, She had *faces*. Dozens of them: hundreds. Features articulated the rising puissance in lurid succession, all of them different; all so huge that only three or four of them were formed at a time; all stretched and frantic as if they were howling in torment. And all women. They modulated constantly, harshly, changing from one tortured visage to another without surcease. But they were all distinct, recognizable. If Linden had known them, she would have been able to say their names.

Instinctively she understood that if the bane caught her and her companions, the men would be slaughtered; torn to scraps. But the women would be devoured, every one of them. She and the Swordmainnir and Pahni would become part of that—that—

She Who Must Not Be Named was the source of Kevin's Dirt. Manipulated and shaped by Kastenessen and Esmer, Her energies cast the pall that hampered percipience. She emitted the sorcery which disguised Law and obstructed Earthpower: to Her, the natural forces of life were mere detritus. Yet She was not drained or diminished. She had the power to uproot mountains. Apparently She lacked only the intention.

So close to that evil, Linden's efforts barely kept her Staff alight. After the battle of First Woodhelven, she had dreamed of being carrion. The bane made her feel that she was already dead; dead and rotting.

One after another, Giants emerged from the portal, flanked by snarling clusters of ur-viles. The ur-viles beckoned raucously for the company to cross the Hazard; but Coldspray and Kindwind paused beside Grueburn and Linden. The Humbled kept watch over Covenant. As Stonemage followed Galesend onto the ledge, she asked why her comrades had stopped; but no one answered. Like Linden, the other Giants were transfixed by the bane's virulence.

Glancing downward, Stave remarked impassively, "Mayhap it was for this that the Unbeliever spoke of Diassomer Mininderain. Mayhap he wished that we might comprehend our peril."

The Ardent must have heard Stave in spite of the distance. From high above the crest of the span, the garish man called, "She is the Auriference as well! One of the

Insequent suffers among those who will destroy us! It was to avoid her doom that so many of my people have eschewed the Land."

Sternly Esmer added, "Kastenessen's mortal lover also participates in She Who Must Not Be Named. She was Emereau Vrai, daughter of kings, and she dared to draw upon this ancient need for the creation of the *merewives*. Therefore she was consumed."

Linden could believe that the bane was Diassomer Mininderain as Covenant had described her, *The mate of might*—If so, its powers—Hers—were beyond measure. She had gone mad and slumbered, instead of tearing Her way out of the depths to ravage the Earth, because She did not crave simple destruction. She hungered instead for mortal lives that could love and be loved.

And She was too close. Surely She was too close? Linden and her company would never be able to cross the Hazard in time.

She needed to persuade or banish Esmer. Now or never.

Many of the ur-viles had run up onto the span. Those that remained gathered in a wedge to ward themselves from the Staff. They all gestured furiously, cawing or snarling for the company to ascend the bridge.

"Linden!" Liand shouted, pleading with her. "We must run!"

Grimly Linden turned to Esmer. Inspired by the distraught legacy of her parents, she asked the most cutting question that she could imagine.

"Does it bother you that Cail would be ashamed of his son?"

Esmer faced her like crashing surf. His eyes seemed to weep storms. "And does it trouble you, Wildwielder," he countered, "that you have at hand the means to end my interference, and yet do not avail yourself of it?"

Linden gaped at him, dumbfounded.

Groaning, he explained, "The *krill* of the High Lord, Wildwielder. It is puissant to sever my life."

In spite of their peril, the Swordmainnir stared. Linden felt Liand's distress. The shock of the Ramen slapped at her nerves.

"If you do not crave the deed for yourself," Esmer continued, "command some *Haruchai* to perform it. With my death, the effects of my presence will end. The Insequent will recover his efficacy. The Timewarden's notice will emerge from its confusion. The gift of tongues will return to the Giants. White gold will become capable in your hands.

"Slay me, Wildwielder. Grant an end to my suffering. If you find worth in your life, mine must cease."

"You're—" Amid the distress of her companions, Linden floundered. "That's—" But then she rallied. "Oh, sure. Kill you. With the *krill*. Perfect. Except that then the *croyel* gets away." Freed, the creature might be strong enough to shove her and even the Giants over the precipice. "I'll lose my son."

Esmer shrugged. "As you say." His gaze did not relent. "No deed is without cost or peril. But you must act *now*. Have I not said that I yearn for an end? And the opportunity fades with every passing moment. My death will not turn She Who Must Not Be Named from Her prey."

For no apparent reason, he added, "The ur-viles and Waynhim still desire to serve you. They are not without cunning."

"Linden Giantfriend!" snapped the Ironhand. "I do not seek to sway you. But you must choose quickly! The bane draws near!"

For a moment—no more than a heartbeat—the implications of Esmer's appeal paralyzed Linden. She could recover Covenant. She could recover wild magic. The Ardent's given powers would return. Then her heart beat again, echoing the life-pulse of dozens or hundreds of tortured women; and she saw that her choice was no choice at all. All of her options were intolerable.

Murder Esmer in cold blood. Lose Jeremiah again. Or face unanswerable carnage.

The Demondim-spawn still urged her toward the Hazard.

"*Go!*" she cried at Rime Coldspray. "Covenant first! Then Jeremiah! Get as many of us across as you can! I'll go last. I'm no match for that thing, but maybe I can distract it."

Instantly the Ironhand wheeled away; rushed Kindwind and Covenant onto the span. As Kindwind and the Humbled sprinted ahead, Coldspray ordered Stonemage and Galesend to follow one at a time, with Cabledarm, Bluntfist, and then Latebirth behind them.

Barking tumult, the rest of the ur-viles ran as well. In moments, only Stave and Esmer remained with Grueburn and Coldspray; Linden, Jeremiah, and the *croyel.*

"Coldspray—!" Linden protested.

"*No*, Giantfriend." The light of battle shone in the Ironhand's eyes. Her grin was ferocious. "You have chosen. I also choose. While the *mere*-son abides with you, I will do what your need requires of me.

"Mayhap," she added quickly, "your son is safer at your side than elsewhere."

Linden thought that she understood. If Coldspray struck Esmer while she, Jeremiah, and the *croyel* were exposed on the span, the creature would have no chance to harm anyone else. And with the Staff, Linden might be able to contain the *croyel's* magicks long enough for Coldspray to regain control.

A slim chance.

Better than none.

"Go," Linden panted, choking on nausea. "Now. I'll do what I can."

With a nod, Coldspray ran for the Hazard.

Grueburn and Stave followed immediately. Esmer stayed near Linden.

She had forgotten how narrow the span looked; how fragile— She had forgotten the mass of the stalactites, tremendous and threatening. As Grueburn carried her onto the bridge, the gulf seemed to leap open as if it sprang from her darkest nightmares. And the bane: God, the *bane*! Excoriated faces gaped upward in insane succession, straining to devour fresh life.

She Who Must Not Be Named did not rise swiftly, but Her approach was as ineluctable as the forces which had riven *Melenkurion* Skyweir.

With the Staff's insignificant light in her hands, Linden ascended into an altogether different dimension of feeling and perception: a dimension of undiluted irrefragable terror.

She understood now why her parents had preferred death. Any other end would be better than a fall into this unfathomable abysm; this corrupt distortion of love and lust.

Somewhere the Ardent screamed for haste. From the fan of obsidian—the cavern's only egress—Giants shouted encouragement. Struggling for courage, Linden tried to tally the members of her company who had reached momentary safety; tried and could not. The yowling of the ur-viles and Waynhim sounded like despair.

At the crest of the Hazard, some signal passed between Coldspray and Grueburn. They were not *Haruchai*: they could not hear each other's thoughts. Nevertheless they had trained together for centuries. They moved as if they shared one mind.

Suddenly Coldspray spun. At the same instant, Grueburn jerked to a halt, jumped backward a step.

Keeping her hold on Jeremiah, gripping the *krill* less than finger's width from the *croyel*'s throat, the Ironhand flung a kick at Esmer.

Apparently he also could not read minds, despite his many powers. Coldspray's kick caught him squarely. And she was a Giant, twice his size, far heavier. In the Verge of Wandering, he had endured Stave's blows with visible ease; but he could not withstand the Ironhand of the Swordmainnir.

She knocked him off the span, sent him tumbling headlong toward the voracity of Diassomer Mininderain and Emereau Vrai and uncounted numbers of other betrayed women.

In a different reality, one of them could have been Linden's mother. Or Joan.

Coldspray did not pause, not for the flicker of an instant. Finishing her spin, she sprang into a run. Behind her, Grueburn started forward again, pounding for speed.

Linden heard shrill alarm in the baying of the Demondim-spawn. Involuntarily she watched Esmer's plummet. She saw jaws stretch to bite him out of the air—

—saw him vanish before the teeth could close.

The Ironhand could not have believed that he would perish. He was descended from *Elohim*: she must have known that he would evade the bane. She was simply trying to create an absence that might allow Covenant or the Ardent to recover themselves.

But before she and Grueburn or Stave had taken two strides, a hand of theurgy flashed upward to grasp the Hazard. Irrefusable might closed around the slim stone and *pulled*.

For an instant, less than an instant, no time at all, Linden felt the span quiver and shriek. Then the whole crest of the bridge exploded into splinters.

Substantial reality seemed to disappear as though it had ceased to exist. The recoil of the bane's power pitched Coldspray, Grueburn, and Stave upward. When they came down, there was nothing under them.

Nothing except a rain of shattered granite—and She Who Must Not Be Named.

Coldspray, Jeremiah, and the *croyel*, Grueburn and Linden, Stave: together they fell like rubble.

Esmer had already reappeared at the foot of the bridge between Covenant and the Ardent.

Someone wailed. The *croyel*? Linden herself? The chasm was full of voices. She had looked into the heart of the bane: she knew that she was not going to die. Stave and Jeremiah would be slain instantly. The *croyel* would be torn apart. Linden's end would be worse.

In those screaming faces, all of them, she saw her fate, the outcome of her failed choices. The bane's victims had fallen to evil, not because they sought evil—some had not—but because they had made mistakes. Now their legacy was endless agony for every woman who could love as they had once loved.

They would *eat* Linden and Coldspray and Grueburn, and relish the taste.

Linden's soul was already carrion. She Who Must Not Be Named would savor her more than any Giant.

But faster than she plunged, a torrent of vitriol shot past her. Somehow the ur-viles had formed a wedge to concentrate their lore. Their ebon fluid struck downward.

When the acid hit, the bane released a roar that shook the cavern. The seethe of faces flinched. The hand of theurgy burst into ineffective mist.

At the same time, a frenetic skein of ribbands snatched at Linden and Grueburn; wrenched them back. The jolt cracked through Linden like the snap of a whip: she nearly dropped the Staff. More cloth caught Coldspray, Jeremiah, and the *croyel*: a score of brightly colored strips. Other bands yanked Stave away.

Taut as cables, the Ardent's raiment reeled his fallen charges upward.

Liquid power plunged into the tortured moil of faces. It erupted like thunder amid the screams.

A few dozen ur-viles could not hope to hurt She Who Must Not Be Named: they must have known that. But they distracted her.

And they were not alone.

A smaller blast of power crashed and volleyed among the stalactites. The Waynhim—! They were too few to equal the harsh strength of the ur-viles. And they had modified their lore to match their Weird; had taken it along different paths than those followed by their black kin. Still they hit hard—and the stalactites were fragile, made brittle by weight and age.

In an earsplitting crack and crash, titanic spires began falling like spikes into the faces of the bane.

Any mistake would have rent the Ardent's ribbands; crushed Linden and Jeremiah. But the Waynhim knew what they were doing. Their projectiles fell from the far side of the cavern.

The Ardent's efforts tested the limits of his strength. Linden rose with fatal slowness. Spots of darkness bloomed in her vision like detonations, echoing the yell of stone as stalactites broke. Grueburn hugged her tight: she could not breathe. But she did not notice the corded pressure of the Giant's arms. She had lost the light of her Staff; lost her health-sense. The bane was imprinted on her nerves. Through blackness and bits of distortion, she recognized nothing except shrieks. The lip of the precipice where the rest of her companions stood or crouched was still too far away. She would never reach it.

Then the Insequent had help. Bluntfist and Cabledarm released Bhapa and Pahni. Braced by their comrades, the two Swordmainnir grabbed at the Ardent's ribbands and hauled on them as if they were hawsers.

Thrashing in fury, She Who Must Not Be Named surged upward. Bluntfist, Cabledarm, and the Ardent heaved harder.

A moment later, other Giants were able to catch hold of Grueburn and Coldspray. Trusting Mahrtiir to hang on, Latebirth gripped the edges of Grueburn's cataphract and tugged her past the edge of the chasm. Onyx Stonemage held Liand with one arm while she helped the Ironhand. When the weight of the Giants was taken from him, the Ardent pulled Stave to safety.

In spite of his weakness, Liand summoned radiance from his *orcrest*. Its pure light pushed against the bane's savagery. With Earthpower, he supported the Swordmainnir and the Ardent.

The Insequent gasped as though he had borne Giants on his shoulders. A dangerous pallor sickened his face: his legs wobbled under him. Reflections of the bane's power made the sweat streaming on his cheeks look like cuts.

For a moment, Linden did not realize that she could breathe again. No doubt her ribs would hurt later: she could not feel them now. Black blossoms expanded across her sight. The roaring of She Who Must Not Be Named filled the world.

Esmer stood among the Giants, regarding them with disdain.

From somewhere nearby, Galt announced, "We need no gift of tongues to comprehend that the Demondim-spawn beseech flight. Already the Waynhim run to guide us. We must follow swiftly."

The Ironhand may have panted, "Aye." Linden was not sure. Serpents of nausea and dread writhed in her guts. As Grueburn struggled upright, the blots on Linden's vision grew until they covered everything, and the world was gone.

≈

For minutes or hours, Linden lived in a realm of death. She had seen too many agonized faces. They left her at the mercy of carrion-eaters. For her, the bane had become crawling things, venomous and noisome. They gnawed their way out of her flesh, reveling in rot: centipedes and spiders, long worms. She wanted to claw off her skin to be rid of them. But her nightmares had claimed her. She was dead: she was death. Responsible for slaughter—

Then she was roused by the jolting of Grueburn's strides, the stentorian rasp of the Swordmain's breathing. In terror, she returned to herself. Sensations of crawling and poison clung to her like muck sweat. Pincers and fangs bit into her under her clothes. She wanted fire; ached to scour herself with flame. But there were no spiders, no centipedes, no vile insects. She only felt them. Grueburn's stubborn struggle did not redeem what Linden had become.

Past Coldspray's bulk, and Cirrus Kindwind's, white flickers of Liand's Sunstone reached Linden. He and Stonemage were leading the company after the Waynhim. But they no longer ran. The tunnel leading away from the chasm and the Lost Deep had become a narrow split with a floor like strewn wreckage. The Giants still carried all of their human companions except the *Haruchai*; but they had to move with care. At intervals, protrusions of rock constricted the passage, forcing them to squeeze through sideways.

Linden had no health-sense and no power. Stave still carried Covenant's ring. She was being eaten alive: everyone she cared about was going to die. Devoured faces and centipedes were promises that would not be broken. And Esmer stayed close to her, ensuring her futility. His many wounds looked as septic as plague-spots.

She expected to sight the Ardent ahead, with Liand. But the Insequent was not there. Only the Humbled escorted Liand and Stonemage, Covenant and Kindwind, Jeremiah and the *croyel* and Coldspray.

Without percipience, Linden could not gauge Covenant's condition. She could not cleanse herself of corruption. But she had no reason to think that he had escaped the chaos of his memories: not while Esmer remained nearby.

Grueburn's broad chest and thick shoulders blocked Linden's view to the rear. But when the Swordmain turned to push past an obstruction, Linden scanned the figures behind her.

She saw them limned in fire and apprehension, dark shapes lurching ahead of the bane's rage. Apparently the constraints and twisting of the split did not hinder She Who Must Not Be Named. Despite Her terrible size and Her throng of identities, She seemed able to alter Her form as She wished. She was like spiders, roaches, beetles: there was no crack too small for Her to enter, no cave too immense for Her to fill. No mere physical barrier could restrict Her. The things that fed on carrion were venomous in every crevice and cranny. The width of the passage might compel Her to pick off Linden's companions one at a time; but it would not hamper the bane's seething energies.

In silhouette, Linden saw Stormpast Galesend carrying Anele, Cabledarm with Pahni, other Giants—presumably Bluntfist and Latebirth bearing Bhapa and Mahrtiir. As far as she could tell, none of the Swordmainnir had fallen. But her impressions were too indistinct for certainty. The jagged path of the crevice cast too many shadows. The Giants fleeing behind her resembled stilted menhirs, distorted and ungainly.

Of the Ardent—or the ur-viles—she saw no sign.

Then Grueburn turned ahead to move more quickly, picking her path over the refuse of ages, and Linden could not look back.

"The Ardent?" Hysteria scraped her voice raw. Uselessly she slapped at the crawling inside her shirt, her jeans. "Where is he? Have we lost him?"

Esmer would know, if Grueburn and Stave did not.

Without the Ardent's powers—

Cail's son did not answer. "The Insequent," panted Grueburn, "vowed to aid the ur-viles. How he thought to do so, I cannot conceive." He could not resist She Who Must Not Be Named with ribbands. "Nevertheless he remains behind us."

"Can you tell what he's doing?" Linden asked.

"I cannot. The bane fills my senses."

"He exceeds all expectation," stated Stave. *Orcrest* or his inborn wards against Kevin's Dirt preserved the former Master's percipience. "His fright is plain. Nonetheless he joins his knowledge to the efforts of the ur-viles. His apparel does not harm the bane. The ur-viles do not. Yet when it extends its force, their lore and his garment turn the theurgy aside. Together they slow the bane's advance."

Linden understood fright. She could not have done what the Ardent was doing. She was covered with gnawing and toxins; hungry ruin. Whenever she closed her eyes, she saw horror below her; watched hideous strength destroy the Hazard; felt her fall—

She had killed her own mother. She deserved whatever happened to her.

Staring wildly, she tried to focus her attention on the rough walls of the crevice. She wanted to believe that it would hold. That the world would hold. But she could not. Soon a monster that relished anguish and despair would consume the roots of the mountain. She slapped at her chewed skin and achieved nothing.

Beyond the fragments of Liand's light, the entombed darkness was absolute.

Immeasurable leagues of granite and schist were veined with obsidian and quartz and strange ores like the slow blood of Gravin Threndor. Long ago, she had believed that the Wightwarrens ran deep; that the cave of the EarthBlood was deep. But until now she had failed to grasp the true meaning of depth. Breathing should have been impossible. The air here must have been trapped for eons, too stagnant to sustain life. It was no wonder that Grueburn had to fight for breath.

Presumably Liand was refreshing the atmosphere with Earthpower. But he could not do enough. Moment by moment, suffocation crowded around Linden. The stone itself was reified asphyxia. Her lungs labored in her chest as if they were being crushed by panic and granite.

In Revelstone long days ago, Liand had taught her that she could draw Earthpower and Law from her Staff even when Kevin's Dirt had blinded her completely. At that time, however, Kastenessen's bitter brume had hung high above her; and she had been perhaps two hundred leagues from its source, protected by enduring barricades of gutrock. Now She Who Must Not Be Named was *close*— Frayed and terrified, Linden did not believe that she would ever be able to overcome the bane's dire magicks.

And without the benign fire of her Staff, she could not drive the sensations of insects from her nerves and skin. Before long, she would go mad.

She needed help, but no one could help her: not now. The progress of the Giants was too arduous to permit succor. And her fragmented glimpses of the way ahead suggested that the crevice was about to become impassable. It was beginning to cant to the side, narrowing and twisting as it followed a line of weakness through limestone and brittle shale. Beyond Liand's Sunstone, the split tilted at an angle that became sharper by sudden increments.

Linden trusted the Waynhim. She tried to trust them. But they appeared to be leading the company along a path which only they could follow. Perhaps she, the *Haruchai*, and the Ramen might contrive to creep after the smaller creatures when the crack leaned close to the horizontal. But the Swordmainnir would be trapped. And if Coldspray released the *croyel*—

"Ha!" Liand's call echoed down the split: a shout of relief. "The Waynhim have not misled us! Here is the way!"

As the crevice tilted farther, Rime Coldspray squatted abruptly, set her back against the lower wall. Clutching Jeremiah and the *croyel* with one arm, and holding the *krill* with the other, she used her legs to thrust herself headfirst along the split. The stone looked too rough to permit skidding in that fashion, but her cataphract served as a sled. She was able to keep moving.

Ahead of the Ironhand, Kindwind used one shoulder and her maimed arm to shove herself forward, still clasping Covenant. At a word from Grueburn, Linden turned so that she could grip the Swordmain's breastplate with both hands, hook her heels around

Grueburn's waist. The Staff she carried pressed between her chest and Grueburn's as the Giant braced her hands on the lower wall and scuttled along on all fours.

Every point at which Linden's body touched Grueburn was a torment of maggots.

Behind them, Galesend followed Grueburn's example. Anele's eyes glared in brief glints from the *orcrest* and the *krill*, but he appeared to understand Galesend's intent. The constriction of the split did not allow Linden to see past the old man's protector.

Then Liand's light was cut off as though he and Stonemage had fallen out of reach. A rush of failure filled Linden's lungs. Sickening swarms of creatures had burrowed too deeply into her: she feared that she would never breathe again.

Somehow she clung to Frostheart Grueburn.

"Here!" Kindwind shouted. "A clear passage! If the Ardent and the ur-viles endure, they will gain a more defensible path."

Through bites and squirming that had no tangible form, Linden seemed to catch a memory from Covenant, as if pieces of their past had leaked out of his chaotic recollections. When they had first come to the Land together—when they had been gaoled in Mithil Stonedown—Sunder had touched Covenant's forehead with the Graveler's Sunstone at Covenant's urging. By that action, Sunder had awakened Covenant's ring, triggering wild magic with *orcrest*.

Linden might be able to do something similar—if she could get close to Liand. Any hint of health-sense might rebuff her dismay; her accumulating collapse. Then she might be able to choose Earthpower and Law instead of carrion. She could use the flame of her Staff to scour her flesh clean.

If only she could breathe—

"As soon as you can," she gasped with her last air. "Take me to Liand. I need his *orcrest*."

Grueburn nodded. She was panting too hard to speak.

Kindwind and Covenant were gone. With her arms rigid around Jeremiah and the *croyel*, Rime Coldspray skidded farther. The monster gazed straight at Linden. Its grin showed its fangs.

Then Coldspray stopped. When she heaved herself and her burdens upright, she did not collide with the upper wall of the split. Instead she and they vanished into a break in the stone.

Half a dozen heartbeats later, Grueburn carried Linden there; and Linden snatched scraps of better air from the Sunstone. As Grueburn turned her back to the lower wall, Linden shifted to face upward. Past the Giants ahead of her, she caught a brief dazzle of purity.

Here a wider fault intersected the split. The new crevice was level at first: then it ascended steeply into the immured dark. Shards of *orcrest*-light showed the Waynhim scrambling at the slope. Their hands and feet dislodged clots of ancient dirt like scurrying beetles. Stonemage and Liand had already neared the foot of the climb. But behind them, behind Kindwind and Covenant, Coldspray had paused to rest. There she held her burdens with the *croyel*'s visage turned away from Linden. The Ironhand's grip on the *krill* did not waver.

She must have heard Linden's appeal. Linden would have to pass her in order to catch up with Liand.

He was too far away.

In that position, the dagger's argence shone straight into Linden's face. It shed stark streaks along the stone; found sudden gleams like inspirations on facets of mica and quartz; exposed the sullen sheen of moisture oozing downward.

The sensations of scurrying in Linden's clothes intensified. Scores of biting things sought tender flesh hidden from the light. She could not endure it; could not wait for Grueburn to reach the Stonedownor.

Halfway between Kindwind and Coldspray, Esmer stood watching as if he had no real interest in anything that transpired among Mount Thunder's roots.

"Hurry," Linden pleaded: a raw cough of suffocation.

Groaning for air, Grueburn thrust herself upright, strode toward the Ironhand.

Millennia ago, wild magic had destroyed the original Staff of Law; but Linden was too desperate to care. As soon as she could, she extended her own Staff. Frantically she jabbed one iron-shod heel into the heart of the gem's radiance.

For a terrible instant, she felt nothing. After all, why should she? The *krill* was not *orcrest*: the Staff was not white gold. And she had no health-sense. She could not focus her needs. She could only try to pray while imminent wails bubbled in the back of her throat.

Then a gentle surge of energy touched her hands, a palpable warmth—

Quickly she jerked back the Staff, hugged it to her chest; concentrated every supplication of her life on the runed black wood.

Hindered by proximity to the bane's magicks, flickers of new life leaked into her aggrieved nerves.

She clung to that vitality, stoked it. Demanded. Cajoled.

By small increments, it grew stronger. A flame as evanescent as a will-o'-the-wisp slid along the shaft. Too frail to be sustained, it evaporated. But another took its place, and another—and the third spread. Briefly it traced the runes as if the wood had been etched with oil. Then it lit other fires. A tumble of flames leapt out as if they sprang from Linden's chest.

Light as kindly and sapid as sunshine cascaded into the crevice. Soon she stood in the core of a pillar of fire; of Earthpower and life.

On all sides, Kevin's Dirt restricted her strength. Her power was a pale mockery of the forces which she had summoned on other occasions. Nevertheless it fed her spirit; implied possible transformations. It would suffice.

It had to.

Febrile with haste, she pulled flame tightly around her; clad herself in conflagration. Then she began scrubbing every distressed inch of her body with cleanliness.

The gnawing and pinching, the crawling, the quick slither of hysteria: they fell away one by one, incinerated or quashed. When she had burned them all to ash, however, she found that nothing had changed. The conviction that she had become carrion, that she bred only death—her true despair—lay too deep for any anodyne that she knew how to provide for herself. A sickness of the soul afflicted her; and the devouring faces of She Who Must Not Be Named drew closer by the moment.

Nevertheless she could breathe easily again. She could see. The revulsion of centipedes and spiders had been banished. Her companions sucked fresh air into their lungs. Coldspray offered her a grin of gratitude.

Stave's flat mien betrayed no sign of doubt. But Esmer regarded Linden as if her ailment were his.

Climbing higher, the Waynhim had ascended past a bulge in the fissure's wall. Below them on the slope, Stonemage waited with Liand, beckoning urgently. In the illumination of his Sunstone and her Staff, Linden saw that Kindwind and the Humbled had also stopped. They must have felt Coldspray and Grueburn halt.

Linden studied Covenant long enough to confirm that he remained lost in the world's past. Then she turned to gauge her other companions.

Anele's fright cried out to her nerves. Galesend's alarm mounted as her comrades gathered at her back. Nevertheless Linden ignored them; forced herself to cast her senses farther.

Beyond the Giants, she tasted the rank vitriol of the ur-viles in rabid bursts. Among them, the feverish gibber of the Ardent's incantations added his support against the baleful gnash of teeth and pain—

She Who Must Not Be Named was too close.

Fresh panic stung Linden. "Oh, God." She had taken too much time for herself. "We have to *go*."

"Aye," growled the Ironhand. She needed no urging. Bearing Jeremiah and his doom and the eldritch threat of the *krill*, she headed for the slope. In spite of her long weariness and her exigent burdens, she managed a brief sprint.

Grueburn followed immediately, hurrying over the damp grit and scree of the crevice floor. At her back came Galesend and the rest of the Swordmainnir.

As Grueburn heaved her bulk up the loose surface of the ascent, Linden felt the Ardent squeeze out of the canted split. She perceived him clearly now. His wheeze of effort scraped along her nerves as he lifted himself into the air on strips of fabric that clung to the crude walls. Rising, he made way for the ur-viles below him.

Then Linden smelled burning—

—from the Insequent. His raiment had lost many of its colors. Scores of his ribbands had been charred black, or scorched to brittle threads. She tasted his sweating frenzy like iron on her tongue; his sharp fear and fraying resolve; his desperation. Yet he did not flee ahead of the ur-viles. Instead he braced himself high above them, guarding their retreat.

As they straggled out of the split, the creatures seemed ragged and unsteady; routed. The narrowing of the passage had forced them to disperse their wedge: they had been unable to combine their theurgies. As a result, some of them had been horribly damaged. Linden sensed creatures with cleft hands or feet, missing limbs. She felt a few ur-viles collapse on the damp dirt and fail to rise. Through the bane's ferocity, she smelled the acrid pulse of unnatural blood.

They were the last of their kind. One by one, they were being decimated.

Floundering, they formed a new wedge in the crevice. She could not guess how many of them had been lost. Ten? More? Nevertheless they prepared to continue fighting. After a long moment, their loremaster appeared out of the split, wielding its ruddy jerrid. As the largest and strongest of the creatures reclaimed its position at the point of the wedge, the power of the whole formation snapped into focus.

A turmoil of screaming faces thrust into the crevice. It filled the fault from wall to wall.

The ur-viles responded with a spray of fluid force, bitter and corrosive. Their magicks were too puny to injure the bane; but they made the faces pause—

While She Who Must Not Be Named summoned Her many selves in pursuit, the creatures backed away.

The bane must have been certain of Her victims. She did not deign to hasten. The Demondim-spawn were able to put a little distance between themselves and their chosen foe.

Distracted by alarm, Linden's concentration slipped. Her fire faltered.

At once, she felt renewed squirming inside her boots, along the waist of her jeans, across her breasts. Nightmare spiders and centipedes as avid as rapine resumed their interrupted feast.

She heard herself whimpering: a thin frail sound like the cry of a dying child. She tried to stop, tried to close her throat against a surge of hysteria as sour as bile, and could not. She was an unburied corpse ripe with rot, helpless to refuse any dire appetite.

Abruptly a different scream shocked the air: a howl of such extremity that it seemed to draw blood from the Ardent's throat. In a display of strength that staggered Linden, his ribbands wrenched huge chunks of rock out of the walls.

No, he did more than that. He did not merely tear boulders loose. Somehow he pulled the walls themselves toward each other, heaved on them until they shattered.

In an instant, an avalanche destroyed the entire opening of the crevice. The sheer mass of the rockfall shook the standing walls. Moist grit and debris slid under the feet of the Giants, poured them downward. The very gutrock groaned like an echo of the Ardent's scream.

Tons of granite and malachite, schist and travertine, crashed onto the bane. Rubble buried every raving face.

In panic, Linden forgot the Ardent and the ur-viles; forgot the bane and insects and gnawing; forgot her failing grasp on Earthpower. Without transition, she became an eruption of flame. If the slope slipped too far, it might bury the Giants. Certainly it would make the ascent impossible. Unless she caught it with fire and Law, forced it to hold—

The earth slide should have been too heavy for her; but she ignored its fatal weight, its impending rush. Hardly aware of what she did, she anchored the slope until the convulsion of the avalanche passed.

Mahrtiir tried to shout Linden's name, but air thick with new dust clogged his throat. Gasping, Latebirth called upward, "We are unharmed! As are the ur-viles!" A tattered breath. "I cannot discern the Ardent!"

More strongly, Stonemage responded, "We also are unharmed!"

The bane was not gone. She had not perished or suffered. She had only been thwarted. Already Her puissance reached through the rockfall; yowled against Linden's abraded nerves. In moments, She would force open a passage—

Crawling things in the privacy of Linden's flesh brought her back to herself. Oh, God, they were everywhere! They did not exist. Nevertheless they relished her dead flesh as if she had perished long ago. Dozens of devoured faces raged to consume her, uncounted women in limitless torment.

Somehow she held on until the slope settled. Then she withdrew her power. Weakly she called out for the Ardent.

The company could not escape these depths without him. The ur-viles and Waynhim obviously knew the way. But the Lost Deep was too far below the lowest reaches of the Wightwarrens. None of Linden's companions could climb so far, or follow the paths of the Demondim-spawn. They needed the Ardent's ability to translate them elsewhere.

In the distance, an exhausted voice replied, "I am spent. Naught remains."

"Are you capable of movement?" shouted the Ironhand. "If we must, we will contrive to retrieve you!"

"Nay." The Ardent's response was a sigh of utter weariness. "Your strength is required for flight. I will follow as I can."

"We will not forsake you!" Coldspray countered.

"Nor do I wish to be forsaken." He sounded too frail to go on living. "You must flee.

Therefore I must follow. I cannot confront She Who Must Not Be Named again." A moment later, he added, "If the lady will but cleanse the air—"

Choking down revulsion for her own body—her own existence—Linden swept dust aside; burned away stagnation. Then she wrapped theurgy around herself until she was sheathed in cerements of flame. Whimpering again, she tried to root roaches and centipedes out of her revolted flesh.

That was as much as she could do.

Ahead of and behind her, Giants flung themselves at the climb, fighting for purchase on the weakened slope. Raggedly Grueburn staggered upward. Above the Swordmainnir, the Waynhim chittered encouragements or reprimands. At the rear of the company, the ur-viles hurried to ascend.

Lights tried to fill the space: Liand's Sunstone in the lead, Loric's *krill*, Linden's personal fire, the dour glow of the loremaster's jerrid. But they were too small to cast back the dark. Midnight and vast stone crowded around them; threatened to smother them. Within the crevice, the slope appeared to climb indefinitely, as if here dirt and damp and stale air clawed for an unattainable sky.

Linden clung to her concern for the Ardent until she felt hints of his presence, brittle as desiccated twigs, trailing after the Giants and the ur-viles. He was indeed spent, too tired for terror. Nonetheless he still supported himself on his ribbands, bracing them against knuckles and knags in the old rock. Some vestige of fear or determination impelled him onward.

When she was sure of him, Linden closed her attention tightly around herself and tried not to moan aloud. She needed all of her resources to fend off abhorrence and crawling. Behind her, the bane burst through the rockfall: a rupture that stained the air; made the walls tremble. Ahead the slope seemed to strive toward inconceivable heights. But she did not want to know such things. Wrapped in flame, and crooning to herself so that she would not groan or mewl, she struggled against the sensations of biting and pinching; the seductions of despair.

She could not defeat them. At the bottom of her heart writhed the conviction that she deserved this. The bane was right. She had killed her mother and failed her son. There was nothing left for her to do except wait to be eaten.

∽∞∾

B y slow degrees, however, the rich benison of Earthpower permeated her. Implied denunciations receded from her nerves. The core of her distress remained unrelieved; incurable. But using her Staff granted her a degree of superficial remission.

Tentatively she began to look outward again.

Now she heard Grueburn's exhausted breathing rattle in her chest; felt Grueburn's muscles quiver. Ahead of them, the Ironhand ascended, steady as granite, holding Jeremiah and the *croyel* and the *krill*; but her steps had slowed to a grim plod. Between Rime Coldspray and Onyx Stonemage—between the *krill*'s gem and Liand's *orcrest*—Cirrus Kindwind floundered like a woman who had never fully recovered from her maiming. She seemed to batter her way along, lurching from wall to wall to thrust herself and Covenant higher.

The surface underfoot might not have supported the Giants at all if the shale and scree and dirt had not been damp, clotted by moisture oozing incessantly down the crevice.

Yet Esmer strode easily at Kindwind's back. The slope seemed to require nothing from him. Stave kept pace with Grueburn as if he were impervious to fatigue. Around Kindwind and Covenant, the Humbled moved like men who could not be daunted.

Behind Linden, the other Swordmainnir followed in succession: Stormpast Galesend cradling Anele, Cabledarm holding Pahni, Halewhole Bluntfist with Bhapa, Latebirth with Mahrtiir. Then came the ur-viles in a dark surge, ravaged and scrambling. Above them, the Ardent rose between the walls. Too weary to walk, he wedged his way upward with his ribbands.

In the distance, She Who Must Not Be Named raved and glowered. The mad roil of faces followed without haste, as slow as a rising tide, and as inexorable. The evil that had consumed Diassomer Mininderain and Emereau Vrai and countless others was certain of its prey.

The bane's unhurried stalking seemed to imply that the company was trapped; that the Waynhim were leading Linden and her companions into a cul-de-sac. Linden wanted to believe that the grey creatures knew what they were doing. *They are not without cunning.* But she did not know how to reassure herself.

She had been passive too long; had allowed herself to feel too badly beaten. Now she needed to become something more than just another victim. *Attempts must be made, even when there can be no hope.* Transformations were possible. It was time.

Risking maggots and worms, Linden reached out with Earthpower; spread her fire up and down the crevice until it touched all of the Giants. As fully as possible under the bane's bale, and without endangering the ur-viles, she shared the Land's essential bounty with women who struggled to surpass themselves so that she and Covenant and Jeremiah and the Earth might not perish.

The *croyel*'s abhorrence and Jeremiah's vacancy impeded her, but she did not let them stop her. When vile things resumed their avid feast inside her clothes, she strove to ignore them, at least for a few moments. They were not *real*. They were only a disturbance in her mind, or in her soul: a spiritual disease. Gritting her teeth, she refused to heed them.

Briefly—too briefly—she bathed each of the Swordmainnir in light and flame, washing some of the fatigue from their muscles, cleaning some of the gall from their sore hearts. While she was still able to resist the noxious biting of centipedes and spiders, she extended a small touch of renewal toward the Ardent: a gift which he accepted with fearful eagerness.

Then she heard herself whimpering again, and her self-command crumbled. Frantically she turned her fire against beetles and worms and pinchers which did not exist.

Bit by bit, she was being driven closer to Joan's madness. Her Staff was losing its effectiveness—or she was losing her ability to wield it. Transformations were impossible. Soon she would be crept upon and stung beyond endurance, pushed past the point of sanity. Eventually she might begin to crave the bane's cruel embrace.

But not yet. God, please. Not yet.

Then she heard Liand's voice echo down the fault. "Here the ascent ends! The walls open! Beyond them our passage appears less effortful!"

A rustle of tightened resolve scattered along the crevice. "And not before time," gasped Cabledarm or Latebirth. "Stone and Sea! Am I not a Giant? Aye, and also a fool. I had credited myself with greater hardiness."

"Fool indeed," someone else responded hoarsely. "Have you numbered the days during which we have run for Longwrath's life, or for our own? Truly, it appears that we have persisted in this exertion for an age of the Earth."

Hang on, Linden told herself as if she were trying to encourage a cowed child. Hang on.

Somewhere above her, the light of Liand's Sunstone vanished.

"It is a cavern"—the Ardent's voice was a frayed groan—"immense, damp, and cluttered. I discern naught else."

"Aye," Kindwind answered, struggling for breath. "Immense. Damp. Cluttered. A pool, long stagnant." She may have said more; but her voice was cut off as she left the crevice.

Linden writhed against the intrusion of spiders, the intimacy of centipedes. She Who Must Not Be Named rose like floodwaters.

"Linden Giantfriend is beset!" Frostheart Grueburn announced between fervid gulps of air. "I descry no ill, yet she suffers."

"Mayhap," suggested Stave stolidly, "it is an effect of the bane. I also perceive no bodily hurt, though her distress is plain. It is my thought that the strengths which have enabled her to exceed us time and again are also a weakness. Her discernment exposes her to the bane's evil."

Linden tightened her grip on herself. Involuntarily she tried to twist away from heinous things that scurried and nipped. Stave was mistaken. She had never exceeded her companions. She was weak because she was *wrong*. She belonged among the bane's excruciated fodder. Each spider and insect and worm was an accusation. *Good cannot be accomplished by evil means.* She felt like carrion because she had committed Desecrations.

Ahead of her, Coldspray lurched out of the crevice, taking the *krill*'s argence with her. A moment later, Grueburn reached the opening of the walls; stumbled through it.

A sudden impression of imponderable space spread out around Linden. Stagnation seemed to clog her way as though Grueburn had carried her into a quagmire. And at every distance, water dripped and splashed and ran, an immeasurable multitude of droplets and trickling so extensive that it sounded like rain within the mountain. In Grueburn's arms, Linden entered a drizzle devoid of boundaries. Simple reflex caused her to fling her fire upward.

The cavern was indeed immense. To Linden's abused sight, it looked large enough to contain all of Revelstone, although surely it was not. The company's lights reached the ceiling dimly, but failed to find the far wall: she had no way to gauge the scale of the cavity. However, her immediate vicinity resembled a shallow basin tipped slightly to one side, so that the lowest point of the curve lay somewhat to her left. There eons of dripping water had gathered into a pool so old and unrelieved that it no longer held any possibility of life. Across the millennia, the water had gone beyond mere brackishness to a toxic mineral concentration.

The pool seemed small because the cavern was so broad. In some other setting, it might have been considered a lake.

From its center outward, it trembled to the pulse of the bane's approaching hunger. Ripples fled in circles, sloshing timorously onto the travertine sides of the basin.

The water fell from the tips of stalactites the size of Revelstone's watchtower. And below each pending taper of stone rose a stalagmite. Cluttered—In some places, the stalagmites had met and melded with their sources, forming misshapen columns with constricted waists. In others, the calcified residue of ages appeared to strain for union, yearning upward drop by incessant drop, and infinitely patient. And everywhere around the monolithic deposits, water fell like light rain from lesser flaws in the porous ceiling. Within the reach of the company's illuminations, every wet surface had been cut or sculpted into scallops and whorls delicate as filigree, and keen as knives.

Grueburn stuck out her tongue to catch a few falling drops, then spat in disgust. To the Giants around her, she shook her head sourly.

Rain splashed onto Linden's forehead; ran into her eyes and stung. Blinking rapidly, she searched the cavern for some sign of egress or hope.

To her left, the basin narrowed. Beyond the pool there, at least a Giant's stone's throw distant, a concave wall of granite too obdurate to be eroded by mere moisture formed the lower end of the tremendous cavity. But she could not descry the cavern's limit opposite her. As far as she knew, it reached forever into darkness. To her right, however, the side of the basin rose slowly, and continued to rise in gradual increments, until it was swallowed by midnight.

In the crevice behind the company, the bane still poured upward without haste, confident of Her craved prey. Heartbeats agitated the surface of the pool more and more. Nevertheless the Giants paused to gasp for breath, straining to imagine endurance which they no longer possessed. At the same time, the noxious crawling on Linden's skin intensified. She needed every scrap and fragment of her remaining will to refuse the torment of small creatures that did not exist. Hundreds of them, or thousands, crept everywhere to savor her illimitable faults.

Under Esmer's scornful gaze, the Waynhim had halted off to Linden's right, apparently waiting for the Ardent and the ur-viles. But now all of the Swordmainnir stood on the slope of the basin, fighting to breathe and looking urgently around them. Soon three or four score ur-viles arrived in a black torrent. Limping badly, the Ardent tottered toward Coldspray and Grueburn. Strips of his raiment dragged after him like beaten things, and his head hung down as if he had lost the will to meet anyone's gaze.

At once, the grey Demondim-spawn ran at the slope, beckoning and barking for Linden's company to follow. Without delay, the ur-viles joined the Waynhim. Led by their loremaster, the black creatures snarled demands like curses. Esmer trailed after them as though as he assumed that everyone else would do the same.

But the Giants did not move. Perhaps they could not.

Among them, the Humbled and Stave stood, patient and implacable. Perhaps Linden's crumbling defenses troubled them. Or perhaps not. If they debated decisions that they might need to make for themselves, they did so in silence.

"*Now* what must we do?" asked the Ironhand thinly. "The bane's evil is itself a mountain. We have beheld no more than hints of its true extent. It was for *this*"—she gestured around her—"that it has pursued us at such leisure. Here it will expand to consume us.

"We will run again, if run we must. But we cannot run far, or swiftly. And this cavern appears to have no end. Surely She Who Must Not Be Named will pounce upon us at Her pleasure."

Her voice fell flat in the cavern, echoless and defeated.

From Latebirth's arms, Manethrall Mahrtiir rasped, "It is said that the Ramen have an instinct for open sky. That is sooth. But our gifts will not serve us here. This stone is too great. It thwarts our hearts. If we would flee farther, we must trust to the Waynhim.

"Their fidelity is certain. And Esmer *mere*-son has averred that they are cunning. I will believe that they have guided us hither—aye, and that they now urge us onward—to some worthy purpose. I cannot think otherwise."

Moisture trickled like insects down the sides of Linden's neck. She had as much reason as anyone—more—to put her faith in the Waynhim. But she was too distracted to speak.

"Attend!" commanded Branl abruptly. "The bane is not our only peril."

He and the other *Haruchai* had turned. They were gazing with something akin to alarm at the lower end of the cavern, beyond the pool.

Through Jeremiah, the *croyel* sneered, "You aren't paying attention, Mom. The real fun's about to start."

With the *krill*, Rime Coldspray drew a thin line of pain across the creature's throat. Through her teeth, she hissed, "While I live, beast, I will have your silence."

Jeremiah made a small mewing sound like an echo of the *croyel*'s fright. Then his jaw dropped, and his mouth hung open.

Dumbly Linden peered down the side of the basin. Water dripped onto her head, trickled hideously through her hair. A light rain spattered the features of her companions. When she contrived to focus her attention on the curving granite, she saw that Branl was right.

In at least half a dozen places, *wrongness* had already begun to suppurate in the stubborn stone. With appalling celerity, a thick reek like the stench of gangrene bruited its way through the stagnant air.

She recognized what was happening as if beetles and maggots had whispered the truth in her ears.

"Mane and Tail!" cried Bhapa.

"Linden!" Liand called fearfully. His grasp on the *orcrest* wavered. "*Linden.*"

Linden ignored them. Sicknesses that crawled and stung demanded her attention. One way or another, she would be to blame for the deaths of her friends, all of them.

"Ringthane!" Mahrtiir barked once. Then he shouted at the Giants, "Set us upon our feet! Coldspray Ironhand, hear me! We must do what we can to conserve the last of your strength. We are useless here. Only your weapons and valor may hope to ward us. Release your burdens! Free us to run unaided! I do not fear that we will outpace you."

Attempts must be made—

The clamor of the Waynhim and ur-viles complicated the sound of drizzling water, the implied shrieks of chewed granite. But even the tension of the Demondim-spawn could not contradict the mounting labor of the bane's advance.

For a moment, Coldspray faltered as if her courage had failed. Then she clenched her teeth, squared her shoulders.

"Swordmainnir, the Manethrall counsels wisely. I will continue to bear the boy and the *croyel*, but you must entrust Linden Giantfriend and Covenant Timewarden to the *Haruchai*. The Manethrall and his Cords will watch over the Stonedownor and the old man. You must be able to wield your swords."

Promptly her comrades obeyed. As Grueburn and the other Giants put down their charges, Coldspray turned to the Ardent. "Do you require—?"

He shook his head. "I will not hamper you. If the powers of the Insequent do not suffice to preserve me, doubtless I will perish. Yet while I may, I will strive for life." He attempted a wan smile. "Mayhap a surfeit of terror will amend my deficit of hardiness."

Stave grasped Linden's right arm. Liand held her left. The Humbled accepted Covenant from Cirrus Kindwind. Pahni flung an imploring look at Liand, then took Anele's hand and drew the old man to join Bhapa with Mahrtiir. The older Cord hooked elbows with the blinded Manethrall to guide him.

Centipedes had crawled into Linden's ears. She heard them gibbering. She clung to her Staff as if it might keep her sane. But Law and Earthpower had no will of their own. They could accomplish nothing that she did not ask of them; and the rain leeched away her ability to ask. In spite of Caerroil Wildwood's runes, the wood's bright flame began to gutter and die.

"Go!" the Ironhand ordered harshly. "I will not lag." She may have thought that Linden would understand her. "My comrades will follow as swiftly as our straits permit."

Lit by *orcrest* and the *krill*'s gem, and by unsteady gusts of Staff-fire, the company fled after the Demondim-spawn.

Galt, Clyme, and Branl rushed Covenant into motion. Almost immediately, Bhapa and Mahrtiir caught up with them, as did Pahni and Anele. The old man was not loath to run. In spite of his imperfect comprehension, he was intimately familiar with flight. On any form of rock, he had no need for vision.

Tugged along by Stave and Liand, Linden trotted so that she would not fall. But she could not turn her head away from the end of the cavern; the sick and rotting stone; the rising violence that disturbed the pool. The stink of disease accumulated around her until it filled her lungs with every breath.

Suddenly putrefaction and magma exploded outward, shedding a spray of granite shards. In the eaten gaps, *skurj* appeared: first five or six, then ten; fifteen. Kraken-jaws gaping hellishly, they slithered into the cavern. Their many rows of teeth, their rending scimitars, blazed with the ferocity of lava. Implications of disease howled among the clutter of columns. Briefly the creatures paused, apparently searching for the scent of their prey. Then, fluid as serpents, they squirmed in pursuit.

"Did I not forewarn you?" asked Esmer bitterly.

They were fast: God, they were *fast*. Linden had forgotten—

Ahead of the monsters, the crevice burst open in a blast of incandescent hunger. Some brute instinct caused the *skurj* to shy away as She Who Must Not Be Named tore Her way into the cavern.

A mass of terrible energies with dozens or hundreds of faces surged forward. The bane's savagery shattered stalactites and stalagmites, pelting the surface of the pool to chaos, bludgeoning the *skurj* with blows which they did not appear to feel. Dripping water hissed instantly into steam as it struck the hides of the beasts. But no rain could touch She Who Must Not Be Named.

Through the confusion of her affliction and floundering, Linden received the impression that the bane and the *skurj* paid no heed to each other. In their dissimilar fashions, they were ruled by hungers that defied distraction. After their initial flinch, the *skurj* squirmed swiftly after their prey, twisting past plinths and fallen stone undeterred by the bane's greater might and malice. And when the bane quickened Her advance, expanding as She moved, She did so simply to satisfy Her feral craving.

Led upward by Waynhim and ur-viles, the companions ran as well as they could. The Giants managed a shambling plod that almost matched the strides of the Ramen and Anele, the best pace that the *Haruchai* and Liand could demand from Covenant and Linden. Jagged spires threw shadows that jumped and flared in the garish radiance of fangs and malevolence, the shining of the *krill* and the Sunstone, Linden's guttering flames. Everywhere water dripped delicate streaks of reflection. Stalagmites loomed and were passed while evils yowled in Linden's ears. She wanted to stop breathing the sickened air, yearned to smother her infested flesh in conflagration, and could not.

Struggling, the company ran and ran, to no avail. The bane and the *skurj* gained ground slowly, a few appalling strides at a time; but the outcome was inevitable. The cavern and the ascent seemed endless—and the Swordmainnir were already exhausted. Linden herself was too weary to run without support. Liand had not had enough time to recover from his wounds. Eventually even the *Haruchai* would weaken.

Maggots fed on Linden's eyes. Spiders filled her ears. Centipedes crawled between her legs while beetles enjoyed her breasts. She did not—she could not—notice that the Demondim-spawn were pulling ahead; or that they led the company closer to the near wall of the cavern. She did not hear Mahrtiir's ragged shout, or Rime Coldspray's gasped answer. Her grasp on Earthpower was failing; and she was aware of nothing except agonies, real and unreal, until Liand shook her frantically, crying, "Linden! The Waynhim! The ur-viles!"

Through a haze of distress and gangrene and hate, she made a dying effort to peer ahead.

Somewhere beyond the Ramen, the creatures had found a ledge in the wall of the cavern. From high above and behind the company, a shelf angled down to meet the floor. The Waynhim and ur-viles had already begun to scamper upward. To Linden, the ledge looked dangerously narrow, but it must have been wider than it appeared. When the creatures had ascended to three or four times the height of a Giant, they stopped. There the Waynhim were able to gather in a tight cluster. The ur-viles had room to form a fighting wedge.

They gestured like deranged things at the company. The tumult of their barking matched the bane's fury, the ravening of the *skurj*.

The Ramen did not hesitate. With Anele, they reached the ledge and climbed. A moment later, the Humbled impelled Covenant to follow. Limping heavily, the Ardent went after them.

At the foot of the ledge, Esmer paused to wait for Linden, Stave, and Liand. The rampage of fires behind the company echoed like madness in his eyes.

Linden understood nothing. The ledge ran back in the direction of the bane and the *skurj*. Its elevation would be a trivial obstacle to Kastenessen's monsters—and no obstacle at all to She Who Must Not Be Named. Nevertheless Stave and Liand man-handled her grimly toward Esmer. When he moved to join the rest of the company, they hurried at his back.

Now she could see the bane and the *skurj*. She could not look away. Trailing clouds of steam, the creatures flowed like molten stone among the pillars. Expanding, the bane had grown large enough to scatter stalagmites, break off stalactites. She seemed to roll as She advanced, a world of pain presenting new faces and teeth and screams at every moment.

Her raw force made Her appear closer than She was; closer than the monsters. Clinging to mere shreds of sanity, Linden strained to gauge the true distance.

The bane and the *skurj* were still at least a long stone's throw away. But the bane approached more slowly, savoring the helplessness of Her prey.

All of the Giants would have time to ascend the ledge, reach the place where the Demondim-spawn had halted. They would be able to anticipate and dread the moment when they would be torn apart.

Linden thought that she would rather fling herself into the jaws of the *skurj*. Their blazing fangs would spare her every other hurt. She did not want to participate in the bane's immortal pain.

Coldspray would protect Jeremiah as long as she could. Soon, however, they would both be slain.

Surely the *croyel* would die as well? Even if the bane had no taste for such food, the *skurj* were incapable of thought or scruples: they would eat anything.

No. Linden gripped the Staff and her waning mind until her knuckles burned. No, she was wrong. Esmer was still here. Capable of more treachery. If Kastenessen com-manded it, he could snatch the *croyel* and Jeremiah away whenever he chose.

Then Jeremiah would at least survive. And perhaps one of the Earth's other powers would take pity on him before the end.

That bleak possibility was not enough. Linden needed more.

Her frangible concentration was fixed on the bane and the *skurj*. She hardly noticed that she was no longer moving. Stave and Liand had brought her to the clustered

Waynhim; but her friends and the creatures and her own immobility lay outside the bounds of her awareness. The remnants of her heart were full of Jeremiah, and she saw nothing except the bane and the *skurj*; felt nothing except imminent death and corruption.

Her companions might have time to say goodbye to each other before they were slaughtered.

Liand was shouting in her ear, but she did not hear him until Stave lifted *vitrim* to her lips and tilted her head for her so that she would drink.

The dank liquid filled her mouth, forced her to swallow. Then it ran down her throat: a tonic sting insignificant in the face of She Who Must Not Be Named and Kastenessen's monsters, but suffused with vitality nonetheless, and unaccountably numinous. Reflexively she gulped until she emptied the iron cup; and as she did so, carrion-eaters seemed to scurry out of her eyes and ears, skittering down her neck into the comparative sanctuary of her clothes. At the same time, better fire bloomed from the Staff. Jolted by given energy, she became suddenly conscious of the people and creatures around her.

Rushing, the Waynhim distributed *vitrim* to her friends: to the Giants first, and to Liand; then to the Ramen and Anele and the Ardent. Grueburn held iron, tiny in her huge hands, to Coldspray's lips. While Esmer muttered darkly as if he were reinforcing his power, the grey Demondim-spawn gave a cup to the Humbled and watched as Branl held Covenant's head so that Galt could pour *vitrim* into his mouth.

The Waynhim were exhausting themselves: Linden could see that now. Nonetheless they persisted in their service. Although the draughts were little, the Swordmainnir grew visibly stronger. Fresh energy lifted the Ardent's head, straightened his sagging shoulders. A few of his ribbands flicked out, breaking off their charred ends. Even Covenant seemed to gain focus, as if the outlines of his presence were being etched more sharply. But he did not emerge from his memories.

Together the ur-viles howled in consternation or rage. As one, they pointed at the ceiling of the cavern. Their loremaster used its jerrid or scepter to indicate a precise spot of dampness among the stalactites.

Galvanized by *vitrim*, Linden was finally able to estimate her own condition. Percipience informed her that the strength which she had received was not enough. It restored only a small portion of her resources—and it would not last long. The proximity of the bane sucked at her ability to wield Earthpower. She might manage one final blast of fire. But her poor vehemence would not harm She Who Must Not Be Named—and would have no impact at all on the *skurj*.

Soon those evils would be close enough to attack.

Still the ur-viles chattered and yelled, demanding—

—demanding something that Linden could not identify.

"*Linden!*" Liand shouted at her. "You must *act!* No other power will suffice! I cannot comprehend the ur-viles!"

His Sunstone had become meaningless. Mere swords and muscle had no value. The Ironhand might conceivably strike one effective blow with Loric's *krill*. Then she would be lost—and the *croyel* would escape with Jeremiah.

Now or never. Esmer had deprived the Giants of their ability to grasp what the ur-viles wanted.

Already Linden felt *vitrim* turning to ash in her veins.

"God damn it, Esmer." She could not spare the strength to raise her voice. "You've done more than enough harm. The least you can do is translate."

Cail's son studied her with shame like crimson spume in his eyes. Disdain and anguish buffeted each other across his visage. His wounds wept unassuaged blood.

Renewed nausea twisted through Linden's guts; but she did not look away. With her ruined gaze, she commanded Esmer to consider the cost of his betrayals.

A spasm of revulsion knotted his features. In disgust, he announced harshly, "The ur-viles desire you to recognize that the waters falling here must have a source. Doubt-less you"—his tone said, Even you—"are aware that the Soulsease pours the greater portion of the Upper Land's streams and rivers into the depths of Gravin Threndor. Later those same torrents emerge, besmirched, as the Defiles Course. But have you never contemplated the path of that vast weight of water during its millennia within the bowels of the mountain? The ur-viles assure you that the Soulsease plunges deep among the Wightwarrens, and still deeper, until it has passed beyond the knowledge of all but the Viles and their makings. There it gathers in lakes and chasms, filling utter darkness until it rises at last to its egress on the Lower Land."

Esmer glanced upward. "The ur-viles proclaim that they have discerned a point of weakness in the high stone of this tomb."

Then he clamped his mouth shut, biting down hard on his own misery.

The ur-viles gibbered and gesticulated like incarnations of mania. Below them, She Who Must Not Be Named reared higher, extending Her maleficence as if She dreamed of feeding until She filled the cavern. Some of the *skurj* approached directly. Others arced around the company's position, perhaps to close off any possible retreat, perhaps to ascend the ledge themselves.

"Linden!" cried Liand. "Water! *Water!*"

She hardly heard him. Her gaze followed the line of the loremaster's iron jerrid toward the ceiling. In the radiance of fangs and ferocity, she seemed to see the exact place that the jerrid indicated; see it as if the loremaster had marked it for her by sheer force of will.

The last of the Demondim-spawn had sacrificed themselves for her repeatedly; extravagantly. Nevertheless they wanted to live.

As she did. As long as Jeremiah needed help, and Covenant remained to redeem the Land.

One blast: that was all she had left. Just one. Then she would be finished, for good or ill.

Make it count.

Her parents would not have approved. They had chosen death. But for a moment longer, she refused their legacy. Spiders and worms could not cause more torment than they had already inflicted.

Saving her energies for flame, she whispered the Seven Words as she flung Earth-power toward the ceiling.

"*Melenkurion abatha.*"

Tenuously balanced on the brink of herself, she aimed fire at the damp patch of stone which the ur-viles indicated.

"*Duroc minas mill.*"

Every remaining shred of her love and need and fear, she committed to the written wood of the Staff until they formed a blaze of theurgy as brutal as a battering-ram.

"*Harad khabaal.*"

Centipedes and horror hampered her. The bane's nearness drained her. The example of her parents promised futility; abject surrender. Defying them, she struck—

—and the ceiling held.

But she was not alone. A heartbeat behind her blast, a great gout of vitriol rose from the wedge and its loremaster. Strange magicks as corrosive as acid, and sour as self-loathing, smashed against the rock where her power burned.

Smashed and detonated.

Together the concussion of dire liquid and hot flame tore a cascade of stone from the ceiling.

From the breach, water trickled as though Linden and the ur-viles had partially unclogged a rainspout.

A rumble as throaty and unfathomable as the bane's livid beat resounded among the spires. Tremors ran through the rock, shook the ledge. Clots of damp debris fell, loosened by a subtle convulsion among the mountain's roots. The entire cavern groaned like a wounded titan.

Still some distance away, tortured faces wailed at Linden. Her father had killed himself in front of her. Her mother had begged to be slain. The excruciation of beetles and maggots intensified.

"Ware and watch!" shouted the Ironhand. "This perch may fail!"

She Who Must Not Be Named screamed from a dozen throats. The *skurj* paused as though they were capable of surprise.

An instant later, the damaged ceiling ruptured.

A tremendous fist of water flung great chunks of gutrock downward. From the breach, an immured sea began to fall in a staggering crash like all of the Land's waterfalls joined into one. Thunder filled the air like the ravage of worlds. An avalanche of forgotten waters slammed down onto the *skurj*; pounded against the hideous bulk of the bane.

The tumult drew weight from other caverns above it. Scalding steam erupted from the impact of waters on Kastenessen's monsters; but instantly those bursts were swept away by the torrential plunge. The bane tried to lurch aside, and failed. The plummet of water bore Her down, dragged Her under.

Groaning in granite agony, Gravin Threndor emptied its deep guts as though a firmament of water had been torn open.

Coldspray roared warnings which no one could hear. Other Giants yelled soundlessly, as if they had been stricken dumb. Jeremiah appeared to howl, uttering the *croyel*'s inaudible dismay.

Spray acrid with minerals drenched the company. It bit into Linden's sight. She could not blink fast enough to clear her eyes. Dropping the Staff, she scrubbed at her face with both hands; slapped her neck and chest and legs.

Before the mountain's tremors shrugged the Staff out of reach, Liand stooped to catch it.

Abruptly the ledge shook. It began to sheer away.

Esmer stopped it. The force which he had used on other occasions to raise spouts like geysers from the ground, he exerted now to stabilize the stone. A shudder ran along the steep shelf; but the ledge held.

Water hammered into the cavern, poured like a tsunami down the slow slope. Already it had immersed the bane and the *skurj*. Lurid fires and violence lit its mounting depths as the monsters fought to survive; as the bane strove for purchase among the inundated stalagmites. Shivering feverishly, Linden feared that the *skurj* would survive. Buried in floods, their fangs flamed as if they chewed minerals from the water to feed their furnace-hearts. Fighting for life, they tumbled down the cavern.

Whatever happened to them, Linden could not imagine that a power as enduring and virulent as She Who Must Not Be Named would simply drown. Nevertheless she wiped her eyes, and slapped herself, and prayed—

Betimes some wonder is wrought to redeem us.

Even if the bane failed to gather Herself and return, Linden and all of her companions would soon perish. The vast rush of water smashed against the lower end of the cavern. Then it boiled and frothed back onto itself. And as it accumulated, it rose. Scores or hundreds of centuries of the Land's springs and rainfall would fill the space until every gasp of air had been forced out.

In the distance, fires still burned under the flood. Crimson streaks stained the water: the *skurj* or the bane, Linden could not tell which.

As the new lake mounted, however, the thunder changed. Water pounding onto itself rather than on stone softened the edges of the roar. Dimly Linden heard the Ironhand's voice.

"The *skurj* perish! They *perish*, although the bane does not! But these waters have found the descent to the Lost Deep! They rise more slowly now!"

Coldspray added something about time and Esmer that Linden did not understand. The Ardent appeared to argue with other Insequent who were beyond hearing. Both Liand and Stave shouted pleas or warnings at Linden. But inflicted imaginary beetles had crept into her ears again. She could not distinguish individual words from the adumbration of ancient torrents.

If the rate of the flood's accumulation had indeed slowed, that small reprieve was insignificant. It made no difference.

Through the bite of bitter spray, Linden thought that she saw a few submerged fires fail and die. But she was sure of nothing. Crawling things fed on her; took her life in small nips and stings. Thunder and failure became lassitude. Her parents spoke more loudly than any of her friends. In the bane's voices, they assured her of despair.

Like them, she deserved her end. She had earned it with woe and wrongs and weakness.

No one had the right to make Jeremiah suffer. No one except Thomas Covenant could hope to save the Land. But there was nothing left that she could do for them.

She was not even surprised when the whole surface of the surging flood burst into flame.

Mere water could not harm She Who Must Not Be Named. The ancient poisons which fouled the torrents appeared to nourish Her. Now She had found Her own answer to the inrush of ages.

Below the precarious ledge, boiling currents and chaos were lashed with conflagration as though they had been transmogrified into oil. Waters crashing against stalagmites and walls flung spouts of fire at the wracked ceiling.

Voices cried for Linden, but they conveyed nothing. Weary and tormented beyond bearing, she surrendered at last to the paralysis from which she had fled throughout her life: the helplessness which had permitted Covenant's murder ten years ago, and had left her at the mercy of *turiya* Raver: the ineluctable doom of her parents.

Carrion.

As the bane arose from the waters halfway between the company and the end of the cavern, Linden fell to her knees. Deep inside her, something fundamental succumbed.

12.

She Who Must Not

 Like a ghost, Thomas Covenant occupied discrete realities simultaneously, and had no effect on any of them.

In one, he saw everything that happened around him. He recognized every event from the moment when Esmer touched his forehead until he stood near Linden's collapse above a rabid lake of fire, gazing at She Who Must Not Be Named. He felt everything, feared everything. But he had no volition, no power to act. He could do nothing to help his companions. He could only care and grieve and groan and dread. In that dimension, the part of him that made choices was out of reach.

It wandered elsewhere, among his memories, where nothing was required of him because everything had already happened. Perhaps he needed to recall those people and places and deeds: perhaps he did not. But they did not need him. He was merely a spectator, as oneiric as a figment, amid the fragments and rubble of things past; shattered stretches of time. And because his memories were broken, he did not know how to find his way through them. They were out of sequence; could not lead him back to himself.

Esmer had cast him into a realm of contradictory knowledge and bewilderment where every impulse of his heart was thwarted. Instead of responding to the company's plight, or to the killing deluge which Linden had unleashed in the cavern, or to her final failure in the face of the bane's emergence, Covenant remembered.

Earlier, while the company fled from the Lost Deep, he had observed ur-viles reconsidering their Weird millennia ago. The Demondim had not been fools: they had not made the ur-viles to be fools. Even the Waynhim—the accidents or miscalculations of breeding—had been discerning and lorewise, capable of recondite insights. Their black cousins had been far too intelligent for the contemptuous use which Lord Foul had made of them.

Their Weird as they had first understood it expressed their self-loathing: better to die promoting the end of all things than to live flawed and hateful in a world meant for beauty. Perishing by the thousands in the Despiser's wars, however, the ur-viles had recognized that the logic of their servitude could reach only one conclusion. And in battle at the gates of Lord's Keep, the Waynhim had demonstrated by valor and commitment that other choices were possible. Thus the Waynhim had prodded the ur-viles to question themselves.

When the Despiser had been defeated, therefore, the black Demondim-spawn had withdrawn to the Lost Deep to search their lore and their oldest legacies for a reply to the challenge posed by the Waynhim. Among the ineffable achievements of the Viles, the ur-viles had probed the history of their makers, and of their makers' makers, until they reached an era before the Viles had ventured across the Hazard and been swayed by the Ravers.

In the Lost Deep, miracles of old lore had reminded the ur-viles that they had sprung from creatures not ruled by disgust for their own natures. There the ur-viles found that their first progenitors had conceived truths which spanned Time: truths which in turn enabled the ur-viles to estimate distant outcomes. They saw clearly where their service to the Despiser would lead them in the end—and what would be required to counter the syllogisms of Lord Foul's scorn.

They hesitated. For centuries, they contemplated what they had come from, and what they were, and what they might wish to be. And eventually they reached new conclusions. As a result, they began the assiduous studies and exhaustive labors by which they created Vain.

Vain and manacles.

But while the Swordmainnir carrying Linden and her human companions followed the Waynhim, Covenant fell deeper. Other memories took the place of the ur-viles.

In a different fissure, he regarded an image which did not exist: an image which had never existed, except as a symbol or metaphor for a more profound and inarticulate truth. The image of a young woman. A woman fresh with loveliness and self-discovery. A woman brimming with new passion, ready to give and receive the kind of adoration which would define Her days. In his eyes, She was the reason that men and women had discovered love; the cause of every whole and holy desire.

Studying Her, he saw Her betrayed.

Hers was the tale which had given rise to that of Diassomer Mininderain, seduced and misled; abandoned to darkness. During the creation of the Earth, She had been cast down. By the sealing of the Arch of Time, She had been imprisoned. She was Mininderain and Emereau Vrai and the Auriference and scores or hundreds of other women. Indirectly She was Lena and Joan. At its core, Hers was the tale of every love which had ever been used or abused and then discarded.

The tale of She Who Must Not Be Named.

Heart-wrung by Her plight, Covenant watched Her arise amid water and flames, a lake of conflagration; and he understood that behind Her appalling malice and hunger lay a quintessential wail of lamentation, forlorn and deathless: the devouring grief of a heart that knew no other response to absolute treachery.

Perhaps deliberately—perhaps cruelly—Esmer had sent Covenant to this place among his riven memories. They might have been precious to him, had he been able to act on them. But they were the past: he could not change them.

Remembering love and loss, he, too, was lost.

Nevertheless he knew everything that happened around him. He saw and heard and felt: he cared so much that the straits of his companions rent him. Above all, uselessly, he understood Linden's protracted ordeal. He regarded the effect of finding her son, and of being unable to free the boy from the *croyel*. He saw the hopelessness of her decision to flee the Lost Deep. When she had found the strength to treat his hands, his pride in her had been as poignant as yearning. During her fall from the Hazard, the futility of his desire to leap after her had filled him with anguish. With the ineffable discernment of a spectre, he had witnessed the consequences of her plunge toward agony. The despair that had crawled and fed on her failing sanity, he had experienced as though it should have been his.

Still she had continued to struggle and strive. When the thews of her resolve, of her essential self, had parted at last, his most acute reaction had been relief for her. Later, if she lived, she would think the worst of herself. For the moment, however, she had found a small escape from pain.

Yet she was not likely to survive. She and Covenant and everyone with them were about to die.

He saw no great harm in his own demise. Linden esteemed him too highly. But the others— For reasons that he could no longer recall, Linden and Jeremiah were essential to the Land. Dire futures hinged on Liand and Anele. Manethrall Mahrtiir and his Cords were needed desperately. There was no hope without Stave and the Masters and the Giants. And Covenant did not discount the Ardent, who alone knew how to rescue the company. Nor did he dismiss the Demondim-spawn, who still yearned to relieve their instinctive self-disgust.

Everyone who had come so far in Linden's name, or in the Land's, had a part to play. Even Esmer might find within himself the will to become his father's son rather than Kastenessen's minion. Even Covenant—

He would have given much to believe the same of Roger. But Roger was his mother's son, not his father's; and Joan had chosen the path of her doom long ago. Like Elena, she could no longer escape what she had made of herself, except through extinction.

Covenant had been removed from the Arch of Time. His responsibility for it had been taken from him. But Joan and Roger remained. They were his burdens to bear.

Therefore he, too, needed to live.

She Who Must Not Be Named had no intention of letting any of Her victims survive. Doubtless Esmer would avoid Her hungers. The *croyel* would certainly try to do so, taking Jeremiah with it. And the ur-viles and Waynhim might be able to evade destruction. But everyone else—

Through Esmer's treachery, they also had become Covenant's burdens. And Covenant loved Linden. In different ways, he loved all of her friends and companions: even the Masters, who had misled themselves to the brink of the Land's annihilation. There was no one else who could save them.

Yet he remained lost.

As he examined his circumstances, however, he began to imagine that he was not altogether impotent. Almost by definition, betrayals had flaws. Esmer's were no different.

The Humbled had caused Covenant to swallow *vitrim*; and that musty liquid was an unnatural approximation of hurtloam. It provided a partial mimicry of hurtloam's sovereign healing.

When he had been offered hurtloam in Andelain, he had refused it. He had insisted on numbness and leprosy. *It doesn't just make me who I am. It makes me who I can be.*

Now the dour taste and energy of *vitrim* galvanized his desire to be himself: a leper and pariah who knew better than to heed Despite. Because it was an artificial elixir, it could not bring new life to his nerves. But it made him stronger—

And there was another flaw as well.

Esmer's effect on him bore no resemblance to the stasis which the *Elohim* had once used against him. The *Elohim* had severed him from thought and concern; from any kind of reaction. Esmer had merely knocked him off balance, tripping him into the maze of broken time. He could still think and care and strive. In that sense, he was only lost, not helpless. And anything that could be lost could also be found.

If he climbed high enough, or used his memories in the right way, he might conceivably rediscover his physical present by his own efforts.

If Esmer did not cast him down again.

If.

He had to try. The bane was coming closer.

After uncounted ages within the Arch, Covenant did not have enough time.

She Who Must Not Be Named lifted Herself like a pyre from the burning waters. Even at a distance, She appeared to tower over the company. Her fury shook the ledge in spite of Esmer's efforts to steady it. For no clear reason except that they were Giants and courageous, all of the Swordmainnir except Rime Coldspray stood at the edge of falling and flames with their weapons ready. They must have known that no mortal blade would cut their foe; yet they confronted Her simply because they refused to accept defeat.

In that respect, they could have been Saltheart Foamfollower's daughters.

Behind them, the Ironhand still supported Jeremiah with one arm, holding the *krill* against the *croyel's* throat. Despite the bane's ferocity, Jeremiah's muddy eyes gazed at nothing. Spittle slid from one corner of his mouth. But the *croyel* had lost its feral grin. Squirming its talons deeper into the boy's flesh, the creature seemed to brace itself for one last ploy, some act of power or cunning that might save its life.

Without hesitation, Stave scooped Linden into his arms and carried her to the wall, leaving the Giants room to swing their swords. Glimpsed past lank, untended strands of hair, the slackness of her mouth and the unfocused glaze of her eyes told Covenant that she had become as unreactive as her son. She had endured too much— He could only pray in silence that something within her still lived and loved, and could be reached.

Clyme and Branl had already dragged him back from the edge of the shelf. Galt stood in front of him like Bannor or Brinn: a display of resolve as brave as that of the Giants, and as wasted. At the same time, the Cords had taken Liand and the Staff, their Manethrall, and Anele as far from the rim of the ledge as they could. There Anele squatted against the wall as if he sought to curl his emaciated frame into the stone. Whispering aimlessly, he slapped at his old cheeks.

Nearby the Ardent wrapped every shred of his marred raiment around himself as though he hoped irrationally to ward his plump flesh with cloth. Panic glistened among the reflected fires in his eyes.

Higher up on the ledge, the ur-viles and Waynhim barked feverishly, strident with imprecations or despair. Their baying and yells appeared to be directed at Esmer.

Clad in wounds and tatters, Esmer ignored the Demondim-spawn. Apparently his efforts to scorn the people whom he had betrayed had failed. Dismay twisted his visage as he regarded the bane.

Relishing its immanent feast, She Who Must Not Be Named glowered higher and howled like a call for vengeance. Soon She would loom over the company.

Abruptly the *croyel* croaked in Jeremiah's voice, "Esmer. Get us out of here. *Esmer.*"

Coldspray tightened her grip threateningly; but the monster was too frightened to heed the pain of the *krill.*

"It wasn't supposed to come to this," the *croyel* gasped. "She wasn't supposed to be able to stop the *skurj.* You have to save us."

Only Jeremiah's loose features and silted gaze confirmed that the boy was not pleading for himself.

"You won't regret it. Kastenessen will forgive you. He'll heal you. If he doesn't, we'll *make* him. But you have to *get us out of here.*"

There it was: the path out of himself that Covenant needed. If Linden had been able to hear the *croyel,* its use of Jeremiah would have clawed her soul. In her present state, she was spared that immediate hurt. But Covenant felt it on her behalf. Her pain was his.

It reminded him—

Hit me. Hit me again.

In Andelain, his first taste of corporeal pain had brought him back to himself, albeit temporarily. It had confirmed the bond between his body and his spirit.

Now the thought of what Linden would suffer when she regained consciousness was enough. *Vitrim* had given him strength. And he was a rightful white gold wielder. He stood in the indirect presence of wild magic that Esmer would not or could not block.

Defying Esmer's influence, Thomas Covenant stepped out of the Land's past and became present.

Instant consternation lashed in Esmer's eyes. He shrank back as if he dreaded what the Unbeliever had become.

Ignoring Cail's son, Covenant turned away. His hands and feet were still numb; dead. But they were not useless. Thanks to Linden, he could flex his fingers. When the time came—if he lived that long—he would be able to grasp the *krill*.

But he did not need Loric's dagger now. It would not daunt She Who Must Not Be Named. He required other suasions.

How much time had passed? The bane had not reached the ledge yet, but She had the power to strike whenever She wished.

Had She felt the change in him? Did She mean to destroy him first? Did She see in him an image of Her first betrayer?

Perhaps. That was possible. He did not doubt that the stains of what he had done to Lena—and, in a different fashion, to Elena—still clung to him. She Who Must Not Be Named may well have discerned his resemblance to the Despiser.

But if She wanted terror from him, retribution for his crimes, she was going to be disappointed.

The Humbled met Covenant's return with widened eyes, raised eyebrows. They did not resist as he pulled his arms free of Branl and Clyme, stepped past Galt.

In two strides, he reached Stave and Linden.

"Attend, Swordmainnir," called Mahrtiir softly. "The first Ringthane stands among us once more."

His voice should have been too small to pierce the bane's fiery clamor. Yet the Giants heard him. Kindwind, Grueburn, and Latebirth turned sharply to peer at Covenant. Their comrades took a step back from the rim of the ledge.

Linden lay limp in Stave's arms. She saw nothing, heard nothing. In her snagged and punctured shirt, her stigmatized jeans, she looked as forlorn as a waif; too weak to continue breathing. Just for an instant, Covenant remembered that he had seen her like this before. When he had rescued her from the Clave, she had been as unreactive;

as beaten. *Turiya* Herem had touched her, and she had fled into herself to escape the implications of the Raver's malice.

But she had recovered. After a while, she had come back to Covenant. He had to believe that she would so do again.

Lord Foul had proclaimed that her fate was written in water. Perhaps the Despiser had spoken more truly than he knew.

Cursing the ease with which he was distracted, Covenant refused other memories, less immediate prayers. He had no time. Grimly he forced himself to look at Stave rather than Linden.

He did not need words. He saw swift comprehension in the gleam of Stave's eye. For the sake of their companions, however, so that he would not be misunderstood, Covenant forced himself to say, "I want my ring. I'll give it back. If any of us live through this."

Solemn as an icon, Stave nodded. Cradling Linden, he opened one of his hands; offered Covenant's wedding band and its chain to the Unbeliever.

Unaccustomed to his recent amputation, Covenant clutched at the chain. Awkwardly he hooked it with two fingers to ensure that he did not drop it. Then he lifted it over his head so that the ring hung against his chest.

Muttering again, "I'll give it back," he turned to confront She Who Must Not Be Named.

She heaved closer. Heat beat against his face, parched his eyes: the fury of the burning lake and the bane's passion. If he had not been drenched, his clothes might have caught fire. Her mouths gaped and gnashed, brandishing their teeth. Their shrill roar overcame the thunderous plunge of waters. The bottomless thud of Her heartbeat made his bones tremble.

At the end of the cavern, the flames began to die as the flood extinguished the last of the *skurj*. But the bane fed the conflagration around Her huge bulk. Fire lapped at the jutting tips of stalagmites, the fanged ends of stalactites, the stubborn travertine and granite and limestone of the walls. Covenant's jeans and T-shirt steamed until he seemed wreathed in mortality; but the heat hurt only the exposed skin of his face and arms.

While She Who Must Not Be Named readied Herself to attack, he raised his voice against Her.

"Listen to me!" he shouted with all the authority at his command. "You can kill us whenever you want! But first you should listen to me!"

"You've forgotten what you are!"

Looming high, the bane paused as though he had taken Her by surprise.

In indignation or yearning, Esmer hissed, "You are *demented*. I know not how you have won free. I care not. But do you dream that you are able to *reason* with She Who Must Not Be Named?"

Covenant kept his back to Esmer. He had no attention to spare. No attention—and no time.

"You've forgotten *who* you are!" he called up at the eternal being. "But that's not all. You've forgotten who trapped you here! It wasn't the Creator. He loved you then. He loves you now. And it sure as hell wasn't *us*. Or any of your other victims. It was the Despiser. A-Jeroth of the Seven Hells.

"You've forgotten that *he* made you like this. You've forgotten that he tricked you. He's your worst enemy, but you serve him because you've *forgotten*!"

Faced with Covenant's audacity, the bane writhed as though his words were blows. Tortured visages in wild succession bared their teeth and shrieked and vanished, rolled under or absorbed.

In a voice so immense that the cavern itself seemed to shout, She answered, "You speak to me! *You speak to me!* I will devour you—*I will devour you all*—and gain no ease for my hunger! If I fed upon *worlds*, I would not be sated!"

Gritting his teeth, Covenant refused to admit that he was appalled. "You aren't listening!" he countered as if he were fearless. "You should. You should at least *notice* that the Despiser has made you his lackey."

Fires danced and gibbered. "Do you think to resist me?" With every countenance, the bane sneered. "Then do so. I revel in the struggles of my viands."

Covenant shook his head. His voice echoed her vehemence. "I said, *listen to me.* I'm not going to fight you. Of *course* I'm not going to fight you." Even he might not be able to overcome Esmer's ability to suppress wild magic. And if he succeeded, the consequences might be disastrous. A battle on that scale would wreak vast havoc. It might breach the Arch of Time. But he had other hopes for his ring. "I just want to show you something."

"*Show?*" retorted his antagonist. "You wish to *show*? If I have forgotten what or who I am, I have forgotten the import of any mere object or display."

"Not this, you haven't." With the back of his halfhand, Covenant lifted his ring. "You'll recognize it as soon as you *look*." His passion for Linden and the Land and life skirled among the flames: it seemed to resound from the pronged vault of the cavern. "I'm not talking about white gold or wild magic. I'm talking about what it *is*. A *wedding* band. It's a symbol of everything you've ever wanted. Everything you've ever lost.

"Look!" he urged her. "*Look* at it. You know what it is. It's every love and every promise that were never broken. It's fidelity and passion that *endure*. It's what you thought you were getting when the Despiser whispered in your ear."

Searching for words that She might heed, he insisted, "Trying to destroy the Earth isn't his worst crime. No. The worst was *lying* to you. Lying to *you*. No mortal atrocity can ever be that bad because mortals die. *Your* suffering never ends."

His asseveration—or the implications of his ring—appeared to shock the bane. Rising higher, She reared back from the ledge. The anguish written on Her many miens became more pronounced. Women who could have been Lena or Joan whimpered and keened. Their voice sank to frayed whispers.

"Little man. Human. Fool. You know nothing of woe."

"That's true," Covenant admitted, although his experience of loss was as old as the Arch. "Our lives are too short. Nothing that dies can understand eternal pain. But we're willing to try. And we intend to put a stop to it.

"Let us go. We'll set you free."

Some promises were too terrible to be kept. This was one. Nonetheless he prayed that he was telling the truth. Beyond question, the destruction of the Arch of Time would release She Who Must Not Be Named. But he doubted that the ruin of creation would relieve Her plight. She needed something more than mere devastation. Her torment would continue until the Despiser's evil had been answered. Until She learned to love again, and forgive.

"Free?" She cried bitterly. "You will set me *free*? I cannot *hear* you, little man. You are too small to appease my pain."

Scrambling for arguments, Covenant replied, "Then give me a chance." If his wedding ring did not sway her, he had other ideas. "Maybe I'll find something you *can* hear."

While hunger and flames seemed to hesitate, he turned his back.

"Esmer."

Esmer flinched. "Timewarden?"

Mute with incomprehension, the Giants stared. Awe or dread shone in Liand's eyes. Ignoring Esmer, the *Haruchai* studied Covenant impassively. Perhaps they thought that he knew what he was doing—

Like Linden and everyone else, they deserved more from him.

Facing Esmer, Covenant said, "She's forgotten who she is." Deliberately he took risks that terrified him. "Why don't you tell her? Why don't you tell her her true name?"

Cail's son was descended from *Elohim*: he shared many of the Earth's secrets.

"No!" Esmer's chagrin shook the ledge. Storms whipped alarm like foam from his eyes. "I cannot. I *will* not! Do you not grasp that her forgetting is necessary? It is imperative!

"Recall the convulsion which caused the rift of Landsdrop. It arose from Her imprisonment. Her betrayal and wrath and weeping as She was cast down sundered this region of the Earth to its foundations. If Her name is restored to Her—if She is enabled to remember—the result will be a cataclysm of such rage that it shatters the whole of Gravin Threndor.

"She will remain. I will depart. But you and all who accompany you will perish. Doubtless your son also will perish. Yet Kastenessen and a-Jeroth and the Ravers will endure. The *skurj* and the Sandgorgons and your former mate will endure. And the shattering of Mount Thunder will not slow the Worm of the World's End."

"Tell me!" the bane howled eagerly. "I care nothing for you! *Tell me who I am!*"

Through his teeth, Esmer finished, "Do not ask such folly of me. I will not comply."

"Then I will devour you!" Roaring. "I will gnash your bones and suck their marrow! I will make morsels of your flesh to feed my eternal lament! I will—!"

Covenant interrupted Her as if he had passed beyond death into utter fearlessness. "No, you won't."

Fire and rage tried to override him. "*Also* I will ensure that consciousness lingers within you, so that you may share the excruciation of these others whom I have consumed!"

Face after face wailed like the damned, and found no relief.

Covenant swung back to confront the bane again. "No," he repeated sternly, "you *won't.*" He had no reason to think that She would listen to him. Nevertheless he spoke with the strength of Time, as though all the ages of the Arch made him irrefusable. "I'm not done. There may be other answers. I just need a little time. We aren't going anywhere. You know that. All you have to do is give me a little time."

Feigning an assurance that he could not feel, he turned his back on Her again.

She Who Must Not Be Named may have been astonished at his impudence. Or perhaps he had struck a spark of yearning for Her true self into the fierce tinder of Her heart. Women yowled threats from many throats, but did not advance to kill him.

Slowly he looked around at his companions, meeting each gaze in turn. Then he said with an ache of sadness, "I'm sorry about this. I hate doing it. But it's my last shot. If it doesn't work, I'm out of ideas."

That was not true. A strange certainty gripped him: an assurance which he could not have justified, even to himself. He had another gambit in reserve. But he wanted the bane to believe him. He wanted Esmer to believe him. So that they would wait.

Abruptly Jeremiah squirmed against Coldspray's grasp; attempted to twist free. "You bastard!" The fear and fury of the *croyel* burned in his gaze. "You sonofabitch! If you aren't going to at least fight, just kill me! Mom would *beg* you, if she knew what you're doing. If she wasn't so pitiful. If she ever figured out the real reason you surrendered to Foul all those centuries ago is, you're *afraid* to put up a struggle."

Muttering to herself, Rime Coldspray shifted her grip to prick the creature's throat with the point of Loric's *krill*.

Quick fright glared in the *croyel*'s eyes. The creature let Jeremiah subside.

Manethrall Mahrtiir cleared his throat. "Pay no heed to the *croyel*, Covenant Time-warden." In spite of his blindness—or perhaps because of it—he appeared to have shrugged off the massive intimidation of Mount Thunder's gutrock. "We comprehend your rejection of combat. I cannot speak for the Masters. Doubtless the Swordmainnir will speak for themselves. But we who have been the Ringthane's first companions and friends in this time are content to abide the outcome of your efforts."

"As ever," growled the Ironhand, "the Manethrall is well-spoken. It is a cause for wonder that one so combative of heart is possessed of such courtesy."

"I appreciate that," Covenant replied through his teeth. "But right now, I don't need you. I need Anele."

Pahni stared in alarm, clearly frightened for the old man. As if to himself, Liand asked, "Anele?"

"He's part Earthpower," Covenant explained. "It's inherent in him," the legacy of his transubstantiated parents. "He can do things even Berek and the other High Lords couldn't."

Fearing that at any moment the bane's hunger might overcome Her desire to hear Her true name, Covenant faced the old man.

The Humbled watched him as if they were trying to gauge the likelihood of Desecration. If Her name is restored to Her—Esmer regarded Covenant with bafflement and nausea. —the result will be a cataclysm—

"Anele," Covenant said more harshly than he intended. "You're on rock. You're so full of its memories, you hardly know what's going on. But I think there are still some things you understand.

"I want you to ask for Liand's *orcrest*. I need to talk to you sane."

Anele's moonstone eyes glistened. They flicked toward Covenant and away as if Covenant were as fearsome as She Who Must Not Be Named. His head jerked roughly from side to side. His wrinkled hands seemed to pluck pleading from the air.

"I hear." His voice quavered. "I do not comprehend. This stone knows too much of evil. It remembers horror. Its supplication fills my ears."

Abruptly he slapped himself hard, first with his right hand, then with his left, as though he sought to silence the confusion of his thoughts. Then he extended one scrawny arm, rigid as a demand, toward Liand.

Liand did not hesitate: he gave Anele the Sunstone.

As Anele's fingers closed on it, he jerked back his head and screamed as if a dagger had been driven through his chest. Behind Covenant, the bane's raw countenances paused in their wailing as though they had been startled by the sheer desolation of Anele's cry. As though they recognized it—

An instant later, a rush of theurgy from the *orcrest* swept away the old man's illucidity.

Between one heartbeat and the next, his manner cleared as if he had become suddenly deaf to the myriad hoary murmurings of granite and limestone and madness.

When he lowered his head, his blind gaze held Covenant's. Slowly he straightened his back and shoulders. As he did so, he appeared to acquire the dignity of a Lord.

Through a tumult of fire and ferocity and plunging waters, he said, "Timewarden." Alarm and severity blurred together in his tone. Spray dripped from his straggling beard. "I implore you. Do not."

"I'm sorry, Anele." Mutely Covenant cursed himself. "You've been through too much already. And you aren't done. But I'm running out of choices here. We need your help."

Clutching the *orcrest* like a talisman, Anele protested, "It is not for this that I am made mad."

"I know." Intuitively Covenant understood, although he could not have said how or why. Those memories were gone. He remembered only that Anele held some portion of the Earth's fate in his gnarled grasp—and that his time had not yet come. "But if we don't survive now, you'll never get the chance to finish what you started.

"I think you can talk to the Dead. I think Sunder and Hollian can hear you." Covenant paused to swallow pity. "And I think it's possible they know how to help us."

For the moment, that was all he wanted: a way to distract the bane from slaughter. Somehow.

Dismay twisted Anele's visage. "My father and my mother speak only in my dreams." He sounded forlorn, rent by prolonged sorrow and abasement; by a lifetime of disappointment in himself. "There I am mute. Yet in Andelain I did not dream, and still they counseled me. Here I am not mute. I will ask. If I am not answered, I can do nothing."

Covenant wanted to say, Neither can I. But he kept his dread to himself. Aloud he told Anele, "They'll answer. They love you. They love the Land. Hell, they even love me. And they haven't forgotten what Linden means to them."

To all of us.

Anele nodded vaguely: he was no longer listening. His eyelids fluttered. Then they closed. He began to mutter prayers or invocations too frail to be heard over the cacophony of floods and devoured anguish.

"Timewarden?" Liand's query was an accusation. "To our sight, the recovery of his mind by *orcrest* causes acute suffering. If the Dead do not bring us to destruction by naming the bane, what can they offer to justify his hurt?"

"Peace, Stonedownor." Wrapped in his ribbands, the Ardent was barely audible. "It is a worthy attempt. I deem that the Dead possess no fatal knowledge of this evil."

Covenant held up his truncated halfhand. Wait. He did not glance away from Anele. Just wait.

Above him, She Who Must Not Be Named held Herself in abeyance, anticipating revelation.

Then Bhapa gave a wordless shout. Covenant spun away from Anele as the spectres of Sunder and Hollian took shape on either side of the Despiser's first victim.

Dim against the burning of the waters, the fiery vehemence of the bane, and the writhen stalactites, the Dead were limned in silvery evanescence: the Graveler and the eh-Brand. Amid the forces rampant in the cavern, they looked incomplete, as if they lacked the strength to manifest themselves fully. Nonetheless they were like their son, rife with Earthpower. Though they were little more than silhouettes, they withstood the flames, endured the thunder of torrents.

Briefly they gazed at Anele with aching regret. Before he or Covenant could speak, they turned to each other and nodded as if they had reached an agreement.

We have no value here. Covenant heard them in his mind. Perhaps everyone heard them. We serve only to confirm Her woe and wrath. Yet your need is plain. We will insist upon other aid.

As suddenly as they had come, they vanished—

Wait! Covenant shouted voicelessly, not to Sunder and Hollian, but to his companions.

Frantically Anele thrust the *orcrest* at Liand. As soon as Liand accepted it, the old man crumpled to the lurching stone.

An instant later, Stormpast Galesend swept him into her arms.

—and High Lord Elena appeared directly in front of She Who Must Not Be Named.

When Elena saw the bane, she began to shriek like every damned woman who had ever been consumed.

As if in surprise or recognition, the bane replied with Her own cries. Elena was brighter than Sunder and Hollian: a cynosure of pain wracked by the harm that she had done, and by the use which Lord Foul had made of her. Together the bane's howling and hers scaled higher, louder. They were a firestorm of screams. The tortures of the doomed scourged the air; lashed Covenant's hearing. Liand and the Ramen covered their ears. Several of the Giants flinched. Blood spread from the corners of Esmer's eyes.

Covenant understood. Oh, he *understood*— Sunder and Hollian had made the right choice. Elena had loved, and been betrayed, and suffered. And she was Covenant's daughter, excruciated by self-abhorrence for millennia: the bane's perfect food. The perfect bait. The bane could not ignore such ripe anguish.

But when She Who Must Not Be Named opened Her maws, Elena fled toward the end of the cavern. Covenant's daughter was a Law-Breaker; but she had once been a High Lord. Long ago, she had been consumed by evil—and had been freed by her father. Her horror of being devoured was greater than the punishments which she had exacted from herself. Frantically, as if she remembered being her father's daughter, she tried to escape.

Ravening, the bane thrashed in pursuit; flung out long arms of theurgy to snatch Elena from the air. Somehow she eluded them.

And while She Who Must Not Be Named gave chase, Covenant forced himself to turn away. With his partial fists clenched, and his heart pounding out rage and rue, he faced Cail's son.

Through the chaos of screams, he snarled, "I guess you finally picked a side."

His last gambit.

Blood stained Esmer's cheeks. "I have not." His tone echoed Elena's dismay. "I serve the Wildwielder as I serve Kastenessen."

"Then you've got it wrong. This is all treachery. Sure, you've told us a few things that might have been useful, if we weren't as good as dead. But under the circumstances, they hardly count."

Desperation and shrieks accumulated in the cavern. Wails broke stalactites from the ceiling, sent turbulence across the rising flood. The Swordmainnir retreated to form a tight cluster around their companions. Some of them watched Elena's flight. Others searched Covenant as though he had appalled them.

"I do as I must." Like Anele, Esmer seemed to plead for mercy. "You cannot save me. Earlier I averred my wish for death. That course is no longer open to you."

"I know," Covenant retorted. "But there's a way out." Elena's cries rent his heart. "A way to serve both sides of who you are. Aid and betrayal at the same time."

Esmer shook his head, scattering red droplets. "I cannot comprehend why you have not been redeemed. It is madness! I have granted those who wish to serve you ample opportunity. *That* is my aid to the Wildwielder. Yet I am spurned."

Covenant had no idea what Esmer meant. But he could not afford to pursue the question. Tendrils of power had already grasped the Dead High Lord. The bane's mouths gaped to rend Elena's spectre.

Linden had refused her the gift which Berek, Damelon, and Loric had given Kevin. Now she was being sacrificed—

Covenant had no *time*.

"Don't change the subject," he snapped. "*Look* at us, Esmer. We're finished. If this is how you *aid* Linden, it's just pathetic. You can't hurt her now. You can only make sure we all die.

"That's probably good enough for Kastenessen. But you haven't thought it through. You haven't thought about what happens when She Who Must Not Be Named gets my ring.

"That isn't just betrayal." Swallowing dread like bile, Covenant insisted, "It's *the* betrayal. Treachery pure and absolute. With that kind of power—"

"She is complete in herself," Esmer countered. Blood rimmed his eyes. It formed streaks like shame down the sides of his face. "She cares naught for such theurgies.

"You are indeed betrayed, but not by me."

Abruptly the bane gave a vast roar of triumph. An avid pounce and gnash slashed Elena's voice from the air.

Elena!

Involuntarily Covenant turned. But Giants blocked his view. He did not see his lost daughter eaten by the many maws of She Who Must Not Be Named. He saw only the bane's towering savagery as She consumed Elena—

—who had never been forgiven.

This was his fault, *his*. Not by me. Then by whom? He could not think of anyone to blame except himself. Who else had failed Linden and her companions and Elena badly enough for the failure to be called treachery?

Fiercely he faced Esmer again. With his own rage and grief, he rasped, "Sure. She's complete. I understand that. She wants my ring because it's a *wedding* ring. She doesn't care about white gold. Wild magic can't make Her any more eternal.

"But it'll make Her victims into monsters." It was the symbol and instrument of everything that they had ever desired; everything that had been taken from them. "They'll be capable of endless butchery. They won't have to wait for the Worm. Hell, they won't even *need* the Worm. And they'll probably start with Kastenessen just because he's *using* Her. But they won't stop there.

"It's going to be the end of everything, and *it's your doing!*

"You can't want that. Not if you're still Cail's son."

Almost as an afterthought, he added, "If you let us go now, you can always get us later. If Kastenessen doesn't like it, you can tell him you saved his life."

Mouths and teeth and fire advanced on the ledge again. Esmer's chagrin was as vivid as the bane's hunger.

"I remember my father."

"Then do something about it. *Don't let her get my ring.*"

For an instant, Esmer appeared to hesitate. Storms scattered the blood in his eyes. Winds and screaming whipped at his hair, tugged his torn cymar, stung his damaged flesh. Out of nowhere, hail pelted the company like a fall of stones.

Then he wrapped himself in nothingness and disappeared.

The bane's glee seemed to deafen the world. Excoriation and rage reared over the ledge. Covenant did not have time to see the Demondim-spawn race away, fleeing for their lives; barking incantations of concealment.

But Esmer was gone.

As though he had spent his entire life waiting for this moment, the Ardent flung his ribbands around the company and snatched them all into darkness.

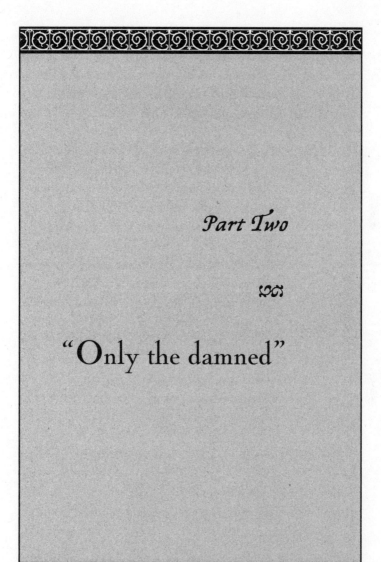

Part Two

Only the damned

1.

Those Who Endure—

Holding Linden against him, Thomas Covenant sat leaning on a boulder half buried in the sandy bottom of a shallow gully. Most of the terrain around him looked barren, stripped of vegetation by thirst and ancient misuse. But a few stunted trees, twisted as cripples, still gripped the edges of the gully. Here and there, tufts of bitter grass clung to some scant source of moisture. He hoped for *aliantha*, but he had not seen any.

His mind was still full of shrieks and fire and torrents: his heart was woe. Whenever he looked at Linden's slack face, he saw Elena's unassoiled horror, pursued by She Who Must Not Be Named. He did not know how to lament for his daughter.

In the east beyond the rim of the gully, the sun was rising. When it ascended high enough, he would have to move; use the boulder for shade. But this patch of sand would lie in shadow a little longer. While he could, he remained where he sat, gently stroking Linden's hair.

It was filthy, soiled with sweat and grime and dust. She had been through too much—And in her present condition, she could not care for herself at all. But the state of her hair made no difference to him. His hands were too numb to feel it.

Only one night had passed since she had restored him to life, maimed him with mortality, and roused the Worm of the World's End. How much time remained until the Worm brought its hunger here, to feed on the ichor in the depths of *Melenkurion Skyweir*? Four days? Six? It was not enough.

If it is not forbidden, it will have Earthpower.

If someone had asked him why he sat in that position, caressing her hair when his own nerves were dead and he had no way of knowing whether she felt his touch, he might have said that he was praying.

As soon as the Ardent had brought the company here from the Lost Deep, Covenant had claimed Linden from Stave. Neither the former Master nor any of Linden's friends had objected when he had seated himself spread-legged against the boulder so that he could hold her, curled into herself and unconscious, against his chest. Then he had lifted the chain holding his ring over his head, and had settled it around her neck.

The Humbled had expressed their disapproval; but he told them, "I never wanted all that power. When I died, I finally succeeded at giving it away." He had tried to surrender it several times before then, and had been refused. "I don't want it back. Not like this."

Most of his companions were weary beyond bearing. None of them argued with him. The Staff of Law they placed on the sand near Linden so that she could reach it if Covenant managed to rouse her. Then they stumbled away to rest.

He recognized where he was. Of course he did. The shock of his reincarnation had not cost him simple things like his knowledge of the Land's geography. He did not need to turn his head and peer past the edge of the boulder to confirm that the jagged cliff of Landsdrop jutted high into the dawn less than half a league away.

Instead of returning the company to Andelain, the Ardent had deposited them on the Lower Land, between Landsdrop and the dour fens and seepage of Sarangrave Flat. The foothills of Mount Thunder—and the dark throat of the Defiles Course—were at least sixty or sixty-five leagues to the northwest. At that distance, the mountain itself was no longer visible.

Vaguely Covenant wondered whether the waters that fed the Defiles Course and Lifeswallower and most of the Sarangrave had been completely cut off. Likely there were other springs within Gravin Threndor, streams that joined the polluted Soulsease beyond its deepest subterranean lakes. And in any case, the Great Swamp and Sarangrave Flat would not soon empty their rank life-blood into the Sunbirth Sea. The Worm of the World's End would find its way to *Melenkurion* Skyweir long before the vast demesne of the lurker began to run dry.

He wanted to ask the Ardent why the compelled Insequent had delivered the company here. But he could wait. The Ardent had been profligate with his given strength. The exertion of translating everyone except the Demondim-spawn out of Mount Thunder's depths had left him chalk-faced and trembling. As soon as he had set his charges down in the dry streambed, he had wrapped his garments around his whole body, swaddled himself until even his face was covered. Then he had collapsed where he stood.

Covenant let him rest. The Ardent had earned it. And Covenant could guess at one or two explanations for the Insequent's choice. Kevin's Dirt did not impend over the Lower Land. Kastenessen—or *moksha* Raver—had foreseen no need to cast the brume eastward. Here Linden, Liand, and the Ramen would retain their natural percipience. And the Staff would be stronger.

In addition, the Ardent had placed the whole bulk of Mount Thunder between the company and both the *skurj* and the Sandgorgons. Speaking of the Sandgorgons, Esmer had said, *Already they have begun the slaughter of Salva Gildenbourne.* And he had promised worse—But the threat they posed was not immediate: they were too far away. Kastenessen could send his *skurj* more quickly, but even those monsters would need time to travel through so much earth.

The Ardent had given Covenant and Linden and their friends the necessary gift of a respite.

Still they had no defense against the Worm of the World's End. Perhaps no defense was possible.

And the problem of Roger remained. *Even now, he summons an army of Cavewights to join his efforts*—If he knew where the Ardent had taken Jeremiah, he might be able to muster an attack more swiftly than Kastenessen could. Certainly he would do everything in his considerable power to recapture Jeremiah and the *croyel*. They were his portal to eternity.

But Covenant did not dwell on such concerns. Though she hardly moved, except to breathe, Linden held his attention.

He saw echoes of Joan in her aggrieved face. The small muscles at the corners of her closed eyes winced occasionally, implying pains which she could not escape. Because of him, Elena had been consumed by She Who Must Not Be Named. Reminders of his ex-wife seemed to demand more from him than did the last crisis of the Earth. Her efforts to destroy his hands demonstrated that she was a burden which he could not refuse.

Therefore he would need Loric's *krill*. If he confronted Joan without some potent weapon, she would incinerate him. But the *krill* was also needed here. It alone controlled the *croyel*. Freed, the creature would escape in an instant, taking Jeremiah with it—and killing everyone it could.

Restoring Covenant to life, Linden had sacrificed the Earth. He refused to sacrifice both her and her son merely to ease his own responsibilities.

Torn within himself, he stroked her hair, and prayed, and waited.

Apart from Clyme, Branl, and Stave, who watched the horizons from the rims of the gully, and Galt, who had accepted the task of restraining the *croyel* and Jeremiah so that Rime Coldspray could rest, Mahrtiir was the only member of the company still standing. Earlier he had sent out his Cords to scout the terrain and search for water in spite of their weariness. They had not yet returned; and everyone else had stretched out on the sand to sleep while they could. Now, alone, the Manethrall faced the east as though he expected the touch of the sunrise on his eyeless face to offer him an obscure revelation.

Fortunately Stormpast Galesend had not neglected to remove her cataphract and set it out as a cradle for Anele: protected by stone armor, he slept like the Giants. And

Liand slept as well. His efforts with his *orcrest* so soon after Linden had healed him had exhausted even his youth and Stonedownor stamina.

Stoic as a plinth of brown marble, Galt held Loric's dagger against the throat of the *croyel*. The blade prevented the fatal creature's teeth from reaching Jeremiah's neck; prevented the *croyel* from feeding. But Covenant could not tell whether the succubus was growing weaker. He knew only that Jeremiah looked like a rag doll, boneless and beaten. The boy's muddy, disfocused gaze was as empty as an unfilled grave.

From Jeremiah's back, the *croyel*'s bitter eyes studied Liand's supine form. The creature's gaze conveyed the impression that the *croyel* craved Liand's death.

At intervals, Mahrtiir glanced toward Jeremiah and the *croyel*; regarded them with senses other than sight. Then he resumed his examination of the east as if he awaited an epiphany.

When the sun gilded his forehead, however, and warmed the begrimed bandage that still covered his eye sockets, he shrugged slightly. Stiff with disappointment, he turned to face Covenant and Linden.

"There is an old tale among the Ramen," he began brusquely, "concerning Hile Troy. He was a stranger to the Land, as you know, and eyeless from birth. According to the tale, the Land's sun gifted him with true sight in spite of his blindness.

"Here Kevin's Dirt does not corrupt the light. For that reason, I permitted myself to imagine that my vision might be restored." He had contributed nothing to the company's escape from the Lost Deep and the bane. Clearly his uselessness galled him. "But my hope was delusion. I am Ramen. We are given no gifts except those of service to the Ranyhyn."

Covenant expected him to add that even that service would be denied him if he returned to his people. Without sight, he would not be considered worthy of the great horses. Instead, however, he changed the subject.

"The Cords will soon return, bearing word of water. The season's rains have been abundant. Our old tales inform us that there are few springs in this region—and fewer still which do not draw some venom from the earth. Battles have been fought between Sarangrave Flat and Landsdrop. Many of the Land's defenders have perished here— aye, and many of Fangthane's servants also. Their blood and magicks stain this ground across the millennia.

"However, this watercourse was formed by rains gathering from the Upper Land. If the stream does not run here, it will flow nearby. We will be able to quench our thirst, though we appear to lack *aliantha*, and have no other sustenance."

Covenant nodded. His own thirst was real enough, but he felt sure that it was trivial compared to the deprivation suffered by the Giants and the Ramen, Liand and Anele; Linden herself. They were able to sleep only because their exhaustion was greater than their need for water.

But he did not know why the Manethrall was talking to him; telling him things that he already understood. Stroking Linden's hair tenderly, he waited for Mahrtiir to continue.

After a moment, the Manethrall nodded toward the southeast. "A *caesure* moves there. I had thought that the absence of Kevin's Dirt would diminish the virulence of such evils. Yet its emanations"—he lifted a hand to his face—"suggest that its force is enhanced."

He was probably right. Long before Lord Foul fashioned and occupied Ridjeck Thome, an insidious miasma had hung over portions of the Lower Land. Baleful creatures had arisen from the corrupt waters pouring out of Mount Thunder. The lurker of the Sarangrave had come to life in the effluvium of bitter theurgies. And the Ravers had taken form among the malign spirits of the region. Interdicted by the Colossus of the Fall, they had spread much of their harm south and east toward the Despiser's eventual seat. Over time, they had done such damage that those lands had come to be named the Spoiled Plains.

Covenant could well believe that *caesures* flourished across the Lower Land, fed by a history of *wrongness*. Especially south of Mount Thunder—

"Is it coming this way?" he asked the Manethrall.

Mahrtiir shook his head. "At present, it tends northward, delivering havoc among the sloughs and mires of Sarangrave Flat."

"Then don't worry about it." Briefly Covenant remembered the Spoiled Plains as they had once been, before they were tainted. Then the rubble of his recollections shifted, and the memory was gone. "We have more urgent problems."

The movement of his hands indicated Linden's apparent catatonia; but he was thinking of Joan. He no longer knew with any certainty where *turiya* Raver had hidden her. That memory, unfortunately, was gone as well. But he could guess.

Mahrtiir's manner sharpened. More harshly, he replied, "I have not forgotten the Ringthane's plight, or that of her son. Indeed, her spirit appears broken by all that she has endured." His tone was bile. "Nor do I discount our own peril. I have neither aid nor counsel to offer. I speak merely to hear myself and know that I remain among the living."

The fierce lines of his face suggested that he would have preferred death.

Covenant sighed to himself. There was so much pain all around him; and he could relieve none of it.

"Don't underestimate Linden," he said gruffly. "Too many people make that mistake." Including Sunder and Hollian, who should have known better. "Hell, even she does it. She's come back before. Give her time. She'll find her way again."

If his numb touch gave her any comfort or aid, it lay beneath the surface, hidden.

The Manethrall confronted Covenant squarely. "I do not fear for her, Timewarden. I fear you."

Covenant waited. He was not surprised: he feared himself. His new humanity had too many flaws.

"I acknowledge," Mahrtiir continued, "that you are mysterious to me. You surpass my comprehension. For that reason, among others, my fealty belongs to the Ringthane rather than to you."

Covenant started to say, I know, but Mahrtiir did not pause.

"Nonetheless I am able to grasp that the spectre of High Lord Elena has been devoured by She Who Must Not Be Named."

"Yes."

"She is your daughter."

Covenant ached with memories like old wounds. His grief rose like keening. But he kept it to himself. "Yes."

"The deed of her undoing was yours. Do not protest to me that you merely requested Anele's sanity and service. I will not hear you. I grant that you did not or could not foresee what would follow." The Manethrall seemed to bite down on each word, restraining an impulse to shout. "Still the deed was yours."

Covenant faced Mahrtiir as steadily as he could. "Yes."

Like an indictment, Mahrtiir proclaimed, "The Waynhim teach that 'Good cannot be accomplished by evil means.' I do not fault you for removing the *krill* from Andelain. You enabled the capture of the Ringthane's son. Nor do I question your valor. Your hands are proof enough that you do not fear to bear the cost of your choices. But for millennia, from the moment of her conception until her last fall beneath Gravin Threndor, you have brought only ruin upon your daughter. Upon your *daughter*, Timewarden."

"Therefore I fear you."

Because he ached, Covenant objected, "We're still alive—"

The Manethrall cut him off. "By evil means. Do you name the expenditure of your daughter good? The Ringthane would not do so. Nor would she sacrifice her son for any purpose."

"No, she wouldn't," Covenant admitted. "I wouldn't either. He's still alive.

"But," he insisted, "I did not know what was going to happen." He needed to be clear about this. He already had more burdens than he could carry. "Sunder and Hollian picked Elena. I didn't.

"And I'm not done."

"Not done?" Mahrtiir barked a humorless laugh. "Do you intend to confront She Who Must Not Be Named again, for High Lord Elena's sake?"

"Don't put it past me," Covenant growled. Linden's weight against his chest was an accusation that he did not mean to deny. Her soiled shirt, plucked and torn, had endured as much as his old T-shirt and jeans. In his time, he, too, had worn stains that should have guided him. "I've done more harm than I can stand. I always have. But *we're still alive*. That means we still have a chance." More quietly, he finished, "*I* still have a chance."

Abruptly Branl jumped down from the edge of the gully to approach Covenant and Mahrtiir. "We will hear no more of this, Manethrall," he stated in a tone like polished obsidian. A threat— The loyalty of the Humbled ran deep. "You are unjust, both to the Unbeliever and to the Dead."

Mahrtiir's bandage emphasized his scowl. "How so?" He seemed to need conflicts. His sense of his own uselessness required an outlet.

"That the crime of High Lord Elena's conception was costly to her," answered Branl, "cannot be denied. Yet the ur-Lord may not be held accountable for the use which she made of her life. The fault of her chosen deeds cannot be excused by the circumstance of her birth and parentage. She elected to summon Kevin Landwaster from his rightful place among the Dead. The ur-Lord did not. Her subsequent enslavement by Corruption ensued from her own folly, not from any choice or desire of the Unbeliever's.

"That her spirit has not served Corruption from that time to this was the ur-Lord's gift to her. Aided by powers invoked by a Forestal from the Colossus of the Fall, he ended her thrall when she was unable to free herself."

Covenant had not forgotten his physical life. He remembered that he had released Elena by destroying the original Staff of Law. If he had not done so, she would have killed him. But in turn, that act of desperation had facilitated Lord Foul's return to strength and the horrors of the Sunbane.

Apparently evil could be accomplished by good—or at least necessary—means.

The Manethrall's jaws worked, chewing possible retorts. Before he decided on a response, however, Covenant told Branl, "No. Mahrtiir is right. Elena doesn't deserve more torment. We all make choices, and none of us can guess how they'll turn out. But we have to live with the consequences anyway. I didn't know what would happen when I asked Anele to speak to the Dead, but that doesn't make me any less responsible."

"And did the Dead not choose?" countered Branl. "Did Elena Law-Breaker herself not choose?"

Covenant nodded. "They did. She did. And she paid for it. She's paying for it right now. But that doesn't change what *I* did. I asked for help. My part in this doesn't go away just because I didn't choose the kind of help I got."

As Covenant spoke, Mahrtiir sagged. His anger became an air of recognition and defeat. He remained silent while Branl searched for a weakness in Covenant's reasoning. But when Branl found none, the Manethrall said unsteadily, "I cry your pardon, Timewarden. I am answered. The judgments of these self-maimed *Haruchai* do not sway me. But I discern now that I have misdirected my ire.

"In sooth, I have no cause to accuse you. I do so only because the Lost Deep has deprived me of myself. I have learned that I am naught, unfit to serve either the Ring-thane or the Ranyhyn. Such knowledge is bitter to me. I do not bear it with grace."

I know, Covenant thought sadly. Mahrtiir's pain was only one of many needs for which Covenant had no anodyne.

Branl looked at the blinded man; raised an eyebrow in inquiry. After a moment, he said, "We do not comprehend. How is it that any mere place can diminish a Manethrall of the Ramen? You are who and what you are, unlessened in strength, forethought, or valor by the loss of ordinary sight. Nor have you been diminished by impenetrable stone or ancient banes. To think otherwise is to heed the blandishments of Corruption."

In a motion too fluid for Covenant to follow, Mahrtiir's fighting garrote appeared in his hands. Through his teeth, he asked, "Do you accuse me, sleepless one? Do you deem that my perception of myself betrays this company, or the Ringthane, or the Land?"

Anticipating a provocative rejoinder from Branl, Covenant groaned.

However, Branl answered flatly, "I have not said so. Nor was that my meaning. You are a Manethrall of the Ramen. For their devotion to the Ranyhyn, the Manethralls have been esteemed by every *Haruchai* since the time of the Bloodguard. Though you revile our Mastery, you cannot question my word. If any accusation stands between us, it arises from within you, not from any judgment of the Humbled, or of the Masters."

In spite of his numbness, Covenant continued stroking Linden's hair. "He's telling the truth, Mahrtiir. You know that. He's *Haruchai*. He doesn't lie.

"I understand feeling useless. But I've been weaker than you are. When I first came to the Land, I clung to the idea I was helpless. I *counted* on it. I didn't want to carry the load that comes with being able to stand for something. It took me a long time to get over needing to believe I'm weak."

He had learned that only the damned can be saved.

"Of course," he conceded, "I had help. A *lot* of help." Atiaran. Mhoram. Bannor. Saltheart Foamfollower. Triock. Even Lena, whom he had raped and abandoned. "But so do you. And you still have a long way to go." Covenant had said that once before, although he no longer remembered why. "You still have to come back."

The muscles of Mahrtiir's jaw knotted. Cords of tension defined his neck. As if he were delivering or receiving a blow, he rasped, "Master, I find that I must cry your pardon also. If joy is in the ears that hear, as the Giants avow, not in the mouth that speaks, then blame and rue must likewise be found in the ears that hear. Condemning the Masters for their judgments, I have vaunted myself worthy to judge them. The fault is mine."

Branl considered the Manethrall briefly. His mien revealed nothing as he acknowledged Mahrtiir's apology with a bow.

Mahrtiir faced Covenant again. "If I am granted an occasion to heed your counsel, Timewarden, I will do so."

Then he walked away as if he hoped to conceal his self-recrimination by turning his back.

With a delicate *Haruchai* shrug, Branl rejoined Clyme and Stave on the rim of the gully, standing guard.

For a few moments, Covenant studied the strict set of the Manethrall's shoulders. He ached for Mahrtiir: hell, he ached for everybody. Maybe, he mused sourly, it was a good thing that most of his former memories lay in ruins. Maybe it was crucial. If he could have remembered *why* he had spoken to Mahrtiir on the plateau of Revelstone— or to Liand, or to Pahni and Bhapa—he might not be able to resist the impulse to explain himself. Doubtless Mahrtiir would be comforted to hear that he still had an important role to play. But the knowledge would shape his decisions, affect everything about him. Directly or indirectly, it would affect the whole company. And Covenant would be responsible for the change. Linden and her friends would be guided by insights which they should not have been able to glean, except by their own efforts. In effect, they would no longer be truly free.

But Covenant had been spared by his imposed mortality, for good or ill. He was in no danger of saying too much—

Hellfire, he muttered in silence. No wonder only people like Roger and creatures like the *croyel* wanted to be gods. The sheer impotence of that state would appall a chunk of basalt—if the basalt happened to care about anything except itself. Absolute power was as bad as powerlessness for anybody who valued someone else's peace or happiness or even survival. The Creator could only make or destroy worlds: he could not rule them, nurture them, assist them. He was simply too strong to express himself within the constraints of Time.

By that standard, forgetfulness was Covenant's only real hope. No matter how badly he wanted to remember, he needed his specific form of ignorance; absolutely required it. Nothing less would prevent him from violating the necessity of freedom.

By slow degrees, sunshine crested the rim of the gully. It reached Covenant's face: a touch that might be a curse in this desiccated region. Still in shadow, the Giants slumbered among the sand and stones and sparse grass of the gully-bottom. Liand and Anele slept. Galt gripped Jeremiah's shoulder, holding the *krill* at the *croyel*'s throat. The boy stood as if he were too vacant to feel thirst or fatigue. The *croyel*'s mouth moved, perhaps yearning for Jeremiah's neck, perhaps shaping some invocation or summons. Above the rest of the company, Stave and Galt's comrades stood like statues, carved and voiceless.

Covenant shifted so that his eyes avoided the sun. Soon he would have to move

Linden into the shade of the boulder. But shade was not water. It would not shield her for long.

She had been through too much: Covenant understood that. And when she found her way back to consciousness, she would judge herself harshly for her temporary escape. She would believe that she had failed her son and her friends and the Land. But he knew better. Her absence was the opposite of failure. Like Jeremiah in the aftermath of his maiming by fire and Despite, she had found a way to survive when every other form of continuance had become unendurable.

And Covenant grasped a truth that she might not recognize, even though she had experienced it before. When she returned to herself, like a butterfly she would unfurl different strengths than those which she had possessed earlier. She would be an altered woman. Even she might not know what she had become.

It was conceivable that her sense of inadequacy would shape her into an empty vessel fit only to be filled with despair. But he refused to believe that of her.

I do not fear for her, Timewarden.

In this, as in other things, Covenant sided with Mahrtiir.

Avoiding the direct stare of the sun, he watched Linden's face for signs that she might be ready to awaken.

She looked ashen and abused, almost drained of blood. The fine lines of her features had become a kind of gauntness. At intervals, the muscles at the corners of her eyes were plucked by pains too intimate for his ordinary sight to interpret. Beneath their lids, her eyes flinched from side to side, wincing at nightmares. Occasionally her fingers twitched as though she sought to grasp her Staff. Her lips shaped words or whimpers like pleas for which he had no answer.

The longer she remained unconscious, the more she would be changed by the experience of hiding among her dreams.

The sun heated his cheek. When he blinked, his eyes felt raw, abraded by the effects of convulsions and rank minerals deep under Gravin Threndor. Dehydration blurred his vision. He thought that the time had come to move. Then he thought that he would wait for Bhapa and Pahni a little longer. Linden lay like a millstone against his chest; but he was reluctant to disturb her.

Hardly aware that he had reached a decision, he began to talk. Bowing his head, he murmured her name softly. Almost whispering, he tried to find words that would reach her.

"I love you, Linden," he said like a sigh. "Do you know that? So much time has passed, you might find it hard to imagine. But it's true. I've spent three and a half thousand years remembering how much you mean to me—and wishing I'd done a better job of telling you.

"That's why I kept trying to warn or advise you, when I should have kept my damn mouth shut. I didn't know how else to tell you I love you. If you've made mistakes—which I do not believe—you can't blame yourself. You only made them because I couldn't leave you alone."

Above him, Stave, Clyme, and Branl stood with their backs to the gully, facing Landsdrop and the more distant vistas of Sarangrave Flat. They may have wished to grant Covenant the illusion of privacy. Guiding Jeremiah by the shoulder, Galt turned the boy and the *croyel* away so that Covenant would not be distracted by Jeremiah's emptiness and the creature's malevolence.

Apparently the Humbled and the former Master understood what Covenant was trying to do.

"Linden," he went on, "I think you can hear me." He kept his voice low to mask his sorrow and regret. "I think that because you're like Jeremiah right now, and *he* can hear me. The *croyel* isn't the only one listening. But that's not all. I think he's *always* heard you. Nothing you ever said to him was wasted.

"That's one reason I believe he doesn't serve Lord Foul. He's been listening to you. You gave him a life that wasn't all pain. It was also years of your care and devotion. You showed him he wasn't alone even though he couldn't tell you he was listening.

"Sure, Lord Foul got to him first. The Despiser marked him in that bonfire. But Jeremiah is like all the rest of us. He's more than the sum of his hurts. One damaged hand doesn't make him anybody's property. And after that, you claimed him. You claimed him in the only way that matters, by loving him the whole time. Whatever Lord Foul has done to him since is too late. I believe that. Someday you'll believe it, too. You've already taught him the difference between love and Despite."

Some of the Giants slept restlessly, fighting old battles in their dreams, or fleeing beyond exhaustion in the deep places of the world. Rime Coldspray snorted defiance or desperation softly through her teeth. Cirrus Kindwind clutched the stump of her severed arm until her knuckles whitened and the thews stood out on her hand. But none of the Swordmainnir seemed likely to awaken.

"And since then—" Covenant tried to speak more strongly, and found that he could not. His throat was too dry, and lamentations filled his chest. "Hellfire, Linden. When I told you to do something they don't expect, I didn't know you were going to surprise me so often."

He did not want her to hear his grief. She would hold herself accountable for it.

"It's quite a list, the things you've accomplished that should have been impossible. I don't know if you realize just what you've done, or how hard it was, or how many different forces were trying to stop you. I could start with escaping Mithil Stonedown and the *kresh* to find the Ramen, or risking a *caesure* to look for your Staff, or finding a way to bring the Demondim with you when you escaped the past." He could have started with the imponderable use of wild magic by which she had saved herself and

Anele from the collapse of Kevin's Watch; but he no longer knew how she had achieved that feat. "But you won't take credit for any of that. You'll say you didn't do it on your own, you had help, you couldn't have done it alone.

"Well, I'm not going to argue with you. Of course you had help. We've all had help. It doesn't diminish what you've done."

The rising sun had reached her face. Her head rested against his chest in a way that allowed the light to strike her troubled eyes, although their lids were closed and clenched. Hoping to ease her, he cupped one hand to provide a patch of shade.

"But think about it, Linden. We only have Jeremiah now because you broke the construct hiding him. Nobody helped you with that. Nobody else could have saved Liand," whose fate seemed to thicken around him as he slept. "And I only have hands I can still use because you healed them. For that alone, I'm so grateful I don't know how to contain it."

Everything that he required of himself while life remained in his body depended on his ability to grip and hold.

Gradually a low breeze began to blow, drawn by the warmed cliff of Landsdrop. It cooled the mounting pressure of the sun; but it could not ease his thirst. His voice had become an effortful scrape of sound. His tongue felt stupid in his mouth, and sand seemed to clog his attempts to swallow.

"But you didn't stop there. You're the reason we survived She Who Must Not Be Named."

With his peripheral vision, he saw that Stave had turned to study him. The Humbled had set aside the pretense that they were not listening.

They wanted to know what he meant.

He was thinking of Elena, agonized and frantic. She was his daughter by rape; and he had not stopped her from drinking the Blood of the Earth, even though he had suspected that her intentions were distorted or dangerous. Now her pain had been consumed by the bane's larger and more rabid torment—

—because Linden had not granted her the compassion which Kevin Landwaster had received from his forefathers.

He wanted to tell Linden that she had done the right thing. —*something they don't expect*. Something no one could have expected. In effect, she had rubbed salt in Elena's wounds. She had left Elena's anguish so fresh and naked that She Who Must Not Be Named had been unable to ignore it.

He wanted to say that sometimes good came from cruel means.

But he could not. The words hurt too much. And they would not help Linden forgive herself. Certainly they did not ease his own remorse.

Yet he believed that they were important. Saying that good could not be accomplished by evil means implied a definition of evil which excluded Linden's particular desperation.

Nevertheless he did not speak of Elena. He did not wish the *Haruchai* to hear him. They would judge him as well as Linden in the same way that they judged themselves. Instead he murmured, faltering, "You've saved us in more ways than I can count. None of us would still be alive without you."

Then he was finished. He had nothing more to say, and very little strength. She would wake, or she would not. Either way, the choice was hers.

Lifting his head, he saw Stave nod before resuming his watch on the horizons. Perhaps the former Master approved. Or perhaps his nod merely acknowledged that Covenant had tried.

〰

L ater Covenant asked Stave to help him move Linden back into the shade of the boulder. He was too weak to shift her gently by himself. As Stave complied, however, the former Master remarked that the Manethrall's Cords were returning.

"They appear stronger. I deem that they have found water."

Covenant did not know how much longer he could wait. Like his concern for Linden, his thirst had become a kind of fever, so hot that it parched his thoughts.

Muttering to himself, he moved as far into the boulder's shade as he could while Stave lifted Linden. Then he accepted her again, settled her against his chest.

Through the haze in his eyes, he saw the Cords approaching, accompanied now by their Manethrall. Pahni and Bhapa had been gone for what felt like a long time. They must have walked far. He could not imagine where he, or the Ardent, or even the Giants would find the stamina to do the same.

While Covenant tried to believe that he was capable of walking at all, Clyme said brusquely, "Stave."

With a small shrug for the affront of being commanded aloud, Stave returned to the rim of the watercourse. At the same time, Clyme and Branl leapt down to greet the Ramen. As soon as the Cords announced their success, Clyme said, "If it can be done, this company must be spared further exertion. We will endeavor to bring water here."

"We have no vessels," Mahrtiir observed.

"And we have seen no *aliantha*," added Bhapa.

Clyme ignored the Cord. "We will contrive a means," he told Mahrtiir. With one hand, he gestured at Anele sleeping cupped in Galesend's cataphract. "Shaped as it is, the armor of the Giants will serve. We need only rouse one of the Swordmainnir."

"It is stone," the Manethrall objected. "Its weight alone—"

Branl cut him off. "We do not ask this of you, Manethrall. We will bear the burden. Stave will stand watch in our stead."

Mahrtiir hesitated for a moment, as if he doubted even the great strength of the *Haruchai*. Then he nodded. "Cord Bhapa and I will accompany you. When Cord Pahni has bestirred the Ironhand, she will join her wariness to Stave's."

Pahni obeyed promptly. Casting a worried glance at Liand, she knelt beside Rime Coldspray. From a small pouch at her waist, she took a little *amanibhavam*. After rubbing the dried leaves between her fingers, she held them to Coldspray's nose.

Covenant had once eaten raw *amanibhavam*: an act of madness which may nonetheless have saved his life.

Coldspray snorted at the smell, twisted away as though it stung her nostrils. A moment later, she raised her head, blinking at the film of fatigue and thirst in her eyes.

Satisfied, Pahni climbed out of the gully toward Stave.

"Ironhand," Clyme stated, "we require your armor to carry water."

Coldspray regarded him with an air of stupefaction. Briefly she struggled to understand him. Then she managed a nod. Fumbling, she undid the bindings of her cataphract. When that was done, she rolled across the sand until she left the breastplate and back of her armor behind.

Freed from the heavy stone, she labored unsteadily to her feet and watched as Clyme and Branl each stooped to lift half of her cataphract. Seeing that they were equal to the task, she took a small stone flask—*diamondraught*—from a slot or notch in her breastplate and drank the last of its contents: a few drops. Then she tucked the flask under her belt and stumbled toward Frostheart Grueburn. Without making any effort to wake her comrade, she knelt to release the clasps of Grueburn's armor.

By increments, she succeeded at rolling Grueburn to one side.

Grueburn opened her eyes, peered at Coldspray. A frown knotted her features as she fought to moisten her mouth. "Ironhand," she rasped painfully. "What—?"

"Rest if you must," Coldspray replied, hoarse with thirst. "If you are able to do so, arise and aid me. We must make use of your cataphract as basins for water."

Grueburn shook her head, staring dully. "Able?" she croaked. "Have I not named myself the mightiest of the Swordmainnir? If you are indeed able to carry water, surely I can do no less."

Goading herself with Giantish curses, Frostheart Grueburn began to climb upright. When she had found a measure of balance, she, too, retrieved her flask and poured her last drops of *diamondraught* into her mouth.

Covenant saw their heavy muscles tremble as Coldspray and Grueburn picked up Grueburn's armor; and he almost slipped. Images tugged at him: Saltheart Foamfollower bearing him into the unendurable magma of Hotash Slay; Grimmand

Honninscrave straining to contain *samadhi* Sheol. His memories spanned too much time. And he had too many lives on his conscience. Linden's destitution against his chest was only one burden among a clamoring host.

"Hang on," he murmured, speaking to himself as much as to her. "It won't be long now. We'll have water soon."

Somehow the Ironhand and Grueburn stood in spite of stone and exhaustion. They looked weaker than Branl and Clyme, but they managed to support the shaped rock of Grueburn's cataphract.

"Now," Coldspray panted to Mahrtiir. "Ere this tattered mimicry of vigor fails us."

The Manethrall turned quickly toward Covenant; bowed like a promise. Then he wheeled away. Guided by Bhapa, he led Clyme and Branl, Coldspray and Grueburn away along the gully. Both Swordmainnir tottered as though they were about to fall; but they did not. From some deep reserve of indomitability, they drew the resolve to stay on their feet and walk.

Covenant watched them go with a pang in his heart, as if he had failed them—although he could not have said how. His sense of disappointment in himself seemed to have no name.

He had certainly failed Linden.

For a time, he forgot to stroke her hair. His shoulders slumped, resting his incomplete hands on the sand. Like his memories, their stiffness threatened to drag him into the fissures of the past. But then he muttered, "Hellfire," and forced himself to lift his arms again.

The sensations of touching her were denied to him. Only the repetitive gentleness of caresses comforted him. But he knew how badly he had hurt her, both by his silence among the Dead and by his recurring absences. He knew that he would surely hurt her again. And he knew what he had done to Elena. He did not seek solace for himself.

Other people needed consolation more than he did.

‿◌‿

He could not measure time. He was not yet attuned to mundane circadian increments—or he was too badly dehydrated. The sun moved: the shadow of the boulder dwindled. Landsdrop seemed to shrink as the angle of the light changed. But such things did not tell him how long Mahrtiir and the others had been gone, or when they might come back.

The season was still spring: he remembered that. Nevertheless the sun's heat leaned down on him until he forgot that he had been drenched only a few hours earlier. It made Linden heavier. The day was going to be hot. Too hot—

More and more as haze blurred his sight, he saw Landsdrop as a barrier. A forbidding—Unattainable. It made him think that he would never see the Upper Land again.

His desire to walk in Andelain once more before the world ended was a new kind of ache, unforeseen and immedicable. He had no anodyne for any of his woes.

When Galt said firmly, "Ur-Lord, the others return. They bear water," Covenant needed a moment to understand him.

Peering down the gully, Covenant eventually made out six figures, four of them small. Their shapes wavered and bled, as uncertain as hallucinations dissolving in the sun's glare. But they became more solid as they approached. Walking with slow care, they took on definition until he could believe that they were real.

Clyme, Branl, and two Giants. Mahrtiir and Bhapa.

Covenant leaned forward in anticipation, but Linden did not awaken.

Clearly the two Swordmainnir had gained much by drinking their fill. Their movements were steady, articulating their stubborn vitality. Nevertheless the Humbled carried their laden basins almost as easily.

The halves of the cataphracts were large enough to hold substantial quantities of water.

Abruptly the *croyel* said, "That isn't going to help you." Jeremiah's voice was harsh with scorn. "This isn't over. The Ardent hasn't done you any favors. Drink as much as you want. Congratulate yourselves for staying alive. It won't make any difference. That fat Insequent isn't as smart as he thinks."

A frown creased Linden's forehead. The *croyel*'s words in her son's mouth appeared to trouble her. The muscles at the corners of her eyes flinched more urgently. Still she did not rouse.

"Be silent, creature," Galt replied. "Do you fancy that I will scruple to sever your foul head from its body? This youth whom you torment has no worth to me. And in her present state, Linden Avery cannot plead for him. It will not grieve me to cause your death."

Covenant wondered whether Galt would carry out his threat. Fortunately the *croyel* did not test the Master.

Stepping among the sprawled forms of the company, Manethrall Mahrtiir said as if his blindness gave him the right to command, "Offer drink to the Insequent. We are in sore need of his powers." Plainly he had quenched his own thirst and become stronger. But he could not appease his sense of futility, or his resentment of it. "If any *diamondraught* remains, grant it to the Ringthane. Her plight demands water, but while she remains as she is, she will drink little. Mayhap the greater potency of *diamondraught* will succor her."

"Aye," assented the Ironhand. The strain of her burden showed in her voice, in spite of her nascent recovery. With elaborate care, she set down her half of Grueburn's armor. Then she went to where Latebirth lay snoring: a husky sound in the back of Latebirth's throat, distressed and uneven. Coldspray opened Latebirth's cataphract, lifted the breastplate aside, and took Latebirth's flask. However, a quick shake of the flask told Coldspray that it was empty. Dropping the wrought stone in vexation, she moved to search Onyx Stonemage.

At the same time, Grueburn carried her vessel to the Ardent's side; Clyme placed his near Latebirth; and Branl approached Covenant. Only Branl's slow caution as he lowered Coldspray's breastplate to the sand betrayed that the armor and its weight of water were heavy for him.

Bhapa had already left the watercourse to join Pahni. Now Stave descended to stand over Covenant. Extending his arms, he said, "You must drink, Timewarden. I will hold the Chosen."

Through his thirst and eagerness, Covenant thought that he heard an undercurrent of concern in the former Master's tone.

But Covenant did not move. The debris of effort and mute rue filled his throat. He had difficulty speaking. "Linden first. I can't—After what she's been through."

He had told her to *find* him. What had he expected her to do? Passively accept his silence?

"Ur-Lord," Branl began, then stopped as the Ironhand walked toward him holding Stonemage's flask.

"Here is *diamondraught*," Coldspray said. "Mere drops remain, I fear. But it is distilled for Giants, and Linden Giantfriend is human. Perchance mere drops will suffice."

Stupid with thirst, Covenant stared at Coldspray. For a moment, he did not understand why she seemed to be waiting for him; why Branl and Stave were waiting. Then he realized that he was holding Linden with her cheek propped on his shoulder. She could not drink in that position.

"You're right," he croaked to Stave. "You'd better take her."

At once, Stave stooped to Linden. Frowning slightly around the scar of his lost eye, he lifted her in the cradle of his arms so her head tilted back enough to open her mouth.

Covenant felt her absence from his chest like a bereavement. Instead of moving to drink from Branl's basin, he watched as Coldspray unstopped Stonemage's flask and shook half a dozen amber drops past Linden's lips.

Linden appeared to swallow autonomically. She gave no sign that she felt the effects of the liquor.

"I can't see into her," Covenant rasped. He was a leper: he had no health-sense. "What's happening? Is it helping her?"

The Ironhand scowled like a wince. "Linden Giantfriend baffles discernment. As do you, Timewarden, and also her son. *Diamondraught* is a sovereign roborant. I will trust that it aids her. But I detect no sign of awakening."

Both Stave and Branl nodded in agreement.

Indicating the flask, Coldspray added, "Doubtless water will provide some further benison."

Covenant thought that he said, Good idea. But he could not be sure. He had too many memories. Long ago, Atiaran had told him, *You are closed to me—I do not see you.* Others had made similar comments. *I do not know whether you are well or ill.*

Ill, of course, he had answered with a bitterness which Lena's mother had not deserved. *I'm a leper.*

She had quoted an ancient song.

> "And he who wields white wild magic gold
> is a paradox—
> for he is everything and nothing,
> hero and fool,
> potent, helpless—
> and with the one word of truth or treachery,
> he will save or damn the Earth
> because he is mad and sane,
> cold and passionate,
> lost and found."

Beyond question, he felt *mad and sane*. Increasingly bewildered. He had surrendered his ring, and did not mean to take it back. In one form or another, his leprosy defined him.

He was slipping—

But Branl had gripped him by the shoulders. Irresistibly the Humbled drew him to his knees beside Coldspray's cataphract.

Thirst and water anchored Covenant. Plunging his whole face into the basin, he drank as long as he could hold his breath.

When he pulled himself back, with water streaming down his cheeks onto his shirt and cooling in the breeze, he felt that he had been baptized; made new in some ineffable fashion. His mouth and throat had been washed clean. None of his griefs or regrets or responsibilities had passed from him. But he could bear them.

And he was not alone. As he mustered the strength to stand, he found that all of the Giants were stirring. They drank sparingly: the company's supply of water was small for women of their size. Yet they drank enough to ease their weakness. Those who still carried any *diamondraught* swallowed it, little though it was. The others allowed Frostheart Grueburn to encourage them by rubbing their arms and shoulders.

Awakened, Liand followed Covenant's example until the blur of prostration faded from his eyes. Then he labored awkwardly to his feet and peered at Linden, scrutinizing her to convince himself that she was physically unharmed. Briefly he watched Coldspray tilt water from Latebirth's flask down Linden's throat. His open nature concealed none of his apprehension.

A moment later, however, he shook himself and turned away. Summoning a fraught smile, he waved reassurance at Pahni. When she waved back, he paused to confirm that his Sunstone had been returned to the pouch at his waist. Then he began to look for a manageable ascent so that he could join the young Cord.

As Stormpast Galesend nudged Anele, Covenant warned her, "Keep him on that armor. I don't know enough about him." He had forgotten too much. "This sand—It used to be stone. Maybe it's safe. Or maybe it'll show Kastenessen where we are."

In any case, Kastenessen was not the only dire being who might notice or enter the old man if he stood on sand baked dry.

"Indeed, Timewarden," Galesend agreed. "Having borne him so far, and at such cost, I have grown fond of our Anele. There is valor concealed within his derangement. I pray that the day will come when the same may be said of Longwrath."

Holding Anele in place, she tugged her armor across the gully-bottom toward the nearest water. Fortunately he did not try to jerk free, in spite of his eagerness to drink. Weakened as she was, she might not have been able to control him. But he seemed content to sit in his cradle and let her pull him along.

The Ardent had been the first to thrust his face into a basin; but he was among the last to struggle upright. For a while, he simply stood, unfurling his ribbands tentatively; studying his damaged raiment. The flesh of his face sagged, and depletions more profound than thirst dulled his gaze.

Eventually, however, he mustered a semblance of resolve. Tottering on his wrapped legs, he came effortfully toward Covenant and Linden, Coldspray and Stave and Branl.

He may have meant to bow, but he managed only a dip of his head. Some of his ribbands trailed like exhaustion across the sand as he braced himself to speak.

"A pitiful end to my former pride," he began. "Doubtless I should name myself gratified. While the Earth endures, no other Insequent will assert that their deeds have equaled mine, or that they have witnessed the wonders which I have beheld. In all sooth, however, I am mortified. Aye, mortified, and also grieved. My many fears and insufficiencies have proven costly. As I near my end, my life comes to naught but this, that you and your companions endure to meet further trials without my aid. In itself, it is a fine accomplishment. Oh, assuredly both fine and fitting. I must crave your pardon that I am not gladdened by it."

Covenant stared. He was about to say, You saved our lives. What more do your people want from you? But the Ardent continued without pausing.

"Here our paths part, Timewarden, though there remains one service which I hope to perform for you, should the Insequent consent to prolong my life. When I have gathered myself, I will depart, praying that I will return, albeit briefly."

In sudden alarm, Covenant protested, "Wait a minute. Don't go anywhere. We have too much to talk about." Inwardly he winced whenever someone called him Timewarden. He had too many titles. They were prophecies which he could not fulfill.

But the Ardent had just said, As I near my end—What the hell was going on? What had Covenant missed?

Temporizing as he tried to gather his scattered thoughts, he asked, "Are you going to abandon us? Now?" While Linden remained unconscious; irreducibly vulnerable? "When we haven't even started looking for a way to resist the Worm?" She had swallowed some of the water that Coldspray had given her. The rest had spilled from the corners of her mouth. Beneath their lids, her eyes continued their nightmare dance. "Have you actually completed your *geas*? Is that all your people care about? Imposing scruples on the Harrow and making sure he kept his promises? Is that all *you* care about?"

The Ardent fluttered his hands uncomfortably. "Timewarden, no. But as you are not Insequent, you cannot be aware that the various oracular visions of my people have been rendered meaningless. On one matter, those who possess the knowledge to scry have been in accord. As one, they have foreseen that the lady's fate is writ in water. Thus it transpired that when she and the ur-viles released floods within Gravin Threndor, all auguries were washed away."

While Covenant and Coldspray studied him, the Ardent explained, "Electing to unite their strengths, the Insequent foresaw many eventualities, but the Harrow's death was not among them. Nor was the lady's deed. For his death, there is a cost which need not concern you. Her valor is another matter. Unleashing torrents, she has altered the course of every heuristic effort. The outcome of both—of the lady's extremity as of the Harrow's passing—is that I have no further purpose at your side, or at hers.

"By my weakness on behalf of the Insequent, the most necessary stricture of our lives has been violated. Now the fate of all things has become undecipherable. The Insequent will not intrude themselves when every road has been made fluid and they have no knowledge to guide them."

"How?" Covenant scowled in bafflement. The sun seemed to have become suddenly hotter. Sweat stood on his forehead as if he were straining every muscle. "I don't understand. You're saying the last thing Linden did before she collapsed changed everything? How is that possible?"

The Ardent lifted begrimed bands of fabric in a shrug. "I know not. The Insequent know not. We know only that some uncertainty too profound for our interpretation has been wrought. You sail uncharted seas, Timewarden. In this, the last crisis of the Earth, I can no longer stand at your side."

"Stone and Sea!" the Ironhand rasped. "These are riddles, Insequent. You mock our incomprehension. Do you conceive that we will content ourselves with chaff when the Earth's last crisis, as you have named it, demands true knowledge?"

"Giant," replied the Ardent mildly, "I expect neither content nor discontent. With respect, assuredly—with grave respect, finding worth in all that you have done— I merely request recognition that I am honest. I proffer no true knowledge because I possess none. The auguries of the Insequent have been swept aside. Therefore the counsels of your own hearts must suffice to chart your courses."

"Thus," Branl stated, "wisdom comes at last to the Insequent." To Covenant and Coldspray, he added, "We have misliked his presence from the first. We will not grieve his departure."

Covenant stifled an impulse to reprimand the Humbled. The Ardent's efforts on the company's behalf were beyond aspersion. But the Unbeliever had too many questions. He was beginning to suspect—

Grinding his teeth, he commanded the Ardent, "Then tell me. Why *here*? Why didn't you take us to the Upper Land? That's where most of our enemies are. What's the point of bringing us here?"

"Aye," assented Rime Coldspray. "This region is unknown to us. The tales of the Giants of the Search do not speak of it. We cannot estimate its perils. It obscures our purposes."

"The Lower Land is known to the Humbled," Branl stated flatly. "We will estimate its perils." His manner dared Coldspray to contradict him.

Stave nodded in confirmation.

But the Ardent brushed past interruptions. "Ah, Timewarden." For a moment, regret colored his weariness. "Do you wish me to concede that I have failed you as I failed the Harrow? Alas, that is to some extent sooth. It was my wish to convey you a number of leagues farther."

"Why?" Covenant insisted.

"Sadly," the Insequent continued, "my strength did not equal my intent. Also the powers of the *croyel* opposed me, hampering my endeavors." Uncoiling a few ribbands, he gestured around him. "Yet this region has virtues which you will assuredly discern.

"First, you are spared the diminishment of Kevin's Dirt. To you, Timewarden, this is a gift of small import. Nonetheless true discernment has great worth to your companions.

"Second, I have attained for you an interval of safety, brief though it may be. Both upon the Upper Land and within Gravin Threndor, it is to the north and west that your foes have gathered their ferocity. Here they cannot immediately fall upon you. They must first bypass Mount Thunder and traverse some three score leagues. You are foolhardy, Timewarden, but you are also wise. In your present straits, you will not disdain any respite."

In that, Covenant knew, the Ardent was right. But the absence of Kevin's Dirt was counter-balanced by the difficulties of the terrain; by the comparative scarcity of water and the complete lack of food. If his companions were forced to forage near the Sarangrave—

Linden's condition, and his inability to relieve her, goaded Covenant to anger. Yet his ire was wasted here, unless he directed it at himself: a defense against mourning. With an effort, he softened the edges of his voice.

"You said you were trying to go farther. You must have a reason. If you can't tell us anything else, you ought to be able to tell us why. What would we gain if you'd succeeded?"

The Ardent sighed lugubriously. "To that question, Timewarden, you must provide your own reply. Have I not said that I am unable to guide you? As the Dead were silent in precious Andelain—as you yourself were silent—so must I be silent now."

Before Covenant could object, the Insequent added, "I may observe, however, that *caesures* flourish in abundance across the Spoiled Plains. Betimes they afflict Horrim Carabal, that wight which is known to you as the lurker of the Sarangrave. Thus the marshes and wetlands of Sarangrave Flat are provoked to heights of menace without precedent in the ages of the Lower Land."

Covenant groaned to himself; but he was not surprised. The Ardent spoke of things which he should have been able to remember. Indirectly the Ardent may have been trying to prod his memories. *You need the ring*, Covenant had told Linden in the Verge of Wandering. *It feeds the* caesures.

If Falls flourished "in abundance" on the Lower Land, there might be more than one explanation.

"This lurker is named in our tales," growled the Ironhand. "The Giants of the Search encountered its might. Speak of this, Insequent, if you will reveal naught else. Does the lurker threaten us now? Is that evil able to extend its many arms across the barrenness of this region?"

The Ardent studied Covenant, apparently waiting for his permission to answer Coldspray. When Covenant said nothing, however, the acolyte of the Mahdoubt turned to the Ironhand.

"Assuredly it cannot. Horrim Carabal is a creature of waters and swamplands, and of the bitter effluence of Gravin Threndor's banes. Its demesne is vast, yet it is bound by its enlivening poisons. The lurker may inhabit any of Sarangrave Flat's currents or stagnancies. Nonetheless its might is greatest among the snares and chimeras of Lifeswallower, and it has revealed no theurgy to reach beyond its borders."

If his reply eased Coldspray's mind, her mien did not show it. Nevertheless she bowed to him somberly. "Never doubt our gratitude, Insequent. We have given scant thanks for your labors, but that is solely because we are worn and afraid, knowing that our own fate is now written in water. If ever we are granted opportunity to speak of you in full, as Giants do, our tale will make plain what is in our hearts. For the present, I name you 'Rockbrother' in friendship and homage. While we live, no iota of your valor and service will be forgotten."

The Ardent bowed, exhibiting his raiment like war-torn pennons; hiding his face. His posture seemed to suggest that he might weep.

Linden needed the *krill* to restrain the *croyel*.

Without Loric's blade, Covenant was helpless.

Grimly he shook off the confusion of his memories. They were too damaged to be useful.

"Oh, hell," he muttered to the Ardent as though he had no cause to share the Iron-hand's gratitude. "Let's pretend I understand what we're doing here. Your auguries must be good for *some*thing. Otherwise we wouldn't still be alive. But we have a more immediate problem.

"Can you help Linden? Can you reach her? I don't know what she's doing to herself. Maybe she's healing. Or maybe she thinks she failed, and she torturing—" The thought choked him for a moment. "I'm afraid the longer she stays like this, the worse it's going to be when she wakes up." If she woke at all. "Can you help her find her way back?"

"That reply, also," sighed the Ardent, "you must discover within yourself." His tone was wan with fatigue or sorrow. "The lady has gone beyond my ken. I can neither aid nor counsel you." He hesitated, then offered as if he were forcing himself, "I perceive only that her need for death is great. Or perchance the need is her son's. But do I speak of her death, or of her son's? Does her plight, or his, require the deaths of others? Such matters have become fluid. Every current alters them. I am able to appease none of your fears.

"If I do not depart, Timewarden, I cannot return."

Deliberately he took a step backward, trying to forestall protests or interference.

But Covenant strode in pursuit. "Stop! We aren't done."

Long ago, Linden had told him about her parents: he already knew enough about her need for death—or for an answer to it. Nevertheless the Ardent had left too many hints in the air.

"Timewarden?" The Insequent's eyes glistened in his flushed face.

"None of this is as simple as you make it sound," Covenant rasped. "You have something at stake, something you don't want to talk about. You said you're nearing your end." —*my life comes to naught but this*— "You've done everything for us, more than we could have hoped for, but there's something else going on for you. Something about the Harrow." *For his death, there is a cost which need not concern you.* "I want to know what that is. If you've doomed yourself somehow, don't you think we have a right to understand what your help is costing you?"

The Ardent squirmed. "You inquire into private matters, Timewarden. They are my burden, not yours. I wish to bear them with some semblance of dignity."

"In that case," Covenant retorted, "you have a misplaced sense of dignity. We aren't dead yet. Someday these Giants hope to tell your tale. Hellfire, I want to be able to tell it myself. If that day ever comes, we owe it to you to tell the truth."

The beribboned man scanned the sides of the gully as if he were looking for an escape. "You search me, Timewarden, to my great discomfiture. And I say again that I cannot return if I do not depart." Then, hesitantly, his gaze met Covenant's. "Yet I must acknowledge my shame. My fault cannot be pardoned if I do not speak of it."

"Briefly, then."

Bracing himself on strips of fabric, the Ardent began.

"When our seers and oracles had cast their auguries, and had conceived of their *geas* concerning the Harrow's purpose, they saw at once that their course was perilous. I have cited the reasoning by which my people justified their intent. But that reasoning was flawed. Oh, assuredly. It rested upon a specious distinction between mere imposition and true interference, a distinction too readily effaced by events.

"To lessen the peril, therefore, the *geas* was made twofold, first to impose the lady's interpretation of his oath upon the Harrow, and thereafter to assist in the fruition of his designs. By such aid, the Insequent hoped to appease or counteract any violation of the most necessary stricture of our lives.

"Yet even then, none consented to undertake the task. The hazard of interference was deemed too great. The most valorous and mighty among us declined to shoulder such jeopardy. Therefore I claimed it in their stead."

The Ardent sighed. "I am young as the ages of Insequent are counted, blithe and self-satisfied withal, as you have assuredly observed. But you have also noted that I am timorous. In my hunger for the singular and unprecedented, I have heretofore eschewed all things which affrighted me. Thus I had no apt conception of my danger, or of yours, or of the sorrow which might ensue from my choice. Instead I rejoiced in my acquired stature among the Insequent.

"I am an acolyte of the Mahdoubt," he explained as he had in Andelain, pleading to be understood—or perhaps to be forgiven. "My intent was kindly. My particular greed is ever unsatisfied. And being young, I was complacent in my ignorance. I claimed the will of the Insequent without regard to its cost.

"Yet I did not complete my task. I failed my *geas* and you and the wide Earth. Lost among the entrancements of the Viles, and appalled by the horrors of the Lost Deep, I left the Harrow to confront his foes without my aid. Thus I permitted his death and the defeat of his designs. By timidity and weakness, I created true interference from the sophistry of imposition.

"Now I must meet the doom which I have wrought for myself. When the last powers of my people are withdrawn from me, I will pass away, leaving naught to vindicate my life except your continuance among the living."

Oh, hell! Shaken, Covenant tried to find a response. He had guessed—But he had also hoped that he was wrong.

Weakly he protested, "It doesn't have to be this way."

"Indeed?" The Ardent fluttered his clothes in disbelief. "How not, Timewarden?"

Covenant scrambled to muster an argument. "If your people can keep you alive for one more service, they can keep you alive indefinitely. Tell them we *need* you. Tell them we aren't going to survive without you. Damnation! Tell them *they* aren't going to survive if you don't help us. The whole Earth—"

"Timewarden." Gently the Ardent reproved Covenant. "That also is sophistry. Have I not spoken of fate and water? The Insequent will not credit such an avowal. I myself do not.

"Our strictures are necessary to us. Without them, we cannot be who we are."

Before anyone else had a chance to object, the Ardent swirled his apparel and vanished as if he had been disincarnated.

—the doom which I have wrought—

At some point in the distant past, Covenant had heard someone say, *There is no doom so black or deep that courage and clear sight may not find another truth beyond it.* But he could not imagine what that truth might be.

∞

After the Ardent's departure, Covenant found himself thinking obsessively about water. —*writ in water.* —*currents and stagnancies*—The basins of armor did not suffice. They could not. Only the Ironhand, Grueburn, and the Ramen had been able to drink directly from the stream, wherever it was. Like Covenant and— presumably—Linden, the others remained raw with thirst.

He tried to distract himself by remembering as much as he could about the lurker,

Sarangrave Flat, and the Spoiled Plains. But he flinched away when his efforts led him to Kurash Qwellinir and Hotash Slay; to the ruins of Foul's Creche. He was not ready, and had no power.

Water was life.

It was also erosion. Terrible storms. Downpours and floods with the force to rive mountains. Tidal waves.

And in the pellucid refreshment of Glimmermere: baptism.

Aching, Covenant wished that the Ardent had been able to take him there. With Linden. So that she might return from her suffering to something clean and Earth-powerful; redolent of love.

Wishing accomplished nothing.

Fortunately Manethrall Mahrtiir was more pragmatic. When he had assayed the company for a while, he announced, "We also must depart. Though this terrain is tainted, the stream which the Cords found is fresh from the rains of spring. And the distance is not great. It seems far only because we are weak. There we may sate our thirst entirely, and bathe, and rest. When we have done so, mayhap we will be better able to confront the conundrum of our straits."

"Aye," said Rime Coldspray. "The Manethrall counsels wisely, as he has ever done. I regret that we"—she gestured around at her comrades—"are too much wearied to bear any burdens but ourselves. Nonetheless the stream is goodly, as the Manethrall has said, and plentiful. Also its environs will afford us a measure of shade."

Covenant nodded. He had nothing else to suggest. Nothing at all.

But Stave looked up at Coldspray. "What of Anele? You have not witnessed the hurts which he endures—or which he inflicts—when he is possessed. On barren ground, he becomes the receptacle and expression of Kastenessen's fury. He cannot walk to the stream. We cannot ask it of him."

Coldspray looked away. "The Humbled—"

"He fears them," Stave stated. "He will not willingly suffer their touch."

As if to confirm Stave's assertion, Anele cowered; covered his head with his arms; moaned through his teeth.

The Ironhand sighed. "Then I will carry him, if the Masters will consent to bear my armor."

Branl agreed without hesitation. He, Galt, and Clyme knew as much as Stave did about the dangers that crowded around Anele when he stood on any surface except stone.

"In that case," Covenant said vaguely, "we should get started." The sun seemed unnaturally hot; unfamiliar to his nerves. "I sweat too much. I need more water."

He wanted to carry Linden himself. He yearned to hold her, protect her—and had no desire to shirk his responsibility for what she had undergone. But he did not have the strength. Stave could have taken her to the stream at a run: Covenant would probably collapse under her within a hundred steps.

Around him, the Giants readied themselves. Coldspray lifted Anele from Stormpast Galesend's cataphract, supported him as gently as she could. Frostheart Grueburn helped Galesend don her armor: then Galesend helped Grueburn. At Mahrtiir's command, Bhapa, Pahni, and Liand positioned themselves to watch the horizons while Clyme and Branl accepted the weight of Coldspray's stone. Gripping the *krill*, Galt impelled Jeremiah into motion.

Covenant took Linden's blackened Staff for himself. He could not use it, and did not mean to try. But he could support himself with it. It might keep him on his feet. And he hoped that its inherent participation in Earthpower and Law might lessen the likelihood that he would stumble into a mental crevasse.

Arduously the company began to move.

ဟ

For a time, they trudged across an uneven flatland like an ancient floodplain long desiccated: bleached soil streaked with ochre and dun, crystalline white and hints of verdigris, veins the color of rust; small hillocks and the remains of creek-beds; lonely interruptions of harsh grass. Gradually the breeze mounted until it raised delicate plumes of dust like feathers from the heels of Covenant's boots, the feet and sandals of his companions. That was a blessing and a curse. Cooling his face, it increased his loss of moisture. By degrees, his vision blurred until he could no longer identify Coldspray's and Grueburn's earlier trail.

But then the Ironhand indicated a line of low hills sculpted by ages of wind and the hard use of armies until they resembled the contorted bones of titans. There, she explained, lay the barrier which had turned the stream from its former course. Among those hills, running crookedly along shallow valleys like furrows plowed by a drunkard, was the stream: water in abundance.

"In another season, mayhap," she added hoarsely, "the flow from the Upper Land would not suffice for our needs. But the rains have been bountiful, as we observed during our pursuit of Longwrath. Hereafter we will doubtless fear many things. For the present, however, we need no longer fear thirst."

Covenant may have nodded. Or not: he was not paying attention. Instead he kept his gaze fixed on Stave's back as if he expected to see the former Master's shoulders slump; see Stave drop Linden—

Stupid, he muttered to himself. If necessary, Stave would keep on walking until the world ended. Reflexively, however, Covenant gauged his companions by the standard of his own weakness; and so he dreaded the worst.

Water, he insisted in silence. Water was the answer. How? He did not know. Perhaps he had not truly understood anything since Esmer had allowed the company to escape from She Who Must Not Be Named. Nevertheless he chose to believe in water. Hell, he had to believe in *some*thing. Didn't he?

If he could not save Linden, he would not be able to save anyone.

But Bhapa and Pahni had served their companions well. When the Cords had located the stream, they had also scouted an easy route through the hills. Although Covenant and some of the Giants stumbled occasionally as they ascended from the plain, they did not lose their footing.

Above them, Liand and the Cords scrambled from crest to crest, keeping watch. Liand stayed to the left, the south. More skilled than he, Bhapa and Pahni studied the north: the direction from which any threat was likely to come.

Coldspray carried Anele with her teeth set and defiance in her gait, daring the old man to become too heavy for her. A few paces ahead of her, Jeremiah trudged upward, Galt's hand on his shoulder and the *croyel*'s cruelty on his back. The boy's steps were as unsteady as Covenant's, but Jeremiah gave no sign of flagging. As long as the creature dreamed of rescue, its host could probably out-walk everyone except the *Haruchai*.

A gradual descent. Another rise. Twisted by the shape of the hills, bursts of dust as transient as wraiths skirled around the legs of the company. Here and there, stubborn granite and weary bits of sandstone protruded through their cloaks of dirt, grit, and shale.

"Soon," Coldspray panted through her teeth. "Soon." But no one responded.

Whenever Covenant shambled into a stretch of shade, gloom thickened around him as if his eyes were failing. Courage, he thought. Clear sight. Ha! Such things were figments: he could no longer recall them. Yet he did not allow himself to fall behind Stave. Linden needed him. Or she would need him eventually. Or she would need her Staff. Weakness was only weakness, after all: he remembered that. It was as human as thirst, and as compulsory. But it was nothing more. Like pain, it could be endured.

If he did not intend to endure, why was he here at all?

There may have been more climbing, more descents. He had lost track. Voices carried along the eddying breeze like the distant cries of ghosts. Then he found himself standing in a gap like a rounded trough between hills pale with age. Through a smear of dehydration, he gazed down at the stream.

Under the wide sky and the sunlight, it looked like chrism.

A short way below him, the current hastened around a curve in a small canyon, muttering irritably against the rock wall on its far side. Here the watercourse was little more than a ravine, but wide enough to leave a swath of ground like a shore within the stream's curve. Where the trough leaned down to the water, opening its arms as though to embrace the current, lay a wide expanse of sand interrupted by weather-softened boulders.

Impelled by the pressure of the sun, Covenant descended as if he were falling.

Stave and Linden were ahead of him. Coldspray and Anele. Galt with Jeremiah. Mahrtiir. Two other Giants. At a word from the Manethrall, Liand scrambled down the hillside, abandoning for the moment his watch on the south. But Covenant regarded none of them. Stiff-kneed and ungainly, he dropped Linden's Staff on the sand, stumbled to the water's edge, and lurched into the stream as if his legs had eroded under him.

How had he been reduced to this? How much of himself had he lost?

Golden boy with feet of clay

Plunging face-first into the Upper Land's runoff, he drank. To his parched nerves, the water tasted as pure as rain. It felt like bliss.

Let me help you on your way.

When he needed air, he found the sand and stone of the streambed, pushed himself upright. Anointed with relief, he gasped words that made no sense. They may have been promises or prophecies—or castigations. Splashing in the current, he scrubbed at his arms, his face, his hair; washed away as much strain as he could.

A proper push will take you far—

Then he ducked his head and drank again. The Land's rich blessings had found him even here.

But what a clumsy lad you are!

Water was the answer. It *was*. He did not understand it, but he was sure.

Finally he raised his head, wiped streams from his eyes, and took stock of the company.

As far as he could tell, Liand and most of the Giants had already swallowed their fill. Branl had assumed the Cords' watch so that they could rejoin their Manethrall. Now Galesend accepted Anele from Coldspray, freeing the Ironhand to drink again. With flasks empty of *diamondraught*, Halewhole Bluntfist supplied Anele while Latebirth tilted Jeremiah's head back and poured water into his slack mouth. In spite of his dissociation, Jeremiah gulped eagerly. When Latebirth refilled her vessel, he drained it again. Clearly the *croyel*'s magicks did not meet all of his body's needs.

Of course, Covenant thought as he studied the boy. Why else had Jeremiah required the attendance of the *skest*? The *croyel*'s power to keep him alive had limits.

Finally Covenant turned his attention to Linden.

She still hung, dream-ridden and whimpering, in the cradle of Stave's arms. Near the water's edge, the former Master stood as if he were prepared to bear the cost of her mortality until the end of Time. But his fidelity would not save her: Covenant was sure of that. Like her son, she would remain lost within herself until someone or something intervened.

That was Covenant's task. He could not ask anyone else to attempt it for him. He was alive because of her.

If he did not act soon, her nightmares might claim her permanently.

Sodden and dripping, he sloshed out of the stream. Strange that he was still weak. He had forgotten too much about being human—His flesh needed time to recover from its ordeals. It trembled for rest and food.

But he did not believe that Linden could afford to wait.

Facing Stave with water in his eyes, he said, "Let me take her."

The *Haruchai* cocked an eyebrow. "Ur-Lord?"

Quickly Rime Coldspray stepped forward. "Is this wise? What is your intent, Covenant Timewarden?"

Clyme drew closer. He may have thought that Covenant wanted or needed his support.

Covenant did not glance up at the Ironhand. "I'm going to carry her downstream," he told Stave. "Out of sight." Beyond a bulge in the hillside that looked too rugged for his wan strength. "I should be alone with her when I wake her up. She won't like having an audience."

He was confident of that. But he also desired privacy for his own sake. What he had in mind would be hurtful enough without witnesses. And no doubt Stave would stop him, if no one else reacted swiftly enough.

"Ha!" grunted Coldspray. "Sadly I fear that your weakened frame is unequal to the task. I foresee falling and broken limbs. No doubt inadvertently, you may both meet harm."

"I know that," Covenant retorted. "But I can't reach her unless we're alone. I need that." I love her. "So does she." With more ire than assurance, he added, "When I've brought her back," if he succeeded, "she'll tell you I did the right thing."

Surely she hated where she was? Loathed and feared it?

"Then," suggested the Ironhand, "permit Stave to bear her to a place of your choosing. There he will part from you, that you may do what you must."

Covenant braced himself to accept this compromise; but Stave said without hesitation, "I will not."

Ignoring the apprehension around him, Covenant looked at no one except the former Master. "Are you sure? How far are you willing to go with this? Are you ready to say you don't trust me? After everything your people and I have been through together? Hellfire, Stave! She needs me. I have to be alone with her."

Stave met Covenant's glare. "Nonetheless." Nothing in the *Haruchai*'s mien hinted that he could be moved. "I stand with the Chosen. Come good or ill, boon or bane, I will not forsake her."

"Stave," Mahrtiir interposed quietly. His tone did not imply a reprimand. "There is no test of devotion here. The first Ringthane's desires do not lessen you. The question is one of weakness, not of intent. I, too, deem that his strength does not suffice to bear her. Yet it is certain that she must be restored to us. If he seeks to be alone with her, where is the hurt? You do not forsake her if you assist him to strive for her return as he sees fit."

"Nonetheless," Stave repeated.

Cursing to himself, Covenant offered, "Pahni can come with us. She can watch from a distance." He might be able to bear his shame and chagrin if he believed that the young Cord was too far away to interfere. "She'll call for help if Linden needs it."

Roughly he asserted, "It would be better if you just let me take her."

He knew that Coldspray and Mahrtiir were right. He was not strong enough. But the struggle to carry Linden over the rocks would be of use to him. It would prepare him—

Flatly Clyme averred, "The Humbled stand with the Unbeliever, as we have declared. If you oppose him, Stave, we will counter you. We will bear Linden Avery in your stead, enforcing the ur-Lord's seclusion with her."

"No, you won't," Covenant snapped immediately. Wheeling away from Stave, he raised his maimed fists at the Humbled. "Bloody damnation! We're not going to *fight* about this. There's too much at stake, and we're all needed."

Clyme's straight stare gave nothing; surrendered nothing. But he did not contradict the Unbeliever.

Trembling, Covenant turned back to Stave. "You trust me," he said as steadily as he could, "or you don't. I respect that. I don't *like* it, but I respect it. If you can't leave me alone with her, we'll just have to wait for her to wake up on her own."

Liand had approached until he reached the Manethrall's side. There he clasped Pahni's hand. "Stave," he said like a plea. "I comprehend nothing here. I grasp only that you are Linden's friend, entirely true to her. For her sake, will you not relent?

"Both she and Thomas Covenant are closed to me. Yet I believe that there is love between them. She did not draw him back from death merely because he was silent before her, or because she feared for her son, or because she considered herself inadequate to the Land's doom. She restored him to life and the living for this reason also, that she loves him. Can you not conceive that his wish to restore her in turn is no less loving—and no less needful?"

Stave held Covenant's gaze like a challenge. "And if he has other motives as well, as she did? What then, Stonedownor?"

"Stone and Sea!" muttered the Ironhand. "You judge too severely, *Haruchai*." Her tone was heavy with impatience. "All who live have other motives as well. Of a certainty, my comrades and I do. We do not serve Linden Giantfriend alone—or Covenant Timewarden with her. In addition, we seek the meaning of our own lives. We wish to measure ourselves against the perils of these times. For the survival of our kind, also, we must strive against ruin with our whole hearts. And we have not forgotten Lostson Longwrath. We crave some reply to his pain.

"I do not doubt that something similar may be said of the Ramen. The Stonedownor's heart is conflicted within him, though his loves are as pure as any. And the old man, whom we have learned to cherish, is a snake's nest of disturbed motives.

"Therefore Giants seek to tell tales fully. We desire to scant no portion of the rich complication of lives and hearts. Joy is in the ears that hear, not in the mouth that speaks."

With her fists on her hips, Coldspray asked, "For this reason, Stave, I urge you to examine yourself. I cast no shadow upon your lealty. It is as untrammeled as the sun. But is it not also plausible that your present contention lies, not between you and Covenant Timewarden, but rather between you and these Humbled? Having been spurned by them, do you not now spurn them in his person?"

Several of the Swordmainnir murmured their agreement. In contrast, Mahrtiir scowled as if he were vexed on Stave's behalf. Bhapa studied the stream, concealing his opinion. Liand and Pahni held each other tensely.

But Covenant sagged as though he had been defeated. He had not intended to subject Stave to this. Concentrating on Linden's plight and his own rue, he had not considered that his need to be alone with her would test the former Master. And he knew the strict pride of the *Haruchai* too well.

Like Linden, apparently, he could not endeavor to accomplish good without questionable means.

Stave's countenance revealed nothing. The scar where he had lost his left eye seemed to preclude any expression. When he spoke, his reply took Covenant by surprise.

"You gauge me justly, Giant. I do not recant my concern. I mislike it that the ur-Lord does not name the nature of his intent. How will he retrieve the Chosen from her travails? He does not say.

"Yet I acknowledge that I'm prideful, though I have been taught much regarding humility. And I have learned that pride is a false guide. I will accede to the ur-Lord's wishes. If the Humbled perceive my consent as submission—" He shrugged, lifting Linden slightly. "They are Masters, misled by mistaken devoir."

A sigh of relief breathed among the gathered companions. For a moment, Covenant felt unaccountably weaker, as if the sun had already begun to leech the fluid from his veins. Nevertheless he forced himself to respond as if he trusted himself.

"In that case," he said hoarsely, "we should go now. The sooner the better. I don't know what's happening to her in there, but it scares me."

Stave's nod seemed to imply an unbegrudged bow.

The Manethrall cleared his throat. "Cord Pahni, when the first Ringthane has found a place which satisfies his purpose, you will do as he instructs. Until then, you will watch over his weakness. No harm can befall Linden Avery in Stave's arms, but Thomas Covenant is vulnerable to misstep. Your first task is to ward him."

Pahni cast a troubled glance at Liand; but she did not hesitate. "As you command, Manethrall."

At last, Covenant remembered that he was no longer holding Linden's Staff. Awkwardly he reclaimed it from the sand. "In case she needs it," he explained to no one in particular. Then he told Stave and Pahni, "Let's go. I'm not getting any stronger."

He would need a certain kind of weakness: the kind that inspired desperation.

Turning downstream, he started toward the hillside bulging with rocks which blocked the eastward watercourse from view.

As both Pahni and Stave joined him, the Giants parted to let them pass. Stave bore Linden with familiar ease. Some dark emotion cast a shadow across Pahni's features, but she did not allow it to interfere with her attentiveness.

As Covenant neared the first rise, he heard Anele's voice. Instinctively he turned his head; saw Anele sitting in the basin of Stormpast Galesend's breastplate. With one hand, the old man stroked the inner surface of the armor. The other he brushed back and forth through the sand, making trails like glyphs or sigils.

Pronouncing each word distinctly, Anele said, "This stone does not recall Linden Avery, Chosen Earthfriend. Yet Anele does. The world will not see her like again."

The old man's words followed Covenant like a prediction of failure as he began clambering along the hillside. —not see her like again. If he failed to rouse Linden, he would make a prophet of Anele.

Distracted, he stumbled; might have fallen. But Pahni caught his arm. After a moment like imminent panic, he remembered the importance of paying attention to where he was and what he did; of watching where he set his feet, being ready to use his hands. As he worked his way among the rocks, he reverted to the neglected disciplines of his disease, the care required by leprosy.

His eyes told him that some of the stones had been weathered smooth while others remained rough and jagged; hazardous. His hands did not. He could not be confident of his grip when he tried to secure his balance on a rock, or on Linden's Staff. Among the obstacles of the slope, he saw patches of dirt parched to the hue of straw; slides of shale so old that they had forgotten their original colors. Gradually his life contracted until it contained little except places to put his feet and hands. He hardly noticed

Stave's progress above him on the hillside, Pahni's watchfulness, the gentle twisting of the breeze, or the vexed mutter of the stream.

For a time, he did not think about Linden or fear.

Laboring, he crested the first rise. As he started down the far side, the rest of the company fell out of sight behind him. Beyond this slope, the next hill looked easier. Already he felt weak enough for any amount of desperation. Nonetheless he was not ready.

Perhaps he would never be ready: not for this. Beyond the shallower climb of the second hillside, past the second writhe of the watercourse, he found what he sought. Below him, the stream curved into and then away from a narrow scallop of sand at the foot of an empty arroyo. And as the current ran onward, it was constricted between bluff facets of granite. There, where the flow tumbled against stone, it had spent long ages of runoff gnawing at its bed until it had formed a pool of deeper water.

From his position above the stream, the pool's depth made the water look dark; almost bottomless. It might have been a well that reached into the heart of the Lower Land.

Ah, hell, he thought. Bloody damnation. But he did not stop. Supported by Pahni and the Staff of Law, he accompanied Stave down to the sand at the stream's edge.

Golden boy with feet of clay.

Chary of hesitation, he dropped the Staff unceremoniously and turned to scan the northern ridgeline. After a moment, he spotted a squat boulder the size of a hut propped against the horizon.

"That big rock," he told Pahni. His voice rasped in his throat. "You can watch from there." For her sake, he added, "Trust your instincts. If you think we need help, call Stave."

She was Ramen; but Stave was *Haruchai*. He would respond more swiftly.

Doubt and determination flitted like spectres across the background of the Cord's gaze. "I will abide by your desires," she replied, "as my Manethrall has commanded." Then her expression sharpened. "And I will heed the counsels of my heart."

At once, she spun away and began to ascend the hillside. Lithe and graceful, she appeared to glide upward in spite of her weariness.

Now, Covenant ordered himself. Now or never. Do it.

If he became any weaker, he would fall on his face.

Extending his arms, he faced Stave. "Out of sight," he said like a man who could hardly stand. "Behind Pahni's boulder, if you want. With your senses, you'll probably know what happens as soon as she does. But I want you to wait until she warns you. Trust me as long as you can. Or trust her.

"You can't care about Linden any more than I do. And you don't need her as badly."

Stave regarded him. "You believe that the Cord will call out. You are certain that I will sense peril."

Covenant met Stave's gaze, and held out his arms, and said nothing further.

After a moment, Stave surrendered Linden to Covenant's unsteady clasp. Without pausing, the former Master turned and strode after Pahni. Like her, he seemed to move more effortlessly than Covenant could imagine.

Apparently he trusted Covenant that far. At least as far as the boulder. Perhaps his *Haruchai* intransigence would unbend enough to let Covenant succeed or fail.

Trembling with strain, Covenant watched Stave and Pahni mount the slope. Ignoring his frailty, he stood where he was until the Cord reached the boulder he had indicated; until Stave disappeared behind it. Then, one small wrenched step at a time, Covenant started toward the stream.

His feet were numb: he could not feel his way. Instead he simply assumed that the sand shelved down gradually. Relying on blind luck or the Land's providence, he lurched into the current.

As directly as he could, he headed toward the pool of deeper water. The well—

Fortune blessed him. His boots did not begin to strike unseen rocks until the stream had accepted a portion of Linden's weight. With that assistance, he was able to keep his balance when he stumbled.

He did not look at her face. If he allowed himself to gaze upon her helplessness now, to regard the loved lines of her nose and mouth, the fraught tension of her brow, he feared that his resolve would crumble. The taut dance of her eyes behind their lids would unman him. He would lock his knees, stop moving, call for help, and weep.

Clenching his teeth until his jaws ached, he kept his eyes straight ahead and walked deeper.

As soon as the water reached his biceps, and he guessed that the streambed was about to drop away, he released Linden's legs. Clamped his hand over her mouth. Pinched her nose with his truncated fingers.

Took a deep breath and dropped with her into the darkness.

When she finally began to struggle for air, he did not let her go.

Trying to Start Again

Linden Avery was drowning in She Who Must Not Be Named. She knew the truth, and her terror was absolute. She had released a flood among the roots of Mount Thunder. Because of her, ancient poisons and the accumulated weight of millennia had thundered into the cavern. They had swept her companions out of existence, carried Jeremiah and Covenant like flotsam to the bottom of the world. Everything that she had ever loved was gone.

But mere water could not harm her now. She had not accompanied her son and her only true lover to their deaths. Instead she had been swallowed by shrieking and hunger. She Who Must Not Be Named had claimed her. Simultaneously preserved and excruciated by betrayed desire and rage, Emereau Vrai and Diassomer Mininderain and the Auriference and Elena and a host of lost women had taken Linden. She had been consumed by the reified outcome of her actions in Jeremiah's name, and in Covenant's. Her own name had become agony.

She did not understand Elena's presence. Nor did she question it.

While the Arch endured, her name would always be agony. And even then—Ah, then! Voices like her own wailed of torments that could never end. When all of creation had been unmade, She Who Must Not Be Named would remain. Her anguish would remain. She was an eternal being: a concept as essential and illimitable as Creation or Despite. Tortures would expand beyond the swallowed stars, beyond the salvific definitions of Time, beyond comprehension, until they filled the reaches of infinity. They could not die, and so they could not stop. The treachery which had formed the bane could not be healed.

Linden knew those women, those victims, in their damnation. They were one with She Who Must Not Be Named; but they were also themselves, as distinct as their spiritual wounds. Helplessly Linden participated in their goaded horror, their compelled craving for food and slaughter. But she knew Elena best because Linden, too, had betrayed Covenant's daughter. With the example of Berek and Damelon and Loric to guide her, she had nevertheless denied Elena Law-Breaker, child of Lena and rape. Linden had withheld compassion where it was most desperately wanted. A Law-Breaker herself, she was intimately familiar with the exigencies and passions which had driven Elena. And yet Linden had refused or failed—

Now she deserved her fate. She could not pretend otherwise. Nevertheless she screamed like all the others, multitudes of them: screamed with her whole being, and raged to cause more pain, and was lost.

On Gallows Howe, she had become the woman who had resurrected Thomas Covenant. But she had also become a woman who had no pity to give Elena.

Soon she would be Emereau Vrai as well: the woman forcibly bereft of her *Elohim* lover; the woman who had conceived the *merewives* in fury and mourning. She would be the Auriference, whose greed had made her as daring as the Harrow, and as foolish. Eventually she would be Diassomer Mininderain and know the truth.

It was that Covenant had not betrayed her. Never. That was Roger's doing. But since then, she had betrayed herself. And her friends. And the Land.

And her son.

She had brought her doom upon herself.

When her body first began to strive for breath, she did not understand. She had been consumed. How was it possible, then, that she could starve for any sustenance except ruin and release? Yet her need gripped her: an autonomic struggle which recognized no relief except air. Spasms clenched her muscles; fought against constraint, blockage, weight. The tissues of her lungs seemed to burst and bleed. Instinctively she tugged at the arm that hugged her chest, the hand that sealed her mouth and nose. Failing to break free, she dragged her nails across skin that must not have been hers because she felt nothing.

There may have been a head pressed to hers, a cheek tight against the side of her face. She tried to reach eyes and gouge them out so that she would be given a chance to *breathe*—

Then hands lifted her. They were stronger than She Who Must Not Be Named. Strong enough to be the foundation-stones of reality: strong enough to draw her out of despair. Through a fading chorus of screams, they released her from the killing embrace, the smothering clasp.

While she tried to gulp water into her lungs, the hands raised her into air and light.

The air and light of the living.

Frantically she gasped to fill her chest with survival.

Now she was upheld by a single hand that gripped the back of her shirt. Amid the receding cacophony of torrents, she seemed to hear an urgent voice pant, "Ringthane! Linden Avery!"

A voice that she may have known restored her name.

Was that possible? It was not. She Who Must Not Be Named would never tolerate it.

Nevertheless the voice was Pahni's. The light on Linden's face was sunshine: she was breathing air. The fluid in which she floated was water instead of anguish.

Clean water. *Fresh* water.

"Ringthane, hear me!"

Beyond question, that voice belonged to Pahni.

Streaming hair covered Linden's eyes. Water splashed inadvertently into her mouth. While she coughed, nightmares endeavored to pierce the daylight, breach the presence of her saviors. They tried to drag her back into the depths. But their grasp on her had frayed. It grew weaker with every won breath.

She was in water somewhere, saved and sustained.

"Ringthane! Here is the Staff!"

The bane could not reach her.

At her side, Stave said, "When Linden accepts the Staff, Cord, will you be able to preserve the ur-Lord? Does your strength suffice? He has fallen within himself once more, and cannot swim. Your aid will ease my task."

"We must escape this current. It hastens, and we may tumble upon rapids beyond those stones."

Linden felt no current. It was gentle—or she had not entirely returned to her body. But she recognized Covenant's ring on its chain around her neck.

"Aye." Pahni's voice was clear over the complex plaints of running water. "The Staff is indeed wondrous. I have held it for moments only, yet already I have become more than I was."

"Then assist me," Stave instructed, "while she regains her senses. We must swim in their stead."

Linden heard them plainly enough. Now she began to understand what they were saying. The Staff. *Her* Staff. The current. Swim.

And Covenant.

They were alive. God, they were *alive*!

Quivering at the exertion, she forced her chin upward, took a long breath free of spattered water. Then she managed to lift her hands long enough to push the hair out of her eyes.

Sunlight. Not the fatal blackness of caverns: sunlight. The pale shapes of hills. A blue sky like a gift, untainted by violation.

Somewhere among the secrets of her spirit, the bane's wailing still echoed. But it was only a memory.

When she blinked her eyes clear, she saw Pahni swimming near her. With one hand, the young Cord offered the Staff of Law, black as a shaft of ebony, and written in runes. With the other, she held Covenant's shoulder, helping Stave keep his head above water.

Opposite Pahni, Stave kicked strongly to support both Linden and Covenant.

Covenant hung limp in the water, drifting. His head lolled back. He looked unconscious; abandoned.

Beneath the surface, faint flowers of blood bloomed from his forearms; blossomed and dissipated. Linden must have scratched him. Like Joan—Long ago, when Linden had first met Covenant, Joan had dragged her nails across the back of his hand, tasted his blood, and become briefly sane.

Feebly Linden began trying to move her legs. She needed Covenant. She wanted to reach out.

But she was too weak. Too full of shared screams. Floundering, she clutched at her Staff.

It was the Staff of Law, articulate with Earthpower. Under *Melenkurion* Skyweir, she had used it to channel more power than she could imagine. She had transformed it to blackness. She had never been able to read its runes. Nevertheless she could interpret its fundamental rightness. It was *hers*. In its own way, it was as natural to her as the blood in her veins. When she closed her fingers on it, it seemed to call her back from a terrible absence.

The sky became brighter: the water, colder. As the Staff's vitality ran along her hands and arms into her chest, Stave and Pahni gained substance until they were as definite as promises. Gradually the sounds of torment sank back into their abyss. The sunshine on her face felt like the light of resurrection.

Holding the Staff after her immersion in the bane, she could almost believe in hope.

Instinctively she began kicking against the water. Then she reached out to grip one of Covenant's arms. Perhaps she helped Pahni and Stave prevent him from sinking.

She did not know how his ring had been restored to her, and did not care. She did not want to think about anything, remember anything, except Covenant and sunlight, Pahni and Stave.

Then Pahni accepted Covenant's slack weight from Stave. While Stave impelled Linden across the current, the young Cord swam away from the rocks, drawing Covenant after her on his back.

With Stave's aid, Linden rose higher in the water; high enough to see that Pahni was headed toward a swath of sand like a beach in a bend in the stream. Moment by moment, her health-sense absorbed strength from the Staff. Vaguely she understood that she had been plunged into a pool deeper than the rest of the flow. Covenant must have done that. Why else were his forearms bleeding? He must have submerged her and held her down because every other effort to retrieve her from her nightmares had failed.

He had found a way to save her when she had been unable to save herself.

She would have clung to him if she could have done so without hindering Pahni. Her rescued heart ached to throw her arms around him. Hugging him would not fill Jeremiah's place in her clasp, or in her love. But she was a woman who needed to touch and embrace. She yearned for the comfort of contact. And Covenant had saved her: she believed that. In his arms, she might begin to recover from her participation in She Who Must Not Be Named.

He was Thomas Covenant: he would forgive her. In spite of what she had done to him. And to Elena.

Like her, he might not forgive himself.

Then she saw Pahni's feet find the streambed. The Cord's shoulders broke the surface: she was able to pull Covenant along more easily. A moment later, Stave began to propel himself and Linden step by step. Linden's boots scraped clusters of stones.

As soon as she gained purchase on the bottom, she tugged away from Stave and surged after Covenant. In a flurry of water, she thrashed forward, leaning against the current.

Ahead of her, Pahni paused.

Linden closed the small distance as if she were frantic. Still waist deep in the stream, she tossed her Staff to Pahni so that she would not inadvertently violate Covenant with Earthpower. The girl's eyes sprang wide in surprise, but she released one hand from Covenant to catch the Staff.

In a burst of grief and longing, Linden pitched forward. As she fell onto Covenant, she wrapped her arms around him. Her embrace closed as though she had been starving for the touch of his body on hers; and her weight drove both of them underwater.

She hardly felt the stream sweep over them. Instead his leprosy jolted her nerves. The dismemberment of his mind and memories hurt her like the gelid misery of emptiness within a *caesure*. Nevertheless he was *here*. He was real and alive: the Thomas Covenant who had nurtured her with his love until she had grown able to love him in return. For a few moments, at least, that was enough.

Entire worlds might be redeemed, as long as Covenant remained alive.

His vacancy hurt her. Of course it hurt her. Lost as he was, he could not reply to her clasp. Parts of him were too numb to recognize her. Nevertheless she clung to him as though he were the rock to which she had anchored her own life, and Jeremiah's, and the Land's.

And as she held him, a spark of silver fire gleamed briefly where her breasts met his chest. It seemed to shine through her damaged shirt until it filled his face, and hers, with argent possibilities. Then it vanished.

Wild magic. Only a hint, but—wild magic.

With a palpable wrench that nearly drove the breath from her lungs, Covenant returned to himself and began to struggle.

An instant later, hands snatched them upward. Quickly Linden released Covenant so that Pahni and Stave could lift him to the surface before he inhaled water. Then she raised herself. Braced on Stave, she gained her feet in a cascade bright with sunshine and sorrow.

When she wiped her eyes clear of rills and lank hair, she saw Covenant aghast in front of her. He seemed barely able to stand; so weak with relief and dismay that he could not find his balance.

"Oh, Linden—" he panted. In the sun's light, the scar on his forehead looked like a denunciation. "Damnation. I nearly—"

"Don't say it." She, too, was panting. Some of the fetters had been struck from her heart: it seemed to fill her chest, leaving too little room for breath. "It doesn't matter. You saved me."

"Chosen." Stave's harshness hurt Linden's hearing like a remembered shriek. "He endangered your life."

Dumbly Pahni nodded as if she shared Covenant's consternation.

Linden shook her head, pushed her dripping hair behind her ears. "I don't care." Memories of Elena and screaming clogged her throat: she could not continue until she swallowed them. "You don't know where I was."

Stave's tone changed. "Chosen?" His irrefusable hands turned her to face him. "Linden?"

Because she had no words for what she felt, Linden reached out for the Staff. Without hesitation, Pahni released it; and at once, Linden pulled it to her, wrapped her arms around it as though it might shield her.

"The bane got me," she said, still panting. "Or I thought it did. I was part of it, and I couldn't get away. I couldn't. Until Covenant—" In spite of Stave's insistence, she looked at Covenant again. "I don't care how you did it. You were my only chance, and you saved me."

Her affirmation eased him. She could see the lines of his self-judgment soften. He made a twisted effort to smile. Opening his hands, he indicated himself: his physical incarnation or his mental presence. "Then we're even."

Even? Never! Linden wanted to launch herself at him again; to feel him return her embrace of his own volition. A part of her had spent years dying to be held as well as to hold; withering like a plant that could not live much longer without sun and rain. He was not Jeremiah: he could choose—

Before she moved, however, she saw a quick flaring of alarm in his eyes. He raised his hands to ward her away; stumbled backward. "Don't touch me." Some private conflict undermined him: she felt its emanations. He was barely able to make himself heard over the fretted susurration of the current. "Linden, please. I'm not ready. I've lost too much of myself. I'm afraid of what I'm becoming. Or what I might have to be. I need to find that out before—" His voice faded. Pain blurred his gaze. The muscles of his jaw clenched. Obviously forcing himself, he finished, "Just don't touch me. There's too much at stake."

Stung, Linden jerked her gaze away. Without transition, the clarity of the light and the cleanliness of the water seemed to become sterile and comfortless, uncaring. He might as well have said in chagrin, *What have you done?* Irrationally she believed that he could see the bane within her still, crouched ready to emerge as soon as She found an opportunity to do harm.

It was more than she could bear.

After a moment, however, she found that she was not surprised. What had she expected? An eager welcome? Immediate love? For the woman who had forced him back into his damaged mortality? The woman who had roused the Worm of the World's End?

It was fitting that Covenant did not want her touch. It was fitting that her Staff was as black as the Lost Deep.

And it changed nothing.

Rigid with self-coercion, she nodded. "All right." The air had turned to ash in her throat. "I think I understand that much." She did not look at Covenant again; avoided Stave's steady regard. Instead she followed the stream with her eyes as it curled around her waist and swirled past her. "So tell me what happened. Why are we still alive? Where is everyone else? Where is Jeremiah? How is he?"

"For the moment, Chosen," Stave replied promptly, "you need not fear. All are safe. By cunning and desperation, the ur-Lord persuaded Esmer to depart. Thereafter the Ardent transported us here, beyond the bane's grasp. Though I am not certain, I deem that even the ur-viles and Waynhim eluded the bane's wrath.

"We stand now upon the Lower Land south and east of Mount Thunder, between the great cliff of Landsdrop and the perils of Sarangrave Flat. Your companions and comrades await you upstream. Only the Ardent has departed, promising a final service upon his return. All have suffered no further hurt, apart from weariness and privation. Your son is as he was, warded by Galt and Loric's *krill*. The Unbeliever's ring he himself restored to you.

"To this place, you were borne at his urging. His intent he did not reveal."

It was too much: Linden could not absorb it all. And it, too, changed nothing. Just don't touch me. She did not lift her eyes from the restless wash of the stream. For the moment, she only cared that Jeremiah was nearby.

When Stave's silence told her that he was done, she released one arm from the Staff, bent to the stream, and splashed water onto her face, trying to rinse the despair from her skin.

"There's more," Covenant said roughly, "but you don't need to hear it right now." His tone implied distress like a premonition. "I just want you to know that we're not safe from Esmer. I didn't convince him to stop betraying us. He'll try again when he figures out how to serve you and Kastenessen at the same time."

That, too, was more than she could absorb. Without thinking, she repeated, "I don't care. I'm just glad that you managed to save Jeremiah." Learning now that he had been lost would have destroyed her. "Everything else—" She shrugged instead of weeping. "You can explain it all later."

Don't touch me.

"That is wisdom," Stave stated firmly. "The ur-Lord's suasion of Esmer was needful, as it now appears that your immersion was needful. Continuing to speak of such matters serves no purpose."

His manner suggested that he was addressing Pahni, advising her not to reveal what Covenant had done. If so, Linden approved. She owed Covenant that much. His rejection made gratitude impossible; but it did not change the fact that he had broken the bane's grip on her mind. Because of him, she could still hope to rescue her son from the *croyel*.

"Chosen," Stave continued, "will you not withdraw from the stream?" With one hand, he gestured toward the patch of sand at the water's edge. "There you may dry your raiment, and accept the sun's warmth, and speak of whatsoever you desire."

Linden shook her head. Her sodden clothes did not trouble her. And she was not ready to face the decisions that awaited her; the impossible futures. Her memories of the monster on Jeremiah's back were bad enough: the actuality would be worse.

Like Covenant, her son was someone whom she could not touch.

"I need a bath," she explained, groaning to herself. More than that, she needed to recover some semblance of emotional balance. "If you don't mind, Stave, you can take Covenant back to the others." She could not bear to look at him yet. "Pahni can stay with me. When I don't feel quite so disgusted"—her mouth twisted at the thought of her filthy hair and rank clothes—"she'll help me find you."

"By my Manethrall's command, Ringthane," Pahni answered, "I must comply with Thomas Covenant's wishes. If the Unbeliever will grant it, however, I will abide with you gladly." Her tone hinted that she might choose to defy Mahrtiir's orders.

"Ah, hell," Covenant sighed. "Why not?" Linden heard regret in his voice. "After what you've been through, the least you deserve is a chance to be left alone."

"Come on, Stave." He lifted a hand in the direction of Stave's shoulder. "I'm exhausted. I probably won't make it without help."

"Go on," Linden murmured automatically. She wanted him gone; wanted to forget him if she could. In self-defense, she had fixed her mind on the idea of a bath: she was impatient to take off her clothes. In the absence of soap, she could use sand to rub away the most tactile of her many soilures.

Pahni shot Stave a quick glance. "If you will, Stave, assure Liand that I am"—she caught herself—"that we are well."

Linden was vaguely surprised to hear the Cord use Stave's name. Her closest friends had become more comfortable with each other than they had once been. For that, she gave Stave most of the credit. He had taught the Ramen and Liand to regret their initial distrust.

"Be certain of it," Stave replied as he drew Covenant's arm across his shoulders. "Return to us when the Chosen desires it. There is no present need for haste."

"He means," Covenant muttered, "we don't have any food, so you might as well do what you can to save your strength."

Then he and Stave turned away, heading for the small scrap of beach and the nearest hillside.

Was that north? Linden wondered briefly. Yes, her health-sense assured her. Or rather northwest. But she dismissed such matters almost immediately. Her percipience had become as precise as Loric's *krill*; and she was acutely conscious of muck and strain staining her hair, her skin, her clothes. While Covenant and Stave rose dripping from the stream and began to angle across the littered hillside, she confirmed that Jeremiah's healed racecar still rested deep in her pocket. When she explored her sore ribs, her cracked kneecap, her battered shin, she found that they did not demand care. She dismissed them as well.

As soon as Covenant and Stave disappeared beyond the ridgeline, she braced her Staff on the streambed, bent close to the water, and began trying to pull off one of her boots.

She could not move it. Full of water, it stuck to her; or she was too weak.

At once, however, Pahni came closer. "Permit me, Ringthane." Before Linden could reply, the girl ducked beneath the surface. Able to use both hands, she tugged off Linden's boot and sock.

Grateful at last, Linden put her foot down, raised her other boot to Pahni. Then the Cord stood up; took a breath; tossed the water from her eyes.

"If you will grant me a moment, Ringthane, I will set your footwear upon a rock to dry." She nodded toward the shore. "Then I will return to wash your garments while you bathe."

Linden was already unbuttoning her shirt. "Just throw them. I'll do something about it later if they're uncomfortable."

"As you wish." Turning, Pahni flung the boots to the scallop of sand. Then she held out a hand for Linden's shirt.

The red flannel was damaged in a variety of ways. Ruefully Linden eyed the bullet holes, front and back. She was fortunate, she supposed, that the slug had passed straight through her. Even now, she did not know how she had healed herself. If the bullet had remained in her—

Making so many mistakes, taking so many risks, she had apparently given Lord

Foul exactly what he wanted. But she refused to second-guess herself now. Regret was costly; as draining as battle. If Covenant did not want her love, he could go to hell. She had found her son. Now she intended to concentrate on learning how to free him from the *croyel*.

Passing her shirt to Pahni, Linden crouched to the challenge of peeling off her jeans.

When she finally succeeded at removing them, she discovered that some trick of wet or color emphasized the green script left by the tall grasses of the Verge of Wandering. Her jeans were like the Staff, inscribed in a language which she could not read.

In Garroting Deep, Caerroil Wildwood had said of her, *She wears the mark of fecundity and long grass. Also she has paid the price of woe. And the sigil of the Land's need has been placed upon her.* For that reason, he had spared her life.

And he had given her *the burden of a question*—

How may life endure in the Land, if the Forestals fail and perish—? *Must it transpire that beauty and truth shall pass utterly when we are gone?*

Linden had promised the ancient guardian of Garroting Deep an answer; but she had no idea how to keep her word.

Frowning, she tossed her jeans to Pahni as though she meant to spurn their implications. Inadequacy and loss: needs that she would never be able to satisfy: loads too heavy for her to bear. The Staff she wedged between rocks so that it would not float away. If it drifted, Pahni would retrieve it.

Regret could be refused. Despair was a different issue.

As if in abnegation, Linden sank into the stream, scooped up sand, and began rubbing handfuls of grit into her hair, onto her scalp. Scouring herself—

The abrasion hurt, but she welcomed it.

ဤ

Later Linden sat on a flat stone near the sand, wearing her wet clothes but not her socks and boots; resting with her feet in the cool caress of the current. Her skin felt scraped raw, and there were patches on her scalp where she had drawn blood. But she did not mind. Those pains were trivial by comparison.

Her socks lay drying beside her. For the time being, she left her boots where Pahni had thrown them. The Staff of Law she held across her lap. With her fingertips, she stroked the incused runes. They could have signified anything; but she wanted to believe that they were a prophecy of hope.

Unhindered by Kevin's Dirt, she ought to be able to accomplish almost anything with her Staff and Covenant's ring. Surely she could do more for Jeremiah here than in the Lost Deep?

Cross-legged and straight-backed, Pahni sat on another stone nearby. She, too, had bathed thoroughly. Now she gazed into the stream with tension in her shoulders and shadows in her eyes.

Linden was not ready to resume thinking and caring; not really. But the conflicted purity of Pahni's spirit pleaded for her attention. Sighing to herself, she said quietly, "Talk to me, Pahni. Something is troubling you. I could try to guess, but it's better if you just tell me."

"Ah, Ringthane," the girl replied with a sigh of her own. "I am a small creature among the great beings and terrors of the world. My concerns do not merit your heed."

Don't touch me.

Then the Cord turned. Gazing nakedly into Linden's eyes, Pahni said, "Yet Liand is not a small creature. He is not. He is the first true Stonedownor in uncounted centuries, wielder of the Sunstone's wonder"—she faltered for a moment—"and my beloved. His valor and daring are worthy of Giantish tales. Indeed, they are worthy of the Ranyhyn. For his sake, I will speak."

Linden knew what was coming. Nevertheless she required herself to wait in silence.

Carefully Pahni said, "It becomes ever plainer that when Anele addressed us on the plateau of Glimmermere, he spoke at the Timewarden's behest. His pronouncements were given to him by the Timewarden's spanning consciousness."

Linden nodded. "I remember."

I wish I could spare you. Hell, I wish any of us could spare you. But I can't see any way around it.

"Then you will recall," the Cord continued, "that Anele's words led Liand to the *orcrest* which has exalted him. But they also suggested some arduous and mayhap fatal outcome which can not or must not be evaded.

"Ringthane—" Again Pahni faltered. Lowering her eyes, she asked over the background whisper of the stream, "Do you now comprehend the Timewarden's prophecy? It lies beyond me, little as I am. By bravery and foresight and love, you have grown to stand among the mighty of the Earth—aye, and to defy them when you must. Do you possess any light that may dispel the darkness which knots my heart? For Liand's sake, I ask it—he who has been your friend and companion from the start, and has never wavered."

Oh, Pahni, Linden wanted to say. You're going to break my heart. She had been afraid for Liand since the day when he had insisted on aiding her escape from Mithil Stonedown. But she had no idea what Covenant's assertions meant.

She can do this. Tell her I said that. And there's no one else who can even make the attempt.

Stroking the Staff for courage, she answered, "I'm sorry, Pahni. I just don't. No matter what you think, I'm not brave, and I sure as hell don't have any foresight. The future is as dark to me as it is to you. You'll have to ask Covenant," although he had probably lost that memory. "Or I will, if you want."

Pahni set her teeth. Blinking furiously, she stared out over the watercourse. "I discern sooth in your words," she said after a moment. "But I do not grasp how they can be sooth. You are Linden Avery, Linden Giantfriend, the Ringthane, the Chosen. How does it chance that you are able to offer me naught?"

"You don't understand," Linden replied more severely than she intended, "but you should. You called yourself a small creature. That's how *I* feel. All the time." She gestured around her. "I'm too little for all this. I want to save my son. If I can't do that, I want to keep him safe as long as possible. That's as far as I go. The rest of it—" She had made too many promises which she could not keep. Even resurrecting Covenant was a promise she had already broken by failing to resurrect him whole. "The rest is too much for me. It's someone else's problem."

A frown complicated the Cord's mien. "I discern sooth," she repeated. Then she said more strongly, "Nonetheless I deem that you are mistaken in yourself. Time and again, you have vindicated the Timewarden's faith in you. Time and again, you have wrought miracles for our redemption. If you name yourself a small creature, as I am, you gauge yourself unjustly."

"No, I don't," Linden retorted with more vehemence. "You still don't understand what I'm trying to say. Liand isn't small, and neither are you. If there's any greatness left in the world, it's *yours*." And Covenant's. "Greatness isn't about power. It's about who you are. You're so unselfish that it staggers me. You make yourselves greater every day. I'm just shrinking."

Stricken by horror and weakness, she had drowned in She Who Must Not Be Named: she knew the truth.

Why else did she need Covenant so badly?

Why else had he refused her?

Now the girl faced Linden again. With none of her familiar unassuming shyness, she said, "Then truly, Ringthane, you have no choice—you who are called the Chosen. You must relieve your son from the toils of the *croyel*. If you do not, you will founder in bitterness, and Fangthane's triumph over you will be complete."

Linden ground her teeth. "In that case"—abruptly she withdrew her feet from the stream and stood up—"we should get started on—on whatever it is we're going to do. I hope you're wrong. But I doubt it."

Where her son was concerned, she had made the only choice that mattered when she adopted him.

Graceful as water, Pahni also rose. Her eagerness to return to Liand was palpable as she went to retrieve Linden's boots.

But Linden was not eager. She was simply vexed. Yet behind her ire lay an ache of dread. Covenant had already pushed her away. If he also pushed away the decisions and responsibilities that she had trusted him to assume—if he repudiated *all* of her reasons for restoring his life—

She was not sure that she would be able to face him.

෴

P lodding through arid heat over the baked hills, Linden was sweating in spite of her soaked boots and damp socks as she rejoined the company.

From the hillside above them, she saw Covenant and Stave, Jeremiah and Galt, Liand and Anele, the Giants and Manethrall Mahrtiir and Bhapa. A glance was enough to assure her that they had rested and drunk their fill. Temporarily, at least, most of them had recovered a portion of their natural toughness. Now they sat waiting in the shade among the boulders close to the stream.

On nearby ridges, Clyme and Branl stood watch. This far from the Land's foes, Linden could not imagine that the company faced any immediate danger except hunger. Nevertheless she was glad for the wariness of the Humbled.

She also could not imagine why the Ardent had brought her companions here, where they could do nothing. Nor did she understand why the Insequent had abandoned them.

Liand greeted her and Pahni with a glad shout. Wasting his scant stamina, he sprang to his feet and hurried up the hillside to meet them. With a warm smile for Pahni, he wrapped his arms around Linden.

His hug was brief, a momentary taste of the deeper embraces for which she was starving. Nevertheless it steadied her. It reminded her sore nerves and her hidden wounds that she was not alone, in spite of Covenant's rejection. She still had friends who were strong and faithful, friends who had earned every bit of her esteem. If Covenant refused to lead the company, perhaps someone else would do so.

The salutations of the Swordmainnir were less impulsive, but they all rose from their resting places and spoke Linden's name with evident relief, pleased to see for themselves that she had escaped her nightmares.

Anele sat in Galesend's armor without acknowledging Linden. In contrast, Mahrtiir gave her a bow of approval; and Bhapa waved, grinning crookedly. But Jeremiah did not react, and the *croyel* ignored her. For reasons of its own, the creature's gaze followed Liand. As usual, the Humbled revealed nothing.

Depending on the Staff and Liand for balance, Linden made her way down the slope. As she descended, she studied Covenant's twisted effort to smile for her. Protecting herself, she tried to think, Go to hell. But she could not look at him and feel that way. At least for the time being, he was *present*. In spite of his rejection, she prayed that his absences would grow less frequent as his long past leaked away.

Like her, he was becoming less than he had once been. To that extent, at least, she understood his desire to distance himself.

She would have preferred to avoid looking at Jeremiah. She did not want to be reminded that nothing had changed. But even a brief glance at his slack stance and muddied gaze, the droop of his mouth, and the stubble like grime on his cheeks confirmed that he was still the *croyel*'s prisoner. And the monster's possessive malice was unabated. Despite the eldritch keenness of the *krill*'s edge only a breath from its neck, its eyes glared with unspecified threats, and its jaws champed steadily, avid to sink its fangs into Jeremiah's throat once more.

The sores on his neck where the creature had fed were raw and open; but they did not bleed, and showed no sign of infection. For the present, at least, Linden lacked the courage to risk treating them.

If the *croyel* had some concrete reason to hope for rescue, she could not perceive it: not without wielding the fire of her Staff. But soon, she promised herself. Soon she would make the attempt. Earlier she had been appalled by what she had discerned of the *croyel*'s mind—and of its intimate bond with Jeremiah's. Now she had other resources.

If her Staff did not suffice, the unobstructed penetration of her health-sense might enable her to wield wild magic with enough precision to threaten the *croyel* without harming her son.

But not yet. She was not ready. Inanition and helpless screaming had left her frail; too weak for extravagant hazards. She needed time to gather herself before she confronted the challenge of her son's straits.

Apart from Covenant and Anele, all of Linden's companions were on their feet. When she sank down to sit leaning against a rock a few paces from Covenant, however, the Giants also seated themselves, sighing gratefully. Liand and the Ramen did the same. Perhaps deliberately, they formed a wide circle that arced from Linden to Covenant and back without excluding Anele.

Uncertain of what to say, or how to begin, Linden asked awkwardly, "Have you decided anything?"

"Without you?" Covenant snorted; but his scorn was not directed at her. Instead he seemed angry at himself. "You forget who you're talking to. One way or another, we're all yours." Abruptly he grimaced. "Or they are, anyway." With one truncated hand, he indicated the circle. "In any case, none of us is going to make plans without you."

I know this is hard. I know you think you've come to the end of what you can do. But you aren't done.

Earlier he had commanded the Humbled to support her; but she was not confident that they would do so.

And his effort to distinguish between himself and the rest of her companions pained her. She was not ready for this. Oh, she was *not*. She needed him to tell her and everyone what to do.

Yet she had to say *some*thing. Shading her eyes from the clarity of the sunlight, she did what she could.

"Then we should probably start with the obvious. Maybe Stave can tell us how to find food." He knew this region. The *Haruchai* as a race forgot nothing. "But what I really want to know—" She swallowed thickly: her throat was already dry again. "Why did the Ardent leave us? And why did he leave us *here*?"

Covenant twitched his shoulders: a shrug like a flinch. "He left because he thinks he's doomed. Interfering with the Harrow is going to destroy him, and he wants to do one more thing for us before he falls apart. I guess he's hoping his people will hold him together a little longer.

"As for *here*—He talked about a respite. Distance from our enemies. A chance to recover and maybe even think." A scowl deepened Covenant's gaze. "He hinted at something else, too, but he wasn't clear about it."

While Linden tried to accept the shock of hearing that the Ardent had sacrificed himself for her and Jeremiah—that he had followed the Mahdoubt's example to his own ruin—Rime Coldspray continued Covenant's answer as if she wanted to spare him.

"In addition, the Ardent conceives that the flood which you released under Gravin Threndor has wrought some profound alteration among the hazards of these times. He deems that it has washed away the auguries of his people. Now your fate is 'writ in water.' Therefore he can offer no more guidance."

Writ in water. Involuntarily Linden winced. During her escape from Mithil Stonedown, the Despiser himself had informed her that her fate was *written in water*.

Nothing made sense to her. Her companions had only begun talking, and already they had said too much. How had what she and the ur-viles had done changed the logic of the Land's plight, or of Lord Foul's manipulations? Surely that was impossible?

The Ardent interrupted her confusion. "And therefore," he announced in the blank air, "I return to fulfill my given word."

Swirling his ribbands, he incarnated himself within the circle of the company.

"The Insequent," he informed the astonished companions, "have elected to honor your need for my aid to this extent." His voice was a wracked shadow of his former plump lisp. "By their powers and knowledge, I am spared to perform my promised service."

Clasped or cradled in his raiment, he bore burdens of all sizes, at least a score of them: bedrolls, heavy sacks, bulging waterskins. Wearing his bundles like a penumbra that almost filled the circle, he was as laden as a caravan. Swift as intuition, Linden recognized that the sacks were packed with food and flasks of wine.

A moment later, she noticed that he was even more besmirched and ragged than he had been when she had last seen him. In fact, he looked like he had been dragged through mud and beaten. The hues of his raiment were stained with mire: most of his peculiar apparel hung in tatters. Seen by sunlight, his once-complacent features appeared haggard, diminished, as if he had lost an unconscionable amount of weight.

Nevertheless he stood erect, feigning strength he did not possess. His strained smile may have been meant as reassurance.

"Here," he said hoarsely, "is a feast to sate even Giants." One at a time, he set down his burdens. "Among the Insequent, the Ardent is not the only acolyte of the Mahdoubt. Your plight has been heeded. Unsparingly consumed, such viands will provide for two or perhaps three days. If you enforce a wise restraint, you need not fear hunger while you confront the last crisis of the Earth."

Covenant stared, almost gaping. For a moment, the Swordmainnir seemed too amazed to react. Then, all together, they surged to their feet and reached for the Ardent's sacks. With a jerk, Anele sat up, snatched alert by the prospect of food.

"Heaven and Earth!" Liand crowed. Springing upright, he rushed to embrace the Insequent.

Just for an instant, the Ardent looked entirely startled; taken aback as though Liand had attacked him. Then, however, he wrapped his strips of fabric around the Stonedownor. His round face beamed with surprise and delight.

In moments, the Giants had unpacked enough food to nourish a multitude: roasted legs of lamb and whole fowl, slabs of cured beef, a bounty of fruits both fresh and dried, wheels of cheese, rich breads still fragrant from the ovens. Smells and appetite rushed over Linden until she was scarcely aware of anything except her own emptiness.

"You must have told them," Covenant rasped. He, too, was on his feet. "You must have told them how much we need you."

"Oh, assuredly, Timewarden." The Ardent tried and failed to sound airy; unconcerned. "You behold the outcome." He indicated his bundles. "For your sake, I am preserved yet awhile."

"Then tell them again. Hellfire! You're dying right in front of us. Tell them we're *useless* without you."

"Timewarden, desist." The Ardent's eyes were sunken. He regarded Covenant like a man consigned to starvation. "Do you wish us self-condemned? Be content as you are. While I can, I will linger among you. Then I must depart. The alternative—" He shuddered. "The alternative is the loss of use and name and life for our race. If we defy who we are, we must become naught."

Quickly Coldspray and her comrades set out supplies in their wrappings: squares of an unfamiliar fabric treated to ward off spoilage. As the Giants readied a meal for their companions, they helped themselves to lamb and cheese, fruits, large flasks like urns. The scent of the wine reminded Linden of springwine's crisp tang without its distinctive suggestion of *aliantha*.

In spite of her hunger, Stormpast Galesend remembered to place food near Anele so that the old man would not be tempted to leave the protection of stone.

While Bhapa and Pahni joined the Giants, gathering viands for their Manethrall as well as themselves, Covenant glared at the Ardent. "Content, is it? We're supposed to be content? And you think that's *likely*? Damn it, I'm not asking them to give up who they are. I just want them to make an exception.

"God in Heaven!" Covenant's eyes glistened as if he were on the verge of tears. "You're dying, and we don't even know your name."

Around the sand, everyone listened while they ate. Even the *croyel* appeared to be listening. Linden fixed her attention on every word—and tried to remember the physician's detachment that shielded her from grief. Covenant was right: the cruel necessity which had drained the Mahdoubt's mind and life had already begun for the Ardent. She could see it. She ached for him as she had for the Mahdoubt. But she did not stop eating. Her own needs compelled her.

Squatting beside trays of waxen fabric, she filled her mouth with cheese and fruit, chunks of beef; swallowed gulps of wine as heady as liquor; took more food and tried to force herself to chew slowly. In its own way, eating was also a defense against grief.

It contradicted despair.

Answering Covenant, the Ardent mused, "In itself, my life is of little consequence. Though I grieve for it, my passing will deprive you of neither power nor purpose. And it is condign that the fate of the Earth is borne by those whose lives began beyond the bounds of our knowledge. The Worm of the World's End also lives and moves beyond those bounds. Doubtless the service of the Earth's peoples is needful. In that service, I have played the part of the Insequent. Yet the last task is yours, assuredly so."

He might have said more, but the *croyel* spoke first. "Somebody feed me," the succubus snarled plaintively. "I can't live on air and wishful thinking. None of you can stop the Worm."

Instinctively Linden jumped to her feet; snatched up her Staff. At once, the creature fell silent. Jeremiah's gaze remained stilted and vacant, as though he had not made a sound.

Trembling, Linden faced Galt's captives. God, she wanted the *croyel* dead! Clinging to her son's back, it seemed to falsify everything that she had ever done for him. Its bitter malice—Only the fact that she did not know how to hurt it without harming him prevented her from striking.

But soon, she promised the monster. As soon as I'm ready. I'll find a way to cut your heart out.

Almost involuntarily, however, she saw that Jeremiah indeed needed food. Avoiding looking at him, she had failed to recognize his inarticulate hunger. Now she discerned it clearly.

Nevertheless she shied away from feeding him herself. The *croyel*'s eyes and fangs held too many threats. And she could not estimate the scale of its desperation, or the extent of its powers and lore. It might cause Jeremiah to grab for her Staff or Covenant's ring. It might believe that it could raise theurgy and free itself before the *krill* severed its neck.

She did not want to take the chance.

Over her shoulder, she asked reluctantly, "Liand, will you help me?"

He responded without hesitation. But before he could approach, the *croyel* snapped viciously, "Keep that whelp away from me." Fury and fear sawed against each other in Jeremiah's tone. "If you don't, I'll teach you what *real* pain feels like."

In the Lost Deep, the monster had attacked Liand rather than Linden. She did not know why—but she heeded the warning.

She stopped the Stonedownor with a gesture. "I forgot. Apparently you scare that thing more than I do."

"That is strange," Liand replied tensely. "I pose no threat to a being of such might. Yet the creature's actions proclaim its fear. I must consider—I do not aspire to a second injury. Yet mayhap—"

Linden shook her head. "Not right now." She had no intention of risking him. She understood Pahni's dread too well. "Right now, Jeremiah just needs food."

"Bhapa? Do you mind?"

The older Cord promptly collected a handful of fresh fruit, a wedge of cheese, and a waterskin, and joined Linden in front of Jeremiah. "I am willing, Ringthane," he told her. "Have I not said that my life is yours, subject only to the commands of the Manethrall and the will of the Ranyhyn? Ask, and it is done."

Linden took a deep breath to steady herself, held it for a moment. "In that case," she said, "I hope you can feed him. I'm afraid to get too close." Afraid to get too close to her own son. "I don't know what that thing can do if it gets its hands on my Staff. Or Covenant's ring."

Bhapa nodded. "As you say, Ringthane." His nerves were strung taut, but he did not delay. A step took him to Jeremiah's side. Carefully he placed a bit of melon in Jeremiah's mouth.

For a heartbeat or two, the boy appeared unaware of the food on this tongue. Then, abruptly, he closed his mouth. When he had chewed and swallowed, his jaw dropped open again.

He accepted a piece of cheese; and a moment later, a few sections of a tangerine. He let Bhapa tilt his head for water. Soon he was eating as quickly as Bhapa could feed him.

Hating her own weakness, Linden turned her back on her son and went to confront the Ardent.

He still stood in the center of the circle, holding himself erect with difficulty. She had the impression that he was dwindling—that he had already lost more weight—and her heart twisted. In the Lost Deep, he had striven prodigiously to keep her and her companions alive. He had snatched her back from the jaws of She Who Must Not Be Named. This was the result.

Like the Mahdoubt—

But Linden's needs outweighed her concern for him. She did not know where else to turn for answers. Biting her lip, she compelled herself to ignore his plight.

"Can you explain it?"

The Ardent regarded her anxiously. "Lady?"

"Why is the *croyel* afraid of Liand? Why not me?"

"Sadly, I have no insight." By slow degrees, his voice was fading. "In their auguries, the Insequent did not concern themselves with the Stonedownor. And now their prescience has become water, as I endeavored to explain to your companions. I have no more to give, lady. There is no more of me."

"Then tell me while you still can," Linden demanded, hating her own selfishness. He was her only chance. "You said that flood changed everything. Now my fate is 'writ in water.' But that doesn't make sense. Breaking open the ceiling wasn't my idea. I didn't even know it *could* break. I sure as hell didn't know where to break it. I just did what the ur-viles wanted," her last effort before she succumbed to the bane. "That flood wasn't really my doing. How did it change *anything*?"

"Ah, lady," sighed the Ardent. "My end crowds close about me, and I have no true answer. The Insequent have none. Perhaps the flood was in sooth the ur-viles' deed rather than yours. They are a mystery in all things, and their strange lore has no equal.

"But if you will accept mere speculation—" He sighed again. "Lady, I have observed that your true strength lies in neither the Staff of Law nor in white gold. Rather it lies in the force of self which attracts aid and allies wherever you are, even from among a-Jeroth's former servants. You inspired the Mahdoubt's devoir as you did mine, and that of the Demondim-spawn as well. You do not have such friends"—he gestured around him—"because you wield magicks, but rather because you are Linden Avery the Chosen.

"This power defies both augury and foresight. Assuredly it surpasses the cunning of a-Jeroth, who knows no fealty which is not derived from possession or other mastery."

Such friends—Appealing to her, the Ardent almost succeeded at making Linden weep. But her heart was too desolate for tears.

Before she could summon a response, he turned away. "Fare you well," he breathed thinly. "I must depart."

With a visible effort, he dragged the scraps of his apparel from the sand, unfurled them around him. Briefly his ribbands seemed to drift aimlessly in all directions, as if they had forgotten their purpose. But then he made a small sound like a sob, and they rallied.

Fluttering, they erased him from sight.

After a long moment like an open wound, Covenant looked at Linden. "He's right, you know," he said roughly. "Lord Foul is cunning as all hell, but he's never been able to guess what we'll do when he has us trapped. No matter how carefully he plots and manipulates, he's never ready for us."

But his assertion did not comfort her. It could not: it came from a man who would not let her touch him.

∞

Eventually Linden resumed her meal. Her companions did the same. None of them seemed inclined to talk: she certainly was not. If she had the ability to attract aid and allies, the price was too high. The Land and everyone around her would be better served by despair.

To that extent, at least, she was learning to understand High Lord Kevin.

Seeking numbness, she drank too much wine; and soon she began to drift on a current as slow and necessary as the stream. God, she was tired—Every price was too high. While the Giants were still eating, she stretched out on the sand and fell asleep.

During the heat of the afternoon, she awakened briefly, sweating in direct sunlight. For a few moments, she studied the sky, watching for some indication that the weather might change. Then she moved to a patch of shade and settled herself for more sleep.

This time, she did not awaken until she was roused by the stirring of her companions. With her eyes closed, she felt the Staff of Law propped against a rock nearby. Shadows covered her, easing the pressure of the sun: they covered the watercourse and the swath of sand and the lower hillsides. Among the movements of the company, she smelled food again; heard the Giants murmuring to each other. And when she extended her attention, she sensed Covenant's absence. Claimed by memories and mortality, he wandered among the broken places of his mind; and his features knotted and released as though he were remembering horrors.

If Linden had dreamed, she did not remember it. But she had not forgotten terror and shrieking, or the scurry of centipedes.

After a few moments, she raised her head and sat up to look around. Jeremiah still stood in Galt's uncompromising grip. The blade of the *krill* still kept the *croyel*'s fangs away from her son's neck. The Cords had gone somewhere, no doubt at Mahrtiir's command. But the Manethrall stood with Stave, watching Covenant blindly. Mahrtiir seemed impatient, as if he were waiting for a chance to talk to the first Ringthane.

Covenant's white hair looked stark in the dim shade; so distinct that it almost seemed to glow.

Anele sat in the curve of Galesend's breastplate, gnawing with apparent content-ment on a chunk of cured beef. In contrast, Liand leaned restively on the same rock that supported the Staff, studying Linden sidelong. His black brows arched above his eyes, ominous as the wings of a raven. As she blinked the blur of sleep from her sight, she considered the tension moiling within him, and realized that she recognized it.

When he had determined to offer health-sense to the destitute villagers of First Woodhelven, and again when he had conceived the idea of summoning rain against the *skurj*, his aura had revealed the same growing apprehension and resolve, the same impulse for self-expenditure.

Linden could guess what he had in mind. But it would be dangerous for him in ways that she did not know how to predict. And she had her own arguments to make first; her own gambits to attempt. She hoped to forestall his intentions until they were no longer needed.

Fortunately he was not ready to announce a decision. Trying to sound casual, he remarked, "Pahni and Bhapa have been sent to seek out firewood, for the night will grow chill when these hills surrender their heat. Yet I do not foresee success. In this severe landscape"—he gestured around him—"they will search far and find little."

She cleared her throat. "Along the stream?" Surely runoff brought wood as well as water?

"It is possible," he conceded. "I would welcome the solace of a fire. We have known too much darkness." Then he shrugged. "But I will not rely upon the prospect."

Privately relieved, Linden nodded. Reclaiming her Staff, she climbed to her feet.

Her friends had reached the watercourse in a low canyon too wide to be called a ravine. Much of the ground was sand worn down from the hillsides; but boulders of various sizes jutted from the grit. She had slept behind one such thrust of stone: Covenant sat against another. However, the stretch of sand where the company had sat earlier was comparatively clear.

Without haste, several of the Ironhand's comrades were setting out a second meal. Clearly they had eaten and rested well. Remembering their exhaustion under Mount Thunder, Linden was glad to see that they had regained much of their vitality.

Rime Coldspray gave her a sharp grin. Frostheart Grueburn greeted Linden with a Giantish bow; and Latebirth grinned as well, loosening her longsword in its sheath:

a gesture like a promise. The other Swordmainnir concentrated on the Ardent's bundles.

When Linden turned her gaze to the west, she saw the high cliff of Landsdrop above its foothills. The sun lay behind the precipice, leaving a blaze of late afternoon glory along its age-etched rim. From that angle, it cast its shadow across the whole company, leaving only Branl and Clyme on the hilltops lit.

Soon, she reminded herself, thinking of Jeremiah. She could not delay much longer.

Tightening her grip on herself, she tried to think of a way to unpuzzle the dilemma of Covenant's absence: a way that did not involve holding him under water, or hitting him, or threatening to heal him. Or possessing him. She had learned to view such deeds with dismay. Like the *croyel*'s hold over Jeremiah, if with very different intentions, they would violate his essential freedom.

In addition, he had made it abundantly clear that he wanted to remain a leper, broken and numb and floundering. For reasons that surpassed her, he clung to his plight as if it defined him—or protected him.

If she tried to impose her health-sense and healing on him, she might damage him somehow; perhaps cost him some vital memory. Or she might become as lost as he was.

She could not allow herself to forget the warnings of the Ranyhyn again.

Unsure of herself, she went to join Stave and Mahrtiir. The former Master did not appear to be paying any specific attention to Covenant's fissured sleep; but the Manethrall studied the Unbeliever with sharp intensity.

"We have to reach him somehow," she said without preamble. "We're helpless where we are, and this respite can't last. We have to make some decisions. We can't do that without him."

"By your leave, Ringthane," Mahrtiir replied in a low voice, "I will make the attempt. I have searched the Timewarden as deeply as my senses permit. And I have not forgotten the Ramen tales of his long past. It may be that I am able to rouse him."

"Please," Linden said without hesitation. "Almost anything is worth a try."

Nothing that Mahrtiir did would violate Covenant.

The Manethrall nodded. Around his neck, he still wore his woven garland of *amanibhavam*. It was shredded and blood-stained, and its yellow blooms had withered, but it had not fallen apart. The fibrous grass had been as tightly braided as rope. Carefully he pinched the nub of a dead blossom from the strand, rubbed it against one palm until it was little more than powder. In spite of its condition, the grass gave off a whetted odor that made Linden's nose itch.

"Fresh and living," said Mahrtiir formally, "*amanibhavam* may be safely consumed only by the Ranyhyn. Yet its virtues are many. According to the tales, the first Ringthane once ate of it, and did not perish. True, he fell into madness. But in the forest of Morinmoss, he was restored. It is my thought that the scent of this grass may awaken him to himself."

Kneeling beside Covenant, he nudged Covenant's mouth shut. Then he held the *amanibhavam* in his palm under Covenant's nose, and waited.

The effect was swift. Scowling in his sleep, Covenant jerked away, knocked his head against the rock behind him. His eyes sprang open. "Hell and blood," he breathed. "That woman healed me. I think it killed her."

In Salva Gildenbourne, Anele had told Linden, *Morinmoss redeemed the covenant, the white gold wielder*. Apparently the old man had been right. Again.

While she watched, Covenant blinked memories out of his eyes and became present. *Now those days are lost.*

"Linden," he said thickly. "I'm glad you're all right." Then he winced. Ruefully he rubbed the back of his head: he almost smiled. "Maybe next time you won't hit me quite so hard."

All vastness is forgotten.

An instant later, he scowled again. "No, wait. You didn't hit me. That was *amanibhavam*. I remember the smell. And Morinmoss." Still rubbing his head, he muttered, "I must have done this to myself."

After her first rush of relief, Linden told herself that she should not have been surprised. On other occasions, she had seen *amanibhavam* work its wonders. Among the Land's many blessings, the grass was just one more. The only surprise was that Mahrtiir's garland retained so much potency.

"I'm glad, too." Like Covenant, she tried to smile. But she could not. *Just don't touch me.* "I don't enjoy hitting you." She meant, I need you. Please help me. "And holding you under water feels like overkill."

She meant, Please love me. In spite of everything.

Covenant's mouth twisted: a grimace of wry humor. Mutely he extended a hand to Stave. When the *Haruchai* pulled him to his feet, he said, "We have a lot to talk about." Then he glanced at the waiting food. "But maybe we should eat first. I can't believe I'm already hungry again."

A moment later, he rested a hand on Mahrtiir's shoulder. "Thank you, Manethrall. I don't think any of us would survive if Linden didn't have friends like you."

The Manethrall responded with a Ramen bow. His bandage concealed his expression, but his aura revealed a fierce glimmer of accomplishment.

As Covenant and then Linden turned to the rest of the company, she saw that all of the Giants were grinning broadly. Several of them chuckled, shaking their heads. And Rime Coldspray acknowledged Covenant and Linden with a sweeping gesture like a flourish, welcoming them to the Insequent's provisions.

"It is now," said the Ironhand with muffled humor, "as it has been since we first encountered Linden Giantfriend in Salva Gildenbourne. The brevity of your tales tests our hearing. 'Overkill,' forsooth. We must greet such utterances with amusement. When entire lives are thus compressed, their significance named in one mere word—" Clearly she found the notion risible. "Ah, my friends, we must respond with mirth. How otherwise can we suffer your cruelty to yourselves?

"Sadly," she continued, striving to sound grave, "we have grown accustomed to the haste of folk who measure their span in decades rather than in centuries. Also an intimate acquaintance with peril in many guises has taught us that upon occasions such as the sinking of *dromonds* and the destruction of worlds, we must accommodate the vagaries of circumstance."

Around her, Giants chuckled again, and Frostheart Grueburn laughed outright. Apparently they heard a jest in the idea that they were familiar with the destruction of worlds.

"We would prefer," concluded Coldspray, "to expend the remainder of this season— or of this year—reveling in tales. Nonetheless we are able to recognize an exigency when it tweaks our noses, though we are Giants indeed, and by nature foolish. While the last crisis of the Earth looms, we will endeavor to emulate your concision. When we are fed once more, we will attempt a Giantclave scant enough to appease your impatience."

With that, the Ironhand bowed flamboyantly, seconded by loud applause from her fellow Swordmainnir.

Linden regarded them, bemused. Strange, she thought, that she had forgotten what Giants were like in high good humor. And stranger still that they were able to laugh and clap so soon after their ordeals. But Covenant advised her in a feigned whisper, "Don't worry. They'll calm down. Sometimes they just need to get speeches like that out of their systems."

To a chorus of laughter and a few whistles, as if he had delivered a particularly telling riposte, he sat down near one of the cloth trays.

Feeling suddenly estranged, like a ghost at a banquet, full of sorrows and fears that no one else recognized, Linden hesitated. Covenant knew Giants better than she did: he seemed to belong with them. And she was unable to match him. She had never been his equal.

For a moment, she considered taking some food and standing apart with Jeremiah. Her son's emptiness and the *croyel*'s malevolence and Galt's distrust suited her mood. But then Liand made the decision for her by taking her arm and pulling her down to sit between him and Covenant.

Sighing, she accepted a cloth tray from Grueburn.

Before long, Pahni and Bhapa came down a hillside into the dusk. Pahni dropped to the sand at Liand's side and gave him a quick hug while Bhapa informed Mahrtiir that the Cords had failed to find enough wood to sustain even a small fire during the night. Bhapa's posture suggested that he expected a reprimand; but the Manethrall replied mildly, "Have no concern, Cord. This region is too barren. A fire would have comforted our counsels, but its lack will not sadden us." He indicated the ready meal with a nod. "Eat and rest while you may."

Then his manner sharpened. With a familiar edge in his voice, he added, "Remember that you will be Manethrall when I have passed away. You will be denied the proper ceremonies and homage, but you must bear my duties nonetheless. You are better suited to do so than you believe."

As he spoke, an involuntary shiver ran down Linden's back. She understood Mahrtiir. He had been told, *You'll have to go a long way to find your heart's desire. Just be sure you come back.* The Manethrall was trying to prepare Bhapa.

Like Pahni, Mahrtiir burned to know what Covenant's prophecies meant.

The Land needs you.

Bhapa felt the same desire: Linden saw it in his eyes as he bowed to Mahrtiir and seated himself. But he was also afraid. Through Anele, Covenant's spirit had addressed both Bhapa and Pahni by name. *In some ways, you two have the hardest job. You'll have to survive. And you'll have to make them listen to you.* Linden guessed or feared that this was a reference to the Masters; but she could not imagine what its import might be. From the Lower Land, Revelstone and its guardians were effectively out of reach.

They won't hear her. She's already given them too many reasons to feel ashamed of themselves.

When she began eating, she chewed slowly, too troubled to enjoy what she tasted. And she avoided the wine. In retrospect, giving the Masters *any* reason *to feel ashamed of themselves* seemed like a mistake; perhaps a fatal one. They were too well acquainted with humiliation, and did not know how to grieve.

Around her, the company ate well, but sparingly, at least by the standard of their previous meal. Being Giants, Coldspray and her comrades took longer to satisfy themselves. But when they had finished the last of the Ardent's rich wine, they were done. Together they rose to pack away the rest of the supplies.

Having stored the food in its wrappings and bundles, and set aside the bedrolls and waterskins, the Swordmainnir sat down again. As before, they arrayed themselves in a circle. At the same time, Covenant moved to resume his seat leaning against his chosen boulder. As if she saw him as an antagonist, Linden positioned herself opposite him. He had pushed her away: she needed to keep her distance.

Like a shaft of midnight in the thickening gloom, the Staff rested on her crossed legs. Holding hands, Liand and Pahni took places near her: a subtle declaration of allegiance. And Stave stood behind the rock that supported her back. But Mahrtiir and Bhapa sat among the Giants. Once again, the circle included Anele in his protective cradle.

Beyond the company, Jeremiah stood silhouetted by the light of the *krill* as if he and the *croyel* were wrapped in their own gloom. The argent glow illuminated Galt's face, reflected in his flat gaze, but cast the rest of his form into darkness. Streaks of silver reached across the circle, shifting slightly as Jeremiah breathed, until they found Covenant. There they seemed to ignite his white hair; but they left his eyes in shadow.

As far as Linden could see, the Ardent had left the company in an untenable position. They were too far from their foes. And here, or anywhere, they could do nothing to stop the Worm.

"Well, then," began the Ironhand abruptly. "A Giantclave tailored to the brevity of humans, and to the stoicism of *Haruchai*. It is an arduous task in all sooth. Yet we must prove worthy of it. Doubtless there are needs and queries nurtured within each of us. How shall we consider them?"

Directly or indirectly, the whole circle seemed to refer Coldspray's question to Linden. While her friends waited for her, however, Covenant spoke.

"We're too weak the way we are. Anywhere on the Upper Land, Kevin's Dirt cramps Linden and her Staff. And as long as there are *caesures*, she can't afford to risk the ring." He did not call it his—or hers. "We need power.

"Kastenessen is responsible for Kevin's Dirt. He gets its force from She Who Must Not Be Named, but it's his doing. His and Esmer's and *moksha* Raver's. We have to do something about him."

"And about Joan," Linden put in harshly. She needed to be angry. *Don't touch me.* Otherwise she could not face him now.

"I know." Covenant rubbed his cheeks with his foreshortened fingers; ran them through his hair. Dusk cut by slashes of argent emphasized his maimed hands. "And Joan."

"And Roger," Linden continued.

"Yes," Covenant sighed. "My son. I know that, too."

"Also," Mahrtiir added, "the Ardent has spoken of Sandgorgons and *skurj* in rampage against treasured Salva Gildenbourne. And it is his word that the first Ringthane's son has amassed an army of Cavewights."

"But how may we counter such evils," asked Liand, "when we are few and weak, and the distance is great? Surely we cannot journey so far before the coming of the Worm? And can we deny that the Ardent has been our great ally? He has kept hidden his reasons for placing us in this region. Yet surely those reasons exist. Do we not dismiss them at our peril?"

Without hesitation, the Manethrall replied, "We need have no fear of distance. The Ranyhyn will answer when they are summoned. And these Giants have demonstrated beyond all question that they can run. The leagues are an obstacle, aye, but they are not our peremptory concern."

The thought of Hynyn roused an ache in Linden's chest. Mahrtiir was right. The horses would answer. And Hynyn's devotion was a poignant argument against the dire images which had filled Linden's participation in the horserite.

But the help of the Ranyhyn could wait. They had cautioned her—and she had failed to heed them too often.

With iron in her voice, Rime Coldspray was saying, "Our peremptory concern is with the Worm of the World's End. By that measure, both Kastenessen and Thomas Covenant's former mate are of small import, as are mere Sandgorgons and *skurj*. And in the matter of the Worm, we must give close consideration to the insights imparted by Anele. Though his madness is evident, there can be no doubt of his gifts."

Covenant shook his head. But if he had any reservations, he did not express them.

Thinking about the old man, Linden winced. Sprawled on obsidian at one foot of the Hazard, the son of Sunder and Hollian had articulated the mourning of the mountain's oldest rock.

Even here it is felt. Written. Lamented. The rousing of the Worm.

"We are Giants," murmured Cirrus Kindwind, massaging the stump of her forearm, "lovers of both Sea and Stone. We well recall the old man's words. He spoke of the Worm's compelled hunger, as necessary as death is to life."

When it has consumed lesser sustenance, it must come to the Land.

"Aye," assented the Ironhand. "And in his revelation lay no scope for uncertainty."

Here it will discover its final nourishment.

"I remember," Covenant muttered darkly. "We all remember. It's not the kind of thing anybody forgets."

If it is not forbidden, it will have Earthpower. The very blood of life from the most potent and private recesses of the Earth's heart. Like the tolling of the world's last heartbeats, Anele had pronounced its doom. *When the Worm of the World's End drinks the Blood of the Earth, its puissance will consume the Arch of Time.*

"Well, then," repeated Coldspray grimly. "If it is remembered, then it lacks only explication. Our comprehension of 'the Blood of the Earth' does not suffice. We have no tales of such fell mysteries. And Linden Giantfriend has revealed little more than the skeleton of her sojourn in the Land's past. Since we must oppose or forbid the Worm, we would know more of its 'final nourishment.' "

Covenant ducked his head. Recalling Roger and Jeremiah under *Melenkurion* Skyweir, Linden felt too much turmoil to answer. None of this was relevant to Jeremiah or the *croyel*. But Stave replied with his usual stoicism.

"Only one *Haruchai* has borne witness to the Blood of the Earth and lived, the

Bloodguard Bannor. Thus our awareness of EarthBlood is not limited to the overheard converse of the Lords."

Linden seemed to see memories of Bannor flit like spectres across Covenant's darkened gaze. But he did not interrupt Stave.

Characteristically terse, Stave told the Giants what Linden and Covenant—and, indirectly, Liand and the Ramen—already knew. He spoke of Earthpower in its purest and most concentrated form: magic so potent that it conferred the Power of Command. And he described what his people knew of its hazards.

"Therefore High Lord Damelon Giantfriend deemed it too perilous for any use. Such absolute might exceeds mortal conception. Any Command outruns both foresight and control. It may prove ruinous to the one who utters it."

"In sum," growled the Ironhand, "you deem that we must not seek out this Earth-Blood and Command the Worm to resume its slumber."

Stave shrugged. "If Earthpower is the Worm's food, then the Worm is itself Earthpower. Can Earthpower suppress Earthpower? Will you Command the cessation of all life and death?"

For a long moment, the company was silent. Linden felt distress skirling among her companions, sensed their thwarted desire for comprehension. They needed to know what to *do*. None of them were people who could remain passive in the face of calamity. But they had no outlet for their passion and resolve.

And Linden could not guide them. She could speak only for herself—and she had already chosen her immediate path.

When no one else responded to Stave's challenge, Liand ventured hesitantly, "Mayhap the insight we require lies elsewhere in Anele's utterance. Did he not state that the Worm will bring destruction 'If it is not opposed by the forgotten truth of stone and wood—'? What is this truth?"

Covenant's reply was a grimace. "Beats the hell out of me. If I ever knew, it's gone now. There's just too much. I've lost most of it. And every time I come back, I lose more."

Sternly Mahrtiir said, "Yet other aspects of Anele's pronouncement invite consideration as well. He did not speak only of 'forgotten truth' and EarthBlood. He also urged 'forbidding.'"

"The Forestals knew how to do that," Covenant admitted. "They made the Colossus of the Fall. The Interdict against the Ravers. But it failed eventually." His frown kept his eyes hidden from the *krill*. Only his transubstantiated hair held the light. Over the centuries, the Colossus itself had crumbled. "Too many trees were slaughtered. Every one that fell made the Forestals weaker.

"And that brings us back to power. Even Berek wasn't strong enough to do what they did. Before Kevin's Lore was lost, the Lords used what they called a Word of Warning. But their version of forbidding was trivial compared to the Colossus."

All vastness is forgotten.

"If the knowledge endures among the Insequent," Stave stated with a hint of grimness, "the Ardent did not speak of it."

Frostheart Grueburn lifted her head. "Doubtless the *Elohim* possess that which we lack."

"And you expect them to answer?" countered Covenant. "If you can think of a way to ask them?" He shook his head. "They're too busy running for their lives. They probably won't even notice us unless we do something that scares them worse than the Worm—"

He left the obvious futility of the idea hanging. According to the tales that Linden had heard in various forms, the Forestals had created their Interdict by imprisoning an *Elohim* within the Colossus. Now, she felt sure, Infelice's people were done with self-sacrifice. They were already dying.

"Then," Rime Coldspray said like a growl, "since we have named the *Elohim*, I will add one more to our litany of concerns.

"The Swordmainnir do not forget Lostson Longwrath, who remains abroad in the Land, driven by purposes which we do not comprehend. With the resurrection of Thomas Covenant, the *geas* inflicted upon him by the *Elohim* has been thwarted. Has he now been released? Does rage still compel him to insanity and murder? We are Giants, and his people. We cannot forget him."

Longwrath had tried to kill Linden. More than once. But what could the *Elohim* possibly gain by her death now?

A moment later, Manethrall Mahrtiir rose to his feet. Impatiently he stepped into the circle. Through his teeth, he said, "This accounting of perils accomplishes naught. At one time, a measure of guidance was proffered to us. In the absence of other counsel, we must rely upon it. Will you speak of *that*, Timewarden?"

Covenant flinched. "What do you mean?"

Linden winced as well. She knew what was coming.

"On the plateau of Lord's Keep," Mahrtiir stated, "you addressed those of us who are the Ringthane's first companions. In Anele's voice, you delivered prophecies and counsel. We have forgotten none of your words, yet their import eludes us.

"Will you shed some light upon them now, that we may see our paths before us?"

Again Covenant scrubbed his unfeeling hands over his face as if to remind himself that his palms and the remains of his fingers still existed. Briefly he avoided the Manethrall's bandaged scrutiny. Then he raised his head, met the stare of Mahrtiir's empty eye sockets. Compassion or regret blurred his gaze.

"I'm sorry. I don't remember. And I'm afraid to try. Sometimes digging into the past makes me slip. When that happens, I don't know how to bring myself back."

At once, the Manethrall retorted, "*Amanibhavam* will restore you."

"Sure," Covenant answered like a curse. "And whenever you do something like that, another piece of what I'm trying to remember disappears. Permanently, as far as I can tell. Then there's less of me, and I can't recover what I was."

He appeared to bear the attention of the company as long as he could. Then he punched his fists against each other.

"See?" he snapped. "*This* is why I shouldn't have said anything while I was still part of the Arch. It's why I didn't say anything until I was brought back to life. It makes you look at me like you think I know what to do.

"But I'm *human* now. As fallible as anybody. And I haven't lived—" He groaned in frustration or protest. "I haven't experienced the same things you have. I haven't learned what you've learned. Just watching it happen doesn't teach the same lessons.

"Hellfire and bloody damnation!" he cried suddenly. "Have we been through all this"—the reach of his arms seemed to imply the world—"without convincing you unearned knowledge is *dangerous*?"

He glared around the circle, defying anyone to contradict him. When no one replied, he continued in a low voice like the rasp of a file, "Even if I remembered absolutely everything, I couldn't make your decisions for you. And I couldn't explain things. I'm not qualified because I haven't lived through it. Until you figured it out for yourselves—whatever it is—the only thing I could possibly do is mislead you.

"I *need* to be a leper. I *need* my mind the way it is. I don't have any other defenses." *Don't touch me. I'm afraid of what I'm becoming.*

While Linden twisted her hands together and chewed her lower lip, the Ironhand let the silence of the company accumulate until it seemed as dense as the advancing twilight. Then she pronounced as if she were settling an argument, "We are Giants, acquainted with the hazards of unearned knowledge. And if we were not, Linden Giantfriend's fleshless tale is rife with admonishments.

"In one matter, the Manethrall has spoken sooth. Belaboring our many ignorances, we achieve naught. The time has come for trust, both in ourselves and in her whose heart has piloted us to our present Sargasso.

"Linden Giantfriend, we will gladly hear any word that you choose to offer."

As one, Linden's companions turned toward her as though she had the authority of an oracle.

She wanted to hide her face. More than that, she wanted to cry out, What makes you think *I* have the answer? Do you *like* what I've accomplished so far? But such plaints were as useless as self-pity. And she had long ago surrendered her right to shrug decisions and consequences aside. From the Verge of Wandering to Andelain, she had persuaded or coerced her friends to follow her. She could not pretend now that she had not already determined her own path.

In a small voice, she answered, "I can't tell any of you what to do. I've made too many mistakes, and you didn't deserve any of them. I can only tell you what *I'm* going to do."

She took a shuddering breath, held it until she thought that she might be able to speak steadily. Then she said, "Sometimes I think that I learned everything I know in emergency rooms. I've been taught to take one problem at a time. And to start with the one that's right in front of me.

"We have Jeremiah now. He's right here. And it's obvious that he's important. I'm going to start with him."

Did the Staff of Law wield the wrong kind of power to extinguish the *croyel* without killing her son? Fine. She still had her health-sense, unfettered now by Kevin's Dirt. And if it did not suffice, it might nonetheless enable her to make some use of Covenant's ring.

Kasreyn of the Gyre had believed of white gold that *Its imperfection is the very paradox of which the Earth is made, and with it a master may form perfect works and fear nothing.* She had no reason to think that he was wrong.

"First," she murmured, "I'm going to get more sleep. Then I'm going to do everything I can think for Jeremiah." Knowing that the *croyel* could hear her, she added more sharply, "If I'm strong enough to rouse the Worm of the World's End, I ought to be able to at least *scare* that damn monster."

"There!" Covenant's tone seemed to express satisfaction and alarm simultaneously. "One of us has a plan. First things first. That makes sense to me. The Ironhand is right. It's time for some trust.

"You heard the Ardent. Somehow she's changed everything. Even Lord almighty Foul doesn't know what's going to happen now. And maybe she actually can save Jeremiah. Maybe he's the only one of us who *has* to be saved.

"In any case—" He spread his hands. "She's the only one who could have brought us this far."

Because she had friends—

Linden recognized an undercurrent in his voice; a hint of complex intentions or desires. An ulterior motive? A specific hope or need which he kept to himself? She did not know—or other implications had more significance for her.

He had given her his approval. Again. Nevertheless she bit into her lip as if he had just pronounced sentence on her.

3.

—Whatever the Cost

After a while, the Giants stirred from the circle. Rime Coldspray was the first to rise; but Grueburn, Cabledarm, and the others soon followed her example. Their frustration was obvious. Nevertheless they conveyed a clear unwillingness to demand more from Linden—or from Covenant. Instead, at a word from the Ironhand, they drew apart. When they had walked a short way up the shallow canyon, they seated themselves again, facing each other. In low voices, little more than a susurrus carried by the twilight breeze, they spoke together, holding their own less condensed Giantclave.

Linden could not make out what they were saying, and did not try. They were Giants: she trusted their hearts more than she trusted her own.

She still sat against her chosen rock, facing Covenant without looking at him. Liand and Pahni remained near her: a show of solidarity that she valued, but did not want. And Stave stood at her back as if his devotion had indurated him against uncertainty. Such deliberate faith relied too heavily on strengths which she did not possess.

Farther away, Galt controlled the *croyel* and Jeremiah. Barely visible against the purpling sky—as remote and uninflected as outcroppings—Clyme and Branl watched for threats in all directions.

Around the sand where the Swordmainnir had been sitting, Manethrall Mahrtiir paced, unable to contain his tension. Linden caught flashes of vexation from him, a gnashing ire at his own uselessness. His tight strides resembled an iteration of protest. He seemed to want more than he had received from the Unbeliever.

Squatting near Linden, Bhapa made a studious effort to mask his anxiety from Mahrtiir. He kept his head down, tried to cast no shadow on Mahrtiir's attention. Yet whenever Bhapa's eyes caught the glow of the *krill*, Linden saw them flick toward the Manethrall and away again.

Mahrtiir ached for a sense of purpose: Bhapa did not. He wanted his Manethrall to make his decisions for him.

Anele had fallen asleep, apparently oblivious to impatience. Mouth hanging open, he snored and snorted at intervals; twitched occasionally; shifted his limbs as if in dreams he sought to become one with Stormpast Galesend's armor. Nevertheless his slumber was deep: the long collapse into unconsciousness of the aged, the over-wrought, and the appalled. Studying him, Linden suspected that he would not hear her if she called his name.

Let him sleep, then, she thought. He had endured enough to earn any amount of rest.

In that, she knew, he was not alone.

She meant to sleep soon herself. But unresolved concerns still crawled along her nerves. After a while, she realized that some part of her was waiting for Covenant to speak. Covenant or Mahrtiir. Irrationally she hoped to hear something that would shed illumination into the gloom. But the only light came from the *krill*, and from the dwindling glow of dusk.

Sighing to herself, she rose to her feet. When Liand moved to join her, she rested a hand on his shoulder to stop him. With a glance, she asked Stave to accompany her as she crossed the sand toward the stream.

At the water's edge, she picked out a flat stone and sat down. Gazing out over the current, she settled the Staff in her lap and tried to find names for a few of her many needs.

The Staff was an ebon shaft across her legs, as stark in its blackness as the Earth's deepest caverns. Caerroil Wildwood had given her runes like commandments, but she did not know how to obey them.

Standing beside her, Stave waited in silence.

After a moment, she murmured like the low voice of the stream, "Escape has a price. I learned that a long time ago. There's always a price. Getting out of the Lost Deep"—she did not want to remember the bane—"was hard, and I think we're still paying for it. Maybe that's why everything looks so murky right now. We haven't finished paying."

"Chosen," replied Stave quietly, as if her title were a commentary on what she had said.

Linden gave him a chance to say more. When he did not, she resumed.

"You told me that Covenant convinced Esmer to leave. But you didn't tell me how he did it." *By cunning and desperation*— "Or how he had time. The last thing I remember"—she clenched herself against nightmares— "we were all about to die."

Stave's tone became harder as he answered, "The Unbeliever's efforts were made possible by Anele."

Linden turned her head to study the former Master. Anele—?

"First," Stave explained, "the Unbeliever endeavored to sway the bane directly. Then he sought aid from the old man. Perhaps because Anele stood upon stone, or perhaps because our peril clarified his madness, he met the Unbeliever's appeal by claiming the sunstone. Then he reached out to his parents among the Dead. In response, Sunder

Graveler and Hollian eh-Brand appeared before us as the bane prepared to strike. At once, however, they withdrew. In their stead, the spectre of High Lord Elena came or was compelled to our succor.

"Such was her anguish, Chosen, that she drew the heed of the bane. While the bane sought to consume her, the Unbeliever gained an opportunity to dissuade Esmer from our immediate ruin."

Within herself, Linden staggered. *Anele* did that? He did *that*? At Covenant's urging? How had the old man managed it? And how had Covenant known that Anele was capable of such things?

At least now she knew why she had encountered Elena in her nightmares. God in Heaven! Covenant had sacrificed his own daughter. Indirectly, perhaps: he may not have foreseen exactly what Anele would do, or what the outcome might be. Nevertheless—

But Linden could hardly blame him. In Andelain among the Dead, she had refused Elena's tormented shade any form of absolution. Inadvertently she had ensured that Elena's spirit would be the precise sustenance that the bane craved most.

Linden was as much responsible as Covenant—or as Anele and his parents—for the lost High Lord's terrible doom.

Profoundly shaken, she could not find words for the questions which followed from what Stave had told her. And in his own fashion, he was surely aware of her distress. Nevertheless his voice did not soften as he added, "The arguments by which the ur-Lord banished Esmer ensured that Cail's son will strike again."

Ah, God. Trying to understand, Linden asked, "Do you know how Covenant did it? What did he say that convinced Esmer to leave?"

Stave hesitated momentarily. "I am uncertain, Chosen," he admitted. "The Unbeliever spoke of the peril to Kastenessen if the bane obtained possession of white gold. Yet the degree to which Esmer heeded him was unclear. Rather Esmer appeared to expect that some other powers or beings would balance the scales of aid and betrayal on his behalf. He averred, 'I cannot comprehend why you have not been redeemed. I have given those who wish to serve you ample opportunity. Yet I am spurned.' Also he said in protest, 'You are indeed betrayed, but not by me.' The import of his words, however—" The *Haruchai* shrugged.

—those who wish to serve you— Linden groped for meaning, and found none. Surely every possible friend and ally had been present while the bane loomed? She did not count the Ranyhyn. They could not have accompanied her into the Lost Deep.

Then who—? "Oh, hell," she muttered. Not the *Elohim*: that was out of the question. "I don't get it. And I am tired to death of people who seem to think that being cryptic is their life's work." Even Covenant on occasion. "Just once, I want to meet someone who calls a spade a damn shovel."

Stave could have made a claim for the *Haruchai*; but he surprised her by saying,

"The Demondim-spawn do so. That we cannot comprehend their speech is a lack in us, not in them. It is not their intent to thwart understanding."

Slowly Linden nodded. He was right, of course. The shared resolve of the ur-viles and Waynhim may have been inexplicable in human terms, but they had done everything in their power to make their purposes clear. If not for Esmer—

Damn Esmer.

After a moment, she said unsteadily, "All right. I wasn't being fair." Then she added, "And the Humbled aren't cryptic. They're just reticent. And suspicious." They stood on ground that shifted under them like quicksand. Everything that they had done in her company had taken them farther from their essential commitments. "What do they think about all this?" She waved an aimless gesture as if she meant the stream and the dusk-clad hills. "They've been putting up with me for days—presumably because they don't expect me to survive. But they sure as hell don't *approve*.

"What are they going to do?"

They had been maimed to resemble Covenant. In a sense, he was all that they had left.

Stave considered briefly. When he answered, his tone hinted at vehemence in spite of his native stoicism.

"To say that they mislike all that has transpired does them scant justice. At the heart of their Mastery lies a desire"—he corrected himself—"nay, a compulsion to forestall Desecration. The deeds of Kevin Landwaster, following as they did upon the humiliation inflicted by the Vizard, have hardened the hearts of my kinsmen in ways which they do not discern. Indeed, I did not perceive the hardness of my own heart until my thoughts were transformed in the horserite. I was not conscious of this truth, that for us shame and grief have become more terrible than any other fate.

"If the Land is crushed under the heel of Corruption, the Masters will not fault themselves. They will give of their utmost, and will bear the cost without shame or sorrow. But if they permit some new Desecration when prevention lies within their power, their loss will efface all meaning from their lives. From this seed grows the Mastery of my kin in every guise."

In different ways, Stave had told Linden such things before. However, his perspective on his tale had shifted.

"They weren't always that way?" she asked carefully. Like the Humbled, the *Haruchai* that she had known long ago had seemed as intransigent as basalt.

"They were not," Stave stated. "When our ancestors first entered the Land, seeking some anodyne in combat for the lessons learned from the Vizard, they remained susceptible to gratitude. There the generosity of High Lord Kevin and his Council gave them cause to believe that the wound of their humiliation might be healed by service. Therefore they swore the Vow of the Bloodguard. And therefore they complied when

Kevin Landwaster commanded their absence. They did not grasp that he did so in order to preserve them from the dictates of his despair.

"Even in the time of new Lords, some"—the former Master appeared to search for a word—"some softness endured within them, though it was concealed. But their perception of service, and of themselves, had been slain when Korik, Sill, and Doar became the minions of Corruption. And their hearts were further hardened by the abhorrent use made of them by the Clave.

"Now they are the Masters. Those with us are the Humbled. Their greatest desire is to bereave you of your powers so that you will not haunt them with images of some new Desecration."

Oh, God. Linden wanted to defend herself, to argue on her own behalf, and could not. Long ago, *turiya* Raver had told her much the same thing. As if the final truth about her were beyond question, he had said, *You are being forged as iron is forged to achieve the ruin of the Earth. Descrying destruction, you will be driven to commit all destruction.*

And the Despiser had already succeeded with her. She had awakened the Worm—

But Stave was not done. Stiffly he continued, "Yet you have brought the Unbeliever among us. The ur-Lord Thomas Covenant. For the Masters, as for all *Haruchai*, he is the true Halfhand, Illender, Prover of Life. We have no experience of High Lord Berek Heartthew. We have merely heard his tale. But Thomas Covenant the Unbeliever is another matter altogether.

"He has forbidden the Humbled to oppose you. Indeed, he has demanded their fidelity to you. And his deeds in your name—his very manner toward you—confirm his desires.

"Thus the Humbled are caught in a contradiction for which they have no answer. They execrate those actions which they perceive as Desecration. Yet the Unbeliever himself stands before them, he whom they have been maimed to emulate. By his mere presence, he falsifies their understanding of Desecration.

"Now they must refuse him and grieve, or they must accept you and be shamed. Either choice is intolerable. Nevertheless they remain *Haruchai*. Therefore they must choose. Yet they cannot—and must—and cannot—and must."

Finally the undercurrent of ire in Stave's tone left him. He sounded almost gentle as he said, "For this reason, Linden, if for no other, they will withhold their opposition from you. Rather they will serve the Unbeliever. He is the ur-Lord, the Halfhand. They will trust in him to answer their contradiction."

His assertion was like a promise of hope. Yet it did not comfort her. She was not one of the Land's true heroes. Her loves were too small, too specific; too human. And she carried a burden of anger and darkness too heavy to be set down. Covenant had rejected her love. How could she trust any hope that depended on his support?

As calmly as she could, she asked, "How did you do it, Stave? How did you become so different?" In Revelstone, he had answered that question. Nevertheless she needed to ask it again. "You see things that the other Masters don't. And you care differently." He had called her by her given name. "How did that happen?"

He did not hesitate. As if the truth had become easy for him, he replied, "The Ranyhyn have laughed at my pride and shame. And the kindliness of their laughter has eased my fear of grief. Made one with them, and with you, by the eldritch waters of their tarn, I was resurrected to myself."

After a moment, Linden was relieved to realize that her eyes were full of tears. They flowed like the stream, and with the same offer of solace. If nothing else, she had recovered her ability to weep.

Perhaps her bedrock despair was not as unyielding as she had feared.

∞

L ater she returned to the stretch of sand where Covenant sat with Liand, Pahni, and Bhapa. While Mahrtiir paced, and Anele snored to himself, Galt stood with Jeremiah and the *croyel* like a carving in the Hall of Gifts, a close grouping of conflicted figures as unreadable as the first dim gleam of stars. Farther up the canyon, the Swordmainnir continued their Giantclave, speaking quietly so that they would not disturb their companions.

Knowing that she needed rest, Linden stretched out on the sand with one arm folded beneath her head for a pillow. But then she decided that she would not sleep. She feared her dreams. Instead, she told herself, she would only relax and think until she was ready to face the challenge of Jeremiah's straits.

But the sand seemed to settle around her, adjusting to her contours as comfortably as a bed. Between one thought and the next, she dropped like a stone into a soothing river of slumber.

When she awoke, she knew at once that midnight had passed. Dawn was still some hours away. And there was no moon. Apart from the impersonal glitter of the stars, the only light was the ghostly illumination of High Lord Loric's *krill*. Its gem shed silver streaks past Jeremiah and the *croyel* as if Linden had awakened in the insubstantial realm of the Dead.

From his seat across the sand, Covenant regarded her with argent like instances of wild magic in his eyes. Linden could not tell whether or not he had slept. She was only sure that he was present, concentrating on her as though she embodied futures which had no reality without her.

Around the floor of the canyon, several of the Giants slept like Anele, abandoned to their need for rest. Liand and Pahni had gone somewhere, apparently seeking a degree of privacy. Alone among his human companions, Bhapa had hidden from his doubts and dreads in slumber. However, the Ironhand, Frostheart Grueburn, and Onyx Stonemage remained watchful, although they lay propped against boulders in attitudes of rest. Barely visible against the heavens, Clyme and Branl stood motionless on their respective hillcrests. And Mahrtiir still paced, measuring out his frustration in bearable increments. To avoid disturbing the sleepers, he had gone down to the water's edge, where he fretted back and forth beside the stream.

As quietly as she could, Linden grasped the Staff of Law and rose to her feet. While she brushed sand from her clothes, she confirmed that Jeremiah's racecar still nestled in her pocket; that Covenant's ring hung on its chain around her neck. The time had come. She was not ready for it. Perhaps she had never been ready for anything. Nevertheless she had made up her mind.

Now or never.

How often had she said that to herself?

But when she turned toward Galt and Jeremiah, Covenant spoke. In a low rasp like the subtle scrape of a saw on rotted wood, he said, "Linden, listen to me."

She faced him. After an instant of hesitation, she went to stand over him so that he would not need to raise his voice.

"What is it?" she asked softly. Had he remembered something? Something that might help her with Jeremiah?

"I want you to understand," he replied. "Whatever you have to do, I'm on your side. For what it's worth, I think you're doing the right thing. You said it yourself. First things first. Everything else can wait." With a touch of grim humor, he added, "It's not like any of our problems are going to solve themselves."

"But—" His voice caught. When he continued, he seemed to be forcing himself. "Wild magic is like a beacon. Especially now. If you decide to try it—and remember I'm on your side—any number of our enemies will know where we are. They'll *feel* it. Even if they aren't *Elohim*."

Awkwardly he spread his hands as if to show her that they were full of darkness. "Please believe me, Linden. I'm not *advising* you. I'm not trying to tell you what to do—or what not to do. Just be aware. There's more than one kind of danger here. *Caesures* aren't the only bad thing that can happen when somebody uses white gold."

Linden heard the tension in his tone; but she was not really listening. As soon as she realized that he had nothing to offer except a warning, her attention shied away. She could not afford to be *even more* afraid. Not now. Not while her first and most necessary commitment was to Jeremiah.

She had already been given enough warnings.

As if she were answering Covenant's appeal, she said, "So Kastenessen knows where Joan is."

"That's not—!" Covenant began with sudden ferocity. But then he caught himself. More mildly, he said, "Of course he knows. Hellfire, Linden. I'm starting to think even *I* know. Or I would, if I could just remember. Or I should be able to guess.

"All I'm trying to say is, I'm on your side." He may have meant, Whatever happens. "I trust you."

His response struck a sudden spark into the tinder of her heart. Before she could stop herself, she retorted in a whisper as scalding as tears, "You keep saying that, but I don't know what it *means*. You told me not to touch you!"

Do you think I love *anyone* enough to leave Jeremiah the way he is?

Just for an instant, he looked so stricken that she thought he might cry out. But then the lines of his face resumed their familiar strictures. Masking the reflections in his eyes, he said gruffly, "I'm broken, Linden. I told you. I don't know what I'm becoming, and I don't know what I'll have to do about it. I trust you. It's me I'm worried about."

With one truncated finger, he pointed at Jeremiah. "Try everything you can think of. We need him."

Then he withdrew into himself. He had not fallen into his memories: that was plain. Nevertheless he had erected a barrier against her.

For a moment longer, she glared at him, striving by force of will and need to make him meet her gaze. God, she wanted—! But there was nothing that she could say. And she had no right to rail at him. Not after doing him so much harm.

Aching, she turned toward Jeremiah, Galt, and the *croyel*.

Briefly she paused to rally her resolve. Then she said to Galt, "Come on. We should let the others sleep as long as they can. Let's climb out of this canyon."

From an open ridge or hilltop, she might find some form of guidance among the stars.

The hairless skull of the *croyel* cast Galt's face into shadow: she felt rather than saw him nod. At once, he drew Jeremiah away from the sleepers toward one of the easier slopes on the northern side of the canyon. As he walked, the *krill*'s gem cast shifting gleams like omens across the bare dirt and shale of the hillsides.

Linden followed, bracing herself on the Staff. Stave fell into step at her side. Together Coldspray and Grueburn rose to accompany her, leaving Stonemage to watch over the others. With the nerves of her skin, Linden tasted Mahrtiir's indecision; knew the moment when he made up his mind. Leaving the stream, he went to Covenant and stood there until Covenant muttered a familiar curse and heaved himself to his feet. The two men trailed after Coldspray and Grueburn.

As Galt started upward, picking a careful path in the darkness, Stave said quietly, "Chosen, there remains one matter of which you have not been apprised." Then he paused.

Concentrating on the uncertainties of the slope, Linden asked, "Yes?" to prompt him.

"While you were absent within yourself," he replied, "the Unbeliever sought aid for you from the Ardent. He desired your return, as did all who accompany you. But the Ardent professed himself unable to succor you."

Again Stave paused. When he resumed, Linden heard hints of anger and apprehension in his tone.

"Here I must be exact, for I cannot interpret his words. To the Unbeliever, the Ardent answered, 'The lady has gone beyond my ken. I perceive only that her need for death is great.'"

Instinctively Linden flinched.

"'Or perchance,'" Stave continued, "'the need is her son's. But do I speak of her death, or of her son's? Does her plight, or his, require the deaths of others? Such matters have become fluid. Every current alters them.'"

Without inflection, the former Master admitted, "I have scrupled to speak of this. If it is indeed sooth that your fate is now 'writ in water,' of what worth are further pronouncements? The import of the Ardent's words may be vast or trivial. Unable to distinguish augury from emptiness, I thought to spare you added alarm."

"But now?" Linden asked more sharply than she intended. Why tell me now?

"Now," Stave answered, "I fear for you. Should you fail, the outcome will be heinous to you. And should you succeed"—he appeared to consider the night's implications—"we cannot know what will emerge from the clutches of the *croyel*. In this matter, I now perceive that I resemble the Unbeliever. I seek both to assure you of my place at your side and to caution you against every form of peril."

"All right," Linden muttered. "Fine." The ascent that Galt had selected was not difficult: she was breathing harder than necessary. "So the Ardent thinks that one of us needs death. Or deaths. Or we did. Or we will. So what? How is that a surprise? The Worm of the World's End is coming. Everything is about death."

Her father had killed himself in front of her. She had ended her mother's life. For her, becoming a doctor had begun as an attempt to reject the legacy of her parents. If she turned her back on Jeremiah's plight, she would have nothing left except warnings and doom.

Stave's only response was a firm nod, as if his acceptance of her had become complete.

Now I fear for you. That scared Linden. Its mere simplicity made it more ominous. But in her former life, she had faced innumerable emergencies: she knew the dangers of panic. Since that time, she had fallen so far from herself that Linden Avery the physician no longer seemed to exist. Climbing the hillside with a clog of dread in her throat, however, she felt old reflexes return to life. Her sense of peril triggered responses so deeply trained that they were almost autonomic. Gradually calm settled into her nerves. Step by step, she shed her fears, and began to breathe more easily.

She could do this, she told herself. As long as she refused to panic. And here she was not alone. Several of her friends accompanied her, of course—but she was not thinking of them. No, where Jeremiah's possession was concerned, she was not alone because the Land itself stood with her. Its gifts were her aides, her surgical team: health-sense, the Staff of Law, Loric's *krill*, even wild magic. In spite of a landscape left arid and stricken by ancient warfare and bloodshed, she and Jeremiah ascended a hillside in a place where health and self-determination and even sanity were his birthright.

In addition, she had other help, aid for which she had not asked. Roused by Pahni's skilled instincts, or by his own empathy, Liand trailed behind Covenant and Mahrtiir. In one hand, the Stonedownor held his piece of *orcrest* shining in the dark like a sustained moment of sunlight; a small display of wonder, human and ineffable. Already his light blurred the crisp precision of the stars.

Linden wanted to send him away. She intended to spare him. For Jeremiah's sake, she did not.

More friends. More support. More Earthpower.

Here, if nowhere else in the Land, she could *do* this.

As long as she was careful.

Her pulse was strong in her veins, hard but unappalled, as she and Stave topped the rise a few paces behind Galt and Jeremiah, and reached the crest of a ridge like a contorted spine twisting east and south away from the distant loom of Landsdrop.

Here the whole ridgecrest was an exposed seam of gypsum, sickly white against the darker terrain: a pale road into the east. Around Linden, the wan glitter of starlight lay like immanence on the friable crust. On one side, the hills piled higher against the south. On the other, they canted slowly lower, apparently slumping toward the fens and marshes of Sarangrave Flat. From her vantage, she seemed able to see for leagues in spite of the darkness; yet she descried no sign of the Sarangrave itself. Its ominous sprawl was still occluded by hills, or it was simply too far away for her senses. The breeze blowing over the baked slopes was cool, almost chill, and slightly moist; but it suggested none of the Sarangrave's verdure and rot, or of the lurker's bitter appetites.

Black against the softer hues of minerals and sandstone, Clyme stood atop a hill a long stone's throw to the north. From the far side of the canyon, Branl watched the south.

Galt had stopped Jeremiah at the highest point of the ridge. Now he turned the boy to face Linden. As Linden and Stave halted as well, the Ironhand and Frostheart Grueburn arrived behind them. Outlined by the glow of Liand's Sunstone, Covenant plodded upward in stark contrast to blind Mahrtiir's lighter, more confident strides. Soon Liand and Pahni would reach the foot of the ascent.

All right, Linden said to herself. The time had come.

Placing herself so that the shadow of Jeremiah's head protected her eyes from the *krill*'s piercing silver, she leaned on the Staff and considered her options.

Long ago—and without the enhancement of her Staff—she had reached deep into Covenant, in spite of his organic resistance to percipience. On one occasion, she had triggered a release of power from his ring. On another, she had entered him to free him from the machinations of the *Elohim*. And more than once, she had gone to the extreme of attempting to possess him. Terrified by his willingness to hazard himself, she had striven to stop him—

She could try something similar for Jeremiah. In the Lost Deep, she had seen that the *croyel* had made its mind and life inextricable from her son's. She could not simply separate them. But there were other possibilities. Without question, the *croyel* would fight her. With the Land's best instrument of Earthpower and Law in her hands, however, she might be able to penetrate the creature's defenses. One thin neural strand at a time, she might be able to sever or extirpate the malign tangle of the *croyel*'s grasp. And if she could do *that*—if she could do it without harming or tainting or even touching Jeremiah's own sentience—

The Ranyhyn had warned her against possessing her son.

Galt would cut the creature's throat for her without hesitation. The *krill* would slice through the *croyel*'s theurgies as readily as ordinary flesh.

If.

She might fail. The task would be as challenging as her efforts to protect Revelstone from the Illearth Stone in the hands of the Demondim. At the same time, it would require far more delicacy. She would need an almost supernal degree of precision and care. One mistake, *any* mistake, might harm the core of Jeremiah's consciousness for as long as he remained alive.

And the *croyel* might prove too strong for her. She doubted that: here nothing hindered her access to health-sense and Earthpower. Yet the sheer sickness of the monster's nature might be more than she could suffer. It would hurt her as intimately as the Sunbane, but it would do so with intent. While she reached into Jeremiah, the *croyel* might reach into *her*—

If it were capable of possessing two distinct minds at once, the monster might endeavor to rule her as well as Jeremiah.

Galt would not permit that. Liand and Covenant would not.

And if her first efforts did not relieve Jeremiah, she still had Covenant's ring.

In the Lost Deep, Esmer had said that only white gold could oppose She Who Must Not Be Named. Surely wild magic might sweep aside the *croyel*'s magicks? With raw force, Linden might be able to accomplish what subtlety and precision could not.

All right. Behind her, Liand and Pahni gained the spine of gypsum. *Orcrest* spread its forgiving light across Jeremiah's slack form and scruffy cheeks. It humanized the silt that defined his gaze. Again Linden confirmed that Jeremiah's racecar rested in her pocket, as ambiguous as runes. Then, gripping her Staff until her knuckles ached, she readied herself to examine the nature of the *croyel*'s hold over her son.

"Pay attention," she murmured to no one in particular. "I don't know what I'm getting into here. I'm going to try to make that thing let go. If I succeed, things might happen fast." The *croyel* would seek another host, or defend itself in some other fashion. "And if I don't, I might need help breaking away."

Unexpectedly Jeremiah raised his head. Despite the emptiness of his eyes, he spoke with mordant sarcasm. "Do your worst." Sarcasm or fright. "Or your best, if you think that'll help. You can't even read those runes. When it comes to power, you're like a kid playing with bonfires. You're too ignorant to do anything except kill your son. If that's what you want."

"Oh, stop," Linden replied impatiently. "Have you forgotten the last time you tried to fight me? Have you already forgotten that you were terrified? *You* did your worst, and I'm still here."

Unfurling cornflower fire like an oriflamme from her Staff, Linden Avery the Chosen cast herself into the core of Jeremiah's enslaved mind.

Entering him was easier than she had imagined. The *croyel* could not ward against this specific manifestation of Earthpower and health-sense—or it did not wish to oppose her. And Jeremiah's natural barriers were too weak to resist her. Between heartbeats, she found herself in a place like a graveyard at dusk, in twilight so dim and grainy that it might never have known full sunshine; a place littered with the poorly tended memorials of a fallen army.

Veiled in greyness as if a fine powder of midnight filled the air, the writhen mounds of graves sprawled in all directions as far as her senses could reach. At first, she did not understand them, or know where she was. The gloaming was pervasive and depthless, as if the failed light had no source. No stars shone overhead. The black sky was impermeable, as blank as the lid of a tomb. Nothing stirred the air, neither cold nor heat nor recognition. Nothing grew, or gave off scent, or implied life. Despite the wan illumination, there was nothing here except an innumerable clutter of graves: the buried remains of a multitude utterly decimated.

Bewildered and suddenly afraid, Linden extended the reach of her senses. She pushed hard against the flat vault of the heavens, thrust discernment down into the ground; strove to relieve the illimitable bereavement of the gloom.

By slow degrees, she began to *see*.

At first, she perceived only that there was more to the lid or sky than she had initially realized. Some weight or power worked there, holding it down; sealing it shut. At the boundaries of her health-sense, she felt the presence of a dark resolve.

Driven by fear, she pushed harder.

Yes: resolve. Concentrating her percipience, she smelled or heard its bitter force and malevolence; its hatred; its atrocious strength. It was a web, at once tangled and thetic, sequacious; deliberate in its snarled confusion. It lay tightly bound across the sky as if to preclude any possibility that the lid would lift. But it did not cover only the heavens. When she had tuned her nerves to the hue and thrum of its fierce theurgies, she saw that it enclosed the wide landscape of graves completely. It squirmed far beneath her feet as well as far overhead, a sepulcher of magicks from which neither life nor death would escape.

And it was warm: as warm as the force of repulsion which Jeremiah had wielded when Roger and the *croyel* had lured her into the Land's past. Warm and malign.

Hesitantly she risked drawing the fire of her Staff into the twilight. But her flames were invisible. They seemed as ineffective as dying breaths.

Yet she felt their presence, discerned them with her health-sense. Apparently her power could not cast back the gloaming. Nonetheless it was *here*. She could use it.

Remembering horserite visions and supreme care, she extended her strength to pluck gently at one clenched strand of the web.

It responded instantly. From that precise spot, a shaft of lightning blazed down.

Lurid and obscene, it lit the thronged burials from horizon to horizon. Instinctively Linden recoiled; and dusk closed back over the landscape like a clap of inaudible thunder, too loud to register on any mortal hearing.

But the blast did not touch Linden. Instead it struck a grave perhaps a dozen paces distant. At once, the mound of barren ground began to seethe. Briefly it appeared to moil and bubble as though the force of the lightning had liquefied the dirt. Then the mound scattered in clumps as something under it struggled to claw free.

Oh, God! Something *alive*—

A hand thrust clear of the dirt. The right hand, a halfhand. Missing the index and middle fingers.

More dirt was shoved aside. Clods slid off the mound. Dust drifted in the vacant air; thickened the gloom. Straining, a head forced its way into view.

Jeremiah's head.

Appalled and paralyzed, Linden watched as her son labored out of the dirt: first his head and one arm; then the other arm and his chest. When he could brace his hands on either side of him, he rose in a frenzy of effort, shedding clots of earth.

He was naked. And he was whole; untouched by the ruin of bullets. Standing at last, swaying unsteadily with his calves and feet still buried, he flung his gaze toward her like a wail.

His eyes retained the color of old mud. But they were clear. And conscious. He seemed to see her as vividly as she saw him.

For a moment, his jaw worked as though he had forgotten speech. Then he said, "Mom," in a voice like the drift and settle of dust. "Help me."

Linden knew then that he had never belonged to the Despiser. No servant of Lord Foul would beseech—

But before she could summon an answer, he began to fray and fade. Impalpable breezes tugged through him as if he had as little substance as mist; as little meaning. While she fought herself, floundering to call out or rush forward, Jeremiah slowly dissipated like a banished ghost.

Soon he had dissolved completely; become as crepuscular and eternally lightless as the air that absorbed him.

As the last residue of his plea evaporated, the earth of his grave re-formed to cover him again. Soon there was no sign that he had ever emerged from life or death.

As though the harsh flare of lightning had been a revelation, Linden understood. She *understood*.

She was inside an incarnation of her son's mind, a reification of his imprisonment made corporeal by health-sense and Earthpower. The tangling web of magicks knotted around the graveyard was the power of the *croyel*; the power that ruled him. With cruel bolts of energy, the monster unleashed what it needed from the boy: the ordinary language and movement and memory which enabled the *croyel* to carry out its charade of being Jeremiah. And the graves, the endless graves, careless mounds scattered beyond the farthest extent of Linden's senses—

Sweet Christ! The graves were Jeremiah's thoughts. They were the workings of his trapped mind moment by moment, each as solid as a corpse, and as transient as mist—and all buried alive within him.

Buried.

Alive.

Within him.

In that flash of comprehension, she forgot everything that might have been fear or paralysis. Horror she remembered—horror and unendurable rage—but every emotion that might have limited or constrained her vanished as though it had been exorcised. *Jeremiah!* If mere lightning could raise discrete fragments of her son's self, she could resurrect them all with Earthpower and fury. She could set every grave ablaze, arouse in fire every instance of the identity which he had never been able to manifest as his own. In their thousands, their myriad thousands, she could gather them into herself before they evaporated and were reimmured. And then she could—

Possessing Jeremiah, she would remain in his crypt. And the *croyel* would fight her. Oh, it would fight! With every scrap of its native puissance, with every particle of its gleaned lore and cunning, it would do battle to make her its prisoner as well.

Within the smaller world of Jeremiah, the creature's magicks were as vast as firmaments.

But *she*: ah, *she* existed *outside* her son's mind. She had a separate identity and a physical self which the *croyel* could not grasp. And she was not the monster's only foe. Galt would not hesitate to cut its throat. Fear would hamper its efforts to contain her.

She could *do* this!

She, Linden Avery, who had already roused the Worm of the World's End.

All she had to do—*all she had to do*—was exert enough Earthpower and outrage within Jeremiah's mind to *possess* him.

But she had experienced possession. She knew its cost.

In her metaphysical hands—the clasp of health-sense and revelation—she felt the runes which defined her Staff awaken and burn. They seemed hot enough to scour the flesh from her bones. She could not read them. Nevertheless her nerves interpreted them as if their meaning were written in pain.

She had enough power. She could retrieve Jeremiah's mind. But would her son thank her for replacing one form of possession with another? Even if she only violated the integrity of his deepest self in order to rescue him?

She might forget everything else; but she could not forget the Ranyhyn horserite. Not again. Not while runes of fire burned Caerroil Wildwood's irrefragable anguish into her hands.

The Forestal's ciphered bereavement had assisted her efforts to call Thomas Covenant back from death. She had thought then that she had stumbled upon the sole purpose of the runes.

Now she knew otherwise.

Must it transpire that beauty and truth shall pass utterly when we are gone?

She had made a promise to Caerroil Wildwood on Gallows Howe. He did not mean to let her forget it. Her unfurled fire had become visible; but it did not shed yellow light or smell of cornflowers. Instead it spread sheets and gouts of utter blackness through the caliginous air. In her hands, the runes demanded remembrance, and even Earthpower had become despair.

Her own extremity took her to the horserite. Surrounded by graves, she recalled the blending of minds which she had shared with Hynyn and Hyn; the images which had appalled her—

First the Ranyhyn had told her High Lord Elena's tale from their perspective, as they now saw it. They had acknowledged the flaws in their foresight, the reasons why their efforts had achieved the opposite of their intended effect. Then—Ah, God. Then they had told the same tale again as though it described Linden herself rather than Elena. They had shown Linden her own inherited capacity for Desecration. And when they had appalled her to the core of her spirit, they had gone further—

Drawing upon her experience of *turiya* Herem and *moksha* Jehannum, the Ranyhyn had described Jeremiah's plight as it appeared to them. They had reminded her that blankness was his only defense: he could only retain the beleaguered fragments of himself by concealment. And when she could bear no more, they had gone still further.

They had caused her to see herself as if she were Jeremiah possessed. On that image, they had superimposed Thomas Covenant lost in the stasis imposed by the *Elohim*. And they had shown her the consequences of her yearning to set them free.

In compelled visions, Linden had seen the Worm of the World's End emerge from her resolve to restore Covenant. More than that—worse than that—she had seen her beloved son's visage break apart and become despicable: as vile as the Despiser's malevolence, and as irredeemable.

With every resource at their disposal, the Ranyhyn had assured her that possession was not the answer. If with fire and need she breathed her life into every one of Jeremiah's uncounted corpses and gathered them into herself, she would commit a crime for which there was no possible exculpation.

Remembering, she wanted to howl at the unrelieved sky of her son's suffering. But she did not.

Like the Ranyhyn, she was not done.

The flame of her Staff had become blackness—but it was still *power*. She could still try to break through the *croyel*'s bitter mastery. She could do that without touching Jeremiah's soul.

As soon as she made the attempt, however, she discovered that she was wrong. Her first flagrant blast elicited another strike of lightning from the *croyel*'s defenses. A second bolt sizzled into the heart of a second grave. Coruscation moiled and spat in the mounded earth. Again Jeremiah fought free of the ground. When he gained his feet, he said like the gloom and the wafting dust, "Mom, don't. This is what Lord Foul wants."

Then he was gone, dissipated; returned to living death.

She began to shout the Seven Words—and another incinerating blast inscribed horror across the twilight. Another avatar of Jeremiah's misery arose; uttered its brief, forlorn supplication; dissolved back into its grave.

Realization dropped her to her knees among the incoherence of the mounds. She could not—oh, she *could not!* Not like this. She could not strive for her son's release: not while she remained within him. Her efforts would break down his defenses. Struggling against the *croyel*, she would exacerbate his agony until it became damnation.

He did not belong to the Despiser. Not yet. Linden had seen him, heard him. His graves both imprisoned and protected him.

But if his own mother destroyed that protection— Violated heart and soul, he would become Lord Foul's. Whether or not she succeeded at freeing him.

Kneeling, Linden felt the same aghast anguish which had sickened her after the horse-rite. The idea that she might do *that* to her son, not in visions, but in tangible truth—

It could have broken her. Perhaps it should have. But it did not. She still was not done. She had other sources of power. She could make other choices.

In a rush like a sudden fever, she surged back to her feet. Deliberately she tightened her grip on burning runes.

Contained within Jeremiah's mind and the *croyel*'s malice, she tried to make her physical throat and mouth and tongue cry aloud.

Liand, help me! Get me out of here!

She may have succeeded: Liand may have heard her. Or he may simply have seen her peril and understood.

Like a burst of sunlight, the salvific radiance of *orcrest* touched the back of her neck and the side of her face.

Touched and took hold.

An instant later, she staggered for balance as her boots rediscovered the bare gypsum of the ridgecrest under a wilderness of stars. Jeremiah stood, unclaimed, in front of her. The *croyel* bared its fangs in a feral grin. Struck by the shining of the Sunstone, the creature's eyes glared yellow triumph.

Stave caught her at once; steadied her. In her hands, flames as black as the Staff crawled across the surface of the wood, elucidating the runes. But the fires had already begun to fade. They had already faded. Only the pain deep in her palms and fingers retained Caerroil Wildwood's admonition.

Shocked by ebony, Giants called her name. Manethrall Mahrtiir muttered curses under his breath. Liand grasped her arm with his free hand, seeking some assurance that she was unharmed.

Linden flung him off. She flung them all off. She had no time for explanations—and no language for what had happened. She needed to act now, *now*, while images of her son's plight remained as precise and piercing as shards of glass in her mind.

Covenant tried to say something, but his voice sounded as cut as the runes, impossible to scry.

Because she did not plan to channel her attack through the *krill*'s gem, she feared to hold and wield two instruments of power at the same time. *Either alone will transcend your strength*—Febrile with haste, she thrust her Staff into Stave's hands. Liand might try to use it: Stave would not.

Then she pulled the chain that held Covenant's ring over her head. Shoving her index finger into the band, the way Covenant had worn it, she closed her fist on the chain. With her other hand, she tugged Jeremiah's racecar out of her pocket; held it up in front of him like a talisman.

She did not know how to carry out her intentions. The ring did not belong to her:

she lacked Covenant's inherent relationship with wild magic. But for that very reason—
and because her health-sense retained its crystalline clarity—she trusted herself. Her
limitations as well as her senses would prevent her from committing any grievous
harm. And if her efforts announced her to Kastenessen—or to Joan—she did not care.
Jeremiah's straits outweighed every other fear.

Racing within herself as though she had become sure of her passage, she reached
the secreted chamber where her access to wild magic lay dormant. Without a pause,
she threw open the door.

In that instant, the ring released a shaft of argent incandescence like the lightnings
which had roused brief avatars of her son from their graves.

It was too much: too potent; too dangerous. She knew that immediately. It was *wild
magic*: it resisted control. Its brilliance blinded her. Its sheer force seemed to efface the
night. Yet the ring's potential for ruin did not daunt her. She had invoked this fire in
the past, more than once. She believed that she would be able to master it.

It was only too strong because she had called upon it so fiercely. When she had
gauged every dimension of its strength, she would refine it to suit her purpose.

Its imperfection is the very paradox of which the Earth is made—

Obliquely she saw avarice throbbing in Loric's *krill*. Covenant's bitten curses confirmed it: the grim consternation of the Giants confirmed it. Joan—or *turiya* Herem—
had already noticed Linden. In moments, the *krill* might grow hot enough to damage
Galt's hands. It had nearly destroyed Covenant's. But Linden ignored that possibility.
She intended to work quickly; to finish her task before the Master suffered.

—and with it a master may form perfect works and fear nothing.

While Liand and the Ramen stared at her, Linden pulled her power out of the heavens and began forging it into a spike like the flame of a cutting torch, a nail with a
point as precise as a star and as piercing as a dagger.

At the periphery of her awareness, she felt the rest of the Swordmainnir surge
onto the ridgecrest, bringing Bhapa with them. In the shaped rock of her breastplate,
Stormpast Galesend carried Anele. The old man was awake now, taut with alertness,
apparently watching Linden. Her wild fire and the shining of Loric's gem seemed to
catch and burn in his blind eyes.

But Linden ignored her companions. Her whole heart was concentrated on fury
and white gold; on energies chaotic enough to rend the heavens, and pure enough to
savage the *croyel*'s brain.

It was hard—Ah, it was *hard*. More difficult than creating a *caesure* to escape the
Land's past: more arduous than summoning the sheer might to resurrect Covenant.
Long ago, he had warned her that wild magic accumulated, that it gathered force with
every use; that its fire always resisted containment. She had experienced the danger
herself.

But she was not merely Linden Avery the Chosen. She was the by God Sun-Sage! Unfettered, her health-sense made her capable of perceptions and evaluations which Thomas Covenant himself could not match. She did not need to fear true havoc: the ring was not hers. And the blood in her veins was *rage*. It had transformed every other passion of her life.

For Jeremiah's sake, she could muster a degree of control that might have surpassed any rightful white gold wielder.

With every resource at her command, she formed a knife of argent which would coruscate through the *croyel*'s brain without laying waste to the graveyard of Jeremiah's consciousness.

When her weapon was ready, she moved closer to her son. Holding up the racecar so that he could see it—so that it might serve as an anchor or lodestone for his buried thoughts—she aimed wild magic like a honed scream at the monster's face.

At the same time, however, she sent percipience like tendrils of supplication and tenderness back into Jeremiah. She did not reach so deeply now; did not enter him entirely. Instead she extended her senses only far enough to gauge his condition while she threatened the *croyel*.

Rigid with strain, she panted through her teeth, "This is it, you vile bastard. I'm done with you. Let him go or die, one or the other. *I will not—!*"

The creature's gaze interrupted her. Its eyes glared yellow terror. Sweat as rank as the halitus of a charnel glistened on its hairless skin. For an instant, Linden believed that she would succeed. Surely the *croyel* understood that she would kill it without remorse? Surely it wanted to live?

But then she realized that the monster's stare was fixed, not on her, but on Liand.

The *croyel* still feared him more than it feared her. It had done so from the first.

A heartbeat later, Jeremiah howled in agony. Within him, energies from all directions began to scourge his interred sentience. Bolts of ferocity lashed dozens of graves at a time, hundreds. Molten earth boiled around aspects of himself as they writhed to their feet. But this time, the blazing shafts did not raise him and then withdraw. No, this time each strike was sustained— It burned and *burned* him until each risen avatar was reduced to whimpering and ash; true death.

The *croyel* was not merely excoriating moments of Jeremiah's mind: it was incinerating them entirely. Dozens or hundreds of his lost thoughts had already been destroyed.

How many of them could the monster slaughter before Linden killed it? Thousands? *Tens* of thousands? Then her son's mind would be crippled. The damage would be irretrievable.

In horror and fury, Linden wanted to punch wild magic straight through the *croyel*'s skull. She could halt Jeremiah's torment almost instantly. She would lose a thousand pieces of him, or ten thousand, or a hundred thousand. But the graveyard was immense; almost limitless. Like any mind. A gently nurtured brain could recover from appalling amounts of harm. In her former life, she had seen such things happen. And there she had lacked the healing powers of her Staff—

Nevertheless she stopped herself. Jerked backward a step. Quenched Covenant's ring as rapidly as she could. Wrenched the band from her finger; shoved both the ring and the racecar deep into her pockets.

Withdrew her threat.

Because the *croyel*—

Her whole body trembled until she felt the barrage of lightning inside Jeremiah cease.

—feared Liand more than it feared her.

Liand and *orcrest*.

Covenant was shouting her name. How long had he been trying to get her attention? She had no idea. She was crying again, and could not stop. Hellfire, Linden! he may have yelled. You can't do this! Wild magic is the wrong kind of power!

She knew that now.

Stave's strong arms held her until her initial rush of trembling faded. Unable to stanch her tears for her, he did what he could by pushing the Staff of Law into her hands.

He had said, *Should you fail, the outcome will be heinous to you.* And she had certainly failed.

Nevertheless he was wrong. As long as *Liand* did not fail—

For a moment, stars seemed to reel around her, wheeling overhead as if she had thrown them into turmoil. The Sunstone still shone, refusing the immediate dark. The light of Loric's *krill* throbbed with intimations of greed and murder. Yet to Linden the black sky felt as heavy and fatal as a cenotaph.

Stepping back from the brink of Jeremiah's fate, she had made herself small again: too small to have any meaning among the forlorn immensities of stars and night, the hard truths of barren hills and crumbling gypsum. But she could bear her own littleness. It was enough for her.

As long as Liand did not fail.

Still quaking in the marrow of her bones, she accepted the burden of herself from Stave. The touch of the Staff's runes continued to hurt her hands, but the burn was receding. Soon she would be able to find comfort in the clean wood again.

Around her, eight Giants loomed like menhirs against the nightscape. Liand stood poised at her side, gripping his *orcrest*, eager to talk to her; as eager as a man who had identified the import of his life. A few steps away, blind Mahrtiir appeared to watch over Covenant. The Humbled could not: Clyme and Branl remained on their chosen hillcrests, and Galt's hands were full.

Behind Liand's far shoulder, Pahni waited with sun-yellow and silver lights like fears in her wide eyes. A stride or two behind the other Swordmainnir, Galesend still bore Anele in her armor. The old man watched Linden and Liand, Jeremiah and the *croyel*, with his head jerking fearfully from side to side as if he had stumbled to the edge of an inner precipice. With one hand, he made plucking motions in Liand's direction as though he wanted the Stonedownor's attention.

Halfway between Anele and Mahrtiir, Bhapa fretted, unsure of his duty to men who could not see.

"Linden Giantfriend—" began Rime Coldspray. But she appeared to have no language for what she wanted to say, or to ask. Her strong jaws chewed emotions which defied expression.

"I was afraid of this," Covenant muttered. "Linden, I'm so sorry. Sometimes we just have to—"

He did not complete the thought. Like Jeremiah, he sank into silence as if it were a grave.

Quietly intense, Liand said, "Linden, I grieve for you, and for your son. Yet there is an admixture of eagerness in my sorrow, though it is selfish to feel thus. While the boy remains among us, hope also remains."

"And I have not yet tested my strength."

His Sunstone glowed like a promise. He was the first true Stonedownor for millennia. There was no one like him in the Land.

Linden wanted to cry out, Don't talk about it! Don't explain it! Just *do* it! My God, he's *buried alive* in there!

But she stifled her demand. Like her, other people needed to make their own decisions. Liand would do what he could. Somehow she contained herself while he sought words for his excitement.

"In Revelstone," he said, almost whispering, "you spoke of *orcrest*. I had learned that it gives light at need, and has the virtue to find wholeness among the fragments of Anele's thoughts. To this, you added other knowledge, lore which has proven its worth. And you spoke—"

He seemed to swallow wonder and anticipation that bordered on exaltation. "Linden, you spoke of *healing*. When you had informed me of *orcrest*'s power to wash away the effects of Kevin's Dirt, you made mention of healing. Healing of the spirit rather than of the flesh. From this surely arises the ancient use of Sunstone as a test of truth."

While Linden ground her teeth, Liand said more strongly, "It is in my heart that your son's plight, first and last, is an affliction of the spirit. If *orcrest* is puissant to bind together Anele's incoherence, mayhap it is able also to seal your son's soul against ravage. How may such a creature as the *croyel* endure any test of truth? I am uninstructed in the ways of Earthpower." As he spoke, he seemed to become taller in Linden's sight; more solid. "Yet both my heart and my eyes assure me that the magicks of *orcrest* are anathema to this hideous being.

"Linden Avery, I ask your leave to attempt your son's release."

Before Linden could reply, Onyx Stonemage countered, "And if the *croyel* exceeds your strength? What then? We have seen Linden Giantfriend's flame transformed to blackness. I pray that the alteration proves fleeting. Yet if she who is adept at Earthpower can be tainted thus, how will you endure?"

"Liand of Mithil Stonedown, I honor your willing valor. I am proud to name you among my companions. But when you gaze into this lost boy's heart, his possessor will gaze into yours. Then mayhap no admixture will remain to ease our own lament."

Linden started to say, *Do it, Liand*. At some better time, she might have added, *I trust you*. While urgency clogged her throat, however, she felt the sickening migraine aura of a *caesure* slam into existence among the hills.

Whirling, she scrambled to focus her senses. Around her, Giants turned, scanning the horizons swiftly. Groaning to himself, Bhapa hastened toward Manethrall Mahrtiir.

"Protect Anele!" the old man gasped frantically. "He is the hope of the Land! *It* seeks him!"

"It is there, Chosen," Stave announced, pointing into the northeast. "It writhes a league or more distant. At present, it does not threaten us. Yet it seethes toward us. If it does not veer aside or disperse itself, you must oppose it."

He was right. As soon as Linden located the Fall, she felt it clearly: a miasma of corruption as vicious as a swarm of hornets, and as massive as Revelstone's watchtower, chewing its way through the Law of Time. It lurched from side to side, apparently reacting to the whims and impulses of Joan's madness rather than to the terrain. But it was coming—

Damn it!

"Stave's discernment is certain," growled the Ironhand. "A great evil advances against us. Its path is erratic, aye, yet it hastens in its own fashion. If we do not scatter before it, we must have some other defense.

"Is this a *caesure*? A Fall? You have spoken of such wrongs, but ere now we have not beheld their like."

No one answered her. "Whatever you're going to do," Covenant snapped at Liand, "do it soon. Joan won't stop with just one. *Turiya* won't let her. She'll keep trying until she finds the range."

Linden jerked a look at the *croyel*—and nearly wailed. The creature's whole face radiated triumph like a cynosure.

For the space of a heartbeat, she froze while her entire reality split into fragments. A dismembered part of her recalled inhabiting Joan's mind in the core of a Fall: a lorn figure who should have perished long ago; a madwoman so weak and wounded that only *turiya* Raver's compulsion and the ministrations of the *skest* kept her alive. Standing between thrashing seas and a wilderland of rubble, she used blasts of wild magic to destroy small pieces of stone and Time, creating *caesures* from the riven remains of granite; of sequence and causality. Nothing except her broken humanity and her inability to make her own choices prevented her from tearing the whole Arch from its foundations.

At the same time, another part of Linden gaped mutely at the *croyel*, crying, Why aren't you *afraid*? Surely the creature was in the same danger? Surely the merest touch of a Fall would destroy the *croyel* as effectively as any physical death?

Why was *turiya* Herem willing to risk the destruction of a monster that both Roger and Lord Foul wanted alive?

But Linden had no time for this. When her heart beat again, her scattered mind sprang back into focus.

"*Go!*" With a shove, she sent Liand toward Jeremiah. "Save him if you can! *Caesures* are *my* problem!"

Then she swung the Staff of Law and begged it for fire.

If Joan struck again, and closer—If the Raver could impose that much coherence—

A moment later, dark flames bloomed from the Staff; and some of the aftereffects of wielding white gold left her. This conflagration was hers in spite of its compelled blackness: it felt right in her hands. And she was not Joan. She could choose. Earthpower and Law could heal the harm of wild magic. As long as Joan did not contrive to strike the exact place where Linden stood, the exact moment, Linden would be able to protect Liand.

"Ringwielder, no!" Pahni cried. "You must not permit this! I implore you! The peril is too great!"

She meant the peril to Liand.

"Cord!" barked Mahrtiir harshly. "Be silent! This matter is not ours to adjudge."

Pahni ignored her Manethrall. "Liand, *please*. You are my love! I will beseech you on my knees, if that will sway you. Leave this hazard to those who are not so loved."

Linden watched the coming storm of evil and readied herself. But she studied Liand more closely than she regarded the *caesure*, praying that he would not falter. That the Sunstone would not crumble to dust in his fist.

Liand turned from Jeremiah to wrap his arms around Pahni. So quietly that Linden barely heard him, he told the Cord, "Fear for me, my love. I fear for myself. Yet in Linden Avery's company, and in your embrace, and in *orcrest*, I have found myself when I had not known that I was lost. If I do not give of my utmost here, I will become less than my aspirations. I will prove unworthy of the gifts which I have discovered in you."

"But if you are slain—!" Pahni moaned.

"If I am slain," he replied so tenderly that Linden's heart lurched, "you will remain to serve the Land, and the Ranyhyn, and the Ringwielder, as you must. My love will abide with you. Grief is strength. The use that you will make of it vindicates me."

While Liand held Pahni tight, a second *caesure* violated the night.

It opened its destructive horrors to Linden's left—and closer than the first; much closer. Like an eruption, it split the air no more than half a dozen paces from Clyme's position north of the ridge. Then the chaos of instants lunged toward him. But he sprang away, preternaturally swift. Scanning the hills for other threats, he kept his distance from the Fall.

Like the first, this *caesure* swarmed toward Jeremiah and the *croyel* as if it were drawn by the bright passion of Loric's *krill*.

Through his teeth, Covenant rasped, "Soon would be good. Now would be better."

He may have been speaking to Linden as much as to Liand.

Gently Liand separated himself from Pahni, raised his Sunstone high; strode toward Jeremiah.

The *croyel*'s look of triumph was gone. The nausea in the creature's eyes echoed the sick squirming in Linden's chest.

As he advanced, Liand made his light brighter, and still brighter. It lit Jeremiah's slack features like a small sun, challenging the night; burned like ruin on the monster's sweating face. Impossibly torn, Linden tried to concentrate on the *caesures*, and could not. She needed to stop those gyring evils. But her need to witness what happened between Liand and the *croyel*—what happened to her son—was greater.

"Hellfire, Linden!" Covenant shouted. "Pay attention! Joan isn't done. Look at the *krill*! Saving Jeremiah won't do any good if a *caesure* gets us!"

The gem around which High Lord Loric had forged his dagger was throbbing like a heart in ecstasy.

Caesures *aren't the only bad thing that can happen*—

Joan's attacks were Linden's doing: she knew that. She had announced her location. But the effort of turning her back on Jeremiah and Liand surpassed her.

She had to do it. If Liand failed now—If he failed because of *her*—

Shaking with strain, she lifted ebon flame to meet savagery and madness.

—when somebody uses white gold.

Nearly in tears, she faced the Fall squirming toward her from Clyme's hilltop. It was closer. Again she tried to believe that she could do this. She had quashed other *caesures* by affirming the structures of Law and the passion of Earthpower. She could do the same here. Surely she could do the same here?

But Liand was reaching out to touch Jeremiah's forehead with his Sunstone; and there were no ur-viles or Waynhim nearby to help Linden transcend herself.

The crash of the third *caesure* would have sent her sprawling if Stave had not caught her. It struck the ridge directly behind her. In the midst of the company.

While alarms squalled in her nerves, Stave spun her to confront the assault.

Virulent sickness nearly undid her. The *caesure* was not large: not by the measure of other evils which she had encountered. But it boiled and twisted right where—

God in Heaven!

—right where Covenant and Mahrtiir and several of the Giants had been standing.

In the first rush of panic, Linden could not count her companions. She did not know whether any of them had been taken. The Fall was no more than ten steps from Liand and Jeremiah.

Then her heart hammered once; and she saw Covenant plunge down the side of the ridge wrapped in Mahrtiir's arms. Grueburn snatched Pahni aside. On all sides, Swordmainnir sprang out of the *caesure*'s path.

Frantic with haste, Stormpast Galesend staggered backward—

—and tripped—

—spilling Anele out of her armor.

With the second thud of her heart, Linden became flame.

God, she hated *caesures*!

She knew this evil; knew it in every nerve and sinew of her being. She had experienced it too often. She needed only percipience and dread to focus Earthpower on the complex distortions shredding Time's necessary Law. If she had been stronger, or better, or clearer, she might have been able to reach straight through the Fall into Joan's excoriated heart. But she did not require that much force to counter the storm itself. While she believed in the commandments of linear cause and inevitable effect, she could stitch them together as she had once sewn a patch of her shirt onto the Mahdoubt's gown.

Watched by the abandoned stars, she flung black fire into the *caesure* and began its unmaking.

She did not have to grasp every severed instant and restore its proper sequence. The Staff's rich outpouring performed that repair for her. And Caerroil Wildwood's runes made the wood's theurgies more specific than her own instincts for health and wholeness; more definite. Almost immediately, the *caesure* started to implode. The collision of energies within Joan's maelstrom caused a deflagration which shrank as it burned.

In moments, the Fall vanished as though it had been sucked away, inhaled by the sovereign *rightness* of healed Time.

Yet encroaching evils still wailed in the night. The *caesure* which had struck near Clyme surged closer. Joan's initial attack continued the hard wrench-and-lurch of its advance.

And Anele had risen to his feet on bare dirt: crumbling sandstone and gypsum, exposed chunks of shale, the friable detritus of erosion and ancient wars.

Anele!

He radiated raw power as horrendous as the *caesures*, but far more conscious; full of intention and screaming rage. With gestures like shrieks of lava, he dismissed Giants, swept obstacles aside. A fulvous crimson like primal brimstone blazed in his blind eyes, the hue of fangs in the maws of the *skurj*.

Howling, he rushed at Liand.

Kastenessen had taken possession of the old man. In agony, the *Elohim* had come to rescue the *croyel* and claim Jeremiah.

Linden could not react quickly enough. She was too human; too horrified. But Stave had already left her side to stand in Anele's path.

Long days ago, the former Master had lost an eye to the horde of the Demondim. Nevertheless he had struck down Anele then, borne the old man to safety. Now he did not hesitate to confront Kastenessen's charge.

A slash of power flung Stave aside as if he were a handful of desiccated bones.

Standing in the heart of the *orcrest*'s clean light, Liand seemed unaware of his peril. Oblivious to every darkness, he touched Jeremiah's forehead with his Sunstone: the sum and incarnation of his Stonedownor birthright.

Galt saw the threat. Of course he saw it. His flat eyes watched Anele. Yet the Master remained motionless, uncharacteristically trapped by conflicting commitments. He gripped Loric's *krill*. And he was swift. He could have driven death into the center of Kastenessen's fury. Could have killed Anele. Distrusting the old man's heritage of Earthpower, Galt might have slain him without a qualm.

But he could not do so without releasing the *croyel*.

Freed from the blade at its throat, the monster would surely support Kastenessen. It might destroy or deflect Galt before the Humbled could harm Anele.

Perhaps Galt considered killing the *croyel* and Jeremiah before confronting Kastenessen. Perhaps he did not have time to weigh every implication, Covenant's commands against the cause of Kevin's Dirt.

Screaming like Elena, Linden finally hurled black Earthpower against the *Elohim*. But she was too late. Anele shed her fire like water as he slapped his hands to the sides of Liand's head.

Compelled by Kastenessen's strength, the old man filled Liand's fragile skull with lava.

In a spray of blood and bone and tissues, Liand's head was torn apart.

Then Stormpast Galesend hurtled forward. She slammed into Anele; wrapped her arms around the old man's incinerating force; carried him past Liand and Jeremiah, Galt and the *croyel*. Ignoring the murderous heat in her clasp, the instantaneous burn like a furnace-blast, she somehow remembered to roll as she fell so that Anele's flesh lost contact with the ground.

In the instant before Galesend hit him, however, Anele contrived to catch the *orcrest* as it dropped from Liand's dead fingers. Linden saw the old man clearly. Kastenessen was trying to destroy the Sunstone—

—until Galesend snatched Anele off the dirt.

When Galesend landed on her back in a welter of stones and snarled pain, Kastenessen's power vanished. The *orcrest* went dark. Night seemed to crash down onto the ridge like the sealing of a sepulcher despite the hungry throb of the *krill*'s gem and the swelling rapacity of the *caesures*.

Galt remained as rigid as a carving in the Hall of Gifts. Jeremiah stood like an empty husk while the *croyel* gibbered and spat on his back. Gushing blood, Liand slumped to his knees; leaned forward until he rested like an act of contrition against Jeremiah's legs.

When your deeds have come to doom—

Unconscious in Galesend's arms, Anele still gripped the inert Sunstone as though his life depended on it.

—remember that he is the hope of the Land.

The impending Falls were all that kept Linden from wailing like a maimed child.

4.

Attempts Must Be Made

Storms of time and anguish filled the night. Somewhere *turiya* Raver imposed purpose on Joan's weakness by sheer brutality; compelled her to direct her blasts. Moments after Linden quenched the nearest *caesure*, a fourth made madness of the stream at the foot of the canyon, spun the sand where she and her companions had eaten and slept into a migraine tornado. A fifth nearly claimed Branl as he sprinted toward the company. He saved himself only by diving headlong down a bouldered slope. A sixth found the ridge a stone's throw to the east and staggered closer.

After that, there were no more. The Raver must have exhausted Joan. Still five fierce instances of chaos converged on Jeremiah—or on the *krill*. Linden could not answer them all. Other storms raged through her, leaving her concentration in shreds.

Liand.

She had brought this upon him. In spite of his youth and ignorance, she had allowed him to accompany her when she fled from Mithil Stonedown. She had taken him to Revelstone, where he had become the first true Stonedownor in many millennia. And she had practically commanded him to risk his life for Jeremiah.

Liand!

She had seen Anele gesture at Liand, asking for the *orcrest* and sanity: his only defense against possession. But in the frenzy of other pressures, she had ignored the old man's plea.

Liand!

Here was the result. Still on his knees, Liand leaned against Jeremiah's legs, resting there with his skull torn open as though he prayed to the idol of a false god.

In a sense, Handir had foretold this. Speaking of Anele, the Voice of the Masters had said, *Yet the Earthpower within him cannot be set aside. Therefore his deeds will serve Corruption, whatever his intentions may be.* Now Anele had killed Liand.

It was too much. Linden needed to hold Liand in her arms and wail her bereavement; weep herself out of existence. Yet *caesures* lurched closer. Toward Jeremiah. Joan sent no more; but these five did not dissipate. Instead they raved like hurricanes trapped in spaces too small for them. Joan or *turiya* Herem had made them strong. And Thomas Covenant's spirit no longer defended the Arch of Time.

If Linden did not set aside her horror and grief—and if she did not do so *now*—everyone she loved would be destroyed. Swept away into a future of unrelieved absence and cruel cold. *The eventual outcome of Joan's craziness.*

Voices shouted tumult at Linden, but she did not hear Covenant's among them. Stave said her name with something like urgency. She did not hear him at all.

Battered by storms, she could not look away from Liand and Jeremiah.

The hunger echoing like exaltation from the *krill*'s gem had begun to ebb. Now the *croyel* struggled for freedom. Finally it feared the *caesures*. Jeremiah jerked up his head; his arms. Reaching behind him, he clawed at Galt's forearm, tried to drag it away from the throat of the creature.

If he shifted Galt's grasp, the blade would bite into his own neck. Nevertheless he strained to free the *croyel*.

The Humbled did not move. He betrayed no hint that the heat of wild magic had hurt him. Unyielding as Loric's dagger, his forearm defied Jeremiah's efforts.

The Ironhand barked orders, rallied the Swordmainnir. Still on her back, Stormpast Galesend hugged Anele as though she meant to squeeze out his life. Swift as a hawk, Pahni threw herself at Liand.

Through the confusion, Mahrtiir yelled Bhapa's name.

Instantly obedient, the older Cord rushed to Linden's side. But she hardly noticed him. She only remained on her feet because Stave held her.

Caesures yowled at her from every direction. Their sheer *wrongness* made her want to puke up her soul.

Bhapa may have rubbed something under her nose. He may have dabbed a powder as fine as dust onto her tongue. Nothing made any sense—

—until she closed her mouth and swallowed; inhaled through her nose.

At once, the acrid sting of *amanibhavam* ignited flames in her as if she were tinder, apt only for bonfires and lightning, conflagrations that would consume the housing of her entire life.

She needed flame. Oh, she *needed* it!

With an inadvertent slash of Earthpower and despair, Linden sent Bhapa tumbling down the slope. Involuntarily her gaze followed his plunge; but she could not afford to watch what happened to him. The Fall which had routed Clyme was only heartbeats away. Bhapa was not swift enough to catch his balance and sprint aside.

This, too, was her doing.

There were four other Falls. They were all advancing. But she did not look at them. Crying curses as if they were the Seven Words, she flung dire Earthpower and Law like a shriek into the abomination which threatened Bhapa.

Perhaps she extinguished it. Perhaps she failed. She did not wait to observe the outcome. Like a surgeon surrounded by carnage, she did not pause to check her work or watch for intimations of survival. With Stave's help, she whirled away.

Four more *caesures*. Four unconscionable rents in the necessary fabric of time.

Her Staff was a streak of midnight in Linden's hands as she wheeled it around her head; lashed ebon fire like the scourge of a titan in every direction. Her theurgy had changed, but she did not feel the difference. It was an exact reflection of her spirit.

Blinded by fury and woe, she did not know whether she snuffed the Falls, any of them. Her own flame consumed her. Moments ago, she had been helpless; paralyzed. She had simply watched while Liand was slain; watched and done nothing. But if Lord Foul, or Joan, or Roger, or any abhorrent bane had stood before her now, she would have striven to tear them apart.

I perceive only that her need for death is great.

God damn *right!*

Shouting accompanied her grief-stricken rage, her inconsolable slash of flame. She may have been yelling herself. The only voices that she could hear clearly were the cries and excoriation of She Who Must Not Be Named's victims. Around herself and her companions and the ridgecrest, she created a whirlwind to answer the seethe and distortion of the Falls. But she no longer knew what she did. Exalted or broken by pain and loss, she whipped blackness into the dark heavens until it seemed to erase the stars.

Until Stave reached out to catch hold of the Staff.

Until her vehemence and Stave's grip nearly ripped the Staff out of her hands.

Then the energies of *amanibhavam* and fury failed her. In an instant, her lash of Earthpower vanished, leaving only Loric's *krill* to answer the irreparable night. Panting like sobs, she sagged into Stave's clasp.

"It is done, Linden." His voice sounded as unrelieved as the Earth's deep rock. He seemed to know the cost of what she had done—and had failed to do. "There is no more need. Wild magic and Desecration have passed. We endure."

Word by word, he brought Linden back from storms. Every sentence restored some riven piece of her. Leaning against him, she believed that he had stopped her at the brink of a catastrophe as intimate as her immersion in She Who Must Not Be Named.

But he could not heal her.

"When you are able," he continued as if he spoke for the darkness, "you will observe that we have lost only Liand. Bruises and gashed flesh we have in abundance. And Kastenessen's fires were bitter to the Swordmainnir. But they are Giants, hardy against any heat or flame. They will prevail over their hurts. Also the Manethrall has preserved the Unbeliever. He is absent once again, but unharmed. And your son stands unscathed"—Linden felt Stave shrug—"apart from the many cruelties of the *croyel.*

"Six Falls assailed us, Linden. Nonetheless we endure."

He may have meant to comfort her. But she could not be comforted. She felt like a derelict in his arms, wracked beyond repair.

Nevertheless her health-sense returned by increments. As her vision cleared, she saw that Stave spoke the truth.

Above her on the ridge, Giants towered against the benighted sky. The dagger's gem lit their forms with silver streaks like cuts. Cirrus Kindwind had taken Covenant from Mahrtiir. Vaguely Linden recognized that Covenant had again collapsed into his crippled memories. Kindwind carried him in one arm as if to protect him from himself.

Frostheart Grueburn trod heavily toward Linden and Stave while Bhapa scrambled upward. The Swordmain's face and arms radiated a scalding pain, and a deep contusion ached on one side of her forehead. Her right hand and forearm bled from various scrapes. Yet she was essentially whole.

As was Bhapa. Patches of skin had been torn from his limbs, but those injuries were superficial. At some other time—perhaps in another life—Linden would be able to treat them.

Both Grueburn and the Cord peered at Linden, perhaps seeking to assure themselves that she was still sane. Then Grueburn called a few words over her shoulder to Rime Coldspray; and the Ironhand passed them to the other Giants. Linden Giant-friend remains among us. She has suffered no bodily wound.

Galt and Jeremiah were likewise untouched. The *croyel* had ceased its struggles. The boy stood slack and vacant, as if the creature had relaxed his puppet-strings. Blood and gore stained his pajama bottoms from thigh to hem.

Careful to keep Anele from touching dirt, Stormpast Galesend climbed to her feet. Unconscious, the old man dangled in her arms as if every possible meaning had been taken from him. But he still gripped Liand's *orcrest* as though it might restore what he had lost.

—*the hope of the Land*.

Fresh wailing strained for release in Linden. Biting down on her lower lip, she held it back. Any cry that she permitted herself to utter now would be Elena's screaming, and Emereau Vrai's, and Diassomer Mininderain's. It would be the compacted rage and ruin of Gallows Howe.

Dark in Jeremiah's shadow, Pahni had taken Liand into her arms. She knelt on gypsum and shale, hugging her lover against her while his sundered skull oozed its last blood onto her shoulder. She seemed as motionless as the Stonedownor, as unable to draw breath. Nevertheless the young Cord emanated distress as loud as keening. Her pain struck blows at Linden's heart.

Gently Galesend bore Anele to the spine of the ridge where Coldspray and Kindwind stood with their comrades. At Grueburn's urging, Linden forced herself to step away from Stave's support. With Stave and Bhapa ready to catch her if she stumbled, she trudged toward her gathered companions.

Her friends. Who had loved Liand as much as she did.

Mahrtiir had placed himself like a guardian in front of Kindwind and Covenant. Blindly he scrutinized Linden's approach. In his stance, she saw a raptor's acute ferocity.

Clyme and Branl now stood poised on either side of Kindwind. But their attention was fixed, not on Linden, but on Anele, and their hands were fists. The *krill*'s reflections in their eyes resembled threats. They had stood watch over the company to no purpose. And they had foreseen the peril in Anele from the first.

Instinctively Linden feared them. They were *Haruchai*, Masters, the Humbled—and they had failed. If they did not fault Galt for Liand's death, they would accuse Anele.

Hoping to forestall them, Linden said in a hoarse rasp, "You can't blame him. He didn't choose this."

Days ago, Anele had urged his companions to give him the Sunstone when he requested it.

"The Earthpower is his," Branl replied without glancing at her. "It alone enabled him to endure such possession. Also the madness is his. The openness to Corruption is his. Such flaws conduce always to Desecration. Who will accept the burden of his deeds, if he does not?"

"I will," Linden answered through the turmoil of remembered cries. "It's my fault." She deserved this. "I only cared about Jeremiah. I stopped paying attention to Anele."

Together Clyme and Branl turned to regard her sternly.

You hold great powers. Yet if we determine that we must wrest them from you, do you truly doubt that we will prevail?

Mahrtiir ignored the tension in the Humbled. Standing between argent and darkness, he retorted, "Do not speak of *fault*, Ringthane. The deed was Kastenessen's. His and no other's." Suppressed mourning fretted the Manethrall's wrath. "To assert otherwise is to urge despair in the guise of blame."

"I stopped paying attention," Linden insisted. "I let it happen. Anyone here could have told you what Kastenessen would do if Anele touched bare dirt without—" Her voice caught in her throat. Oh, Liand! She could not say his name. "Without the Sunstone. I caused this when I ignored him."

Galt might conceivably have warned Liand. But she had seen Cail beaten bloody by his kindred. She had watched Stave's expulsion from the communion of the Masters. For Galt's sake as well as her own, she insisted that she was culpable.

But Mahrtiir did not relent. "And I will not hear of fault!" he shouted. "*Attempts must be made.* We have spoken of this, Ringthane. Even when there can be no hope. Your son requires redemption. Therefore Liand strove to succor him. To claim fault demeans the Stonedownor's sacrifice."

With a visible effort, the Manethrall lowered his voice. "Mischance alone released Anele from Stormpast Galesend's protection. Thereafter Kastenessen's deeds could doubtless be foreseen. Yet the assault of such *caesures*—aye, and of *caesures* invested with such purpose—could not. And it was not inattention which caused the mischance of Anele's release. Stormpast Galesend's stumble was the consequence of unprecedented hazards. If you wish to assign fault, you must name her also. Indeed, you must name every Giant among us, and cast aspersion upon all who have learned to love the Stonedownor. Like you, we knew of the old man's plight, and of his desire to be given *orcrest* when some aspect of his madness demanded clarity.

"Hear me well, Ringthane," Mahrtiir demanded through his teeth. "You tread paths prepared for you by Fangthane's malice. Speaking of fault, you bind yourself to his service."

Linden bowed her head under the weight of his ire. As if to herself, she sighed, "You don't understand." No one except Covenant had truly understood her. Lord Foul knew her better than Mahrtiir did. She Who Must Not Be Named knew her better. "What I've done is all I have. Without it, I'm nothing. I ignored Anele. I roused the Worm. I followed Roger when he was pretending to be Covenant." Despair made sense. The new blackness of Earthpower in her hands suited her. "If I don't take responsibility, I might as well be dead."

All three of the Humbled watched her as if she had justified their deepest distrust.

She felt Bhapa's desire to protest. Stave also seemed ready to object. But Rime Coldspray spoke first.

"Enough." Like an appeal for forbearance, she rested one hand on Clyme's shoulder. "Linden Giantfriend, it is enough. If joy is in the ears that hear, then I must answer you with laughter. I do not only because I fear to augment your dismay."

Frostheart Grueburn murmured her assent. Several of the other Giants nodded.

"You demand perfection of yourself," Coldspray continued, "when mischance and error are the lot of all who live and die. You have assumed burdens sufficient to cow even Giants. For doing so, we honor you. If betimes you chance to stumble, as did Stormpast Galesend—

"Well." The Ironhand tightened her grip on Clyme momentarily, then released him. "Among Giants, you would perhaps be named Blunderfoot." Frowning, she nodded toward both Latebirth and Galesend. "Thereafter you would doubtless be often teased. But you would not be faulted. In the *caamora*, you would allay your pain and lamentation. Then you would arise, and shoulder your burdens again, and be held in undiminished esteem by all who accompany you.

"I myself," she admitted, "have upon occasion assigned blame to myself. Now I cede that I erred in doing so. There was no harm in my heart when I delivered the blow which gave rise to Lostson Longwrath's madness. There was no harm in Latebirth's heart when by mischance she permitted Longwrath's escape and Scend Wavegift's death. There was no harm in Stormpast Galesend's heart when she stumbled. And there was no harm in your heart, Linden Giantfriend, when you fixed your attention and yearning upon your son rather than upon Anele. If I grieve for you, I grieve only because your flesh cannot suffer the healing hurt of flames.

"There is wisdom in the Manethrall's words." Coldspray shook her head sadly. "You have spoken with the voice of despair."

If the Ironhand had shared Linden's nightmares, she would have recognized that voice. It was the scurry of noisome things that feasted on carrion; the shrieking of the bane's victims. Ever since Linden had surrendered to the horror of She Who Must Not Be Named—no, ever since she had stood on Gallows Howe—she had forgotten forgiveness.

She did not choose to remember it now.

With the surface of her mind, however, she understood Coldspray. She understood Mahrtiir. Superficially she could acknowledge their arguments. And she had succeeded in her immediate aim: she had deflected the recriminations of the Humbled from both Galt and Anele.

"All right," she muttered without lifting her head. "I get it. Liand is dead." She said his name as if it were as dangerous as the *krill*. "The *croyel* still has Jeremiah. That's what matters. Talking about me right now is just a distraction.

"We're wasting time." Grimly she forced herself to look up at her companions. "We ought to concentrate on what's important."

The Giants had no wood for a *caamora*. Like Linden and the Ramen and even Stave, they would have to find some other way to anneal their loss.

Apparently Pahni had been waiting for Linden to acknowledge Liand's death. Now she lowered him to the ground. Gently she settled his limbs as if to make him comfortable. Then she surged to her feet and flung herself at Linden.

With the *krill*'s light behind her, the Cord's visage was masked by shadows. Nevertheless her anguish outran her. Pain as raw as an objurgation stung Linden like a blow. Before Pahni reached her, she flinched.

Quicker than the girl, Stave stepped forward to intercept her. But Pahni wrenched to a halt before he touched her. Her garrote she gripped taut between her fists, although she seemed unaware of it. For a moment, her chest heaved so hard that she could not shape words.

"Cord," Mahrtiir said sharply. "Compose yourself." Ire and compassion struggled in his tone. "This is unseemly."

Pahni ignored him. "Ringthane!" she cried: a ragged shout rife with imminent hysteria. "Restore him!"

"Pahni!" Now the Manethrall's voice cracked like a whip. "*Compose* yourself! Is this the conduct of a Cord?"

Still she ignored him. In jagged gasps, she demanded, "You must *restore* him!"

Shaken, Linden hardly heard herself protest, "I can't."

"You *must!*" yelled Pahni. "He is my love! And his death is needless! He has given himself in your name, and *it is needless!*"

"Pahni!" Mahrtiir urged. With both hands, he reached out to restrain or embrace her.

So fluidly that Linden scarcely saw her move, Pahni snapped her garrote around the Manethrall's wrists, jerked them together. In the same motion, she sprang past Mahrtiir and raised her arms over her head; used her fighting cord to flip him off his feet.

Branl caught him before he struck the ground. Clyme positioned himself to ward off a following attack.

But Pahni had already returned to Linden. She held her garrote ready for Linden's throat.

"You will *heed* me, Ringthane!" she shouted like pelting hailstones. "In Andelain, you restored your own love! Now you will return mine to me! Every instrument is present. White gold. The Staff of Law. The *krill* of High Lord Loric. And *there*"—she did not drop her hands—"lies Liand slain!

"Are you heartless? I know that you are not! *Therefore you must renew his life!*"

Mahrtiir had regained his feet. Now he showed his own speed. Blind, he moved unerringly to grasp Pahni's garrote between her fists. Then he was behind her. Pulling on her cord, he bent her arms until he could pin them with his own.

"Pahni," groaned Bhapa. "Oh, Pahni." Refused weeping clogged his voice. "You must not. You must not."

"Ringthane!" The young Cord thrashed against Mahrtiir's clasp. "*You will heed me!*"
Her every word left wounds like the scoring of claws.

"I can't," Linden said again. Abruptly she dropped her Staff. As if she were striking herself, she snatched Covenant's ring out of her pocket and hurled it to the dirt. Then she went to wrap her arms around Pahni and Mahrtiir.

"I would if I could," she breathed like a moan in Pahni's ear. "For you, I would. Even if I didn't love him myself." Even if she had not already violated so many Laws. "But I can't. I just can't.

"I don't know where he is."

For a moment, the Cord paused to listen. Then she began to fight again. "He is *there!*" she cried as if she wanted to sink her teeth into Linden's throat. "His body lies *there!*"

"I know." Like Bhapa, Linden refused weeping. "I know that. But I don't know where his spirit is.

"In Andelain, Covenant was right in front of me. I didn't need his body because his *spirit* was there." It implied every aspect of his lost flesh. "He was still himself. But all I have now is Liand's body. I can't call his spirit back," even if she could have repaired his skull, "because I don't know where it is.

"Maybe he's among the Dead in Andelain. I hope so. But I can't reach that far. I can't locate him, never mind ask him to live again. And I can't create a new soul for his poor body out of empty air. I don't know *how*." She had learned none of the lore of the Old Lords. Even the meaning of Caerroil Wildwood's runes mystified her. "Whatever I made—if I could make anything at all—it wouldn't be Liand."

This time, the sound of his name in her own mouth went through her like a spear. It seemed to repeat the moment of his destruction: the brutal slap of Anele's hands;

the sudden rage of lava; the ravage of bone and blood and brain. Gasping, she clenched her teeth, bit down on her pain, so that she would not cry out in Pahni's ear.

Briefly Pahni continued to writhe against Mahrtiir's embrace, and Linden's. Then, so suddenly that she appeared to stop breathing, the Cord went limp.

Imagining that Pahni had fainted, Linden released her. The Manethrall eased his clasp; shifted his feet so that he could scoop the Cord into his arms.

In that instant, Pahni spun free. Fiercely she threw a punch at Linden's face: a blow that would have staggered Linden if Stave had not deflected it. Instead Pahni's knuckles only clipped Linden's cheek; jolted her. Phosphenes like lightning flashed across her sight and were gone.

Wailing, "*He is my love!*" Pahni fled.

Mahrtiir made no attempt to stop her. When Cabledarm moved to catch her, the Manethrall barked, "Do not!" and Cabledarm let the girl pass.

Sprinting into the night, Pahni headed down the southward slope of the ridge. Almost at once, she dropped beyond the reach of the *krill*'s illumination.

"Manethrall," Bhapa protested: a muffled plea.

Mahrtiir faced Pahni's flight. In his fist, he held her garrote. After a moment, he gestured Bhapa into motion.

"Follow, Cord," he commanded softly. "Do what you may to ward her from harm. But do not intrude upon her sorrow. She has lost her first love. Such attachment is sometimes deep and lifelong, but always as rending as fangs."

Linden had done nothing to relieve Bhapa's hurts. She had treated none of her companions.

While the older Cord hastened away, the Manethrall addressed Linden obliquely. "She is Ramen. She will become herself again when she is needed."

Then he turned to study Linden through his bandage. "Ringthane," he said stiffly, withholding anger, "I crave your pardon on my Cord's behalf. She would not suffer so, had she not heard the Timewarden imply Liand's doom."

I wish I could spare you.

"Nonetheless she *is* Ramen, and has committed insult. To raise her hand against the Ringthane is inexcusable. Yet I must excuse it. Therefore I will bear any consequence which you may choose to require."

Mahrtiir—Unable to master her voice, Linden simply went to the Manethrall and hugged him: the only language she had.

At first, he stood rigid, affronted; as unyielding as one of the *Haruchai*. But then she felt him soften as though she had won his assent.

She wanted to sob on his shoulder, and could not. Her emotions were too extreme. Liand's death and Jeremiah's plight left no room in her heart for other forms of surrender.

After a moment, she stepped back.

"The consequence," said Cabledarm gruffly, as if she expected an argument, "is that all must excuse Pahni of the Ramen."

"Our regard for her is assured," the Ironhand answered, mildly reproving. "We need no urging to countenance her grief and ire. Therefore I ask a more exigent consequence.

"Linden Giantfriend must also excuse herself."

Before Linden could find words, Clyme spoke.

"The Humbled do not excuse her. All that has transpired results from her transgressions. We sought to prevent her violation of Law in Andelain, but were opposed. That failure cannot be undone. And because we are the Humbled, we now honor the Unbeliever's return. Yet some action we must take against Desecration. We are *Haruchai*. We are Masters. In a former age, we were Bloodguard. We do not condone. Nor will we permit."

"Permit what, sleepless one?" asked Mahrtiir sharply. "What is it that you will not condone?"

Around him, several of the Giants moved closer, ready to intervene. Cirrus Kindwind withdrew slightly to keep Covenant out of harm. But Stave did not react.

He knew what the Humbled were thinking.

Without inflection, Clyme replied, "You have beheld the blackness of Linden Avery's flame. You have witnessed her taint. You can no longer doubt that Earthpower is perilous. Therefore we will retrieve the Sunstone from the old man. We will allow him no further access to its magicks. In his hands, *orcrest* may also be turned to Corruption."

As if their rectitude were self-evident, Clyme and Branl started toward Stormpast Galesend and Anele.

"No!" Linden cried out. God, she had misunderstood the Humbled. Again! Fearing for Galt and Anele as well as herself, she had jumped to the wrong conclusions.

With one arm, Coldspray barred the path of the two Humbled, although she did not touch them. In a granite voice, she announced, "Nevertheless you will do Linden Giantfriend the courtesy of hearing her objection. You propose to wrest Anele's only sanity from him. Yet he has served us well—and has been much abused. We will not stand aside while he is harmed."

Out of respect for the Ironhand, perhaps, or perhaps simply because Linden no longer held her instruments of resistance, Branl and Clyme paused; waited.

Silent as the heavens, Stave moved to stand with Galesend.

"Name your objection, Linden Avery," Branl commanded. "We will consider it."

Linden felt her companions watching her. Deliberately she left her Staff and Covenant's ring where they were. If the Humbled were *caught in a contradiction for which they have no answer*, as Stave had told her, they might be susceptible—Hell, they might be almost human. Her voluntary powerlessness might do more to sway them than any words.

When she had swallowed as much of her despair as she could, she answered carefully, "Maybe what's happened to the way that I *use* Earthpower is corruption." She could not tell. "Maybe it isn't. But it's an effect of the runes." An expression of Caerroil Wildwood's power. The legacy of Gallows Howe. "They seemed to come alive while I was inside Jeremiah. Maybe they changed my Staff." Reinterpreted it. "Or they changed me. I don't know how," although she could guess why. "But they didn't change Earthpower. You saw me snuff those *caesures*. You saw that Earthpower hasn't changed.

"The Sunstone is what it is. It won't serve Lord Foul.

"Anele needs it. It's his only real protection. And it protects us at the same time." Trying not to mourn, she insisted, "If we had given it to him when he wanted it, Kastenessen wouldn't have been able to touch him. Liand would still be alive."

She could not imagine what use Anele might have made of the Sunstone, or of his resulting lucidity. In Andelain, he had spent time alone with the spectres of his parents. For all Linden knew, they had shared insights which she desperately needed.

For all she knew, Covenant had urged the doom of the Sunstone on Liand so that it would eventually be inherited by Anele. The old man certainly could not have found or taken the *orcrest* for himself. The Masters would never have allowed it.

The flat faces of the Humbled concealed their reactions; but Linden did not stop. "As it is, we almost lost Galt and Jeremiah. And Kastenessen is still Kastenessen. As soon as he gets a chance, he'll slaughter us all.

"If you can't trust Anele, trust Sunder and Hollian. Your ancestors knew them. You remember that. If Sunder and Hollian thought that he might ever commit Desecration, they wouldn't have called him 'the hope of the Land.' And they made it possible for us to escape the bane. How is letting Anele have the Sunstone worse than leaving him open for Kastenessen?"

Clyme and Branl gazed at Linden. *Krill*-shadows shrouded their faces: they looked as dangerous as darkness, and as unpredictable.

Trembling with self-restraint, she finished, "Before you make any decisions, why don't you ask Covenant what he thinks? Sooner or later, he'll come back. Finding the *orcrest* was his idea. Maybe he'll remember why he wanted Liand to have it."

The Ironhand of the Swordmainnir nodded. "Well said."

"Aye," growled Frostheart Grueburn as if she were clenching her fists. "Linden Giantfriend reasons wisely. I have felt my flesh scalded by Kastenessen's touch, Giant though I am. I applaud her caution."

For a long moment, the Humbled did not speak. They may have been considering Linden's appeal. Or they may have already dismissed it. She could not read them.

But Clyme and Branl made no move toward Galesend and Anele.

From his place behind Jeremiah and the *croyel*, Galt stated, "I serve no purpose as I am, except as bondage for this fell creature. If a Giant will consent to assume my task, I do not fear to confront Kastenessen once more."

With an unfamiliar asperity, Stave asked Galt, "And are you, Humbled and *Haruchai*, the equal of any Giant against the puissance of an *Elohim* who has merged with the *skurj*?"

"I repeat," Galt retorted, "that I do not fear—"

Stave cut him off. "You are also a Master. That service presumes that you do not fear. Therefore it demands your concern for the larger well-being of others, for the preservation of your companions as well as of the Land.

"In this, you have already failed. You did not warn the Stonedownor of his peril. You made no attempt to evade Kastenessen, either for Liand's sake or for that of the Chosen's son. Do not speak of fearlessness when you have withheld your full service from this company."

The *krill* blazed in Galt's eyes, implying anger that his countenance concealed. Instinctively Linden feared an attack on Stave. For several heartbeats, there was no sound apart from the restless tension of the Giants, Mahrtiir's vexed respiration, and the delicate waft of the breeze.

Then, in unison, the three Humbled nodded.

"We are answered," Clyme announced. "For the present, we will await the counsel of the ur-Lord. If thereafter we determine a different course, we will speak of it plainly. We desire no animosity with the Giants, whom we honor. Also the Unbeliever has commanded our acquiescence to Linden Avery."

In spite of her personal darkness, Linden felt a moment of relief. Rime Coldspray sighed: a gust of released pressure. Then she acknowledged, "That also is well said." Other Swordmainnir broke their silence, commenting quietly to each other. Mahrtiir turned away as if he were biting his tongue.

After a brief exchange with Onyx Stonemage, the Ironhand said formally, "We are Giants. We crave the release of a *caamora*. Here, however, we have no fire for our grief. How then shall we lament Liand of Mithil Stonedown's passing?"

Lament? Linden's chest tightened at the thought. If she allowed herself sorrow now, she might not be able to contain it.

Yet how could she refuse to grieve for Liand, when he had given so much of himself?

She had done nothing to ease the burns and hurts of her companions.

"In a distant age," Stave offered after a moment, "when each Stonedown was nurtured by the lore of the *rhadhamaerl*, Liand's forebears raised cairns to honor their fallen."

Coldspray considered the idea; nodded sharply. "Then we will do likewise. Perhaps it is fortuitous that we have no abundance of worthy stone." She indicated the ridge. "We must delve and strain to wrest condign rock from the earth of these hills. By that labor, we will attempt to articulate our woe."

One at a time, her comrades expressed their approval.

But Linden said, "No." Then she corrected herself. "I mean, not right away. If you don't mind, I want to be alone with him for a while." She could not ease her heart by carrying rocks. "I need a chance to say goodbye. Before you cover him up."

She read the emanations of the Giants clearly, though they did not speak. They were not reluctant to respect her wishes. They simply had no words suited to her distress. Stave and the Humbled said nothing. For its own obscure reasons, the *croyel* withheld its bitterness or mockery. But Mahrtiir reached up to touch Cirrus Kind-wind's arm.

"Come, Giant," he urged quietly. "Let us discover if any of the Ardent's largesse remains. The Ramen also must lament Liand's death. But it is our nature to do so running, as Cord Pahni now runs, and perhaps Cord Bhapa also. I will expend my own sorrow when we have learned the full extent to which we have been harmed by *caesures*."

Mutely Kindwind accompanied the Manethrall, taking Covenant with her, as he turned to descend the ridgeside toward the stream where the companions had left their supplies.

Together the other Giants bowed their heads and followed. But not in silence now. Instead, softly, their Ironhand began to sing.

"There is no death that is not deeply felt,
    No pain that does not bite through flesh and bone.
All hurt is like the endless surge of seas,
The wear and tumbling that leaves no welt
    But only sand instead of granite ease."

Frostheart Grueburn's voice joined Coldspray's for the second line, and Cabled-arm's for the third. Line by line, each Giant added her sadness to the song until all of them were singing. Before the end of the second stanza, the Ironhand's threnody had risen to become a shared hymn.

"Yet stone endures, endures, against the surge:
    It comes to sand, and still the world is stone.
While shores are gnawed, new mountains elsewhere rise.
And so the seas' lament is not a dirge:
    It is a prayer for rock that fronts the skies,

"The calm of rock that always meets the seas,
    A harmony that is both song and groan.
This music is the Earth's reply to pain,

The slow release that lifts us from our knees.
  By this, harsh death becomes both loss and gain."

Stormpast Galesend still carried Anele, still unconscious, still clutching the Sunstone as though his fate depended on it.

While the last Giants left the ridge, Clyme and Branl separated, heading north and south to resume their insufficient watch. Stave also walked out into the night, although he did not go far. And Galt trailed after the Swordmainnir, taking Jeremiah carefully down the uneven slope. Soon Linden was left alone with Liand's body.

Alone and lightless, regarded only by the bereavement of the stars.

Briefly she considered her Staff and Covenant's ring, but did not retrieve them. Instead she moved slowly toward Liand's ruined form. Thinking, Gain? Oh, Liand! she sank to her knees beside her friend and bowed her head to the pebbles and crushed gypsum.

There is hope in contradiction.

Maybe that was true. But she could not see it. Her only consolation was that Jeremiah did not belong to Lord Foul. If he had indeed been claimed, as the Despiser apparently believed, he would not need to hide his thoughts in graves.

☾◯☽

W hen Linden returned to the canyon at last, with the Staff of Law in her hand, Covenant's ring hanging from its chain around her neck, and sorrows engraved like galls on her countenance, the first pallor of dawn had touched the east, emphasizing the crooked horizon of the hills. Stave had joined her when she had walked partway down the first slope, but he had said nothing; asked nothing. And she had not spoken. What could she have said that Stave had not already heard?

In silence, they made their way across the shale and slippage of the hillsides until they reached the thick sand of the canyon-bottom and the impatient mutter of the stream.

There they found their companions organizing the supplies left behind by one of Joan's *caesures*. In the light of the *krill*, Linden saw that several bundles remained. Most of the bedrolls were gone, as well as a few waterskins and two or three sacks of food. But a substantial portion of the Ardent's providence was intact.

That was good fortune, better than she had imagined. But it did not touch her.

Anele was awake now, eating a sparse meal that Latebirth had set out for him. Protected in Galesend's armor, he ate with one hand, clutching Liand's *orcrest* with the other. However, he showed no sign that contact with the Sunstone had relieved his madness. When Linden studied him more closely, she saw that he had buried his legacy of Earthpower deep within him, as if he feared its interaction with *orcrest*. Not for the first time, she thought that he did not want to be sane. Not now: not yet. He dreaded what coherence would impose on him—or require from him.

Mahrtiir also was eating a little food. Jeremiah chewed and swallowed whatever Cabledarm put in his mouth, drank whatever she offered, without any perceptible reaction. But the Giants had apparently decided to save their rations for an occasion of greater need. And Covenant's absence was as plain as a seizure. Broken memories held him, leaving him as uninhabited as Jeremiah.

As if Linden's silence were a commandment, no one spoke. Rime Coldspray and the other Giants watched her with shrouded eyes, keeping what they saw to themselves. The Manethrall finished his food, swallowed a little water. Then, severely, he gestured for Linden's attention and pointed her toward Covenant.

When she did not respond, he sighed. Breaking the night's quietude seemed to cost him an effort as he said, "Like the Cords, Ringthane, I must run my grief. I await only your word. Shall I endeavor to rouse Thomas Covenant? Whether his plight is cruel or soothing, I cannot discern. Therefore the choice is yours."

Part of Linden wanted to leave Covenant alone. She wanted the same thing for herself. But her need for him was greater.

"All right." She sounded awkward to herself, as if she had forgotten how to use her voice. "Give it a try. We have too many decisions to make, and I don't know where to start. Maybe this time he'll remember—"

Her throat closed. Her last decision had led to Liand's death.

Mahrtiir nodded sharply. He was in a hurry. Pinching the nub of a withered bloom from his garland, he rubbed it between his palms as he approached Covenant. There he squatted. With a mute glance up at Cirrus Kindwind, he asked for her aid. The last time that he had used *amanibhavam* in this fashion, Covenant had hurt his head on the boulder.

Kindwind responded by kneeling beside Covenant and cupping her hand behind his head. The stump of her forearm she held ready to catch him if he flung himself to one side or the other.

In slashes of argent from Loric's gem, Linden saw Mahrtiir close Covenant's mouth and press powdered grass to Covenant's nose. She saw Covenant inhale; felt the lingering potency of *amanibhavam* spread like a pang into his bloodstream.

With such suddenness that Mahrtiir jerked backward, Covenant slapped his hand away.

"You aren't here," Covenant snapped. "You don't see what Kastenessen's Durance costs him." His vehemence was as startling as a shout. "The *Elohim* think he deserves it. I don't know how it's *possible* to deserve this kind of pain."

Linden's health-sense recognized the truth. Covenant was still lost in some fissure of recollection. He spoke as though he stood at Kastenessen's side while the horrific task of containing the *skurj* drove the *Elohim* mad.

Shaking his head, Mahrtiir rose to his feet. "Accept my regret, Ringthane," he said gruffly. "He has fallen too far. *Amanibhavam* cannot restore him now."

Linden sighed. "Then go." In her own way, she was as displaced as Covenant. "Do what you have to do. When you come back, we'll try to figure out"—she had no language for her sense of helplessness—"something."

The Manethrall replied with a grave bow. Then he left the company, heading east along the floor of the canyon. As he moved, he gradually quickened his pace until he was sprinting blind. Soon he had faded beyond the reach of Linden's senses.

He, too, had loved Liand.

Without meeting Rime Coldspray's gaze, Linden murmured, "If you still want to do it, Liand deserves a cairn."

The Ironhand nodded. "In a moment. First there is a question that I must ask. Linden Giantfriend, your discernment surpasses ours. Perhaps you will be able to answer."

Done with apportioning and securing the Ardent's supplies, several of the Giants gathered around Coldspray and Linden.

"We were informed," Rime Coldspray began, "that the touch of *orcrest* inspires sanity in Anele. Yet now he holds the Sunstone—and is not transformed."

"I know," said Linden sadly. "I see the same thing."

"Then my question is twofold. If *orcrest* no longer wields the virtue of sanity, does it yet ward him from possession? If it does not, what purpose is served by his grasp? In another's hands—in the Timewarden's, perchance, or in yours—it might aid us well."

It might force Covenant to remain present. If so, he would reject it.

"And if Anele no longer finds himself in *orcrest*," Coldspray continued, "are you not blameless for Liand's death? While the skein of his mind remains confused, the deeds which ensued from your heedlessness would not have been altered. Does his state not demonstrate the unwisdom of claiming fault? Does he not give you cause to excuse yourself?"

Linden shook her head. "No." Still she avoided Coldspray's eyes. "He's even more vulnerable like this." She had found no forgiveness while she was alone with Liand's body. "*Orcrest* isn't affecting him right now"—she scrutinized the old man to confirm her perceptions—"because he isn't letting it.

"Usually it triggers the Earthpower bred in his bones—or his magic triggers Earthpower from the Sunstone. Then he's sane. But now—" Linden shrugged stiffly. "He's hiding himself somehow. I didn't know he could do that. But he needs his madness."

Like an answer, the old man muttered, "Anele fears."

His voice snatched at Linden's attention. Cautiously she moved toward him. "Anele?"

He sat in the curve of Galesend's breastplate, jerking his head from side to side.

Occasional glints of argent accentuated the milky hue of his eyes. One hand gripped the Sunstone against his stomach as if to appease his incessant hunger. The other punched a rhythm at the cataphract, bruising his knuckles.

"He fears to fail—and to succeed." With every phrase, he rocked back and forth in time to his blows. "He wears shackles of horror and shame. Murder. Futility. Error. Greater spirits speak of hope. They do not grasp that he is old and weak. Unable. He must, and cannot. Must. Cannot."

Repeating, "Must," and, "Cannot," like a mantra, he hit the stone, oblivious of his audience.

"Anele?" Linden asked again softly, as if she were crooning to a child. "Anele?" The idea that he knew what he had done to Liand ached in her chest. "Just let it happen. Let it happen. I know that it hurts. But it might help us understand. We might be able to take better care of you."

"Must," Anele replied like an echo of himself. He may not have heard her. "Cannot."

Gritting her teeth, Linden swallowed curses. She was intimately familiar with at least some of Anele's emotions, and they ravaged her.

"I don't know what else to do," she admitted unhappily to Coldspray. "Trusting him is the only thing that I can think of. His parents were my friends. And they were talking to him in his dreams before he ever got to Andelain.

"Sometime long ago, he decided to be crazy—not to mention blind—because he couldn't stand what was happening to him, or how he looked at himself, or what he thought he might have to do. But he's still the son of his parents. I have to believe that his heart is as good as theirs. Eventually he'll prove himself."

So far, everything that Anele had contributed to the company, and to the Land, had been imposed on or wrested from him. In effect, insanity, blindness, and survival were the only choices that he had made for himself.

The Ironhand had come to stand near Linden. Now she rested a gentle hand on Linden's shoulder. "We believe as you do. The old man has become dear to us. And we see no point of resemblance between his plight and Lostson Longwrath's. For his sake, we pray only that 'eventually' will not be long delayed."

Thus she sanctioned Linden's desire to leave Liand's birthright in Anele's hands.

Then Coldspray stepped away. To her comrades, she said, "Come, Swordmainnir. A task awaits us. We must grieve with effort and stone, having no other *caamora*."

At once, the other Giants readied themselves to depart. They seemed grimly eager to confront their own pain and loss. Only Cirrus Kindwind did not join them. Indicating her maimed arm with a grimace, she rose from her knees to stand near Covenant.

Linden smelled sunrise in the air. Soon dawn would find its way into the canyon. Of course the Giants needed to grieve. How could they not, being who they were? Nevertheless she felt a primitive desire to hold them back. When they had honored

Liand with their sorrow, the company would need to make decisions. But she had no idea what to do—or how to face being asked to choose. She had failed Jeremiah. And she had sacrificed Liand in the name of her failure. How could she answer her friends when they posed their questions again?

Forcing herself, she nodded to Rime Coldspray. "I'll wait here. Maybe Covenant will recover. Or Pahni and Bhapa will come back. There might be something that I can do for them."

Certainly she had done nothing to heal the Giants' burns and gashes, or Stave's. In spite of her assertions to the Humbled, she feared the blackness of her power.

"That is well," assented the Ironhand. "We will return when we are content."

Without more words, the leader of the Swordmainnir turned her back on the stream and strode away. Flanked by her comrades, she rose into the first gloom of dawn until she and they became one with the gloaming, discernible only by their troubled auras.

Sighing to herself, Linden considered the radiance of Loric's *krill* for a moment; looked at Galt's rigid stoicism and the *croyel*'s quiescent malice and Jeremiah's emptiness. Briefly she wondered whether Stave might be able to offer some insight into her dilemmas, as he had done before.

But his chance to speak would come, as would that of the Humbled. All of Linden's companions would be free to say what they wished, to no purpose.

Without Covenant—

Her need for some loving touch throbbed like a deep bruise. Covenant had forbidden her; but his mind was gone. After a moment, she went to him. Setting down her Staff, she seated herself beside him; leaned her futility against his boulder.

Cirrus Kindwind had turned away. Her attention was fixed on her comrades in the distance, sharing indirectly the ambergris of their efforts. Stave's manner conveyed the impression that he was listening to Galt's thoughts, or to Clyme's and Branl's, rather than standing watch over Linden and Covenant. The *croyel* had closed its eyes, presumably resting. Jeremiah's unfocused stare resembled the windows of an abandoned dwelling.

Linden almost felt that she was alone with Covenant.

For a time, she studied his vacant profile: the strict line of his jaw, the distinct assertion of his nose, the potential empathy of his mouth. Illumined by the *krill*'s argent, his silver hair looked like reified wild magic.

Tentatively, ready to snatch away her hand, she reached out and stroked his cheek with the backs of her fingers.

He betrayed no reaction. Under her touch, his skin gave off a faint hint of fierce cold and absolute blight: a sensation so diffuse that it was barely palpable. She could imagine him trudging across the gelid heart of a *caesure* within himself, trapped in a wilderland where her caress had no effect.

Oh, Covenant. She had never called him Tom, or even Thomas: only Covenant. In her eyes, pacts and promises defined him. Without them, she could not have learned to love him.

Leaning closer, she said in a low voice as soft as a breath, "I wish that you would come back. I need you. I can't do this without you."

Still he did not react. After a moment, an autonomic shiver ran through him as if he were indeed chilled; freezing in the white void of destroyed life.

He had warned her not to touch him. But surely that prohibition was meaningless while his memories ruled him?

Surely his flesh would welcome her human warmth?

With great care, Linden shifted closer to him. Timidly, as if she risked violating a bond as fragile as trust, she lowered her head to his shoulder.

When he did not flinch or spurn her, she allowed herself to snuggle against him; nestle her forehead in the hollow of his neck. Later she stretched her arm lightly across his chest.

In that position, his absence was vivid to her, as hurtful as a wound. Nevertheless she did not pull away. The sense of cold in him was growing stronger: she hoped to help him resist it. And she needed this contact. Since she could not rescue Jeremiah, Covenant's involuntary embrace, vacant and fraught, might be as close as she would ever come to the touch of true tenderness.

Some time later, her hopes were answered. The wedding band between her breasts began to emit a gentle heat, responding naturally to his need. And soon the ring's soft warmth eased his chill. He did not return to himself; but perhaps he had found his way into some less bitter region of his memories.

After that, the metal cooled again. Apparently he had stopped calling upon it, or he had slipped beyond its reach. Still his ring's brief energy reassured Linden, as if she had been given a sign. Some of her fears receded as she waited for daylight, and for the completion of Liand's cairn, and for decisions that she could not make.

∽∞∾

Seeming as reluctant as Linden, the sun finally rose above the constricted horizon of the hills. If she had looked westward, she might have glimpsed daylight on the dour cliff of Landsdrop earlier. But she had remained pressed against Covenant, unwilling to surrender any precious moment of contact with him, until she felt the sun shining directly on her. When he recovered from his fall, he would push her away.

With the sun's rising, however, she became self-conscious. Stave had heard Covenant forbid her to touch him. In daylight, she could not ignore the former Master. With an effort, she forced herself to shift until she leaned on stone rather than on Covenant's unwitting support.

The sun was pleasant on her cheek, a balm for the night's coolness. Later, she knew, it would gather warmth until it seemed too hot for the season. But by then the heat would be the least of her problems.

When she had stretched her arms and her back, she reclaimed the Staff of Law and climbed stiffly to her feet.

Stave greeted her with a bow. If he—or Galt and Cirrus Kindwind, for that matter—had any opinions about what she had done, they kept their reactions to themselves.

Kindwind had not moved. Her attention remained focused toward her comrades, although the shape of the terrain blocked them from ordinary sight. Apparently her health-sense was strong enough to discern what they were doing. With percipience, she shared their grief in the only fashion available to her.

Linden could have extended her own senses to the place of Liand's death, if she had drawn upon the Staff to do so. But she did not want to observe the Giants at their labors, or to discern the shape of their lament: not until she had no choice. When the cairn was complete, Liand would be sealed away; entirely gone.

Instead she asked Stave quietly, "Are they almost done?"

He considered her question for a moment, then replied, "I deem that they are not." Through Branl and Clyme, he could see the Giants. "Much of this region's stone is porous and eroded, too friable to content them."

"Aye," Kindwind sighed without turning her head.

"Therefore," Stave continued, "they search widely for boulders adequate to express their respect for the Stonedownor, and to expend their lamentation. I question whether they will name their homage complete before the sun approaches midday."

"Aye," Kindwind repeated. "By the measure of the Land's need, and the Earth's, they are too meticulous. While they labor, the time remaining to us drips away. Yet we are Giants. By the measure of our grief, their haste is great.

"And"—for the first time, she looked at Linden—"there is this to consider. We have not yet found our path. The perils arrayed against us are many, and we have not deter-mined our course among them. By the measure of our indecision, the efforts of my comrades impose no delay."

Midday? Linden thought. Good. She was not ready. She did not know how to make herself think about anything except Covenant and Jeremiah.

ဿ

She prayed for Covenant, but he remained absent. The crevasse into which he had fallen was deep. The sun rose high and hot enough to draw sweat from his forehead, and still he seemed vacant, as though he had forgotten the Land and Linden and his own flesh. For him, Time had become a maze without an egress.

Instead Manethrall Mahrtiir was the first to return.

He came from the east along the shallow canyon, trotting as if his health-sense were as precise as vision. His chest heaved, and his garments showed dark patches of sweat; but Linden could see that he had begun to recover from his sorrow. He appeared calmer, soothed by physical strain. In spite of his bandage, he looked as keen for strife as ever. But his aura of anger and self-recrimination was gone.

Approaching Linden, he paused to offer her his familiar Ramen bow. But he did not address her, or wait for her to speak. Rather he continued down to the water's edge, flung himself into the stream's embrace, and let the current carry him along as he scrubbed dust and grime from his limbs.

Until he floated out of sight, Linden did not realize that she wanted to ask him if he had encountered Pahni.

Before long, however, the young Cord emerged from a gully among the southward hillsides. Moving slowly, with a tremor in her legs and a shudder in her respiration, she picked a cautious path toward Linden. Dust clung to her skin, a pale dun that resembled the hue of her leather jerkin and leggings. Caked with dirt and sweat, her features were a mask. From it, her eyes stared, white and stricken, like those of a woman who no longer recognized herself.

Before she reached the sand, she stumbled. Goaded by loss, she had pushed herself until she had nothing left—

Instinctively Linden started toward her. But Stave was faster; much faster. As Pahni fell to one knee and sprawled forward, he reached her, caught her. But he did not lift her in his arms. Careful of her pride, he only supported her until she forced her legs under her and regained a semblance of balance. Then he released her.

Expressionless at her side, he accompanied her while she finished her fragile descent to the floor of the canyon.

Then Bhapa appeared on a hilltop behind them. To Linden's percipience, he looked less weary than Pahni—and less relieved than Mahrtiir. Concerned for the young Cord, he had run more to watch over her than to appease his grief. As a result, he was both stronger than Pahni and more troubled.

For Pahni's sake, Cirrus Kindwind turned away from the labor of her comrades. As wordless as the Cord, the Giant set her hand on Pahni's shoulder and steered her toward Anele, then urged her to sit. Uncharacteristically Anele had not touched his food since he had last spoken. Instead he crouched in Stormpast Galesend's cataphract, staring blindly at nothing, and clasping the Sunstone in both hands as though he both needed and refused it.

Faced with the remains of Anele's viands, Pahni seemed no more inclined to eat it than the old man did. Her gaze may have been as sightless as his. But Kindwind left the

Cord there and went to retrieve a waterskin. When she held the waterskin to Pahni's lips, Pahni took it and drank urgently.

Linden sighed in private relief. Apparently the girl still wanted to live, in spite of her bereavement.

There Bhapa joined Linden, Kindwind, and Stave. Descending the last slopes, he had regained a measure of control over his breathing. To Linden he bowed as Mahrtiir had bowed, gravely and in silence. But to the Giant, he said hoarsely, "Accept the thanks of a Cord, Cirrus Kindwind. Your care and kindness toward the least of your companions is a gift for which I have no adequate guerdon. I have long been a Cord, and have witnessed sorrow that would test the fortitude of a Manethrall." Then he nodded toward Pahni. "Ere now, however, I have not seen grief threaten to extinguish any Raman."

Pahni had begun eating. With painful slowness, she lifted small morsels to her mouth and chewed them as if they had no meaning except survival. She did not appear to hear Bhapa.

"In the lives that we have known," the older Cord continued, "our love for the Ranyhyn is an anodyne for mourning. How can our hearts not lift when we behold the great horses in their glory? But in this circumstance Pahni is thrice bereft. Her joy is slain, the Ringthane has of necessity refused her, and here there are no Ranyhyn."

"My gratitude for your consideration—"

Bhapa swallowed fiercely, unable to find his voice again. He looked like he might weep, although his body had no moisture to spare for tears. As if he were ashamed of his emotions, he ducked his head.

More harshly than she intended, Linden asked, "Did you think about calling her Ranyhyn? Naharahn would have answered. Pahni wouldn't have come so close to the edge—"

Then Linden stopped, cursing herself. She was not angry at Bhapa. It was her own role in Pahni's pain that vexed her.

Before she could apologize, Bhapa raised his head. For the first time since she had known him, she saw ire in his eyes.

"The Ranyhyn do not live to serve us," he said like sand scraped by stone. "They are not ours to command. We live to serve them. Until you came among us, no Ramen had ever ridden them. Enabling us to accompany you on your dire quests, they do us too much honor. None but a Manethrall may ask more of them."

"I'm sorry," Linden replied as gently as she could. "I shouldn't have said that. I know better. I'm just upset that there's nothing I can do for Pahni."

Bhapa's glare did not soften: he seemed unwilling to accept her apology. She had awakened his Ramen pride. But Cirrus Kindwind rested her arm across his shoulders and drew him away from Linden. "Come, Cord," she said to soothe him. "If you deem me considerate, permit me to be so now. Your need for aliment emulates Pahni's. Join her, I beseech you, and nourish your strength. We must soon depend upon yours, and hers, and every heart among us."

Firmly Kindwind guided him to the meal that she had offered Pahni and seated him beside the young Cord.

"Thank you," Linden murmured. Little as it was, it was as much as she could do. The comfort of resting against Covenant was gone, eroded by the effects of the Liand's death. Pahni's distress triggered reminders of She Who Must Not Be Named.

Cirrus Kindwind nodded; shrugged. Briefly she glanced at Stave, perhaps asking him with her gaze to watch over the Cords. Then she turned her attention toward her comrades once more.

The *croyel* kept its eyes closed. Jeremiah continued to gape at nothing as if he did not need sleep—or could not tell the difference between slumber and wakefulness.

Ah, God, Linden thought. Resurrected spiders and centipedes scurried on her skin. Covenant, please. I'm falling apart here.

But Covenant did not hear her prayer, or did not heed it. Sweating slightly, he slumped against his boulder as if he were as trapped as Jeremiah; as if his memories were graves.

After a while, the Manethrall returned, wading against the current. As he drew near, Linden saw that he had washed his garments as well as his limbs and hair. He had even scrubbed his bandage. Then he had retied it around his head, concealing the ruin of his lost eyes.

When he had surveyed Linden and her diminished company, he turned to his Cords. At once, Bhapa surged to his feet. Perhaps ashamed of his lingering anger, he bowed as if he were accepting a reprimand. But Mahrtiir did not address the older Cord. Instead, standing with his feet in the stream, he spoke to Pahni in a tone of quiet authority, confident that he would be obeyed.

"Cord Pahni, Bhapa requires your aid. He must bathe. You must insist upon it. He is a Cord deprived of his Maneing only by the absence other Manethralls. His appearance is unseemly."

Linden had expected Mahrtiir to respond to Pahni's pain more directly. But he knew the girl's Ramen nature better than Linden did. In Pahni's present state, attempts at consolation might only weaken her. Instead he directed her awareness outward; away from her woe and exhaustion.

Linden could not see Pahni's face, but she felt the girl flinch. A moment later, however, the young Cord climbed, tottering, to stand upright. Wavering on the frayed edge of her balance, she bowed to her Manethrall. Then, weak as a foal, she turned to Bhapa.

"Come, Bhapa." Briefly her voice seemed to stick in her throat, clogged by sorrows. "Ramen do not protest when a Manethrall commands."

Taking Bhapa's hand, she led him into the stream as if he, too, had been blinded.

As Mahrtiir had foreseen, she responded when she was given reason to believe that she was needed.

If Linden had thought for an instant that Covenant would do the same, she might have tried to slit her wrists.

ৎOঌ

E ventually Rime Coldspray and the rest of the Swordmainnir came back from the ridgecrest, carrying their armor. After their fashion, they seemed as tired as Bhapa, and as unresolved. Yet their fortitude ran deep. Although they adored stone and sea, they were timbers, able to flex instead of shattering. To honor Liand, they had spent much of their endurance. But much remained.

When they had greeted Linden, Stave, and the Ramen, and shared their condolences with Cirrus Kindwind, they went first to the stream to wash off the grime of sweat and digging, and to drink their fill. Afterward they ruefully doled out an inadequate meal for themselves. Then, while the other Swordmainnir began to resume their armor, Rime Coldspray turned to Linden.

"Linden Giantfriend," said the Ironhand formally, "we have spent too long in sorrow. The day advances, and doubtless the Land's foes do the same. We must delay no longer.

"We"—she indicated her comrades—"wish to display our handiwork. Will you ascend to the place of Liand's passing? From his cairn, we may set our course, for good or ill."

"All right," Linden answered. She did not want to see it. "I don't have any better ideas." Trying to be clear, she added, "About anything. I was counting on Covenant. I was counting on being able to free Jeremiah. Now I'm as lost as they are. If Covenant doesn't come back, you'll have to make our decisions for us. You and Stave and Mahrtiir. I'm done choosing."

The results of her inadequacy were all around her. She had already done too much harm. And she had been changed by her nightmares; by mistakes and weaknesses beyond counting.

The Ironhand frowned. "You mis-esteem yourself. It is plain that indeed you do not forgive. Yet heretofore you have assumed great and fearsome burdens, as I have averred. Therefore I acknowledge that you require a greater respite. With Stave's consent, and that of the Ramen, we will take upon ourselves the task of choice.

"If the Masters protest, they must name their own desires."

"We will do so," Galt stated flatly.

The Manethrall studied Linden and Coldspray. After a moment, he nodded. "It will be as you have said, Ironhand of the Swordmainnir. Nonetheless I must affirm that the Ramen stand with the Ringthane. When she becomes Linden Avery the Chosen once more, as she must, her word will command us, whatever the cost."

Ah, God. —as she must—

Stave indicated his own commitments by shifting closer to Linden. His single eye watched Galt impassively.

The Master had already implied that he was not content to simply restrain the *croyel*. Like Clyme and Branl, he might soon feel compelled to act on other priorities.

Coldspray answered Mahrtiir's nod with her own. "We are in accord, Manethrall. We also wish to follow Linden Giantfriend until the end. I seek only to ease her present distress."

This time, the Manethrall bowed. "Then let us go now to honor Liand's cairn as well as we may. We will make of the Stonedownor's steadfastness a lodestone to guide our purposes."

Bowing in turn, Coldspray stooped to retrieve her armor.

Frostheart Grueburn, Latebirth, and Halewhole Bluntfist had already fastened their cataphracts around them, loosened their longswords in their scabbards. Now Bluntfist lifted Anele's unresisting form out of Stormpast Galesend's breastplate.

The old man did not react. He seemed oblivious to the activity around him. His thoughts remained fixed on something that no one else could see: the dilemma of his personal contradiction, *Must* and *Cannot* in unrelieved succession.

Soon Galesend was ready to reclaim Anele. The rest of the Giants had secured their armor and shouldered their bundles of supplies. Unasked, Galt turned Jeremiah and the *croyel*, and began to impel them carefully up the hillsides toward the gypsum ridge. Cirrus Kindwind offered to carry Covenant, but Manethrall Mahrtiir stopped her. "Other attempts have failed," he explained. "Mayhap the exertion of walking will reassert the claims of his flesh upon his mind."

Then he instructed his Cords to take Covenant's arms, raise him to his feet, and support him on his way. In spite of their weariness, they obeyed at once. Pahni's dull stare conveyed the impression that she was too numb to care what she did.

Acquiescing with a shrug, Kindwind joined her fellow Swordmainnir. Shortly Linden and all of her companions were in motion, repeating their angled ascent to the place where Liand had perished.

Her friends intended to make her decisions for her—but only until she felt able to become the Chosen again: the woman in whom they elected to believe. They did not understand that Liand's death, and the state of Jeremiah's mind, and the bane's screaming power had taught her the truth about herself. At her heart, she was carrion. Food for maggots and vultures. She was done with choosing.

She had no other defense against the Despiser's machinations.

5.

Inheritances

Carrying her Staff and Covenant's ring and Jeremiah's healed toy as if they were empty of import, Linden climbed the slopes with Stave and Mahrtiir like a woman ascending Gallows Howe.

The hills seemed high to her now; more difficult than she remembered. A kind of moral weakness dragged at her muscles. She did not want to see Liand's cairn—and could not refuse. Like the company's circumstances, the outcome of her efforts to save her son called for more courage than she could imagine.

Only Thomas Covenant had it in him to meet the challenge of doom and death: she believed that. Only his instinct for incalculable victories—But she did not know how to reach him.

She wanted to turn and simply walk away forever. —*as she must*—Unfortunately she had abdicated her right to choose. Her friends had promised to make her decisions for her. Looking at Liand's monument was only the first of them. Obedient to her own surrender, she forced her way up the shale and grit of the hillsides until she reached the ridge.

There the desiccated browns of the surrounding terrain made the white spine of gypsum appear unnaturally stark, almost pure; as distinct as chalk. Along the ridge, bits of quartz and mica caught the sun and flashed like implied omens. No doubt dust would have billowed from the strides of the Swordmainnir in any breeze; but the air was as still as a tombstone. Arid heat and haze rather than dust gave the sky a tan hue.

Immediately in front of the company, the handiwork of the Giants dominated the east, a long oval mound towering over the ridge from slope to slope. With sweat and strength and love, Rime Coldspray and her comrades had piled rocks the size of *kresh* and Cavewights and even mustangs to cover Liand's death with homage. A few of the boulders were as big as huts. In an abstract way, Linden had understood that the Giants were mighty, and that they had labored long. Nevertheless she was taken aback by the scale of the cairn. Liand had been given a barrow suitable for a king.

It seemed more final than his ruined corpse.

Oh, Liand. Through her reluctance and shame, Linden felt her eyes burn with unattainable tears. Nothing could comfort her for the Stonedownor's passing. Still she felt that the Giants had done him justice.

"A small gesture only," explained Coldspray as if she were embarrassed. "Being Giants, we had it in our hearts to dig away this stretch of the ridge, and that beyond as well, thus forming a pediment for the cairn. But time pressed against us, and we abandoned our first intent."

"Nonetheless," Mahrtiir stated after a moment, "what you have done is well done. Be assured that it is well done."

Instead of speaking, Stave bowed in the manner of the *Haruchai*, first to the Ironhand, then to the high mound of stone.

Still Covenant did not react. Creviced memories held him.

On a hilltop some distance to the north, Clyme stood with his back to the company. In the south, Branl also faced away. The two Humbled seemed to disregard their companions; but Linden understood their vigilance. They had not forgotten their many enemies. Joan's attack during the night had demonstrated that even here, tens or scores of leagues from more obvious dangers, the company was not safe. Clyme and Branl did not assume that the Land's last defenders would be safe anywhere.

"If it is well done," Rime Coldspray said finally, "we are content. I name our grief and honor complete. Now let us consider our course. We cannot remain as we are while the Worm threatens to unmake all that we have known and loved and needed."

Her words may have been addressed to Linden; but Linden stood with her head bowed and did not respond. What could she have said?

"Our foes are easily counted," replied Mahrtiir grimly. "The Timewarden's former mate craves our ruin. Only her madness preserves us from endless *caesures*. Further we are told that his son amasses Cavewights to claim both the Ringthane's child and the *croyel*. Given opportunity, Kastenessen may strike again, as we know to our great cost. Also it is his theurgy which shapes Kevin's Dirt, hampering Earthpower across the Upper Land. And we are told as well that both Sandgorgons and *skurj* assail Salva Gildenbourne. Indeed, they may dare the ravage of Andelain, for the *krill* no longer defends the heart of the Land's loveliness."

That one detail, at least, had been Covenant's doing, not Linden's. It was all that had enabled the company to capture Jeremiah.

"These are fearsome perils in all sooth," Mahrtiir observed, "terrible and heinous. In addition, however, Esmer endures, compelled to treachery. And we must not forget the Worm itself as it seeks the roots of *Melenkurion* Skyweir."

The Manethrall paused briefly, then said, "I do not regard such lesser wights as *kresh* and *skest*. In themselves, they are mere servants. Nor do I consider *turiya* Raver. If he does not remain with his victim, she is nothing. Contemplation of Lostson Long-wrath I leave to the Swordmainnir, who are better able to comprehend his plight. The Insequent have turned aside. And I do not cite the lurker of the Sarangrave, though we stand nigh unto its demesne. Ancient tales suggest that it is little more than a monstrous appetite devoid of thought or aspiration.

"However, I must speak of *moksha* Jehannum. Where he toils, and what he strives to gain, are hidden from us. I cannot discount She Who Must Not Be Named. Aroused, the bane may rise still farther, wreaking vast torment. And I must not neglect the purest abomination, dire Fangthane himself, Despiser of Land and life. It is by his will that all other perils and evils have awakened. There can be no reply to the Worm unless Fangthane also is answered."

Mahrtiir paused again; turned his bandaged face toward each of his companions one by one. Explicitly he did not spare Linden his scrutiny. After giving them a moment to absorb his summation, he asked, "What say you? Is my tale complete?"

The Giants shifted their feet uncomfortably. Some of them looked daunted in spite of their native resilience and courage. Pahni stood like a woman in shock. Bhapa fretted as if he wished to flee. Between them, Covenant mumbled something that sounded like a list of all the trees in the One Forest. But Anele had fallen silent in Galesend's arms, apparently conscious of nothing except *orcrest* and dread.

Linden did not want to speak. She felt beaten down by Mahrtiir's toll of troubles, almost immured, as if his words were stones. When no one else responded, however, she forced herself to say, "One of us ought to at least mention the *Elohim*. They're probably all scrambling to save themselves. But Infelice sure as hell didn't want us to rescue Jeremiah. Now that we have him, she may be desperate enough to interfere."

Like the Manethrall, Coldspray scanned the company. Having ascertained that no one wished to offer a comment, she nodded once, harshly. "Then we are agreed. The tale is complete, though its unadorned brevity resembles a wound. Now we must make known the counsels of our hearts."

Looking directly at Pahni and Bhapa, she continued, "And here none may keep silent. Every thought and insight and apprehension must be heard." She seemed to think that the Cords might be too diffident or weary to express themselves. "Any word may serve to inspire guidance, but it cannot if it *is* not uttered."

Like Coldspray, Mahrtiir faced the Cords. "Harken well. The Ironhand's command is also mine. I comprehend the hurt of speaking only to be countered or dismissed. But our straits require this of us. Naught can be gained without risk of hurt."

Bhapa nodded with a nauseated grimace. But Pahni surprised Linden by answering, "The Ardent has said that the Ringthane's need for death is great." She sounded vague, almost stupefied. Nothing flickered in her eyes to indicate that she was aware of her own bitterness. "I see no promise that her need has been sated."

Restore him!

I can't. I would if I could.

Mahrtiir's wince was visible in spite of his bandage; but he did not reprimand the girl.

As if in Linden's defense, Frostheart Grueburn said, "The withdrawal of the Insequent is lamentable. Our grief over the Ardent's passing is whetted by our inability to seek further explication of his auguries."

After a moment, Onyx Stonemage added, "Nor are we able to ask aid of the ur-viles and Waynhim. Doubtless their lore is great. Certainly we have witnessed their strange puissance. While Esmer lives, however, we are deprived of our gift of tongues. It may be that Linden Giantfriend remains able to call upon them. But if so, we would not comprehend their counsel."

More sternly, the Ironhand stated, "It is bootless to dwell upon queries which cannot or will not be answered. We must consider deeds which are within our compass."

"Then, Ironhand," said Cabledarm, "let us begin by discarding deeds which are not within our compass." Her tone suggested a dour jest, although her expression was somber. "Neither the Sandgorgons nor the *skurj* merit concern. Our mere strength and swords cannot defeat such creatures."

Halewhole Bluntfist agreed. "And let us discard also the Worm itself, and She Who Must Not Be Named, and Fangthane Despiser. Doubtless such evils must be answered. There again, however, strength and swords will achieve no worthy effect. Those who wield wild magic and Earthpower"—she glanced at Galt—"aye, and Loric's eldritch *krill* must devise our course. We cannot."

Linden swallowed an empty protest. Clearly Bluntfist and the others were still counting on her; and they were wrong. Yet she could frame no real objection. The Giants were being practical: their reasoning made sense.

Coldspray considered her comrades briefly. Then she admitted, "Nor do we suffice against Esmer *mere*-son. There we must place our trust in the ur-viles and Waynhim. As for the *Elohim*, their plight is beyond our ken. Thus our deliberation is simplified. We need contemplate only the Timewarden's former mate—their son and his army of Cavewights—and mad Kastenessen."

Only? Linden thought. *Only?* But before she could find her voice, Mahrtiir put in sharply, "And also the Ringthane's son and the *croyel*. That burden has not been relieved by Liand's death."

"Aye," Rime Coldspray assented. "I hear you, Manethrall. Nonetheless his plight is a matter of theurgy. While Linden Giantfriend remains thwarted by the *croyel*, and Covenant Timewarden is absent, we can do naught to ease the boy."

"Aye," grumbled Mahrtiir in turn, conceding the Ironhand's point.

Linden gnawed her lip and tried to guess what conclusion the Giants and the Ramen would reach.

"Thus," Coldspray said again. "The Timewarden's former mate. Their son. Kastenessen." She looked around at her comrades once more. "Upon another occasion, I will require your condolences for such concision. For the present—" Then she faced the two *Haruchai*. "Master. Stave. You have not spoken. Do you consent to the nature of our counsels? Is there aught which we must add or discard ere we continue?"

A glance like a knife passed between the Humbled and the former Master, although their miens were impassive; and a spatter of tension ran down Linden's spine. She could not see beneath the surface of either man, but she felt—

As if to the air rather than to Coldspray or Stave, Galt said, "I will speak when your deliberations are done."

"And I will answer you," promised Stave.

Without explanation, he shifted his gaze to the Ironhand.

"I would urge," he told her, "that some forewarning must be conveyed to the Masters in Revelstone. Yet I cannot conceive how my desire may be accomplished. If the word of an *Elohim* is to be believed, scant days remain to us, and even a rider Ranyhyn-mounted must have more than a few to gain Lord's Keep."

He shrugged delicately. "Thus my wishes for my kindred come to naught." With an air of formality, he concluded, "Ironhand of the Swordmainnir, I am content with your counsels."

Rime Coldspray replied with a nod as grave as a bow. Then she said to everyone, "Now we must further simplify our course. To my mind, the choice has become one of urgency. Which of the three perils that we have selected poses the most severe or immediate threat?"

Involuntarily Linden shook her head. She did not mean to interfere with Coldspray's leadership, or with Mahrtiir's; but she answered without thinking.

"Urgency isn't the problem. They're all urgent," Jeremiah more than anything else. "The problem is finding them. I can't even guess where Joan is. But Esmer and the Ardent told us that Roger is in Mount Thunder." Somewhere among the Wightwarrens. "And Kastenessen has to be there, too, since he's drawing on the bane to power Kevin's Dirt. Locating them sounds impossible, but it probably isn't. If we get close enough, we won't have to find either of them. They'll find us."

Abruptly she stopped. This was not what she wanted. She had good reason to avoid more responsibility. And she doubted that the Humbled would respect any choices except their own.

In dismay, she argued against herself. "At least we know where Jeremiah is."

We need to help him somehow. Please.

After a quick consultation with her comrades, the Ironhand mused, "The distance is not insurmountable. The remaining portion of the Ardent's largesse may be stretched to sustain a trek of several days. Yet qualms disturb me. I fear the suddenness with which Covenant Timewarden's former mate is able to strike. And within the Wight-warrens of Mount Thunder, of which we have heard tales, we will traverse passages and confusions unknown to us, yet intimately familiar to the Cavewights. Doubtless the Timewarden's son and his forces will offer battle at a time and place where every circumstance is unfavorable to us."

Linden said nothing.

"Also," continued the Ironhand, "I am reluctant to turn my back upon the intent of the Ardent. Aye, he did not name his purpose. Yet the great cost of his service has won my regard. I cannot conclude that our presence here is without value."

"By your reasoning, then, Ironhand," Mahrtiir concluded harshly, "we are returned to our starting place. We cannot choose a path toward any point of our compass. In my heart remains the belief that what has transpired here"—he pointed at Liand's cairn—"must serve as our lodestone. Yet its import eludes me." In frustration, he muttered a Ramen curse. "Therefore I can offer no further counsel."

Abruptly Bhapa took a step forward. "Perhaps—" he began, then stopped, staring as though his own thoughts shocked him.

"Speak, Cord," the Manethrall commanded at once.

Please, Linden repeated, if only to herself. Somebody think of something.

Bhapa appeared to fumble for words. "Earlier." He swallowed hard. "When Cord Pahni returned to us." He glanced, flinching, at Linden, then forced himself to meet Mahrtiir's eyeless scrutiny. "The Ringthane asked why we did not summon the Ranyhyn to ease Pahni's sorrow. I replied"—again he swallowed—"with disrespect, hearing no esteem for the Ranyhyn in her. Yet now—"

Once more, he faltered.

The Manethrall waited. Carefully Rime Coldspray prompted, "Yet now—"

A flush spread like shame across the Cord's face. In a rush, he said, "If we summon the Ranyhyn, and entrust ourselves to their wisdom, perhaps they will consent to select our path.

"They are the *Ranyhyn*," he insisted as if his companions had objected. "Though they have ever allowed both the Ramen and their riders to choose their roads, they share insights which surpass us. Perhaps they can discern the whereabouts of the

Timewarden's former mate. Or they may recognize the Ardent's purpose. They may elect to resume the journey which he was unable to complete.

"Surely any destination deemed condign by the Ranyhyn is preferable to our present bafflement."

There Mahrtiir silenced Bhapa. "Enough, Cord," the Manethrall said, unexpectedly mild in spite of his palpable excitement. "This is unforeseen counsel. I now comprehend your hesitation in speaking of it. Ramen do not presume to such thoughts. Before the Ringthane's coming, however, no Raman had presumed to ride the Ranyhyn. Yet when that occasion presented itself, they made plain their approval. I do not doubt that they will approve once more."

His eagerness stirred the company. The Giants lifted their heads as though they had caught the scent of hope.

Hyn! Linden thought. Hynyn. Naharahn and Bhanoryl and Mhornym and the others. In their sparse horserite, Hyn and Hynyn had found a way to share their concerns without manipulating her choices. And they were responsible for persuading Stave to alter his allegiance despite the combined indignation of the Masters. Her many mistakes had taught her to trust them.

Suddenly she missed Hyn with all her heart: the mare's proud carriage and fleetness, the affection in her soft eyes, the certainty of every step. Hyn would know—

With a clarion note in his voice, Mahrtiir asked, "What say you, Ironhand of the Swordmainnir? Lacking other wisdom, we are baffled. And I conceive that Liand's steadfastness came as near as any human may to the fidelity of the Ranyhyn. If we determine to abide by their guidance, his openness and valor will indeed be made our lodestone."

Again Rime Coldspray spoke quietly with her comrades. When she was ready to answer, her eyes shone.

"The Swordmainnir," she announced, "are content in all sooth. Our knowledge of the Ranyhyn is scant. Yet we have witnessed their glory and service. To our sight, they resemble the wonder and mystery of Andelain made flesh. And we have seen the reverence in which they are held by all whose experience of them exceeds our own. When Galt has revealed the will of the Humbled, we will gladly hear the call which summons such horses—aye, and gladly be led by them."

As she spoke, Bhapa squared his shoulders. His shame was transformed: it became a glow of pride that Linden had never seen in him before. And Pahni's expressionless stare lost some of its dullness. The prospect of seeing the Ranyhyn again seemed to ameliorate her deep exhaustion and grief.

But Linden's own anticipation faded almost immediately. She had forgotten Galt's promise to speak—and she feared what he might say.

Brusquely Stave told Galt, "The time has come. Your silence is both unjust and hurtful. You demean companions who have entrusted their lives to your honor and service."

His tone doused the rising spirits of the Ramen. A frown gathered on Coldspray's brow, and Halewhole Bluntfist looked like a woman about to take umbrage. Latebirth betrayed a small wince of surprise.

To Stave, Galt nodded. "I will do so." Then he turned his head to address the company.

"In the Unbeliever's absence from himself," he said as if his words were without portent, "we approve your wish to rely upon the Ranyhyn. Knowing them of old through our memories of the Bloodguard, we do not doubt that they will guide us well."

Nothing in his tone betrayed the nature of his intentions as he added, "When they have come, and have given their consent to your desires, I will slay the *croyel*."

At once, a jolt like the touch of a *caesure* struck the company. Bhapa cried out in protest, and Mahrtiir's garrote seemed to leap of its own accord into his hands. "Stone and Sea!" roared Coldspray. "Are you mad, *Haruchai*?" Two other Giants reached for their swords, but did not draw them.

Stillness clogged the air, making it difficult to breathe. Instinctively Linden sprang toward Jeremiah, drawing obsidian like panic from the Staff of Law. Flame gusted into the sky, as stark and black as the Staff itself: a blare of darkness against the heavens. But she did not see it. She saw only Galt's impassive mien, and the fraught gnashing of the *croyel*'s fangs, and the ferocity in its acid eyes.

Mahrtiir and the Ironhand called Linden's name simultaneously. A stunned turmoil gripped the rest of the company. Galt's fist tightened on the *krill*. He gripped Jeremiah's shoulder harder; studied Linden like a man who never blinked. But Stave reached past her power to set his hand like a barrier between her and Galt.

"Withhold, Chosen," he said sharply. "I will implore you if I must. He is *Haruchai*, a Master, one of the Humbled. If he chooses death, your power cannot stop his hand."

"Must," Anele echoed almost inaudibly. "Cannot."

Spreading midnight fire like sheet-lightning over the ridgecrest, Linden whirled to confront Covenant.

"*Stop* him!" she cried in a voice as dark as her flame. "You've told them and told them! You've supported me ever since I brought you back!" And Esmer had healed Jeremiah's crumpled toy. Surely that implied some possibility of salvation for her son? "Don't let him do this!"

Covenant stood unsteadily between Bhapa and Pahni. He did not so much as glance at Linden. Lost in memories, he looked as forlorn as a disturbed grave. The muscles of his jaw knotted and released, knotted and released, like the struggle of his mute heart.

"Linden Avery." Stave was almost shouting. "Quench your fire. The Unbeliever cannot reply. Were he able to do so, I do not doubt that he would forbid the Humbled. But he cannot. And such stained Earthpower is surely a beacon to every lorewise being who seeks our harm.

"I have said that I will answer Galt. I will do so. But you must end this dire display."

At last, Linden's mind seemed to catch up with her actions; her desperation. In spite of the fury pounding in her ears—fury or despair—she understood Stave. Covenant could not respond: not as he was. And she had never meant to oppose any *Haruchai* with Earthpower or wild magic. Stave's people were the Land's friends, if they were not hers.

—your power cannot stop his hand.

Trembling as if she were feverish or freezing, Linden panted, "All right. All right. Answer him. Do it now."

Every sinew in her body shuddered as she forced herself to swallow her frenzy and her Staff's fire.

Momentary relief spattered among the Giants, the Ramen. Then it was gone. Even Anele's blind gaze seemed to follow her as she faced Galt again. Only Jeremiah showed no sign that he was aware of his peril: only Jeremiah and Covenant.

"Speak, Galt," Stave demanded. "Account for your intent so that your companions may comprehend it. Then hear my reply."

"I will do so," Galt repeated. "Betimes others have concealed their purposes. But we are the Humbled, and Masters, and *Haruchai*. We scorn such conduct."

To Linden, his every word sounded as heavy as the beat of a dirge.

"Our reasons are many," he began. "Least among them is that I will not bear this monstrous being upon the back of Bhanoryl, or upon that of any Ranyhyn. All *Haruchai* honor the Ranyhyn. I will not impose the evil of the *croyel* upon them."

Immediately Mahrtiir retorted, "You impose nothing, Master." His scorn was as harsh as Galt's. His garrote he held taut between his fists. "The Ranyhyn will bear you and the boy and the monster, or they will not. Their choices are not yours to make."

Galt ignored the Manethrall. More to the Giants than to Stave, the Ramen, or Linden, he said, "A weightier reason is that my present task fetters me. Against the assault which slew the Stonedownor, I could not act without risking the *croyel*'s release. I will not again suffer this waste of my strength when every strength is needed."

As steady as a boulder, Stave replied, "If your impatience surpasses your flawed restraint, cede the *krill* to me. I will bear the burden in your stead."

Stave also Galt ignored. "A still greater argument," he continued like the thud of funereal drums, "is that the boy's plight cannot be redeemed. That has been demonstrated beyond question. It has been amply witnessed."

No, Linden insisted. *No.* But the Humbled did not heed her silent protest.

"Linden Avery's mad quest for her son has met its irreparable doom. Lacking any good cause, we have endured many bitter hazards in her name, and have gained naught but an increase of sorrow. Now our need for the *croyel*'s death exceeds the value of the boy's life. The Unbeliever has commanded us to honor Linden Avery's wishes. In his present state, we cannot. We must serve according to our avowed Mastery."

"There your reasoning falters," Stave pronounced. "You arrogate to yourselves a foresight which you do not possess. One failure does not foretell another. That the Chosen has not found some means to relieve her son does not ordain that she can not or will not. To claim otherwise is to assert certainty concerning events and deeds which have not yet occurred."

Yes, Linden thought. Please. I'm going to try again. As soon as I think of a way to do it. I just need time.

But still Galt ignored Stave. Now he appeared to speak exclusively to the Giants as if he considered the rest of the company suspect; flawed by their loyalties.

"However, the greatest reason is this. When the time comes to confront our foes, the Unbeliever will require the *krill*. High Lord Loric invested this blade and this gem with a mighty theurgy. Like my own strength, that theurgy is wasted in its present use. It is wasted utterly, though it will be utterly needed.

"The Unbeliever did not wrest it from its place merely to capture and preserve the boy. He foresaw far graver exigencies, else he would not have surrendered all of Andelain to ravage and ruin. It cannot be his intent that Andelain should perish for the sake of Linden Avery's irretrievable child."

To this, the Swordmainnir responded with silence and glowering. Linden felt their anger rise. The set of Rime Coldspray's jaw seemed to rebuff Galt at every point.

For centuries or millennia, the Masters had rebuffed the Giants—

But if Stave felt any frustration at Galt's attitude, he did not show it. Instead he continued to answer. Now, however, he spoke so slowly that he seemed to drawl, emphasizing every assertion.

"Then, Humbled," he said as if he had assumed Covenant's authority, "you will stay your hand while you await the Unbeliever's return to himself. Your other persuasions are chaff. They are mere impatience misnamed devotion. But the reason of the Unbeliever's need has merit. It is incontestable. Yet his absence is also incontestable. He cannot require the *krill* while he remains as he is. And it is neither honest nor honorable to kill the boy when no purpose is served. It is murder.

"Have the Humbled come to this? Do they commit murder, when the *Haruchai* have always refused assent to such crimes?"

Now Galt met Stave's single gaze. Briefly he flexed his fingers on the haft of the *krill*, eased the pressure of his grip on Jeremiah. When he replied, Linden thought that she heard a subtle discomfiture in his tone.

"It may chance that the touch of the *krill* will restore the Unbeliever to himself."

Still slowly, Stave said, "Or it may chance that it will not. Then the son of Linden Avery the Chosen will have been slain, and you will have accomplished nothing, and your vaunted devoir will be made a mockery of itself."

Linden hung on Stave's response. Inwardly she burned to hear what Galt would say next.

But he did not reply.

Without warning, he and Stave both stiffened as if they were about to leap at each other's throats. Then Stave grabbed her arm, snatched her away from Galt and Jeremiah—

—turned her in time to see Clyme launch himself off the crest where he had stood watch.

In his right hand, Clyme gripped a long spear by its shaft. Blood marked the point of the spear and the side of his left shoulder. His tunic there had been rent.

"Ware and ward!" Stave shouted. "We are assailed!"

As Clyme plunged downward, the hilltop of his vantage-point exploded in a blast of heat and fury like brimstone.

Oh, God—!

Around Linden, Giants wrenched their swords from their scabbards. Rime Cold-spray gave them no commands: they were Swordmainnir and knew their tasks. Long strides swept them into a defensive arc to protect their smaller companions. Those Giants carrying supplies threw their bundles southward off the ridge. The Ironhand brandished her glaive, loosening her arms and wrists.

As the Giants readied themselves, Stave called, "The Unbeliever's son brings Cavewights against us! Concealed by some glamour, they eluded Clyme's senses. Only the spear in its flight forewarned him!"

Linden wanted to protest, They can't be here. We're too far from Mount Thunder. But she could not breathe, and had no voice.

Once again, Roger Covenant had caught the company by surprise. Cavewights charging closer should have raised a cloud of dust—unless the air was too still for dust, or the creatures ran entirely on stone. Or Roger's glamour was so complete that it masked every sign of his coming.

Grimly Manethrall Mahrtiir ordered his Cords to protect Covenant. "Doubtless Branl will aid you! Entrust the Ringthane to Stave, and to me!"

For a moment, Linden saw nothing except Clyme's pelting haste. The spear was stone, massive and ungainly; yet he carried it with ease. Several hills intervened between him and the ridge, all lower than the crest he had left. He dropped into a valley, then reappeared, still some distance away.

Then she felt a silent shock. With her health-sense rather than her ears, she heard a shredding sound like the rip of claws through fabric. An instant later, her foes became visible as if they had been translated here by some immense magic.

A wave of Cavewights had already broken over the hill where Clyme had stood, scores of them. More poured around the slopes on either side, tall and gangling, with disproportionately long limbs, club-heads, eyes like molten crimson, too much strength. They all wielded weapons: swords as crude as claymores, truncheons like battering-rams, heavy spears, axes chipped from blocks of flint. Like the creatures that had attacked after the destruction of First Woodhelven, they wore slabs of armor fashioned from the benighted stone of Gravin Threndor. And they kept coming, more Cavewights than the rocks of Liand's cairn; more than Linden had ever seen before: more than enough to sweep even Giants away like debris in a flood.

How—?

Unable to match their pace on his own legs, Roger rode the shoulders of a Cavewight. Glee and triumph distorted his features, effacing any resemblance to his father. His right fist was a blaze of power like deep magma. He seemed to hold the savagery of a dozen *skurj* in one hand: a piece of Kastenessen's essential agony and rage.

How had he and the Cavewights come so far in so short a time?

Alone among the Giants, Stormpast Galesend held back. She held her longsword ready in one hand. With the other arm, she cradled Anele's flinching terror.

"Ironhand!" she yelled through the advancing clamor. "What must I do? The old man hampers me!"

Swiftly Coldspray scanned the company's formation. She glanced at Linden's dismay, then turned away, cursing.

"Set him upon the cairn! Its stone will ward him! Against so many, we must trust that he will evade spears!"

Perhaps Anele would draw enough sanity from Liand's *orcrest* to duck and dodge.

As Galesend obeyed, the Ironhand snapped at Linden, "We cannot prevail against so many—or against such theurgy! We must have your aid!"

Linden understood. Oh, she *understood*. Still she felt paralyzed, overtaken by confusion and dread. Kastenessen must have told Roger where she was; where Galt held the *croyel*. But how had Roger and his Cavewights arrived so soon? As far as she knew, he could not transport himself or anyone else magically without the *croyel*'s help.

Anele appeared to recognize his peril. He clambered frantically up the boulders until he gained the crown of the cairn. There he searched for a niche or covert between the rocks; a place to hide himself.

Crossing the lower hills toward the base of the ridge, the Cavewights howled like ghouls. Their lust for blood was ancient, especially the blood of Giants. In their own eyes, at least, it was justified. The First of the Search and Pitchwife had done much to prevent the resurrection of Drool Rockworm.

Clyme and Branl reached the gypsum ridge well ahead of the creatures. For an instant, they considered the formation of the Giants, regarded Bhapa and Pahni holding Covenant's arms, consulted mind to mind with Galt. Then Clyme joined the Swordmainnir. Branl stood between Covenant and the coming onslaught. To the Cords, he said flatly, "Flee with the Unbeliever when you must. He must be preserved."

"How—?" Linden tried to ask Stave. The question stuck in her throat.

Over his shoulder, Stave told Galt, "Again I offer myself in your place. Acquiescence is preferable to murder. If you would give battle, release the *krill* to me."

Without hesitation, Galt answered, "I will not. You will retain it when it is required by the Unbeliever. And you will not slay the *croyel*, whatever the cost. You will name it preferable to see every defender of the Land butchered."

Stave looked toward Anele, glanced sidelong at Linden. Then he shrugged. Relaxed and ready, he prepared to defend her.

Her friends needed her. And she would never be able to resurrect Covenant again: not if he fell here. She would have to burn as many Cavewights as she could. She would have to oppose Roger with every scrap of her strength.

In the absence of Kevin's Dirt, she could be mighty—

Yet her greatest fear was for Jeremiah. It shackled her. She could too easily imagine the fluid motion of Galt's arm as he pulled the *krill* across the *croyel*'s throat—

"How," she managed to croak, "did they get here so fast?"

"I am uncertain," Stave told her without apparent curiosity. "However, I speculate that Kastenessen has wielded his strange magicks to aid them. Through Anele, he has become certain of our location. And there is precedent. The attack of the ur-Lord's son and his Cavewights at First Woodhelven defied mundane forms of travel. The distance from Gravin Threndor was too great, and the Cavewights know little of theurgy. Yet the ur-Lord's son contrived to strike when we were vulnerable, as we are here.

"If we judge by Esmer's condition, Kastenessen does not ease the straits of his servants when they have displeased him. Perhaps this accounts for the ur-Lord's son's flight on the shoulders of a Cavewight when he had failed against us."

The cacophony of howling became a kind of ululation, a full-throated demand for killing. In their eagerness, several Cavewights flung their spears. But they had not yet reached the foot of the ridge, and their shafts fell short. Those that struck within reach, the Giants snatched up and returned with startling vehemence.

The company had the advantage of elevation. Roger and his forces would have to fight an uphill battle. Nevertheless half that many Cavewights would have been enough to overwhelm the ridge eventually.

More sharply, Stave urged, "Ready yourself, Chosen." But she was already too late.

Shouting avidly, Roger hurled a second blast of brimstone and lava. In a frenzy, Linden tried to haul fire from her Staff, impose concentration on her conflicted heart.

She could only persuade Galt to stay his hand by driving back the assault: she had no other argument that he would heed. But distress slowed her efforts to summon Earthpower.

Unimpeded, Roger's fury slammed into the side of the cairn.

Anele!

Heavy stones erupted outward, shattering as they slashed the air. In a welter of rubble and spraying shards, nearly a third of the cairn was torn away. A few smaller fragments pelted the Giants and Clyme; but most of the wreckage carried beyond the company.

Roger had attacked the cairn, the *cairn*. He was trying to kill Anele. Or destroy the Sunstone.

For the duration of a heartbeat, no more than that, Linden searched the crown of the pile for the old man, her first companion, *the hope of the Land*. She spotted him almost instantly, crouched and gibbering on the south side of the cairn.

Then she reached far down into herself for Jeremiah's sake, and for her friends, and brought up a cyclone of flame from the willing wood of the Staff.

Her fire was as black as the shaft itself; as the lightless depths of mountains. And as it gyred into the pale sky, the runes written into the Staff shone like purest silver, articulating Caerroil Wildwood's ire and grief. Arcane symbols gave their consent.

They made Linden stronger.

Her counterattack was a driving gale that nearly unseated Roger. If he had defended himself with anything less than Kastenessen's desecrated hand, her outrage and despair would have charred the marrow of his bones. But his magma caught her blow; held it back as if he were equal to every aspect of her.

Bhapa was panting, "Ringthane, Ringthane," as though she had appalled him. Stave regarded Earthpower transformed to fuligin with a suggestion of chagrin in his eye. Apparently they had not grasped the true scale of her transubstantiation. Liand's death had completed a change begun in the graveyard of Jeremiah's mind; an alteration inspired by She Who Must Not Be Named, and by dreams of being carrion, and by Gallows Howe.

Below her, the first Cavewights reached the foot of the ridge. Mad as a rabble, and vicious as *kresh*, they charged upward, a rising scend of slaughter.

The Ironhand gave them a moment. Then, crying, "Stone and Sea!" she and Frostheart Grueburn and Halewhole Bluntfist sprang to meet the rabid rush.

From the tumult of creatures, spears streaked the air. A few crossed the path of Linden's black flame and became powder, harmless amid the howling. Stave caught one, used it to deflect another, then threw it back, all in the same motion. Pahni and Bhapa jerked Covenant away from a shaft which would have nailed him to the crumbling gypsum. Branl grabbed two more out of the air. When he returned them, one burst into slivers against the rough armor of its target; but the other took a Cavewight in the throat and sent the creature sprawling backward, sweeping half a dozen more off their feet as it fell.

Coldspray, Grueburn, and Bluntfist did not waste their swords on armor. With wheeling strokes as fatal as Linden's fire, they hacked at arms and legs, at exposed necks and skulls. Then, as their first assailants fell, tripping Cavewights lower on the slope, the three Swordmainnir allowed themselves to be driven back. Deliberately they retreated to higher ground.

At the same time, Latebirth, Cabledarm, and Onyx Stonemage flung themselves into the battle, protecting their comrades with their own attack. Stonemage had claimed a spear. Now she fought with two weapons, swinging her longsword and jabbing with the spear as though she had spent centuries training to do so.

That quick succession of countering assaults, three and then three, disrupted the initial charge; blunted it. More and more Cavewights stumbled over their fallen. Some lost their footing. Others staggered aside. When Coldspray, Grueburn, and Bluntfist rushed downward again, they drove their foes back.

In the confusion of toppling bodies and spraying blood, the first onslaught of the Cavewights became a rout.

But they were thinking creatures in spite of their bloodlust. Too many of them had tried to attack the company's position directly. Now they adjusted their tactics. From the rear of the army, scores of Cavewights turned to challenge the ridge in the west, beyond the reach of swords. Others pounded upward in the east, apparently intending to use the remains of the cairn for cover while they massed against the Giants.

Linden saw what they were doing, but she paid no attention. With her whole heart, she sent an unremitting torrent of ebony at Roger. Runes shone like inscribed wild magic as she strove to batter down Roger's defenses, repay his bitter betrayals; fought to prevent Galt from deciding to kill the *croyel*.

In Galt's grasp, the monster yowled encouragement or instructions at Roger and the Cavewights. Froth splashed from its fangs like venom. Despite its desperation and malice, however, it did not dare to press its throat against the *krill* in order to chew on Jeremiah's neck.

One-handed, Cirrus Kindwind left her comrades and went to confront the surge of Cavewights in the west. Apparently satisfied by the chaos immediately below him, Clyme joined her. Alone, Stormpast Galesend began to fight her way around the cairn toward the eastern threat. Entrusting Covenant to the Cords, Branl took Clyme's place among the other Swordmainnir.

A doomed struggle. Only a few score of the Cavewights had attempted the ridge, and more came as if they were numberless. To an extent, the Ironhand's alternating sallies downward had succeeded. The surface below her was already slick with blood and gore, churned to mud. The creatures climbing there slipped and skidded, rose arduously: they were vulnerable. But to the east and west, throngs of weapons and red eyes gained ground. Soon Coldspray would be forced to send Swordmainnir to support Kindwind and Galesend. Then direct assaults would become more effective.

From his hilltop, Roger seemed to ignore the rest of the battle. Like the Cavewights, however, he changed his tactics. Sitting the shoulders of his mount, he blared magic like scoria at Linden's black fire until he had formed an angled wall of power that caused her flame to glance away. Then, with the suddenness of a convulsion, he flung eldritch lava at the cairn again.

Roaring, Cirrus Kindwind charged her foes. At her side, Clyme struck hard and deep. Blood ran from cuts on Grueburn's arms and legs. Latebirth bore similar wounds. Spear-points and blades had scored Coldspray's cataphract: truncheons smashed the shaped stone away in flakes.

Linden was almost too late to protect the mound that shielded Anele. At the last instant, however, she realized what Roger was doing. Frenzy pounded in her temples as she nudged his bolt aside. It ruptured the far corner of the pile, sent a small rain of boulders and shards onto the Cavewights in the east, but did no serious harm to the stones where Anele cowered.

The old man looked like he was screaming, but Linden heard nothing except the loud rage of the creatures and the vicious sizzle of Roger's onslaught.

Retreating by increments, Pahni and Bhapa tugged Covenant from side to side to avoid spears and hurled axes, thrown scraps of rock. Even now, he showed no sign that he would ever return from his memories. Nevertheless Linden thought that she felt Galt's grip tighten on the *krill*.

With nothing to guide him except his health-sense, Manethrall Mahrtiir suddenly dove headlong down the slope; hit fouled mud and rolled; collided with the legs of Cavewights scrambling for purchase on the slick ridgeside. Instead of trying to hurt single creatures, he twisted among them, kicking at their ankles and knees, fighting beneath the reach of their weapons to knock them off balance. On a slope made treacherous by blood and spilled guts, he was impossibly successful. Below the Ironhand and her comrades, a small swath of Cavewights went down as if he had scythed them from their feet.

He would be dead in moments, suffocated under the weight of falling bodies if no weapon pierced him. While he lived, however, he wrought such turmoil that two of the Swordmainnir were freed to fight elsewhere. Heaving for breath, Latebirth ran to join Cirrus Kindwind and Clyme. Drenched in blood, Bluntfist followed Stormpast Galesend around the cairn.

Nonetheless more and more Cavewights reached the long spine among the hills. Then they no longer had to struggle upward. On gypsum crushed to dust, they gathered from east and west. Only the comparative narrowness of the ridge kept them from over-running the Giants immediately.

With Clyme, Kindwind and Latebirth fought like berserkers. Their great strength and uncounted years of training wrought devastation. But the Cavewights were too many—

Linden could not see Galesend and Bluntfist past the cairn; but she did not doubt that they would soon be overwhelmed.

Branl needed no request to go after the Manethrall. Like a boulder pitched from a rampart, he plunged out of sight into the melee around Mahrtiir.

Stave did not so much as glance at Galt as he moved to take Branl's place with Cold-spray and Stonemage, Grueburn and Cabledarm. Screams and shrieking punctuated the battle-howl of the Cavewights—and still they came.

Inspired by dread for Jeremiah, Linden adjusted her attack on Roger. Instead of opposing him squarely, she lowered her aim. In a flash of black puissance, she inciner-ated the Cavewight carrying Covenant's son; reduced the creature to instantaneous ash. And as Roger fell, cursing, in a flurry of limbs, she turned her fire like a scourge against the Cavewights around him. Before he could flounder to his feet, she set ablaze every creature that might have shielded him. When she resumed flailing at him again, he stood alone on his hilltop, an eyot of absolute ferocity above the tide of Cavewights and the carnage.

Cabledarm fell to one knee, an axe embedded in her thigh, with her longsword thrust through the throat of her attacker. Before other creatures could inundate her, Stave wrenched loose the axe and spun among them, delivering hacked limbs and gashed necks on all sides. Snarling in pain, Cabledarm cleared her sword; hobbled to follow Stave with Frostheart Grueburn at her shoulder. Together the two Swordmain-nir and the former Master cleared a space at the gore-streaked edge of the ridge.

Into that space climbed Branl with Mahrtiir hanging on his back. The Humbled wore blood as thick as a cloak: cuts covered the Manethrall like fretwork. But they were still alive.

With a word, Coldspray sent Onyx Stonemage to join the fighting beyond the cairn. The Ironhand seemed to wade through blows and bodies, whirling her glaive in a fierce blur, as she labored to support Grueburn and Cabledarm.

In another moment, or perhaps two, they would all be hacked down. Every Giant. Every *Haruchai* except Galt. Manethrall Mahrtiir. There would be no one left to defend the Cords and Covenant, or Galt and Jeremiah, or Anele, except Linden herself.

Seeing what was about to happen, Bhapa and Pahni began to drag Covenant down the far side of the ridge.

They would not get far.

Surely Galt was ready to slice open the *croyel*'s throat so that he could carry Loric's *krill* into the fight? He would need it. Linden could hardly believe that he had waited so long.

No! she yelled to herself, harsh as vitriol, bitter as the dirt of Gallows Howe. *No! I will not allow it!*

Screaming the Seven Words, she redoubled her pitch-dark assault on Covenant's son. Flame as black as the core of an eclipsed sun struck at him from both shod heels of her Staff. Between the iron bands, Caerroil Wildwood's script flared with unconstrained possibilities. If she could stop Roger, kill him, his Cavewights might falter. Galt might refrain from causing Jeremiah's death.

But she was the one who faltered. Caught by surprise, her concentration broke when she sensed Anele's descent from the cairn. In one fist, he held the *orcrest* blazing as if it were a remedy for possession. His moonstone eyes shone like sunlight, articulating his inheritance of Earthpower.

Anele, *don't!*

Already he was exposed to any blow that she failed to intercept. Through the clang of weapons and pain, she heard the iterated refrain of his compulsions.

"Must."

"Cannot."

As he worked his way down the last boulders, however, his "Cannot" sank to a whimper. "Must" became a cracked-voiced shout.

Cavewights fought forward from the east and west; closed like the jaws of a trap. More creatures gained the ridge just beyond the reach of Rime Coldspray's glaive, Grueburn's and Cabledarm's longswords. Even with the strong support of Stave and Branl, three Giants were not enough. Weak with wounds, Mahrtiir could no longer stand or struggle. In the west, Kindwind, Latebirth, and Clyme fell back involuntarily. Together Stonemage, Bluntfist, and Galesend appeared around the edge of the cairn, slashing fervidly as they retreated.

None of them were enough.

Linden had no choice: she had to swallow her desire to kill Roger Covenant. She and all of her companions were about die. If Galt slew the *croyel* now, he would be too late: even the undefined magicks of the *krill* could not hold back so many assailants. But if he did not, he would be slain himself, and the monster would escape with Jeremiah.

In either case, Covenant would fall soon after the rest of the company.

Raging the Seven Words like curses, Linden turned the black fury of her Staff against the nearest Cavewights. Struck by her force and frenzy, they burst into flame like kindling; staggered away screaming in agony as they perished.

But while she scorched the bones of her immediate assailants, she could do nothing to hinder Roger. He was free at last to strike in any manner that pleased him.

Yet he did not. Instead he withheld his virulence. Standing alone on his hilltop with his hands braced on his hips, he yelled triumph at the battle.

More Cavewights surged closer, and were set afire, and died. The heat of their burning scalded Linden's eyes. It drove the Giants, Stave, and the two Humbled back to form a final cordon around Linden and Galt, Jeremiah and the *croyel*. Nevertheless Roger's army continued to surge through the bonfires of dying creatures. The Ramen and Covenant were given up for lost.

Pure and dazzling as a cynosure of coercion or doom, Anele thrust his way into the center of the cordon.

Through Linden's torrents of flame, he said distinctly, "It was for this. Sunder my father and Hollian my mother urged me to it, but I have always been conscious of my fate. I live only because I am the Land's last hope."

His eyes were the precise hue and brightness of *orcrest* as he confronted Jeremiah. With both hands, he reached for the sides of Jeremiah's head. In one, he gripped the Sunstone urgently. The other he held open as though he meant to stroke the boy's cheek.

Possessed by Kastenessen, he had approached Liand in a similar fashion. Now he was sane. The interaction between the *orcrest*'s Earthpower and his native magicks warded him.

Terror burned in the *croyel*'s yellow gaze. Yet Jeremiah did not struggle. He regarded Anele emptily, understanding nothing.

But the old man did not touch the boy. He was interrupted.

Without warning, Esmer plunged out of the sky like a falling meteor.

Covenant had accused him of choosing Kastenessen's legacy over Cail's. *You are indeed betrayed*, Esmer had replied, *but not by me.*

His arrival shattered Linden's power. It seemed to stun the nerves of her hands, leaving them numb on the Staff. Nausea writhed in her guts. He was a mass of wounds, rank and suppurating. Odious infections stained the tatters of his cymar, and his mien was anguish. Pain splashed from his eyes like spume. Nevertheless he came bearing concussions which tossed boulders from the cairn, caused upheavals like eruptions in the ridge. Quakes staggered the Giants. Linden nearly fell. Yowling in alarm, Cavewights sprang backward. Anele was flung aside. He collapsed like a bundle of rags on the gypsum.

Screaming, "*Havoc!*" Esmer strode after the old man. Anele brandished the Sunstone frantically, but he could do nothing. Unanswerable as a hurricane, Esmer raised his arms as if he meant to crack open the heavens; rain down chaos on *the Land's last hope.*

As abrupt as Esmer's coming, a score of ur-viles and Waynhim appeared within the cordon as though they had been incarnated by his vehemence. His hands fisted the sky, ready to hurl ruin. But before he could strike, the loremaster sprang at his arms.

With a jolt of force that seemed to shift the world, the loremaster clamped iron manacles onto Esmer's wrists; sealed the bands.

In that instant, Linden's nausea vanished. All of Esmer's power vanished. The concussions endangering the ridge ceased. Bound together and helpless, his hands fell. They held nothing that could threaten Anele. When he plunged to his knees, he was sobbing.

To Linden, his cries sounded like relief: a release too long desired and denied for words.

In the distance, Roger gave a shriek of rage. At once, he began mustering a blast to shred the flesh of the Swordmainnir, hammer lava into the heart of their last defense.

Cavewights yammered in response. Roger's fury rallied them. Swinging their weapons, they surged forward.

He would not care how many of them were slain.

But Anele scrambled back to his feet. Brushing past Esmer, he hastened toward Jeremiah again with his eyes and his *orcrest* as bright as little suns.

Linden felt Roger's power gather like the force of a volcano. She tasted Anele's urgency and the *croyel*'s terror. As if Galt's hand were etched in the air, she saw their tension on the haft of the *krill*. Around her, the Giants wheeled for a final effort. At the same time, the Demondim-spawn rushed to form a fighting wedge with their loremaster at its tip. But she could not help them. Everything was happening too quickly. Esmer and manacles. Ur-viles, Waynhim, Anele. —*the hope of the Land*. Jeremiah passive as a puppet. The massed throng of Cavewights. Roger Covenant.

The *krill*'s gem began to blaze as Joan poured wild magic through it. In another moment, the blade would grow hot enough to sear Galt's skin. Joan—or *turiya* Raver—wanted him to drop the dagger; wanted the *croyel* set loose.

Linden needed enough sheer force to counter every attack simultaneously, and she did not know how to find it in herself.

She heard combat rage around her; felt the wedge of ur-viles and Waynhim summon their lore in a killing gout of vitriol; sensed Roger's desperation to attack through too many intervening bodies. But she did not see the hurled axe spinning across the sunlight toward Anele.

Galt saw it. And he was *Haruchai*: he had time to consider the axe, the press of Cavewights, the company's vulnerability. He had time to regard the distrusted old man and choose.

Instead of pulling Jeremiah and the *croyel* to either side—and instead of killing the monster so that he could fight for his companions with Loric's *krill*—he spun in place. As swift as thought, he turned his back to the axe without taking Jeremiah beyond Anele's reach.

Almost that quickly, Anele sprang in front of the boy.

The axe was flint, heavy as a bludgeon. Its jagged blade bit deep into Galt's back between his shoulder-blades, deep enough to slice through the intransigent rectitude of his heart. Blood and life gushed from the wound, taking with them every pulse of determination. As his dead fingers uncurled, the *krill* rolled out of his grasp and fell. Then he folded to the ground as though all of his joints had been severed.

For an instant—no more than an instant—the *croyel* was free.

But its escape came too late; or it had misjudged its opportunity. It still clung to Jeremiah. Rather than flinging itself aside, it pounced at his neck with its fangs, seeking the nameless magicks hidden within him.

Too late. Too slow.

Anele had already pressed his hands and the Sunstone to the sides of Jeremiah's head. Now he poured his birthright into the boy, using *orcrest* to channel his long-preserved inheritance into Jeremiah's vacancy.

As he did so, the *orcrest* fell to powder in his grasp. It could not endure the forces streaming from it and through it.

Nevertheless it served its purpose.

Immediate Earthpower became a kind of fire in Jeremiah's veins. It entered him utterly, blossomed in his chest, raced along his limbs, shone out of his skin.

And from the graveyard of his mind and the enduring throb of his heart, the rich essence of health and Law was sucked into the *croyel*'s mouth.

Belated realization filled the creature's eyes with horror as its own malign ichor caught flame and *burned*—

In unison, the *croyel* and Roger squalled as if they were answering each other; suffering together. Then a conflagration for which the monster was entirely unprepared tore through it like a wildfire through brittle deadwood. On Jeremiah's back, the succubus burst apart, consumed from within by energies that it could neither contain nor suppress. Gore and viscera sprayed out over the slope, and steamed in the hot sunshine, and did no hurt.

Jeremiah still stood slack-mouthed and dull, as unreactive as a husk. Nevertheless he rather than the *croyel* was free. The creature which had used and excruciated him had been destroyed.

By Anele, who lay at his feet gasping for breath. In the old man there remained no flicker or pulse of Earthpower to stitch together the rent remnants of his spirit. Yet he was sane at last, and smiling.

Linden wanted to sob like Esmer; wrap Jeremiah in her arms; wail over Anele's dying body. But she had no time.

6.

Parting Company

Fighting raged around Linden and Jeremiah. Within the frantic protection provided by Stave, Clyme, Branl, and the Giants, Galt lay dead, and Anele was dying. Esmer's sobs had faded, made impotent by manacles. The ur-viles and Waynhim had thrust their wedge between two of the Swordmainnir. Joined by the surviving remnants of their kind, the creatures flung liquid blackness to shield Linden's company from Roger. Within that dark theurgy, Cavewights fell and died in agony.

Yet the cordon was failing. The Cavewights were too many; and Roger's blasts struck the ridge like convulsions.

At the feet of her comrades lay Onyx Stonemage, clubbed senseless. Cabledarm fought on one knee, unable to support herself with her damaged leg. Frostheart Grueburn did the same, hamstrung by the thrust of a spear. But their longswords were being beaten down by the rabid savagery of their foes. Halewhole Bluntfist had lost the use of her right arm: she was forced to wield her blade with her left. Battered by too many blows, Latebirth's broken cataphract hung from her shoulders in fragments. The Ironhand, Cirrus Kindwind, and Stormpast Galesend had all been hacked until they were weak with blood loss; but they continued to struggle, desperate as the doomed.

Like the Swordmainnir, the remaining *Haruchai* had been badly wounded. Still they punished their assailants as if they were as mighty as Giants, and as unyielding as granite. They shattered brute armor with punches and kicks, broke necks, snapped limbs, cracked skulls—and could not prevail.

Without the intervention of the ur-viles and Waynhim, every *Haruchai* and Giant would already be dead, scorched lifeless by Roger's withering magma. But acid magicks intercepted a portion of his fury; deflected a portion. And he hurled his power like a madman, too crazed for thought or care. He seemed deranged by the loss of the *croyel*, and therefore of Jeremiah. Cavewights who chanced to stand in his path perished. His screams echoed everywhere as if the sky were a vault, featureless and sealed.

Mahrtiir had crawled to the edge of the battle. He could no longer defend himself, and there was no one left to guard him except Bhapa. The older Cord had abandoned Covenant to Pahni. Now Bhapa stood over the Manethrall with bleak determination in his eyes and his garrote in his hands.

But at the focus of the carnage, Jeremiah stood exactly as he had stood while he was possessed, slack and vacant, with nothing that resembled awareness in his muddy gaze; as unreactive as a corpse. His whole body thronged with Earthpower, Anele's last gift. Yet his new strength changed nothing. It did not restore his mind.

When Roger had killed everyone else, he would go after Covenant: Linden did not doubt that. Lord Foul would consider her death, and Covenant's, a victory, if Roger did not.

Covenant's son needed the *croyel* and Jeremiah. *The* croyel *can use your kid's talent. He'll make us a door. A portal to eternity. —to help us become gods.*

For Roger, that hope was gone. Now he would have to trust the Despiser.

It was too much. Too much. Linden could not suffer it. All of her friends. Jeremiah and Covenant. She had felt overwhelmed and frantic earlier. Now her despair had no limits.

Unable to make any other choice, she became Gallows Howe: a killing field made flesh.

In the gypsum and dirt where it had fallen, High Lord Loric's *krill* still shone. Its brilliance throbbed to the beat of Joan's madness. And she was a rightful white gold wielder. Only her abjection and *turiya* Raver's mastery restricted her access to wild magic.

Linden was done with hesitation, with paralysis, with weakness. Done with humanity. Deliberately she dropped the Staff of Law at Jeremiah's feet. Then she lifted Covenant's ring on its chain over her head. Closing the chain in her fist, she slipped the ring onto the index finger of her right hand.

With no more preparation than that, she stooped to touch the avid gem of the *krill* with Covenant's wedding band.

Long ago, she had seen him do something similar when he had needed a trigger or catalyst; a source of power to overcome his instinctive reluctance. *She* was not reluctant: not now. And Esmer's influence no longer blocked her. It would never hinder her again. But she had no right to white gold. She needed help.

In the instant that the ring made contact with the gem, she became a holocaust of silver flame.

When she had spent one heartbeat, or two, measuring her borrowed power with her health-sense so that she could be sure of her control, she left the collapsing defense of her friends and began to wreak havoc as if she had been born for butchery and death.

☙☙

S o quickly that she appalled herself, the battle was over. While her friends and the Demondim-spawn watched, too stunned or horrified or injured to react, she ravaged every Cavewight on the ridge; rent asunder the hilltop where

Roger stood; brought down cascades of fire from the blank sky. When surviving creatures turned to flee, she let them go. But she would have harried Roger until she had scorched every drop of his blood with wild magic, if he had not first hidden behind blunt hills and then warded himself with lava while he raced away on the shoulders of a Cavewight.

At his escape, she raised a scream of her own into the air; a shriek of unconstrained wild magic that seemed to challenge the Despiser himself. She yelled for Liand, and howled for Anele, and cried out for the pain of her companions, until her strength failed. Then at last her world went dark. All of her burdens fell away, and there was no more power anywhere that could hurt her.

∽∞∾

W hen she recovered consciousness, she was sitting propped against a boulder at the base of Liand's cairn. Someone must have put her there. Must have hung Covenant's ring around her neck again, rested the Staff of Law across her lap. Stave, probably. He stood over her now, watching her while blood dripped from the ends of his fingers and the hem of his rent tunic.

Her entire being flinched at what she had done. But she could not undo it.

"Your absence has been brief, Linden," the former Master answered before she found the will to question him. "We have only begun to tally our wounds." His voice was strangely congested, thick with an emotion which she did not recognize. "Had you not bestirred yourself, however, I would have roused you. Our need for your aid is grievous. Among us, only the Unbeliever, the Cords, and your son lack any dire hurt."

Then he turned and walked away as though he could no longer bear the sight of her. Oozing blood, he went to join the figures kneeling or supine near Jeremiah, Galt, Anele, and Esmer.

Thinking, Anele? she tried to pull herself to her feet. Is he still alive? Tried, and could not. If she managed to stand, she would see bodies. Hundreds of them. Thousands. She would be forced to confront the outcome of her despair.

Peering through a blur of weakness, she saw the black shapes of ur-viles and the grey forms of Waynhim moving among her companions. Dimly through the reek of spilled guts and gore, she caught the dank scent of *vitrim*. The Demondim-spawn were still trying to help. Their musty drink appeared to be all that kept some of the Giants and Mahrtiir alive. As far as she could tell, however, *vitrim* did nothing for Anele, although he did not refuse it. And Esmer laughed at it softly, without scorn, as if he had passed beyond the reach of any sustenance.

That the ur-viles and Waynhim offered kindness to Esmer confounded Linden. In a distant age, they had forged their manacles, foreseeing this day. Ever since she had first encountered them, the Demondim-spawn had come to her aid whenever Esmer had posed a threat. Yet now they showed him compassion?

For centuries or millennia, they had been among the most feared of the Despiser's servants—

Closing her fingers on the warm wood of her Staff, she tried again to rise.

The bright silver of Caerroil Wildwood's runes had vanished. They were inert again, as inarticulate as sigils. But the shaft retained the stark blackness of her fire. She could not imagine that any blaze would ever burn it clean. Still it was the Staff of Law, an instrument of Earthpower and health. When she asked it for a little strength, it replied with its familiar gifts.

Trembling, she braced herself on ambiguous commandments until she gained her feet.

Everywhere she looked, the ground had been desecrated by blood and offal, mangled limbs and bodies. Weapons and shattered armor littered the ridge. In the vicinity of the battle, the friable gypsum had been fouled until only a few random patches of whiteness remained to punctuate the carnage.

Above her, the voiceless sky seemed to retain echoes like memories of screaming and slaughter.

For a moment or two, she thought that she ought to cleanse the ridge. That should have been her next responsibility. A pyre for the dead: some form of sanctification for the betrayed hills. But then she sensed Thomas Covenant striding fiercely from the south as if he meant to deliver a burden of wrath and repudiation. At the same time, she felt Anele slip closer to his life's last precipice. When he fell, others would follow him soon—and they, too, were her friends. Like Liand, they had given her more than she had ever given them.

Squaring her shoulders against the recrimination of the dead, Linden Avery left the cairn to resume the pretense that she was a healer.

Because she needed to do so, she went first to Jeremiah. With one hand, she stroked his flaccid cheek, confirming that he remained lost inside himself. That fact hurt her. Nevertheless it was true that he had been released from the *croyel*. Freed—To that extent, at least, the promise of his mended racecar had been kept. Received Earthpower enriched him with vitality. He gave no sign that he could use his new strength. Yet the grisly sores of the monster's feeding had already begun to heal themselves.

Briefly Linden hugged him. She had been too long denied the simple comfort of touching him. Then, while Covenant was still too far away to judge her, she turned to acknowledge the sufferings of her friends.

Among the Giants, only Rime Coldspray and Frostheart Grueburn met the rue in Linden's eyes. Stormpast Galesend knelt with her hands clamped on Cabledarm's thigh, trying to slow the bleeding. In spite of her injuries and maiming, Cirrus Kindwind pressed repeatedly on Onyx Stonemage's chest as if she feared that Stonemage would stop breathing. Stonemage's breastplate hampered her efforts; but Kindwind clearly did not have the strength to remove it. Laboriously, like a woman with fractured ribs, Latebirth struggled to tie a tourniquet above the spear in Grueburn's upper leg. After a glance at Linden, Coldspray continued working on Halewhole Bluntfist's right arm, trying to reset dislocated bones.

The ur-viles and Waynhim gave *vitrim* to all who could or would accept it. Nourished by their weird lore, Manethrall Mahrtiir had recovered enough to stand facing Covenant's approach. And Bhapa stood with him. They kept their backs to Linden. But she saw in the stiffness of their spines, the clench of their shoulders, that they were readying themselves to confront the Unbeliever's ire on her behalf.

She might have said something, although every word that she knew how to utter had been burned away. The sight of Stave stopped her.

He sat spread-legged in the dirt and clotting blood, so motionless that he hardly seemed to breathe. With both arms, he held Galt against his chest. The last slow drops of Galt's life joined the stains that stigmatized Stave's tunic. Pain had curled Galt's hands into claws. But Stave did not look at the body in his arms. Instead he regarded Landsdrop as though in his heart he gazed past the high cliff and Salva Gildenbourne and the plains and Revelstone toward the Westron Mountains. Tears spilled from his eye. They ran down his cheek into the cuts that marred his visage.

He did not glance at Linden. In a low voice as taut as choking, he said to her, or to the distant home of the *Haruchai*, "He is my son. To the last, he remained himself."

As if that were Galt's epitaph.

—*it is their birthright*—

Ah, Stave. Linden wanted to weep with him, and could not. Your son? I didn't know. Neither he nor Galt had allowed any hint of their kinship to pass between them. Yet it was Galt who had chosen to protect Jeremiah's life with his own, so that Anele might expunge the *croyel*.

In the end, Galt must have heeded his father.

The rest of the Masters, or all of the *Haruchai*, may have suppressed their vulnerability to sorrow. Stave had not.

While his tears ran, Linden yearned to stay with him. She owed him that much. To her percipience, however, the injuries of her other companions were as audible as cries. She could taste the onset of infection and fatality, the fiery gnash of pain. Even in gratitude for Jeremiah's life, she could not pause to share Stave's grief.

Fortunately none of the Giants were as close to death as Anele. Even Clyme and Branl were not, although they rejected the aid of the Demondim-spawn. Stonemage's heart beat on its own under Kindwind's steady pressure. The shreds of Esmer's raiment fluttered as though impalpable winds tugged through him, but his old wounds did not appear to trouble him. When Linden had studied the company, she decided that the Swordmainnir could wait for her a little longer. If she felt compelled to walk away from Stave, she could nonetheless afford to spend a few moments with the old man who had sacrificed himself for Jeremiah.

Anele lay on the churned ground a few paces from his companions. Somehow he had crawled that short distance, or someone had dragged him, seeking safety during Linden's cataclysm of wild magic. Now he sprawled on his back with his arms outstretched, gazing sightlessly at the sun, and straining for breath as if he had inhaled a pool of blood. The *orcrest*-light was gone from his eyes: his eyes themselves were gone. Yet he was not afraid.

Kneeling beside him, Linden tried to say his name. But her throat closed against her.

"Linden Avery," he gasped wetly. He must have felt her presence. "Chosen and Sun-Sage. Accept my gratitude—and my farewell."

Gripping the Staff, Linden fumbled for Earthpower. But Anele panted, "Do not. Do not heal. Make no lament. My time is past. I was the hope of the Land. Now I have given that gift to another. I have kept faith with my inheritance." Small spasms of suffocation wracked his chest, but he fought to speak. "Now I may stand with Sunder my father and Hollian my mother, and feel no shame. If you slow my end, you will delay my spirit from their embrace."

In sorrow, Linden acceded. It was intolerable that she had no good farewell to give the old man. After a moment, she forced herself to reply.

"I don't know anything about hope." Her heart was full of darkness. "But I'm sure that Sunder and Hollian have always been proud of you. As proud as I am." Her voice caught. She had to struggle to finish. "You could have just let Jeremiah suffer, but you didn't. You didn't."

"Thus I am made whole," Anele sighed. The words were a hoarse rattle of fluids. "I am content."

Then his eyelids closed on all that he had lost or surrendered. Slowly his body settled until it seemed to belong to the Earth.

There is no death that is not deeply felt,
No pain that does not bite through flesh and bone.

Now Linden understood the necessity of his madness. Without it—without that form of concealment—Kastenessen or Lord Foul might have realized that Anele was far more dangerous to their intentions for Jeremiah than Liand or *orcrest*. More dangerous than Linden herself. Kastenessen might have killed the old man at his first opportunity, in the Verge of Wandering.

All hurt is like the endless surge of seas,
The wear and tumbling that leaves no welt
  But only sand instead of granite ease.

As she had with Stave, Linden wanted to stay with Anele awhile. Her debt to him was boundless: he deserved more than her paltry sentences. But there was nothing left that she could do for him, and other needs demanded her care.

Feeling as blood-stained and barren as the hills, she climbed upright, secured her grasp on the Staff, and turned to the Giants.

Some of them were close to joining Anele and Galt. And Liand.

One of the Waynhim stood in front of her, snuffling damply to ascertain her scent. The creature lifted a small iron cup of *vitrim*. She took it gratefully, drained it in three unsteady swallows.

While the piercing tonic of the Demondim-spawn raced along her nerves, she raised fire from the heartwood of her Staff: fire that should never have been used to deliver death. Though her flame was black, it was still Earthpower. It still articulated Law. Setting aside her despair, she faced the Swordmainnir and reassumed the forsaken task of healing.

As she did so, she heard or felt Covenant's ascent on the ridgeside. He came wreathed in an air of ferocity that she had seen before, long ago—although she had never seen it expressed in bloodshed like hers. Behind him, Pahni trailed numbly, still preoccupied by Liand's passing and her own woe.

Linden ignored him; left Mahrtiir and Bhapa to greet or forestall him. She had already kept the Giants waiting too long.

With a quick sweep of her health-sense, she assessed the urgent clamor of wounds, some more immediately cruel than others, all potentially fatal. Then she wrapped a cocoon of Earthpower and Law around Onyx Stonemage to stabilize the Giant's heartbeat while flames as poignant as lamentation massaged healing into cuts and deep gashes, severed thews, bitter contusions.

But Linden could not tend Stonemage thoroughly: not yet. There were too many other hurts. As soon as she had eased the most dangerous of Stonemage's injuries, she gave Cirrus Kindwind a quick burst of kindness, then turned to spin fire around Cabledarm's mangled leg.

Before Covenant was halfway to the ridgecrest, Esmer called softly, "Wildwielder. I must pass soon. To do so, I crave your consent. Will you not pause to acknowledge that I am justified at last? Good has been accomplished by evil means."

Linden did not glance at him. When she had burned away the worst effects of Cabledarm's wound, she coiled black flames around Latebirth's chest so that none of the Swordmain's shattered ribs would shift to puncture her lungs or her heart. Earthpower was still Earthpower. Linden's health-sense enabled her to mend and cleanse in spite of her essential bitterness.

Through her teeth, she told Esmer, "You finally picked a side. You chose betrayal." If the ur-viles and Waynhim had not come— "How does that justify you?"

In her soiled state, each new effort of healing felt more like an act of violence.

As Latebirth began to breathe more easily, Linden moved to Frostheart Grueburn. Carefully she sealed rent vessels and ligaments so that Rime Coldspray could draw out the spear without too much loss of blood.

"I did not choose here," Esmer replied like the soughing of winds that touched only him. "At Kastenessen's behest, I endeavored to preserve the *croyel*. For your sake, I also strove to preserve your son. By imprisoning the boy's gifts, I would betray you. By leaving him alive in your care, I would thwart Kastenessen. Thus I endeavored to perfect my excruciation."

And Jeremiah's torment in the *croyel*'s possession would have continued. Bitterly Linden began to lash out, flailing at Rime Coldspray's hurts, and at Halewhole Blunt-fist's, as if she sought to punish them.

The Giants bore her vehemence in silence. Her harsh succor they endured as if it were a *caamora*.

"Yet on one occasion I did choose," Esmer continued. "When I brought the ur-viles and their manacles to this time, I repudiated my grandsire. Will you deny that I have suffered for my deeds?"

He may have been asking Linden's forgiveness. Helpless, he knelt with pleading like rain in his eyes. The fetters on his wrists bound every expression of his power.

Incensed and shaken, she tried to restrain herself. The Swordmainnir had hazarded their lives for her. For Jeremiah. For Covenant. They needed to be caressed with healing, not whipped. While she struggled to bind her heart to its task, she bathed Stormpast Galesend in swift flames. Then she returned to her starting place with Onyx Stonemage and began to work more meticulously, striving now for completeness.

Will you deny that I have suffered—?

Together Mahrtiir and Bhapa left the ridge to meet Covenant, followed by Clyme and Branl. The two Humbled were too sorely injured to walk without limping. In spite of their great strength, they looked like they might pitch forward onto their faces. Yet the Manethrall—badly hurt himself, and sustained only by *vitrim*—did not refuse their company.

They accosted Covenant a dozen paces below the crest; but Linden could not hear what they said. Whatever it was, it caused him to pause and listen.

In spite of her concentration on Stonemage, she wanted to ask Esmer, How did the ur-viles know what was going to happen? How did you? But another question leapt into her mouth.

"Why does Lord Foul care about Jeremiah? With or without the *croyel*, he's just a boy," ensepulchered and inaccessible. "What difference does he make to the Despiser?"

Like a dying breeze, Esmer breathed, "A-Jeroth's designs are hidden from me. I know only that his hunger concerning the boy's gifts festers within him. Perhaps he perceives an obscure peril. Or perhaps those gifts are necessary to his intent. In either case, he craves possession of your son.

"Such concerns matter naught to Kastenessen. Though *moksha* Raver hints of them, Kastenessen does not heed him."

Roger wanted *A portal to eternity*. But Linden was too weary to pursue the idea. The next injury, and the next, required too much of her attention. A certain amount of Stonemage's recovery could be entrusted to her native toughness. The rest, however—

Abruptly Covenant's voice carried up the slope: a bark of outrage or dismay. "Bloody hell! Why didn't one of you *hit* me? Break my arm? Do *something*? I might have been able to help!"

"How?" retorted Mahrtiir. Linden heard him clearly. "You are no warrior. You hold no implements of power."

"I know that," Covenant almost shouted. "But I would have been one hell of a distraction." More quietly, he added, "If nothing else, I could have held the *krill* for Galt. He might still be alive."

Grinding her teeth, Linden finished her work with Stonemage. She closed her eyes for a moment, wrestled for self-control. Then she turned Earthpower and Law on Cirrus Kindwind.

Kindwind was not in more danger than her comrades. She was simply closer to Linden.

"Wildwielder." Esmer's appeal sank as if he had lost hope. Nevertheless he continued to insist. "I cannot endure as I am. Nor do I wish to do so. An end I must have, if you will grant it. Still I beseech your acknowledgment that I am justified. If you cannot hear Cail's voice in any other deed of mine, will you not concede worth to the presence of the ur-viles in this time? By their hands, I am undone. And your son's release betrays both Kastenessen and a-Jeroth."

Crushed nerves. Shredded veins and arteries. Muscles and tendons and ligaments torn or severed. Infection everywhere. Raw contusions. Bruises as brutal as knife-thrusts. The profligate reek of blood and dirt and too much killing.

Linden wanted more *vitrim*. Without it, she feared that the needs of the Giants would outlast her. And she had not yet done anything for Stave or Mahrtiir. Or for the Humbled.

An end I must have—

Ragged with strain, Branl answered Covenant, "We deemed the preservation of your life paramount, ur-Lord. In this, we concur with Linden Avery. You are necessary. We saw no cause to endanger your life in combat."

"Then why," demanded Covenant, "didn't you at least take Jeremiah somewhere safe?" But before the Masters could reply, he snapped, "No, don't tell me. I already know. You were waiting for an excuse to kill the *croyel*. So you or Linden or *somebody* could use the *krill*."

A weapon which had enabled her to rouse the Worm.

Like an act of self-flagellation, Branl said, "Yet Galt was swayed by Stave, as he was by Linden Avery."

Covenant did not relent. "Some of this is still your doing." He may have meant the battle, or Galt's death, or the company's multitude of wounds. "For once in your lives, I want you to accept the consequences."

Now Clyme spoke. His voice sounded weaker than Branl's; closer to prostration. Bitter with blood loss and old indignation, the outcome of a humiliation which his people had never forgotten, he asked, "When have the *Haruchai* ever declined the cost of their deeds?"

"I'm not talking about your damn *deeds*," Covenant snarled. "I'm talking about being *mortal*. About not being equal to all things. This is what you get. You're both too badly hurt. Now you're going to let Linden heal you. *That's* the consequence you have to accept. If you don't, I am going to by God *leave you behind*."

The Humbled or the Manethrall may have offered an objection too soft to reach the crest. In a harsh growl, Covenant responded, "It won't be as hard as you think. I'll just tell the Ranyhyn not to let you ride. You can't possibly believe they won't do it. They *reared* to me, for God's sake!"

Linden drew strength from his misplaced wrath. In another time and place, she had learned to love his anger. She knew what it meant. It was recognition and compassion disguised as accusation. And he had come back, for the Land if not for her and Jeremiah. If he fell again, he would find a way to return.

She owed her life to the *Haruchai*. Because Covenant insisted upon it, Clyme and Branl would swallow enough of their pride to let her repay a portion of her long debt.

When she had staunched Kindwind's bleeding, and had extinguished the last taint of infection, she did not take the time to seek sustenance from the Demondim-spawn. Turning to Cabledarm's injuries, and Latebirth's, she found that she could answer Esmer.

"All right." She spoke without interrupting her ministrations. "I accept that. Bringing the ur-viles here wasn't just a way to balance the scales. They were a gift. You saved Jeremiah, even if you didn't do it yourself. You made it possible."

On her own, she had failed terribly. And she had seen the price that Esmer paid for his one true choice.

Remembering that she had denied Elena, she added, "As far as I'm concerned, what you've accomplished is practically a miracle. Maybe it's enough to compensate for everything else."

Esmer's face twisted: he may have been smiling. "Then grant me an end, Wildwielder."

In spite of her determination to continue healing, Linden nearly froze. "How?" With one sentence, Esmer restored her despair. "You can't—" Liand and Anele were dead. Stave's son was dead. She had killed— "You can't expect—"

"The *krill* of the High Lord lies there." Esmer tilted his head toward Jeremiah. "It will suffice to slay me. You need only pierce my heart, and I will find peace."

Joan's intensity no longer pulsed in the gem. Nevertheless the jewel still shone, responding to the distant theurgy of her ring.

"*Damn* it, Esmer!" Linden cursed so that she would not wail. Earthpower slipped from her grasp. She almost dropped her Staff. "You can't ask me to just *murder* you!"

Not after she had committed such slaughter—

Among themselves, the ur-viles and Waynhim chittered incomprehensibly.

Esmer's eyes oozed like his sores. "Then I must remain as I am, a husk of life, until the Worm devours me."

That, Linden wanted to protest, is not my problem! Too many other injuries ached for her care. All of her companions—She should have simply turned her back on Cail's son.

But she could not. She had butchered thousands of living creatures. He was the only one who actually needed death.

"Linden Giantfriend—" the Ironhand began like a groan. Then she stopped, unable to find words.

Suddenly Stave lifted Galt's body aside. When he had settled his son gently on the stained ground, he rose to his feet and picked up Loric's *krill.* Then he strode toward Esmer.

Without a flicker of hesitation or doubt, he drove the dagger into Esmer's back.

Stave!

For an instant, joy broke across Esmer's tormented features. He had time to lift his eyes to the heavens in gratitude. A heartbeat later, he vanished like dispelled smoke, leaving no sign that he had ever existed except manacles: the symbol and resolution of his compelled nature. If any hint of his spirit lingered in the air, Linden could not sense it.

As one, the ur-viles and Waynhim raised a tumult of barking. As one, they fell silent again.

With an air of scorn or disgust, Stave dropped the knife. His gaze met Linden's consternation squarely.

"It is not murder," he pronounced, as rigid as any of his kindred. "It is mercy."

When he had shown her that he was prepared to accept her reaction, whatever it might be, he turned away.

For a moment, the manacles lay where they had fallen in the mire of drying blood and gypsum. Then they began to corrode. The purpose for which they had been forged was done. Now the effects of millennia seemed to dissolve the black iron. While Linden watched, the last makings of the ur-viles slumped into rust and crumbled. Soon they were just one more blot on the ruined whiteness of the ridge.

She wished that she, too, could sag into flakes of rust. She yearned to be done— But she was supposed to be a healer, and she had already permitted Liand's death. She had failed her son. In Andelain, she had refused simple kindness to Covenant's woe-ridden daughter. On this ridge, she had torn apart more Cavewights than she knew how to count. The legacies of her parents were wrapped like cerements around her soul.

She could not pretend that she was done.

And Stave had spared her a burden. His mercy was for her as much as for Esmer. She understood his disgust.

Scornful of herself, and grieving, Linden Avery recalled black flames from her Staff and resumed her tasks.

Stave would need her soon. So would Mahrtiir, if to a lesser extent. But the Sword-mainnir came first for the sufficient reason that they were closer.

ಊ

S he had treated all but the most superficial of Frostheart Grueburn's wounds, and was working deep within Halewhole Bluntfist's hacked frame, when Covenant arrived on the ridgecrest, trailing the Humbled and the Ramen behind him like a cortege.

The force of his appearance jolted her to a halt. Her mouth was suddenly dry: the air felt too thick with carnage to breathe. Struggling to remember that she had once been a physician, she had forgotten how much he meant to her—and how much she feared his repudiation.

Apart from the Cords, she was the only member of the company who did not wear the stains of her actions. Even Jeremiah had been splashed by Galt's blood, and by Liand's. How could Covenant look at her without feeling sickened?

Yet her relief that he was unharmed pushed that concern aside. And when he met her gaze, she saw that his wrath was gone. He had expended it on the Humbled. Now he looked ashamed, as though he had failed her and everyone with her. His eyes held a kind of moral nausea, but it was not directed at her. Emphasized by the pure silver of his hair, the scar on his forehead suggested an instinct for self-blame that had grown pale with time, but had never entirely healed.

In that, he resembled her. The difference between them was Gallows Howe. It was She Who Must Not Be Named and limitless killing. With the Earth at stake, Thomas Covenant would not have done what she had done. He would have found some other answer.

"I'm sorry," he said thickly, as if he rather than Linden had cause to expect recrimination. "I spent too long in the Arch. I don't have any defenses against wild magic." With one hand, he gestured at the *krill*. "It's like Joan has me on a string. This time, she brought me back. She wants me where I can be hurt. But before that—" He winced. "Maybe she was holding me down. Or maybe I just don't know how to climb out of what I remember."

The Swordmainnir studied him gravely. Mahrtiir regarded Covenant through a drying crust of blood. Bhapa considered the killing ground with chagrin. Pahni looked around as if she had become a wasteland; as if the life in her eyes had been slain. For a moment, no one spoke. The Demondim-spawn stood motionless, as attentive as a salute.

Then Rime Coldspray found her voice. "Yet you live, Timewarden." She sounded precise in spite of her hurts, like a woman stroking a whetstone along the edges of her glaive. "Nothing more was needed. Linden Giantfriend sufficed."

Covenant scanned the company. Gruffly he replied, "I can see that. I would have thought all this"—with a jerk of his head, he indicated the battleground—"was impossible. Kastenessen and Roger and poor Joan and even Lord Foul must be tearing their hair right now."

With that simple statement, he seemed to honor a victory that appalled Linden.

Then he shook himself, ran the stubs of his fingers through his hair, frowned ruefully. "Unfortunately we can't afford to wait here for another attack." To the loremaster, he said, "I hope you'll stick around, at least for a while. You've already saved"—he spread his hands—"practically everything. As much as it could be saved. But Linden needs more *vitrim*. We all do. And we have questions you might at least try to answer."

The loremaster merely nodded. After a moment, Waynhim began to move through the company again, offering their iron cups.

Hoping that she would someday be able to draw at least one clean breath, Linden accepted a cup. Instead of drinking, however, she continued to watch Covenant's every movement, clutch at every word. He was right: she required sustenance. She felt so weak that she could barely stand. But she needed something more from him as well. Something more personal than his willingness to accept the crime of carnage.

After a moment, he told her directly, "You have to keep working, Linden. You're still the only one who can do this. When you're done with the Giants, Stave needs you. Mahrtiir needs you. And the Humbled are going to let you treat them." His tone sharpened. "They won't like what happens if they don't."

Sighing, he added, "We're the last. We can't afford to lose anybody else."

Now he avoided Linden's gaze. Scowling, he moved to stand over the *krill*. "I've been waiting for this."

He bent to retrieve the dagger, then stopped. The gem no longer pulsed. Instead it shone with a steady radiance made pale by sunshine. Joan's concentration had broken: she was too frail to sustain any intent. Clearly, however, she—or *turiya* Herem—could sense his touch on Loric's weapon. She might strike again.

He had already been severely damaged.

Hesitating, he searched for some form of protection. But he seemed reluctant to take any scrap of cloth or leather from the corpses of the Cavewights. At last, he forced himself to approach Anele's body.

Awkward with self-coercion and inadequate fingers, he rent strips from Anele's aged tunic. The fabric was tattered and filthy, soiled by unrelieved decades of privation and neglect; but it was cleaner than anything worn by the Cavewights. As if he were violating the old man's sacrifice, Covenant tore enough cloth to cover the *krill*; shield his hands: Anele's last gift, taken without his volition. Then Covenant went to reclaim Loric Vilesilencer's supreme achievement.

Shaken, Linden abruptly lifted *vitrim* to her lips and drank. She needed—Oh, she had too many needs. Covenant's actions shocked her. They seemed uncharacteristically callous. And yet she had no idea what else he could have done.

He had shown that he could be callous when he had told her not to touch him.

As soon as her depleted body began to absorb vitality from the dust-scented liquid, she returned the cup to the Waynhim and called fresh fire from her Staff.

While Linden finished caring for Bluntfist, Rime Coldspray spoke to her comrades. The Ironhand was profoundly weary; but her voice was clear, founded on granite.

"Recover our supplies," she told those Swordmainnir who were able to comply. "Return to the stream. Covenant Timewarden descries a need for haste. Yet some food and cleansing we must have. By the stream we will gather to drink and bathe, and to reconsider our course. And if these valiant ur-viles and Waynhim accompany us, mayhap they will consent to answer or advise us."

"Aye," assented Frostheart Grueburn and Onyx Stonemage together. Stiff with exhaustion and newly mended tissues, they limped down the ridge to collect the company's bundles.

Weakened more by bleeding than by any single wound, Manethrall Mahrtiir could barely stand. Nevertheless he retained his authority. Leaning on Bhapa, he instructed Pahni to take Jeremiah and follow the Giants. "Ready viands for them," he added, "and for us, while they drink and wash and rest."

The girl obeyed without hesitation; without any sign of emotion whatsoever. Clasping Jeremiah's hand in hers, she drew him away, passive and unaware. At once, Covenant joined her, tucking the wrapped *krill* into the waist of his jeans as he went.

Branl and Clyme started after him; but he snapped, "I *warned* you," and they halted.

Linden approved the Manethrall's instructions and Pahni's compliance. She wished that her son had never been forced to witness such slaughter. She would breathe more easily herself when he was no longer forced to inhale the stink of what she had done. But she also felt a pang at Covenant's manner. He was still keeping his distance from her—

Striving for thoroughness, she continued to work.

Fortunately the Cavewights had not damaged any of Rime Coldspray's vital organs or arteries, or of Stormpast Galesend's. They had not caught the force of Roger's wild blasts. Their worst dangers came from infection and the sheer multiplicity of their hurts. Linden could afford to spend less time with them than she had with the other Giants.

As soon as their condition satisfied her, she turned to Mahrtiir. Stave, Branl, and Clyme she postponed simply because they were *Haruchai*, inherently hardier than any Raman.

As Linden tended Mahrtiir's many cuts and the poisons which dirty weapons had left in his wounds, Coldspray's comrades headed for the stream until only the Ironhand remained. Briefly she scanned the area for something with which she could clean her glaive. Then, growling Giantish epithets under her breath, she dropped the stone sword at her feet.

In spite of her long exertions, and the strain of imposed healing, she went to the litter of boulders bestrewn from Liand's cairn and began shifting them.

Alone Rime Coldspray labored to raise a smaller grave mound for Anele.

It was for this. I have kept faith with my inheritance. In his madness, Anele had endured more than Linden could imagine.

She was losing her ability to distinguish between grief and failure.

"It is enough, Ringthane." Mahrtiir's tone contradicted his words. Blood still seeped from some of his cuts. Nevertheless he took a step backward, plainly asking her to leave him as he was. "Stave has lost a son so that yours might live. And my fear for the Humbled is greater than my distrust. Were I sighted and whole, I could perform no service to equal theirs." At the edges, his voice frayed into sorrow. "Humbled myself, if in another fashion, I implore your succor for them."

Linden let her fire fall away. She could not refuse his plea. Just for a moment, she caught him in a tight hug; gave him an embrace which she could not share with Covenant; accepted the responsibility of his blood on her clothes and skin. Then she went to face Stave's more intimate wounds.

The ur-viles and Waynhim stayed where they were. Having put away their cups, they appeared to study Linden by scent and sound as if they were waiting for her.

Quietly but firmly, Mahrtiir sent Bhapa after Pahni and the rest of the company. But the Manethrall himself did not depart.

Linden was not brave enough for this. Like Anele and Liand, Stave had sacrificed too much in her name. She might have guessed that the passions of fatherhood ran strongly in him. —*a fire in us, and deep.* But nothing in her experience of any *Haruchai* had prepared her to see tears in his eye—

He had slain Esmer without hesitation.

Yet his life was ebbing from him in spite of his preternatural toughness. If she did not intervene, he would eventually perish.

Bracing her Staff on the dirt's burden of bloodshed, Linden stood in front of him. With her health-sense, she studied his gashed face and blade-bitten shoulders, his arms and torso brutally cut. But when he met her gaze, she bowed her head.

"Does it help," she asked in a small voice, "if I say that I'm sorry? Stave, I am so sorry. I didn't see that axe coming. If I had—" With an effort, she caught herself. She had been about to say, *I would have tried to stop it.* But he deserved better honesty. Wincing, she admitted, "I would have prayed for Galt to do what he did. But I'm still sorry. I didn't want him to die. I regret everything that's happened to you."

For her sake, he had been spurned by the Masters.

"I wouldn't change anything," she insisted to the unspoken protest of his injuries. "For the first time since Roger took him, Jeremiah isn't being tortured. He might even have a chance to come out of himself." And Covenant was alive, although he no longer wanted her love. "But I wish—"

Stave interrupted her. "Do not, Linden." His voice was little more than a sigh; yet it silenced her. "Wish for nothing. Regret nothing. Has your long acquaintance with *Haruchai* not taught you that my pride in my son is as great as my bereavement?"

Linden had no answer except the power of the Staff. She had stood on Gallows Howe; had become an incarnation of that benighted mound, barren and bitter. She had refused Elena in Andelain, and had succumbed to the irremediable savagery and suffering of She Who Must Not Be Named. Her only reply was fire.

She scrutinized how his wounds closed as she cared for them, seeking to ensure that she missed no hidden damage, no site of infection. At the same time, she burned blood and grime from his skin, and tried to believe that she was doing enough.

When she was done, she turned away as if she were weeping, although her eyes were parched, as tearless as the landscape.

Now she saw why Mahrtiir had not left. Defying his weakened condition, he was trying to help the Ironhand. His residue of strength was an infant's beside hers. Yet he moved smaller stones to clear her way; steadied boulders while she lifted them; settled Anele's limbs to receive the weight of his makeshift tomb.

Rime Coldspray was no longer alone.

While Linden watched, helpless to intervene, Stave raised Galt in his arms. Saying nothing, he moved toward Coldspray and Mahrtiir; placed his son's body beside Anele's. Then he, too, joined the Ironhand's efforts. Stubborn as any of his people, he contributed his own homage to the new cairn.

Damn it, Linden thought. Damn them. They deserved better. The Worm of the World's End was coming. It would destroy them all. Yet they persisted in being true to their own natures.

Aching for her friends, Linden Avery forced herself to meet the challenge of the Humbled.

Both Clyme and Branl stood like crumbling monuments. When she faced them, Clyme said like the voice of his injuries, "We do not require your aid." He was close to collapse, to death and the world's ruin, but there was no fear in his eyes, or in Branl's.

Their unrequited pain brought back Linden's anger. "I know," she retorted. "You would rather just die. That way, you won't have to resolve any more contradictions. But Covenant needs you, so shut up about it. Either stop me or let me work."

Neither of them raised a hand against her as she filled them with flame as if Earthpower and Law were her only outlet for ire and shame, the essential components of her despair.

ΩΩΩ

When Linden finally descended to the stream, the ur-viles and Waynhim followed her, a ragged procession better suited to running on all fours than walking upright. In the Lost Deep, nearly a third of them had died. But among the survivors, most of their wounds had already been healed, mended by their uncanny lore.

Ahead of Linden strode Clyme and Branl as though they had never been hurt, never questioned themselves. The shreds of their tunics and the latticework of new scars belied their assurance; yet they held their heads high and gazed about them like men who did not relent. Nearing the stretch of sand where Covenant paced back and forth with storms brewing in his gaze, the Humbled bowed to him as though he had not tarnished their *Haruchai* estimations of rectitude. Then they separated to climb the nearby hills in order to stand watch over the company once more.

Linden saw at a glance that the Swordmainnir had bathed and eaten. Their washed armor lay drying in the sun, and they were visibly stronger. Among them, Jeremiah chewed reflexively on some morsel of food. Pahni or Bhapa had cared for him in his mother's absence. Nonetheless the silt of his stare remained unreactive, empty, like a wall against the hurts of the world.

"Linden—" Covenant began, then stopped. Conflicting emotions seemed to close his throat. The muscles of his jaw bunched as he fought what he was feeling, but he did not say anything more than her name.

Avoiding his congested gaze, Linden nodded to the concerned faces of the Giants, Bhapa's more troubled expression, Pahni's numbed mien. Hoarse with weariness and too many needs, she explained, "Coldspray is building a cairn for Anele and Galt. Mahrtiir and Stave are helping her. They'll be here soon."

Even their strength and determination would not last much longer.

Then she strode past her companions. At the edge of the water, she dropped her Staff as though it entailed more responsibilities than she could bear. Empty-handed, she walked out into the stream until it filled her boots, reached her knees, rose to her waist. When it was deep enough, she plunged beneath the surface.

Like a small child, irrationally, she prayed that the water would feel as clean and cleansing as Glimmermere.

But it could not wash away what she had seen and done and felt. The darkness in her was immiscible. No mere spring runoff could dilute it. Like the healing that she had given to her companions, the stream had no power to expunge her sins.

In Andelain, Berek's spectre had said of Lord Foul, *He may be freed only by one who is compelled by rage, and contemptuous of consequence.* Since then, she had proven herself an apt instrument. If Jeremiah had not been rescued from the *croyel*—

But her son had been set free. If the current's gentle urging did not ease her heart, she had other answers. For years, she had made a study of despair: as a physician, she knew it intimately. In addition, she could still hope that Jeremiah would emerge from his graves, if he were given time. And the imponderable implications of Covenant's instinct for redemption might somehow counteract the lessons that she had absorbed from Gallows Howe; the horror that she had shared within She Who Must Not Be Named.

Underwater she scrubbed at her hair, tried to claw the disgust and lamentation off of her arms and face. Gradually she grew calmer. When she broke the surface and wiped the water from her eyes, she was able to meet the anxious glances of her companions without flinching.

Sodden, and glad of it, she left the stream to reclaim her Staff and the rest of her burdens.

As she approached, Bhapa held out food for her: bread that had not had time to grow stale, grapes and a little cheese, some cured beef. He offered her a bulging waterskin. She accepted his care and thanked him. Then she began to eat.

She was hungrier than she would have thought possible. In spite of everything that had sickened or appalled her, her body had not forgotten its own needs.

Covenant stopped his pacing to watch her. She sensed the pressure rising in him like a fever, but she did not know how to interpret it. After a moment, he began again, "Linden—We're running out of time. I know you've been through hell. You've lost too much. You all have. But we should—"

He seemed eager to get as far away from her as he could.

Chewing, Linden held up a hand to interrupt him. When she had swallowed, she asked, "Have you remembered something that makes a difference? Something that we can understand?"

He shook his head. Shadows like thunderheads complicated his gaze.

"Then we should wait for Stave, Mahrtiir, and Coldspray." She rebuffed him because she felt rebuffed herself. "They need food and a chance to wash. And they have a right to hear whatever you want to say."

She expected him to overrule her. He had that authority: he was Thomas Covenant. But he did not. Briefly he scowled at her as if he wished that he could read her heart. Then he resumed his pacing.

The ur-viles and Waynhim had spread out around the Giants, enclosing Linden and her companions in a half-circle. Now they began growling like creatures who wished to be heeded.

Frostheart Grueburn jerked up her head. Surprise lit the features of the Giants: surprise and sudden gladness. While Onyx Stonemage and her comrades whispered excitedly to each other, Grueburn turned to the loremaster and bowed with the formality due to a sovereign among invaluable allies.

"Our ears have been opened," she said with as much gravity as her eagerness and relief allowed. "We hear you and attend, honoring your great valor and service."

The loremaster replied in a guttural snarl that conveyed nothing to Linden—or to Covenant and the Cords. But Grueburn bowed again, grinning as if something within her had been set free. Latebirth and Stormpast Galesend laughed softly, full of pleasure. Other Giants beamed, smiling with their whole bodies.

"Linden Giantfriend," Grueburn said, "do not misapprehend our joy. It is the restoration of our gift of tongues which lifts our hearts, not the words of these brave creatures. Yet there is no hurt or harm in those words. The loremaster merely desires us to comprehend that the ur-viles and Waynhim must depart. For the present, they have fulfilled the dictates of their Weird." The Swordmain broke off. Aside, she explained, "Among them, 'Weird' has several meanings, none of which are plain to me." Then she resumed. "Now they wish to seek out a deeper understanding, for their deeds here do not content them.

"Ere they depart, however, they will answer any questions that you may choose to ask, if the answers lie within their ken."

Linden stared. Now? When she and her companions had barely survived Roger's attack? The list of things that she wanted to know seemed endless. But she was close to exhaustion: she could not think clearly enough to remember them all.

Nevertheless the loremaster's offer was a precious opportunity. It might not come again.

Covenant's eyes seemed to catch fire in the sunlight. He turned sharply; strode toward the loremaster as though he meant to hurl a volley of queries. When the black creature sniffed in his direction, however, and proffered an awkward mimicry of a human bow, he did not speak. Instead he bowed in return, then looked at Linden.

Not for the first time, he appeared reluctant to take command in her presence.

All of the Demondim-spawn had fallen silent. The Giants gathered more closely around Linden, Covenant, and the loremaster. Torn between diffidence and a desire for comprehension, Bhapa joined them. But Pahni stayed with Jeremiah. As if she had no interest or purpose in life except to carry out assigned tasks, she busied herself feeding the boy as long as he was willing to chew and swallow.

Pressed by Covenant's gaze, Linden asked the first question that came to her.

"How did they know?"

Grueburn cocked her head quizzically. "It may be, Linden Giantfriend, that the creatures comprehend you. Alas, I do not."

Linden dragged a hand through her hair. She wanted to slap herself, sting a measure of acuity into her thoughts.

"Esmer said that they forged their manacles in the Lost Deep. They must have done it thousands of years ago. He saved the last of them—but they were ready for him. How did they know that they were going to need those manacles? How did they know that he would even exist?" If she understood what Esmer had told her, he had urged the creatures to accompany him before the time of his own birth. "How did they know what he would be like, or what he would do, or how he could be stopped?"

At once, the loremaster began to bark a lengthy response. Scrambling to keep up, Grueburn attempted a simultaneous translation.

"These are matters of lore. They cannot be contained by your speech. We labored in the Lost Deep, where the Snared One could not discover us, for our presence was masked by the hunger and somnolence of the nameless bane. Thus we were not taken by the purge which destroyed all others of our kind. In our fashion, we witnessed the Snared One's defeat, and the union of the *Haruchai* with those beings whom you name *merewives*, and the first stirrings of the mad *Elohim*'s struggle to escape his Durance. From these gravid portents, we inferred what must follow. We could not be certain of it, just as we could not be certain when we created Vain to serve against the Snared One. But we saw—"

Abruptly Grueburn winced in frustration. "Loremaster, I cry your pardon. You speak in concepts beyond my grasp."

The Waynhim replied with low growls and snarls as if they were making suggestions. But the Giants shook their heads in bewilderment, and the grey Demondim-spawn fell silent.

Abandoning literal translation, Frostheart Grueburn endeavored to paraphrase instead.

"Linden Giantfriend, the ur-viles saw *possibilities*. I have no better language. They saw possibilities and prepared themselves.

"However, the loremaster states plainly that they did not foreknow Esmer's coming to bear them across the millennia. But they do not age and die as we do, and they conceived themselves secure in the Lost Deep. It was their intent to simply wait out the centuries until possibilities became certainties, or proved to be chimeras. In the forgotten caverns beneath Gravin Threndor, and in their loreworks, they had much to occupy them.

"Yet when Esmer appeared, they *knew* him. Again the word is not adequate to their meaning. They saw possibilities made flesh. Therefore they consented to accompany him, perceiving that his nature might one day require the constraint of their manacles."

Increasingly stymied by unfamiliar rationales, Grueburn betrayed a surge of agitation. "Here also," she continued, hurrying, "the loremaster states plainly that the ur-viles did not foreknow events. They merely—"

She stopped short. As if to herself, she protested, "Stone and Sea! I am a Giant, am I not? How does it transpire that I have no sufficient speech?"

"Don't worry about it," Covenant murmured gruffly. "You're doing fine." And Hale-whole Bluntfist added, "We are not *Elohim*, Grueburn. That we are not more than Giants does not imply that we are therefore less."

Clenching her fists, Grueburn swallowed her vexation. Uncomfortably she finished, "They merely followed the path of possibilities, and awaited culmination."

The loremaster may have been satisfied. It made no effort to explain further.

Possibilities? Linden thought. That's *all*? Her own mind and experiences were alien to those of the ur-viles and Waynhim; too alien. Their thoughts were like Caerroil Wildwood's runes: they surpassed her ability to interpret them.

Covenant watched her with a complex intensity in his eyes; but he did not interject his own questions.

All right, she told herself. All right. It is what it is. One step at a time.

Studying the stark ebony and eyelessness of the loremaster's visage, she asked, "So what changed? For a long time, they served Lord Foul. Then they didn't. They started working against him instead." Something had inspired them to redefine their Weird. "Why did they do that?"

The loremaster responded with a string of sounds like harsh choking. But this time Grueburn seemed more at ease with the creature's reply.

"Two—insights? recognitions?—caused them to reexamine the import of their Weird. The first is this.

"They were drawn to the Snared One's service by promises of fulfillment. When his designs were accomplished, he assured them, they would achieve every aspiration, and the strictures of their Weird would be appeased. Like him, they would perceive themselves as gods, far greater in form and substance and lore and worth than the Demondim, their makers. For this, they strove in his name."

Through the low mutter of barking and growls from the Waynhim and several of the ur-viles, Frostheart Grueburn's voice carried more strongly. The creatures may have been encouraging her.

"By increments, however, they became acquainted—how could they not?—with his insatiable contempt for all beings other than himself. They deemed themselves the foremost of his servants, mightier and more necessary than even the Ravers, for the Ravers required stolen forms and did not honor the vast lore of the Demondim. Still less did the Ravers esteem the spanning knowledge and theurgies of the siring Viles. Also the enslavement of the Ravers was such that they had lost themselves. They had grown incapable of any clear aspiration not commanded by their lord. And the ur-viles were many, the Ravers few. Surely, therefore, the ur-viles were the most prized of the Snared One's adherents.

"Yet they were not. Rather they were despised. Indeed, his contempt for them seemed as unfathomable as the deepest secrets of the Earth. And no promises were kept. At last, they saw that his contempt exceeded their self-loathing. Thus they became disposed to turn aside from their service."

Urged by soft calls and snarls, Grueburn added, "Yet to turn aside is also to turn toward, and they lacked any new purpose, any new vision of their Weird, toward which they might turn."

There she paused, apparently trying to follow the strands of the loremaster's involuted speech.

As if to prompt her, Covenant remarked, "That's where the Waynhim came in. That was their real gift to the Land. A different interpretation."

"Aye," Grueburn assented as the loremaster barked. "You speak of the second insight or recognition which guided the ur-viles to their present course.

"In the unyielding opposition of their smaller, weaker, and fewer kindred, they discerned strength of a kind which lay beyond their emulation. It was neither lore nor puissance. But it may have been wisdom, and it surpassed them."

Sadly Grueburn admitted, "Mere *wisdom* is too small to suggest the scale of the loremaster's meaning. The creature implies a discernment of the underlying nature of existence. However, the pith of the matter is this. The Waynhim no longer loathed their own forms. They had surrendered that self-disgust, or they had transcended it. They were impelled to the Land's service by—I have no more fitting word—by love. They were driven, not by abhorrence, but by affirmation."

Again the Swordmain paused, wrestling with ramifications. Several of her comrades seemed to want to help her, but they kept their ideas to themselves.

After a moment, Grueburn sighed like an admission of defeat. "This," she resumed, "the ur-viles did not comprehend. They could not. Yet they saw that there was no ire in the opposition of the Waynhim. Again I lack needful language. The Waynhim fought, and were overwhelmed, and perished—and felt neither rage nor protest. Rather they comported themselves as though their service alone sufficed to vindicate their interpretation of their Weird. To both vindicate and achieve it.

"Though the ur-viles did not comprehend, they recognized that their own service to the Snared One offered no such reward. They were given promises, and they were sacrificed, but they were denied the calm certainty of the Waynhim. Thus they were led to the arcane study of possibilities. And when those possibilities were confirmed in Vain—in Linden Giantfriend's Staff of Law, and in Covenant Timewarden's transubstantiation—these ur-viles now among us pursued their study further."

As the loremaster's answer ended, Linden saw Covenant watching her sidelong. He appeared to be biding his time, as if he hoped that she would eventually ask a different question.

Perhaps he wished her to seek guidance. If so, he was going to be disappointed. At that moment, she did not want advice. She wanted an effective way to thank the ur-viles for stopping Esmer.

"Then tell me what their Weird *is*," she said. "What does it *mean*?" A moment later, however, she shook her head. "No. That isn't what I'm trying to ask."

Weird, Wyrd, Würd, Word, Worm: she had heard too many explanations. More would not improve her comprehension.

"Before we left Revelstone, I made a promise. I told them that if they ever figured out how to tell me what they need from me, I would do it. I want to keep that promise." She yearned to keep at least one of her promises, and she had already failed Anele. In truth, she had doomed everyone who had ever trusted her. Facing the loremaster, she concluded, "You've done so much for me. For all of us. Tell me how I can repay you."

Dozens of voices replied simultaneously, as insistent as the clamor of hounds on the scent of their quarry.

Frostheart Grueburn tried to follow them all. Then she punched her fists against each other: a gesture of protest. "I implore you," she groaned. "I cannot encompass so much. When I am given more than I am able to heed, I receive none of it."

At once, the tumult of the creatures was cut off. Testing the air with its wide nostrils, the loremaster fell silent.

Abashed, Grueburn turned to Linden. "I am unequal to this task. The Waynhim in particular strive to account for their Weird, but I hear little that I am able to convey. Some cite *worth* and *otherness*. Some make reference to *transfiguration* or *rebirth*. But their true meaning eludes me."

She looked around at the Swordmainnir, mutely asking for aid. But they shook their heads, admitting their own confusion.

Glumly Grueburn told Linden, "They appear to conflate concepts in a manner baffling to me. Do they equate their own worthiness with that of the wide Earth, or do they attempt some obscure distinction? Do they crave an alteration of themselves, that they may be condign in the world, or do they desire the world's transformation in their own image? They appear to set their course by many headings. I cannot follow them."

Now the loremaster spoke again. When it was done, Grueburn squared her shoulders; gazed at Linden more sharply. "To one aspect of your question, however, their response is plain. The nature of the Staff of Law is inimical to them, though they possess a limited virtu to ward themselves. In this circumstance, Linden Giantfriend, they require naught that you may provide."

To herself, Linden groaned. She needed a different answer. Something tangible, attainable: something that she could actually do to balance the scales of her long debt.

Something to lighten the weight of her growing darkness.

But before she could find words for her regret, Covenant moved closer to the loremaster. "In that case," he informed the creature, "I have a question."

His tone suggested potential wrath held in strict abeyance.

"Esmer said he wasn't the one who betrayed us in the Lost Deep. But hellfire! He was the only one *there*. The Harrow was already dead, and Roger was gone, and Kastenessen sent the *skurj*, and the bane just is what She is.

"So what was Esmer talking about? How were we betrayed?"

Frowning at the question, or at Covenant's attitude, Grueburn turned back to the loremaster.

For a long moment, all of the ur-viles and Waynhim replied with silence. Then the loremaster uttered a quick, raucous burst.

Translating literally, Grueburn announced, "The son of *merewives* and *Haruchai* spoke of us."

Covenant waited, stiff and demanding.

Another burst of noise like the yowling of a penned dog.

"He was cognizant of our purpose. He abhorred and desired it. He considered you betrayed because we did not impose our manacles then. Had we done so, you would have been freed to flee without further peril or striving."

Under his breath, Covenant muttered, "Now we're getting somewhere." Then he asked harshly, "So why didn't you? You could have spared us almost any amount of suffering. I won't even mention what I did to Elena." For an instant, his self-control broke. "*She's my daughter!*" Almost immediately, however, he mastered himself. "But we came close to losing Linden completely. Hell and blood! You know what's at stake. Why did you take a chance like that?"

Linden wanted to object. Surely the creatures did not merit this? But Covenant's passion—and his question—held her.

There was a storm building in him. It gathered somewhere beyond the horizon of her comprehension. When it broke, people or beings or creatures were going to die.

Indirectly the ur-viles had doomed Elena. Her sacrifice in the Lost Deep must have appalled him.

This time, the silence was longer. When the loremaster finally replied, it spoke at some length, voluble and urgent. But Grueburn did not attempt a translation until the creature was finished.

"Your pardon," she said at last. "I wished to confirm that I have understood the loremaster." Puzzlement and speculation were eloquent in her gaze. "It responds thus."

"Had your efforts to forestall the bane failed, Timewarden, we would have attempted intervention, knowing that we must. Earlier, however, other possibilities constrained us.

"Their form and substance as we comprehend them cannot be expressed in your speech. The Giant has made the attempt. We do not fault her. Yet our tongue wields connotations and meanings which are not accessible to her. We cannot explain.

"Yet consider one matter. We could not be certain that the son of *merewives* would not counter us. He knew the intent of our manacles. He named you betrayed because we did not act to prevent him. Yet his nature was contradiction. He both craved and abhorred each of his deeds. Desiring the absolution of our manacles, he might nonetheless have forestalled us. Therefore we deemed it needful to ensnare him when he was unaware of us.

"Also there is this. Had we acted otherwise, how might the immeasurable strengths of the Vilesilencer's instrument have been released for your use? The instrument was necessary to restrain the *croyel*. He whom you name Esmer had not yet revealed his purpose against the old man, the inheritor of Earthpower. Nor had the old man's own purpose been revealed. And we had cause to fear that the *Haruchai* would oppose him. Inadvertently, perhaps, they might have precluded the *croyel*'s death.

"We see possibilities, Timewarden. We do not foreknow events. Yet portents abound. Guided by them, we saw no path to the present outcome which did not rely upon both the defeat of Esmer and the acquiescence of the *Haruchai*. For such reasons, we accepted the peril of the bane, and of white gold made impotent, knowing that events might prove fatal to you, and to the fruition of our Weird."

When Grueburn was done, her posture—her whole body—seemed to plead for Covenant's understanding; or for Linden's.

Linden could not reply. The complexity of the creatures' thinking stunned her. They read portents which were opaque to her; effectively invisible. How could they have guessed that Esmer's attack might sway Galt?

For a moment, Covenant, too, seemed stunned. But then he turned a whetted grin on Linden and the rest of the company.

"There!" he said like a paean. "*That's* why we aren't doomed. No matter what Lord Foul has planned. He isn't the only one who knows how to *think ahead*. He can still be taken by surprise."

His affirmation seemed to hang in the air as he faced the loremaster once more. "I hope you'll accept my gratitude. As far as I'm concerned, you've already shown you're worthy of anything you might ever want." He swallowed roughly, then added, "What happened to Elena was my doing, not yours."

When the creature replied, Frostheart Grueburn translated gruffly. "The ur-viles and Waynhim crave naught from you, Timewarden. Your tasks do not concern them. They desire only Linden Giantfriend's leave to depart."

Linden had the impression that every Waynhim and ur-vile was watching her. Waiting for her to say something that might imply comprehension. Something that might vindicate—

But she was not Covenant. Like the Demondim-spawn, he saw reasons for hope that she could not. Like Jeremiah, if in an entirely different fashion, she was trapped inside herself.

Nevertheless her own gratitude was as real as Covenant's. And she did not believe that the creatures could have spared her any whit of the distress inflicted by She Who Must Not Be Named.

Deliberately she set aside her sorrow that she could not repay the Demondim-spawn; swallowed her surprise at Covenant's reaction. Once again, she forced a hand through her tangled hair.

"Oh, go ahead," she said like a sigh, "if that's what you need to do. And take my blessing with you." What else could she possibly offer them? "I agree with Covenant. You're worthy of anything." Then she added, "I stand by my promise. If you ever do think of some way that I can help you, just tell me."

Her response seemed to release the creatures. Quickly the loremaster bowed to her as it had bowed to Covenant. Every Waynhim and ur-vile bowed. Then they dropped to all fours and began to run, heading like a pack of wild animals along the floor of the low ravine.

Soon they were gone. Nevertheless their departure left Linden with the sensation that she had disappointed them. Too late, she realized that she could have asked them to translate Caerroil Wildwood's runes. Once again, she had failed—

Jeremiah and her friends and the Land needed the kind of calm certainty that the ur-viles had found in the Waynhim; but she had none.

ꕥ

S oon Covenant resumed his pacing. The Swordmainnir spent a while discussing the Demondim-spawn. Then they settled themselves on the sand to tend their weapons or rest. When Jeremiah no longer chewed or swallowed, Pahni stopped putting food in his mouth. With Bhapa's help, she readied meals for Rime Coldspray, the Manethrall, and Stave. After that, the Cords repacked the company's supplies. While Bhapa occupied himself with that simple task, obviously fretting, he watched the horizon where the absent companions might appear.

But Linden turned away and went to sit alone near the edge of the stream. There she gazed vacantly at the unresolved tumble and contradiction of the current, and tried to convince herself that her use of Covenant's ring was not an abomination.

Good cannot be accomplished by evil means.

She and everyone with her would have been slain if she had not killed so many Cavewights. And when Roger had finished with her and the Giants and the Humbled and the Ramen, he would have hunted down Covenant to complete his victory.

What else could she have done?

But she was not persuaded. Surely other answers had been possible, for someone else if not for her? She was so much less than she needed to be: too ignorant of lore and Law and her own powers to defend her friends without butchering their foes.

At her back, heat accumulated in the sand and on the hillsides: a mixed blessing. It eased sore nerves and muscles, dried her clothes—and made her thirsty again. The stream's voices called to her, but she ignored them.

Stuck in a round of emotions and flaws that she did not know how to escape, she became as restless as the waters, as anxious as Bhapa. As impatient as Covenant. When the Ironhand, Mahrtiir, and Stave finally came within the range of her senses, she surged to her feet like a released spring and began striding toward them before she realized that they were not alone.

The Ardent followed close behind them, stumbling as if he were too weak to stay upright much longer.

For obvious reasons, Coldspray, Mahrtiir, and Stave were desperately tired, although Stave's stoicism concealed much of his fatigue. The Ironhand and the Manethrall trembled as they walked, unsteady on their legs; severely dehydrated. In contrast, Stave seemed only dull, numbed, unable to focus. He did not react to Bhapa's greeting or the calls of the Giants.

Nevertheless the condition of the Insequent was worse. His ribbands hung from his frame like long shreds of flesh; soiled streamers of suffering and loss. Inside his raiment, his former corpulence had melted away until he looked more than gaunt: he resembled a man in the last stages of a wasting disease. Emaciation or caducity made hollows of his cheeks, his eyes, even his mouth. Loose wattles hung from his jaw. As he lurched along, his gaze rolled from side to side as if he no longer had the strength to choose what he saw or thought.

He seemed oblivious to his own deranged chuckling. The sound scattered around him like broken bits of melody; disarticulated sanity.

The Ironhand and the Manethrall ignored him. With no more than nods for their comrades, they shambled forward until they had gone far enough to fall face-first into the stream. But Stave managed to halt among the company. He bowed to Linden, gave Covenant a vague nod. In a husk of a voice, a sound as desiccated as the hills, he said, "It is done. We have raised a cairn for Anele and Galt. The Ardent appeared when our task was complete."

Linden stared at him, tried to say his name. But she succeeded only at gaping.

Without waiting for a reply, Stave followed Coldspray and Mahrtiir. In the stream, he did not stop until the water was deep enough to let him sink beneath the surface.

"Hellfire," Covenant rasped to no one in particular. "Hell and blood."

Instinctively Linden moved toward the Ardent with her Staff ready. But as soon as she looked at him closely, she saw that he was beyond help. The forces unbinding him were inexorable, as cruel as too much time. He needed the kind of mercy that Stave had given Esmer. Any other anodyne was impossible.

Grueburn and two of the other Giants came closer to scrutinize the Ardent's ravaged form. Then they shook their heads. With pity in their eyes, they stepped back, leaving the Insequent to Linden and Covenant.

"They got it wrong." Covenant's voice was choked with pity. "When I told you I wanted them to make an exception, I didn't mean *this*." His compassion gathered until it resembled outrage. "They didn't by God *listen*."

"Told," chortled the Ardent. "Listen. Tell." His voice scaled high; sank low. "The Insequent are not *told*. One stricture for all. One allowance unmakes all. Every life. They listen. Oh, they listen! Some grieve. But you do not *tell* the Insequent to end every life."

"What?" Linden protested, unable to stop herself. "*Every* life? Are you saying that *every* Insequent dies, the whole race *dies*, if they let you live?"

"Listen," he repeated. "The Ardent tells. You do not listen." Ribbands flinched around him. "One stricture for all. One stricture for *all*."

412 Stephen R. Donaldson

His condition was yet another consequence of Linden's need to rescue her son.

While Covenant floundered in chagrin, Onyx Stonemage murmured thickly, "It is a *geas*, is it not? He has spoken of such matters. The will of the Insequent rules him still, though he stands at the outermost verge of his life."

As if he were answering her, the Ardent said, "Such carnage." He giggled softly. "Great death, aye. Great and needful. Incondign." His gaze veered from place to place as if he were watching motes of fine dust circulate. "It does not suffice."

Groaning to herself, Linden tried not to imagine what he meant.

"If this is indeed a *geas*," Cirrus Kindwind suggested, "surely it is incomplete. I do not wish to conceive that the Insequent have imposed his presence here merely to demonstrate that he suffers a compulsory doom. They cannot lack all heart."

None of her comrades responded. Covenant gritted his teeth, restraining himself until the muscles at the corners of his jaw bunched like knuckles.

The Ardent had done so much more than Linden could have asked of him. This was his reward.

Behind her, Stave emerged from the stream. A moment later, Rime Coldspray and Manethrall Mahrtiir did the same. Dripping, Stave approached Linden and Covenant while Coldspray walked stiffly to join the Swordmainnir. At the same time, Bhapa hurried down the slope with food for the Manethrall.

Linden feared that Mahrtiir's aggrieved pride would require him to ignore Bhapa. But apparently the Manethrall was determined to accept that he, too, had been humbled. Leaning an arm across Bhapa's shoulders, he acknowledged the Cord's concern by taking a little food. However, he did not stop moving until he stood beside Linden.

Among her people, the Ironhand shared collective embraces, hugging the other Giants in clusters of two or three. From Latebirth, she received a double handful of fruit and meat, and began immediately to eat. Then she turned her attention to Linden, Covenant, and the Ardent.

Linden had no words for what she felt and feared; but Covenant seemed unable to contain himself. "Kindwind is right," he growled to the Ardent. "Your people didn't send you back just to convince us they can't save you.

"There's something you came to say. Something you still need to do."

Abruptly the Ardent spasmed as if he had been struck by a galvanic shock. His head jerked up: his whole body flinched. In a completely different voice, compelled and straining, he said, "While you remain apart, events elsewhere conspire to thwart your defense of the Land."

He seemed to quote someone else, mimicking someone else's speech. "To the north of ancient Gravin Threndor, the Sandgorgons and the *skurj* have come together. It was our hope that they would expend their ferocity in mutual extermination. But our hope misled us. We misgauged the degree of Kastenessen's mastery over the *skurj*, and the cunning of *moksha* Raver's counsels, and the potency of those shreds of *samadhi* Sheol which endure among the Sandgorgons. Against all expectation, those monstrous beings have conjoined their strengths. Now they rampage together within Salva Gildenbourne, wreaking such a ruin of trees and verdure that you would weep to gaze upon it."

For an instant, the *geas* of the Insequent appeared to slip. The Ardent slumped; staggered like a man scarcely able to stand. He chuckled softly as if his own grief amused him.

His announcement shocked Linden out of her recursive dismay. The truth was vivid in his voice.

—those monstrous beings—

"Stone and Sea!" growled Rime Coldspray: an appalled imprecation. Several of the other Giants cursed as well. A few moved to begin donning their armor.

—have conjoined their strengths.

Almost immediately, however, a fresh convulsion clenched the Ardent. "The devastation is wide and bitter," he continued, "leaving naught but the reek of fouled ground in its wake. But it is not without purpose. Kastenessen may indeed be lost to forethought or tactic. *Moksha* is not. And *samadhi* comprehends his brother. The *skurj* and the Sandgorgons do not seek mere ravage. Nor is their savagery directed against sacred Andelain. Rather they strive toward Gravin Threndor.

"Do you comprehend this? They strive toward Gravin Threndor because you cannot meet the Worm of the World's End while the vile theurgies of Kevin's Dirt hamper the lady. But if you wish to quench Kevin's Dirt, you must first master Kastenessen—and he has secreted himself within the Wightwarrens, where he draws upon the illimitable vehemence of She Who Must Not Be Named. Therefore—"

Harshly Covenant muttered, "I get it."

But the distant Insequent did not heed him. "—when you attempt the mountain, you will find the Sandgorgons and the *skurj* arrayed against you. And doubtless a host of Cavewights will join with them. Your foes will be many and terrible."

"I said," Covenant snapped, "I *get* it." His hands clutched the wrapped bundle of the *krill*, although he seemed unaware of it. "Hellfire! You don't need to beat me over the head. And you didn't come here just to warn us. You have something in mind."

Reflexively Linden held her breath. The Swordmainnir watched the Ardent with warrior intensity. Mahrtiir stood at Linden's shoulder as if he were poised for battle.

Now the Ardent's people kept their grip on him. Apparently expending the last shreds of his life, he panted, "The lady's fate is writ in water. All auguries are swept aside. Yet her need for death remains. We conclude that you must have allies."

Linden forced herself to exhale; but she could not still the hammering of her heart.

"Though powers abound in the Earth, we have no means to summon them. The *Elohim* will not aid you. And for this purpose, the Insequent themselves cannot serve. We are largely defenseless against Ravers, as we are against She Who Must Not Be Named. The hazard that we will turn against you is too great."

Covenant's air of storms increased. "Get to the point. Who else is there?"

This time, the Ardent appeared to hear him. "We see no alternative other than the *Haruchai*. Yet they will not heed us. No Insequent will sway them. Should we appeal to them, they will close their ears and remain as they are."

"It's suicide," Linden breathed without thinking. "Of course they'll refuse. They can't fight Sandgorgons and *skurj*."

But Mahrtiir's voice rode over hers. "To whom will the sleepless ones attend?"

At the same time, Covenant countered, "What's the point? Even with the Ranyhyn, none of us can get to Revelstone fast enough. The Worm will be here before the Masters even know we need them. After that, whatever they do will be wasted."

Rigid as the last clench of death, the Ardent waited for silence.

Glaring at him, Covenant muttered, "Oh, hell. Do it your way. I'll shut up."

Through their coerced vessel, the Insequent replied, "This is our last requirement of the Ardent. The *Haruchai* are capable of much. Select those among you who will be most readily heeded. He will transport them to Revelstone, where they may plead on the Land's behalf. Then he will depart from life and suffering. Perchance some measure of hope will remain."

Before anyone else could respond, Mahrtiir announced, clarion as the call of horns, "If that is your word, Insequent, my Cords will accompany you."

At once, Pahni jerked up her head, spun away from Jeremiah. Bhapa's sudden pallor made him look faint; appalled.

The Manethrall's assertion appeared to satisfy the Ardent—or his people. "That is well," he or they observed. "The *Haruchai* would not refuse the Timewarden. Nevertheless he has another purpose. He must not step aside from it."

Then the *geas* left the frail man. As if he were crumpling, he folded to the sand. Propped on his hands and knees, no longer able to call on his apparel for support, he gasped small bursts of broken laughter.

The Cords? Linden thought. The *Cords*? Oh, God!

Covenant had foreseen this—

He scowled at the dying man as though he wanted to hear more. —another purpose. But the Giants turned to regard Manethrall Mahrtiir. Studying his bandaged visage, Rime Coldspray said uncertainly, "It is much to ask. Surely Stave or one of the Humbled—?"

Without a flicker of hesitation, Stave stated, "My kinsmen will not harken to me. And the Humbled will not part from the Unbeliever. It is bootless to inquire of them."

"Then a Giant?" asked the Ironhand. "The Masters have made their unwelcome plain for many centuries. Nonetheless I will believe that they have not forgotten their ancient esteem, first for the Unhomed and later for the comrades of the Search."

"No." The Manethrall spoke as if his word were Law. "My Cords will bear this burden. It was foretold for them. They will not refuse it."

—you two have the hardest job. You'll have to survive. And you'll have to make them listen to you.

For the same reason, Mahrtiir could not accompany them. Covenant had counseled him to take a different path.

You'll have to go a long way to find your heart's desire. Just be sure you come back.

Shaken, Bhapa cried softly, "Manethrall, *no*. I implore you!"

Instinctively Linden wanted to add her voice to the Cord's. She feared Covenant's prophecies. They all seemed to mean death.

She's already given them too many reasons to feel ashamed of themselves.

But Pahni swept forward as if she were pouncing. "*Yes!*" The eagerness of a hawk shone in her soft eyes. "I will lay Liand's death at the feet of the Masters and compel an answer. They deem themselves the descendants of the Bloodguard. I will require of them a comparable service.

"Come, Bhapa," she commanded. Passionate and peremptory, she extended her hand to the older Cord. "No Cord may refuse when the Manethrall speaks and the Land's need is clear."

The Ardent made aimless sounds in the back of his throat. He was too weak to chuckle.

With something like sympathy in his voice, Mahrtiir asked, "Will you gainsay me, Bhapa? Were you selected to accompany the Ringthane along the path of her many travails because you were counted unfit for lesser duties? Did not Whrany consent to bear you, when until that day no Raman had ever ridden the Ranyhyn? And did not Rohnhyn freely offer himself when Whrany was slain? The Timewarden has spoken of trust. The time has come for Cord Bhapa of the Ramen to trust himself."

Panic filled Bhapa's mien: alarm glistened in his eyes. The skin of his face was the color of sun-beaten dust.

But then, trembling, he bowed to his Manethrall. His hand quivered like an aspen leaf about to fall as he accepted Pahni's clasp.

With a visible effort, Covenant unclosed his fingers from the *krill*. "I'm sorry," he muttered to no in particular. "If this was my idea—" He grimaced. "I can't imagine what I was thinking. You deserve an explanation, but I don't have one."

Bitterly Linden swore to herself. Under other circumstances, she might have protested. She did not know how to bear Liand's death, or Anele's, or even Galt's. She did not want to lose Bhapa and Pahni as well.

Panting, the Ardent said hoarsely, "Timewarden."

Covenant moved closer. "Yes?"

Stretched thin with effort, the Ardent urged as clearly as he could, "Remember Mishio Massima."

Covenant stared. "Is that your true name?"

Could he be invoked? Even when he was so close to collapse?

The dying man gave a cracked laugh. "It is my steed."

A moment later, the *geas* of the Insequent gripped him for the last time. It wrenched him to his feet with his head thrown back as if he needed to scream. Ribbands coiled spasmodically around him; fell to the ground; twisted upward again. His hands clutched at the air like claws.

"It is enough," he said as if the words were torn from his throat. "We are content. Here ends the Ardent. If the Earth endures, he will be honored as the greatest of the Insequent."

A moment later, his raiment reached out to clasp Pahni and Bhapa. So quickly that the Cords had no chance to say farewell, he gathered them to him and vanished.

Involuntarily Linden staggered as if she wished to follow them. Their departure seemed to leave a gap in the air that she needed to fill. But Stave caught her instantly; and of course she had nowhere to go.

At her side, Mahrtiir sagged like a man unexpectedly bereft. Now that his Cords were gone, his aura revealed a pang of uncertainty, as if he had sent them to be humiliated. Nothing that Handir and the other Masters had done in Revelstone gave the Manethrall cause to believe that Bhapa and Pahni would succeed.

Linden hoped that one of the Giants would say something to reassure Mahrtiir. She could not. But Covenant had already flung himself into motion; resumed his pacing. "Hellfire," he growled to himself. "His *steed*?" Briefly he appeared to count the number of times that he could repeat those words between one slope of the canyon and the other. Then he wheeled to face the company.

His manner compelled their attention in spite of the abrupt loss of Pahni and Bhapa—and of the Ardent.

"I don't need to know the name of his damn horse," he rasped. "I have to go." Then he swore again, a string of curses so familiar that they sounded like pleading. To Linden's startled dismay, and the small lift of Stave's eyebrow, and the open surprise of the Swordmainnir, he repeated, "I have to *go*."

Brusque with self-coercion, he added, "I know this is sudden. Never mind that I'm usually useless. You still think you need me. You went through too much to bring me back in the first place. Probably the last thing you want right now is to watch me leave. Hell, if I were you, that's how I would feel. But I *have* to go.

"And you can't go with me. Before I worry about anything else, there's something I have to do alone."

—he has another purpose.

While Linden reeled within herself, he shrugged awkwardly. "Well, not absolutely alone. I'm taking Clyme and Branl with me. You'll have to manage without them until I get back."

With both hands, he held the bundled *krill* as if his life depended on it.

He must not step aside from it.

Disconcerted, the Giants struggled to muster a response. Mahrtiir stared at Covenant in unconcealed chagrin. Even Stave's flat visage gave hints of disapprobation.

"Is this some new recollection?" the Ironhand inquired finally. "Do you now possess knowledge or understanding which you have not revealed?"

But Linden noticed none of her companions; no one except the man who had once loved her—and now would not let her touch him.

"Covenant," she panted, unconsciously fighting for breath. "Covenant." He was rejecting her. "What are you talking about?" God, he was *rejecting* her. "I need—We need—" Her sins had become too much for him. "God damn it, Covenant! If you don't care about anything else, the *Land* needs you."

She had awakened the Worm for his sake. She could not suffer the consequences of her desperation or folly without him.

"Linden, *listen* to me." His gaze was flagrant with emotions for which she had no names. His eyes were blurred fires of loss or pity or pure rage. "I'm talking about Joan."

For an instant, he raised the *krill* as if he meant to drive it into Linden's chest. Then his features twisted. Roughly he shoved the shrouded weapon back into his jeans. Empty-handed, as if he were defenseless, he tried to explain.

"She's not just a white gold wielder who can make the whole created world into a wasteland if she lives long enough. And she's not just going through the tortures of the damned because bloody *turiya* and the bloody *skest* won't let her die. She was my *wife*. She's Roger's *mother*. I owe her for that." He may have meant restitution or retribution. "She's my problem. I can't do anything else until I deal with her."

While Linden struggled for air, Rime Coldspray stepped forward. To counter Covenant's intensity, she spoke with the steadiness of stone.

"Covenant Timewarden. I perceive now that you have awaited this opportunity, when the *krill* is no longer needed to secure Linden Giantfriend's son. For your restraint, I honor you.

"But the Ardent has spoke of Sandgorgons and *skurj*, and of the imperative need for some response to the manner in which Kastenessen has shackled the Staff of Law and all Earthpower. Is this not more urgent than the plight of a lone madwoman?"

"Hell and blood!" Uselessly Covenant brandished his maimed fists. "I heard the Ardent. I know what's at stake. But I've already sacrificed my own daughter. I can't go on until I've faced Joan. Sometimes we have to do things that are more important than saving the world. Sometimes we can't save anything else until we've cleaned up our own lives."

"Then why," objected the Ironhand, "must you refuse our aid?" Her tone did not waver. "Here are eight Giants, a Manethrall of the Ramen, Stave of the *Haruchai*, and Linden Giantfriend. Surely our combined strengths are not too paltry to be of service."

But her reasoning or her calm seemed to infuriate Covenant. "God in Heaven!" he retorted. "Are *none* of you paying attention? You can't go with me because it's *too dangerous*. Joan makes *caesures*. Just one of those things in the wrong place at the wrong instant, and there won't be anybody left who can even *try* to defend the Land.

"Besides—" With a visible effort, he caught himself; swallowed his extremity. Squaring his shoulders, he faced Linden. "You have other things to do."

"Like what?" Light-headedness had become a roaring in Linden's ears. Black spots danced across her vision like inverted Wraiths. She had no argument except her own weakness. "What do you expect us to do without you? We barely survived Roger and the Cavewights." And Esmer. "We don't even know how to help Jeremiah. What do you think that we can accomplish against Kastenessen and *skurj* and Sandgorgons and *moksha* Jehannum? Against Lord Foul and the damn Worm of the World's End?"

Why do you want to get away from me so badly?

"Linden, stop," Covenant urged. His quiet restraint resembled a kind of flagellation. "You're just intimidating yourself. Everything is simpler than you make it sound. I expect you to do what you've always done. Something *unexpected*. Which you are by God good at. You've surprised me more times than I can count. There's no one else like you.

"Just trust yourself. That's all. That's *all*. Everything else will take care of itself.

"If it doesn't—" Sighing, he shrugged again. "There was nothing you could have done anyway."

Linden found a deep breath, and another. Stave was still holding her. "It's not that easy." Slowly the spots faded from her eyes. "Do you even know where to look for Joan?"

Covenant did not look away. "I can guess. The Ardent brought us this far for a reason. I figure all I have to do now is go farther. If I don't find her, she'll find me."

Before Linden could manage another protest, Manethrall Mahrtiir demanded without preamble, "Will you journey afoot?"

"Hell, no." Now Covenant shifted his attention from Linden. In his mind, apparently, he had already turned away. "We don't have time. Clyme or Branl can summon the Ranyhyn."

In a burst of indignation, the Manethrall asked, "What then becomes of your vow that you will not ride? Must I name you an oath breaker? Did you not once aver to the great horses rearing that you would not ask them to bear you?"

"I did," Covenant admitted. Ignoring the dismay and uncertainty of the company— ignoring Linden—he walked stiffly across the sand, heading along the floor of the ravine. "How often do I have to talk about trust? They're *Ranyhyn*, for God's sake. They'll think of something."

Linden watched him go as if he were forsaking her.

After a few tense strides, he shouted up at the hilltops, "It's time! Call the Ranyhyn!"

But he did not pause for a response from Branl or Clyme. Quickening his pace, he passed between boulders and ragged slopes on either side as if he were eager to confront Joan.

Eager to be done with life.

The Humbled must have heard him. A lone whistle smote Linden's heart. Among the barren hills, it sounded as forlorn as a wail in a lightless cavern.

Clyme or Branl whistled a second time. A third.

In the distance beyond Covenant, three horses came trotting down the shallow canyon.

Two of them were Ranyhyn, Naybahn and Mhornym. The stars on their foreheads gleamed in the thick sunlight.

The third was the Harrow's destrier. Tossing its head in vexation or alarm, the tall brown stallion trotted between Naybahn and Mhornym with a glare of resentment in its eyes, as if the Ranyhyn had compelled it against its will.

As the horses neared Covenant, Clyme and Branl appeared, sprinting down the treacherous hillsides to join him as if nothing could undermine their steps. They reached him moments before the Ranyhyn and the destrier stamped to a halt.

With an air of ceremony, the Humbled greeted their mounts. They may have been speaking welcomes or rituals which had been ancient when Covenant had first visited the Land; but Linden refused to hear them.

Until she saw Covenant heave himself into the Harrow's saddle, she did not realize that he had not taken any of the company's supplies. He had no food, no water, no blankets.

He had said that he would come back; but he behaved like a man who did not expect to return.

He was doing it again; sacrificing himself to spare the people he cared about most.

Was there no one like her? Truly? She did not believe it. But beyond question there was no one like him.

Perhaps that was why he had turned away from her. She had never been his equal.

7.

Implications of Trust

Among eight Giants who towered over her, and Stave and Mahrtiir, who had never wavered, and Jeremiah, who remained as abandoned as a derelict, Linden Avery stood alone, staring hopelessly at the writhe of the ravine where Thomas Covenant, Branl, and Clyme had ridden out of sight.

If she had been able to look at herself, she would have seen a bedraggled figure, worn and unkempt. Her hair had not known the touch of soap or brush for more days than she could count. After her attempts to wash it, it had dried into matted, impossible tangles. Her features had been eroded by care and loss until they resembled Covenant's flensed countenance, but without his indomitable strictures. And the red of her shirt had lost much of its vividness, its clarity. The flannel was a mess of plucked threads and little rents dominated by the bullet hole over her heart. The swatch of fabric which she had torn from the hem for the Mahdoubt no longer seemed to have any significance: it merely made her look even more like a refugee from a better life. The grass stains on her jeans below the knees were as indecipherable as Caerroil Wildwood's runes.

And the Staff of Law, stained to fuligin when its shaft should have been as clean as the One Tree's heartwood— *Its import lies beyond my ken.* Even her use of its flame had become darkness, echoing the condition of her soul: stark and irredeemable.

Covenant's departure was an open wound. Without his ring, he had no defense against *caesures* and chaos. He could not even control the seduction of his broken memories. And Joan *knew* him: she—or *turiya* Raver—could sense his touch on Loric's *krill*. Linden urgently wished to believe that he was not riding to his death; but that hope eluded her.

His abandonment left her with nothing to shield her. In spite of his vulnerabilities, she had counted on him in ways that were too profound for language. Yet he considered his ex-wife more important, or more urgent. *It's like Joan has me on a string. I can't do anything else until I deal with her.*

He had told Linden, *You have other things to do,* but she could not imagine what they might be.

Because Jeremiah was all that endured of the loves which had shaped her life, she dropped the Staff and went to him. With both arms, she hugged him hard, trying to anchor herself on the form that she had nurtured and tended for so many years. He was only a husk of the young man he should have been; an empty hull. But he had always been like this: his vacancy did not diminish his hold on her. And now she knew how he had concealed himself. She had stood in the graveyard of his mind. In some sense, she understood how he had resisted the *croyel*'s torments, and the Despiser's.

But she did *not* understand why Anele's gift of Earthpower had failed to rouse her son. That mystery surpassed her. The vigor of his new theurgies was clear to every dimension of her health-sense. It should have sufficed—yet it was not enough.

While Linden clung to her son, Rime Coldspray cleared her throat. "Linden Giant-friend." Her voice was husky with weariness. A little food and a sufficiency of water could not replenish her spent strength. Nevertheless she sounded grimly determined. "The day flees from us. Soon the sun will near the rim of Landsdrop, and still we stand in this harm-ridden region. We must not delay longer. The Worm of the World's End will not await our readiness to meet it."

Linden tightened her grip on Jeremiah for a moment. Then she let him go. The Ironhand was right. The sunlight slanted from the west, casting shadows like omens after Covenant. The fact that the Worm seemed like an abstraction, a mere word rather than an imminent threat, did not lessen its significance. Turning away from her son, Linden faced the leader of the Swordmainnir.

As if for the first time, she saw how deeply exertion had chiseled Coldspray's visage. The Ironhand bore the marks of strain and imponderable effort like galls on her forehead, around her eyes, along the sides of her mouth. Faint tremors shook her muscles whenever she moved.

Apart from his bandage, Manethrall Mahrtiir's features reflected Coldspray's. His posture slumped uncharacteristically: he carried himself like a man who had cut off his hands by sending his Cords away. Of the three who had labored to honor Anele and Galt, only Stave showed no sign that he had paid a price. His hurts were internal, masked by his *Haruchai* mien and his stoicism.

Fortunately the other Giants had recovered more fully. They had fought as hard as Rime Coldspray; had suffered as much from their wounds. And the healing which Linden had provided for them had been as swift as cruelty: it had its own cost. Latebirth still moved gingerly, protecting her ribs. Both Cabledarm and Frostheart Grueburn were limping, and Onyx Stonemage looked unsure of her balance. Nevertheless they had rested longer, and eaten more, than their Ironhand. They looked ready to wear their armor and carry supplies and travel, at least for a while.

For that Linden could be grateful.

"All right," she sighed to Coldspray. "I'm sick of this place anyway. But there's still the question of where we're going, or what we think that we can do when we get there." Bitterly she added, "Assuming that no one attacks us on the way.

"Covenant—" She swallowed bile and grief. "Abandoning us like that. It changes things." It changed everything. "Maybe we should rethink this whole situation."

Rime Coldspray opened her mouth to reply; but Mahrtiir spoke first. "Ringthane." Fatigue thickened his voice until he seemed to be groaning. "Ere we consider such matters, will you not make some new attempt to bestir your son?" Without his Cords, he was a different man: smaller in some way; perhaps more fragile. Time and again, he had relied on Bhapa and Pahni to compensate for his blindness. "As he is, he remains helpless. And much has been altered since you last strove to retrieve his mind. Can you not now discover some means to restore him to himself?"

Linden shook her head; but she did not respond at once. She had to search for words to describe perceptions which had become plain to her. *How often do I have to talk about trust?* She had made too many mistakes. Worse, she had made the same ones too often. She needed to believe that better solutions existed; but she did not know how.

With an effort of will, she forced herself to say, "He isn't helpless in there. Not really. He's like Anele. He *chose* this. It's his only defense. Or it was. That deserves some respect. I can't think of any other way that he could have protected himself.

"So maybe he's stuck there now," she conceded to forestall protests. "He's been like this for a long time. Maybe he wants to come out and just can't find the way. But I can't help him unless I go deeper than I did before." Much deeper: deep enough to drag him from his graves. "I'll have to *possess* him. And that's just wrong. The Ranyhyn warned me. They showed me how bad things can get if I insist on violating people who have the right to make their own decisions."

More than once, in differing ways, Anele had opposed her impulse to heal him. Before the horserite, Stave had done the same in spite of the injuries that he had received from Esmer.

"I used to be a doctor. A healer for people with broken minds. And the one thing I learned is that I *couldn't* heal them." God, this was hard to admit! She had learned to accept the truth where her patients were concerned. But to say the same about her own son— "They had to heal themselves. My only real job was to help them feel safe so that maybe they would believe that they could risk healing themselves.

"I'm not much of a healer anymore." She had committed such slaughter— "But *possession* is still wrong. I know because it's been done to me." By *moksha* Jehannum. "And I've done it myself." To Covenant. "Covenant keeps telling me to trust myself, but that doesn't make much sense." She meant that it was impossible. "Not after what I've accomplished so far. What does make sense to me is trusting the Ranyhyn.

"They went to a lot of trouble to warn me." She did not want to remember the images with which they had filled her thoughts. "I think it's time that I stopped ignoring them."

Attempts must be made, Mahrtiir had told her days ago, *even when there can be no hope*. But he had also said, *And betimes some wonder is wrought to redeem us*.

She anticipated objections. How could her companions grasp what she was trying to say? None of them had been taken by Ravers, or had participated in Joan's lurid agony, or had become carrion. But Coldspray's only reply was a frown of consideration. None of the other Giants offered an argument. Stave regarded Linden impassively; accepted her. And Mahrtiir—

The Manethrall relaxed visibly. She had eased some unspoken doubt or burden for him. His shoulders lifted as he announced, "Then I see no cause to alter our intent. Earlier we resolved to entrust our course to the will of the Ranyhyn. That choice I have approved. I do so again. Few as we are, we can select no better path. Let Stave of the *Haruchai* summon the great horses. Let us renew our intent to abide by their guidance."

His counsel was a gift. Linden did not want to make more decisions. And in one respect, she was like the Ramen. The prospect of the Ranyhyn eased her spirits. She could find a kind of solace, comfort as visceral as a caress, in the kindness of Hyn's eyes, the security of the mare's strong strides.

Briefly the Ironhand considered Mahrtiir's advice. For a moment, she scanned the reactions of her comrades. When she returned her attention to the Manethrall, and to Linden, her countenance opened into a broad grin.

"Manethrall, your words are folly. By some measure, they are madness. For that reason, they are a delight to us. Are we not Giants? Fools all? And do we not desire to cast our strength against the utter ravage of the Earth? What fate, therefore, can be more condign for us, than that we must commit every passion and every life to the will of beasts that cannot reveal their purposes? Earlier we assented to this course because we saw no other. Now we do so because it gladdens our hearts.

"If it should chance that the Earth and Time endure, tales will one day be told of Giants who dared the destruction of all things at the behest—I mean no offense, Manethrall—at the behest of mere horses."

Mahrtiir also was grinning. Unlike Coldspray's, however, and those of the other Giants, his expression had a whetted edge, fierce and eager, like a promise of vindication.

If Roger or Kastenessen, Linden thought, or even Lord Foul had seen the Manethrall at that moment, they might have felt apprehension writhing in their guts.

"All right," she said again. She tried to sound stronger, and may have succeeded. "Let's see how much ground we can cover without getting into trouble." She meant, Without running into another attack. But she also meant, Without asking too much of the Giants. "I'll never be any readier than this."

Nodding to Linden, Mahrtiir, and the Swordmainnir in turn, Stave raised his hand to his mouth and began the ritual summoning which his ancestors had used during the time of the Bloodguard, and of the Council of Lords.

Three whistles, each as piercing as cries; each separated by half a dozen heartbeats. Linden scarcely had time to shake her head in wonder at the inexplicable magic which enabled the horses of Ra to know hours or days or seasons in advance when and where they would be called, and to arrive when they were needed. Then she heard the muted impact of hooves cantering on packed sand.

She should not have been able to hear it at that distance. Perhaps the sound carried simply because the horses were Ranyhyn, majestic and ineffable, as vital as the Land's pulse of Earthpower, and as numinous as the Hills of Andelain. Soon, however, she saw them. Constrained by the litter of boulders and the quirks of the slopes, they came in single-file: first proud Hynyn, roan and magisterial, then Hyn dappled grey with her star like heraldry on her forehead, then Narunal, palomino and eager—as eager as Mahrtiir, with the same air of fierceness. Just for an instant, Linden thought that there would be no more. But another Ranyhyn followed behind Narunal, another roan, as like to Hynyn as a son, but less heavily muscled, less broad in the chest, and somewhat smaller.

Hynyn, Hyn, and Narunal: Stave, Linden, and Mahrtiir. The last of the ten that had set out from Revelstone with the begrudged permission of the Masters.

And a mount for Jeremiah.

A mount for Jeremiah, who had never ridden and would not throw himself off balance, and could therefore sit his Ranyhyn as safely as if the beast were made of stone.

Linden had watched Naybahn and Mhornym carry Branl and Clyme away. She believed that she would never see Rhohm, Hrama, and Bhanoryl again: their riders were dead. As for Rohnhyn and Naharahn, Bhapa and Pahni, she did not know what to think. She could hardly believe that they would be able to sway the Masters.

But Jeremiah had a mount! He would be better cared-for aback a Ranyhyn than he would have been in her arms. And maybe—Oh, maybe! The experience of riding might serve to guide or lure him out of his dissociation.

She had seen stranger things during her years at Berenford Memorial. Sometimes a simple touch was enough, if it were the right touch given at the right moment—by the right person.

Her hugs were not the reassurance that Jeremiah needed; or she was not. The knowledge was anguish. Nonetheless she told herself that she could be content with any form of consolation that restored his mind.

In their disparate fashions, Stave and Mahrtiir greeted the approach of the Ranyhyn. As the Giants watched, simultaneously bemused and entranced, the former Master spoke formally of *Land-riders and proud-bearers, sun-flesh and sky-mane.* At the same time, the Manethrall prostrated himself, pressing his forehead to the sand in a manner that seemed both self-effacing and exultant.

Clearly none of the horses had run hard or suffered trials: a dramatic contrast to their state when they had been called in Andelain. They must have left the Hills in plenty of time, and known of a comparatively direct descent from the Upper Land.

With his neck imperiously arched, Hynyn stamped to a halt in front of Stave and whinnied like a shout of defiance. Prancing, Hyn moved among the Giants toward Linden. The mare's affection was plain as she nuzzled Linden's shoulder, asking to be petted. Linden complied willingly; but she did not look away from Hyn's companions.

Narunal stopped near Mahrtiir's out-stretched arms and nickered a soft demand. Apparently the stallion was impatient with Mahrtiir's obeisance and wanted him to rise. The fourth horse paused a few paces behind the others. The younger roan's eyes were fixed on Jeremiah, but Linden could not interpret their expression. Was that pride? Anticipation? Dread?

When Hynyn whinnied again, Mahrtiir rose to his feet. For a moment, he stroked Narunal's nose and neck, communing in some intuitive fashion with his mount. Then he turned to Linden.

"Ringthane," he pronounced distinctly, "here is Khelen, young among the stallions of the herd. Youth to youth, he has come to bear your son—if you will consent. But he requires your consent. He has not yet inherited his sire's pride, and he is cognizant—as are all of the great horses—that he offers to assume a charge both perilous and exalted. Will you grant him leave to care for your son? He will do so with his life."

Linden could not imagine how the Manethrall knew such things. Nevertheless she believed him. Carefully courteous, she replied, "Please thank Khelen for me. He has my consent."

Mahrtiir answered her with a Ramen bow; but he said nothing. Doubtless he had reason to trust that the Ranyhyn understood her. Instead of relaying her words, he whirled away and sprang onto Narunal's back. Indeed, he seemed to flow into his seat as though he had spent all of his life riding; as though he and his Cords were not the first Ramen to ever sit astride Ranyhyn.

Tentatively Khelen moved a few steps closer to Jeremiah.

"Again with your consent, Linden Giantfriend," said Stormpast Galesend briskly. But she did not wait for Linden's response. Lifting Jeremiah, the Swordmain set him down on Khelen's back.

Hoping, Linden held her breath.

For a long moment, Khelen stood utterly motionless. If the fouled scent of Jeremiah's pajamas disturbed him, the young stallion did not show it. Instead he appeared to be waiting for some reaction from Jeremiah: some flinch of fright or hint of relaxation.

But Jeremiah gave no sign of consciousness. His mind was too deeply buried. He sat exactly as he had stood a few heartbeats earlier, slack-lipped and silt-eyed, oblivious to the saliva gathering at the corners of his mouth.

Oh, well, Linden sighed to herself. Maybe when Khelen started to walk—or to run—

Finally Khelen tossed his head, made a whickering sound like a query. Hynyn answered with a snort of command; and the younger roan began to move away from the stream, carrying Jeremiah as if the boy were a treasure.

At last, Linden looked away. When she glanced at Stave, he came to boost her onto Hyn's back.

Almost at once, Hyn's familiar ability to communicate ease and stability settled into Linden's muscles, although she had not ridden for days that felt as long as seasons. As Stave mounted Hynyn, Linden nodded to Rime Coldspray, who answered with a grin as wide as Pitchwife's.

"Thus we turn to a new heading," the Ironhand proclaimed, "foolishly, and glad of it. Many have been the vagaries of our journey, and extreme its trials. Each new course has been as unforeseen as the Soulbiter, as unforeseeable—and betimes as reluctant to permit passage. Yet never, I deem, have we sailed seas as chartless as those now spread before us.

"Had we the strength for exuberance, we would announce with songs our pleasure that in the Sargasso of the Earth's fate we will be guided by the innominate mystery of these Ranyhyn."

"Aye," assented Frostheart Grueburn gruffly. "And if we reserve our breath for wheezing, we will trust that joy is in the ears that hear, not in the mouth that does not sing."

Chuckling, Cabledarm shouldered a sack of supplies. In spite of her unsteadiness, Onyx Stonemage took another: the last of the Ardent's foodstuffs and waterskins. Cirrus Kindwind hefted the only bedroll. Then, laughing softly, she tossed it to Stave: a feigned admission that it was too heavy for her. The Haruchai caught it as if it were weightless and set it across his thighs.

"Ringthane?" Mahrtiir asked with something of Hynyn's brazen assurance in his voice.

"Sure," Linden muttered. She was watching Jeremiah again as if her attentiveness might serve to rouse him. "I assume that you can tell the Ranyhyn what we want." Somehow. "If they refuse, we'll know soon enough."

The Manethrall barked like one of the ur-viles. Then he bent low over Narunal's neck, stroking the stallion as he whispered words in a language that sounded like nickering. Linden thought that she caught Kelenbhrabanal's name, but the rest escaped her.

If the Giants understood, they only grinned, and checked their weapons, and readied themselves to leave the stream.

Narunal responded with a neigh as clarion as Hynyn's. At once, Mahrtiir's mount turned to retrace his path along the floor of the ravine. Without any sign from Stave that Linden could discern, Hynyn followed. And Khelen went next, stepping with such care that Jeremiah was not jostled or disturbed in any way.

Snorting soft reassurances, Hyn took a position behind Khelen. And after them came the eight Swordmainnir led by Rime Coldspray, with Bluntfist in the rear.

Clearly the Ranyhyn had elected to accept at least this much responsibility for the company's role in the Land's fate.

ↂↄ

W hile the ravine twisted westward, and its floor formed a comparatively clear path, the Ranyhyn followed it. But as the company moved beyond the region of battle, beyond the cairns, the hills on both sides began to slump. At intervals now, Linden glimpsed more distant landscapes to the north and south: barren slopes interspersed with swaths of dirt and gravel like long-desiccated swales.

When Narunal and the other Ranyhyn finally turned away from the fading trail of sand onto a broad field of grit and fine dust made hazardous by shards of flint, they surprised Linden by heading into the southeast.

Surely they should be going northwest? Toward Mount Thunder, if not toward Salva Gildenbourne? In that direction, the *skurj* and the Sandgorgons were laying waste to the forest as they moved to defend Kastenessen. Yet the horses chose the southeast, picking their way warily among flint splinters and knives.

Were they following Covenant? Linden's heart squirmed at the thought. He had suggested that he intended to look for Joan along the same heading that the Ardent had taken from the Lost Deep: *this* heading. Did the Ranyhyn believe that Covenant would need Linden's help when he faced his ex-wife at last?

If so, she wanted to hurry. She feared losing him to a *caesure* more than his rejection; his efforts to spare her.

But the company could not hasten: not yet. The horses had to be careful where they placed their hooves. And the Giants—They plodded doggedly ahead as if they were impervious to sharp stones, raising small puffs of dust with every heavy step; but weariness clogged their strides. They moved like women carrying boulders on their backs.

"Stave?" Linden tried not to raise her voice or sound apprehensive. "Did Covenant go this way? Can you tell?"

Stave said nothing. Instead Mahrtiir answered, "The Ranyhyn have diverged from their path toward us. Yet ahead of us lie the marks of three horses, one shod. I judge that we trail after Naybahn, Mhornym, and the Harrow's mount.

"Lacking ordinary sight," he admitted, vexed by his limitations, "I am no longer capable of true Ramen scoutcraft. Yet the Timewarden's passage with the Humbled is plain here. For the present, his way is ours."

"Can you tell—?" Linden began. She did not know the extent of Mahrtiir's communion with Narunal and the other horses. "Can you tell if we're going to keep on following him?"

"Ringthane, I cannot." His assertion clearly did not trouble the Manethrall. "The bond between the Ranyhyn and their Ramen is not"—he seemed to search for the right word—"explicit in that fashion. We are the servants of the great horses, nothing more. And the essence of our service is *service*. We do not vaunt ourselves by endeavoring to comprehend more than we are given."

"So you don't know what they have in mind?"

"I do not," Mahrtiir stated calmly.

Linden scowled at his back. "Then how do you know that they understand what we're asking them to do?"

"Ringthane." Now the Manethrall's tone revealed an edge of asperity. "That we do not strive to grasp the thoughts of the Ranyhyn does not imply that they cannot grasp ours. How otherwise are we able to serve them, if they cannot comprehend us?"

"The Timewarden has spoken of trust. And you have given your assent. If you now wish to recant, do so. Ask of Hyn what you will. *Command* her according to the dictates of your heart. I will await the outcome with interest."

Just for a moment, Linden considered taking the dare. She wanted another chance to be with Covenant. To protect him if she could. To understand why he had turned his back on her.

But then she shook her head; resisted an impulse to slap herself. —spoken of trust. She needed some way to control her accelerating descent into darkness; and she knew from long experience that she could not refuse the logic of despair if she became incapable of trust. Eventually she would succumb—

Days ago, she had urged her companions to doubt her. All well and good, as far as it went. She had doubted herself: therefore she had needed to believe that her friends made their own choices freely. But the ultimate implication of her insistence then was that *she* had doubted *them*.

Was that not why Kevin Landwaster had committed the Ritual of Desecration? He had blamed himself for the Land's plight—and had not trusted any other power to accomplish what he could not.

Now Mahrtiir had effectively challenged her to admit the truth about her doubts; and she could not. She had already done too much harm. She no longer had any real choice except to cling to her friends and the Ranyhyn.

In the end, every other alternative would lead her back to She Who Must Not Be Named.

Her silence seemed to satisfy Mahrtiir. He held his head high and his back straight, concentrating ahead of Narunal as he led the company off the flints into a region of shale and sandstone mounded like barrows or the detritus of glaciers.

There the Ranyhyn could have quickened their pace safely. But they did not. Even at a canter, Covenant and the Humbled might be leagues ahead of them by now. Nevertheless Narunal continued to move as if the Ranyhyn had no purpose other than to conserve the stamina of the Giants. As if Linden and her companions had chosen to put their faith in an illusion.

As if the Ranyhyn intended to let her slip deeper into despair.

ᔓᓂ

As the sun sank past the rim of Landsdrop, casting the abused terrain of the Lower Land into shadow, *caesures* began to appear. At first, they were sporadic and transient; frequent only in comparison to their occurrence on the Upper Land. They danced at intervals across ground that had been laid waste by ancient battles and rapine, storms of theurgy, bitter despoilage: danced and flickered and went out, posing no threat. But as night gathered over the extended litter of mounds, the Falls came more often, and lasted longer. They hit with the force of a concussion, stirred time and stone and air into turmoil. When they vanished, the sudden vacuum of their absence tugged at the breath in Linden's lungs.

Somewhere Joan's hysteria appeared to be approaching a crisis. Watching the horizons anxiously, Linden could only surmise that Covenant was headed in the right direction—and that Joan knew he was coming.

Joan, or *turiya* Herem: there was no useful distinction, apart from the fact that Joan was weaker than the Raver.

As far as Linden could see, Joan's weakness was Covenant's sole hope. The *krill* and the Humbled could not protect him from gyres of chaos more destructive than tornadoes. Even the Ranyhyn could not—and he was mounted only on the Harrow's destrier.

Despite the erratic stutter and squall of *caesures*, however, Narunal, Hynyn, Hyn, and Khelen retained their ability to find forage and water. Somehow they discovered small rills in cracks among the rocks, stubborn clumps of grass in hollows that looked too dry to sustain vegetation. Without turning aside from Covenant's trail, they located occasional clusters of *aliantha*.

In the aftermath of the Despiser's wars and workings, treasure-berries grew too sparsely to meet the needs of the Giants. Still, a little of the viridian fruit, and a sparing use of the Ardent's supplies, and a few opportunities to refill the waterskins kept the Swordmainnir on their feet.

Lit only by the stars, by the first faint suggestion of moonlight, and by the wild glare of *caesures* as uncounted centuries of day and night were flung together, the company kept moving. Apparently the Ranyhyn had decided that they could not afford rest.

Disturbed by the unpredictable eruption of Falls, Linden became less and less sure of her surroundings. Details of stone and terrain blurred into vagueness. In addition, she felt a storm coming. The nerves of her skin tasted confusion in the air, abraded winds rising, ambient pressures shifting in response to the violence of the *caesures*. But she made no attempt to estimate the severity of the storm. The effects of Joan's madness demanded her attention. If a Fall came too close, she had to be ready.

Concentrating on dangers, she was taken by surprise when the horses stopped. They had entered a low vale between outcroppings of basalt so smooth and slick that they hinted at the distant abandonment of the stars. A tentative trickle of water ran down the vale-bottom, tending eastward; and tough grasses clung to life there, interspersed with more *aliantha* than the company had found elsewhere.

There the Manethrall and then Stave dismounted. As Narunal and Hynyn trotted away, Mahrtiir announced quietly, "Some rest we must have. The Ranyhyn will watch over us."

In a chorus of soft groans and sighs, the Giants gathered around Linden and Hyn, Jeremiah and Khelen. Some of them loosened their cataphracts, dropped the shaped stones to the grass. While Stormpast Galesend lifted Jeremiah from his mount, Cabledarm and Onyx Stonemage began to unpack a meal. All of the Swordmainnir were uneasy, troubled by the possible burgeoning of *caesures*, the approach of bad weather. But they could not refuse a chance for food and sleep.

As Khelen cantered away after Narunal and Hynyn, Linden slipped down from Hyn's back; let the mare go. Stave had already set out the bedroll for her, but she ignored it. Of Mahrtiir, she asked, "Did Covenant stop here?"

Like the Manethrall and the Giants, she spoke softly. She did not know the Lower Land; did not know what waited in the night. Loud sounds might attract notice—

"I gauge that he did," Mahrtiir replied, almost whispering. "Hooves have preceded us. Treasure-berries have been plucked. But his pause was brief. Had he lingered here, more sign of his mount would be evident."

"How far ahead is he?"

"Perhaps five leagues." Now the Manethrall sounded less assured. "Certainly no more than ten. At greater speed, the marks of his passing would be more distinct, the strides longer."

Linden tried to consider the implications of Covenant's progress. But she could not imagine them: her scant experience of the Lower Land did not extend this far south.

Keeping her voice low, she asked Stave where she was.

Around her, the Giants gave no obvious sign that they were listening. Instead they prepared a meal, or gathered *aliantha*, or shed their armor and massaged each other's sorest muscles. Yet Linden felt the weight of their oblique attention.

Only Jeremiah appeared to hear and understand nothing.

The shared memories of Stave's people were precise. "At present," he said without hesitation, "we travel the arid marge which separates the foothills of Landsdrop from the wetlands of Sarangrave Flat. This terrain is not wide. Its constriction may account for the fact that our path follows the Unbeliever's.

"Where we now rest, Landsdrop continues to the southeast. If the Ranyhyn do not quicken their pace, we will remain much as we are for perhaps another day. Then, however, we will attain both the easternmost cliffs of Landsdrop and the southern reaches of the Sarangrave. In that place, the broken plinth of the Colossus will stand high above us, while beyond it the River Landrider plunges from the Plains of Ra to become the Ruinwash."

"Aye," Mahrtiir put in: a muffled growl. "And along the leagues of Landsdrop which demark the Plains of Ra are many ascents. There the armies of Fangthane breached the Upper Land in an age long past, bringing their savagery first to the Ranyhyn and their Ramen."

Stave nodded. "Beyond the Sarangrave, the Spoiled Plains fill the Lower Land both eastward to the Sunbirth Sea and southward beyond the ken of the *Haruchai*. There the purpose of the Ranyhyn may diverge from the ur-Lord's, if they do not first turn to essay Landsdrop. Our path and his will no longer be constrained by the perils of the Flat, and of the lurker.

"From the Colossus," he continued, "the shattered site of Foul's Creche lies somewhat south of east, torn from a promontory of cliffs which front the Sunbirth Sea. Between the Colossus and that rent habitation are arrayed the Spoiled Plains, still rife with the effects of Corruption's malice, then the Shattered Hills, a maze and snare for the unwary, and last the long-cooled floes of lava which were once Hotash Slay. In the time of the Unbeliever's first triumph over Corruption, Hotash Slay formed the final defense of Foul's Creche, ancient Ridjeck Thome. After the destruction wrought by the ur-Lord's victory, however, the lava spilled into the Sea until its sources were drained.

"The Masters seldom journey there, seeing no purpose in the visitation of sites where memories of Corruption's cruelest evils linger. But upon occasion they have confirmed the lifelessness of his former abode."

For a moment, Linden no longer heard what Stave was saying. He had triggered a memory that stopped her ears; that almost stopped her heart.

Joan.

A wasteland of shattered stone, the rubble of a riven cliff.

The unmistakable tumble and flow of surf crashing forever on rocks.

And *turiya* Herem.

Oh, Covenant! He was going—He was going *there*.

Then the abrupt glare and seethe of a *caesure* snatched at her. Instinctively her heart clenched: she scrambled for Earthpower.

An instant later, however, her senses snapped into focus, and she realized that the Fall was too far away to harm the company. If it came closer—

It did not. For a few heartbeats, it writhed eastward, increasing the distance. Then it vanished with the suddenness of a thunderclap.

Linden took a deep breath, loosened her grip on the Staff; tried to calm her hammering pulse.

God in Heaven! Covenant—

The storm brewed by so many temporal disruptions was growing stronger. But that threat was easier to ignore.

She had to force words between the mallet-strokes of her heart. "That's where Covenant is going."

Stave seemed to understand her. "Mayhap," he said with a shrug. "Or mayhap his goal lies more to the south. Or—"

Linden cut him off. "He's going to Foul's Creche."

"Are you certain, Ringthane?" Mahrtiir asked tensely. And Rime Coldspray added, "How have you derived this knowledge?"

"She's *Joan*," Linden replied as if that were answer enough. "Where else would she be?" But then she compelled herself to explain. A promontory jutting into the sea. Torn apart when Covenant destroyed the Illearth Stone. "I saw her. I was there."

"You weren't," she told Mahrtiir. He had said so when they had spoken of this in Revelstone. "I'm talking about that first *caesure*. The one that took us to the Staff. The Ranyhyn and the ur-viles protected you." She turned to Stave. "And you didn't let yourself get sucked in. You recognized the Raver. You were strong enough to stay away.

"But I couldn't do that. I was caught in Joan's mind. I saw what she saw, heard what she heard. That was part of what made the whole thing so terrible." In the spaces between her heartbeats, the memory was more vivid to her than any of her companions, more immediate than the coming storm, or the night's unfathomable implications. "I saw the remains of a broken cliff. I heard waves.

"Covenant is going to Foul's Creche."

The Giants studied her closely. But they said nothing: they had not shared her experiences within Falls.

Stave considered Linden's assertion, then nodded. "I cannot gainsay you. If the Unbeliever must confront his doom at Ridjeck Thome, it is fitting that he should do so. Yet this insight does not elucidate our own path.

"Chosen"—abruptly his manner intensified, although he did not raise his voice—"the Ardent spoke of a need for death. Recalling his words, I must observe that no region of the Land has endured more carnage than the Spoiled Plains. The ravages inflicted upon the Upper Land pale beside the multiplicity of blights and bloodshed which the Spoiled Plains have endured. Their condition is the unredeemed outcome of Corruption's malice.

"Is it not therefore plausible that the answer to your purported need lies there?"

Linden ignored him. Another *caesure* glared and crackled in the west. A league away? Less? It extinguished itself quickly; but it made her flinch nonetheless. God, Joan was driving herself crazy—

She knew Covenant was coming.

A storm of her own gathered in Linden. "*Damn* it!" she cried. "We have to stop him." Letting him go, she had made another hideous mistake. "We have to catch up with him and stop him!"

The Ironhand stared at her. "With our strength as it is, and the Ranyhyn content walking? How shall we accomplish such a feat? And did the Timewarden not forbid our presence?"

"He said it was too dangerous," Linden retorted. An excuse for leaving her. "But he got it backward. It's too dangerous *for him*. He's gambling that Joan's need to hurt him is going to break her before she can destroy him." What else could he do? Loric's *krill* could not ward him from wild magic. "But he isn't just gambling with his own life. He's gambling with *everything*." She hardly noticed that she was shouting. "And he's *doing it without me!* I'm the only one who can protect him, and he couldn't wait to get away!"

"Madness," assented Coldspray equably. If Linden's vehemence troubled her, she did not show it. "Utter and undoubted folly." She may have been chuckling. "Indeed, were I not myself deranged, made so by the sad truth that I am a Giant withal, I might venture to suggest that his conduct is very nearly as demented as our own. He merely knows with whom he wagers, and how, and why. The same cannot be said of us. We have gone further, for we can name neither our foe nor our intent."

Before Linden could respond, Frostheart Grueburn advised in an amiable grumble, "Do not heed her, Linden Giantfriend. The Ironhand jests lamely, like a Swordmain with one foot cleft. She means to aver only that in straits as extreme as ours, one gamble is much like another.

"Thomas Covenant wagers all things on his own strength and resource, and on the friable extravagance of a possessed white gold wielder. We have chosen to entrust our fate, and the Land's, and the Earth's to the Ranyhyn. Time—if it endures—will reveal who has been wiser."

"And is it not also true," Mahrtiir suggested, "that we are in greater peril from *caesures* and other evils than the Timewarden? We are many by comparison, and commensurately vulnerable. He and the Humbled are few. Surely their need for protection does not exceed ours."

"It addition," Stave stated flatly, "it is the word of the Unbeliever that you have a separate task to perform. If you strive to preserve him, you may thwart some greater purpose which we do not yet comprehend."

Protests clamored in Linden. You don't understand. She was running out of ways to fend off the darkness that filled her heart. I want to do something that *makes sense*. I can't let Joan kill him.

But that was not what he desired of her. *I expect you to do what you've always done. Something* unexpected. And she had already missed her chance to help him: she knew that. When she had let him ride away, she had surrendered her right to share his fate—or to ask him to share hers. It was too late to change her mind. None of her mistakes could be undone. If Joan killed Covenant, Linden would have no one to blame except herself.

Trust was a bitter joke—and she had forgotten how to laugh.

Avoiding the concerned stares of her companions, she tried to pretend that she had recovered her emotional balance. "All right. I understand." She did not want their misdirected reassurances. "I just wish I could be with him."

"Don't worry about me. You should get some rest, all of you. Sleep if you can. I'm going to find someplace where I can see farther. The Ranyhyn can't save us if a Fall gets too close."

Then she turned away, hoping to forestall arguments. Unsure of her ability to climb the basalt in such darkness, she began to walk along the vale after the horses.

She heard the Giants murmuring anxiously to each other, felt Mahrtiir's troubled regard and Stave's blunt gaze. Jeremiah's emptiness made it plain that he did not need her. Tightening her grasp on the Staff, she pushed herself to walk more quickly.

Her parents had taught her how to meet despair; but there were other answers. She had learned a few from her patients in Berenford Memorial.

Soon she found a southward slope beyond the basalt. But when she climbed to the hillcrest, she was not high enough to scan the dark horizons for more than a stone's throw in any direction; so she moved toward the nearest obstruction and plodded upward again.

That rise afforded her a clear line of sight for perhaps a third of a league on all sides. Was it enough? She did not know. But the vantage suited her. Here she could no longer feel the emanations of her companions. And the ground was littered with loose stones, some of them sharp enough for her purpose.

She was as weary in her own way as any of the Swordmainnir, yet she needed to stay awake. Hunger and thirst might suffice to keep her from dozing for a time. Cold might help. But she needed more, and had other plans.

Somewhere in the night, one of the Ranyhyn nickered a query. Surely that was Hyn? But Linden did not know how to respond; and the soft call was not repeated.

She needed to be left alone. When she had seated herself on uncomfortable rocks exposed to the accumulating turbulence in the air, however, her nerves recognized Stave's approach. He held a waterskin and a handful of treasure-berries. Over one shoulder, he carried the bedroll.

Sighing, she composed herself to endure his company, at least for a little while.

Fortunately he said nothing. Instead he gave her the waterskin, dropped the bedroll nearby. Then he stood motionless beside her, holding *aliantha* in his cupped fingers so that she could accept the fruit at her own pace.

He had lost his son so that hers could be saved. He may have understood more of her emotions than she cared to consider.

For his sake, she made an effort to drink and eat slowly; to convey gratitude by savoring the vitality of the berries. But the strain of his presence was too much for her. Soon she began to gulp from the waterskin. A moment later, she scooped the fruit from his hand so that he would have no excuse to stay with her.

He did not leave. He was Stave: he had declared his allegiance in spite of its extreme price.

After a moment, she begged him to go. "Let me do this by myself. Please." Her voice was little more than a croak. "I'm lost. Too many of us have died, and I've done too much killing. I'm like Jeremiah. I need to find my own way out."

She prayed that he would not speak. At first, he did not. Then he advised sternly, "Heed the Ranyhyn, Chosen. Their gifts are many. It may be that they are able to divine coming disturbances of Time, or to perceive Falls in the instant of their creation. If so, they will forewarn you."

After that, he was gone. With her health-sense, Linden watched him until she was sure that he had returned to the Giants and Mahrtiir. Then she finished her small meal, drank more water, and turned her attention to other things.

She needed a response to despair that did not require her own death; and she could not think of a way to help Jeremiah.

Fumbling, she searched around her for a stone that she could use: one with a raw edge or a jagged point.

The sky overhead was a glittering loveliness of stars, profuse and forsaken. Covenant had gone to face Joan without her. She had no way of knowing what the Ranyhyn wanted from her—or for her. The Worm of the World's End was coming to the Land. If the stars were sentient in any sense, their bereavement was too vast and irreducible for comprehension.

Finally her fingers found a stone that suited her. It seemed sharp enough. It had a good point.

She rolled up her left sleeve, studied the faint pallor of her skin. But her father had killed himself by cutting his wrists. After all these years, she still intended to refuse his legacy. Tugging at the fabric of her jeans, she worked one leg up to her knee.

An answer to darkness. A way to control her despair so that she did not sink deeper.

Hunched over herself, she gripped the stone and began scraping cuts into the sensitive flesh of her shin.

That *hurt*. Of course it did. But the pain would also help her. As Berenford Memorial's physician, she had worked with a number of cutters, self-mutilators. Cutting was a common symptom because it was so effective. Voluntary physical hurts suppressed helpless emotional anguish. Cutters damaged themselves so that the pain would calm them. It galvanized their few residual strengths. For some, it provided a relief as exquisite as joy.

It might do the same for her.

Using an edge and point as raw as the teeth of a saw, she tried to cut from memory the inadvertent pattern of the grass stains on her jeans into the human skin of her shin and calf.

Perhaps she would have succeeded. She might have attained the whetted peace that she had witnessed in her patients. Given time, she might even have managed to replicate *the mark of fecundity and long grass*, the sign that she had *paid the price of woe*. But while she gasped at each kind, cruel gouge and tear, she realized suddenly that Hyn was standing over her.

The mare was little more than a silhouette against the blighted horizons. The faint gleam of the star on her forehead was barely visible: her eyes were only dim suggestions. Still her presence shamed Linden.

No cutter wanted to be watched. Being watched reversed the craved effects of the pain. Linden needed those effects. Nevertheless Hyn denied them.

Groaning, Linden cast away her stone. Pulled down the leg of her jeans. Struggled to her feet. She wanted to swear at Hyn, but she had no curses left: none that were as bitter as her life.

Now she could only hope that she had hurt herself enough to stay awake as long as her last companions needed her.

As long as Joan lived and could hurl *caesures*—

‹∞›

When the sun rose at last, it came in a brief blare of crimson, as if the horizon were occluded with dust or ash; omens. Then storms came tumbling over the region, and the light was gone.

They seemed to arise from all directions at random, colliding with such force that their thunder made the ground tremble. Wind and rain slapped at Linden from one side and then the other, a turmoil of spats and downpours that changed more swiftly than she could gauge them. This was no natural battering boil of rains and gusts. Nor was it deliberate, driven by malice. Instead the conflict of squalls and deluges was the oblique consequence of too many Falls.

Its turmoil felt like a presage.

Now more than ever, she had to rely on the senses of the Ranyhyn. Wild modulations of violence confused her discernment. She would not be able to recognize a *caesure* until it was almost on top of her, if Hyn or the other horses did not give warning.

When the company set out again, Linden rode wrapped in the ground-cloth that had covered the last of the Ardent's bedrolls. It gave her a measure of protection, slowed the seepage of cold into her bones. But it did not block the erratic flick and cut of rain that stung her exposed cheeks, her open eyes.

At her request, Stormpast Galesend had wrapped the blankets around Jeremiah. But the boy made no effort to hold them. He did not react to the smack of raindrops in thick gouts and thin spatters, the lash of shearing winds. Galesend was forced to walk at Khelen's side so that she could replace Jeremiah's coverings whenever they slipped from his shoulders.

Perhaps he did not need them. Perhaps his bestowed strength warded him from cold and wet and wind. It had done so for Anele. Still Linden was glad that Galesend did what she could to shield the boy.

Under the circumstances, Linden was not surprised to hear that Mahrtiir had lost Covenant's trail. The Manethrall sounded angry at himself; but she wondered how even the most cunning and sighted of the Ramen could have identified hoof-marks on this sodden ground in this weather. In any case, she knew where Covenant was headed. And Clyme and Branl were with him: he would not lose his way.

Still the Ranyhyn refused to travel faster than the Giants could walk. As the storms closed around Linden, constricting her percipience, they inspired a kind of claustrophobia; and she could not resist asking Hyn for haste. But Hyn ignored her. Together the horses maintained a trot that felt as slow as plodding.

Yet they were not tired. Linden could feel the ready power of Hyn's muscles. And the Ranyhyn did not lack for provender. At irregular intervals, they continued to find patches of sufficient grass for themselves, huddled clumps of *aliantha* for their riders. When they did so, they did not resume their battered trek until both they and their riders had eaten. Stubbornly they allowed Covenant and the Humbled to run farther and farther ahead.

Did they seek to diminish the likelihood that the company would be caught by a *caesure*? Linden did not know. Occasionally Narunal or Hynyn trumpeted a warning.

At those times, however, she felt nothing except the moil and barrage of rain, the incessant to-and-fro of wind. Falls had apparently vanished from this region. Joan was concentrating her madness elsewhere, or she had exhausted her fury, or she was dead—or Linden was wrong. If the mounts were alert to some other peril, Linden could not detect it. Even when she used the Staff to extend her senses, she recognized no threat except the weather and her own frailty.

What could the great horses fear under these conditions, if they were not endangered by *caesures*?

Gradually the terrain changed. For a time, there were mounds, and eroded thrusts of rock like worn-out teeth, and drenched ridges. Then the ground became poured sheets of dark stone as smooth as recent lava. Later the stone gave way to a plain so featureless that it seemed to have been pounded flat. Later still, erosion gullies like cracks in the landscape's flesh complicated the company's path. Then came more hills arrayed in lines like barricades raised to force anyone advancing from the northwest to turn eastward.

Doubtless the mounts and the Giants could have held to their course. Long millennia had softened the contours of the hills. Shaking their heads, however, and snorting in apparent disgust, the Ranyhyn allowed themselves to be deflected. For the first time, they began to travel more east than southeast.

Toward Foul's Creche? Linden had no idea.

Late in the afternoon, the storms finally resolved their contention. The winds became a rough blast out of the west: the rains dwindled. Soon the clouds broke open behind the company, letting sunlight touch them for the first time since dawn. Thunderheads scudded along. In a rush, the sky cleared.

But as Linden watched the clouds race away, she saw with a shudder that the revealed sky was not blue. Instead it had acquired a dun color tinged with grey like smoke as if the gales of an immense dust-storm had found untended flames somewhere on the Upper Land and fanned them into wildfires.

Like the storms, the hues staining the air did not feel *wrong* or malevolent. Nonetheless they were palpably unnatural. The Upper Land was not a desert, or barren: it could not be lashed to produce so much dust. And the season was still spring. Its rains had been too plentiful to permit a conflagration on that scale.

"Stave!" Linden cried. The wind tore his name from her mouth. "What is *that*?" Shivering, she gestured at the sky.

At a word from Stave, Hynyn came to Hyn's side. The former Master leaned closer to Linden.

"Chosen, I know not. The *Haruchai* have no experience of such weather. In a distant age, the Bloodguard saw evils storm from the east, the handiwork of Corruption. But this is altogether unlike those blasts."

"You will observe, however," called Rime Coldspray, "that these strange taints do not ride the wind! They spread from the east. In *Bhrathairealm*, such skies prevail upon occasion. They arise among the nameless theurgies of the Great Desert. Elsewhere we have not witnessed their like!"

The Worm, Linden thought. Oh, God. *Caesures* had not filled the sky with dust and ash. Lethal forces of a different kind were starting to spread—

The refusal of the Ranyhyn to hurry baffled her completely.

Yet the horses were sensitive to the condition of their drenched riders and companions. Without warning, Narunal veered aside into a breach between the nearest hills, a gap like Bargas Slit or the crooked cut of a plow. When Hyn followed the others, Linden soon found herself in a scallop on one side of the breach; a hollow of comparative shelter formed by the wearing away of softer soil from the hill's underlying rock. It resembled a scaur in miniature, barely wide and deep enough to hold Linden, Jeremiah, Stave, Mahrtiir, and eight Giants. Still it offered a degree of protection from the blast's flail.

The Manethrall dismounted; and at once, Narunal cantered away. Khelen did the same after Galesend lifted Jeremiah to the ground. Wearily Linden slipped off Hyn's back. As her legs took her weight, neglected pain stabbed her shin. Unable to hide her reaction, she flinched.

There was still too much wind, too much cold. Nevertheless she was reluctant to call fire from her Staff. She did not want to be reminded of flames as black and lamentable as the wood. And she did not want to announce the company's location to any being capable of spotting her power. But she and Mahrtiir needed heat, even if their companions—and Jeremiah, perhaps—did not.

Gritting her teeth so that they would not chatter, Linden summoned flames.

They were as dark as she had feared: an impenetrable ebony like obsidian which had never seen the light of day. Apparently the change in her was permanent. She could do nothing clean.

Nevertheless her fire was *warm*. Its effects remained benign: a tangible relief. Her chills receded in waves like a withdrawing tide. Around her, the Giants opened their arms to her blackness and smiled. After a moment, Mahrtiir's manner rediscovered its familiar edge, its implied craving for struggle. Only Stave and Jeremiah seemed to derive no comfort from her gentle efforts.

Ignoring her private revulsion, Linden sustained her exertion of Earthpower until every outward sign that her companions had suffered in the storms was eased. When she quenched her flames at last, she found that she, too, felt somewhat eased. Their benevolence was balm to her sore heart. The blackness was in her as it was in the wood, not in the magicks her Staff wielded. In spite of her sins and her despair, she had not tarnished the fundamental vitality of Earthpower and Law.

Not yet—

In any case, the armor of the Giants had absorbed a surprising amount of warmth. It radiated in the hollow, as affectionate as grins and jests. Disregarding the truncated winds, the sodden ground, the promise of a chilled night, Cabledarm and Onyx Stonemage began unpacking food and waterskins. Stormpast Galesend took Jeremiah's steaming blankets, squeezed out as much water as she could, then draped them around him again.

While Stave set out Linden's ground-cloth so that she and a few others would have a dry place to sit, she asked him, "So where are we? How far have we come?"

He appeared to consult his store of memories. "These hills have urged us away from Landsdrop toward Sarangrave Flat. I gauge that we rest some three leagues north of the promontory of the Colossus."

"How close are we to the Sarangrave? Are we in danger?"

Why had Narunal and Hynyn whinnied so urgently during the day, when there were no *caesures*?

Without hesitation, Stave answered, "I estimate the distance at less than a league. However, the Flat's proximity poses scant peril. In this region, the wetland is extensive but shallow, little more than a marsh sporadically snared with quagmires. The lurker prefers the deeper mire within the heart of the Sarangrave, and in Lifeswallower. Its vast bulk and ferocity require more noisome waters.

"It is conceivable," he admitted impassively, "that the monstrous wight which the Ardent has named Horrim Carabal is cognizant of our presence. To the certain knowledge of the *Haruchai*, the lurker is avid to devour all Earthpower"—he paused to glance at Mahrtiir—"including that which the Ranyhyn possess. It may crave any form of theurgy. But its hungers do not respond swiftly. The lurker is fearsome and fatal, but first it is slow, suggesting that its attention must be drawn to Earthpower from a considerable distance or depth.

"Perhaps the lurker has noted your son's passage. Perhaps it is able to discern the Ranyhyn. Perhaps it has sensed your use of the Staff. Nevertheless its reach is not known to extend beyond the bounds of the Sarangrave."

"I am content," the Manethrall announced when Linden did not speak again. "The appetite of the lurker for the Ranyhyn is familiar to us. It elicits a distress among the great horses which other hazards do not. Plainly some alarm troubled them during the day. Yet no *caesure* appeared. Therefore I am inclined to believe that they were disturbed by the scent of the lurker.

"Here, however, their spirits are resigned. For that reason, I likewise deem that there is no present peril."

"Then we will eat and rest while we may," said the Ironhand. "Linden Giantfriend's benisons have renewed our hearts. And no Giant born is fool enough to refuse viands and ease. Nor do we scorn slumber. Many are the storms through which we have slept, at sea and elsewhere. Indeed, Frostheart Grueburn did so in the toils of the Soulbiter"— she nudged her comrade while Latebirth, Halewhole Bluntfist, and Cirrus Kindwind chuckled—"though others aboard Dire's Vessel remained watchful, chary of horrors. Guarded by the valor and vigilance of the Ranyhyn, we fear nothing."

Sighing, Coldspray sank down to sit in her warmed cataphract against the wall of the small space. Other Swordmainnir did the same. But Linden fretted over concerns that did not involve the lurker. The insistence of the Ranyhyn on taking the company farther into this region of wars and slaughter and evil appeared to confirm Stave's guess that the horses were intent on satisfying her *need for death*. Hers, or Jeremiah's.

For her son's sake, she prayed that the need was hers. Nevertheless she feared it. She was sick of killing, morally nauseated, and had no cure. Her leg did not hurt enough.

God, she wished that Hyn had not interrupted her cutting. Shame was the wrong kind of pain.

ಬಂ

As twilight and then darkness thickened like murk over the Lower Land, Linden and her friends ate as much of their dwindling supplies as they could spare. Chewing on her lip, Linden drew more ebon fire from her Staff and used it to heat the stone of the scant shelter. Then the Giants stretched out as best they could. Gradually they drifted to sleep.

Mahrtiir sat on the ground-cloth with Linden, apparently determined to wait with her until she allowed herself to rest. But she kept herself awake by galling her cuts with the damp fabric of her jeans, pretending to massage them; and after a time, the Manethrall began to doze. Then only Stave remained to share her watchfulness and her fears.

Soon the night grew so deep that she could not see the far wall of the breach. Lulled by the warmed stone, she felt her attention fraying. She had not slept the previous night, and her cut shin did not hurt enough to sustain her. Before Stormpast Galesend went to sleep herself, she had wrapped Jeremiah in his blankets—again—and laid him carefully on the ground-cloth between Linden and Mahrtiir. If the boy's eyes had closed, Linden's might have done the same. But he stared upward, gazing at nothing as though he had outlived his need for rest or dreams.

Linden watched him like a mother with a sick child. More and more, the stained tint of his eyes seemed to resemble the milky hue of Anele's blindness. Jeremiah's new Earthpower had done nothing to relieve his dissociation. Instead it appeared to emphasize the silt that defined his sight, as if the ramifications of Anele's gift had driven him deeper into his graves.

For a time, anxiety kept Linden alert in spite of her weariness.

Eventually, however, her concentration faded. She was helpless to stop it. By degrees, her thoughts became so vague that she did not recognize Hynyn's stentorian call until she felt Stave slip silently out of the hollow.

Inchoately alarmed, she jerked up her head, slapped at her cheeks. After an instant's hesitation, she took up the Staff and ground one iron heel against the cuts in her shin and calf until she broke them open; drew fresh blood.

After a few moments, Stave returned. Touching Mahrtiir's shoulder, he said softly, "Manethrall." Then he nudged the Ironhand's armor with one foot, spoke her name more loudly.

Linden struggled to her feet. "What is it?"

At the same time, Mahrtiir came instantly awake; surged upright. Coldspray shook her head as if she were scattering dreams, rubbed her face vigorously to dispel them.

Without preamble or inflection, Stave announced quietly, "We are approached. The Ranyhyn have departed."

Simultaneously Linden said, "Approached?" the Manethrall demanded, "Departed?" and Coldspray asked, "What comes?"

Before Linden could insist on an answer, Mahrtiir stated harshly, "The Ranyhyn do not flee any peril."

"They flee no peril," Stave countered, "except that of the lurker."

The lurker? Linden thought, scrambling to understand. Here? But you said—

The Manethrall's whole body seemed to blaze with anger, but he did not contradict Stave.

"Swordmainnir!" Coldspray barked to her comrades. "We are needed!" Then she confronted Stave. "I await your explanation, Stave of the *Haruchai*."

As the other Giants lurched awake and began to rise, Stave shrugged. "Whether we are threatened is beyond my discernment. I do not sense the lurker's presence. I am certain only that the Ranyhyn no longer watch over us, and that a small throng of wights approaches from the direction of the Sarangrave.

"However," he added, "these creatures are not entirely unknown. Upon occasion in more recent centuries, such wights have been observed by Masters who chanced to be scouting the boundaries of Sarangrave Flat.

"They appear to roam freely among the fens and quags, singly or in sparse groups. They are man-shaped, short of stature, and hairless, with large eyes well formed for vision in darkness. Within sight of the Masters, they have not heretofore wandered beyond the waters of the Flat. Observed, they have betrayed no awareness of their observers.

"And there is this—" Stave paused; almost seemed to hesitate. "To the Masters, they have evinced no theurgy or other puissance. Indeed, they have appeared altogether harmless. Yet those that now draw nigh hold in their hands a green flame like unto the emerald hue of the *skest*. In some fashion, this fire sustains their emergence from their wonted habitation."

Linden scrambled—and could not catch up. She felt stupid with sleeplessness. What was Stave saying? He had not seen any indication of the lurker. But the Ranyhyn feared it: Mahrtiir had not denied that. And the horses were gone.

"My God," she breathed, hardly aware that she spoke aloud. "Are those things *minions*? Servants of the lurker?"

Millennia ago, the *skest* had served the ancient monster. Horrim Carabal? Those creatures of living acid had tried to herd Covenant and Linden, Sunder and Hollian, and a small party of *Haruchai* into the lurker's snare. Their quest for the One Tree would have died there, if Covenant had not risked his life to wound the lurker with Loric's *krill* and wild magic. And if he, Linden, and their companions had not encountered Giants: the Giants of the Search. And if the *skest* had not been opposed by creatures called the *sur-jheherrin*.

Now the *skest* cared for Joan. They had tended Jeremiah.

How many of them were there?

They did not match Stave's description.

Again the former Master shrugged. "Chosen, I know not. I cannot discern their intent, for good or ill. I am confident only that our presence has been marked. Now we are sought."

The Ranyhyn had abandoned their riders.

Oh, hell! Without Hyn— Given room to move, the Giants could survive any force that resembled the *skest*. But without Hyn and Hynyn, Narunal and Khelen—

God, please. Not more killing.

While the Ironhand's comrades chafed wakefulness into their cheeks, and donned their cataphracts, Coldspray commanded, "At once, Swordmainnir. We are too easily contained where we stand. Come boon or bane, we must meet it upon open ground."

"Aye," Stormpast Galesend agreed. "We hear you." Scooping up Jeremiah, she cradled him in one arm; kept the other free to wield her sword.

"Hear, indeed," growled Frostheart Grueburn, grinning. "When the Ironhand speaks in such dulcet tones, she is heard by the Lower Land entire."

As if Coldspray had slapped at her, Grueburn ducked. Then she drew her longsword and ran from the hollow, heading toward the place where the company had first entered among the hills.

Halewhole Bluntfist and Cabledarm followed immediately. The other Swordmainnir arrayed themselves like an escort around their smaller companions. With the Ironhand in the lead, Linden and her friends went after Cabledarm.

Sheltered by the breach, Linden had forgotten the full force of the wind. In the lowland between this line of hills and the next, however, icy air struck her like the rush of a flood. She felt pummeled and tossed as if she had fallen into a torrent. Even in darkness, she would have seen or felt her breath steaming, condensed to frost, if the wind had not torn it away.

Dirt crunched under her boot heels as she walked among the Giants. The ground was freezing—

After High Lord Elena's disastrous use of the Power of Command, when her spirit had been forced to serve Lord Foul, she had used Berek's Staff of Law to inflict an unnatural winter upon the Land. Standing at the Colossus, she had scourged the Despiser's foes with snow and ice.

In Andelain, Linden had unleashed something worse. This day's deranged weather was only the leading edge of a far more savage storm.

Berek's spectre had said of Lord Foul, *He may be freed only by one who is compelled by rage, and contemptuous of consequence.*

Had she done that? Truly? Had she already accomplished the Despiser's release?

If so, she had earned the right to despair.

The cold made her leg ache as though the cuts had sunk into her bones.

The blast struck tears from her eyes: she could not see. Coldspray shouted demands or warnings that vanished along the wind. Cirrus Kindwind, Latebirth, and Onyx Stonemage joined Grueburn, Bluntfist, and Cabledarm to form a partial cordon. The Ironhand and Galesend stayed with Linden, Stave, and Mahrtiir.

Jeremiah still had not closed his eyes. He did not appear to blink. Perhaps he never blinked. If so, he would eventually go blind. As blind as Anele. It was inevitable.

Stave gripped Linden's arm. "Attend, Chosen."

She was already shivering.

She squeezed her eyes shut, scrubbed tears away, opened them again.

At first, she saw only small green flames bobbing like Wraiths in the distance. Their essential *wrongness* was palpable; but they were so little—Too minor to wield much force.

Then she realized that the fires were not affected by the wind. They danced and moved blithely, oblivious to the blast.

That should have been impossible.

Blinking fervidly, she made out the forms of the creatures. As Stave had said, they looked vaguely human. Naked, lacking either pelts or garments. No taller than her shoulders. Cupped in each of their hands, they carried quick flaws of emerald like recollections of the Illearth Stone. Green glints reflected auguries or promises in their large round eyes. Small as they were, they resembled eidolons reeking with malice.

They advanced steadily, but not in a group. Instead they spread out across the lower ground and partway up the hillsides: at least a score of them; perhaps thirty. Straining her senses, Linden saw no bonds of theurgy between them, no reinforced power. Yet she felt certain that they had come with a shared intent.

While the nearest creatures were still a dozen Giantish strides away, Rime Coldspray swept out her stone glaive. "Hold!" she shouted at the caper of fires, the green reflections. "Friend or foe, we require a parley! Name your purpose. Explain your wishes. We mean to defend ourselves if we must!"

The wind carried her voice away as if it would never be heard.

Yet the—eight? ten?—creatures most directly in front of her halted. For a few paces, the others did not. Then, beginning on the lowland and spreading incrementally up the slopes on both sides, those creatures also stopped.

Now the company stood half-enclosed in a shallow arc of handheld fires that defied the wind.

A creature spoke, Linden could not tell which one. Perhaps they all did, using a single voice. Without apparent effort, or any hint of emotion, it said, "We are the Feroce."

Its sound was strangely squishy, damp and ill-defined, like mud squeezed between toes.

"We are Swordmainnir of the Giants," answered Coldspray. Her blade did not waver. "Why have you come?"

The pain in Linden's leg had begun to burn. Without the support of her Staff, she might not have been able to stand.

"There is among you," replied the creature or creatures, "a stick of power." They may all have been discrete instances of the same being. "The cruel metal we will not touch. It is abhorrent. But we claim the stick. Our High God hungers for it."

Linden gasped; felt the breath snatched from her lungs. Christ, her *leg*—!

All of the Giants drew their swords. Stave shifted closer to Linden. With his garrote in his hands, the Manethrall positioned himself near Stormpast Galesend and Jeremiah.

The blast was becoming a gale, as gelid and heartless as the wasteland within a *caesure*.

Who were the Feroce? *What* were they?

Loudly the Ironhand replied, "You cannot have the Staff of Law!" Her tone was firm, but unthreatening. "Yet if you will speak with us concerning your High God's hunger, perhaps we will discover some fashion in which we may be of service. We neither fear nor desire contention. Rather our preference is for amity in all things. Speak, therefore. Let us together consider the nature of your need."

Linden heard a splash of water, an ooze of loam, as the creature responded, "We are the Feroce. We do not need."

Did she see a multitude of verdant fires leap and flare, mounting like disease into the heavens? No: it was only imagination. Hallucination. Not magic.

There was nothing except darkness.

A subtle shift in the air. Realities swept aside; replaced.

A momentary sensation of falling, of vertigo, as if she had lost her balance.

But she caught herself. Her leg held. It did not hurt.

It had never hurt. That pain did not exist. She had already forgotten it. Only her palm stung where she had gouged it with her car keys.

She was in the farmhouse, Covenant's house. It shook around her, battered by angry winds. Outside, lightning glared, an erratic succession of furies from a clear sky. Thunder groaned in the timbers of the building. Joists squalled at the force of the dry storm.

The detritus of Covenant's former life littered the kitchen floor. Blood cooled in coagulating puddles. But she did not stop here. She did not turn and flee. Instead she entered the short passage leading to three doors. Covenant's bedroom. The bathroom. The last room, where he had cared for Joan.

Following splashes of blood and the splayed illumination of her flashlight, Linden went down the hall to the last room. Where else could she go? Roger had Jeremiah.

The weight of her medical bag in her left hand steadied her. It was her anchor against the storm's madness, and Roger's. Her only weapon. Her grip on the flashlight abraded the small wound in her palm, but that beam was too frail to protect her. She had left her coat at home. Deliberately she had put on a clean red flannel shirt, clean jeans, sturdy boots. She had driven here, to Haven Farm, where she knew what she would find.

The door was open: the last room. She smelled ozone and blood. The house trembled. Roger had committed butchery here. But he had not killed some poor animal. Certainly not: not Covenant's heartless son. He had shed the life of one of his hostages.

Linden felt as buffeted as Covenant's abandoned home. A strange disorientation thwarted her. For some reason, she expected there to be crusted dirt on her shirt. Stains, grime, tatters: consequences. She expected a neat hole over her heart. But the flannel was still clean. It was practically new. Her jeans were innocent of Roger's carnage.

Lightning struck nearby, lightning and thunder, a crash like a tall tree shattering. Roger had taken Jeremiah. Jeremiah had driven a splinter like a spike through the center of her hand. The last room was a ruin, wrecked and toxic. There the wan thrust of the flashlight revealed Sara Clint lying on the forlorn bed in the dark residue of her life. She had been cut dozens of times, *dozens of times*. Roger had lashed her wrists and ankles to the bed frame with duct tape. Then, over and over again, he had sliced through the white fabric of her uniform, drawing venous blood. Preparation for a ritual.

Static made a galvanic nimbus of Linden's hair, a halo of desperation. Jeremiah!

Roger had cut Sara with *that* knife, the large cleaver protruding from the pillow beside her desecrated head. When he was satisfied, he had stabbed the blade into her heart before leaving the knife in the pillow: a presentation for Linden's benefit, demonstrating his seriousness.

He was gone now. He had taken Jeremiah and Joan and Sandy Eastwall. To the place where he meant to sacrifice Jeremiah. And probably Sandy as well. He might need her blood to open the way. He might need even his own mother's life.

Linden should have spent a while grieving over Sara's body. Absolutely she should have. No one could say that Sara Clint had not earned at least that much recognition. She was a good woman, and she had been murdered.

But Linden had no time. She knew where Roger was going; where he was taking his prisoners. She knew why. She had to catch up with him before—

Jeremiah!

There was something that she needed to remember.

—before he reached the sheet of rock in the woods where Thomas Covenant had been killed. The place where Lord Foul's bonfire had claimed half and more of Jeremiah's hand.

No, there was nothing to remember.

Yes. There was.

A face.

Whose face was it? Jeremiah's? No. She had not forgotten his lost visage. It was as essential to her as the pathways of her brain. That was why she was here.

Liand's, then? Anele's? Stave's?

Who in hell were Liand and Anele and Stave?

And why did she want to think about Giants? She had not seen them for ten years, and could not afford to be distracted by old love. Not now.

In spite of her haste, she tried to honor Sara briefly. A few heartbeats of sorrow. But she could no longer smell blood. Or ozone. Those scents were heavy enough to cling. Nevertheless the barrage of winds had torn them from the house, through the broken windows and gapped walls.

Instead she smelled smoke: smoke so thick and dire that it could have been the leaping fume of the Despiser's blaze. She saw wisps in the beam of her flashlight. Pressure grew in her chest. Threats of suffocation filled her lungs.

She had to go. She had wasted too much time.

Wait! Her shirt—Her jeans—

Nothing. They might as well have been new. She did not know Liand, or Anele, or Stave, of course not, she had never heard those names before.

Roger had taken Jeremiah and Joan and Sandy into the woods. Linden knew where he was going.

Where had Liand's name come from—or Anele's and Stave's—or Mahrtiir's—if she had never met them?

Lightning had struck the house: it must have. All of this dry wood was going to burn like a pyre.

God, she was hallucinating! Her son needed her, and she was losing her mind. Stave spurned by the Masters. Covenant's hands burning, ravaged by Joan and wild magic. Covenant was dead. Killed ten years ago. Nothing after this moment had happened. She had imagined it, all of it. Every struggle, every nightmare, every loss. Liand and Anele: Stave and Mahrtiir: Pahni and Bhapa: Giants. They were figments, chimeras sent to distract her. To paralyze her. Until the flames took her. So that she would not follow Roger.

So that she would not save her son.

Screams of rage or terror that she could not hear ripped at her throat as she wheeled away from Sara and murder, rushed from the bedroom back into the hall.

Covenant's ring hung on its chain under her clean shirt; but white gold had no power to save her here.

Roger wanted it. He had said so. *It belongs to me.* Otherwise he could have created his portal here, in this house; doomed her where she stood. But he lacked his father's ring.

Lurid flames chewed the edges of the boards, the walls of the passage. The whole house was kindling. A jolt like the impact of a hurricane staggered the entire structure. Swinging her bag, Linden beat at the fires; recovered her balance.

She needed to dash past them before they could catch her. Reach the kitchen, the living room, the front door. Escape into the night. Free Jeremiah.

But she was already too late. Ahead of her, the door to Covenant's room burst outward, blasted from its hinges by a furnace-roar of flame. Conflagration howled into the hall. Smoke as black as midnight struck at her, demented fists of heat. They drove her backward. Soon the fire itself would be as black as—as black as—

She could not flee through the house.

She had nothing with which to fend off the heat except her medical bag. Holding it up like a shield, she returned in a stagger to the room where Sara lay. Sara's cruel pyre.

Linden slapped the door shut behind her, but she knew that it would not protect her. Her bag was her only defense. In a rush, harried by Cavewights and killing, she reached the window.

The glass was broken and jagged: it would cut her to shreds. It would kill Galt.

Who was *Galt*?

Dear God! She had to stop this. Stop *imagining*. Roger had Jeremiah. He had Joan and Sandy. If Linden died here—if she let her delusions trap her—nothing would save her son.

With her bag, she swept daggers of glass from their frame. Her flashlight she tossed outside. She meant to throw her bag as well; but first she braced her right hand on the window-frame.

A shard of glass dug into her palm. Blood pulsed from the cut. She could not let go of her bag. She *needed* it—

—needed it to fight the flames.

Screaming like the storm and the blaze and the bane, she took the bag in her right hand, sealed her grip with blood. Awkward as a cripple, she began to crawl backward through the window.

Stave would have helped her, but he did not exist. None of her friends had ever existed. —*dreaming*, Covenant had once told her. *We're sharing a dream*. If she could not stop imagining people and events and nightmares, Roger would butcher her son.

But going backward through the window required her to brace her shins on the window-frame. She felt half a dozen cuts in one leg, a dozen, more cuts than there were scraps of glass.

And when she dropped to the ground outside the house, she was still in the hallway. Smoke and flame boiled toward her, a tumult avid for the end of all things. But now the last room, Sara's death-chamber, had become an inferno. It roared with ruin like the rest of the farmhouse.

She should have thrown her medical bag out the window with her flashlight. She had lost her chance to escape that way.

Long arms of fire reached out for her. Ebony smoke streaked with bitter orange and unbearable heat tumbled toward her.

Shrieking, she turned and fled; ran frantically as if the hall were the throat of She Who Must Not Be Named. She had to find the end before the bane's mouth closed; before she became horror and torment forever.

Before Roger hurt Jeremiah.

Because she was still trying to save her son, she slapped fire and smoke away with her bag. Floundering and flailing, she ran with all her strength—

—and could not reach the end, the final wall—

Pain throbbed in her leg as if her shin and calf were gushing blood.

—because there was no end. She had been betrayed by her dreams. The hall stretched interminably ahead of her, and flames devoured the walls, growing faster than she could stamp them out, and the furnace squalling at her back had become the heart of a volcano: the savage core of the bane's need, or the brimstone ferocity of Roger's given hand.

Where had Roger obtained a hand that spouted lava and anguish? With such strength, he would not have needed a gun, or Sara Clint, or Sandy Eastwall. He could have claimed Joan and Jeremiah, done whatever he wished to obtain Covenant's ring. No force on this earth could have stopped him.

He did not have that kind of power.

The bane did. She Who Must Not Be Named had seen into Linden's heart and judged her. She was the bane's rightful prey, trapped in a gullet that had not yet swallowed her because uncounted devoured women were screaming.

The bane did not exist. The women did not. Linden knew nothing about Elena except tales.

Only her bag of instruments and vials kept the flames from consuming her. Only the bleeding of her palm gave the bag meaning; kept her alive.

Her lower leg throbbed like an open sore. She had pierced it on the window-frame. She could not run or struggle much longer; but there was no end to the hall and the flames, the smoke, the terrible heat.

This was death. It was hell. It was the agony of all things ending, irredeemable calamity. And she had brought it on herself. She had earned it with anger and folly.

Wind flailed the flames. Smoke thick with sparks gyred upward amid lightnings that came from nowhere and never stopped.

A spasm of pain snatched her leg away. She sprawled along the burning floorboards.

In a frenzy, she flipped over onto her back. Frantically she swung her bag at the rush of the blaze.

Damn it. This was impossible. The hall had an end. It ended at the wall of the room where Sara had died. Linden had not left enough glass in the window-frame to hurt her this badly.

But she had lost her chance to save Jeremiah. Her reason to live.

Trust yourself.

Covenant was crazy. Dead and insane. There was nothing in her that she could trust. The only thing that mattered was power; and her defense was failing. By now, every necessary resource in her bag had been smashed.

Trust yourself.

Trust *what*, you bastard?

She might not have resurrected him and roused the Worm if he had only spoken to her. In Andelain. When any word from him would have been as precious as her son.

She can do this. No, she could not. No one could.

No one except Covenant, who had refused her.

Her hair sizzled and stank. Her eyelashes burned, scorching her eyes. Flame and smoke scoured her mouth, her throat, her lungs. Charred blots like deserved torments marked her shirt.

Now she needed to die. Anything was better than spending eternity trapped in the nightmare of She Who Must Not Be Named.

The world will not see her like again.

But there were also marks on her leg, on her jeans: a tracery of blood-stains below her knee. They formed a pattern.

She did not know what the pattern meant. Still she recognized it.

It could not have been caused by her struggle to crawl over the fanged frame of the window. Beneath the darker script of blood, she saw hints of green. Her eyes were scalded; nearly blind. Nevertheless the green looked as essential as grass.

The pattern—if it existed—was a map.

And *there*, on her shirt, surrounded by smoldering and blackness: a small round hole as precise as the passage of a bullet.

—her like again.

From somewhere beyond the flames, voices shouted her name. They had been shouting for a long time. Too long. Friends whom she had never met because they did not exist, imagined friends, pleaded for her in voices as loud as the conflagration and collapse of the farmhouse.

If she could not trust herself, she might be able to trust them.

Or the map.

It showed the way out.

Out of what? Into what? She had no idea. She could not read the map. She could only follow it.

She knew how. *Do something they don't expect. Everything else will take care of itself.*

Because she had only one real weapon, one defense, and had failed to save herself, she hurled her medical bag straight into the teeth of the fire.

Everything is simpler than you make it sound.

Simpler, hell!

In that instant, a bolt of lightning struck through the blazing house into her chest. The concussion knocked her flat, expelled the anguish from her lungs, stunned every muscle. But the shock was brief. Night swallowed the flames, effaced fire from the world. Before her heart knew that it had died, it beat again. She lay on damp grass while realities wheeled around her, spinning too fast to be understood. When she gasped for breath, the air had become cool bliss.

At once, the shouting changed. Crying, "Linden Giantfriend!" Frostheart Grueburn scooped Linden into her arms. The Swordmain's muscles strained with urgency.

"Is she harmed?" demanded Stormpast Galesend. Her voice was so loud that it covered Mahrtiir's tense query.

Like a blaring horn, Rime Coldspray roared, "*No!* This I will not permit!

"Stave! The Staff!"

Vaguely Linden realized that she was no longer holding the Staff of Law. Her nerves remembered throwing it— Her medical bag: every drug, every instrument. The darkness held a greenish tinge, wan and frail, so faint that it scarcely dimmed the unregarded stars.

The muffled thud of a Giant's strides receded. They became splashing, a rush into water: shallow water that grew deeper at every step.

Other feet sprinted in pursuit. Smaller splashes: a smaller body. Stave? Linden's heart clenched again, and a clamor of water arose. Something greater than a Giant reared and thrashed.

In the distance, aghast children wailed in little voices that sounded like mud.

"*Linden!*" Grueburn insisted. She held Linden hard against her armor. "You must speak! Some horror has befallen you! *Why did you cast away your Staff?*"

Somehow the Manethrall made himself heard through the clamor of Giants, the turmoil of water, the gasp and pound of struggle. "She returns to herself! Ringthane, hear us! Why did you prevent our aid? What madness possessed you?"

Linden did not reply. She could not. She hardly had the strength to lift her head, focus her eyes. But she heard desperation, combat, fear. She should have died. Instead she tried to see.

At first, everything was a blur of darkness. Emerald flames shed no illumination: ordinary vision was useless. With her health-sense, however, her Land-given sight, she discerned sparse grass in damp sandy soil, an agitated boundary of water. Beyond that, details smeared into each other. Shapes bled until they became confusion, a flurry of writhing that flung water in all directions. The water smelled of rot, thick with muck and mold, like a marsh that did not drain.

Why *had* she discarded her Staff? She needed it now.

It was hers. *Hers.* She did not have to hold it in order to call up its strength. As long as she could sense its presence—

She could not. It was gone.

Or it was masked—

Christ!

—by a looming evil as thick as trees, as dense as a grove.

From the verge of the grass, a fen spread farther than her percipience could reach: a wetland clotted with mold and mud and swamp vegetation. Between small eyots of roots and muck, water lay dense and stagnant—and deeper as it stretched into the distance. It had been undisturbed for an age: it was not so now. Its ancient decay was in chaos, scourged and writhing, a welter of froth and spray. And from it came the stench of corpses, bodies by the thousands so long immersed that their putrefaction clogged the air.

The Sarangrave, Linden thought numbly. Sarangrave Flat. What was she doing *here*? Why had her companions brought her? They knew the danger—

Grueburn's chest shuddered at each rank breath. From somewhere nearby, Mahrtiir made retching sounds. Galesend cupped her hand over Jeremiah's mouth and nose as if she hoped to filter the reek with her fingers.

Gagging helplessly, Linden forced her perceptions farther.

Latebirth, Cirrus Kindwind, and Onyx Stonemage stood to the ankles in the edge of the marsh, poised to fling themselves into some fray. Yet they appeared to hesitate, uncertain of their enemy—or enemies. Latebirth faced the fen, aimed her sword toward the struggle that lashed the water; searched for an opportunity to attack. But Kindwind and Stonemage kept their backs to the Flat. Across a gap of a dozen or more paces, they confronted two clusters of the small, hairless creatures, the Feroce, one off to the left, the other on the right of Grueburn and Galesend, Linden, Jeremiah, and Mahrtiir.

Green flames gibbered in the hands of the creatures. Their muddy wailing rose through the stench and clash from the wetland, and was swallowed into silence.

Kindwind and Stonemage seemed to be waiting for the Feroce to attempt an assault.

Rank humidity clogged the air. It filled Linden's lungs like stagnant muck. Her leg throbbed in response to the panicked theurgy of the creatures. But they paid no attention to her.

She had already thrown away her Staff. They had no further interest in her.

Out in the marsh, Coldspray, Cabledarm, Halewhole Bluntfist, and Stave fought the lurker of the Sarangrave.

Oh, God. Linden *knew* that evil, that fierce hunger. She remembered it. She could hardly breathe. Years or millennia ago, it had come close to killing her and everyone with her. In strength and savagery and sheer size, it dwarfed even Giants. Without Covenant and the *krill* and wild magic—

She counted three tentacles standing up from the water, no, four, each as thick as one of the Swordmainnir. Each could have stretched to three times the height of any Giant. To her, they tasted like the Illearth Stone and the shrieking bane; like the effluvium of the darkest deeds of the Viles and Demondim in their loreworks. They were reified corruption: long ages of seeping poisons, acrid and malign, accumulating until they became flesh swollen with craving.

Although the lurker had once commanded the *skest*, it wielded no magicks that Linden could perceive. Its physical bulk and muscle sufficed to feed it. Braced on its own immensity beneath the water, it struck at its opponents with enough force to shatter granite.

Cabledarm and Bluntfist stood against the tentacles, hacking with their swords, fending off blows; floundering through water that reached their thighs when they could not otherwise evade the lurker's limbs. At first, Linden did not see Stave or the Ironhand. They had been driven underwater, were being held down—

No, they were not. The hard intransigence of Stave's aura was *there*. Rime Coldspray's courage shouted against the darkness.

When Linden concentrated on the former Master and the Ironhand, she caught a hint of her Staff.

Her leg hurt as if her cuts had become acid. As if the marks on her jeans were being etched into her bones.

Etched by an acid the hue of malign verdure.

Eruptions of water and violence bewildered her senses; thwarted her efforts to interpret what was happening. But she still had her map. She could still follow it.

Through the tumid obstruction of the air, the untrammeled logic of grass stains and pain led her to Coldspray, Stave, and the Staff of Law.

She had missed them in the rapid flurry of blows, the mad lash and slash of tentacles and swords, because they were not with Cabledarm and Bluntfist. They were not in the water at all.

Supple as snakes, the twisting arms of the lurker had caught them.

One had coiled around the Ironhand's chest, heaved her into the air. Now it held her there, shaking her viciously and *squeezing*—Through the rancid fetor of corpses, the wet bellow of the swamp, Linden sensed the lurker's tremendous might. If the monster could not snap Coldspray's spine or neck, it meant to crush the life from her body.

Coldspray flailed with her glaive; but the tentacle's thrashing kept her blade from its target.

The lurker was powerful enough to kill her. Its clench should already have collapsed her chest, driven ribs into her heart and lungs, sent blood spurting from her mouth and nose. Yet she was not crushed. She still lived and fought.

For the moment, at least, her armor withstood the hideous pressure of the monster's arm.

Another tentacle had taken the Staff. Wrapped several times around the shaft, the arm drew back from the contest. The inner surface of the arm was thick with small fingers: it could *grip*. And Cabledarm and Bluntfist were not near enough to assail it. Other tentacles held the Swordmainnir at bay.

But Stave clung to the Staff. In spite of the lurker's efforts to fling him off, he gripped the wood with both hands. Bracing his feet against the heavy coils, he strove to pull the Staff loose.

He could not out-muscle the tentacle: not directly. To the lurker, his strength was a child's. And the arm had too many fingers. But the Staff was small in the monster's clutch, a mere twig compared to the tentacle's thickness. Stave fought, not to break the lurker's hold outright, but rather to haul the Staff free from one end.

He was succeeding. By increments so small that Linden could barely discern them, he dragged the wood out of the coils.

If the monster tried to shift its grasp, it would lose the Staff altogether.

Nevertheless Stave could not win. Linden saw that. The lurker would change its tactics. Another tentacle would arise to toss the *Haruchai* aside. Or he would be punched down into the water and mud, forced under until he drowned.

He needed help.

The Swordmainnir understood his peril as clearly as Linden did. With a Giantish battle cry, Latebirth charged into the marsh. Three against two tentacles, she, Bluntfist, and Cabledarm fought to create an opening so that one of them could reach Stave. An instant later, Onyx Stonemage abandoned her watch against the Feroce and rushed to Coldspray's assistance.

In response, a fifth tentacle joined the fray.

Linden could not bear it. Covenant had told her repeatedly to trust herself. *She can do this.* The pain in her leg demanded deeds that had no name.

She was too weak to shout. Her lungs held too much water. Stonemage, Latebirth, and the other were too embattled to hear her. Trusting herself meant trusting her friends. It meant trusting Frostheart Grueburn.

"Tell them," she gasped. Her throat felt raw, scorched by flame, scraped by smoke. "Save Coldspray. I'll help Stave."

Grueburn must have heard her. Must have believed her. Clarion as a thunderclap, the Giant roared over the tumult, "*To the Ironhand!* Linden Giantfriend aids Stave!"

They all must have believed in Linden. Crashing like a berserker, Latebirth turned to head toward Rime Coldspray with Stonemage. An instant later, Halewhole Bluntfist did the same, leaving Cabledarm to engage three tentacles alone.

Without hesitation, Cabledarm dove beneath the fouled surface, the scourged spray. Then she surged to her feet near one of the arms. Streaming with muck and fronds, with gobbets of putrid flesh, she swung her sword two-handed; hacked into the thick muscle and sinew of the tentacle.

Her blow bit deep. The Feroce wailed as though they had been pierced. Acid pulsed in Linden's leg.

Another tentacle struck Cabledarm down. But the arm that she had hurt toppled, loud as a scream, back into the fen.

It did not rise again. Instead it fled, plowing a writhen furrow in the water.

At the same time, Stonemage drove a headlong thrust into the heavy mass striving to crush Coldspray—and Latebirth threw her whole body into a horizontal slash—

—and Linden reached out with percipience and desperation for the Staff of Law.

It was hers. It was *hers*, Goddammit! She had fashioned it with wild magic from her own love and bereavement as much as from Vain and Findail. Only its iron heels had once belonged to Berek. And it had answered her call when she had needed Earthpower to heal a dying Waynhim. It would answer her now.

While one tentacle held Cabledarm underwater, and another swatted Bluntfist aside, knocking the Swordmain away as if she were weightless, Linden summoned fire from her Staff.

Panting the Seven Words, she did her best to spare Stave. But she could not afford to concentrate on his safety. To harm the lurker, she needed her fiercest flame. For reasons that she did not try to understand, the monster wanted the Staff. It would not let go unless she made it flinch.

From the Staff, she called one small tongue of fire, flame blacker than the tinged darkness. Then another. Another.

Every sign of Earthpower and Law made Linden stronger. The Seven Words filled her mouth. She could not recover the lost cleanliness of her theurgy; but she could make it hurtful. Between one heartbeat and the next, her little flames became ebon incandescence: a deflagration of condensed midnight.

The wails of the Feroce turned to bereft shrieks as power like a piece of an obsidian sun burned into the lurker's flesh.

Floundering, the tentacle released its grip. Stave clung to the Staff as the monster dropped it and him into the marsh.

Instantly water quenched Linden's fire. Her alarm for Stave extinguished it. A dark wind like an in-rush seemed to sweep every vestige of her power from the Sarangrave.

But she had done enough. A convulsion of pain clutched the lurker. Twisting in anguish, tentacles cudgeled the night. One blade-bitten arm released Rime Coldspray. As the Ironhand fell heavily between Latebirth and Stonemage, Cabledarm gained her feet; broke the surface and whooped for rank air. The tentacle that Linden had burned squirmed away beneath the whipped water.

In flailing pain, the monster withdrew. The suction of massive shapes moving away hit the fen like an eruption. Waves high enough to reach the chests of the Giants crashed in all directions: a thunder of water and rot. The pressure of moisture in Linden's chest eased as if a thunderstorm had passed.

At the same time, the Feroce ran after the lurker. Wailing as one, they dashed for the refuge of the Sarangrave. And as they splashed into the Flat, their fires winked out. In water, they appeared to have no need or use for magicks.

Before the last flame vanished, however, Linden saw Stave stand up from the muck. Clots of mud and bits of corpses stuck to his skin. Rancid fronds and stems hung like vestments from his shoulders. But in his hands he held the Staff of Law as if it could not hurt him; as if even the black savagery with which Linden had wounded the lurker could not touch him.

When she saw him—when she discerned Coldspray upright with Latebirth and Stonemage, and Cabledarm apparently unscathed, and Bluntfist wading vehemently through the swamp—Linden felt relief rise in her like a tide.

Relaxing at last in Grueburn's arms, she hardly noticed that the pain of her cut shin and calf was gone.

8.

The Amends of the Ranyhyn

 Heading into the teeth of a bitter wind, the companions trudged toward the comparative shelter where they had intended to spend the night.

As soon as Stave handed the Staff to Linden, she stroked dark fire from the wood to counter the effects of her eerie ordeal. Then she extended Earthpower to soothe everyone around her.

They did not need it to the same extent that she did. Even Rime Coldspray did not require healing: her cataphract and bulk of muscle had preserved her. And Stave was *Haruchai*. He had been scalded by Linden's burst of incandescence: beneath their coating of muck, his palms and forearms were blistered. Yet he seemed to shed his pain like water until it was gone.

Like Cirrus Kindwind, Stormpast Galesend, and Grueburn, Manethrall Mahrtiir and Jeremiah had played no part in the struggle. They had no discernible hurts.

Nevertheless Linden tended them all. She had put them in peril. Without knowing it, she had succumbed to the theurgies of the Feroce. She did not understand what the creatures had done, or how; but she felt sure that they had sent her mind back to Haven Farm. By some means, their green flames had caused that rupture in her reality. They had broken her connection to her present. And she had *believed*—

Somehow the fact that she had cut herself the previous night had left her vulnerable. Driven by memories, she had led or compelled her companions toward the Sarangrave. Where the lurker could reach them—and her Staff.

Now she tried to make restitution. At least for a time, she was not ashamed of the hue of her power. She felt more chagrin over the immediate consequences of her weakness.

And other issues were more important.

Who or what were the Feroce? What manner of magic did they wield? Why did they serve the lurker? Why did the lurker crave her Staff?

And why had the Ranyhyn abandoned their riders?

Carried in Grueburn's arms, Linden felt Mahrtiir's presence nearby. The long strides of the Giants forced him to trot, but the effort suited his compressed anger, his silent fulmination at his own uselessness. And at the actions of the Ranyhyn? Linden could not tell.

Slack as a discarded puppet, Jeremiah dangled in the cradle of Galesend's clasp. He stared at nothing, as though the sky were empty of stars. Linden still did not know whether he ever blinked. Yet Earthpower pulsed in his veins. It had become part of him, as essential and vibrant as blood—and as devoid of purpose as his sealed thoughts.

Stave had dismissed his pain; but he was still covered in filth, stained from head to foot with mud, despoiled flesh, and the shredded remains of plants that fed on rot. And Coldspray, Cabledarm, and Bluntfist were no cleaner. Fetid water drained from the confines of their armor as they plodded between barricades of hills. Latebirth and Onyx Stonemage had not fallen: only their legs were caked and sodden, roped with mire and stems and putrid skin like vines. Yet their strides were as leaden as those of their comrades, clogged with old death, as if the touch of the Flat's foulness had wounded them emotionally.

Or as if—

Linden groaned to herself.

—they had suffered some spiritual blight while she had floundered to escape the conflagration of the farmhouse.

Why did you prevent our aid?

God, what had she done?

In the confusion of flames and terror, she had thrown her medical bag. Because Covenant had told her, *Do something they don't expect*. And because the marks on her jeans had shown the way. She must have thrown the Staff at the same time; must have believed that the Staff *was* her bag.

Over and over again, she had used her bag to beat back flames while she fled from ruin to ruin along the throat of She Who Must Not Be Named. The lurker's creatures had found such things in her mind. Appalled past endurance, she had wielded her bag like a weapon against incineration. An instrument of power—

Some horror has befallen you!

Oh, hell. She must have used Staff-fire to repel her friends—to keep them away from her—as she ran down the engulfed hallway of hallucination or memory toward Sarangrave Flat.

Fortunately the Giants could withstand flames. Stave must have evaded her desperation. The Manethrall must have kept his distance, knowing himself powerless.

Nevertheless she was a danger to all of her companions.

But Covenant had also said, *Just trust yourself.* She must have done that; must have obeyed her instincts as well as her fears. She had seen a map in the random stains of blood and grass. And she had cast her Staff into the heart of her dismay. If she had not done so, the lurker would have taken her as well. The rupture imposed by the Feroce would have closed too late. No one would have been able to save her.

While she wondered how she would tell her friends what had happened to her, they brought her to the breach in the hills where they had sheltered earlier. When Grueburn set her on her feet in the hollow, Linden spent a quick moment confirming that Stave's burns were not septic; that Rime Coldspray's chest and neck and joints were indeed whole; that Cabledarm, Latebirth, Bluntfist, and Stonemage had no grave hurts. Then she turned the energies of her Staff on the stone around her, tuned Earthpower and Law to the pitch of heat. If Stave and the Swordmainnir did not suffer from the wind, at least she, Jeremiah, and Mahrtiir would be warm. And heat would dry wet garments. Then some portion of filth could be brushed off.

How had the Feroce mastered her so easily? She knew the answer. The cuts that she had made in her lower leg had exposed her true weakness. The gradient of her descent into despair was increasing. *You tread paths prepared for you by Fangthane's malice.* Everything that she did and felt exacerbated her entanglement in the Despiser's designs.

But her cuts had also saved her. *There is hope in contradiction.* They had given meaning to *the mark of fecundity and long grass.* Her own blood had interpreted a script which she had worn since she had visited the Verge of Wandering.

That rich valley was a habitation or resting-place for the Ramen and the Ranyhyn.

As she considered what had happened, Linden grew more troubled by the behavior of the Ranyhyn. The great horses had faced other horrors in her name. Why had they abandoned the company now? When she was becoming weaker?

Sighing, Rime Coldspray unfastened her armor and dropped it. Then she seated herself, resting against the warmed stone. Cabledarm and Halewhole Bluntfist followed her example: the other Swordmainnir did not. Apparently they intended to remain on guard. Scowling with disgust, Latebirth and Stonemage rubbed dirt from their legs. Cirrus Kindwind drew her sword and left the hollow to watch the length of the breach. Stormpast Galesend continued to hold Jeremiah as if she did not want to disturb him. But Grueburn stayed close to Linden. Perhaps the Swordmain intended to intervene if the Feroce returned.

Linden wanted to question Mahrtiir. He or no one would be able to explain the Ranyhyn. But before she could frame her first query, a distant whinny pierced the wind.

It sounded like Hynyn's voice.

It sounded angry.

Another neigh carried into the breach, coming closer. Kindwind looked quickly in both directions; answered her companions by shaking her head. Nevertheless Mahrtiir left the warmth of the hollow to stand beside the maimed Giant.

Linden held her breath until she felt the faint thud of hooves through the hard ground. Then she relaxed slightly. One of the horses was coming closer. More than one had returned.

A moment later, the Manethrall faced the south. Kindwind nodded in that direction. To show her respect, she sheathed her blade. Through the wind, Linden heard hooves more clearly. At last, she saw Hynyn's proud head past the rim of the shelter; saw the glare of ire in the stallion's eyes.

Without hesitation, Mahrtiir prostrated himself. But Hynyn did not regard the Manethrall. The stallion was too angry—or, Linden thought suddenly, too ashamed. Instead Hynyn fixed his attention on Stave. Dim in the night, the star on his forehead nonetheless resembled a demand.

Stave appeared to understand. Perhaps he simply trusted Hynyn. Or perhaps he had formed a desire in his mind, confident that the stallion would heed him. He had done something similar when he, Linden, and their companions had ridden through a *caesure* to Revelstone. Saying nothing, he strode at once to Hynyn's side; vaulted onto the horse's back.

Still ignoring Mahrtiir, Hynyn wheeled in the breach and trotted away.

While Linden and the Giants watched, the Manethrall rose to his feet. His bandage did not conceal the fact that his own wrath was unappeased. Linden knew him well enough, however, to feel sure that he was not angry at Hynyn. Rather he seemed to share the stallion's vexed pride.

"Manethrall of the Ramen," Coldspray asked quietly, "do you comprehend what has transpired here?"

Mahrtiir's hands curled and tightened as if they ached for his garrote. Through his teeth, he muttered, "Hynyn offers amends. By the deeds of the Ranyhyn were we brought into peril. But of those who suffered tangible harm, only Stave rides. Therefore only Stave is suited to receive their first contrition." Bitterly the Manethrall shrugged. "More than that I have not been given to know."

Trying to be careful with his emotions, Linden did not ask why the horses had risked venturing so close to the Sarangrave. Instead she said, "There's too much that I don't understand. If the Ranyhyn are afraid of the lurker, they must have a reason." A good reason. Otherwise they would never have forsaken their riders. "Can you tell us what it is?"

"I cannot," Mahrtiir snapped. He may have meant, Do not ask me. "No Raman has partaken of the horserite. We do not share their thoughts and knowledge in that fashion."

Linden bit her lip; did not pursue an answer. Instead she only gazed at the Manethrall, watching passions writhe beneath the surface of his self-command.

The Giants studied him mutely. He could not discern their faces, except with his health-sense. Yet he must have felt their concern, their curiosity, their desire for comprehension—and their willingness to respect his silence. For a few moments, he appeared to wrestle with himself. Then, by slow degrees, his shoulders sagged.

"Yet we speculate." He kept his voice low. "How can we not? They are the Ranyhyn. It was known even to Bloodguard and Lords that they fear the abomination of the Sarangrave—they who master every other dread. How then can we not endeavor to grasp the nature of their sole frailty?"

He rubbed his cheeks; checked the security of his bandage. As if he were assuming a painful burden, he began to explain.

"The tale of great *Kelenbhrabanal*, Father of Horses, has been widely shared. It is no secret that in a distant age, when an onslaught of *kresh* and other evils threatened the Ranyhyn with extinction, *Kelenbhrabanal* sought to treat with Fangthane. Seeking to spare his failing herd, *Kelenbhrabanal* offered his own life in return for theirs. To this dark exchange, Fangthane consented readily, intending betrayal. Thus *Kelenbhrabanal* surrendered his throat to his foe, and his blood was shed to the last drop—and still the *kresh* came, ravaging, until the Ranyhyn could not survive except by flight. The home of their hearts they forsook. Nor did they return until they had won the Ramen to their service, to fend and fight for them.

"This tale all the folk of the Land once knew. Now it has been forgotten."

Linden had heard the story before: the Giants had not. They listened avidly, with their love for tales in their eyes.

"But among the Ramen," Mahrtiir continued, "the mystery of *Kelenbhrabanal* has been contemplated for uncounted generations." Gradually a tinge of sorrow crept into his voice. "Across the centuries, telling and re-telling our tales, we have wondered, and wondered again. And always we have returned to the same question. *How* was *Kelenbhrabanal* slain?

"In every age of the Lords, we were assured that Fangthane is a bodiless evil. Aye, he is able to master or discard physical substance at will. And doubtless his theurgies are capable of tangible manifestation. Yet his essence is incorporeal. In this, he resembles the Ravers, who wield no direct force when they do not possess a host.

"How, then, was *Kelenbhrabanal's* murder effected?" The Manethrall had slipped into a reverie of sadness. As he spoke, he turned his head slowly from side to side as if he were searching for insight. "If Fangthane assumed flesh to slay the Father of Horses, he risked physical death under *Kelenbhrabanal's* hooves. And *Kelenbhrabanal* was too great a sire to be overcome by the manner of magicks which Fangthane wields indirectly.

"Yet *Kelenbhrabanal* was indeed slain. His blood was shed. Generation after generation, the Ramen have asked of themselves, How? By what means was *Kelenbhrabanal's* life torn from him?

"What crime do the Ranyhyn grieve, apart from betrayal?"

There Mahrtiir recovered his ire. His tone became sharper; more insistent. And as his manner changed, Linden's attention sharpened as well. She had never considered his questions, but she could guess where they might lead.

In the horserite, she had learned that the Ranyhyn felt shame. At the time, she had understood how and why they faulted themselves for Elena's fate. But now she suspected that Mahrtiir would offer a deeper explanation. Obliquely he might reveal why beasts as knowing and sufficient as the great horses gave others the same selfless service that they received from the Ramen.

"We merely speculate among ourselves," the Manethrall stated. He still spoke softly, but his underlying anger was plain. "We possess no knowledge of such matters. Yet the fear which the Ranyhyn evince toward the lurker of the Sarangrave—toward that evil and no other—is certain. Thus in our minds the mystery of *Kelenbhrabanal* has become entwined with the fear of the Ranyhyn, another mystery. And we surmise, having no assurance of truth, that the lurker was the means by which Fangthane slew the Father of Horses.

"Perchance we are mistaken. Fangthane has never lacked servants to do his biding. Yet the pith of our speculation remains. Among those evils which the Ramen have encountered, none but the lurker daunt the Ranyhyn. And we are certain that the great horses have not forgotten *Kelenbhrabanal's* death. Their recall is renewed in every horserite across the generations, mind to mind, until each mare and stallion knows treachery and terror. For that reason, we surmise, they grieve, and cannot rule their fear, and are ashamed."

Hearing the Manethrall, Linden understood his anger—and perhaps Hynyn's as well. Covenant's farmhouse still burned in the background of her mind: she had her own causes for shame. But Mahrtiir's guesswork raised the question that she had not asked.

The Ranyhyn had chosen the company's path. Why had they elected to drift toward Sarangrave Flat? Surely they could have found another route through the barricades of hills? What purpose had been served by exposing the company—exposing Linden and the Staff of Law—to the Feroce, and to the lurker's hunger?

While she searched for a way to pose her query that did not sound like an accusation, however, the Manethrall's manner changed again. As if he expected a rebuff, and did not mean to accept it, he said, "I have replied as well as I am able. Now, Ringthane, I also require a reply. That the Feroce imposed a *geas* upon you is plain. Yet they wielded no force to equal that of the Staff. Any and all of your companions would have intervened to spare you, but you did not permit our aid. With fire and seeming fear, you spurned us as you ran to the lurker's embrace.

"I crave some account of the coercion which ruled you."

Involuntarily Linden winced. She owed her friends an explanation: she knew that. But her vulnerability had not begun with cutting herself. Nor had it arisen from her encounter with She Who Must Not Be Named, or from Roger's treachery, and the *croyel*'s, under *Melenkurion* Skyweir. She had brought it with her from her former life. Ultimately its roots reached past Sara Clint and the savaged ruin of Covenant's home to the futility of Linden's love for her son, to her failure to prevent Covenant's murder, and from there to the plight of being her unforgiven parents' daughter. She did not want to describe the real sources of her despair.

Nevertheless she could not refuse to answer Mahrtiir. His need, and the ache in the eyes of the Giants, compelled her.

Swallowing against a sudden thickness in her throat, Linden said unsteadily, "The Feroce— Whatever they are. They have a kind of power that I've never felt before. A kind of glamour." Even with her health-sense, she had never been able to pierce the theurgy with which Roger could conceal or disguise himself. "But it was all in my mind. It took over"—she swallowed again—"the whole inside of my head.

"It wasn't possession. They didn't force me to think their thoughts. They didn't control what I was feeling. Instead they used who I already am against me. They used my own memories to make me believe—"

She wanted to stop there. Surely her companions could imagine the rest? But no: Mahrtiir's stance demanded more. The expectant attention of the Giants resembled pleading.

When was she going to start trusting them?

With a private groan, she told them as much as she could bear about what the glamour had unleashed within her.

Roger and Jeremiah. Covenant's farmhouse. Sara Clint. The fire. Fighting the flames. She Who Must Not Be Named. Recursive agony and horror. Desperate flight.

Rime Coldspray's eyes widened as Linden spoke. Frostheart Grueburn muttered Giantish oaths under her breath. But Linden did not allow herself to pause.

These people were her *friends*—

She elided as many details as she could. She did not wish to experience them again. But she interpreted the effects of the imposed hallucinations as she had explained them to herself.

"When I thought that I was beating at the flames, I must have been fighting you. Keeping you away while I tried to escape. But when I threw the Staff, the Feroce dropped their glamour. I wasn't what they wanted." *Our High God hungers for it.* The *stick of power.* "All at once, I stopped believing that I was trapped. The house and the fire disappeared, and I was here again."

Finally Linden bowed her head. What more could she say?

Manethrall Mahrtiir regarded her in silence for a moment. Then, gravely, he nodded. "Ringthane, I am content." He may have meant that she had accepted a burden as hurtful as the one he had been asked to bear.

Marveling, Rime Coldspray mused, "Much you have concealed from us, Linden Giantfriend—aye, and much revealed. You say nothing of the reasons for the Timewarden's son's deeds. Yet you make plain that you have long sought your son, at great cost. And though you speak little of your former world, you have allowed us to discern that it is fraught with hazard. With these scant words, too few to contain their own substance, you imply the import of your trials.

"Therefore I salute you, Chosen Ringthane." Sitting, she pressed both palms to her chest, then spread her arms wide as if she were opening her heart. "Once again, you have wrestled life from the teeth of death, as by your own account you have done from the first. Had you not cast away your Staff—"

The Ironhand shook her head in wonder. "I am not shamed to acknowledge that eight Swordmainnir are no match for the lurker of the Sarangrave. We would have spent our last strength, and caused much hurt. But in the end, the monster would have taken your life as well as the Staff of Law, and all hope would now be lost. In Andelain, you surrendered your Staff to redeem your son. Doing so again, you have rescued yourself and us.

"Therefore," she continued more quietly, "I ask your consent in one matter. I wish to forestall the necessity of further surrenders. By your leave, Frostheart Grueburn will assume guardianship of your Staff in the event that the Feroce essay another approach. We cannot be assured that her mind will not also fall into glamour, as yours did. However—"

"It will not," put in Onyx Stonemage. "You speak of Grueburn, whose natural bewilderment excludes other confusion."

Several of the Giants chuckled; and Grueburn retorted, "Fie and folly, Stonemage. Breathes there a Giant upon the wide Earth whose acquaintance with bewilderment is as intimate as your own?"

But Coldspray's manner remained serious. "However," she persisted firmly, "the Staff is not hers. She has neither skill nor aptitude in its use. Should the lurker's minions bemuse her, we will be able to intercede.

"By your leave, Linden Giantfriend," she repeated.

Stifling an instinctive reluctance, Linden nodded. More than once, she had trusted Liand with her Staff. Surely she could trust Frostheart Grueburn?

Her own response if the Feroce returned might be to tear them apart before they could intrude on her mind again. But that would mean more killing—and more despair. Eventually she would become like her mother, begging someone who did not deserve the cost to put her out of her misery.

Too many people had already paid the price for her first failure to rescue Jeremiah.

ॐ

She had not slept the previous night. She did so now. Warmed by the partial shelter's infused Earthpower, she stretched out on her ground-cloth, then wrapped it around her. In spite of the erratic moan and rasp of the wind, and the cut of the unseasonable cold, Linden Avery stumbled into sleep as if she were fleeing.

During the remainder of the night, she dreamed of bonfires and flame-ripped houses; of a crude throne like a gaping maw in the Lost Deep; of centipedes and intimate pestilence. Deep in sleep, she pushed one hand into a pocket of her jeans and grasped Jeremiah's toy racecar as if it were a sovereign talisman, potent to ward off nightmares and malice.

She was still clutching the car when Frostheart Grueburn nudged her awake to meet the dawn of another unanswerable day.

With the distant rise of the sun, a light as grey as ash had drifted into the gap among the hills. When Linden blinked the blur of dreams from her eyes, and sat up staring as if she were dazed, she saw that Stave had returned.

He was clean. Indeed, he looked positively scrubbed. Every hint of marsh-filth was gone from his skin, his strife-marred tunic. Hynyn must have taken him to a source of clean water. There he must have beaten his vellum garment against a rock until even the stains of old blood were pounded away.

Now he stood between Manethrall Mahrtiir and Grueburn, gazing at Linden with his one eye and waiting as if he had never known a moment of impatience in his life.

His cleanliness made Linden consider her own condition. She had not been fouled in the Sarangrave. But she still wore the grime of riding in rain and harsh wind. She, too, needed a bath; needed to wash her hair. As for her clothes—

Nothing had changed. The over-worn flannel of her shirt looked like it had been plucked by thorns. A small hole marked the place where her heart should have stopped beating. The fraying threads where she had torn a patch from the hem were all that remained of her gratitude to the Mahdoubt.

On both legs below the knees of her jeans, green lines explicated her plight in a script that she could not read. Where she had cut herself, small blots of blood complicated the grass stains, altering them to obscure or transform their content.

Aching in every limb as though her dreams had been battles, Linden climbed to her feet. As she accepted a waterskin and a little food from Latebirth, Stave told her, "The Ranyhyn will convey us to a tributary of the Ruinwash. There we will find fresh water and *aliantha.*"

"That is well," muttered Cabledarm sourly. "The muck of the Sarangrave"—she grimaced—"clings. It assails my nostrils yet. I cannot rub it away."

The Ironhand and Stonemage nodded, sharing her distaste.

"But I must counsel against delay," Stave added. "Chosen, I lack the Manethrall's communion with the great horses. Yet in Hynyn I sense a new urgency. The Ranyhyn appear to desire haste."

"Let the beasts desire what they will," replied Coldspray. "We must wash. We will be better able to quicken our strides when rot and malevolence no longer clog our lungs."

Haste? Linden wanted to ask. Why now? After walking for two days? But she was still too groggy to pose questions that none of her companions would be able to answer. Baffled, she drank and chewed and swallowed, and tried to believe that she was ready.

As ready as she would ever be.

Latebirth repacked the company's dwindling supplies, tied the blankets into a tight roll. Apparently the Giants and Mahrtiir had eaten while Linden slept; or they had elected to forgo a meal. Stormpast Galesend informed Linden that she had fed Jeremiah, although he gave no sign of it. When Linden nodded to Stave, to Mahrtiir, to Rime Coldspray, the company set out, led southward through the hills by Cirrus Kindwind.

With the rising of the sun, the wind had ceased. Now the air was as still as a held breath: it was growing warmer. Yet it remained grey, tainted by fires and dust-storms which had never occurred. Overhead the sky was leaden with rue, as if a pall of regret had settled over the eastern reaches of the Land. Through the haze, the dispirited sun shone wanly.

In the dulled light, the company found Hyn, Hynyn, Narunal, and Khelen waiting on open ground. Beyond a narrow lowland rose another crooked barrier, and then another. But Linden did not regard the obstacles ahead. She was simply glad to see Hyn again.

She should have known that the mare would return. Whatever the Ranyhyn had sought near Sarangrave Flat, they had not wished to rid themselves of their riders.

An abashed look darkened Hyn's eyes as she approached Linden; a suggestion of shame. At the last moment, the dappled grey hesitated. She halted just out of Linden's reach, issued a nickering query. In response to Hynyn's peremptory snort, however, Hyn came another step closer, then bent one leg and lowered her head, bowing.

Oh, stop, Linden thought. I don't blame you. I don't know why you did it. But I'm sure you had your reasons. If I knew what they were, I might even approve.

They're Ranyhyn, *for God's sake. They'll think of something.*

To reassure the mare, Linden went to her and wrapped her arms around Hyn's neck.

Manethrall Mahrtiir prostrated himself briefly in front of Narunal, then sprang onto his mount's back. When Galesend set Jeremiah astride Khelen, the boy settled there, passive and unmoved, as if there were no perceptible difference between the Swordmain's care and the young stallion's. While Linden still held Hyn, Stave mounted Hynyn; and the Giants arrayed themselves around the Ranyhyn.

For a long moment, Linden gazed into the softness of Hyn's eyes until she was sure that the mare's abashment had faded. Then she looked up at Frostheart Grueburn.

"All right," she said as firmly as she could. "Let's go. I want a bath as much as you do."

With a fond grin, Grueburn put her huge hands on Linden's waist, lifted Linden lightly onto Hyn's back.

At once, the Ranyhyn began to move, trotting at a pace that the Giants could match without running.

The horses had chosen to approach the next wall of hills at a westward angle, away from the Sarangrave; closer to Landsdrop. From Linden's perspective, the barricade looked impassable, for the mounts if not for the Giants. But within half a league, the Ranyhyn came to a more gradual slope that allowed them to reach a notch like a bite taken out of the forbidding ridge. And as they passed between rocky crests gnarled with lichen and age, she saw that the south-facing hillsides provided an easy descent.

The hills ahead appeared to be the last obstruction plowed to defend the Spoiled Plains.

In the furrow between the ridges, Stave guided Hynyn to Hyn's side opposite Frost-heart Grueburn. Linden expected him to say something about her actions the previous night. But when he had taken his position, he remained silent. Apparently he desired nothing more than to resume his wonted role as her guardian.

She scanned the company; confirmed that Khelen bore Jeremiah easily, and that the Swordmainnir looked able to keep pace with the horses. Then she said to Stave sidelong, "You weren't with us when Mahrtiir talked about *Kelenbhrabanal*. He did what he could to explain why the Ranyhyn are afraid of the lurker. But he didn't say anything about why the Ranyhyn took us so close to the Sarangrave in the first place."

The company's present path demonstrated that the horses could have chosen a different route.

The former Master gazed at her steadily. "Chosen?"

"You probably don't know any more about that than I do. But hearing about *Kelenbhrabanal* made me think about Kevin." Both had sacrificed themselves, if by different means for dissimilar reasons. "I was wondering if you can tell me anything about him."

Again Stave asked, "Chosen?"

Her query was too vague. But clarifying it would require her to reveal one of her deepest fears. Instinctively she wanted to keep the core of her emotional plight secret. Nevertheless the crisis induced by the Feroce had convinced her that she had to rely more on her friends. If she did not, she might never find a way to thwart Lord Foul's intentions.

The next rise still looked insurmountable. Among steep slides of shale, sandstone, and gravel, massive knurls of granite and schist gripped each other like fists, too clenched and contorted for horses. Some of the slopes conveyed an impression of imminent collapse: any slight disturbance might unloose them. In places, slabs of sandstone leaned ominously outward, poised to topple. Yet the Ranyhyn approached the obstruction without slackening their pace, heading into the southwest as though they expected the hills to part for them.

Linden had fled flames in a hallway—a gullet—that had no end and no escape. She had only survived because she had turned to face the blaze; had read the map on her jeans and thrown away her only defense.

Trusting *someone*—

"There's something that I want to understand about Kevin," she told Stave awkwardly, "but I don't know how to put it into words." Grueburn's presence discomfited her. Her friendship with the Swordmain lacked the earned certainty of her bond with Stave. Still she forced herself to proceed as if she and Stave were alone. "Ever since the Ritual of Desecration, he's been called the Landwaster. I guess that makes me the

Earthwaster. Compared to waking up the Worm, his Ritual looks like a petty offense. I want to know what he and I have in common."

She needed a reason to believe that she had not already achieved Lord Foul's victory for him.

"I can see how what *Kelenbhrabanal* did is different. He only sacrificed himself. And he did it because he thought that he was saving the Ranyhyn. He wasn't trying to commit a Desecration. But what I've heard about Kevin sounds like how I feel.

"I mean like how I feel now. I didn't feel this way in Andelain. Sure, I was too angry to think about the consequences. But I also had hope." And need. "I wanted Covenant alive because I love him. But I also believed that he's the only one who can save the Land. If I brought him back, I could afford to concentrate on rescuing Jeremiah. He would take care of everything else."

Covenant was supposed to be her defense against despair. She had counted on that. She had never imagined that he would want to leave her behind—

"So now," she finished like a sigh, "I want to know what Kevin and I have in common." She felt the force of Grueburn's scrutiny at her side; but she tried to ignore it. "He destroyed pretty much everything. I thought that I was saving everything."

Fortunately Grueburn did not speak. If she had questions, she was too considerate to express them.

The Ranyhyn confronted the hills as if they were proof against mundane doubts. To Linden's distracted gaze, the immediate slopes looked ready to slip. Sandstone columns whispered to her nerves that they were friable, too heavy to support their own mass. And beyond the columns stood glowering buttresses without any breach or gap. Nevertheless Narunal and Khelen began an angled ascent as if they were confident of safety. And Hyn and Hynyn followed without hesitation, surrounded by their coterie of stonewise Giants.

Somehow the surface held as horses and Swordmainnir pushed upward.

Stave appeared to dismiss the potential dangers of the climb. For a long moment, he was silent, perhaps probing the ancient memories of the Bloodguard. Then he replied, "*If*, Chosen."

Grueburn nodded as though she knew what he meant. But Linden stared at him. "I don't understand."

Like a man who had resolved a conundrum, Stave stated, "*That* you share with High Lord Kevin Landwaster, who is now forgiven by his sires. *If*.

"Summoned to a parley with or concerning the Demondim, *if* he had not sent his friends and fellow Lords in his stead. Concerned and grieving for your son, *if* you had heeded Anele's desire for the Sunstone. You believe that you might have acted otherwise, and that you are culpable for your failure to do so. Thus you open your heart to despair, as High Lord Kevin did also."

Again Frostheart Grueburn nodded—and said nothing.

"Chosen," Stave continued, "you have rightly charged the Masters with arrogance. They have deemed themselves wise enough, and worthy, to prejudge the use which the folk of the Land would make of their knowledge. After his own fashion, Kevin Landwaster was similarly arrogant. In his damning *if*, he neglected to consider that his friends and fellow Lords selected their own path. He commanded none of them to assume his place. Indeed, many among the Council valued his wisdom when he declined to hazard his own vast lore and the Staff of Law in a perilous vesture. Yet those voices he did not hear. Arrogating to himself responsibility for the fate of those who fell, he demeaned them—and failed to perceive Corruption clearly. Faulting himself for error rather than Corruption for treachery, he was self-misled to the Ritual of Desecration, and could not turn aside.

"So it is with you."

Linden listened as if she were in shock; as if the impact of his words were so great that her nerves refused to absorb it. No, she thought, shaking her head. No. Damnit, I *learned* that lesson.

I thought I learned it—

Leading the company, Narunal and then Khelen rounded the base of the first plinth; altered the thrust of their strides to pass above the next column. In spite of the sun's shrouded light, the day was growing warmer. Already the spires of porous rock appeared to shimmer in the heat as if they were about to shatter.

Hell and blood! Echoing one of Covenant's epithets, Linden reminded herself that she had asked the question. She should at least try to understand the answer.

"Chosen," Stave said again when he had given her a chance to protest, "I do not name the Unbeliever's resurrection a Desecration. The Humbled do so. I do not. Yet there you were yourself arrogant. Fearing that your companions would oppose you, you kept your full purpose secret from them. By that means, you denied them the freedom of their own paths. Yet you were honest enough to acknowledge that you do not forgive. And you insisted upon doubt. So doing, you allowed your companions to estimate the extremity of your intent. Also, as you have said, your heart was filled with rage and love rather than with blame. Therefore your deeds in Andelain differ in their essence from High Lord Kevin's.

"Now, however"—the former Master shrugged—"matters stand otherwise. Now you do not consider that Liand acted according to his own desires, or that Anele did not plainly or loudly or vigorously demand the *orcrest*, or that you had companions who might have been better able to heed the old man at that moment. Nor do you consider that the deed of Liand's death was Kastenessen's. Rather you demean all who stand with you by believing that there can be no other fault than yours, and that no fault of yours can be condoned. Doing so, 'You tread paths prepared for you by Fangthane's malice,' as Manethrall Mahrtiir has said. Thus you emulate High Lord Kevin.

"In your present state, Chosen, Desecration lies ahead of you. It does not crowd at your back."

Linden reeled in her seat. Had her mount been anything less than a Ranyhyn, she might have fallen to the ground. Stave said, Desecration lies ahead of you, as if he meant, *I perceive only that her need for death is great.*

God in Heaven! How bad *was* it? How fatal had her personal failures become? Had she gleaned nothing from Liand's death, or Anele's, or Galt's; or from She Who Must Not Be Named? From the rousing of the Worm of the World's End?

Did you sojourn under the Sunbane with Sunder and Hollian, and learn nothing of ruin?

Yet the world did not reel. The Ranyhyn did not falter, or feel faint. Those weaknesses were hers alone. Narunal and Khelen were moving along the foot of a high wall like a fortification, knuckled and obdurate; visibly impenetrable. After a score of paces, however, they turned upward and disappeared as if the stone had swallowed them. Behind them, Rime Coldspray beckoned to the rest of the company. Then she, too, was gone.

When Hynyn and Hyn reached that spot, Linden found that her companions had entered a narrow defile like a cleft in the gutrock. There the stone was cut as if it had been smitten by a titanic axe. The crevice was too strait to allow either Stave or Grueburn to remain beside her: the company was forced to file upward singly. But the steep clutter of the surface did not impede the Ranyhyn; and the Giants knew stone as if it were the substance of their bones.

Hynyn and Stave must have discovered this route during the night.

Desecration lies ahead of you.

Enclosed by uncompromising walls, she could not have turned aside to save herself from falling rocks or flung spears or theurgy. Jeremiah was beyond her reach in the gloom. Crude rock brushed against her knees. At intervals, she had to lean left or right to avoid an outcropping. Grueburn's tense breathing carried up the crevice, magnified by echoes.

This symbolized Linden's life, this defile. She had never lacked for help and support: not really. In the end, even Sheriff Lytton had tried to save her. Nevertheless she had never been able to turn aside. Ever since Roger had come to claim his mother, Linden had been caught between impossible choices.

And every compelled step took her closer to Lord Foul's ultimate triumph.

Yet the defile was only a cleft in the granite: a passage, comparatively brief. It had an end. Already Linden could see it growing wider. Ahead of her, she sensed that Narunal and Khelen and now the Ironhand had emerged onto a more open hillside.

When Hyn finally surged out of the split, Linden was breathing hard, not from exertion, but from the constriction of her plight.

Desecration lies ahead of you.

She could not contest Stave's reasoning.

Overhead a soiled sky covered the Lower Land like a foretaste of calamity. To her health-sense, the air did not smell of smoke or destruction. Rather it seemed to be the natural atmosphere of the region, characteristically arid, and reminiscent of ancient warfare. Yet no more than two days ago, the firmament had been blue, untainted by Kevin's Dirt or omens. Like the previous day's storms, this ashen sky was a consequence of powers or movements too distant for her to discern.

Linden wanted a few moments alone with Stave and Frostheart Grueburn. At her request, Hyn waited for Grueburn to rejoin her. Then the mare walked away from Mahrtiir, Jeremiah, Coldspray, and the arriving Giants. Without being asked, Hynyn and Stave accompanied her.

When she was confident that she would not be overheard, Linden asked Grueburn awkwardly, "What are you going to tell the others?"

She had revealed and heard truths that filled her with dismay. She was not ready to share them.

Grueburn cocked her head to one side. She appeared to be stifling a grin. "I have no wish to shock you, Linden Giantfriend. Yet I must assure you that Giants are acquainted with discretion. Your words were intended for Stave's ears, not for mine. I cannot say that I did not attend to them, or that I will forget. But Giants tell no tales that have not been freely offered."

For a moment, relief closed Linden's throat. Saving her strength for Stave, she mouthed to the Swordmain, Thank you. Then she turned to the former Master.

He faced her stolidly, as if nothing had passed between them.

He was not merely her friend: he had been her best counselor. She had confided in him when she had felt unable to name her fears to anyone else. And in the Hall of Gifts, he had given her reason to hope for Jeremiah.

Swallowing dust and dread, she said, "You're a harsh judge."

He had named her doom.

His eye held hers. "Indeed. I am *Haruchai*." Then he shrugged. "Yet grief is now known to me. Therefore compassion also is known. And in your company I have learned that I must aspire to humility."

Just for an instant, the lines of his mouth hinted at a smile.

Desecration lies ahead of you. But Giants tell no tales— Obliquely both Stave and Grueburn triggered memories of Anele's excoriated lucidity in Revelstone. She had promised to protect him from the consequences of her desires—and he had refused her.

*All who live share the Land's plight. Its cost will be borne by all who live. This you can-
not alter. In the attempt, you may achieve only ruin.*

Now she understood the old man. *When your deeds have come to doom, as they
must—* She understood Stave. She had spent so many years taking care of Jeremiah, so
many years tending patients too damaged to provide for their own survival, that she
had forgotten how to count on other kinds of relationships. She had allowed herself
to believe only in Covenant—and now she doubted even him. Blind to the implications of her actions, she had in some sense treated all of her friends like children or
invalids.

Even Liand. Even Stave.

Why else had she felt diminished whenever they had risen to challenges which had
defeated her?

She still did not comprehend why the Ranyhyn had risked taking her close to the
lurker of the Sarangrave; but she knew what the experience meant. It had forced her
to cast aside her Staff: the emblem of her arrogance. Perhaps inadvertently, the horses
had shown her that she could rely on her friends to save her and Jeremiah and the
Land when she could not.

Hyn and the others were still trying to show her how to find her way. How to forgive her weaknesses by having faith in the strength of her companions.

ഇ

The company's path upward remained tortuous until the ridgecrest. From that
height, however, Linden could see that the southward descent was more gradual. And she caught sight of Landsdrop. Grey in the depthless sunlight, it loomed two
thousand feet and more above her own elevation: a blunt rampart smoothed by the
ages until it appeared almost blank; too sheer to scale. But she knew from old experience as well as from tales that Landsdrop was more accessible than it looked. There
were trails of all kinds up and down the precipice, although she could not descry them
at this distance.

Ignoring the impatience of the Ranyhyn, Linden studied the vista. Almost directly
to the west, a thin string of water fell as though it had been tossed over the rim by a
negligent hand. Dull against the dim stone, like a strand of tarnished silver, it dropped
in stages, shifting from side to side as its plunge encountered obstacles, and casting fine
hints of spray into the etiolated sunshine.

Was that the River Landrider, tumbling to become the Ruinwash? No, she decided.
The stream was too small. It had to be the tributary that Stave had mentioned. At
its base, it disappeared among the cliff's crumpled foothills. When its twisted length
brought it back into view, it was less than a league away, still tending generally eastward.

There it gathered into a pool, little more than an islet in the barren landscape, before it turned southward, following the contours of the terrain.

In that pool, Stave must have bathed during the night.

The company reached it before a third of the morning had passed. Some of the slopes sweeping down from the ridge were treacherous, on the verge of slippage; but for long stretches, the footing was secure. Palpably eager, the Ranyhyn quickened their pace; and the Giants began to trot, cheered by the prospect of fresh water in abundance. Along the way, Linden watched Jeremiah for signs that he might fall from Khelen's back. But the young roan was careful to ensure that nothing unbalanced his rider. Jeremiah sat the Ranyhyn as if Khelen were motionless.

Linden had a plethora of questions that she could not ask the horses. Why had they risked proximity to the Sarangrave? Where were they taking her? And why were they in a hurry now, when they had insisted on plodding for two days? Nevertheless she had reasons for gratitude. Khelen's attentiveness to Jeremiah's passivity was only one of them.

Urged by Mahrtiir, she and the Giants bathed quickly, drank their fill, washed some of the stains from their apparel. While the Giants gulped a swift meal of cured mutton, stale bread, and *aliantha*, Linden took Jeremiah into the stream and scrubbed briefly at his blood- and gore-streaked pajamas. But she did not linger over the task.

When she was done, the Manethrall announced, "Narunal makes plain to me that the Ranyhyn require greater speed." His tone was raw frustration. "Time grows urgent. Events or perils have acquired suddenness. Why or how this is so, they cannot convey to my human mind. Nonetheless they must run.

"Their pace will be too swift for weary Giants. Yet they do not wish to forsake the Swordmainnir. Therefore I must remain with Narunal to guide the Ironhand and her comrades. With Stave, the Ringthane, and her son, Hynyn, Hyn, and Khelen will strive to accomplish the nameless intent of this quest. We will follow with such alacrity as the Giants are able to sustain."

Before Linden or the others could object, Mahrtiir added fiercely, "Ringthane, I do not part from you by my own choice. More, I am shamed to be apart from you in this exigency. I do not willingly surrender my place in your tale. Yet my service to the Ranyhyn compels me. I cannot flout their will and remain Ramen."

In their own fashion, the Ramen were as severe as the *Haruchai*.

"Hell, Mahrtiir," Linden muttered. "I don't want to lose you either. We've been walking for two damn days—and *now* we're in a hurry? But—"

"But," Rime Coldspray interrupted sharply, "we have agreed to entrust our fate to the Ranyhyn. We were not coerced to this heading. Nor were we able to select a clearer course. And the Manethrall belabors a manifest truth when he observes that we are weary.

"Linden Avery, we are Giants, loath to fail the aid of any and all whom we name friends. Yet we are also sailors. We do not choose the world's winds. We do what we may to seek our own desires, but we do not pretend to rule that which is offered to our sails. Come calm or gale, we gain our sought harborage—when we gain it—by endurance rather than by mastery.

"For our part, we will accept the will of these horses. If they are worthy of the honor which Manethrall Mahrtiir and the Ramen have accorded them, they will not mislead us."

"*But*," Linden repeated, "I was about to say that I've been making too many decisions for other people. And I don't know that the Ranyhyn have ever been wrong." They may have erred when they had exposed her to the Feroce and the lurker; but she no longer cared. Like Hyn, Hynyn, and Khelen, she yearned for speed. *Desecration lies ahead of you.* She wanted to meet it before fear or despair paralyzed her; while she could still choose. "*Something* has changed. I can't guess what it is, but I believe that they know.

"So maybe they're right. Maybe you should eat more. Rest more. Try to build up your strength. Narunal won't hold you back when you're needed."

Then she faced the Manethrall. "Mahrtiir, I'm sorry. I can imagine how you feel." She had watched Covenant ride away without her. "But as far as I'm concerned, nothing makes sense anymore. And we've come this far. Without the Ranyhyn, we're all lost now. I'm just glad that they still know what they want."

Mahrtiir appeared to flinch. But his emotions were too complex for Linden to read clearly. He radiated chagrin, anger, pride, umbrage, all in turmoil.

Stave's reply was to vault astride Hynyn. Sitting the stallion, he bowed gravely, first to Manethrall Mahrtiir, then to Rime Coldspray.

For perhaps the last time, Grueburn boosted Linden onto her mount's back. While Stormpast Galesend did the same for Jeremiah, the boy seemed to gaze at the cemetery of his thoughts as though every grave had been emptied of meaning.

At once, Hynyn, Hyn, and Khelen started away from the pool. For Jeremiah's sake, apparently, they moved slowly at first. But with every heartbeat, they lengthened their strides. Soon they were running at a full gallop.

The Giants let the riders go without a word. Linden suspected that they did not wish to acknowledge that they might never see their companions again. But Narunal whinnied a farewell. As it carried across the uneven ground under the ashen sky, his cry sounded as formal as a fanfare: a call to battle, or a proclamation of homage.

Leaning low over Hyn's neck, and clutching the Staff of Law across her thighs, Linden prayed that she was not making a fatal mistake.

9.

Great Need

From the rumpled terrain south of the pool, the Ranyhyn pounded onto a baked flatland as hard as the surface of an anvil. In spite of the previous day's rain, their hooves raised bleached dust as fine as ash. When Linden glanced behind her, she saw a pale plume trailing after her like a pennon.

The speed of the horses was wind in her face, growing warmer as the morning advanced. The air parched her throat, dried her eyes. She thought that she tasted death on her tongue; but if she did, the scent was ancient beyond reckoning. Uncounted centuries ago, living things by the scores or hundreds of thousands had perished in bloodshed: human and inhuman, sentient and bestial, monsters whose forms were no longer remembered even by the *Haruchai*. Like every shape and kind of vegetation that had once flourished here, they were the forgotten detritus of Lord Foul's wars. Ghosts so long dead that they had lost all substance lingered, mourning mutely. Nothing remained to bespeak their desires and wounds, their fears and furies, except a vague tang pounded up from the iron dirt by the strides of the Ranyhyn.

Without her health-sense, Linden might have thought that the Ranyhyn were giving their utmost. But the smooth flow of Hyn's muscles under her legs assured her that the mare had strength and stamina in reserve. At need, the horses could do more.

Stave looked fluid and relaxed, more like an expression of Hynyn's swiftness than a burden. In contrast, Jeremiah rode characteristically slack, slumped, as unmoved as a sack of grain by Khelen's fleet pace. Linden had not seen him blink since his rescue. Yet his eyes were unharmed, preserved by some implication of the Earthpower that he had received from Anele.

For a portion of the morning, the Ranyhyn headed somewhat east of south across the beaten plain. Before noon, however, Stave pointed out the promontory of the Colossus in the distant west. Over the drumming of hooves, he informed Linden that beyond the promontory Landsdrop curved southward. There the River Landrider fell in a heavy cascade to become the Ruinwash.

Thinking, —*written in water*, Linden wondered whether the Ranyhyn intended to intercept the Ruinwash. But according to Stave, the Ruinwash skirted the Spoiled Plains as well as the Shattered Hills to reach the sea many leagues beyond Foul's Creche.

Although the horses turned south when they had passed the promontory, their goal apparently lay somewhere between the Ruinwash and the Shattered Hills.

As heat mounted from the flat, the sky began to resemble a lid closing over the Lower Land: as grey as a sheet of molded lead, and impossible to lift. How much longer could the Ranyhyn gallop like this? They were mortal. Surely they had limits? To Linden's nerves, Hyn's endurance seemed as certain as the sun. Yet there was froth on the mare's nostrils. Sweat darkened her dappled sides, soaking slowly into Linden's jeans; chafing Linden's legs. At intervals, she thought that she heard an irregular catch and falter in Hyn's respiration.

If the Ranyhyn still had far to go, they would need help. Their destination might be a dozen leagues distant, or a score. Blinking rapidly, Linden tightened her grip on the Staff; readied herself to summon black fire.

But then, on a horizon fraught with haze, she saw the end of the flat. In the east, the terrain tilted toward lower ground. Toward the west, brief hills like afterthoughts interrupted the plain. They wore a scurf of scrannel grass like a beggar's mantle, threadbare and tattered.

If they had grass, they had water—

Responding to Hynyn's authority, Hyn and Khelen followed the roan stallion toward the hills.

Soon they were passing between rises that were little more than hillocks; low mounds of dirt partially clad in patches of grass. As the horses ran deeper into the region, the grass grew more thickly.

Then Hynyn slowed to a canter; to a walk. Ahead of him, Linden saw an erosion gully. She smelled water.

At once, she dropped down from Hyn's back so that she would not impede Hyn's approach to the stream. And she was in a hurry to drink herself; to clear dust and death from her throat. A moment later, Stave also dismounted. Jeremiah he pulled gently but unceremoniously to the ground. Bringing the boy with him, he followed Linden and the Ranyhyn toward the watercourse.

It was, he told her, the same stream in which the company had bathed earlier, pursuing its union with the Ruinwash. But when Linden asked him if he had any idea where the horses were going, he only shrugged. Foul's Creche lay to the east. The Ranyhyn were headed south. More than that he did not know.

The horses drank deeply. They cropped a little grass along the verges of the gully while Linden and Stave quenched their thirst. For a few moments, Linden scooped water into Jeremiah's mouth. With her hands and her health-sense, she assured herself that he was physically well. Then Stave lifted her onto Hyn; seated Jeremiah on Khelen; mounted Hynyn.

Within a few strides, the Ranyhyn were running again.

Soon they left the mounded hillocks behind, still racing south. For a time, they crossed damaged plains. After that, however, they came upon a wide field of broken obsidian, basalt, and flint, the muricated remains of a slagland. Shards as cutting as blades gouged out of the soil at every angle: another consequence of ancient violence.

Linden thought that the Ranyhyn would have to find a way around. Otherwise splintered edges would tear the frogs of their hooves to shreds. But she had underestimated the great horses. As nimble as mountain-goats, they plunged among the rocks; swept and wheeled forward as though they were engaged in an elaborate and courtly gavotte. Somehow they found safe footing that Linden could not see, and passed unharmed.

Beyond the shards, they encountered a rugose region like a delta or malpaís where igneous creeks and rills had branched, burning, through once-arable earth. Some fierce theurgy during a distant era had caused the stone of the area to melt and stream like spilth. There the Ranyhyn ran again, apparently heedless of occasional surfaces as slick as ice, twisted clumps of dirt that masked rubble, friable ground concealing sinkholes like deadfalls.

The heat across the landscape felt more like summer than spring. The sun seemed to lean its leaden aspect close to the Lower Land. It barely cast shadows, but its pressure made the mounts drip sweat as they ran, splashing the complex ground. Linden's shirt clung to her back: her legs rubbed like sores against Hyn's damp flanks. Trickles ran down Jeremiah's cheeks into the soilure of his pajamas, his stained rearing horses.

Early in the afternoon, the riders left the delta behind; galloped onto a slowly rolling plain like a trammeled moor. Guided by instincts more precise than Linden's percipience, the Ranyhyn came to a thicket of *aliantha* clustered around a small spring oozing like blood from the wounded ground. There they paused while Stave dismounted to gather treasure-berries. Linden made a bowl of her shirttail to hold the fruit. With both hands full, Stave leapt onto Khelen's back behind Jeremiah. As the horses cantered away, Stave placed berries one at a time into the boy's mouth. Jeremiah did not chew them, or spit out the seeds; but he swallowed everything.

When Stave was done, he sprang from Khelen's back to Hynyn's; and the Ranyhyn resumed their urgent gallop, racing south.

Linden ate more slowly, savoring the refreshment of *aliantha*; casting aside the seeds. The haste of the Ranyhyn infected her. With every increment of the day's passage, she became more certain that she and her companions would need all of their strength. She had no idea what lay ahead of them. They had to be ready.

Finally she leaned as close as she could to Hyn's ears and murmured, "I want to help, but I don't know how to ask your permission. If I'm wrong, I hope that you'll forgive me."

Hesitant at first, then with more confidence, Linden began to draw Earthpower from the Staff. Concentrated flames uncoiled like dire tendrils, like the Ardent's ribbands, and reached out to wrap sustenance around Hyn, Hynyn, and Khelen.

Hynyn blared a neigh; tossed his head. Khelen pranced for two or three strides, as if he were showing off. Hyn's whickering sounded like affection. In a moment, they increased their pace, thrusting the ground behind them until they almost seemed to fly.

Apparently the horses of Ra approved.

ℜ

By mid-afternoon, the terrain tilted gently downward to both the south and the east. For a time, the running was easier. But then the dirt became sandstone and shale again, a punitive surface made hazardous by outcroppings and loose sheets of rock. Fighting the blur of speed in her eyes, Linden forced her gaze ahead. In the distance, she saw the land begin to rise. By stages and shelves, layers of erosion, the ground climbed to a ragged horizon like a wall of broken teeth. The ascent was neither high nor steep, but it sufficed to block everything beyond it.

Peering upward, she had the impression that she was approaching the rim of the world.

The Ranyhyn raced down the last decline, crossed a flat span like an alluvial plain left behind by some long-forgotten flood, then thundered urgently upward. As they neared the crest, Linden realized that the teeth of the horizon were not boulders. They were flawed sheets of sandstone like mammoth scapulae that jutted, cracked and fraying, from the underlying skeleton of the rise.

At last, Hynyn, Hyn, and Khelen eased their pace. In spite of their weariness, they conveyed the impression that they slowed, not because they were tired, but rather because they were close to their goal. Cantering, then trotting, finally walking, they ascended as if the lip of the climb were the edge of a precipice; as if the sandstone plates were the final barrier between them and an absolute fall. Yet they did not seem apprehensive. Instead their steps were almost stately, and the spirit shining through their sweat and fatigue suggested pride or awe, as if they were nearing a source of wonder, a place potent to transform realities.

"Stave—?" Linden asked hoarsely. "What—?"

Surely he knew where they were? Surely his people had seen what lay beyond the broken teeth?

The *Haruchai* did not answer. Nothing in his manner implied recognition—or comprehension.

The upthrust sheets were taller than Stave on Hynyn's back; taller than any Giant. They reached for the sealed sky as if they had once stood high enough to hold back the heavens; as if eons ago they had formed an impenetrable barrier. Now the Ranyhyn stepped between them, unhindered, and paused.

The riders had reached the ridge of a round hollow like a crater or caldera, although Linden could not imagine what manner of volcanism might have created such a formation. All around the rim rose eroded sheets like weary sentinels, a ragged troop of guards too tired to stand at attention. The caldera itself was so wide that one of the Swordmainnir might not have been able to throw a stone across it. Yet the enclosed hollow or crater was not deep. Indeed, it resembled a basin rather than a pit, with shallow sides and a flat bottom.

This, apparently, was the reason that the Ranyhyn had spent the day running hard enough to burst the hearts of ordinary horses. So baffled that she had no words, Linden stared downward like a woman who had come to the end of her wits.

The bottom of the caldera was filled with piled bones.

They were old—God, they were *old*! Thousands of them, tens of thousands, lay there as though they had been simply tossed aside; as though the crater were a midden in which every other form of refuse had fallen to dust. Or perhaps Lord Foul's armies had never bothered to burn or bury their dead. Seasons of sun and weather beyond counting had scalded the bones to an utter whiteness. Under a brighter sky, they would have been dazzling.

Trying to understand, Linden studied them. Her first thought was that they were human; but they were not. She had never seen their like before. Some had curves or condyles that seemed unnatural. Some were far too long or broad to belong to Giants. Some looked like the ribs of animals much larger than Ranyhyn. Among them, there were too many crooks and bends, too many bones that resembled flames, too many wide sheets that might have been the shoulder-blades of hills or the sides of cromlechs.

They could not be what the Ranyhyn had sought in such haste. They *could not*. They were not merely unimaginably old: they were meaningless. Perhaps this was the graveyard of some species that had gathered together for comfort while it fell into extinction. Or perhaps Lord Foul, for some incomprehensible reason, had discarded his failed or slain creations here. In either case, these bones had no conceivable purpose now. Whatever they had once been, they had become nothing more than the residue of vast time. They might well be as ancient as the gutrock of the Lost Deep, but they were just bones; dismembered skeletons. They remembered only death.

The sheer *waste* of what she and her friends had done since Covenant's departure urged Linden to fill the sky with her frustration.

Yet the Ranyhyn felt otherwise: that was obvious. After a long pause while she scanned the caldera, and her chagrin swelled until it seemed too great to be contained, all three of the horses whinnied loudly: a sound like the clash of swords on shields as a mighty army marched to battle. Then they began to move again. As if they were approaching a seat of majesty, they paced gravely down into the hollow.

"Stave," Linden croaked. Her heart labored toward a crisis of denied needs. "God damn it. What *is* this?"

"I cannot answer," he said flatly. "The Masters have seen this place, but have no knowledge of it. And during the centuries of the Bloodguard, no Lord hazarded this region of the Lower Land. Upon occasion, the Council of Lords spoke of a time before the coming of the Bloodguard, when High Lord Loric risked forays toward Sarangrave Flat and the Spoiled Plains. But within the hearing of the Bloodguard, those Lords described neither the purpose nor the outcome of Loric Vilesilencer's efforts. And no mention was made of these littered bones."

The *Haruchai* turned a searching gaze on Linden. "I will remind you, however, that even here Manethrall Mahrtiir would counsel trust. The ways of the Ranyhyn are a mystery in the Land, and their discernment surpasses ours. I surmise that in this place we will witness some event, or encounter some friend or foe, which they deem needful. Come good or ill, boon or bane, we must hold fast to our faith in the great horses."

An *encounter*? Linden drew a shuddering breath, tried to calm the rapid stutter of her pulse. An *event*? What could possibly happen *here*? She had ridden for leagues across open terrain, but her life was still constrained by stone walls that allowed no turning, no choices: no conceivable escape. No help for her son. Stave was wrong: Desecration did not lie ahead of her. It was here, in this pile of ruined bones. Or the Ranyhyn had followed *Kelenbhrabanal's* example by electing a form of self-sacrifice which she was helpless to alter.

Yet the former Master was also right. —hold fast to our faith— What else could she do? She was here now, with no food or water, no hope for Jeremiah; no chance to make one last effort in the Land's name. What remained, except to pray that she and her friends had not made a terrible mistake by surrendering their fate to the Ranyhyn?

When the horses gained the bottom of the caldera, Linden found that the mound of bones did not rise much higher than her head. And around them lay a clear space perhaps a dozen paces wide, suggesting that the bones had been placed here rather than simply discarded. At some point in the lost past, someone had arranged the scatter of skeletons into a heap like a cairn. But why anyone had bothered to do so, she could not conceive.

In the cleared flat, the horses halted, facing the bones. Their muscles trembled with fatigue. Sweat still ran from their flanks. But they did not shift their hooves or walk around the pile. Instead they stood motionless, waiting, as if they expected something ineffable to manifest itself within the clutter.

It is ever thus. The alternative is despair.

Linden closed her hand around Covenant's ring through her shirt. She was finding it harder and harder to believe that despair was not a better choice. Here her deeds had *come to doom, as they must*—She could not escape their ramifications.

She had violated the Laws of Life and Death to restore Thomas Covenant; but she had failed to bring him back whole. From that moment, it was probably inevitable that he would abandon her. Only his fatal loyalty to other people's mistakes had prevented him from turning his back sooner.

She should have listened—

Without warning, Jeremiah slipped down from Khelen's back; and a *caesure* appeared, seething luridly among the teeth of the caldera's rim.

Christ!

Scrambling in panic, Linden released the ring and snatched up her Staff in both hands, wheeled it around her head. *Melenkurion abatha!* Nausea clawed at her guts. Hornets swarmed toward her. *Duroc minas mill!* She had not faced a *caesure* like this: not since her personal descent into darkness had taken hold. The stain on her soul might weaken her. Some part of her had learned to crave violations of Law.

But she had to try.

Harad khabaal!

If the Seven Words had no outward power unless they were spoken aloud, they still served to focus her desperation. Responding to her frantic desires, fuligin fire erupted from the wood. Blackness scaled upward, baleful and abused, like a scream that she had inherited from She Who Must Not Be Named.

Savage as a tornado, the Fall surged into the crater as if Joan or *turiya* Raver had aimed it straight at the bones. Some effect of fury or madness—or perhaps of lessened distance—had improved Joan's control over her blasts.

Dissociated and vacant, Jeremiah ignored the *caesure*. He may have been unaware of it. Certain of himself, he walked toward the jumbled skeletons.

Into the path of ravaged time.

The Ranyhyn did not react. Stave did not move. Linden wanted him to spring down from Hynyn, catch up her son, run—But he sat his mount as if there were no peril.

As if he did not fear the virulent storm.

As if he trusted Linden Avery the Chosen.

Swinging her Staff, she lashed blazing midnight into the *caesure*'s wild core.

You cannot have my son!

Just for an instant, a staccato heartbeat, she saw herself fail. Her gush of power seemed to exacerbate the Fall—The *caesure* was feeding on her soiled strength.

But her sins had not altered the nature of the Staff, or the import of Caerroil Wild-wood's script. Almost immediately, the fundamental strictures of Earthpower and Law asserted themselves. They existed to affirm the organic integrity of life: Linden's dark-ness did not corrupt them. As the *caesure* squirmed downward, it caught fire from the inside out. Halfway down the slope, it became an ebon conflagration, writhing in hunger. A moment later, it began to collapse into itself.

The force of its inrush nearly tugged Linden from Hyn's back. But she did not stop scourging the Fall with flame, or shouting the Seven Words in her mind, until every severed instant of its violence was quenched.

Then she staggered inwardly; let her power fade. God, that was close—Too close.

"Stave," she panted. "Damnit, Stave. What are you doing? Why didn't you—?"

He did not glance at her. Without any expression that she could interpret, he said, "Attend to your son, Chosen. You have spoken of such things."

Still staggering, she wrenched her attention toward Jeremiah.

He stood at the edge of the pile, regarding it as though nothing had happened. His back was to his mother: she could not see his face. But she caught whiffs of Earthpower from his shoulders and arms; Earthpower and absence, the same emptiness that she had known ever since he had withdrawn his halfhand from Lord Foul's bonfire ten years ago.

One by one, he began pulling bones out of the pile; examining them; setting them on the ground beside him.

At the sight, Linden's mind went blank.

She could not think or feel; could not react. Paralysis stopped her private world. Words seemed to whirl through her like stars and wink out as if every form of language had become incomprehensible. She had no name for what she was seeing.

He had already selected five bones, no, six. Two were twisted into unworldly shapes, but they appeared intact. One resembled the metatarsus of a creature large enough to dwarf a Giant. The others looked like phalanges of various sizes. Now he put his hands on a bone that might have been a mammoth femur.

It was splintered at one end, or perhaps in the middle, obviously broken. Still it should have been too heavy for him to lift. But ages of the sun's heat had cooked out most of its substance, or it was as hollow as a bird's—or he had become supernally strong. Without any visible strain, he took the bone from the heap, tested it in his grasp, then placed it carefully on the ground as if its position required precision.

Jeremiah—

That was as far as Linden could go.

He moved a step to the side, studied the pile. After a moment, he found two more bones like long candles that had been heated in their centers, warped into useless twists. He collected several more phalanges, another metatarsus, a massive lump like a talus. From the abundant clutter, he extracted a second femur, a match to the first. This he set exactly parallel to the first with the space of a long stride between them.

Jeremiah was—

Displaying the same steady lack of impatience or doubt that had characterized his work with Legos or Tinkertoys in his former life, he gathered more bones. Some he found nearby. Others he discovered hidden within the heap. Phalanges by the dozens. Five more femurs that he should not have been strong enough to move, one of them whole. A number of metatarsals. And as he added to his selections, his choices became more diverse: cuboid shapes and tarsal lumps; a variety of scapulae that had apparently belonged to some titan; joint-bones with condyle sockets wide enough to cover Linden's head, or Stave's. All of these he arrayed in an open space like a craftsman readying his materials.

When he was satisfied, he stooped to his parallel splintered femurs and began to balance other bones on top of them as though he intended them to serve as foundations. As though he were constructing walls.

Jeremiah was building.

That's natural talent. Roger's tone had falsified everything he said; but he had told the truth about Jeremiah. *The right shapes can change worlds. They're like words.*

Linden struggled against blankness until her heart felt ready to burst. She had to fight to breathe. She had forgotten any words that were not prayers. Oh my God. Oh my God. OhmyGod.

It was for *this*. The Ranyhyn had brought them here for *this*. So that Jeremiah could build.

Your kid makes doors. All kinds of doors. Doors from one place to another. Doors through time. Doors between realities.

It was all impossible: the unerring instincts of the horses; Jeremiah's blank certainty; his strange strength. It was impossible that he could do what he did without focusing his eyes, or giving any sign that he was conscious of his hands. And it absolutely should have been impossible that those bones stayed where he put them, inconceivably poised on each other, defying gravity and their own lines. Their positions were so precarious, so oblivious to the dictates of mass and fit, that they all should have collapsed as soon as his fingers released them. Yet they remained where he put him: scapulae standing on their ends atop rows of phalanges, or resting off-center along awkward knobs of bone; tarsal blocks supporting rachitic lengths that may never have belonged to any natural creature; metatarsals wedged like afterthoughts between long thin fingers that looked like they would topple at any moment.

First, he has to have the right materials for the door he wants to make. Exactly the right wood or stone or metal or bone or cloth—or racetracks. And they have to be in exactly the right shapes.

Watching her son, Linden could not move. Amazement held her in a grip of stone. Her son was building. He was building! But she had never watched him make a construct like this one. Legos and Tinkertoys and raceway tracks interlocked. The branches and twigs with which he had fashioned his portal into *Melenkurion* Skyweir had been visibly braced on each other. Their own weight had held them in place. But *this*—

Lost in shock, she took too long to notice that his hands were full of Earthpower when he placed the bones on each other; or that he seemed to caress each fragment before he moved on. Or that each new piece was then fused to those it touched: that each bone became one with the others as if he had welded them together.

He was using Anele's gift to keep his structure intact.

And he was definitely making walls.

Something about his use of power was familiar. Somewhere she had seen fused bone in the shape of a Ranyhyn rearing like the horses that ramped across the begrimed blue of Jeremiah's pajamas.

"Chosen," Stave said—and more sharply, "Linden!"

All of her senses were concentrated on her son; on the transcendental possibilities of his talent; on the magic in his hands. Moments seemed to pass while a distant part of her tried to recognize Stave's voice.

Fresh nausea prompted her to hear him. Like an act of abnegation, she forced herself to look away from Jeremiah—

—and saw another *caesure* roaring like an inferno on the rim of the caldera.

It had already torn apart several of the sandstone teeth, swept them into insanity. Now it rushed downward, a stinging holocaust that made havoc of everything in its path. It came from the side of the crater opposite Jeremiah. In another instant, it would begin to devour bones, spinning them toward a future of infinite devastation.

Now Linden had no time for panic: no time and no patience. She wanted to watch her son. *She wanted to watch her son.* Exalted by outrage and frustration, she called a second flail of Earthpower from her Staff.

Instead of the Seven Words, she shouted as if she were yelling at herself, *Damn* you, Joan! Leave us the hell *alone!*

Where was Covenant? He should have stopped his ex-wife by now. Stopped her or died.

Her indignation for Jeremiah multiplied her strength. Her Staff was a howl of theurgy. It thrummed in her hands as she flung stark blackness against the Fall. Hardly aware of what she did, she drove the *caesure* back. Then she incinerated it.

It was gone before she recognized that she had succeeded. Enraged or enraptured, she went on lashing the air with Earthpower until Stave caught her arm, jerked her down from Hyn's back.

He startled her enough to make her stop.

She had not seen him dismount. She had seen nothing except Jeremiah and then the *caesure*. Perhaps he had jumped down as he grabbed her arm. Now he turned her away from Jeremiah; forced her to look at him.

"Chosen!" he said like a slap. "You must attend to our peril as well as to your son. I acknowledge that his efforts are an entrancement. Yet we must not be ensnared." When she finally met his glare, he added, "And we must free the Ranyhyn to provide for their own safety. Mounted, we hinder them."

"That's *your* job," she retorted as though he had interrupted some vital task. "Your senses are better than mine anyway. I need to *see* this."

Roughly she pulled away from him. Freed of their riders, the Ranyhyn remained behind her, far enough away that she would not accidentally strike them with her Staff or her fire.

Two steps took her closer to Jeremiah's construct. Blind and deaf to everything except his own efforts, he had continued to work. Dissociated silt filled his gaze until he looked as sightless as Anele; but he had already balanced a broken femur upright on the base of a plate like a shoulder-blade, sealed it in place. Supported by phalanges, and by bones that mimicked snakes in agony, it rose taller than his head; taller than Linden's. Now he selected another bone like it, splintered at one end, and positioned it standing an arm span beside the first. Together the two femurs looked like doorposts or the scantlings of a wall.

Between heartbeats, Linden's ire became excitement. At one time, she had loved watching him. He had been a wizard with Tinkertoys and Legos, wooden blocks, race-tracks; endlessly fascinating. But now he was more, much more. And long days ago, she had experienced the power of his talent. Whatever he was making here, he would accomplish something wondrous.

"Stave?" she breathed as if she had erased anger from her heart. "Do you know what this is? Do you know what he's doing?"

Standing at her side, the former Master answered with his accustomed stoicism, "No *Haruchai* has beheld its like, apart from that which resides in the Hall of Gifts. Yet I deem that this is *anundivian yajña*, marrowmeld, the Ramen craft of bone-sculpting. Their memory of it has ever been tarnished by sorrow, for the necessary lore was lost. How your son acquired such skill surpasses my conception."

Yes, Linden thought. In the Hall of Gifts. She wanted to believe that she could already feel power accumulating in the early stages of the construct; that its sheer glory would be apparent to Stave. But the bones remained stubbornly inert after each flaring of Earthpower. Their places in his design were still too fragmentary to imply their eventual shape and purpose.

When Stave said her name again, however, she reacted at once. Readying her Staff, she strode away from Jeremiah. She hoped to put at least a few paces between him and anything that she might have to do.

At first, she did not understand why Stave had called her. Under the leaden lid of the sky, she found only the untenable whiteness of bones, the circle of cleared ground, the shallow sides of the basin, the frangible jut of sandstone around the crater's rim.

But the Ranyhyn had skittered away in alarm. Hynyn, Hyn, and Khelen rounded to the far side of the pile and halted there, fretting.

What is it? Linden might have asked the *Haruchai*. What do you sense?

Then she knew. She heard chiming—

In an urgent clamor of bells, Infelice of the *Elohim* arrived like a whirlwind arising from the lifeless dirt.

Imperial and proud, she confronted Linden. Adorned in gems and rich music, and clad in sendaline woven and glittering like the stuff of dreams, the woman advanced like the world's suzerain wreathed in wrath and judgment. The luster of her hair was bright with compulsions in spite of the waning sunshine, and she wore her supple loveliness as though it were an accusation. The gales implied by her eyes reminded Linden of Esmer's sea-storm gaze.

"Now you are thrice a Desecrator, Wildwielder!" Her voice might have been a bitter snarl, but it was tuned to the pitch of beauty and jewels, and every word soared, accompanied by chimes in perfect harmony. "Rousing the Worm, you have doomed all that is precious within the bounds of Time. Acceding to the Harrow, you have bestirred slumbering havoc, avid for horrors beyond comprehension. Yet here you surpass yourself."

Linden glared in response. No doubt she should have been daunted; but she was not. Jeremiah was building— She was eager to see what he would achieve: too eager to flinch or falter.

"By all that your paltry heart deems holy, Wildwielder!" Infelice was a carillon of vehemence. She seemed to assail Linden with song and majesty. And she had placed herself between Linden and Jeremiah. "Releasing the boy from the toils of the *croyel*— That indeed was well done—and no deed of yours. Likewise the Harrow's death was well done, and no deed of yours. But now you enable ruin incarnate. You should not have heeded the Ranyhyn. They have brought you to this place of death, intending dire atrocity."

Linden's eyes widened, but not in dismay. The flagrant indignation of the *Elohim* meant nothing to her. Death! she thought, sudden as an epiphany. *Bones.* For which her need—no, *Jeremiah's* need—was great.

Somehow the Insequent had foreseen this. In their own way, the Ranyhyn had foreseen it. And that flash of insight released Linden's heart.

It contradicted the harsh logic of despair.

With music and consternation, Infelice proclaimed, "If you preserve this vile boy, you will cause eternal woe."

Vile boy? Inspired by revelation, Linden aimed her Staff at Infelice to show the *Elohim* that she was ready for battle. The need for death was Jeremiah's, not hers—and he already lived in graves. If nothing of hers could restore him, perhaps he would be able to resurrect himself with bones.

"Listen to me." Linden pronounced each word as if she were articulating the significance of her love. "I'm only going to warn you once. If you lift so much as a finger against my son, I'll do whatever it takes to stop you."

With her whole heart, she willed Infelice to believe her.

"I'll call up so much Earthpower that it makes another Landsdrop." In some sense, the *Elohim* were embodied Earthpower. Surely Infelice could be harmed by her own form of life? "And if that doesn't work, I'll use Covenant's ring.

"I'm not its rightful wielder. I'm told that I can't actually destroy the Arch. But I can still hurt *you*. There's a reason that you're so afraid of wild magic. I think it's because you don't have any defense. Try me, and I'll burn you until there's nothing left."

Infelice clenched her fists. Bells clamored wrath in the caldera until the bones trembled, all of them—except the ones which Jeremiah had merged.

"And do you conceive that I regard your threat? Wildwielder, you do not desire comprehension. You have inquired concerning the shadow upon the hearts of the *Elohim*, but you do not attend when you are answered. It is *this*." She slapped a gesture at Jeremiah. "His purpose for us is an abomination, more so than our doom in the maw of the Worm. But it is not the worst evil."

"All right." Linden did not waver. The Staff held steady in her hands. "Let's take this one step at a time." Jeremiah was still working, as undisturbed by Infelice as he was by *caesures*. Apparently he had completed one wall of his construct. Now he began to meld a similar structure atop the second of his foundation-bones. He only needed to be left alone. "If there's something that you want me to understand, help me with it."

Before Infelice could interrupt her, she said, "Whatever Jeremiah is making, he needs bone. But why *these* bones? What are they? Where did they come from? How did they get here?"

The *Elohim*'s raiment displayed jewels and exasperation. "Wildwielder, I will not suffer this. You ask for the history of the Earth entire. I will say only that they are the remains of *quellvisks*." Her bells sang distaste under the dulled sky. "It does not concern you that they once made war upon the *Elohim*. In a distant age, they were destroyed. Their bones we deposited here, in Muirwin Delenoth, which signifies the resting place of abhorrence, as an emblem of our disdain for such affronts."

—destroyed. By Infelice and her people.

Linden frowned as though she wanted to understand. "That doesn't help." She had no interest in extinct monsters. "It doesn't matter how long ago you killed them. They're still just bones. I'll try a different question.

"Why were the Ranyhyn suddenly in such a hurry? For God's sake, they spent two days just *walking*. Then they decided to run.

"Maybe if you explain what changed, I'll understand."

Infelice brandished her fists. For an instant, her chiming collapsed into cacophony. Then she mastered herself.

Melodious again, she answered, "An implausible threat approaches the Timewarden's wracked mate. Long and long within her frail confines, she has readied herself to confront him, she and *turiya* Herem with her. But now the minions of noisome Horrim Carabal advance against her. They cannot harm her. However, they endanger the *skest* that ward and sustain her. By so doing, they hope to weaken her.

"This neither *turiya* Herem nor the Ranyhyn foresaw. They could not. It is the unlikely outcome of your encounter with Horrim Carabal. Therefore the Timewarden's mate fears it. She is roused to frenzy, and her *caesures* imperil all who travel here. For that reason, the Ranyhyn have hastened to accomplish their loathsome purpose."

This time, Linden shook her head. Infelice's explanation raised as many questions as it answered. The Feroce had almost succeeded in delivering the Staff of Law to the lurker—and now they moved against the *skest*? But Linden did not allow herself to be distracted. Covenant was still alive: in effect, Infelice had said so. Other issues were more important.

Jeremiah was more important. He was balancing the first layers of his second wall, fusing them with Earthpower—and far from done. He might need hours yet.

He had enough bone here to fashion an entire castle.

"All right," she repeated, speaking slowly; stalling for time. "That's a start. Let's move on. You said that coming here enables atrocity. Jeremiah's purpose is an abomination. What do you imagine his purpose *is*? What do you think he's making?"

She could guess. Roger had said about the *Elohim*, *They're* vulnerable *to certain kinds of structures. Like Vain. Specific constructs attract them. Exactly the right materials in exactly the right shape. Other structures repel them. Or blind them.* By that means, the *croyel* had concealed itself in the Lost Deep.

Jeremiah's edifice of bone might well be a trap of some kind. But Linden wanted to hear the truth from Infelice.

"Did the halfhand not speak of this?" The *Elohim*'s tone was bitter; but a note of sorrow softened the angry harmonics of her music. "The boy will ensnare us. He will deprive us of life and meaning and hope."

Your kid makes doors. Doors through time. Doors between realities. And doors that don't go anywhere. Prisons. When you walk into them, you never come out.

Linden ached to move so that she stood between Infelice and Jeremiah; but she forced herself to remain where she was. As long as she contrived to keep Infelice's attention fixed on her, away from Jeremiah—

Stave watched the *Elohim* with his arms folded as though he had the strength to defy her.

"I'm going to pretend that that makes sense," Linden drawled, "although why Jeremiah would care what happens to you is beyond me. Tell me why—"

"Chosen," Stave said abruptly: a warning.

An instant later, the three Ranyhyn wheeled aside, lunged away from each other; and a *caesure* erupted where Khelen had been standing on the far side of the bones.

It was as ravenous as one of the *skurj*; as irresistible as a Sandgorgon. And it was *close*—! Its proximity filled her throat with vomit. In three more heartbeats, it would surge near enough to swallow Jeremiah.

Noise filled the air like the clatter of dropped bells or swords as Infelice vanished.

No. "*Melenkurion abatha!*" Black fire burst from Linden's Staff, fierce as a volcanic detonation. "*Duroc minas mill!*" Her whole being was flame: she lashed at the Fall with every passion of her life. "*Harad* God damn *khabaal!*"

You *will not* have my son!

She was becoming an adept, elevated by extremity. For a moment, she seemed to hear Joan screaming in the heart of the storm. *I've been good!* Against Linden's onslaught, the *caesure* staggered; flickered. *Make it stop!* Then it lurched backward. *I can't bear it!*

Struck to the core, the time-storm curled into itself and imploded. Scant instants after it appeared, it was gone.

It won't be much longer. Roger had promised his mother that. *We'll make it stop together.*

Covenant! Oh, Covenant, watch out. She's getting stronger.

Jeremiah was still at work as though nothing had happened. Empty of every form of consciousness except concentration on his construct, he sealed phalanges in place, propped crooked bones among them, rested a scapula off-center and left it, imponderably secure. To Linden's urgent glance, this side of his structure appeared to be an exact mirror of the other. If she had looked more closely, she might have noticed that he had set dozens of details deliberately askew. But she did not have time.

Announced by chiming, Infelice incarnated herself between Linden and Jeremiah as though she had never been absent. Her sendaline murmured of disdain and supplication as it moved, stirred by a breeze that Linden could not feel.

"Oh, good," Linden panted, shaken by her own exertions and the *caesure*'s inrush. "You haven't given up. I still have questions."

In scorn, the *Elohim* retorted, "And I continue to reply, imploring you to set aside your opposition. If you will not permit me to deflect the boy from the path of this atrocity, I pray that you yourself will thwart him, for the sake of the Land and the Earth, since you care naught for the *Elohim*. Remove him from his task. Unmake what he has done. Set him upon his beast and ride hence. If you do so, while they live the *Elohim* will ensure that he does not fall under the Despiser's dominion a second time. Thus the worst of all evils may be forestalled."

"Wait a minute," Linden demanded. She no longer held the Staff aimed at Infelice, but she was ready. "You're going too fast for me."

"Never mind that Jeremiah probably doesn't care about you any more than I do. I was about to ask you why getting caught in one of his doors is worse than being eaten by the Worm. They sound about the same to me. Either way, you're finished. Why is a prison worse than dying?"

The music around Infelice sounded like teeth grinding in frustration. Lordly and contemptuous, she answered, "Wildwielder, the Worm is mere extinction. The prison which the boy will devise is eternal helplessness, fully cognizant and forever futile. It will out-live the ending of suns and stars. Which doom would you prefer? Which would you elect for your son?"

Still Stave stood motionless, like a man who had no part to play in the world's ruin. Behind Infelice, Jeremiah had used two more heavy bones like huge femurs snapped in half to complete the frame of his second wall: the side of an entryway, or the start of a corridor. Now he was busy filling the space between the uprights with fingers and limbs and lumps and gnarled boughs of bone. And as he worked, without haste or hesitation, Earthpower flowed from his hands like water, binding together the many pieces of his construct.

By degrees, theurgy swelled in the bones. It was still nascent, still tenuous and vague, but Linden sensed that soon it would start to burgeon. His creation was beginning to resemble the numinous box which he had used to reach the depths of *Melenkurion Skyweir*: it was coming to life.

"All right," Linden said for the third time; perhaps the last time. "I'll give you that one. It makes sense.

"So tell me. I'm ready to hear it now. What's 'the worst evil'? If imprisoning you is worse than the Worm of the World's End, what could possibly be 'the worst of all evils'?"

Infelice had become unalloyed wrath, a tintinnabulation too clangorous to be ignored. "The Despiser," she rang out, "who is called a-Jeroth and Lord Foul and many other names, has placed his mark upon the boy. You claim the boy as your son, but you do not know him. You have not grasped that there is no limit to what he can achieve when he is given suitable aid.

"Assuredly the Despiser desires his escape from the Arch of Time—and to accomplish that end, he does not require the boy. In his secret heart, however, he nurtures a darker intent. He seeks to devise a prison for the Creator, making use of the boy's gifts when the Arch has fallen. This he means to accomplish in the moment of collapse, when all things have become mutable. As the Despiser has suffered, so he wishes all possible Creation to suffer, in unending emptiness and lamentation.

"This you do not comprehend. Your mortal mind cannot encompass such absolute loss. Yet I beseech you to hear me. You have asked after the shadow on the hearts of the *Elohim*. The eternal end of Creation is shadow enough to darken the heart of any being."

Linden stared, shocked in spite of her allegiance to her son. Was it possible? *Possible? Could Lord Foul *do* that? With Jeremiah's help? The eternal end—

—but of my deeper purpose I will not speak.

More power throbbed behind Infelice. Jeremiah appeared to be finishing his second wall, the other side of a doorway or passage. In another moment or two, he would commence the next phase of his construct, whatever that might be.

He needed more time. But Linden was too stunned to think. The eternal end—? Infelice was right about one thing: Linden could not grasp the concept. Lord Foul intended *that*? And she had run out of questions or arguments. Soon she would have no means to delay her antagonist except Earthpower or wild magic.

"Nonetheless, *Elohim*," Stave said unexpectedly, "your own comprehension is flawed." He remained standing with his arms closed across his chest, as impassive as Jeremiah, and as unmoved. "I acknowledge that your undying thoughts surpass mine, or the Chosen's, or indeed those of the Ranyhyn. Yet when you speak of the shadow upon your heart, you speak in contradictions.

"In Andelain, you averred that your spirits are darkened by 'the threat of beings from beyond Time.' You cited the Chosen and also the Unbeliever, and I doubt not that you include this boy in your tale of darkness. You described them as 'beings both small and mortal who are nonetheless capable of utter devastation.'"

Linden remembered. *By his own deeds*, Infelice had said, *the Despiser cannot destroy the Arch of Time. He requires your aid, Wildwielder, and that of the man who was once the Unbeliever.*

"To content you," Stave continued, "I will also acknowledge that the presence in the Land of 'beings from beyond Time' has been chiefly caused by Corruption, if not by his own hand then by the efforts of his servants."

Infelice lifted an elegant eyebrow. The ire of her chiming receded into a more cautious mode. Apparently the *Haruchai* had caught her attention.

At her back, Jeremiah turned away from the walls or sides of his construct. With strength that astonished Linden, far more strength than he should have possessed, he retrieved the largest of his gathered bones, the single intact femur, and raised it over his head. His muddy gaze regarded nothing as he carried the massive bone to his structure and set its length across the tops of the walls like a lintel.

When he had sealed the femur in its position, the vibration of his created magic rose to a higher pitch. Linden felt its hum in her own bones. Waves of power made her skin itch as if every inch were a wound newly healed.

But Stave did not pause; gave no sign that he was aware of Jeremiah or theurgy.

"Yet by your own admission," he said, "the Chosen did not effect the boy's release from the *croyel*. Nor was he freed by ur-Lord Covenant's intervention. And it was neither the Chosen nor the Unbeliever who discovered the boy's covert in the Lost Deep. Furthermore we were not brought to this place at this time by either the Chosen or the Unbeliever—or by her son, or by his son or mate. We are here only by the will of the Ranyhyn.

"Herein lies your error, *Elohim*. Every essential step along the path of the boy's purpose has been taken by the natural inhabitants of the Earth. The Chosen and the Unbeliever and perhaps even the Unbeliever's son have enabled those steps, but have not determined them. Therefore our presence here, and the boy's present display of lore, do not conform to your description of the shadow upon the hearts of the *Elohim*. If we are now threatened by 'the worst of all evils,' it is through no fault or purpose or power of the Chosen's son.

"Thus," the *Haruchai* stated as though his logic were unassailable, "it is made plain even to mortal minds that your protestations are spurious. You appear to believe that this boy is no more than a tool wielded by other beings. But the tool cannot be held accountable for the use which is made of it. And here the hands which wield him are those of the Ranyhyn and the Harrow, the first new Stonedownor and the lost son of Sunder and Hollian. They are the hands of beings who live and may perish within the proper confines of Time.

"Thus it follows that you have no cause to oppose the boy. His present efforts cannot achieve Corruption's designs."

Yes, Linden thought. *Yes.* It was Stave who had first shown her how to believe that Jeremiah did not belong to Lord Foul. Now the former Master dispelled every doubt that had marred her faith.

Apart from the claiming of your vacant son—

He's belonged *to Foul for years.*

Roger had lied to her. The Despiser had tried to mislead her. From the first, one or both of them had striven to teach her despair. And they had succeeded.

Yet Stave answered them for her. The Ranyhyn and Anele had answered them. Jeremiah himself was answering them now.

Trust.

With as much subtlety as she could manage, Linden began mustering Earthpower in her mind.

As her son added phalanges and tarsal blocks like supports for his lintel, the force implicit in his structure scaled still higher. Soon it felt like the gnashing of dislocated realities, a door between worlds. In contrast, the music of the *Elohim* seemed dim and lusterless; as dulled as the ashen sky.

Over her shoulder, Infelice cast a glance like a blaze of gems at the boy. Then she faced Stave for the first time.

"You are *Haruchai*," she said in a tone of regal disdain. "Have you forgotten that your strength is as weak as water to the *Elohim*, and as devoid of import? Yet I have heard you, hoping that the Wildwielder will reconsider her folly while you bandy words. Now you have said enough. I will hear no more."

"If the tool cannot be held accountable for its use, it likewise cannot be used if it does not exist. Hold yourselves blameless, if that is your desire. I have spoken of perils which transcend blame. They must be prevented at any cost."

With a gesture of dismissal, as if she were banishing Stave from her sight, Infelice turned away.

Toward Jeremiah.

Linden was already summoning fire from her Staff when Stave barked harshly, "Chosen!"

Another *caesure*. As soon as Stave called to her, she felt it stinging her flesh, hiving in her guts.

The puissance of Jeremiah's construct ramified into the grey heavens. He stepped back from it as if his work were done. Gazing blankly at his structure, his marrowmeld sculpture, like an artist who had expended every iota of himself, he extended his half-hand in Linden's direction like a request for confirmation. But he did not turn his head, or shift his feet, or give any other indication that he wanted something from his mother.

Infelice was about to destroy him. One way or another, the *Elohim* would put an end to every possibility, every hope.

Nevertheless the Fall was more immediate. And Infelice feared it. She feared it at least as much as Linden did. She might hesitate while she was in danger.

Frantically Linden wheeled away to hurl black fury into the migraine storm of hornets and instants.

But she was wrong. As soon as she spotted the *caesure*, she saw that she was wrong. Joan had missed her aim. Her concentration, or *turiya*'s, was fraying. Vicious as a tornado, the Fall seethed on the far rim of the caldera. From where she stood, Linden could not have thrown a piece of bone to hit it. And it was moving away. Awkward as a cripple, it stumbled onto the outer slope of the crater and began to descend, a blind thing forsaken by its guide. If it did not suddenly change directions, it would drift out of sight and do no harm.

Wrong, wrong, *wrong*. Linden had given Infelice a chance—

And Stave was powerless against the *Elohim*. Long ago, Linden had witnessed the negligent ease with which Infelice's people had refused Brinn and Cail, Hergrom and Ceer, from their demesne.

Swinging the Staff's howl of Earthpower, she spun back toward Jeremiah—

—and was instantly frozen; stopped where she stood, as if every imaginable motion had been stripped from her. Her arms and legs were paralyzed: her heart seemed to stop beating. Blood congealed in her veins. Her fire vanished as if she knew nothing of Earthpower and had never understood Law.

The air of the caldera was full of stars. They winked and spangled in front of her, around her, between her and her son, as evanescent and irrefusable as sun-dazzles. They were the gems of Infelice's raiment, the eldritch jewels of her chiming, and they sang a song of immobility that ruled the basin, dominated the bones. Jeremiah still stood facing his construct with his right arm extended toward Linden: for him, nothing had changed. But Stave had been snared in mid-stride. Impossibly balanced on one foot with the other reaching for its step, he remained like a statue carved from stone.

Linden tried to move, and could not. She had forgotten how to breathe.

Only Infelice moved. Graceful as a breeze, she floated toward Jeremiah with a kind of gentle inevitability, as though his doom had been written eons ago in the materials of his construct.

The Ranyhyn trumpeted warnings that no one heeded.

As Infelice neared Jeremiah, she opened her arms to embrace him with ruin.

In horror, Linden watched as if helplessness were the ultimate truth of her life. She had no answer to it. Perhaps she had never had an answer. It may have been the true source of her despair.

But Stave—

Ah, God.

Somehow he found the will to speak.

"You delude yourself, *Elohim*." His voice was a whisper hoarse with strain. Stars like commandments resisted it. Yet he made himself heard. "Do you deem me helpless? I am *Haruchai*. I do what I must. When you strive to enact your desires against Linden Avery's son, I will strike a blow which will alter your conception of power."

Bright gemstones swirled around him, bursts of suzerain coercion. He could not move: of course he could not. Nothing except wild magic could counter the force of the *Elohim*.

And yet—

—he did move. Slowly, arduously, inexorably, he closed the fingers of his right hand into a fist.

Visibly startled, Infelice turned to stare at him. Her music shaped words which she did not utter. *No. You will not.*

You. Will. Not.

Ignoring her denial, Stave clenched his fist. His arm shook as he raised it.

At the same time, the pressure binding Linden within herself eased slightly.

She could breathe again. Her heart beat.

Stave had given her a gift greater than power or glory.

It would be brief. In another moment, Infelice would gather enough of her vast magicks to crush the *Haruchai*.

Linden had to act now.

She was no match for Stave. She did not try to equal him. In spite of Jeremiah's peril, she ignored her Staff, made no attempt to reach for Covenant's ring. Infelice would react to any effort of theurgy, any overt challenge. Instead, while the ire of Infelice's stars forced Stave to lower his arm, Linden slipped her hand into the pocket of her jeans.

The pocket where she carried Jeremiah's red racecar.

Aid and betrayal. Esmer had healed the crumpled toy for a reason. Linden needed to believe that he had not intended yet another form of treachery.

Her refusal to be helpless was a pale mimicry of Stave's; but it sufficed.

While Infelice concentrated on stifling the last of Stave's intransigence, his fundamental birthright, Linden withdrew the racecar from her pocket and tossed it toward Jeremiah.

Stars flared in repudiation. Bells clamored denial across the caldera. But they had no effect on the toy's passage.

The racecar resembled Stave's fierce stubbornness. It was Jeremiah's birthright; his inheritance.

He still faced his construct, motionless and lost. He had not once turned his head to glance at his mother. He could not have caught even a glimpse of his toy.

Nevertheless he claimed it. Deft as legerdemain, his halfhand plucked the racecar from the air.

In that instant, he appeared to receive the full potential of Anele's gift. His whole body became an exultant hymn of Earthpower, as rich as the *Elohim*'s chiming, and as profound. Grasping the racecar, he looked as mighty as a Forestal.

The deep thrum of his construct repulsed stars and bells and coercion.

Do you see? Linden asked Infelice, too weak to form words aloud. *Do you see him? He's my son.*

Jeremiah's transformation and the loud demand of his portal snatched Infelice away from Stave. "*No!*" she sang, shouted, yelled. "You *will* not!"

Swift as a whirlwind, the spangling of stars and jewels swept around Jeremiah. Infelice left only enough power in the air to hold Stave and Linden where they were; only
enough to prevent Linden from using her Staff or Covenant's ring. All the rest of her
music and her ineffable majesty spun around Jeremiah; bound him like a cocoon.

In spite of his new puissance, he did nothing. Infelice was too strong for him.

Her sendaline whipped about her as she strode toward Jeremiah to complete her
purpose.

But her second step took her directly into the path of the charging Ranyhyn.

She had forgotten about them—or had underestimated them. She may have believed
that mere animals could not resist her compulsions. She may even have believed that
they would not; that they would recognize her supremacy and be daunted.

She should have known better.

Doubtless Infelice's magicks would protect her. Hynyn, Hyn, and Khelen were
Ranyhyn; but they were *only* Ranyhyn. She was *Elohim*. Their inborn Earthpower
could not overcome the forces at her command.

Nevertheless she had noticed them too late.

Khelen was in the lead. He crashed into her, drove her to the dirt, and pounded
away, leaving her to be trampled by Hynyn and Hyn.

Their hooves did not touch her. She vanished in an instant—and almost instantly
reappeared behind them.

During her brief flicker of absence, however, all of her stars vanished with her.

That small release was enough for Jeremiah. Three quick strides took him around
the edge of his construct. Two more carried him into the center of his portal.

Infelice returned like a hurricane. Savage winds slapped Linden to the ground;
flung Stave halfway up the slope of the basin; drove the Ranyhyn to their knees. Gales
of rage and terror hammered at the portal; at Jeremiah. The sheer desperation of the
Elohim staggered him.

Yet the magicks of his construct shielded him. Within its supernal walls, he recovered his balance, straightened his back. Storms ripped at his tattered pajamas, but did
not sway him.

His begrimed face and soiled eyes looked entirely vacant, as empty of consciousness as an abandoned farmhouse, as he reached for the lintel of his doorway.

Infelice blared at him in fraught turmoil as chaotic as a *caesure*, but her powers
failed to stop him.

He resembled an incarnation of Anele's blind essence, ragged and enduring, as he
wedged his racecar between two bones supporting the femur lintel. With Earthpower,
he sealed the toy in place.

Before Linden could guess what he was doing, Infelice began to shriek like a banshee—
and the entire marrowmeld sculpture became a white shout of radiance so pure that

Linden could not look at it. She clapped a hand over her eyes, squeezed them shut; but the light pierced her hand and her eyelids, seemed to stab straight into her brain. She saw every bone of her palm and fingers limned in incandescence. Every phalange and metacarpal, the capitate, the scaphoid, the hamate: they all gleamed as if they were lit by the cynosure of the sun.

For a moment, she believed that she would never see anything else again; that she would be left as sightless as Anele and Mahrtiir. The defined framework of her hand would be all that remained of her world.

Then she felt Infelice disappear again, still shrieking.

The *Elohim* did not return.

Seconds or hours later, the portal's blaze went out. There was no light except the dust and smoke of sunshine. Every sensation of power had left the caldera. Nothing endured to commemorate Linden's lost sight or Infelice's defeat except a wide pile of bones which should have been as white as Jeremiah's innominate triumph.

But Stave was still here. Linden heard him calling her name. He did not sound hurt. And the Ranyhyn had survived. The hard thud of their hooves as they trotted, nickering proudly, around and around the pile seemed to promise that they had accomplished their intent.

Fearfully Linden lowered her hand, blinked open her eyes, and found that she had not been harmed. Dazzles like little suns swirled in her vision, confusing everything; but she could see. Experience and health-sense assured her that soon she would be able to see normally.

Squinting, she searched for her son.

Jeremiah stood in the center of a crude square of ash. His entire edifice had been rendered to powder around his feet. Even his racecar—If any scrap of the red metal remained, it lay buried in the residue of ancient bone.

His legacy of Earthpower had receded into the background. But he was looking at Linden.

At Linden.

His eyes were clear as untainted skies. When she met his gaze, his face broke into a broad grin of excitement and affection.

"I did it, Mom." He sounded like he wanted to crow. "I *did* it. I made a door for my mind, and it *opened*.

"I couldn't have done it without Anele." Gradually his grin fell away, unmade by remembered sorrows. "Or without Galt. And Liand. And the Ranyhyn. Stave was amazing." Nonetheless his eyes shone on Linden, luminous with gratitude. "And I could never have done anything without you.

"But I *did it*."

Then he hurried forward to fling his love around her.

In that moment, Linden Avery began to believe that her rent heart might heal.

Lord Foul always told the truth. *In time you will behold the fruit of my endeavors. If your son serves me, he will do so in your presence. If I slaughter him, I will do so before you. If you discover him, you will only hasten his doom.* But the Despiser's craving for his foes' self-desecration was so great that he never told the *whole* truth.

Perhaps he did not know it.

Do you *see* him? He's my *son.*

Hugging Jeremiah hard, Linden thought that maybe this time Lord Foul's machinations had gone wrong. Like Infelice, perhaps, the Despiser had misled himself.

10.

The Pure One and the High God

From the ravine where he had left Linden and her companions, Thomas Covenant rode the Harrow's destrier south and east into a region of denuded hills interspersed with shallow vales of gravel and dirt.

Clyme and Branl guarded him, Mhornym on his left, Naybahn on his right. And the Ranyhyn set a hard pace, apparently disregarding the limitations of Covenant's mount. The destrier was a heavy warhorse, but it had been bred for endurance as well as power and fury. Covenant sensed that it would strive to emulate its Earthpowerful companions until its heart burst. And by some means, Mhornym and Naybahn seemed to impose their will on the beast, stifling its instinctive loathing for an unfamiliar rider; transforming its trained battle-frenzy into speed. While it could, the horse matched the fluid gallop of the Ranyhyn.

Protected by Ranyhyn and the Humbled, Covenant rode toward his future as if he were absent from himself; as if he were conscious only of other people, other places, other times. But he had not slipped into one of the flaws that riddled his memories. Nor was he distracted by the imponderable prospect of confronting Joan and *turiya*

Raver and the *skest*. Instead he traveled among the hills like an abandoned icon of himself because he was too full of grief and dread to regard the landscape or his companions or his own purpose.

Some distant part of him felt grateful for the Harrow's saddle and stirrups, the Harrow's reins. They steadied him: he was a poor rider. In addition, he was vaguely glad that Kevin's Dirt did not cover the Lower Land. He was already too numb, too inattentive; and Kastenessen's dire brume would aggravate his leprosy. But such details did not deflect his sorrow.

He was galled by the way that he had left Linden; by the manner in which he had refused her.

He knew how Clyme and Branl felt about her. He understood why they distrusted her. But he also understood why she distrusted them. And he was not convinced that she had misjudged the Masters, or that her risks and concealments were mistakes, or that her determination to resurrect him had been misguided. Both in death and in life, he had watched her refusal to forgive harden toward despair—and still he believed in her. In spite of everything, he loved her exactly as she was. Every pain, every extravagance, every compromised line of her beauty: he loved them all. Without them, she would have been less than herself. Less than the mother Jeremiah needed. Less than the woman Covenant himself wanted. Less than the savior the Land required.

Nevertheless he had told her the exact truth when he had pushed her away. He had lost too much of himself. He feared what he was becoming—or what he might have to become.

That was why he had distanced himself from her, why he had kept himself apart from her clear yearning, why he had ridden away without so much as a kind farewell. He could not profess his love—or accept hers—without making it sound like a promise; and he had no reason to believe that he would be able to keep that troth. If Joan did not succeed at killing him, he might return from facing her in a condition which he had not anticipated, and which Linden would no longer recognize. He might find that he had become abhorrent to her; or to himself.

There was indeed a storm brewing in him, and it was dread. Resurrected, his dilemma represented that of the Land, and of the whole Earth; the plight of Linden and everyone he cared about. He was afraid because he had too much to lose.

Long ago, he had told Linden, *There's only one way to hurt a man who's lost everything. Give him back something broken.* In Andelain, he had done that to her. But now he knew a deeper truth. Even broken things were precious. Like Jeremiah, they could become more precious than life. And they could still be taken away.

He was more afraid of making a promise to Linden that he could not keep than he was of Joan.

And he had another reason for treating Linden severely. Any promise—even an implied one—might encourage her to insist on accompanying him. To choose him instead of her son.

Perhaps everything would have been different if he could have explained why her desire to help him face Joan would effectively doom Jeremiah. But he had no explanation. He had told her, *You have other things to do*, but he had no real idea what they were. He only knew that they were crucial. They may have been more important than his own need to confront Joan.

It was conceivable that he could not remember them because he had never known. Even from his perspective within the Arch, the future may have been undefined; less certain than it was to the *Elohim*, whose fluid relationship with time confused linear distinctions. His mortality made it easy for him to believe that he had never possessed any prescient insight into the Land's need.

Then why was he certain that Linden's support against Joan would prove fatal to Jeremiah—and therefore to the Land as well? He had no answer. Yet he was sure of it. And his only justification, although it sounded contradictory, was that he *trusted* her. He trusted her more than he trusted himself.

He trusted the implications of her devotion to her son.

Still the ache of leaving her forlorn seemed to consume his heart. During his participation in the Arch of Time, he had witnessed so much loss and wrong that eventually he had imagined himself inured to ordinary woe. But now—Ah, now he acknowledged that his share of immortality had blunted his perceptions of individual human anguish. Across the ages, his sense of scale had changed to accommodate vaster possibilities.

Watching Linden's struggles, first to retrieve the Staff of Law, then to survive Roger and the *croyel*, then to reach Andelain, he had understood her pain. But he had also seen beyond it. He had known far more than she did about what was at stake, and about how her actions might affect the Earth. Now he was human again: he could no longer see past his own limitations. Like every creature that died when its time was done, he could only live in his circumscribed present.

This was the truth of being mortal, this imprisonment in the strictures of sequence. It felt like a kind of tomb.

In his earlier state, he had recognized that this prison was also the only utile form of freedom. Another contradiction: strictures enabled as much as they denied. The *Elohim* were ineffectual precisely because they had so few constraints. Linden was capable of so much because her inadequacies walled her on all sides.

Now, however, he had to take that perception on faith.

But there were other truths as well, or other aspects of the same truth. His imprisonment had its own demands: it insisted upon them. And one of them was his body. The flesh which reified his spirit was both needy and exigent. He could only spend a certain amount of time in grief before the jarring of his inexpert horsemanship demanded precedence. The gait of the Ranyhyn was as smooth as water: the destrier's was not. Already his joints were beginning to hurt. And when he finally realized that he was sitting too stiffly to endure a long ride, he also became aware that he was thirsty. The first premonitions of dehydration throbbed in his temples, and his tongue felt so dry and thick that he could hardly swallow.

Blinking to compensate for what may have been hours of neglect, Covenant peered around; tried to identify where he was.

He should have known this region. Hell, it probably even had a name. But that was only one of a myriad—no, damnation, a myriad myriad *myriad*—things which he had forgotten.

The hills were gone: he had lost them somewhere. Between Mhornym and Naybahn, his mount was pounding heavily across bare dirt thick with splinters and blades of flint. The beast's hooves were iron-shod: that provided a measure of protection. But how the Ranyhyn avoided hurting themselves—Yet they flowed ahead, sweeping the ground behind them, apparently impervious to the hazards of the terrain.

As far as he could tell with his numbed health-sense, all of his mount's fierceness was focused on endurance. But it was laboring hard. Eventually, inevitably, the beast would begin to founder. Then—

Then what? He had no notion. He had brought no water with him; no food; nothing for the horses. He had made no plans. In fact, he had given no thought to anything except getting away from Linden and heading toward Joan before his courage failed.

They're Ranyhyn, *for God's sake.* He had said that. *They'll think of something.*

He had left himself no choice except to assume that Naybahn and Mhornym would compensate for his improvidence.

He rubbed at his forehead. For some reason, it had begun to itch: a reminder of falling.

"Hellfire," he mused to himself. "This damn mortality—It's enough to humble a pile of rocks."

But he did not realize that he had muttered the words aloud until Branl asked over the rumble of hoofbeats, "Ur-Lord?"

Shaking his head, Covenant blinked at the Master. "Huh?"

Branl rode as if he were one with Naybahn; as if their disparate strengths had merged. His flat gaze was fixed on Covenant. "You spoke of mortality, and of being humbled."

"Oh, that." Covenant dismissed the subject. Jarred mercilessly in his seat, he found speech difficult. "I was just thinking."

He wanted to tell Branl that he needed water. But before he could frame a request, the *Haruchai* observed, "Yet with every word and deed, ur-Lord, you demonstrate that you comprehend neither the Masters nor the Humbled."

Oh, good, Covenant sighed. Just what we need. Clearly there was something nagging at Branl and Clyme; something at which they had taken umbrage.

Past the thickness of his tongue, he mumbled, "Don't tell me. Let me guess. You don't like the way I forced you to let Linden heal you. You don't approve."

Branl nodded. "Nor do we approve of your forbearance toward Linden Avery, when all of her actions conduce to ruin. You do not ask humility of us. You inflict humiliation.

"We are *Haruchai*. The distinction has been made plain to us. In earlier incarnations, you did not seek to diminish us. Since your return to life, you have done so repeatedly."

Don't you think, Covenant wanted to retort, there could be more than one reason why I act this way? Have you considered that maybe you've changed as much as I have? But he was too thirsty to welcome an argument. Soon he would be too hungry.

Stifling sarcasm, he said, "Then explain it to me. If you think I don't understand, give me some help."

Perhaps the justifications of the Humbled would distract him until the Ranyhyn found water.

Branl nodded. "I will speak only of imposed healing," he began. "It is bootless to belabor slights long past recall.

"Ur-Lord, we are the Humbled. By skill and long combat, we have won the honor of embodying the refusal of our people to countenance humiliation. That we live and die does not humble us. It demands neither humility nor humiliation because we make no compromise with failure. We do what we can, and we accept the outcome. If our strength and skill do not suffice, we are content to bear the cost in pain and death. Indeed, the cost of our efforts provides the substance of our lives, and by our contentment we confirm our worth.

"When you demand that we endure Linden Avery's healing, you deny our acceptance. You proclaim us unworthy of our lives."

"Hell and blood," Covenant growled under his breath. Haven't you realized yet that everything isn't about you? But he gritted his teeth, trying to keep his irritation to himself.

Impassively Branl continued, "If you assert that humility necessitates an acknowledgment that we are not equal to all things, as the *Elohim* describe themselves, I reply that we are indeed humble in our acceptance. With Clyme and lost Galt, I am our humility made flesh. But if you avow that humility requires relief from the consequence of being less than equal to all things, I reply that you speak of humiliation, not of humility. Any abrogation of the outcome of our deeds diminishes us.

"If you wish it, ur-Lord, I will describe the self-denigration implicit in Cail's return to the Land. That was the failure for which our ancestors judged him. They did not denounce his seduction by the *merewives*, but rather his acceptance of rescue from the cost of his surrender, and his insistence that in his place his kinsmen would have acted as he did.

"Or if you wish it, I will speak of Stave—"

"No," Covenant interrupted gruffly. He had been goaded too far. "Please don't." He hated the way that Cail had been repudiated. He did not want to hear any accusation against Stave. "Sometimes you people make me crazy." Like Stave, Covenant had a son. "You've accepted *gifts*, haven't you? From High Lord Kevin, if not from anybody else. What's so wrong about accepting a gift from Linden?"

"First," Branl answered without hesitation, "our ancestors accepted no gift from the Landwaster until they had determined how they would repay his largesse, with the Vow by which *Haruchai* became Bloodguard. Thus they preserved the import of their lives. Second, his gifts were not imposed. The freedom of refusal was not denied to our ancestors as it was to us."

"Then don't blame Linden," Covenant retorted. "Your grievance is with me, not her. And I didn't deny you anything. I just told you what I was going to do if you refused. You could have accepted *that* cost.

"If Joan doesn't kill us," he promised, "you'll get your chance to repay Linden. Or me, if you judge me the way you judge her."

When he squinted ahead, he saw the terrain changing. Beyond the flint, sandstone and shale gathered into mounds like barrows or glacial moraines. He had the impression that huge creatures had been buried there: buried, or plowed under by warfare. But he did not try to remember the forces which had shaped that landscape. He did not want to fall into the past again.

As the horses pounded toward the mounds, the Humbled regarded him steadily. "Still you do not comprehend us, ur-Lord," Branl observed. "It is not without cause that you have been named the Unbeliever."

Apparently unwilling to let the matter drop, he took a different approach. "The Ardent has assured us that the Cords Bhapa and Pahni have been conveyed toward Revelstone, where they will strive to sway the Masters. But the Masters will not heed them. Cord Pahni's desire for the Stonedownor's resurrection is abhorrent to us. She has beseeched Linden Avery to demean his death by unmaking the outcome of his life. Thus her every word will be tainted by her craving for the Stonedownor's humiliation, which she misnames love. No Master would hold him in such low esteem. He was courage in life. Why, then, should he be denied the courage of his death? Is that not false honor?"

Covenant rubbed his forehead again. Damnation! Branl's pronouncements seemed to aggravate the itching of the old wound. The Humbled had misjudged Pahni: that was obvious. Was it possible that Branl and Clyme and all of the Masters were unforgiving of loss and failure because they refused to grieve? Because they equated grief with humiliation? If so, then of course their only response to bereavement would be repudiation.

But Covenant had no intention of debating Pahni with Branl and Clyme. Instead he admitted sourly, "That's the Law." The Law of Death. The Law of Life. By that standard, Covenant himself was inherently false. A disease upon the body of the world. "Life depends on death. But there are other things to consider."

The severity of the Humbled ignored the wonders of the Land; the possibility of miracles.

Again Branl asked, "Ur-Lord?"

Covenant did not respond. At the boundary between flint and sandstone, the Ranyhyn veered unexpectedly to the west, guiding the destrier between them. While Covenant tried to relax in the saddle, the horses trotted to a halt at a clear spring hidden by a fold in the ground. The spring's pool was little more than an arm span across. From there, the water flowed away along a minor gully like a scratch in the dirt. But at the sides of the slow rill, grasses grew, punctuated by a few clumps of *aliantha*.

By damn, Covenant breathed to himself. Speaking of wonders—

At once, he flung his aching body down from his mount, staggered when his boots hit the ground, caught his balance. Beside the destrier's avid muzzle, he knelt at the edge of the pool and pushed his whole face into the water to drink.

Branl and Clyme also dismounted. While Naybahn and Mhornym drank, the Humbled scooped a little water into their mouths, then picked and ate a few treasureberries. But the Ranyhyn appeared to disdain the grass. Moving aside, they left the Harrow's charger to crop as much provender as it needed.

When Covenant was satisfied, he scrubbed his face in the pool, splashed water onto the back of his neck. Then he gathered and ate enough fruit to sustain him, cursing at the awkwardness of his truncated fingers. Still he said nothing. When Clyme and Branl were mounted again, he hauled his trembling muscles up into the destrier's saddle.

Concentrate, he instructed himself. Don't fight it. Long ago, he had ridden across the Land with Lord Mhoram, Saltheart Foamfollower, and the quest for Berek's Staff of Law. He needed to remember how to relax in his seat. If he did not, his mount's galloping would batter him until he felt dismembered.

As the horses began to clatter among the barrows or moraines, heading generally southeastward, he returned to the challenge of arguing with his companions.

Unable to think of a graceful way to begin, he said brusquely, "You're both maimed. You fought long and hard to become halfhands. If I remember, you did it because you wanted to be like me." Why else had the Humbled swallowed their judgments of

Linden and Jeremiah? Why else had they accepted healing so that they could accompany him? "What does that mean to you? Why do the Masters need halfhands?"

Now it was Clyme who answered. "Unbeliever, in you we have found the highest exemplar of ourselves. More, we have found our counter to humiliation. Twice you have confronted Corruption, and twice prevailed. These are deeds which no *Haruchai* has equaled. Others who made the attempt were self-betrayed to their dooms.

"Of necessity, therefore, we have considered how it transpires that you who are weak succeed where we who are strong fail. And we have concluded that your victories rest upon a degree or quality of acceptance which once surpassed the *Haruchai*. You do not merely accept your own weakness, defying common conceptions of strength and power. You accept also the most extreme consequences of your frailty, daring even the utter ruin of the Earth in your resolve to oppose Corruption. You cling to your intent when your defeat is certain.

"In you, ur-Lord," Clyme stated, "we have seen that such absolute acceptance of both your purpose and your weakness is mighty against all evil. We have seen the Land twice redeemed. And we aspire to the same willingness, the same triumph. Knowing that they cannot prevail, the *Haruchai* have become the Masters of the Land. For the same reason, we have won the role of the Humbled, to embody the high mission of our people. Thus we give answer to Corruption, and to all who demean us."

Comfortable on Mhornym's back, Branl echoed Clyme with a nod.

Inwardly Covenant winced. He saw more than one fallacy in Clyme's argument. Obviously Clyme gave him more credit than he deserved; but there was another.

The Masters and the Humbled were still trying to *prove* themselves—and that was never going to work. Not against Lord Foul. It was the same mistake that Korik, Sill, and Doar had made: the same mistake disguised in different language. The same mistake that had caused the *Haruchai* to become the Bloodguard. Their fixation on humiliation revealed the truth.

So the whole world is going to die. Let it. Knowing that we've accepted the consequences of our actions is good enough for us. Nothing matters except how we feel about ourselves.

Lord Foul probably ate that kind of thinking for breakfast, and laughed his head off. No wonder he had told Linden that the Masters already served him.

But Covenant could not say such things to Clyme and Branl. Stave might understand him: the Humbled would not.

He let that one fallacy pass. For a few moments, he concentrated on trying to loosen his muscles so that his body would flex with the destrier's movements. As he did so, however, the wrapped *krill* dug into his abdomen. With an exasperated wrench, he moved the dagger to the side of his waist. Then he set about contradicting the Humbled.

"You're forgetting something. I've always had help. I never would have reached Foul's Creche on my own. Foamfollower had to carry me." If the *jheherrin* had not rescued him—if Foamfollower and Bannor had not distracted Elena—if a nameless woman in Morinmoss had not healed him— "And I still would have failed if Foamfollower hadn't given me exactly what I needed," if the last of the Unhomed had not revealed the courage, the sheer greatness of spirit, to laugh in the face of despair.

"Without Linden and the First and Pitchwife, I would never have made it to Kiril Threndor. Without Linden, I couldn't have forced myself to hand over my ring. Without Vain and Findail, she couldn't have created a new Staff. Without the First and Pitchwife, her Staff would have been lost.

"Sure," Covenant rasped, "Lord Foul was defeated. Twice. But *I* didn't do it. *We* did it. Foamfollower and I. Linden and I. The First and Pitchwife and Sunder and Hollian.

"So tell me again," he demanded. "What's so *wrong* about accepting gifts you haven't earned?"

But he did not wait for an answer. "In any case," he muttered, "dying is easy. Anybody can do it. Living is hard."

And living was untenable without forgiveness.

In silence, Clyme and Branl conveyed the impression that they were consulting with each other. For a little while, Covenant allowed himself to hope that they had heard him; that for his sake they had lowered their defenses. But then Branl turned to him with an unmistakable glint of disapprobation in his gaze.

"Is it your belief, ur-Lord, that we must countenance humiliation? That we must subjugate ourselves to powers beyond our ken, and to choices which we have not affirmed?"

Hellfire, Covenant thought. Hellfire and bloody damnation.

"Never mind." Swallowing his vexation, he shrugged. "This isn't getting us anywhere. Think about it another way.

"Down at the bottom, your accusation against Linden is, 'Good cannot be accomplished by evil means.' Breaking Laws is an evil means. Concealing her intentions is an evil means. So of course she has to be stopped. You couldn't block the Fall she used to get to Revelstone. You couldn't make her tell the truth about what she wanted in Andelain. You couldn't get past Stave and Mahrtiir and the Ranyhyn when you realized what she had in mind. But I should have let you stop her when she first resurrected me.

"Well, sure," he went on before the Humbled could respond. "That makes sense. There's only one problem. There are *always* evil means. Nobody is ever as pure as you want them to be. You aren't. I'm not. We all have some kind of darkness in us. So the only way to avoid evil means is to do nothing. And the only way to do nothing—to be innocent—is to be powerless," which in effect was what the Masters had chosen for the Land. "If you have power, any kind of power at all, it always finds a way to express itself. Somehow.

"But *you* aren't powerless." Passion mounted in his tone. He did not try to restrain it. "Practically everything you've done proves it. You don't trust how people use Earthpower—and you have good reason. So you've been trying to keep the Land innocent by making everybody else impotent. And you've succeeded. Liand was a perfect example.

"For all I know, you thought you were giving him a gift.

"That much, at least, I understand." Covenant kept his gaze on the horizon, surveying reminders of devastation. "The first time I came to the Land, I almost turned myself inside out trying to be innocent." After what he had done to Lena— The memory still made him cringe. "What I finally accepted wasn't being weak, and it sure as hell wasn't the consequences of my actions. What I accepted was evil means. Guilt. The crime of power.

"But there's one part of all this *you* don't seem to understand." He was on the verge of shouting. "The thing that makes Earthpower terrible is the same thing that makes it wonderful. Even if innocence is a good thing, which I doubt, you've confused it with ignorance.

"That's what's wrong with being the Masters of the Land. You wanted to stop something terrible, so you stopped everything. Including everything that might have been wonderful. You've even stopped yourselves from being the kind of force that could have changed the world. And you've ensured nobody else changes it. Hell, you've subjugated *everybody* to choices they didn't make.

"If you want to be innocent, that's your right. But you've been so determined to prevent another Kevin Landwaster, you've closed the door on another Berek Halfhand, or another Damelon Giantfriend, or another Loric Vilesilencer.

"Hellfire." Gradually Covenant's vehemence subsided. The impassivity of the Humbled seemed to imply that words were useless. "Sunder and Hollian could have started a new Council of Lords. The Land could have had more Mhorams, more Prothalls, more Callindrills, more Hyrims. All you had to do was tell people what you know instead of keeping everything secret."

Now Clyme and Branl were staring straight at Covenant; and he did not need health-sense to recognize their ire. The hearts of the *Haruchai* were tinder. Beneath their studied dispassion, anger burned like a bonfire.

"You denounce us," Branl asserted as if he were certain of Covenant's meaning. "Do you seek to spurn our companionship? Do you desire our enmity?"

"Hell, no!" Covenant wanted to rage at the sky in simple frustration. "I *need* you. And I respect you." With an effort that made him ache, he restrained himself. The intransigence of the Humbled filled him with loneliness. "I know I don't sound like it, but I respect the hell out of you. If I were in your place, I might have made different decisions a long time ago, but that doesn't stop me from wishing I could be more like you.

"If I were, I wouldn't be so damn terrified of my ex-wife."

And perhaps he would have been brave enough to assure Linden that he loved her.

To his surprise, his reply appeared to content his companions. Their wrath faded as they looked away. For several moments, they rode mutely at his sides. Then Clyme asked as if he were not changing the subject, "Have you considered, ur-Lord, how you will contest your former mate? Ruled by *turiya* Herem, she wields wild magic and Falls. And we have cause to believe that she is warded by *skest*. Also we are concerned that Corruption may summon other forces to her defense.

"With the aid of the Ranyhyn—if the terrain permits—we may perhaps suffice against the *skest*. But against Falls, we cannot shield you. And we have no lore to gauge the uses of the *krill*.

"You have surrendered your rightful ring. How, then, will you oppose her?"

"Don't worry about it." Covenant did not want to dwell on Joan. He was not ready. To prevent the Humbled from insisting, he added, "You have one thing I don't. You remember everything—and you can hold on to it all at once. In fact, you make it look easy. Maybe that'll save us."

The Masters seemed to discuss Covenant's remark privately before Branl answered, "Ur-lord, we are able to contain our memories because we do not do so alone. Across the generations of the *Haruchai*, we have learned together to accommodate an ever-expanding recall. But we cannot gift our communion to others. We lack that power or craft. That we hear and answer the silent speech of Sandgorgons results from the remnants of *samadhi* Sheol within them, not from any outreach of our own minds.

"We are cognizant of your straits. The vastness of Time exceeds you. But we know not how to aid you."

Grinding his teeth, Covenant reminded himself again to relax. "Don't worry about it," he repeated more severely. "One of us will think of something. And if we don't—" He sighed. "The Ranyhyn still know what they're doing."

He had to believe that. He thought that he knew where to find Joan; but he had no notion what he would do when he reached her. He was only sure that she was his responsibility—and that he would never return to claim Linden if he did not first find an answer to Joan's excruciation.

✦

B arrows and shale seemed to stretch indefinitely into Covenant's future and the Land's past: a wracked wasteland like a battlefield where armies beyond counting had slaughtered each other for centuries. Yet eventually that region gave

way to a wide sheet of old lava. Beyond it, the riders found a beaten plain webbed
with gullies. Nonetheless Naybahn and Mhornym continued to discover water and
forage; occasional *aliantha*. Between them, they kept Covenant fed and his mount
running.

Later they came to a protracted series of ridges that lay athwart the south like fortifications, obstructing the course of the Ranyhyn. However, Naybahn and Mhornym
surmounted each line of hills by angling away from Landsdrop to more gradual slopes
in the east.

By Covenant's reckoning, each ridge nudged his company closer to the boundaries
of the Sarangrave.

By degrees, the Ranyhyn turned more directly toward the Sunbirth Sea. According to Clyme, they were passing south of the Sarangrave's verge. If Mhornym and
Naybahn held to this heading, their path would skim the northern edge of the Shattered Hills.

With every league, Covenant became more confident that he knew where the Ranyhyn were taking him. Somewhere among the broken stone and ravaged cliffs of Foul's
Creche, he would find Joan. Why else had the Ardent striven to convey everyone as far
as he could in this direction? And if Ridjeck Thome were indeed their goal, the horses
had chosen the safest route; probably the quickest. Any other approach would force
them into the jumbled maze of the Shattered Hills: an area fraught with hazards, apt
for ambush.

How much farther? Covenant wondered. At this pace? Assuming that the cliffs of
the coast were even passable? But he did not ask Clyme or Branl. He had more immediate concerns. His mount's gait had become labored, a ragged jarring. And as the sun
sank toward distant Landsdrop, *caesures* began to sprout across the Spoiled Plains.

Too many of them: more than he had believed Joan could unleash without causing
her own heart to burst. Instinctively he assumed that she—or *turiya* Raver—was trying to hunt him down.

Yet the Falls were comparatively brief. They flared into chiaroscuro, a swirling stutter of day and night, writhed avidly across the landscape, and then extinguished themselves. Indeed, they seemed somehow indecisive, as if they had lost the scent of their
prey. And none of them came close enough to endanger Covenant's small company.
Instead they searched the region which the Ranyhyn would have crossed if they had
run straight toward Foul's Creche.

As late afternoon became evening, Covenant began to breathe more easily. He was
able to persuade himself that Joan did not know where he was. She and *turiya* were
only guessing. As long as his skin did not touch Loric's *krill*—

Of course, it was possible that he was not Joan's target. This display of violation may have been aimed at Linden and Jeremiah. The Despiser—and therefore his Ravers—surely understood that Linden and her son were at least as dangerous to him as Thomas Covenant. But Covenant trusted the Ranyhyn to protect them. And Linden had her Staff: she could ward herself and her companions.

When darkness had settled over the Spoiled Plains, Naybahn and Mhornym took shelter in a crooked gully. There a slightly brackish stream flowed vaguely northward, perhaps adding its waters to the Sarangrave; and along its sides grew tough saw-edged grasses sufficient for the destrier, as well as clumps of *aliantha* stunted like scrog. And among them grew a scant patch of *amanibhavam* to sustain the Ranyhyn. Clearly the Ranyhyn intended to rest there for the night.

After a sparse meal of treasure-berries, Branl left the gully to stand watch; and Covenant tried to settle himself for sleep by scooping hollows in the loose dirt to form a crude bed. Watching, Clyme remarked that the barrage of Falls would disturb the weather over the Lower Land. The Humbled sensed the approach of storms; of rain and winds in turmoil. But Covenant only shrugged. He could barely resist his memories: he certainly had no control over the weather. If his leprosy and the warmth of the *krill* did not sustain him, he would simply have to endure whatever came.

Huddled into himself, he dozed and roused repeatedly, waiting with as much patience as he could muster for the night to pass.

At dawn, he learned that Clyme was right. The sun first rose into a sky appalled by a taint that resembled dust and ash or smoke; but soon dark clouds came boiling over the Plains, and rain began to spatter down, apparently driven by winds from every direction at once. Before Covenant had finished quenching his thirst and eating more *aliantha*, his T-shirt and jeans were soaked. When he mounted the horse, he saw that the beast's endurance had been reduced to gritted misery. It had not rested not enough to restore its spirit. Nevertheless the Harrow's charger strained to resume its effortful gallop.

In rain and contending winds, Covenant and the Humbled continued their eastward rush.

Sometime during the night, the *caesures* had ceased. Presumably Joan had exhausted herself. Or *turiya* Raver may have been given new instructions. But Covenant refused to think about them. He tried not to think about Linden. Wrapping his arms across his chest, he endeavored to ignore the rain by emptying his mind of everything except the heat of the *krill*: the heat, yes, but not the gem from which it radiated, or the implications of wild magic. If he allowed himself to yearn for anything more than ordinary warmth from Loric's eldritch dagger, Joan or *turiya* might sense his attention. They might even be able to locate him.

Emulating Jeremiah's vacancy, Covenant rode and rode; opened his mouth to the rain when he was thirsty; ate *aliantha* when the fruit was given to him; and accepted his regret whenever Linden slipped into his thoughts.

ॐ

F inally a change in the weather drew him out of his willed somnolence. The day had reached late afternoon, and the rain had stopped. Perhaps because the winds had resolved themselves into a bitter blast out of the west, the storm clouds had scudded away, leaving behind a sky mired with ash and fine dirt like the fug of a distant calamity.

Yet the murk in the air appeared to come from the east. Against the wind—

Now on the horizon to his right Covenant could make out the first jagged outcroppings of the Shattered Hills. And perhaps a league or two ahead of the horses, the terrain rose in a long slow sweep as if the ground were gathering itself to plunge over the edge of the world.

Was that the cliff fronting the Sunbirth Sea? Covenant wanted badly to have covered so much ground; but he had no way to estimate how far he and the Humbled had traveled. And he doubted that his mount would last long enough to reach the top of the rise. He felt exhausted himself, physically battered. His legs quivered trying to grip the destrier's sides. But the beast's condition was worse; much worse. During the day, it had surpassed its strength. Now its heart hardly seemed able to manage a lurching beat. As far as he could discern, only the insistence of the Ranyhyn kept the charger from surrendering its last breath.

The horses' hooves were barely audible over the raw hum of the wind. They were running on grass as thick as turf. Apparently this portion of the Lower Land received more rain than the westward reaches. Covenant and his companions must indeed be nearing the coast, where natural storms would break and tumble on the cliffs, releasing a comparative abundance of rainfall. Here the destrier could have cropped enough grass to refresh a measure of its stamina; but it made no attempt to pause or feed. The beast's spirit was broken. It had nothing left except a primitive desire to perish without more suffering.

Through the bitter plaint of the wind, Covenant called to the Humbled, "Where are we?"

Branl glanced at him. "We approach the cliff above the Sunbirth Sea. There we will seek out shelter ere nightfall, hoping for some covert to ward you from the chill of this wind."

Covenant nodded; but he felt no relief. "What're we going to do when my horse dies? This poor thing won't last much longer. As soon as it stops moving, it's finished."

He needed a mount. He was too far north; too far from Foul's Creche. He could not afford the time to walk that distance.

Branl shrugged. "The beast has labored valiantly. It must be allowed its final peace." A moment later, he added, "Mhornym is well able to bear two riders—as is Naybahn."

"Don't insult me," Covenant growled, even though he knew that the Humbled meant no offense. "You keep your promises. What makes you think I won't do the same?"

Long ago, he had made a pact with the Ranyhyn. He intended to abide by it. How else could he ask them to do likewise?

Briefly Branl consulted with Clyme in silence. Then he asked, "What alternative remains? We have seen no more *amanibhavam.*"

Covenant swore to himself. "Then what about *aliantha*?"

Branl raised an eyebrow: a subtle show of surprise. "It is not a natural provender for horses. Neither horse nor Ranyhyn consumes such fruit."

"So what?" Covenant countered. "It's worth a try."

After only a moment, Branl nodded. "Indeed, ur-Lord."

At once, Clyme and Mhornym veered aside, racing in search of treasure-berries.

Fortunately they soon found what they sought. The destrier was stumbling at the slope. Each time the beast caught itself, locked its knees, and jerked forward, it came closer to falling. With every stride, its muscles trembled like the onset of a seizure. Covenant had to clutch the saddle horn to keep his seat.

Strain throbbed in his temples as he watched Clyme dismount to gather treasure-berries, then leap onto Mhornym's back and return. While the Ranyhyn sped toward Covenant and Branl, Clyme pitted berries deftly with his fingers, scattering the seeds.

Please, Covenant asked Naybahn and Mhornym, hoping that they understood his thoughts, or his heart. Keep this animal alive. Make it eat. I know it's suffered enough, but I need it. I don't know what else to try.

As if in response, Naybahn slowed to a halt. Staggering on the verge of collapse, the destrier did the same. Its chest heaved brokenly, dying for more air than its lungs could hold.

Uselessly Covenant wondered why the Ranyhyn had not taken better care of his mount earlier. But he had no idea how to question the great horses. Perhaps they perceived a need for haste which outweighed lesser considerations. At other times, they had shown that they knew more than they could communicate about the events of the world. Or perhaps they were testing Covenant's determination to keep his promises—

Clyme dropped to the turf at the destrier's head. Firmly he untied the bridle, tugged the reins out of Covenant's hands, slipped the snaffle from the beast's mouth. Holding the horse by its mane, he lifted one cupped hand full of fruit to its mouth.

At first, the destrier only gasped at the berries, too drained to blow froth; too empty of life to scent anything, want anything. But both Naybahn and Mhornym gazed at Covenant's mount with instructions in their stern eyes; and after a moment, a small spasm ran through the beast's muscles as if it had been goaded. Weakly the horse lipped a few treasure-berries from Clyme's hand.

Covenant should have dismounted, but he did not think to move. With as much concentration as he could muster, he focused his senses on the destrier's condition: on the limping struggle of its heart, the shredded straining of its lungs.

Relief left him briefly light-headed when the horse took more *aliantha*. His health-sense was too blunt for precise discernment, but he seemed to feel a faint touch of vitality flow into the beast's veins.

Then he remembered to slip down from the destrier. His own legs throbbed at the unaccustomed effects of two days on horseback; and he felt battered, as if he had fallen from a great height. Standing would do him good: walking would be better.

While Clyme stroked the destrier's neck, encouraging it, Branl rode away. When he came back, he brought another handful of berries. These the horse ate more willingly.

The Humbled both nodded in satisfaction. "Ur-Lord," Clyme announced, "with your consent we will walk to the cliff. Gentle movement will quicken the benison of *aliantha*. Mayhap the beast's awareness of hunger will awaken. If we then discover water—" He shrugged; did not finish the thought.

Covenant knew what he meant. Maybe the horse would live. Maybe it would be strong enough to carry him after a night's rest.

If.

"Sure," he answered. "We can at least hope."

Leaving Clyme and Mhornym with the destrier, Covenant headed up the long rise, accompanied by Branl on Naybahn. At first, he walked stiffly, forcing each stride against the protest of his muscles. But gradually his limbs loosened. And the grass softened his steps. Soon he began to move more briskly, aiming to reach the rim of the slope before twilight.

alf a league from the horizon-line where the ground dropped away, Naybahn adjusted his course slightly to the south.

As Covenant drew closer, he saw that the precipice was scored with cracks. Some of them looked like the results of erosion, the claw-marks of weather and old time.

Others appeared to be deeper faults in the fundamental substance of the cliff. But he still did not smell salt or hear surf. The harsh wind from the west blew away any indication that he was approaching the sea.

Naybahn angled farther south. Instinctively Covenant quickened his strides. Vulnerable in his damp clothes, he was already chilled: he wanted to believe that Naybahn or Branl would lead him to some kind of shelter from the wind.

Tossing his head, the Ranyhyn gave a snort that sounded disdainful. For his own reasons, if not for Branl's, the stallion nudged Covenant with his shoulder. Have you forgotten who I am? Are you foolish enough to doubt us? You who spoke of *trust*? That gentle bump directed Covenant toward a crack or crevice extending perhaps a hundred paces inland.

At the tip of the crack, he found that it was shallow enough for a horse to enter, wide enough to admit a mounted rider. Its floor as it dropped toward the precipice was not dangerously steep. And it ended, not in a plunge, but on a ledge as broad as a road.

There Covenant saw the Sunbirth Sea.

Under a leaden sky at the onset of evening, it looked misnamed. Lashed waves taller than Giants, and as dark as thunderheads, seethed heavily toward the cliff and out of sight. Tumbling winds ripped the crests of the waves to spume, tore them in all directions. Nonetheless the seas heaved closer with the massive inevitability of avalanches or calving glaciers. In spite of his numbness, Covenant seemed to feel a faint tremor as each breaker crashed against the granite coast. Somewhere far beyond the range of his perceptions, storms which had fled eastward earlier hammered the ocean; or some new atmospheric violence was gathering against the Land.

Without hesitation, Naybahn entered the split and bore Branl downward. Cautiously Covenant followed.

As he worked his way toward the ledge, he glimpsed more and more of the sea. Atavistic vertigo began to squirm through him: the waves were a *long* way down— A man who fell from that ledge would have time to repent every misdeed of his life before he died. Reflexively he hugged the stone of the crevice-wall; but its ancient endurance refused to steady him.

Don't, he commanded himself. Don't look. But the plunge was already calling to him. It insinuated itself among the pathways of his brain, urging him to stagger and reel and drop; to pitch the disease of his existence over the precipice. He was in a crevice, and his mind was a maze of fissures. Memories summoned him from all sides. Soon they would become a gyre, a *geas*, and the cliff or the past would take him.

In some other life, Lena would have come to his aid. Foamfollower and Triock would have helped him. Or Linden's presence would have given him the will to suppress this spinning. But in *this* life—

Branl clasped his arm in a grip like a manacle. Beyond the Master, Naybahn waited on the ledge, unconcerned by the fall. But Branl had come back for Covenant.

The *Haruchai* forgot nothing. They had a strength that Covenant lacked, one supreme gift: within themselves, they were not alone. As well as he could, Branl contradicted Covenant's impulse toward isolation and dizziness.

Anchored by the grasp of the Humbled, Covenant moved toward Naybahn without losing his way.

On the ledge, the Ranyhyn stood between him and the precipice. Branl held his arm. Protected in that fashion, Covenant went warily southward.

Now he could hear the waves: an iterated crash-and-roar among the rocks far below him. The turmoil of winds sawing against granite edges everywhere complicated the rush and smash of the breakers, emphasized their timeless hunger. For a few moments, the surf seemed to have a voice, singing of mortality—

All hurt is like the endless surge of seas,
The wear and tumbling that leaves no welt
But only sand instead of granite ease

—until he almost stumbled into his fragmented past. But then the ledge rounded a bulge and became the floor of another split in the battered cliff.

The sun was setting quickly now: he could barely see. This crack led downward without visible limit or end into the heart of the gutrock. After a dozen steps, however, Naybahn and Branl brought him to a break in the left-hand wall of the split, a gap just wide enough to admit the Ranyhyn. Drawn through the break into complete darkness, Covenant sensed that he was entering an open space like a chamber in the stone. Just for a moment, he thought that the chamber was a closed cavity. But almost at once, he discerned a slit of gloom in the direction of the sea; heard the faint plash and susurrus of water.

He could not smell salt. Air-currents flowing into and out of the cave carried away the ocean's scent.

"Here is shelter, ur-Lord," Branl stated flatly. "Thus shielded, you will suffer little of the wind's chill, though doubtless the stone is cold. And beyond us arises a goodly spring, flowing past our feet to drain from the cliff."

Covenant nodded, trusting the Humbled to see what he could not. "What about the Harrow's horse?"

"Clyme and Mhornym will guide the beast to water here." Branl spoke like the darkness. "Thereafter the Ranyhyn and your mount will surely depart to feed above the cliff. When they have cropped their fill, however, I anticipate that they will return to this covert, to share warmth and rest. In that event, the Humbled will stand guard at the rims of the precipice."

Covenant nodded again. He felt perfectly capable of freezing to death if three horses did not suffice to warm the chamber. Nevertheless he was content with his sanctuary. It was better than any covert that he had expected to find. "If you'll guide me to a place where I can sit down—preferably someplace dry—I'll get us some light."

And some heat? He hoped so.

Holding Covenant's arm, Branl steered him to a level surface where he was able to step over the stream. Beyond the spill of water, the chamber's floor rose toward its far wall in stages like steps. There Covenant sat down and carefully untucked the bundled *krill* from his waist.

He had reason to believe that Loric's dagger could cut anything. Long ago, he had stabbed it into the top of a stone table. With as much care as his deadened and fore-shortened fingers could manage, he unwound fabric from the blade without touching the metal. The haft and the gem he kept covered. After a moment's hesitation, he raised his arms and drove the *krill's* point at the rock between his boots.

He expected a hard jolt, a skitter of metal as the blade skidded across stone. But the knife pierced rock as if it were flesh; bit deep and held fast, standing like an icon in the floor.

"Well, damn," he breathed unsteadily. "At least *that* worked."

With the nub-ends of his fingers, he unwrapped the rest of the cloth; let the gem's bright silver shine out.

It resembled a beacon, but he chose to believe that it would not draw Joan's attention if he did not touch it.

The sudden blaze of light filled the cave: it seemed to efface even the possibility of shadows. Branl stood etched in the air beside a brisk stream that caught the radiance and glittered flowing argent as it ran toward a narrow slit like an embrasure in the for-tification of the cliff. As Naybahn drank from the stream, the stallion's coat glowed as if it had been touched with transcendence, and the star on his forehead gleamed.

Apart from the window to the outer world on one side, and the tapering hollow opposite it from which the spring emerged, the chamber was shaped like a dome. Even at its tallest point, the ceiling was too low to let a Giant stand fully upright; but the dome was high enough, and more than wide enough, to admit several horses. Its walls and ceiling were oddly smooth: the eldritch gem's echo of wild magic made them look burnished, almost holy, as if at some point in the distant past they had formed a primitive fane. In contrast, however, the floor was rough and scalloped, composed of a different stone which seemed to insist that it was made for darkness rather than for light.

As Branl had predicted, the rock was cold. Covenant already felt its chill seeping into him through his damp jeans. Fortunately he also felt steady heat emanating from Loric's dagger. White gold in the hands of its rightful wielder made the whole knife too hot for his unprotected flesh. By that sign, he knew that Joan was still alive. Inadvertently her reflected desperation might warm the entire chamber.

"Thank you," he murmured to Naybahn. He needed to express his gratitude, whether or not the Ranyhyn understood him. "I forgot about this place—if I ever knew it existed. You came back to the Land at the right time. None of us would have gotten this far without you." Especially Linden. "And we sure as hell wouldn't get any farther."

Naybahn whickered softly, tossed his head. The silver shining in his eyes looked like pride.

Covenant wanted to ask Branl how Clyme and Mhornym fared with the Harrow's mount. But an answer to that question would not quicken their arrival, or restore the destrier's stamina, or relieve Covenant's underlying fears. Instead he inquired abruptly, "How far are we from Foul's Creche?"

Branl appeared to consult a map of his memories. "In a direct line, ur-Lord, the ruins of Corruption's former abode lie no more than fifteen leagues distant. However, these cliffs are rugged, forbidding clear passage. I gauge that we must traverse a score of leagues—if," he added, "the riven promontory of Ridjeck Thome is indeed our destination." Then he shrugged. "If our goal lies elsewhere, the Ranyhyn know it. The Humbled do not."

With a wave of one hand, Covenant dismissed Branl's proviso. "Assume we're going to Foul's Creche. Where else is Joan likely to be? That place is too damn *fitting*." A wilderness of broken granite between the Sunbirth Sea and the Shattered Hills: enough rubble to symbolize dozens of millennia. Joan's attacks on Time required a physical manifestation. She tore instants into chaos by destroying stones. The Earth was the incarnation of the Laws which enabled it to live: she struck at one by harming the other. And Covenant did not doubt that the Despiser's malice still permeated the wreckage of Foul's Creche. The evil of the Illearth Stone lingered there as well. Such things would enhance *turiya* Herem's possession. "So how long will it take us to get there?"

Branl studied Covenant flatly. "Since you choose to rely upon assumptions, ur-Lord, I will do the same. If your mount regains strength sufficient to bear you, I gauge that we will sight the remains of Ridjeck Thome at nightfall on the morrow."

Another day— Hell and blood, Covenant swore to himself. Too much time had already passed, and the Worm was coming. The Earth did not have long to live. Yet so far he and the Land's last defenders had accomplished nothing except Jeremiah's rescue from the Lost Deep, and from the *croyel*. True, Esmer had been put to rest. But his release had been the gift of the ur-viles and Waynhim, and of Stave. Covenant himself had done little to justify his return to life.

He needed to face Joan.

He needed to be ready. He could not afford to fail.

But he still had no idea how to answer her anguish.

 споﬢ

E ventually Clyme entered the cave with Mhornym and the destrier. While the horses relieved their long thirst, Branl left to search the slopes above the cliff for more *aliantha*. He was still absent when Mhornym and Naybahn led the Harrow's mount back out of the chamber to feed, leaving Covenant alone with Clyme and the *krill*. For a time, the steady tug of air through the cave seemed to draw off more heat than the dagger offered, siphoning every possibility of comfort through the crack in the cliff-face. But then Branl returned with a double handful of treasure-berries; and when Covenant had eaten, the fruit's rich sustenance gave him a measure of protection from the cold.

The seeds he thrust into one of his pockets so that he could scatter them on fertile soil later.

Later the three horses also returned; and Clyme left to stand guard over the covert. The destrier still looked like a living derelict, dull-eyed and shambling. Small convulsions ran through its muscles, and it moved as though it sought to limp with all four legs simultaneously. Nevertheless Covenant saw hints of nascent recovery. Two or three days of rest and abundant fodder might well restore the charger's contentious spirit.

Ah, hell, he sighed. He had no choice: he would ride as long as his mount lasted. After that, he would have to walk—or to run, if he could manage that much haste.

Whatever happened, he was not going to ride the Ranyhyn. Broken promises would not save the Land. *There are* always *evil means.* He had said that to the Humbled. *The only way to avoid evil means is to do nothing.* Nevertheless he had no intention of discarding any more promises. He had already done enough harm to vindicate Lord Foul's expectations. Mere days ago, he had sacrificed Elena to She Who Must Not Be Named. If he had no other choice, he meant to kill Joan: an *evil means* if ever there was one. And he had hurt Linden—

His own humanity would turn against him if he started breaking his promises.

Fortunately Mhornym, Naybahn, and the destrier gave off a surprising amount of warmth in the constricted space. Together they and the *krill* softened the chamber's chill. By slow increments, the air acquired a modicum of comfort, and the stone surrendered some of its cold. After a while, Covenant began to think about sleep.

Stretching out on a step near the *krill*, he closed his eyes and tried to let himself drift. But instead of slumber and dreams, he sank into unbidden memories.

For no reason that he could name, he remembered *quellvisks*.

Monsters as tall as Giants. Six taloned limbs, each gnarled with muscle and theurgy. Eyes all around their crude skulls. Fangs dripping venomous magicks. Minds capable of lore and bitter ambition. Once they had been very different beings, a species of sentient herbivores. The transformation which had created *quellvisks* from such creatures had been Lord Foul's only dangerous achievement during his centuries among the Demimages of Vidik Amar. Doing what he could with monsters both too intelligent and too savage to be ruled, the Despiser had given them an aspiration which might serve his purpose. When the *quellvisks* had rendered the Demimages extinct, Lord Foul had convinced them that they could master the entire Earth if they first slew the *Elohim*.

By that means, the Despiser had hoped to awaken the Worm.

Even in that distant age, the *Elohim* were too self-absorbed to regard the threat. They did not go out to battle because they saw no need: they believed that the *quellvisks* would turn against each other; destroy themselves. Therefore the Despiser considered the *Elohim* ripe for ruin. But they were roused from their rapt immersions when the *quellvisks* found their way to *Elemesnedene*.

When the *Elohim* finally fought back for the first and last time in the Earth's history, they did so without restraint or pity. They had been affronted to the core of their surquedry, and they left nothing of their foes except bones.

Undisturbed, the Worm of the World's End had continued its slumber.

"Ur-Lord."

Involuntarily Covenant remembered what the *Elohim* had done with those bones. Muirwin Delenoth, resting place of abhorrence. Somewhere on the Lower Land west of the Shattered Hills. As if the Land were a midden for everything that the *Elohim* despised.

"Unbeliever," Branl said more insistently. "You must rouse." He shook Covenant's shoulder. "There is peril."

With a startled jerk, Covenant opened his eyes.

For a moment, he could see nothing except the blaze of the *krill*, bright as a tocsin in his blurred gaze. As he blinked, however, his covert took shape around the gem's light. The stream ran, undimmed, across the cave to tumble down the outer precipice. Branl stood stolidly over him, waiting for him to shed the remnants of his dreams.

Outside, the past day's gale still blew. It moaned as it struggled through the cave.

The destrier had folded its legs under it to sleep on the other side of the stream. The beast appeared to be resting deeply. But there was something missing—

With an awkward heave, Covenant pushed himself to sit up. Swallowing sleep, he asked hoarsely, "Where are the Ranyhyn?"

"Creatures approach, ur-Lord," answered Branl, "a score of small beings. When

Clyme discerned their advance, Naybahn and Mhornym appeared to do so as well. They have departed. It is my thought that they mean to watch over us in Clyme's stead, freeing him to join in your defense."

Creatures? Covenant shook his head; tried to clear away his confusion. Defense? His fears were as confused as the previous day's storms. While he strove to knit Branl's words into a sequence that made sense, he asked, "What time is it?"

Branl regarded him without expression. "Dawn lags behind the creatures. We must perforce meet with them in darkness. And we must not await them here. In this place, their advance will be constricted. That is to our benefit. But we cannot flee at need. Therefore we must stand on open ground."

Covenant started to rise. Then he sat down again. "Wait a minute. Let's think about this." The *krill* was his only weapon, but he could not carry it unwrapped. And he might not be able to use it without touching the metal. "These creatures. What are they? What do they want? How do you know they're dangerous?"

If the Humbled felt impatient, he did not show it. "They are human-like in form, but small, little more than shoulder-height, with large eyes well suited to sight in darkness. Though they resemble children, they are naked against the elements, clad neither in garments nor in pelts. Upon some few occasions, the Masters have beheld such creatures, always at a considerable distance, and always within Sarangrave Flat. Indeed, the waters of the Sarangrave appear to be their habitation. And while we have taken note of them, they have betrayed no awareness of us.

"Now, however—" Branl paused as if he were speaking mind to mind with Clyme. "They have strayed far from their accustomed marshlands. And their approach is unerring. It cannot be doubted that they have come to seek you out.

"Also there is this to consider. In each hand, they bear a green flame which does not bend to the dictates of the wind. This theurgy appears to enable their departure from their native waters." Branl's tone became sharper. "It's the precise emerald of the Illearth Stone, and of the *skest.*

"You will recall that the *skest* once served the lurker of the Sarangrave. Now they have become the minions of Corruption. These creatures may be *skest* in some new guise, perhaps altered by the baleful seepages of Gravin Threndor. Whatever their origins, however, the nature of their magicks cannot be mistaken. It is green and malefic, binding their hearts to cruel hungers.

"Their purpose cannot be other than harm. Therefore we must be prepared to give battle, and to flee."

Covenant peered up at the Humbled. He wanted to ask how Branl proposed to save his sleeping mount. And he wanted to remind Branl of the *sur-jheherrin,* creatures that had once saved him and his companions—including several *Haruchai*—from the lurker. The *sur-jheherrin* were descended from the *jheherrin,* the Soft Ones, who had rescued Covenant and Saltheart Foamfollower during their approach to the Shattered Hills and Foul's Creche. Not everything bred in the Sarangrave was evil.

But instead he posed a different question. "Has Clyme tried talking to them?"

The *Haruchai* lacked the Giants' gift of tongues. But the *jheherrin* had been capable of human speech.

Branl raised an eyebrow: for him, a dramatic show of surprise. "He has not."

"Maybe he should do that. Before we get into a fight we don't want."

The Humbled cocked his head in what Covenant assumed was Clyme's direction. After a moment, Branl replied, "Clyme will make the attempt. To his senses, the creatures do not appear to unite their theurgies. Each wields only its own might. He deems it unlikely that they are able to overwhelm or slay him."

Covenant resisted an impulse to hold his breath. How long would this take? He had no idea how far the creatures were from Clyme's position. Would Covenant and Branl still have time to escape the cave? With the charger?

The moments seemed to stretch, mocked by the quickness of the stream. In the absence of the Ranyhyn, Covenant felt colder; more vulnerable. Branl waited, motionless. He did not react to whatever he heard from Clyme.

Abruptly the Master spoke. "The creatures name themselves the Feroce. At the behest of their High God, they crave an audience with the Pure One."

Covenant winced. The Feroce? He had lost any memory of them. But "the Pure One"—

Ah, Foamfollower! Hellfire. He remembered too much about the Pure One.

Without thinking, he told Branl, "They have the wrong man." Then he caught himself. "No, don't say that." In the legends of the *jheherrin*, the Pure One had been their promised savior. If the Feroce believed that Covenant rather than Saltheart Foamfollower had rescued the *jheherrin* from the Maker, the Despiser, they were mistaken. But that error might help him avoid a conflict. "Don't give them an excuse to stop talking.

"Ask them why they want an audience. What do they want to talk about?"

Branl gave no sign that he was relaying Covenant's desires to Clyme, but Covenant did not doubt him. He was *Haruchai*.

A few heartbeats later, the Humbled announced, "The Feroce avow that they intend no subterfuge. They acknowledge their enmity. They acknowledge that they have attempted harm. They acknowledge that their first purpose has failed. In pain and desperation, their High God now seeks alliance with the Pure One."

Covenant's mind whirled as though he stood on a precipice. Attempted harm? *What* harm? If the Feroce had attacked Linden—! Anger and possibilities spun swiftly; too swiftly. The creatures had invoked *jheherrin* legends. Long millennia ago, the *jheherrin* had misjudged Covenant. But if the Feroce knew those legends, they might be descendants of the *sur-jheherrin*: they might believe what the *jheherrin* had believed.

Attempted *harm*?

Apparently they were being honest.

Then who in hell was their "High God"? The *lurker*? If they lived in the Sarangrave—

An alliance with the lurker was impossible. The idea was insane. But he had no difficulty imagining potential benefits.

He was running too far ahead of himself. Grimly he muttered, "I don't know what's going on here. But I'm going to guess.

"If the Feroce want to talk, tell them to come here. Just three of them. The rest have to keep a safe distance. Clyme can decide what that means. And tell them I have High Lord Loric's *krill*. A long time ago, I hurt the lurker with it. I won't hesitate to use it again if I think I'm being threatened."

If the creatures had not come in good faith.

Studying Covenant, Branl hesitated. "Ur-Lord, is this wise? Our covert has no other egress. If the Feroce do not endeavor to slay us, they may nonetheless impose an effective imprisonment. Snared here, you will be prevented from seeking your former mate."

"I know that," Covenant sighed. "Of course you're right. But I can't forget the *sur-jheherrin*." Or the *jheherrin*. "Life in the Sarangrave isn't as simple as it looks. If the Feroce want to talk to the Pure One, I can't ignore them." Without the *jheherrin*, he would have died among the Shattered Hills. "Just tell Clyme what I said. If they try to send more than three—if they do anything he doesn't like—he can warn you."

Frowning slightly, Branl nodded. Then he moved to stand guard against the far wall beside the entrance to the chamber.

The destrier went on sleeping. It seemed too profoundly weary to hear anything; or to care.

A dozen heartbeats later, the Humbled reported, "The Feroce comply. Three of them approach. Their manner is fearful. The others withdraw according to Clyme's instructions." Then he added, "The Ranyhyn stand ready in the night above our covert. Doubtless they will come to our aid at need."

"Good," Covenant breathed. If creatures wielding fires that resembled the bale of the Illearth Stone meant to assail him, he doubted that Mhornym and Naybahn would be able to provide an effective defense. Still their alert proximity reassured him.

He tried to compose himself while remembrances clamored for his attention. The *jheherrin* had called themselves *the soft ones*. *Maker-work*, the occasional failures of the Despiser's efforts to breed armies; suffered to live only because Lord Foul enjoyed their abjection. Their flesh had resembled mud: they seemed to have been molded from clay. But they had shapes— Child-forms. Serpents. Grotesque mimicries of Cavewights. Others. And they had legends, tales of the Un-Maker-made: the stock from which Lord Foul had created monsters and *jheherrin*.

According to the tales, those ancestors were also Makers. Unlike the Despiser, however, they were not seedless. *From their bodies came forth young who grew and in turn made young*. And some of them survived or escaped or avoided Lord Foul's violation. They endured beyond his influence, *still free of the Maker*. Still capable of children.

Those memories were bitter to Covenant. He had been so tormented and sick— To him, and to Foamfollower, the *jheherrin* had described their legends. *It is said that when the time is ready, a young will be birthed without flaw—a pure offspring impervious to the Maker and his making—unafraid. It is said that this pure one will come bearing tokens of power to the Maker's home.* He wanted to forget, and could not. *It is said that he will redeem the* jheherrin *if they prove—if he finds them worthy—that he will win from the Maker their release from fear and mud—* But he had done nothing to redeem the *jheherrin*: nothing except bear the burden of his ring. He was a leper. He would always be a leper. Birthed without flaw? There was nothing pure about him.

No, it was Saltheart Foamfollower who had provided for the Maker's defeat. Cleansed in the savage *caamora* of Hotash Slay, he had laughed in Lord Foul's face and died, giving Covenant the strength to destroy the Illearth Stone. He rather than Covenant had become the Pure One.

That the *sur-jheherrin* thousands of years later still considered Covenant to be their Pure One only exacerbated his grief for Foamfollower—and his sense of his own unworth.

Yet here he sat like a monarch in exile, awaiting creatures who wanted an audience with the Pure One. For the Land's sake, and for Linden's—even for Joan's—he was willing to consider any alliance that the Feroce might mistakenly offer him.

Deliberately he shifted so that he sat cross-legged with the *krill* directly between him and the cave's entrance. For a few moments, he massaged the sore muscles of his lower back. Then he forced himself to sit straight as a sovereign. Let the Feroce be fearful. Let them approach humbly. Trapped in this chamber, he needed every possible advantage of posture or certainty.

He needed to conceal that he feared touching Loric's dagger.

"Ur-Lord," Branl warned quietly. "Three Feroce have gained the outer ledge. Soon they will enter here."

Covenant took a deep breath; held it. The *krill* cast a slash of brilliance through the break that gave admittance to the chamber. Silver light shone like a kind of purity on the far wall of the outer fissure. He fixed his gaze there, counting the thud-beats of his heart; watching for hints of emerald malevolence.

It came first as a slight taint at the edge of the argent, a tinge that might have seemed vernal from some other source. Then the sick green of acid and hunger grew stronger. That hue did not outshine the *krill*. Perhaps it could not. Nonetheless it stained the silver until the darkness beyond it seemed rife with menace.

One at a time, three creatures breached the light and stepped into the chamber.

They were as Branl had described them: no taller than his shoulders, hairless and naked, with large eyes like pools of reflected silver and emerald. Each of them flinched at its first sight of the *krill*: each shied as far as it could from the gem's blaze without touching Branl. When they looked past the light at Covenant, they conveyed the impression that they were cowering.

In the cups of their hands, they carried flames like promises of disease. Despite their alarm, they had an air of malice suppressed or denied. Perhaps they would have flung themselves at Covenant, if they had dared to do so. Instinctively he believed that they had been spawned by Mount Thunder's ancient poisons.

They avoided the *krill* with their eyes and remained silent. They may have been waiting for Covenant to speak.

Scowling as though he had the right to sit in judgment, he said nothing.

Finally one of them of them raised its voice. "We are the Feroce." But he could not tell which one spoke: the words seemed to come from all or none of them. And the voice had a peculiar sound, damp and undefined, like wet mud being forced past an obstruction. Their mouths and throats may not have been formed for language. Their speech may have been an effect of theurgy rather than of physical utterance.

Masking his own anxiety with feigned hauteur, Covenant replied, "I've heard you. You want an audience. You want an alliance for your High God. We'll get to that. Tell me something first. Convince me to trust you.

"You say you've attempted harm. That was your first purpose. What did you do?"

With their flames, the three Feroce made timid gestures like attempts at placation. "Our High God sustains us," they responded in their single voice. "In his agony, he speaks to us. He speaks through us. We obey his commands. Without him, we are dust. We cannot part from the waters of the Sarangrave.

"Havoc draws ever closer." More and more, they appeared to cower. "The havoc of all life. You are aware of this. You cannot be unaware. Our High God has felt it.

"He desires life. He desires *power*. He must have might, and greater might, and still greater might, lest he perish. All other enmity must be set aside.

"A female of your kind wields a stick of immense potency. Of this you are also aware. You cannot be unaware. Our High God yearned for it. At his command, we strove to lure it from her. We failed. He was wounded. He cannot obtain life by that means."

Covenant swore behind his scowl. Linden—! Fiercely he demanded, "Did you hurt her? *Did you hurt her?*"

The Feroce flinched like threatened children. Emerald flames guttered and spat in their hands. "We made the attempt. We failed. Now we are here."

"What, *you*?" he countered to conceal his relief. *We failed.* "I mean, you *personally*?" He did not know where Linden and her friends were, but he trusted that she was many leagues behind him. How had the Feroce covered so much ground so quickly?

He could not afford to wonder how the creatures had tried to snare Linden, or what her resistance had cost her.

"We do not comprehend." Silver and green flared in the wide eyes of the creatures. Behind them, Branl stood like a statue, unmoved and unmoving. "We are the Feroce. We obey our High God. What is 'personally'? We are not one. We are many.

"Do you speak of the Feroce standing before you? We have no answer. At our High God's command, we pursued you from the most seaward extent of the Sarangrave. The female of your kind we approached far to the west. There is no 'personally.' We are only the Feroce. We serve our High God in many places."

"All right." Covenant made no effort to muffle his vexation. He needed to keep his back straight; needed to appear wrathful and dangerous. "I'm going to assume you aren't the same creatures that attacked the woman." If they were, he wanted a better explanation; but he did not know how to obtain it. "Go on. Your High God is right. He can't save himself by making enemies."

The Feroce seemed to hesitate. Perhaps they had lost the thread of their instructions. But then their flames burned brighter, strict with coercion. Timorous as sycophants, they resumed in their single voice.

"You are the Pure One, redeemer of the *jheherrin*, ally of the *sur-jheherrin*. But you are also the wielder of abhorrent metal. The deliverer of agony. Such agony as our High God has never known. We dare not oppose you. We must not. We are dust.

"Havoc awaits our High God. He must have aid. In his name, we now seek alliance."

There the creatures fell silent as if they feared an immediate refusal.

Covenant paused for a moment, thinking furiously. As far as he could tell, the Feroce were sincere. And they had invoked the name of the Pure One: he could not ignore that. But he did not know enough about them.

He wanted to thump himself on the head, jar loose the memories he needed; but he resisted the temptation. "We'll get to that," he repeated. "I still have questions.

"Who or what is your High God? I've never heard of him."

The Feroce gaped as though they were utterly baffled; as though his question made no sense in any language known to them.

"He is the High God," they offered tentatively. "He is our High God. Others do not worship him. We—"

Abruptly they froze as if their minds had been seized by an alien thought. For an instant, their consternation was so plain that Covenant almost took pity on them. But the sickening hue of emerald writhed in their hands; and the moment passed.

"Others," they said more strongly. "You ask of others. We do not comprehend. But they speak of him by false names and affronts. One we are commanded to utter." They rolled their eyes in strange terror. "It is Horrim Carabal."

At once, they ducked their heads as though they expected to be struck down for blasphemy.

Ah, hell! Covenant thought. The lurker— The idea staggered him, even though the Feroce had already implied it clearly enough. The *lurker* had become a deity to these creatures? That was something he should have been able to remember—

"How—?" he began in confusion. "You worship *that*—?" Then he took hold of himself; crossed his arms on his chest to contain his chagrin. "Never mind. I don't need to know. What I need to know is, who are *you*? Where do you come from? And why do you live in the Sarangrave? Were you *made* there? Did you end up there from someplace else?"

Why did they know enough about the Land's history to speak of the *jheherrin*, the *sur-jheherrin*, and the Pure One?

"We are the Feroce," the creatures insisted anxiously. "You are aware of this. You cannot be unaware. You are the Pure One. You bore tokens of power foretold to the *jheherrin*. You brought about the downfall of the Maker and the Maker-place. You redeemed our far ancestors from enslavement and terror."

They nodded together, indicating compliance to some form of command. "You are the Pure One," they said again. "You have spoken with the *jheherrin*. You have been aided by them. We do not comprehend your question. Were you unaware that the numbers of our ancestors were too vast to be counted? Were you unaware that they had no wish to remain in their perilous tunnels when the Maker-place had fallen? They were the soft ones. For an age, they feared to depart. But as the region of their former horror declined increasingly to dust and death, and the Maker's lingering evil waned, they resolved to seek the water and mud of a kinder home."

As they spoke, their voice took on more complex rhythms. In their minds, apparently, their tale required a different cadence. "Many and many of them, *aussat Befylam*, *fael Befylam*, *roge Befylam*, others too fearful to endure your sight, all who sought to repay the gift of life with life—all endured the long labor northward, bitter and loathsome, questing always from water and mud to water and mud in search of a new habitation. Were you unaware of this?"

"The *sur-jheherrin* told me a few things," Covenant admitted reluctantly. "I guessed a few. But that doesn't answer my question."

How had the *jheherrin* in their many forms become creatures like the *skest* and the Feroce?

Why did the Feroce consider the lurker a god?

The idea that he needed allies like the lurker of the Sarangrave filled him with curses.

"You are the Pure One," the creatures repeated as if that name had the force of liturgy, "wielder of metal and agony. You cannot be unaware of the majesty that thrives in the Sarangrave. You cannot be unaware of its glory over marsh and fen and swamp, its grandeur among all that swims and slithers and crawls and burrows and scurries. We do not comprehend how you can be unaware that majesty transforms. Its powers are wondrous. It wrought wonders upon the soft ones. It wrought variously upon the several *Befylam* of the *jheherrin*, but all were transformed.

"From among the *Befylam* arose the *skest*, mindless and servile, too easily swayed to grant our High God his due homage. For an age of the Sarangrave, they followed his command, hearing no other. Then they were called to new service. The Feroce despise them.

"Others of the *jheherrin* begat the *sur-jheherrin*, too fearful to honor their true lord, and too cunning to attract his notice. The Feroce despise them also.

"Wiser, others from each *Befylam* sought oneness with our High God. The Pure One was gone. In his absence, they yearned to repay salvation with surrender. Their wish was granted. Our High God devoured them. They nourished his increase of majesty. The Feroce revere them.

"But among the *jheherrin*, some desired purpose in another form. Humble, they did not aspire to oneness. Grateful for redemption, they craved abasement rather than surrender. Their wish our High God granted as well. From several forms of the soft ones, he brought forth the Feroce to do his bidding. Generation unto generation, we multiply in homage. Thus we complete the redemption of the *jheherrin*."

Inwardly Covenant squirmed. He wanted to protest; wanted to deliver denials as unanswerable as the *krill*. Directly or indirectly, the Feroce held him responsible for their devotion to the lurker. The logic of their gratitude toward the Pure One had led them to adore and serve one of the Land's most enduring evils.

But Covenant was not the Pure One. He was *not*. From the first, the *jheherrin* and their descendants had mistaken him for Saltheart Foamfollower. Yet that was irrelevant here. The Feroce *believed*. Their misapprehension both damned and blessed him.

It was damnable that he had played any inadvertent part in inspiring their service. But it was also a blessing. Because of their confusion, they feared him too much to oppose him. And the lurker feared him enough to offer an alliance.

Horrim Carabal feared the Worm of the World's End more.

He suspected that this was Linden's doing. Somehow her defeat of the Feroce had forced the lurker to recognize that its malevolence was ultimately suicidal.

Pain and mortality could have that effect.

Struggling to contain his shame and ire and repudiation, Covenant clung to the idea that Linden had saved him. It was fitting. As fitting as his certainty that Joan stood among the ruins of Foul's Creche. *There are* always *evil means.* Even a horror like the lurker of the Sarangrave might accomplish something good in the end.

Rigid with internal conflict, Covenant said through his teeth, "I understand. I think you're telling the truth. Now I'm ready to talk about an alliance."

"Ur-Lord," Branl put in, warning him. "You speak of the lurker of the Sarangrave. Even the Ranyhyn fear such evil."

Covenant ignored the Humbled. "What are you offering?"

The Feroce also ignored Branl. Cringing before Covenant or Loric's *krill*, they answered, "Our High God offers safe passage throughout the great Sarangrave for all who resist the end of life. Already he suffers the presence of one who wanders lost within his realm, bearing a token of power which has no worth against havoc. He will suffer more. All who aid you will be permitted freedom and sanctuary in Sarangrave Flat."

One who wanders—? Covenant could not guess who that might be, and did not try. "Go on."

"Also," said the Feroce, malleable as mud, "we will combat the *skest* in your name. The Feroce despise them. Our High God feels the approach of havoc. He feels a lesser power as well. From cruel metal, it brings forth lesser hurts. It has wrought other agonies. And it is served by the *skest.* Our High God commands that lesser havocs must cease. They deflect might from the preservation of his life.

"The Pure One is wise in the ways of salvation. You will end the lesser hurts. If you do not fail, you will do more. Our High God offers the aid of the Feroce. We will clear your path of *skest.*"

Reflexively Covenant rubbed the scar on his forehead. Clear your path—That was a gift worth accepting. He did not want to lose either the Humbled or their Ranyhyn to the *skest.*

Probing, he asked, "Is there more?"

Abruptly the flames of the Feroce grew brighter. They seemed to double in size and vehemence, fraught with intentions which Covenant could not identify.

"There is the matter of your defeated beast," the creatures answered. "Witness a transformation wrought by our High God's majesty."

They did not move. None of them waved their arms, or brandished the lamps of their hands, or glanced away from Covenant. Nevertheless their magicks seemed to accumulate puissance within the argent of Loric's dagger.

Branl took a step forward. He clenched his fists. But he had no one to strike. Like Covenant, apparently, he could not sense a threat.

The destrier raised its head. For a moment, it looked around with an air of puzzlement, as though it wondered what had become of it. Then rage and recalcitrance began to smolder in its eyes.

Snorting angrily, the beast surged to its feet. At once, it wheeled away. Like an animal reborn, it headed toward the chamber's egress. Without regard for the Feroce, it lunged out of sight in the direction of the ledge and the towering cliff.

Gradually dangerous green receded as the flames of the Feroce shrank. "We have not given it strength," the creatures said as if admitting their limitations frightened them. "We cannot. But we have caused it to remember what it is. While it lives, it will not forget."

"That's enough," Covenant breathed. "It'll get me there." He could not ask for anything more: not from the descendants of the *jheherrin*, whose lives had been distorted by mistaken belief. If he were honest, he would have told the truth. The Pure One had died in the destruction of Foul's Creche. But Covenant *needed* this alliance. He was convinced that he needed it.

Still wrestling with himself, he asked unsteadily, "What do you want from me? What does your High God expect in exchange?"

The Feroce hesitated briefly, then countered, "What does the Pure One offer?"

Stop calling me that. "Let me think. I need to be clear."

In fact, Covenant had nothing to offer the lurker; nothing that he could bargain away; no aid that he might provide. Only the *krill* and his air of authority had brought the Feroce this far: those things, and perhaps the manner in which Linden had saved her Staff. What else did he have that the lurker might want? A promise that he would rush to the monster's defense? No. He had already condoned too much misapprehension. He was not willing to compound his faults with lies.

Sitting as if he were as obdurate as the Masters, he answered the Feroce.

"Understand me. I don't promise life. I can't swear to you I'll keep your High God alive. I may not have enough power. There may not *be* enough power." The Worm was coming, the Earth's final apotheosis. He could not imagine stopping it. "That 'lesser power' I'm going to face isn't my only problem. There's Kastenessen. Kevin's Dirt. Sandgorgons and Cavewights and *skurj*." He did not care whether the creatures or the lurker recognized those names. He listed his enemies and obstacles for his own sake. "She Who Must Not Be Named. Ravers. My own son. And the Despiser, who took the *skest*. They all have to be dealt with before I can face the 'havoc' you actually fear.

"I can only promise two things. I'll respect the alliance. Everybody who stands with me will respect it. None of us will turn against your High God. And we'll do our best to save the Land. All of it. If that can be done with the *krill* and wild magic and the Staff of Law," by Giants and *Haruchai* and Ranyhyn; by anything as simple and enduring as mortal stubbornness, "we'll do it.

"If your High God dies," he finished as though he had taken an oath, "I probably won't be far behind. Unless I get myself killed first."

Hearing him, the Feroce did more than cower and flinch. They retreated, trembling, until they stood at the cave's entrance. Their voice or voices became a gibbering noise like a host of whimpers. In a small circle, they faced each other and joined hands; clasped their fires together until argent was banished from the air between them, leaving only emerald fire that stank and throbbed like an old bane resurrected from the abysm of lost Time. Even to the failing nerves of Covenant's cheeks, the bitterness of the creatures' theurgy stung like a slap.

But it also smelled like terror. It felt like supplication.

While the Feroce huddled together, Branl moved around them to stand over the *krill* between them and Covenant, readying himself to snatch up the dagger. But they did not move to menace him or Covenant. Their flames remained contained within their circle.

In the absence of any explicit threat, Branl did not touch the knife.

At last, the Feroce spoke again. "Our High God knows desperation. He is acquainted with agony." None of them looked at Covenant or Branl or the *krill*. "Your offer is accepted. While our High God lives, he and all who serve him will honor the alliance."

Then they fled the chamber. In a moment, every hint of green and flame was gone, swallowed by darkness. For a while, the reek of malice lingered, an augur of calamity and woe. But soon the moiling winds from the sea and the precipice swept the scent away.

Finally Covenant let his shoulders slump. He felt vaguely nauseated, sick at heart, as if he committed a crime against the peculiar innocence of the lurker's servants. But he did not know what else he could have done.

Help against the *skest*. Protection for Linden from further attacks. Such things were necessary. But he had procured them by pretending to be something that he was not.

Long ago, in a different life, he had once written that guilt and power were synonymous. Effective people were guilty because the use of power was guilt. Therefore only guilty people could be effective. Effective for good or evil, boon or bane. Only the damned could be saved.

By that reasoning, life itself was a form of guilt.

At the time, he had believed what he was writing. Now he had to hope that he was right.

11.

Kurash Qwellinir

 Dawn was little more than a faint smudge of grey in the cleft of the chamber when Clyme entered, bearing treasure-berries for Thomas Covenant.

As Covenant ate, again saving the seeds to scatter later, the Master reported that all of the Feroce had fled the vicinity as soon as their emissaries had emerged from the cave. Now, he announced, Mhornym, Naybahn, and Covenant's mount were ready to be ridden. Then he stood with Branl while Covenant consumed fruit as salubrious as a feast.

Chewing, Covenant tried not to believe that this was his last meal; that this day would see the end of his renewed life. The end of Linden's greatest gift—

Ah, hell. He had been alive again for such a short time, and there was so much that he wanted to do; *had* to do. He owed Linden more than an apology: he owed her his whole world. And he loved this world so fiercely that he hardly knew how to contain the pressure. Twice he had been given the credit for saving the Land; but the truth was that the Land and its people had redeemed *him* on more occasions and in more ways than he could name. His only real virtue was that he had striven to prove worthy of *aliantha* and hurtloam. Of Glimmermere and Revelstone and Andelain. High Lord Mhoram and Bannor of the Bloodguard, Triock and Saltheart Foamfollower. Brinn and Cail and the Giants of the Search. Atiaran. Memla. Sunder and Hollian. Broken Lena and her doomed daughter, Elena, whom he and the Dead had sacrificed.

Linden Avery.

He knew that Linden blamed herself for many things. But she was wrong. He wanted to earn the chance to tell her so.

When he was done eating, he rose stiffly to his feet. After two days on horseback and a night on cold stone, his legs and back were aching knots. But he was grateful for that kind of pain. It was ordinary and physical, contradicting his numbness. His leprosy was not the whole truth. As long as he could feel, and care, and resist, he would be more than the sum of his hurts.

After a moment's hesitation, he stooped to retrieve the strips of Anele's tunic that he had used to wrap Loric's *krill*. Draping cloth over the haft, he gripped it with his halfhand.

In Andelain, he would have failed to draw the knife without help—and there it had been held by wood rather than stone. He might need the aid of Humbled here. But first he wanted to find out what he could do and what he could not.

This, too, was fitting; condign.

However, he did not try to drag the blade straight from the floor. Wiser now, he attempted instead to work the dagger back and forth until it came free.

The *krill* cut stone with eldritch ease. After only a moment, he was able to pull the weapon loose.

"Well, hell," he muttered. "I didn't expect *that*."

Briefly he studied the radiant gem as though he sought to see Joan through it; to discern her particular torment. But he could discern only the rare jewel's light and heat, its participation in wild magic. Shrugging, he flipped fabric around the *krill* until the whole dagger was covered, shielded, its illumination hidden. Then he tucked the bundle into the waist of his jeans.

In darkness softened only by the distant approach of the sun, he let Branl and Clyme lead him out of his covert.

Certain as stone, the Humbled guided him up the crevice, guarded him from vertigo along the ledge, and watched over him as he clambered up the split to the grassland above the cliff.

There the horses waited. Mhornym and Naybahn greeted their riders with nickering eagerness and trepidation. The destrier rolled its eyes and champed its bit as if only the authority of the Ranyhyn prevented it from charging at Covenant, pounding him into the turf.

Even with his blunt senses, Covenant could see that the Feroce had told the truth. His mount was still weak, worn down by overexertion: the lurker's creatures had not given it strength. Nevertheless it had recovered its cantankerous spirit.

—*caused it to remember what it is. While it lives—*

Covenant prayed that the beast would live long enough.

Angrily the horse allowed Covenant to mount. Groaning to himself, he settled his sore muscles into the saddle, took the reins in his maimed fingers. With one hand, he wedged the *krill* into a more comfortable position. Then he nodded to the Humbled.

"Let's go. I don't know how we're going to do this. But the sooner we get it done, the better."

The Worm was coming. On some intuitive level, he felt it drawing nearer. Or perhaps what he felt was plain dread. *The making of worlds is not accomplished in an instant. It cannot be instantly undone.* Sure, he thought sourly. Fine. But what did that *mean*? How many more days would the Worm spend feeding on the *Elohim*, devouring them to nourish its search for the EarthBlood?

He wished urgently that he could remember—

As Branl and Clyme turned their Ranyhyn and headed south along the soft slope below the cliffedge, Covenant resisted an impulse to prod his mount into a gallop. By one measure or another, he had lived for something like seven millennia; and now he had no *time*.

But Mhornym and Naybahn set a rolling pace that the destrier could match without exhausting itself quickly. In spite of his impatience, Covenant tried to tell himself that twenty leagues was trivial for the Ranyhyn—and possible for his mount. Yet his doubts weighed on him; and the gait of the horses felt as sluggish as lead.

Gradually dawn spread out of the east, muted and ruddy, like a forecast of storms. As the sky grew brighter, it took on an ashen hue, the ominous grey of smoke from distant wildfires. For a while as the sun crested the horizon, pale streaks of a more welcome blue showed through the pall. But they were soon occluded, and the whole firmament of the heavens became a sealed lid the color of hammered iron, uneven and depthless.

"This bodes ill, ur-Lord," Clyme remarked unnecessarily. "The natural currents of sky and wind and weather are disrupted. They foretell the onset of some great violation."

Instead of responding, Covenant dug in his pockets for treasure-berry seeds. As he and his companions rode, he scattered seeds two or three at a time, sowing the grassland with *aliantha* like a gesture of defiance. And with every toss, he murmured to the Despiser, Come on. Try me. Whatever happens, you aren't going to like it.

In this region between the Shattered Hills and the Sunbirth Sea, turf filled the south for several leagues, interrupted only by occasional fissures in the cliff, chewed scallops of erosion, barren stretches where sheets of stone denied incursion. Provender for the horses was plentiful. Water was not.

But as the sun crossed midmorning, the jagged jumble of the Hills crowded closer. Grasses grew more sparsely as the expanse of fertile soil dwindled. The shape of the terrain pushed the riders more and more toward the rim of the precipice.

By some fortuitous quirk of orogeny, however, freshwater springs became easier to find. The same harsh forces which had raised the twists and ridges of the Shattered Hills had also webbed the underlying gutrock with flaws. There ramified splits and gaps had formed the ancient habitations of the *jheherrin*. The same breaks had supplied the Despiser's armies with lines of march beneath the Hills. And they had tapped sources of water as old as the world. In hollows like denuded swales, or cracks so thin that they were barely visible, or crude basins as unexpected as fonts, springs bubbled forth. The Ranyhyn and the destrier and their riders could at least quench their thirst. Then the horses cantered on, heading more southeastward now than south, and probing for a path across the increasingly obstructed landscape.

Covenant suspected that they were beginning to curve toward the long promontory which had once held Foul's Creche; and he still had no idea what he would do if or when he located Joan.

By noon, the horses were forced to move more slowly. There was no more clear ground. The Hills piled ever nearer to the cliff; and the narrowing space between them was cluttered with rubble, or blocked by boulders, or fretted with fissures like veins of erosion pulsing ever deeper into the heart of the Lower Land's last buttress against the Sea. The Ranyhyn may have been sure-footed enough to run there: Covenant's mount was not.

And the charger was failing. It had exhausted the energy that it had regained during the night. Now only its belligerence kept it going. When it died, it would perish because it had ruptured its own heart.

That was the gift of the Feroce: a mixed blessing, beneficial for Covenant, but fatal for the poor horse. The innocent, he thought bitterly, were always the first to die. They were the first casualties of every struggle against Despite.

Nevertheless he rode as if he had no pity. Joan had nothing left except the sheer extremity of her pain. If he hoped to face her and live, he would have to do things equally extreme.

Then thrusts of granite pushed the riders within a stone's throw of the last cliff, and Covenant smelled saltwater; saw the Sunbirth Sea.

The ocean was as grey as the sky, a tainted seethe heaving urgently against the base of the precipice as if it were desperate to break down the Lower Land's fortifications. No wind lashed the waves: the air seemed preternaturally still, as if the sky were holding its breath. Nevertheless the roll of seas was confused, tossed this way and that by its surge over grim boulders and fraught reefs. Slamming against each other, the wavecrests broke into agitated froth and spray like salt expostulations.

And wherever Covenant looked, the sea was stippled with bursts and splashes as if it were being struck by hail. But there was no hail. Instead he felt an almost subliminal vibration, a mute massive thud like the slow beat of the seafloor's immersed heart; or like the heavy tread of doom.

Premonitions of vertigo tugged at Covenant's thoughts; at his stomach. But the knotted bulk of the cliff still stood between him and falling, and he kept his balance.

Time dragged like difficult breathing. For a while, the horses maintained a jolting trot. Then the rimose terrain compelled them to walk. Boulders complicated their path. And with every stride, they were wedged closer to the precipice.

Covenant doubted that his mount would last much longer. He doubted that he would. His trek to Foul's Creche long ago had taught him that the Hills were a hazardous barrier. And they probably stretched right to the cliffedge. Beyond them, of course, the way was easier. At the base of Ridjeck Thome's promontory, the Shattered Hills were cut off by cooled lava where Hotash Slay had once moiled and poured. There he would be able to walk. He had done it before. But here—

A glance at the sky told him that midafternoon had passed. Under the loom of the Hills, night would fall early.

He tried to assure himself that he and his companions had made good progress. Certainly the charger had endured more than he could have expected. When he asked the Humbled, however, they informed him that the igneous boundary of Hotash Slay was still two leagues away.

Meanwhile his mount was stumbling, unable to drag its hooves clear of the uneven ground. And the gap between the sudden upward lurch of the Hills and the sheer plummet of the cliff had become little more than a taunt. On foot, Covenant could have crossed it in four strides. For safety's sake, Branl had to ride ahead of him on one side, Clyme behind him on the other.

He remembered nothing about this part of the coast. Living, he had never been here before. The *jheherrin* had guided him with Foamfollower beneath the Shattered Hills from a different direction. He and his last friend in that time, the last of the Unhomed, had bypassed most of the bitter maze; had emerged from the passages of the soft ones only a short distance from Hotash Slay. But other things he could not forget—

Foamfollower in vast agony carrying him across the boil of lava. Foamfollower sinking horribly beneath the molten stone. Foamfollower reappearing from his *caamora* in time to clear Covenant's way into Foul's Creche.

Foamfollower laughing with unfettered joy at Lord Foul's malice.

Ah, God. The Giants. They were all of them miracles, every one whom Covenant had known: Pitchwife and the First of the Search, Grimmand Honninscrave and Cable Seadreamer, the Ironhand and her comrades: they were all instances of the transcending valor that made the Land and the Earth precious. Too precious to be surrendered. *Joy is in the ears that hear*—Any world which nurtured such beings deserved to live. Any world which gave birth to people like Berek Heartthew and High Lord Mhoram, Sunder and Hollian. Any world so rich in wonders that it could transform the dark Weird of the ur-viles.

This world *deserved to live.*

Engrossed in remembrance and useless remonstration, Covenant was surprised when the horses stopped.

They had come to an impasse. Directly ahead of them, a jut of stone like a plane of slate taller than one Giant standing on another's shoulders blocked the way. It reached from the louring bulk of the nearest hill to the precipice barely two paces away on Covenant's left. Shaded from the westering sun, he and the Humbled were shrouded in shadows and gloom. But beyond the barrier, cliffs and crags like clenched knuckles curved crookedly from the southeast out into the wan sunlight of late afternoon. They towered higher than his recollection of them. At their far end, he glimpsed the jagged edge where the collapse of Foul's Creche had rent the tip of the promontory, sending uncounted thousands of tons of granite and obsidian and malachite into the insatiable hunger of the Sunbirth. And far below him—

A shock like a jolt of lightning ran through him. Bloody damnation!

Far below him, a simple spin and topple over the precipice, seas no longer thundered against the base of the cliff. When he first looked down, clinging fervidly to his saddle, he saw no breakers at all. The whole of the ocean seemed to have vanished, leaving slick rocks, splintered menhirs, and knife-sharp boulders like the detritus of landslides exposed to the air. Among them, reefs like the spines of cripples reticulated the expanse. Grey water lay in pools that trembled at the slow thud of imponderable heartbeats as though even salt and the smallest creatures of the sea understood fear. Patches of cloacal mud seemed to shiver in anticipation, reeking of ancient death and rot. Draped over and around the chaos of stones and reefs, strands of kelp sprawled as if they were already dying.

But when Covenant raised his eyes, cast his gaze farther, he saw the Sunbirth in retreat. Perhaps half a league from the cliff, waves still toppled onto the ocean floor. But they were ebbing. Ebbing dramatically. With every fall and return, they withdrew as if they were being sucked away. As if they were being swallowed by the depths of the world.

Faint with distance, they sounded vulnerable, as forlorn as a plaint.

Instinctively Covenant understood. His mind reeled, and vertigo was an acute teacher.

Somewhere scores or hundreds of leagues out to sea, a shock like a split in the Earth's crust had begun to gather a tsunami.

The riders had stopped on level stone like a small clearing between the impassable hill and the fatal cliff. There the destrier stood with its legs splayed, gasping out its life. Ahead of and behind the beast, Mhornym and Naybahn fretted, tossing their heads and stamping their hooves.

Had they misjudged the path to their destination? Was that even possible?

Gritting his teeth in a wasted attempt to keep his voice steady, Covenant demanded, "Are we lost? We can't be. The Ranyhyn don't get lost."

"Ur-Lord, we are not," Branl replied inflexibly. "Our passage lies there." He pointed at the rockface behind Covenant.

Covenant twisted in his seat, looked where Branl pointed.

The Master was right. A dozen or so paces behind Clyme and Mhornym, a crack opened the wall of stone: a way into the maze of the Shattered Hills. The Ranyhyn knew it was there. And they could thread the maze: Covenant was sure of that. They could navigate time within *caesures*. Yet they had walked past it.

They must have done so deliberately.

Fearing the answer, he asked, "I don't understand. Why aren't we moving?"

His horse was done. But he could still walk.

"Ur-Lord," Clyme answered without expression, "Mhornym and Naybahn choose to halt here. We are not Ramen. We do not discern the thoughts of Ranyhyn. But we speculate.

"It may be that we near our goal. It may be that we do not. We perceive neither your former mate, who is unknown to us, nor vile *turiya* Herem, with whom we are well familiar. They lie beyond the reach of our senses. However, we have no measure for the Raver's awareness. Perhaps Corruption's servant descries our approach. Perhaps your former mate does likewise.

"In addition"—Clyme appeared to hesitate momentarily—"we believe that we have felt the exertion of wild magic. Of this we are uncertain. The sensation is too distant for clarity. Nonetheless it suggests that we draw nigh to your former mate. For this reason, we conclude that *turiya* Herem and his victim are indeed aware of us"—the Humbled inclined his head toward Covenant—"or of High Lord Loric's *krill*.

"Therefore, ur-Lord, we surmise that the Ranyhyn fear an ambush. Among the Shattered Hills, we will be exposed at every moment to an onset of *skest*."

"But we're trapped here," protested Covenant. If *skest* came pouring from that cleft into the Hills, he and the Humbled and the horses would be caught against the slate barricade. They would have nowhere to run—and no room to defend themselves.

"Ur-Lord," Clyme stated, "I repeat that we speculate. We are not Ramen. Yet we conceive that perhaps the Ranyhyn await the Feroce, the fulfillment of your alliance."

His lack of inflection seemed to imply that he considered the word of the lurker's creatures worthless.

"Hellfire!" Covenant made no effort to mask his frustration. "What're we supposed to do in the meantime? Just stand here? My horse is going to collapse. I'm surprised it isn't already dead.

"I'm useless against *skest*."

Even with Loric's dagger, he could only face one creature at a time. And if any drop or splash of acid touched him—

"You deemed the Feroce honest, ur-Lord," remarked Branl. "You were not compelled to their alliance. You elected to grant your trust, disregarding the lurker's enduring malevolence."

I know that, Covenant thought. I knew it was a risk.

But before he could muster a response, Branl stiffened: a subtle intensification.

"*Skest* advance upon us," the Master announced. "They are nigh." A moment later, he added, "They appear to have no direct path. They follow the dictates of the maze. Its intricacy delays them. Nonetheless they come."

Damnation! Twisting in his seat, Covenant looked past Clyme for some sign of the

Feroce. But of course the senses of the Humbled would recognize the lurker's creatures before Covenant spotted them. Briefly he studied the hill-wall beside him; but he saw no hope there. Its outward face was too steep, too smooth. Given time, Branl and Clyme might contrive to scale it. Covenant could not.

Wincing, he glanced over the cliff; tried to imagine a descent. If he abandoned the Ranyhyn, they might have time to escape.

Then vertigo hit him, a blow to the stomach. He jerked his eyes away.

"Say something," he panted at his companions. "Tell me what to do. Tell me what we're going to do."

They were *Haruchai*. As far as he was concerned, no *Haruchai* had ever failed him. Not even when Bannor had refused to accompany him to Foul's Creche.

Rigid as rock, Clyme began, "We will trust—"

He may have meant the Ranyhyn, or the Feroce, or Covenant himself; but Covenant no longer heard anything. Through the cloth covering the *krill*, he felt a sudden throb of heat.

Joan! Instinctively he flinched. His whole body tried to squirm away from the dagger.

An instant passed before he realized that the rush of heat was not as fierce as he had expected. He could bear it.

Ah, hell. Was she simply unsure of her target? Was she too badly broken to focus her force when she could not sense his touch on the *krill*? Or was she getting weaker—?

His own questions distracted him. A moment passed before he felt crawling on the sensitive parts of his skin; hiving insects; fornication. Things that could bite and sting were on his scalp, under his clothes, in his boots.

With no more warning than that, a *caesure* erupted above and beyond the slate barrier.

The Fall was comparatively minor, a mere flick of wild magic and chaos no more than five paces wide. And it had missed Covenant and his companions. At once, it began to lurch away, chewing westward through stone and time into the confusions of the Shattered Hills. Nevertheless it was as destructive as a hurricane in the substance of the world. Centuries or millennia were superimposed and shredded until the rock exploded, torn apart by the instantaneous migraine of its own slow life. Shards and splinters were flung in all directions like shrapnel, cutting as knives, fatal as bullets.

They may have struck Covenant, pierced him, ripped through him. They may have killed the Humbled and the Ranyhyn and the destrier. But he did not feel them. As soon as he glanced into the savage kaleidoscope of the *caesure*, he lost his inward footing and slipped—

Oh, God! Not now! *Not now!*

—into the broken residue of his memories.

After that, he stood where Ridjeck Thome had once held the apex of the promontory and watched time run backward, incrementally unmaking seven thousand years of ruin.

Ages were erased in instants. Instants were ages. At first, he saw only the ponderous accumulation as a mountain of rubble undid its own erosion beneath the unremitting pressures of the sea. Sand gathered into stones. Stones lost their smoothness, whetted their edges. Reefs melted away around them. But memories were also quick, as swift as thought: they could become more rapid than his ability to comprehend them. The wreckage grew in bulk. At the same time, its area contracted as boulders as big as houses, mansions, temples piled themselves on top of each other. A vast weight of seawater collapsed like an eruption in reverse while riven stones thrust their heads and shoulders above the surface of the waves.

First one at a time, then in a mighty rush, the stones sprang upward to resume their ancient places in the promontory.

In a reality which he no longer inhabited, Covenant observed his mount's panic. Terror summoned its final vestiges of strength. He felt it lunge for the edge of the cliff, bearing him with it. But he could not react. He was hardly able to care. His spirit lived elsewhere.

Instead of fearing for his life, or hauling on the destrier's reins, or shouting for help, he watched the torn tip of the promontory and then Foul's Creche rebuild themselves around him.

Within moments, the Despiser's delved dwelling was complete, immense and immaculate and empty, flawless and useless in every detail except for the jagged jaws which formed Lord Foul's throne.

Covenant stood in the thronehall of Ridjeck Thome. The Despiser was there. Before him squatted the dire mass of the Illearth Stone. Beside the Stone, Covenant's slain self cowered on its knees, craven and powerless. Nearby Foamfollower endured his own helplessness, his final agony.

Lord Foul was nothing more than a bitter shape in the air, a shadow reeking of attar. But his eyes were as eager as fangs, carious and yellow. They seemed to grip the kneeling Covenant's soul, avid for despair.

Begone, spectre, the Despiser said in Covenant's mind. You have no place here. You do not exist. Your time will never come.

That voice violated time and memory. It came from a different version of existence, a brief disruption enabled by the *caesure*. Lord Foul *then* had not known that Covenant's spirit was watching *now* from its remembered place within the Arch of Time. The Despiser had believed himself triumphant.

Nevertheless the intruded command banished Covenant. The thronehall and Ridjeck Thome vanished. Instead he found himself far down in the Lost Deep, far down in the Earth's past, looking sadly at the first spasms of the bane's horror and bereavement as She realized that She had been tricked; snared.

Eventually that horror and bereavement would produce the tectonic upheaval which sheared the Upper Land away from the Lower. It would cause the faults in Gravin Threndor which allowed the Soulsease to pour into the bowels of the mountain. But not yet. At this moment, Covenant could only watch and grieve as She Who Must Not Be Named howled rage at Her betrayer.

It was a hurtful memory in every particular, crowded with pain and foreknowledge. But it was also a relief. Lord Foul did not disturb the integrity of this remembered fragment. Perhaps he could not.

As the destrier plunged over the cliff, Covenant saw every cruel span of the fall below him; felt crushing death in all of its vertiginous seduction. He wanted to close his eyes; but his body had no will of its own, and his mind was absent.

Nevertheless a part of him recognized the impact as Branl landed on the charger's haunches. Branl's hands gripped Covenant's shoulders like fetters, manacles. In the same motion, the Master heaved himself backward, hauling Covenant with him.

For a while, Covenant flickered like a chiaroscuro through fractured scenes, forgotten events. He saw Brinn give battle to the Guardian of the One Tree. He watched Kasreyn of the Gyre forge an eldritch sword to use against the Sandgorgons until he acquired the lore and found the materials to perfect Sandgorgons Doom. Impotent and proud, Covenant studied Linden's fight for her life, and for Jeremiah's, under *Melenkurion* Skyweir.

His mount's plunge had become a plummet. They had fallen too far. Even Branl's supreme strength did not suffice to regain the rim of the precipice.

But Clyme was ready. Outstretched on the stone, he reached down, snatched a handhold in the back of Branl's tunic.

The vellum should have torn. It did not.

An instant later, Branl released one hand from Covenant to catch at Clyme's forearm. Together the Humbled wrenched Covenant back to the cliffedge; pulled him to safety. There he sprawled limp on level stone as if nothing had happened.

Too much was happening. Blundering along flaws and crevices, he tried to find a fragment of memory that would save him. *Skest* emerged from the cleft, gleaming vilely in the shrouded gloom. He saw the Theomach divert Roger's efforts to take Linden and the *croyel* to the time of Damelon Giantfriend's arrival on Rivenrock. He heard the *Elohim* pride themselves on their uninvolvement. At least a score of *skest* thronged out of the maze. More were coming. He saw Joan appear, charred by lightning, on the promontory of Foul's Creche. He watched *turiya* Raver pounce on her, into her; watched the Raver compel her to summon Roger, Jeremiah, and Linden. Because they were dead in their former lives, they would never escape this reality.

Without hesitation, Clyme left Branl and Covenant. He flung himself at the corner where the blockade of slate joined the sheer hill. Somehow he wedged or clawed his way upward. When he reached the top of the slate, he straddled it.

Branl lifted Covenant; threw him upward. Clyme snagged one of Covenant's slack arms, nearly jerked it from its socket. While Clyme settled Covenant beside him, Branl climbed to join them.

Undefended, Mhornym and Naybahn faced the corrosive *skest*.

Blood pulsed from a cut on Covenant's forehead. He recalled striking his head on the edge of a table. Blood formed trails around his eyes, ran down his cheeks, dripped from his jaw. A gash along his ribs throbbed. The side of Branl's neck had been torn: a shallow cut. Clyme wore several minor hurts. The barricade must have shielded them from the *caesure*'s worst violence.

Alone within himself, Covenant strove to locate a recollection that might affect his plight.

Instead he stumbled into Joan's recent past, perhaps moments before his resurrection. She looked worse than he had ever seen her in life: a madwoman unkempt and tattered, gap-toothed with malnutrition, no longer capable of focusing her eyes; so utterly frail that she required a throng of acid-creatures and much of *turiya*'s savagery to keep her alive. For some reason, she was clambering, friable as glass, down the granitic wreckage where Foul's Creche had once stood. By weak increments painful to behold, she descended toward the Sunbirth Sea. Was she afraid? Trying to escape her own future? Did she think that *turiya* Herem would allow her to drown among the waves? Or was she seeking older stone, more fundamental rocks and boulders which she could then destroy to unleash greater *caesures*?

The *skest* massed at the opening of the maze. But they did not move to assail the Ranyhyn. Perhaps they were content to prevent escape. Perhaps their master, the Raver, had assured them that Joan would strike again soon.

Remembering her, Covenant tried to call out. Stop this! Please stop! You've already suffered too much! But of course she could not hear him. He was a wraith, a figment of memory, no longer a participant in the Arch: too insubstantial to intrude on her derangement and *turiya*'s possession.

Grimacing in dismay, he turned aside, staggered into another fissure, and found himself in Andelain.

Not in Andelain itself: not among the tangible Hills. Instead he stood beside the *krill*, beside the withered stump of Caer-Caveral's passing, within an image of Andelain, a semblance composed of recollection and symbolism. And he was not alone.

Berek Halfhand was with him, Heartthew and Lord-Fatherer. Loric Vilesilencer, creator of the *krill*. Saltheart Foamfollower, who had laughed, and Cable Seadreamer, who could not. Mhoram Variol-son, representing the later generation of Lords. Cail of the *Haruchai*. Jerrick of Vidik Amar, wrapped in shadows, who had shared his magicks with a-Jeroth, and had watched in shattering consternation as a-Jeroth had brought forth *quellvisks*. The Theomach, alone of the Insequent, clad in cerements after his defeat by Brinn.

Covenant remembered this. He and these spirits had gathered together in an effort to imagine or devise some form of salvation.

They all deferred to him. His was the only soul unconstrained by the strictures of Time.

But he could only recall pieces of their counsel.

He did not know why the *skest* waited. He did not care.

Branl shook him. "Ur-Lord. You must return. There will be another Fall. We cannot ward you. And we must not abandon the Ranyhyn to this death."

The injuries of the Humbled were trivial. They would heal. The wound of Covenant's mind would not.

It is hazardous, Berek said. Hazardous beyond measure. There is the breaking of Laws to consider. There is the Worm.

I know, Covenant said. And Kevin's Dirt. And Kastenessen. And Cail's son.

A litany more heinous than any number of *skest*.

The lealty of my people, Cail added. They are obdurate and mistaken. Also there are *skurj*. There are Sandgorgons. Kastenessen rules the one. *Samadhi* Sheol entices the other.

Dull-eyed and unblinking, Covenant saw small fires shine greenly in the twilight cast by the Shattered Hills. The Feroce had come at last. With emerald lambent in their hands, they approached from the northwest, beyond the *skest*.

The *skest* seemed to be waiting for them. For an alliance of one kind or another to be revealed. But did they believe that promises would be kept between Covenant and the lurker of the Sarangrave? Or did they expect the sundered descendants of the *jheherrin* to reunite, *skest* with Feroce? Did they believe that the lurker would betray Covenant?

I include the Giant named Lostson and Longwrath, Foamfollower said. He is ruled by a *geas* born of a dire bargain and cannot free himself.

Terrible banes are immured among the bones of Gravin Threndor, Loric said. Even the Illearth Stone must be considered.

Branl or Clyme should have taken the *krill*. They could use it. But perhaps they suspected that the grasp of any hand on Loric's dagger might catch Joan's attention; draw another *caesure*.

A white gold wielder is possessed by a Raver, the Theomach said. That alone suffices to unloose a world of woe.

I know, Covenant said again.

This whole discussion had taken place years ago. It was only a memory. But it had more power over him than any facet of his physical present. He needed to remember it. Parts of it might rescue him.

Parts were already irretrievable.

My friend of old, Mhoram said. It falls to me to speak of your own son. He lacks Esmer's unfathomable powers, but also Esmer's self-torment. His is an unrelieved darkness, born of abandonment and nurtured by Despite. He will do much which Esmer would not.

Also, as the Theomach has said, there is the woman who turned from you, your son's mother. She trusts to him, though she has given him naught. She is a rightful wielder of white gold, yes—and possessed by *turiya* Herem, yes. She will oppose you. Yet she is broken beyond sufferance. Her need for mercy is absolute.

Also there is Linden Avery. There is her child freely chosen. None here can declare which of them bears the greater burden of pain. None here possess the wisdom to estimate the outcome of his loss, or the worth of his recovery. We can be certain only that the Despiser craves him urgently.

Like the surge of the departing sea, the Feroce came upon the *skest*. Hand-held fires like reminders of the Illearth Stone met living green vitriol, another echo of the Stone's evil.

Without sounds or battle cries, without any sign of clashing, they began to obliterate each other. Feroce flared and were consumed. *Skest* slumped into puddles that gnawed like infections at the stone. Gouts and flames slashed the premature dusk.

Foamfollower looked at Seadreamer. When Seadreamer nodded, Foamfollower said, You ask that we repose faith in Linden Avery the Chosen. We are content to do so. We are Giants. We cannot do otherwise.

I have received the gift of her acquaintance, said the Theomach. I also am content.

She will sacrifice the Earth entire for her son, Loric said. And for you, Timewarden. I am not content. We must seek another path.

I know, Covenant said a third time. She'll do anything for Jeremiah. She'll do anything for me. That's the risk we have to take. You were never in her situation. Are you sure you wouldn't have done as much for Kevin, if you ever had the chance?

Thereafter Loric was silent.

An eerie battle burned and spat among the descendants of the *jheherrin*. It was as soundless as a charade. Nevertheless the lurker's creatures and *turiya* Raver's died in each encounter.

The lurker was keeping its promise. Sacrificing its worshippers. For Covenant.

He did not know how many Feroce had come. He did not know how many *skest* waited in the passages of the maze. But he knew the acid of *turiya* Herem's servants. Before long, the entire expanse of stone between his perch and the advancing Feroce would begin to crumble. If the cliff's rim did not fall away at once, it would collapse under any weight.

The Ranyhyn may have already lost their only escape. Clyme and Branl might never be able to reach the cleft into the Shattered Hills.

This, then, is my counsel, Cail said. I speak as one who also has a son, and who is grieved by his wrongs. We must abide by the judgment of the Ranyhyn. They are an embodiment of the Land. We are not. And they are attuned to the Law of Time. While we are in accord, their discernment will guide us well.

The *caesure* had left a hollow behind the sheet of slate. Reaching back, Branl found chunks of stone fresh from the Fall's vehemence. Swift and certain, he threw them at the *skest*.

And that's not all, Covenant said. I've seen things some of you haven't. Sure, the *Haruchai* serve Lord Foul. But they might surprise you. They might surprise *him*. If anything can sway them, the Ranyhyn can. Or the Ramen.

Branl's aim was unerring. With every cast, he ruptured one or more of the *skest*. The skin of its life tore, spilling sickness to the ground. Rank vitriol steamed on the stone; corroded it; left it pitted and fragile.

The Ranyhyn heeded his example. Shards and scree littered the space between them and the struggle, Feroce against *skest*. Turning, Naybahn and Mhornym used their hind legs to kick stones at the *skest*. Fatal as missiles, chunks of rock hurtled among the creatures; slew several of them.

Then Branl appeared to realize that he was hastening the ruin of the cliffedge. The Ranyhyn would be trapped. They would be stuck where they stood until they died.

Glaring, Branl ceased his attacks.

Mhornym and Naybahn did not.

Clyme shook Covenant again, harder this time. "Ur-Lord!" His severity was a slap which Covenant could not feel. "Doom gathers below us. We must act. We must act now!"

My counsel is of another kind, the Theomach said. Time is the keystone of life, just as wild magic is the keystone of Time. It is Time which is endangered. The path to its preservation lies through Time.

And Berek said, The Theomach has been my guide and teacher. His counsel is mine as well.

There, Covenant thought. That was the answer.

He lost it immediately. Eager to understand, he tripped into another fissure. Instead of standing in Andelain, he wandered uselessly through the rich twilight beneath the canopy of the One Forest. He remembered the lazy hum of insects, the mellifluous evensong of birds; the fecund scents of loam and moss and ferns, natural decay, ripe growth.

But he did not lose everything.

Joan had her wedding band. She was using wild magic against the Land. It could be used against her.

Without warning, Clyme struck Covenant, an open-handed blow that snapped his head to the side, sent shocks down his spine.

Around him, the One Forest seemed to ripple as though every tree and leaf and breeze had become water. Monarchs which had held their ground for hundreds of years shimmered like mirages.

The Feroce may have been winning. They appeared to outnumber the *skest*.

Turiya could send more. No doubt he had already done so.

With an effort like a rush of vertigo, Covenant moaned, "Again."

Clyme did not hesitate. A second jolt caught Covenant's head from the opposite side. Repercussions rattled his vertebrae.

It was too late. Covenant could not fight the *skest*. He could not touch the *krill*. Not yet.

He had to try something else.

"Hit me again."

This time, Clyme punched the cut in the center of Covenant's forehead.

Hellfire! That one *hurt!*

While new blood streamed into Covenant's eyes, he found his way back to himself.

Scrubbing at his face with both hands, he panted, "That's enough. I can't take any more. Next time, try the *krill*."

It might sever him from the past.

But he did not pause to thank the Humbled. As soon as he could see, he yelled at the Feroce, "A path! We need a *path!*"

If the clifftop could still hold anything heavier than the turmoil of small creatures—

The lurker's servants must have heard him. Mute as martyrs in the apotheosis of their devotion, they adjusted their approach. Instead of pressing themselves and dying against all of the *skest* at once, they shifted to form a wedge.

Arranged like ur-viles or Waynhim, they began to kill and perish their way into the mass of acid-creatures.

"Now!" Covenant told Clyme and Branl. "I have an idea!"

He was closed to the senses of the *Haruchai*. They could not hear his thoughts; could hardly recognize his emotions. Nevertheless Branl responded as though he understood. Quick as intuition, he dropped from the slate; landed between Naybahn and Mhornym, where the stone was still solid. A heartbeat later, Clyme lifted Covenant, tossed him into Branl's arms. While Branl set Covenant on his feet, Clyme jumped down to join them.

Already most of the Feroce were gone, consumed in fire and vitriol. Many of the *skest* had fallen, reeking as their spent lives dissolved stone, ate chunks out of the cliff-top. Wherever they died, they left deep pits and gouges.

"All right," Covenant muttered as if he were Linden. "Let's see if this works."

He took the *krill* from his waist. Careful not to touch any part of the dagger, he flipped its covering aside until he had exposed the gem.

A blare of radiance stung his sight. It swept back the gloom. The jewel was a cynosure of argence. In that narrow place, it effaced imminent night.

Blinking as if his eyes were still full of blood, he saw *skest* wheel away from the few remaining Feroce. *Turiya*'s creatures knew the *krill*; or they remembered it. They or their distant ancestors had encountered it in the Sarangrave. Now they mewled like frightened young. They flinched and cowered. Then they began to retreat.

As if they shared one mind, a dozen *skest* all crowded toward the cleft and the maze at the same time.

Yes.

The Feroce let them go. Only five of the lurker's worshippers still lived. They clung desperately to the green fires in their hands and trembled, shaken by atavistic dread.

When the *skest* were gone, the Feroce came a step or two nearer. Standing on gutted granite, they stopped. Their small forms seemed to ache with fatigue and defeat.

"We are weak," they said, timorous as if they deserved punishment. "We have come too far from our waters. Distance frays the majesty of our High God. The *skest* are too many. We cannot quell them."

Impassively Branl stated, "The *skest* will await us among the passages of the Shattered Hills." With both hands, he stroked Naybahn's neck. He may have been apologizing.

Or grieving.

Covenant's jaws knotted. "And they'll still be afraid." Flanked by the Humbled and the Ranyhyn, he studied his straits. "They aren't the real problem." He knew how to reach Joan. "First we have to get *there*." With his free hand, he indicated the eaten stone between him and the cleft; the only available entrance to the maze. The rock still steamed and stank as lingering acid bit deeper into its substance. "And we have to think of a way to save the Ranyhyn."

The clifftop looked too badly gnawed to support him. It would never hold Naybahn or Mhornym.

Nevertheless Branl left Covenant's side at once. Pressing himself to the hill-wall opposite the precipice, he side-stepped carefully toward the cleft.

Now Covenant saw that a narrow span of stone at the base of the hill had been left undamaged. It was too slim for the Ranyhyn, but it accommodated Branl.

When the Master reached the cleft, he glanced inward, nodded his satisfaction at the retreat of the *skest*. Then he told Covenant, "Our path is secure." Frowning, he added, "It will not serve the Ranyhyn."

Pale in the *krill*'s vividness, the flames of the Feroce guttered, timid and apprehensive. After a moment, they sighed, "Stone lives. Its life is slow. Its pain is slow. But it lives. It remembers.

"We have failed our High God. We must attempt amends. We will ask the stone to remember its strength. It has been ravaged. It has felt havoc. But if its life is slow, its awareness of harm is also slow. Its memory of strength persists."

Covenant stared at the creatures. What, *remember* its strength? *After* it was broken? The damage to the stone was severe. And he could discern no power capable of mending rock from the Feroce; no power of any kind apart from the frantic dance of their flames.

But the creatures did not wait for a response. Trembling, they moved closer to each other, formed a tight circle. As they had done once before, they joined their hands, clasped their fires together. They may have been praying—

Gradually their strange energies found new force. The nauseating hue of the Illearth Stone grew brighter. It etched itself against the hot silver of the *krill*.

By some means, they had caused Covenant's lost mount to recall its own nature earlier. They had restored the destrier's contentious spirit.

Maybe—

Covenant saw nothing change. His senses were too dull to identify the effect wrought by the Feroce—if they achieved any effect at all. Clyme and Branl watched in silence.

But the Ranyhyn reacted as if they understood the Feroce. They jerked up their heads, shook their manes, snorted fiercely. Emerald and argent contradicted each other in the wide glare of their eyes. Trumpeting defiance, they flung themselves forward; burst into a gallop.

They managed one long stride on undamaged stone—and another, foreshortened. Then they sprang as far as they could stretch out across the wrecked rock.

Both of them, when one would have been too heavy.

Covenant forgot to breathe; forgot to blink at the blood still oozing from his forehead.

At the limit of their leap, their forelegs struck the surface. It crumbled instantly. Of course it did. Much of it had been corroded to the consistency of rotten wood. The rest had lost its foundations. Nevertheless Naybahn and Mhornym snatched their hind legs under them and tried to spring again.

They almost succeeded.

Almost.

But the stone had been too badly chewed. A section of the clifftop collapsed beneath the horses. Chunks of rock fell like jagged gobbets of the Earth's flesh.

Frantically Naybahn and Mhornym scrambled at the failing slope. Somehow their hooves found purchase. Straining, they lunged forward onto stone as ruined and ruinous as the rock that they had crumbled.

Beyond them, the flames of the Feroce rose like screams into the air.

More of the surface broke. More of it fell away. Yet the Ranyhyn were faster—or the invocation of the Feroce had taken hold. Together Naybahn and Mhornym outran the collapse.

Granite wreckage plummeted. A hungry plunge snapped at their heels as they neared the lurker's creatures. But there, impossibly, the surface became stronger. The Feroce stood where the greatest number of *skest* had died, yet the clifftop clung to its former endurance. When the Ranyhyn surged past the creatures, they were able to truly gallop.

"Damnation!" Covenant gasped. "Hell and blood! I would not have believed—"

A moment later, the horses reached solid ground. At once, they skidded to a halt, neighing triumph.

The Feroce unclosed their hands; let their peculiar magicks subside. Their small forms slumped as if they were exhausted.

While he caught his breath, Covenant repeated to himself, Damnation! I would *not* have believed it. But he did not pause for astonishment. Relief only whetted his vulnerability. A large portion of the clifftop was gone. Against the foot of the Shattered Hills lay a gap as inviting and murderous as open jaws. And the drop *called* to him.

Vertigo squirmed through him. Ruling himself with curses, he shouted to the Feroce, "Tell your High God! If it can be done, I'll save him. I'll save the Land. And *thank* him for me. He keeps his promises!"

The Feroce looked too weary to respond; and he did not wait for them. Aiming his voice past the creatures, he ordered the Ranyhyn, "Don't try to follow us! Find some other path. I'm counting on you! We're going to need you."

Under his breath, he added, "If I don't get us killed first."

Hurrying, he turned to Clyme. "We have to reach Branl, and I can't do it. No way in hell." His voice shook as if he were feverish. "I can't keep my damn balance." At one time, he had found calm in the eye of a whirling confluence of possibility and impossibility: he could not do so here. "But it's worse than that. There's something in me that *wants* to fall." His inner Despiser? His yearning to surrender his burdens? "If the two of you can't hold me, we might as well just jump."

In the light of Loric's dagger, Clyme's expression looked subtly scornful. "Secure the *krill*, ur-Lord," he said as if Covenant's alarm did not merit reassurance. "We will require both of your arms."

"Right." Covenant tightened his grip on himself. "Of *course* you can hold me. What was I thinking?"

In a rush, he swung the dagger so that Anele's cloth wrapped itself around the metal, masked the bright gem.

At once, darkness enclosed him. Its suddenness sealed him away from everything except the avid gulf. He could not even see Clyme. The Master was only a sensation of rigidity at his side. Nevertheless Covenant tucked the *krill* into his jeans.

Then his eyes began to adjust. The precipice grew wider, darker; more compulsory. The faint flames of the Feroce did not shed enough light to protect him. Clyme became a more substantial avatar of night.

While Covenant's head reeled, Clyme grasped his left arm and pushed him firmly toward the hard wall of the hill.

Instinctively he wanted to resist. Vertigo sang to him, as siren and alluring as the music of *merewives*. Seductions spun in his head, his stomach, his muscles. Did he trust the *Haruchai*? He had always said that he did. Put up or shut up.

When his shoulder touched stone, he jammed his face and chest against it; clung to it. Not *this* time, he swore at his spinning mind; or at the Despiser. You can't have me now. Wait your damn turn.

Out of the dark, Branl said, "Extend your arm, ur-Lord. We will support you. You will not fall."

The appalled voice of Covenant's alarm sneered, Oh, sure. Extend my arm. Like *that's* going to happen. But he was already reaching for Branl. He had come too far and learned too much: his fears did not rule him.

A hand as trustworthy as granite gripped his wrist, rock that defied corrosion. Between them, Branl and Clyme urged him along the base of the hill.

The cleft was millennia away. Creeping on the verge of panic, Covenant would need an age of the Earth to cross the distance. But the Humbled were oblivious to the impossibility of their task. Ignoring the frenetic stutter of Covenant's heart, they impelled him toward the crack in the hill; the entrance to the maze.

When he stood at last between solid walls with gutrock under his boots, he staggered in relief; nearly stumbled to his knees. Still his companions upheld him.

Here there was no light at all. The drained flames of the Feroce did not reach into the cleft.

Gasping for balance, Covenant panted, "Remind the Ranyhyn. Insist, if you have to. They can't follow us. We need them." Then he managed to add, "Thank you."

"We are the Humbled," Branl answered impassively, "Masters and *Haruchai*. We do not require gratitude."

"On the Plains of Ra, the Ranyhyn reared to you. They will heed your wishes."

"In that case—" Gradually the gyre in Covenant's head eased. By increments, his nerves released their terror and yearning. The *Haruchai* feared grief. It was their one maiming weakness. Naturally they did not want gratitude. "We should keep moving. I need a clearing of some kind. A little open ground. Maybe we can find it before the *skest* come at us again."

Storms of impatience and dread brewed in the background of his thoughts. But he did not protest when Clyme and Branl remained still. He was not steady enough to walk yet.

They waited until he was able to stand without their support; until he took a couple of steps into the cleft and turned to face them. Then Clyme asked, "Ur-Lord, what is your intent? The *skest* await us. A Fall may strike at any moment. Your former mate remains beyond our discernment. We will be better able to serve you if we comprehend your purpose."

Covenant cursed to himself. Summoning as much honesty as he could bear, he admitted, "I'm afraid to say it out loud. You told me you don't know how far *turiya*'s senses reach. If he hears me—if he even *guesses*—" Involuntarily Covenant shuddered. He could be so easily foiled. "I'm going to do something almost as crazy as Joan. And I need you with me. You just saved my life, but you aren't done." In darkness, he spread his hands to show the Humbled that he was helpless. "If you don't want to do it, that's your right. I won't blame you. But I need you with me."

He had always needed companions. Friends. People who cared about him and loved the Land.

For a long moment, the Humbled did not move. They may have been arguing with each other; debating the exigencies of their chosen role. Then they appeared to nod: without light, Covenant could not be sure.

Clyme came forward. "I will lead while Branl wards your back. The *Haruchai* have no knowledge of this snare. Those Bloodguard who ventured here did not return, apart from Korik, Sill, and Doar, who revealed naught. But our perceptions exceed yours. We will search out a clearing or open place, according to your desires."

Instead of thanking the Humbled again, Covenant rested his halfhand in acknowledgment on Clyme's shoulder. After that, he simply followed.

Joan would try to kill him. She had no choice. Long ago, she had betrayed herself as well as him by turning her back. The same future could not hold them both.

The cleft seemed to wander aimlessly, as if it had lost its way. Night had settled over the Shattered Hills. In the dark, Covenant could barely discern Clyme's shape ahead of him. He stumbled on the rough ground, caught the toes of his boots on loose rocks. But he had unforgiving surfaces to guide him on either side, the Humbled to shepherd him. And overhead the first dim hint of stars blinked in a narrow slit of sky like a path. When he missed his footing, he recovered his balance and went on.

At intervals, he passed black holes in the bases of the walls, gaps that may have been small caves leading to tunnels. Each opening increased his tension: he expected *skest*. But he felt no hint of the creatures; smelled nothing except age and emptiness, the stagnant musk of departed immiseration. For some reason, *turiya* Herem was holding back. The Raver had some other ambush in mind.

Ahead of Covenant, Clyme came to a fracture that bisected the cleft at a sharp angle. Off to the left, Covenant detected a vague impression of *skest*; a residual fetor. Instead of continuing along the cleft, Clyme turned to the right, almost doubling back on his course. Trailed by Covenant and then Branl, he strode into the dark, steadfast in his certainty.

Here the way was cluttered with impediments: piles of rock fallen from the sheered rims of the Hills; occasional boulders; heaps of innominate debris. Covenant had to go more slowly, probing for obstacles. Damp blood like fire marked the place on his rib cage where he had been cut. His forehead seemed to burn. Fortunately Clyme soon found another intersection where a wider split like a corridor extended in both directions. The Master appeared to consider turning to the right again. Then he shook his head slightly and went left.

Darkness and the height of the walls confused Covenant's tenuous sense of direction. He could not remember patterns among the stars; and cold stone growing colder filled his scant health-sense. He had no idea whether he was moving toward or away from the promontory where he had remembered or imagined Joan.

Impatience beat in the background of his awareness, an accumulating thunder. He did not question Clyme's choices or instincts; but he felt sure that he was running out of time. How much longer would the Raver withhold his next attack? During the afternoon, the Humbled had sensed *caesures*. Had Joan exhausted herself? Was she tired enough to wait for Covenant?

If she struck now, or the *skest* did, he might miss his only chance to surprise her and *turiya*—

Come *on*, he thought at Clyme. Find what I need. While we're still alive. But he insisted in silence. Without the guidance of the Humbled, he would never discover the space he needed, except by accident or providence.

Another intersection. This time, Clyme turned right into a break so narrow that he was forced to squeeze along it sideways. Groaning, Covenant wedged himself between the walls.

He bruised his cheek; abraded his arms. On an unexpected knob of rock, he reopened the clotting wound on his forehead. He could not feel his outstretched fingers. If Clyme or Branl spoke, they did so to each other, not to him.

Panting in silent frustration, he emerged from the crack into a wider seam. There Clyme chose the left. He strode ahead more swiftly, as if he now felt the need for haste. Awkward on his numbed feet, Covenant scrambled to keep up with the Master.

Finally the seam debouched into a junction where several passages and breaks crossed each other. Together they formed an open space six or seven paces across, perhaps ten wide. Its surface was littered with detritus: old rubble, brittle shards of weapons, splintered scraps that may once have been bones. At every step, Covenant tripped on a rock, kicked something metallic, or crushed a desiccated shape to powder.

Against one high bluff of the Hills crouched a pit as black as an abyss: obviously a cave. Two of the intersecting passages looked or felt as broad as roads. They were too clear to be natural formations. They may have served as corridors for Lord Foul's armies long ago. Or they might be lures—

Clyme stopped; indicated the pit. "*Skest* crowd there. At present, they stand in abeyance. Doubtless they will soon pour forth." Then he nodded at one of the broad passages. "That path ends in blind stone. There we will render ourselves helpless. The other clear way holds more *skest*.

"Ur-Lord, will this juncture meet your need? Other choices are open to us, but along them we may be readily overtaken."

Fears thronged in Covenant's throat. He swallowed hard. "I wanted more room." There was too much at stake. "But I guess we'll have to make do with this."

"Then I ask again," Clyme said like the voice of the darkness. "What is your intent?"

"Stay with me." Covenant's hands shook as he pulled the bundle from his waist. "Don't stay with me." Hell and blood! I don't have the courage for this— "It's up to you." Every choice led to doom of one kind or another. He had already been killed once: he did not want to die again. "I can't stop now. If I had a better idea, we wouldn't be here.

"Sometimes we just have to take the chance—"

How many times had he told Linden to trust herself?

Vehement with self-coercion, he gripped the bundle in his left fist and began to unwrap the *krill*. But he was careful not to touch the dagger. Cursing his many trepidations, he bared the haft of the blade; uncovered the gem.

Avid brilliance burst into the night. It glared on every rock, every shard, every sign of ruin. It limned the crowding hills until they seemed to impend over him, stark against the blinded black of the sky.

"At least this way," he panted through his teeth, "the damn *skest* won't attack us until they see what happens next."

Before Clyme or Branl could protest, he stroked Loric's lore-cut jewel with the numb fingers of his halfhand.

In spite of the danger, he rubbed the gem until he smelled scorching flesh.

Come on, damn it. You know it's me. If you can recognize me all the way down in the Lost Deep, you can sure as hell feel me when I'm this close. And don't tell me you're too tired. You want this. It's the only way to end what you're going through.

Branl grabbed his upper arms, clamped them to his sides. Clyme moved to snatch away the *krill*.

"No!" Covenant shouted; raged. "*Hell*, no! If you stop me now, she *wins*! Lord Foul *wins*!"

Just for a moment, Clyme hesitated.

Then a *caesure* exploded to life directly ahead of Covenant, three or four paces behind Clyme. The Master wheeled away as if he believed himself capable of protecting Covenant from the violence of ruptured time.

Branl released Covenant's right arm. Instinctively? Deliberately? Covenant did not care. He wrenched his left free.

The Fall was big, a tornado of chaos. Most of it had appeared within the substance of the hill. Dismembered instants as devastating as the Worm conflated every moment of the stone's recent millennia. The force of their insanity chewed the bluff to grit and pebbles, flung scree like a barrage at the sky.

The *caesure*'s propinquity stung every inch of Covenant's skin that could still feel pain. Nausea and *wrongness* knotted his guts. If he could have unclenched the muscles of his stomach, he might have puked.

But he was ready for this. He had to be. Why else had he forced himself to leave Linden?

The area around him was clear enough. He had room to move.

This is your mistake, Joan. Not mine. I'm coming for you.

Dropping the scraps of Anele's tunic, he clutched the *krill* in both hands. Its heat was Joan's fury; but he knew how to bear it.

Anchored to everything that he loved by nausea and stings and searing pain, he ran straight into the core of the Fall.

Clyme or Branl may have shouted after him, but he did not hear them. As soon as the gyre caught him, it swept him out of existence.

12.

Sold Souls

Without transition, Covenant staggered onto a featureless plain, infinitely unrelieved, and so cold that it froze the blood in his veins. If time had been possible here, one lurching attempt of his heart to beat would have shattered him. His entire body would have burst into ice crystals and drifted like dust, falling from nowhere to nowhere. But of course his heart did not beat, or he did not shatter, because this gelid moment did not move on to another. It did not imply time of any kind. He could stagger and catch his balance—could turn his head or his whole body to scan the suzerain nothing of the horizons—could walk in any direction if he chose—because this one miniscule fragment of causality and sequence had become the universe. It was all that the Arch of Time contained.

If he wished, he could imagine his breath as frigid plumes and searing inhalations, but such things had no significance. They meant nothing. They would never mean anything.

On some other plane of perception, a dimension simultaneous with the plain and the cold, hornets in their myriads or millions burrowed into his flesh. Each of them was pure excruciation, an instance of agony like being flayed. His leper's numbness did not protect him. Even one of them might have destroyed him; but his absolute pain was eternally suspended within itself, forever caught between cause and effect. Here there was no difference between one insufferable anguish and a thousand. A thousand stings and a hundred thousand were the same. He endured them all for the same reason that he endured one: like his body, his mind was not given a chance to shatter.

It would never have that chance. In this place, there were no chances.

On yet another plane of perception, however, another overlapping dimension, he found Joan. He *was* Joan. He stood where she stood, among wet rocks and reefs which had formed the floor of the Sunbirth Sea only a short while ago. He screamed her horror and rage against the pitiless night. He pounded her abused flesh with his useless fists. He tore out her hair in clumps that did not hurt enough to redeem her.

And he remembered.

He remembered her life. His memories were hers. They were broken and whetted, as sharp as flensing knives, and they sliced through him until every vestige of his sanity was cut away.

They had driven her mad. They did the same to him.

And on still another dimension of perception, he recognized *turiya* Raver, Herem, Kinslaughterer. The Raver wore Joan and him as if they were garments donned at will. In his hands, *turiya* juggled memories and realities like toys. When he found one or another that displeased him, he crushed it; discarded it. The rest he kept aloft so that each possibility and recollection scraped across the whetstone of the air and became sharper.

But the Raver had no effect on Covenant. That sempiternal sickness could not hurt him. He had felt it too often; understood it too well. In Lord Foul's servants, evil was just another form of disease. It could be endured. It could be ignored. And *turiya* was only the juggler. He was only malice laughing in wild triumph. His greed for harm changed nothing. He was not freezing emptiness forever. He was not the swarming hornets of maimed time. He was not madness or remembrance.

He was not Joan.

And he would never be Linden Avery.

An instant or an eternity ago, Covenant had known what he was doing. He had chosen this plight. He knew *caesures* intimately. He had spent an age defending the Arch of Time; helping it heal after each violation. He had realized what would happen to him.

He would be lost, of course: that was obvious. He had no defense against the temporal inferno of the Fall: no lorewise ur-viles, no ineffable Ranyhyn, no rightful wedding band. No Earthpowerful companions. And his mind was already webbed with flaws, a cracked wilderland of unscalable fissures as trackless as the Shattered Hills, and as fraught with vertigo as the precipice above the sea. Of course he would be lost.

But he would also find Joan. He *had* found her. A moment or an eon ago, he had believed that she would be his path. His salvation. His way back to life. Mad or sane, she stood at the center of the Fall's turmoil. The whirl of instants revolved around her; around white gold and wild magic. They reached from the Land's past into an unbearable future, but she held the crux of their devastation. The eye of the paradox. And she was still alive. Still human. Moment by moment, her heart continued its fraying labor. Therefore she was also the *present*, her own and Covenant's and the Land's. She could stand on the drained seabed because the tsunami had not yet come. The Worm had not.

Covenant had rushed into the *caesure* because Joan was there.

She was the only road that might lead him back to life and Linden, and to the last, necessary battles for the Land.

He had known the danger; the acute extremes of his vulnerability. Oh, he had known! He had never learned how to ward off the seductions of lost time, the dizzying call of chasms. For that reason, he had trusted—

But he could no longer remember who or what he had trusted. Alone in an irredeemable wilderness of cold while burrowing agony exposed every nerve, he was Joan. Her torment was his. He remembered nothing that was not her.

Somewhere among the multiplied dimensions of his extinction, his human hands still gripped the *krill*: High Lord Loric Vilesilencer's supreme achievement. But it was wasted here because Covenant himself was helpless. He could not unravel his own mind from the skein of Joan's deranged memories. The dagger's implicit fire had no effect on his torment.

You have sold your freedom to purchase the misery of love, *turiya* Herem told him, laughing. While you remained within the Arch, you were capable of opposition. You enforced boundaries upon the World's End. Now you are naught but fodder for my delight. Here your life is mine.

Covenant heard the Raver, but he did not listen. He was Joan. When the tsunami came, it would destroy her—and him with her. Only *turiya* would survive.

If or when Lord Foul decided that he wanted white gold, his servant would know exactly where to find it.

There every tale that Covenant had ever loved would end.

He no longer wondered why the old beggar had not given Linden warning of her peril. The Creator had recognized his own defeat. He had abandoned his creation.

Yet Joan did not think such thoughts; and so Covenant did not. She experienced only pain and betrayal. She felt only rage, wild and ultimately futile. She wanted only to *make it stop*.

At one time in her life, many years earlier, she had craved the opposite. More than anything, she had desired her life then to go on and on just as it was, sunlit and always content. With Covenant on Haven Farm. Pregnant with Roger. Surrounded by her beloved horses. Training them, not by breaking them to her will, but rather by comforting them until they trusted her. By luring them one gentle step at a time to want what she wanted. Happy. Passive.

She had found pleasure in Covenant's first ecstasy of writing. She had enjoyed his passion for her body. The hurt of childbirth was nothing to her because her husband had written a bestseller, and because she had a son, and because her heart sang in the presence of horses.

Turiya Raver relished those memories. They supplied the excoriation for everything that followed. Without them, she would not have felt so profoundly betrayed by Covenant's leprosy.

From the first instant, she had loathed the maiming of his right hand. It disfigured him; tainted him in her eyes. But perhaps she could have lived with it. It was only his hand. Yet she could not quell her revulsion at what his amputation implied.

Leprosy. Her husband was a leper. His humanity had been cut away. His illness was a form of treachery because it destroyed her contentment. It would make her a leper as well. It would turn her precious, perfect son into a diseased thing; an object of abhorrence. Everyone would shun them, all of them. Even horses might flinch away.

And they would be right to do so. Leprosy was more than an affliction of the flesh. It was a judgment. A condemnation. Thou art weighed in the balance and found wanting. Her husband, *her husband*, would sicken everyone who came near him.

In memories distorted by *turiya*'s malice and her own fears, Covenant's novel was a lie. His exaltation in writing was a lie. His love was malevolence, a hunger to inflict his illness on her. If she had killed him then, she might still have been too late to save herself and her son.

But she could not kill him: not then. She had lacked that kind of courage. Instead the shock of his condition taught her that she lacked *any* kind of courage. Her sense of violation seemed to have no bottom. It had no end. It dug into her, and dug, until it exposed the fragility buried at the core of her ruined life. She was doing her utmost when she abandoned him. When she divorced him. When she went to live with her parents, putting as much distance as she could manage between herself and her cowardice.

Yet distance did not save her. The fumbling inadequacy of her parents did not save her. Just once, she had tried to reach out to Covenant. He had refused to speak to her. In his silence, she had heard the truth. Her husband had betrayed her—and she did not know how to live without him. Forsaking him, she had forsaken herself; had turned her back on sunshine and contentment and horses. He had falsified those things; or her fears had driven her to falsify them.

Excruciated, and unaware of what she did, she had already begun the process of selling her soul.

And whenever she contrived to convince herself that she was seeking help, she went further. Sharing her mind, Covenant relived her misdirected struggles as if they were his. His mind was broken: he could not defend himself. Like her, if in different ways, he had fallen far enough to plumb any depths.

Blank cold so extreme that it seared his spirit.

Hornets denouncing every particle of his mortal flesh.

And Joan.

He had become them all.

Therapist after therapist suggested reassurance, offered guidance back to strength.

Some proposed medications. Others did not. But they were all wasted on her. She had never had any strength to which she might return. Weakness was her only resource. Passivity defined her. In the end, therapy gave her nothing. It asked her to confront the beating heart of her revulsion; and so it pushed her deeper.

And churches were no better. Religion after religion, they proposed redemption; promised grace to efface horror. They did not require confrontations. Instead they insisted on contrition. Another form of abandonment: the surrender of her will and abhorrence to their forgiving God.

That might have saved her. Living her life, Covenant prayed that it would. But she could not distinguish between contrition and self-abasement; between acknowledgment and blame. And she could not surrender her horror. It alone justified her. Within her, Covenant remembered the precise moment when she had first realized that she could see eyes like fangs in the back of her mind. Piercing her defenses, biting deep, the eyes had assured her that there was no difference between therapy and religion. Forgiveness was just another way of accepting the disease, the spiritual leprosy, inflicted by Covenant's betrayal. Like therapy, religion expected her to excuse his crime against her. To take the blame herself.

She embraced revulsion because she understood it. The fangs in her mind approved. Offers of forgiveness only pushed her farther into the Lost Deep of her defining despair, her essential and necessary loathing.

Betrayed, she let everything else go—even her parents—even her son—until she discovered the Community of Retribution.

There she felt that she had found recognition at last.

Among those believers, those fanatics, she reveled in promises of punishment. They made sense to her. She became chattel to the Community's fierce priests. They made sense to her. She spoke every word that came to her from the eyes in her mind. They all made sense to her. And in return, she was given a kind of peace. Not the peace of forgiveness: the Community of Retribution did not forgive. Rather she received the peace of universal condemnation. Within the Community, she was blameworthy only because the whole world deserved denunciation, and she was part of the world. In every other way—so the believers and their priests taught her—she was innocent because nothing was her fault. She simply existed: she had not done anything, caused anything, inflicted anything. And the world needed retribution.

It needed to exact the cost of her suffering from Covenant.

To that extent, she thought as he did. In her own fashion, she believed that guilt was power. But for her, as for him, the guilt was his. Not hers. The power was his. And if he were punished enough, if he suffered enough, if he met destruction for his crimes, his agony would redeem her.

Ultimately that was why she had returned to Haven Farm, and to him. So that he would try to help her. It was why she had tasted his blood and given him moments of lucidity. With her weakness, she had lured him to his doom in exactly the same way that she would have seduced a horse too vicious for any fate except slaughter.

In torment and frailty, she was still fighting for salvation. Everything else—rage and the Raver, wild magic, self-abuse, carnage—was just confusion.

Because of course eventually she had realized that she had been betrayed again. Eyes like fangs had not spared her that knowledge. *Turiya* Herem had not spared her. Covenant was the source of her horror. Her agony and degradation could not end while he lived. But her efforts on Haven Farm had led only to the death of his body. His spirit flourished in the Arch of Time. While she grew weaker, he acquired new strength. He was loved. He was even revered. Retribution was her only conceivable release, and he blocked it. Worse, he *negated* it. Simply by standing against her, he made her less than nothing. His treachery transformed every single moment and slash of her unceasing anguish into a cruel joke.

Turiya did not let her forget that. Contemptuously he ruled her thoughts. He guided her use of her ring. And he reminded her that her son hated her. Her own son. Who could have spared her; could have made it *stop*.

Roger had refused to do so because he scorned her pain. He had come for her only to inflict more brutality. Like his father, he had betrayed her utterly.

If she could have found anything within herself except pain and *turiya* Herem, she would have torn down entire worlds to punish him.

Behold! the Raver chortled to Covenant. His glee was the purest sting, the most perfect ice. *Witness the outcome of your long strife! She is yours. You have made her to be what she is. Are you not therefore culpable for her deeds?*

If Joan's *caesures* had not damaged the Law of Time, Linden could not have resurrected Covenant. She could not have roused the Worm of the World's End. She was not a rightful wielder of wild magic. She did not have enough power. No, the original wounds to the structure of Life and Death had been delivered by Elena, Sunder, and Caer-Caveral. But Falls kept those hurts fresh. Without them, Linden would have failed.

By the inexorable logic of guilt, the fault was Covenant's.

Involuntarily he nodded. He did not have it in him to contradict *turiya*. Like Joan, he had been shattered. The fact that she had fallen too far to be retrieved altered nothing. Indeed, he had not merely made her what she was. By permitting himself to be withdrawn from the Arch, when he could have refused the summons to Andelain, he had removed a vital barrier against her madness and wild magic. To that extent, he had enabled the barren future within which he was trapped.

At one time, perhaps, she had been responsible for herself. Now the burden was his.

Cold and scalding as congealed fire, the flat wilderland ached toward its illimit-able horizons. An infinitude of disarticulated instants burrowed like screaming into Covenant's helpless flesh. Within Joan's mind, he returned to Haven Farm and horses in sunlight. He lived through what had become of her over and over again, as she did. Endlessly they repeated the cycle of her terrible dismay.

Such things held him. They had always held him, and always would. This moment would never lead to another, and so he could neither escape nor die. Nothing would ever change.

Nevertheless Branl and Clyme stood on either side of him. They remained exactly where they had been ever since this specific instant had been ripped out of its natural continuum.

They did not look at him. They had never looked at him. They were unaware of his presence—or they, too, no longer existed.

"Ur-Lord," Branl said: a gust of vapor as gelid and unbearable as stark ice. "You must return to yourself."

"You must," Clyme said. Plumes of frost issued from his mouth. "We cannot ward you."

"We are *Haruchai*," Branl said. "We cannot share our minds with you."

"We are *Haruchai*," Clyme echoed. "We do only what we can. Nothing more. As we have ever done."

They stood beside Covenant. Companions. He was not alone.

Nothing changed. Here there was no possibility of change.

Nonetheless Branl put his hand on Covenant's left elbow. Clyme grasped the right.

Together they lifted Covenant's arms until he could see Loric's *krill* clenched in both of his numbed hands.

Oh, they were *Haruchai*! They lived in each other's thoughts. They could carry the burden of too much time without faltering. And they stayed away from Joan. They had that power; that salvific intransigence. Stave had done the same. Even when he could have witnessed the private writhing of Linden's spirit, he had held himself apart.

The dagger's shining did not pierce Covenant's sight. His eyes were frozen. They had been chewed out of their orbits. Mere radiance could not blind him to what he saw; what he had seen; what he would always see. It was only wild magic. It was not redemption.

But it *was* wild magic, an inherent and inextricable aspect of the Arch of Time. It added a new dimension to the overlapping realities of his helplessness.

While Clyme and Branl supported him—while they upheld the *krill*'s transcen-dence—he saw more than the flat plain; more than swarming hornets; more than Joan's reiterated suffering.

He also saw her as if from the outside. As if he were present in her present.

She stood ankle-deep in muck and water surrounded by jagged rocks and cruel reefs. Somehow she had crept or clambered several hundred paces across the seabed. Now she faced the blasted cliff where Foul's Creche had fallen. Under the sealed doom of the night sky, she faced Covenant and the Humbled.

In her trembling fist, she clutched her wedding band with its chain wrapped around it.

Her knuckles were raw. Blood pulsed from the sore on her temple where she had punched and punched herself. In its own way, her self-abuse matched Covenant's bleeding forehead. Blood made streaks of anguish down her sunken cheek. It stained the filth and tatters of her hospital gown. Rage blazed like the *krill* in her eyes. A rictus bared her few remaining teeth. The gaps in her gums oozed more blood. It marked her mouth as though she fed on living flesh.

From his prison inside her mind, Covenant saw that she also saw him. She saw the Humbled and Loric's bright weapon as if they had all stepped out of her madness to confront her.

Watching himself and his companions while he also watched her, Covenant saw that he and Branl and Clyme were making their way toward her. Awash in silver, they traversed the unfathomable dark. Together they passed around boulders sharp enough to shred their flesh, avoided fingers of coral that reached for them like blades, splashed through puddles and pools left behind by the indrawn ocean.

On all sides as far as the light of the *krill* extended, waters and gasping fish and sea-plants quivered in the shocks of distant convulsions. But such things did not trouble Joan. She *wanted* the tsunami. It could not come soon enough.

Staring through her appalled eyes, Covenant saw himself and the *krill* and the Humbled advance toward her like the approach of horror: the ultimate apotheosis of her despair.

None of this was real: he understood that. It was a mirage of movement and sequence made possible by Loric's lore and Joan's wild magic, nothing more; a mere figment. Nothing had changed. Nothing could change. He remained lost in his last Fall. His own abyss would never release him.

But that did not matter. It was irrelevant. Meaningless. Because Joan believed what she saw. Participating in her thoughts, Covenant knew that she believed he had come for her.

She believed that he meant to finish what he had started when he had married and betrayed her; when he had afflicted her with a cruel son. The man whom she most loathed and feared: the man who haunted her worst terrors. The man who had made her what she was.

And she had no *skest* to defend her. The Raver had sent them all to oppose Covenant among the Shattered Hills.

With a shriek that seemed to split the world, she raised her fist. Striking at her forehead, she unleashed a blast savage enough to incinerate an entire legion of Thomas Covenants and *Haruchai*.

The *krill* accepted her attack. Its jewel became a sun in Covenant's grasp. Some of her force the dagger simply dissipated. Some it absorbed until its edges became sharp enough to cut through the boundaries between realities.

Nevertheless a portion of her fury hit him.

It did not kill him outright because he was not real. He had no physical existence, and so he could not be extirpated from her nightmares. But he was still vulnerable. She created *caesures* with wild magic. She could affect what happened within them.

She could hurt him.

In the multiplied simultaneous instants of impact, Covenant finally understood why Lord Foul had not forbidden *turiya* Raver to endanger Jeremiah with Falls. Yes, the Despiser burned to possess Jeremiah's gifts; to control them. And Linden's son would be forever unattainable if he were lost within a *caesure*. Eventually the destruction of the Arch of Time would destroy him also. But if wild magic enabled Joan to take action inside her temporal maelstroms, *turiya* could do the same through her. In effect, therefore, *turiya* Herem had the power to snatch Jeremiah back from chaos. Lord Foul could recapture the boy and use him.

But no foe of the Land would choose to recapture Covenant. Joan's force hurled him away. It pounded him against rocks and shoals.

The Humbled did not move to catch him. They did not react at all. Instead they stood rigid as death, frozen in timeless ice and hornets.

Their passivity was *turiya*'s doing. The Raver lived within Joan. He ruled her. As much as her madness permitted, he guided her rage. Riding her fire, he had reached into the Fall and mastered Clyme and Branl.

They were done. They did not exist. They had never existed.

But—

Hellfire!

But—

Hell and *blood!*

—Joan's blow had other effects as well: effects which Herem had not intended, and could not prevent. It increased the implicit puissance of the *krill*, yes. That was important. It was necessary. But her violence also cast Covenant out of her mind. It *externalized* him. She could not end his life while he was absent in chaos, and so her hunger for retribution began to make him real. Physically present.

Inadvertently her despair resurrected him in front of her.

And the complex lore galvanized in Loric's blade reinforced Covenant's manifestation. It enhanced his substance. His grip on it quickened his translation out of the *caesure*.

Already the gelid wilderness was fraying; evaporating. The firestorm of severed instants lost some of its ferocity. He was no longer trapped inside Joan.

If she struck him again, she would make him fully present.

But the same blow would also incinerate him. With one more bolt of silver lightning, she would finally rid herself of the ghoul which had haunted her suffering.

Until then, however—until she punched herself once more, transformed her intimate agony into coruscation—

Try it, Covenant panted. *Try* it. Try to survive it yourself. You've been making too many *caesures*. You exhausted yourself getting here. You're so weak you can hardly stand. So go on. *Try* to kill me without burning out your own heart.

While she groped for her last strength, he had things to do.

Shaking in pain, he struggled to his feet.

She had hit him hard. He had landed hard. His chest felt like a jumble of fractured ribs. Rocks and coral had torn strips from his jeans and T-shirt. They had shredded his arms and torso, parts of his legs. Blood ran from his forehead and a score of other wounds. Every beat of his pulse spilled more of his humanity. He was scarcely able to swallow or draw breath or hold himself upright.

Nevertheless he stumbled toward Joan with the *krill* clenched in his fists and his own storm glaring in his eyes.

I'm sorry you've been through so much. I really am. But this is the wrong answer. It's possible to be in pain without hating yourself and the whole world. You don't have the right to make everybody else feel the same way you do.

She blinked at his staggering approach. Her wild eyes were empty of comprehension. She was not alarmed to see him coming closer with his incandescent dagger. Here the power was hers, not his. She would hit herself again. Hurl another bolt of wild magic. Flay the skin from his bones; burn out his soul. As soon as he came close enough. As soon as she was able to lift her arm.

In her own way, she was no longer afraid.

And the Humbled could not help him. They were still caught in the *caesure*. They did not exist in any defined time.

But *turiya* saw more than Joan did; understood more. He knew what was happening to Covenant. He knew what the *krill* could do.

In spite of his eager rapture, the Raver lived within Joan's weakness. With torment and coercion, he could direct her outbursts; but he also shared her physical frailty, her prolonged emotional inanition. That was the price he paid for *possessing* her. He could not exceed her limitations through her.

Nonetheless *turiya* Herem retained his own powers. He could exert them. He delivered his separate assault while Covenant was still ten ravaged paces away.

He did not try to enter Covenant. He was unwilling to relinquish Joan. And he had reason to believe that Covenant knew how to defy him. Covenant had twice defeated the Despiser—

Unlike Joan, however, *turiya* recognized that Covenant had other vulnerabilities. Instead of striving to rule Covenant, the Raver turned Covenant's reincarnation against him.

Reaching out, *turiya* tripped Covenant's mind. A dark hand of thought sent Covenant sprawling into one of the fissures that flawed his ability to stand in his own present.

Instantly Joan and wild magic and *turiya* Herem and the Humbled and the *krill* and the emptied seabed lost their immediacy; their importance. In one form or another, they all still occupied the living moments before Joan summoned the will to complete Covenant's death. Stubbornly Branl and Clyme strained to alter what had happened to them. But Covenant did not. He could not. A wall like leprosy stood between him and his mortality. It was transparent. He could see what lay beyond it. But it was also incurable. It enclosed him until nothing mattered except memory.

For a time, he remembered the stasis which the *Elohim* had once imposed on him. They had rendered him utterly helpless—and perfectly aware of it. By that means, they had sought to prevent him from endangering the Arch while they manipulated Linden; while they tried to make of her their chosen instrument. He remembered *Bhrathairealm*, and Kasreyn of the Gyre, and the Sandgorgon Nom.

Fortunately that recollection was brief. He fell again, or slipped aside, and was set free.

From stasis, he walked with the ease of youth and vigor back into the comfortable shade of a remnant of the One Forest.

He knew this region. After centuries of killing and bitter loss, the Forest here had dwindled until it became Morinmoss between the borders of Andelain and the Plains of Ra. Still this portion of the woodland, like others elsewhere, retained its intended grandeur. These were trees that knew abundant sunshine and rain, enjoyed deep loam. Most of them were hoary monarchs bestrewn with creepers and draped in moss, trees like oak and sycamore and cypress that spread their roots and their boughs wide, crowding out lesser vegetation. There were saplings, certainly. There were deadfalls, and trunks blasted by lightning, and vast kings perishing of old age. But such things were natural to forests. And few of them obstructed the ground. Covenant could walk where he willed without hindrance. Blessed by fecundity and shade, he could have run if he had felt any desire or need to do so.

He was in no hurry. He remembered where he was going, and the way was not far.

Guided by the gentle contours of hills, he came to a rich glade like a coronal display of wildflowers and long grass. Reveling in sunlight, he walked out from among the trees to watch with wonder as Forestals came together in conclave.

All of them. Together. Here. For the first time—and for the last. Some who would soon pass away. Others who endured for centuries or millennia, faithful to their tasks among the trees, and to their growing wrath, and to their woe. All of them.

They were singing a song that Covenant knew by heart.

Branches spread and tree trunks grow
  Through rain and heat and snow and cold;
Though wide world's winds untimely blow,
  And earthquakes rock and cliff unseal,

My leaves grow green and seedlings bloom.
  Since days before the Earth was old
And Time began its walk to doom,
  The Forests world's bare rock anneal,

Forbidding dusty waste and death.
  I am the Land's Creator's hold:
I inhale all expiring breath,
  And breathe out life to bind and heal.

Unseen within the Arch, unknown to the Forestals, Covenant had often stood witness to this scene. He loved it with his whole heart.

Caerroil Wildwood was here, and Cav-Morin Fernhold. Dhorehold of the Dark. One who was called the Magister of Andelain; and another who named himself Syr Embattled, doing what he could to defend Giant Woods. Others. All of them. In their times, they had been the exigent guardians of everything precious in the Land: precious and doomed. Here they were wreathed in music and magic, the poignant, potent sorrow of their striving to slow the ineluctable murder of trees.

Yet something about the scene troubled Covenant: something that was not woe or regret or ire. He was surely entranced; but he was also disturbed. In some fashion that he did not know how to identify, the conclave of the Forestals was not as he remembered it. It had become *flat*: too superficial to be true. It resembled a masque performed by smaller beings, accurate in every detail, yet somehow less than it should have been.

If the trees and the glade and the Forestals had been anything other than a memory, Covenant might have concluded that he had lost his health-sense. He could not *see in*, and so he could not truly see at all.

Joan was too strong for him. *Turiya* Herem was too strong. If they did not kill him, he would never survive the tsunami.

Linden might hang on for a few more days. Then she, too, would perish.

He had abandoned her as though he had never loved her.

Without warning, the Forestals began to transgress his recollection of them.

Together they sang, "Only rock and wood know the truth of the Earth. The truth of life."

"But wood is too brief," Dhorehold of the Dark intoned. "All vastness is forgotten."

"Unsustained," answered Andelain's Magister, "wood cannot remember the lore of the Colossus, the necessary forbidding of evils—"

"There is too much," the Forestals agreed as one. "Power and peril. Malevolence. Ruin."

"And too little time," added Syr Embattled. "The last days of the Land are counted. Without forbidding, there is too little time."

Like an antiphonal response, the Forestals chanted, "Become as trees, the roots of trees. Seek deep rock."

No! Covenant protested. He felt abruptly wounded; pierced to the soul. *No.* This isn't what happened. This isn't what I heard.

While the last notes of their litany faded among the trees, Cav-Morin Fernhold walked away from his comrades to look directly at Covenant.

Directly *at* Covenant.

Who was not there.

"Timewarden," Cav-Morin mused in a melody that wrenched at Covenant's bones, "this is false." He had always been Covenant's favorite among his kind: a gentler spirit who knew when to condone human intrusion even though he did not know why he should do so. In his own way, he had loved the Ranyhyn as much as the Ramen did. "Your presence is false. Can you not discern this?

"Your time lies beyond our ken. You are needed then, not here. You are loved then, not here.

"There must be forbidding. The end must be opposed by the truths of stone and wood, of *orcrest* and refusal."

With those words, he turned his back. Wearing sunshine like song and glory, he went to rejoin the other Forestals.

His counsel lit recognition like tinder in Covenant's veins.

Suddenly Covenant was full of fire. His nerves burned. His muscles blazed. His heart hammered in his damaged chest. All of his senses opened, and he could smell—

Oh, God.

Smell? Damnation! He could practically *taste* Herem Kinslaughterer's evil. It was everywhere around him, everywhere: hidden behind every tree, lurking under every leaf, twisting like mockery and malice around every bough. Concealed by sunlight, it boiled and chuckled, delighted with its own cunning.

This was *turiya*'s doing, this corruption of the remembered past. He had sent Covenant here to distract him until Joan recovered her failing strength; until she was ready to scatter the instants of his life like dust over the seafloor. But the Raver's power showed through the veil of Covenant's recall.

Still the ploy had succeeded. *Turiya* Herem had chosen a memory that Covenant adored. Covenant could have remembered this scene happily until he died. He loved it and the Forestals too much to trust his own discomfort.

Or the ploy would have succeeded. Perhaps it should have. But the Raver had made a mistake. He had underestimated the sheer might and melody of the Forestals. He had not considered that they might be able to detect his influence; that they might sing against it, opening Covenant's perceptions.

Now Covenant burned with his own fire and abhorrence; his own storm of refusal. And somewhere long ages in the future, millennia after the last Forestal had surrendered his life, Covenant's maimed hands still held the *krill*.

The *krill* was life. It was the instrument of his resurrection, as it was of Hollian's before him. And Joan had increased its magicks. Covenant could use it. With wild magic, he could reclaim his heritage.

For centuries, his spirit had extended throughout the Arch of Time. Now he had been severed from it. He would never wield its forces again. But he could understand them. He could grasp the nature and implications of Joan's theurgy. He could call upon them indirectly.

Loric's dagger made that possible. *You are the white gold*. It enabled him to burn as if he wore a wedding band that matched his ex-wife's.

And if he could burn, he could return to the *krill*. To the moment when he still gripped the *krill*. No memory had the power to hold him back.

Bleeding from more wounds than he could count, Covenant found the path that led toward his present self. At once, he began to work his way along it. And while he arose from the Earth's past, he fused fissures behind him. He closed cracks. Rife with silver fire, he healed breaks until all of them were mended.

Deliberately he annealed fragments of his former being, rendering them inaccessible so that he could be whole.

Like an astral spirit done with wandering, Thomas Covenant reentered his body in front of Joan.

He stood unsteadily among rocks and pools under a night sky as gravid and heavy as the stone of a tomb. The only light came from Loric's blade: it may have been the only light left in the world. In the gem's argent, the seafloor looked garish, ghostly: a nightscape illuminated by lightning or phosphorescence. Clyme and Branl remained on either side of him; but now they resembled shadows of themselves, tenuous as spectres or dreams, as though they inhabited a dimension of existence which he could scarcely perceive. When he completed his reality, they would be gone, lost among the effects of Joan's madness.

In the sequences of her life, he had not been absent for more than a few moments: that was obvious. She had not moved. Apart from the uncertain clutch of her fist on her ring, and the tremulous shudder of her breathing, and the pitiless drip of blood down her face, she might have been a corpse so meagerly loved that it had been denied sepulture. Her dulled gaze hardly seemed capable of noticing him.

But then the Raver gave fuel to a spark of awareness within her. Her eyes caught reflections from the *krill*: they rediscovered rage.

Shaking at the force of *turiya* Herem's hate, and of her own repudiation, she readied her arm.

Covenant was still ten paces from her. And he, too, was weak; badly hurt. Blood soaked his torn clothes: they felt like bandages applied in haste. He was barely able to remain on his feet and hold the dagger. He could not reach her quickly enough to interrupt her blow.

In another moment, another instant, she would hit herself again. Then he would die.

Gasping against the pain in his chest, he shouted, "Joan!" His own gambit of distraction. "Don't do this!

"One of us has to die. One of us has to live. You know that! You know why. And I think you've already suffered too much.

"Joan, *please!* Let me live!"

She heard him. She must have: she paused. Reflections accumulated in her eyes, a wild glare of madness. Her body stiffened as though she feared that he would rape her.

Her reply was a scream that clawed its way out of her taut throat.

"*Leper!*"

Straining, she lifted her arm; clenched her fist.

Ah, hell, Covenant groaned in silence.

He could not use his hands. He needed them to grip the *krill*. It was his only conceivable defense. But it was not enough. His life and will and even his love seemed to leak out of him from too many injuries. Tottering on the cluttered seabed, he was too drained to do anything except bare his teeth. And the Humbled could not help him. They had already given him the pure gift of their support. They were not substantial here.

Yet he was not dead. *And betimes some wonder is wrought to redeem us.*

With all of the air that he could force from his rent chest, he made a thin whistling sound through his teeth.

Then he waited for death or life.

Any delay would have been fatal; but he was answered instantly. Somewhere behind him, two Ranyhyn trumpeted defiance into the night.

When he heard Mhornym and Naybahn, he secured his grasp on the *krill* and mustered his resolve.

Joan heard them as well. She heard *horses*. Holding her arm poised, she looked away from Covenant.

A moment later, her face crumpled. Her fury vanished. Even her insanity seemed to vanish. Tears welled in her eyes: they spilled into the blood on her cheek and mouth. Her fist dropped.

While *turiya* Kinslaughterer spat and gibbered within her, she opened her arms to welcome Mhornym and Naybahn.

Careless and quick among the stones and reefs, the shivering pools, the Ranyhyn cantered toward her. As they ran, they neighed again: a kinder call now fretted with compassion and sorrow. Together they came near as if they were eager for her embrace.

On their foreheads, their stars shone like echoes of Loric's eldritch gem; instances of salvation.

Covenant did not hesitate. He would not be able to stay on his feet much longer. He had to act—

In spite of his peril, he sacrificed a moment for the Humbled. Swinging the *krill*, he slapped at Clyme's chest with the flat of the blade. He did the same to Branl. Needy as a supplicant, he touched both of them with the inferred possibilities of wild magic.

A heartbeat later, he lurched into motion, stumbling toward Joan.

The Raver tried to warn her. He howled for her attention; roared to break the enchantment of horses. But in her that magic was older than his mastery: much older. It endured like bedrock beneath the rubble of her madness. Rapt in the face of her one remaining love, she waited with her arms wide while Covenant struggled to reach her.

Five wracked steps. Six.

God help me. Be merciful to me, for I have sinned.

Moments before the Ranyhyn came near enough to take his burden from him, Thomas Covenant gave Joan the only gift that he had left. Nearly falling, he slid his blade into the center of her chest.

With High Lord Loric's *krill*, he accepted her guilt and set her free. Then he plunged to his knees.

As she died, he heard Mhornym and Naybahn cry lamentation into the night.

ॐ

L ater Covenant realized that Branl and Clyme were still with him. Wild magic and Joan's death had removed them from the *caesure* before the Arch healed itself, locking them out of their proper time forever.

And the Ranyhyn were still with him. Killing Joan, he had spared them the necessity of striking down a woman who loved them. Because he was capable of such things, they feared him—and would remain faithful to the end.

Turiya Herem was gone. Covenant did not imagine that he had slain the Raver. Doubtless the *krill* could have killed Lord Foul's servant, if *turiya* had continued to possess Joan. However, the Raver had not done so. He had discarded her like a useless husk, seeking some new being or creature to inhabit.

But Covenant did not think about *turiya*, or about the Ranyhyn, or about the improbable survival of the Humbled. He hardly thought at all. Stunned in the aftermath of delivering death, he was not aware that he had dropped the *krill*; or that Branl had retrieved it; or that the dagger's gem was dark, deprived of wild magic and light. Covenant was only grateful that he was not alone.

He had never been able to bear his crimes in isolation. Without friends and companions and love steadfast beyond his worth, he would have failed long ago.

When Clyme or Branl spoke, he did not hear. He had no room for words. Instead he crawled forward, seeping blood, until he reached Joan. Her arms were still outstretched; still waiting for horses. Her right fist still held her wedding band.

With as much gentleness as he could summon, he peeled back her fingers until he was able to claim her ring.

For a long moment, he peered at it as if it were a mere trinket; something to be tossed aside when it had served its purpose. But finally he accepted it as well. Looping the chain over his head, he hung her ring against his sternum: one of the few bones in his chest that did not feel cracked or broken.

Only then did he begin to listen.

"Ur-Lord," Clyme or Branl was saying, "we must flee. The tsunami comes." One of them added, "We cannot bear you to safety. We are not swift enough. You must consent to ride."

After a while, Covenant found that he had room for one word.

"Never."

If he accomplished nothing else that would serve as restitution, he was going to by God keep his promise to the Ranyhyn.

The Humbled did not object or argue. They did not waste time. Quickly they mounted their Ranyhyn. Then they leaned down to Covenant, one on each side of him, grasped him by his arms near his shoulders, and lifted him into the air between them.

Mhornym and Naybahn needed no urging to run. In perfect step an exact distance apart, they wheeled away and sprang into a gallop, racing toward their only conceivable salvation: the riven cliffs where Foul's Creche had once stood high above the sea.

Hanging helpless while his arms wept with pain, and fragments of bone ground against each other in his chest, Covenant heard it now, the unfathomable rumble of the tidal-wave. He felt tremors like incipient spasms in the seafloor, even though the horses were sure of their footing, and the hands of the Humbled were as reliable as iron. If he could have looked behind him, he might have seen havoc looming against the bleak stars, the fragile heavens—

He did not try to look. He paid no attention to the littleness of the Ranyhyn against the imponderable force of a tsunami. He trusted them absolutely, and had no strength left for fear.

The rumble became thunder, an upheaval as vast as the Worm's movement through the sea. It blotted out the world at his back, making every mortal effort vain. To strive against all things ending was simple vanity, valiant and futile. Like the Worm, the tsunami exceeded living comprehension. It could be neither accepted nor opposed. It required a different answer.

Nevertheless the Ranyhyn ran like figures in dreams, swift as yearning, slow as hopelessness. Their febrile rush tore at Covenant's arms, but they would never reach the cliffs.

Then they had already done so. At the verge of a great fan of rubble that piled massively toward the heights of the promontory, Naybahn and Mhornym pounded to a halt.

Somehow Clyme and Branl dismounted without dropping Covenant; without dislocating his shoulders. At once, Clyme swept Covenant into his arms. As he sprang at the rising wreckage, he told Covenant, "Here we are quicker than Ranyhyn. There is no path. They must ascend with care. If fortune smiles upon them, they may yet survive the onslaught of waters. But we require greater haste."

Covenant did not hear him. The roar of the tidal-wave smothered sound. It smothered thought. The tsunami was a mountain-range of water mounting against the Land. It would hit like the earthquake which had riven *Melenkurion* Skyweir. Its violence might resemble the convulsion which had severed the whole of the Lower Land from the Upper. The Ranyhyn would be smashed to pulp in an instant. Covenant and the Humbled would die in the first impact of the wave.

During the past few days, many regions of the Earth must have suffered similar catastrophes: shocks brutal enough to crush islands, maim continents. Now the Worm was feeding its way toward the Land at last.

Useless in Clyme's arms, Covenant tried to say, "Thank you." Just in case. But his voice made no sound that could be heard through the onset of mountains.

Supernally fleet, the Humbled bounded upward. Covenant tried to sense the progress of the struggling Ranyhyn, but the tsunami filled every nerve, every perception. It felt higher than the cliffs; higher than the unattainable obstruction of the Shattered Hills. It might flood the Lower Land as far as Landsdrop. Unable to discern the horses, he simply prayed that Linden and her companions would receive enough warning—

Then the Humbled were not leaping up rocks, not hurling themselves at unassailable boulders. Instead they ran from crest to crest across the foundation-stones of Foul's Creche. The rubble still climbed toward the comparative flat of the promontory, but more gradually here, allowing them to increase their speed.

Covenant should have been able to remember this place. He should have known how far he and the Humbled were from cooled Hotash Slay and the Shattered Hills. He had not cut himself off from the memories which belonged to his former mortal life. But he was too weak now. He had lost too much blood; had too many broken bones. He had killed Joan. Even his most human recollections were effaced by the impending mass of the tidal-wave.

When the Humbled stopped—when they turned to watch the wavefront—he did not understand why. A moment passed before he realized that they stood on old lava at the western boundary of the promontory. He gaped at the dark bulk of the Shattered Hills only a few dozen paces away, and could not comprehend what he saw.

How had Clyme carried him so far?

Why were they still alive?

Why were they no longer fleeing?

At last, he forced himself to look toward the east; and as he did so, the tsunami struck the cliff. In that instant, his entire reality became thunder and tumult as savage as the destruction of Ridjeck Thome.

Time seemed to pause as though the Arch itself recoiled in dismay. He felt stubborn rock shaken to shards and scattered. He heard cliffs scream as they clung to their moorings. He saw an immeasurable mass of water rise and rise, its surge crowned with froth and luminescence as if it were full of stars. Concussions shook the world. But he could not separate one detail from another. They were all one, all too much for his mind to contain; and they appeared to take no time. No time forever.

Water broke over the promontory; inundated it; plunged from its sides; swept forward. It spouted like a tremendous geyser from the rent where Foul's Creche had once stood. Spray stung Covenant's eyes until he could not see. It soaked his clothes, drenched his many wounds. Yet Clyme and Branl stood where they were, rigid as defiance. Apparently they believed that they had estimated the tsunami's reach exactly; that it would not take them.

Too weak to protest, Covenant lay in Clyme's arms and awaited the fate that the Humbled had chosen.

In front of him, the wave's force was split by the wedge of the promontory, deflected by the shape and bulk of the stone. Higher turmoil crashed against the cliffs on either side. Sweeping over granite toward Hotash Slay, the tsunami parted; recoiled against itself; poured away. At the end of its rush, it climbed to the knees of the Masters. It slapped against the first bluffs of the Hills. Then it began to spill backward. Its sweep would have dragged anyone weaker than the *Haruchai* with it.

When time resumed its inexorable beat, Covenant understood that he was going to live.

After a while, he was able to think again. Eventually he was able to look away from the receding waters. But when he regarded his companions, their flat stoicism made him flinch. It reminded him that they had left the Ranyhyn behind.

Sighing to himself, he wondered whether he would ever again draw a breath that did not taste of salt and death. If the Humbled whistled, other Ranyhyn would come. And they would know how to find their way through the maze. But their fidelity would not make the loss of Mhornym and Naybahn less grievous. It would not relieve the necessity of Joan's end.

By degrees, Covenant regained the sensation of passing moments. Through the star-pricked darkness, he watched the seas subside, thrashing against the cliffs. On either side, sections of stone had calved like glaciers. Slabs the size of Revelstone's prow, or of Kevin's Watch, continued to topple, unregarded by the lashing ocean. And as the waves shrank to the scale of a more ordinary storm, he saw that the end of the promontory was gone, broken by the brunt of the tidal-wave. Every hint or relic of the Despiser's former habitation had collapsed, leaving no sign that it had ever existed.

Still Clyme and Branl stood where they were, as unmoved as icons. For a time, Covenant wondered why they remained, expressionless and dour. Then he realized that they were waiting for the Ranyhyn.

Waiting for Mhornym and Naybahn, and refusing to mourn, until hope became impossible.

Even then, they might not permit themselves sorrow. They were *Haruchai*: they had done what they could. To their way of thinking, grief was a form of disrespect. Any admission of loss would dishonor the sacrifice of the Ranyhyn.

Vexed by the self-inflicted wound that was the *Haruchai* version of rectitude, Covenant twisted against Clyme's arms; asked to be put down. When the Master set him on his feet, he feared that he would prove too weak to stand. But he splayed his legs, braced himself on Clyme's shoulder, and refused to crumble. Then he withdrew his hand, kept himself upright.

He needed at least that much distance from the intransigence of the Humbled. His own mute lament demanded it.

Gradually he became aware that dawn was near. The pallor in the east was faint: he could not be sure of it. Nonetheless his wan health-sense interpreted the darkness. His surviving nerves assured him that this night was nearly done.

Perhaps when the sun rose, the Humbled would consent to leave Hotash Slay so that he could at least try to return to Linden and Jeremiah and Stave; to Mahrtiir and the Swordmainnir.

Linden would recognize his sadness and his sins. Her companions would understand them.

But the sun did not rise.

By tentative increments, the east paled. Slowly a preternatural gloaming spread across the Sunbirth Sea until it diluted the dark over Hotash Slay and the Shattered Hills. In contrast, the stars overhead grew strangely distinct, eerie and fragile. They seemed closer, drawing near to bewail their plight. The Humbled became vaguely visible, as if they stood in dusk or shadow. At their backs, the Hills crouched like megalithic beasts. But there was no sun.

No sun at all.

When he peered upward, Covenant saw that the stars were winking out. One at a time, they vanished from the infinite heavens. A few died in rapid succession, others at longer intervals; but they were all doomed. Within a handful of days, every star would perish, extinguished by the unforbidden hunger of the Worm.

Here ends

Against All Things Ending

Book Three of

"The Last Chronicles of Thomas Covenant."

The story concludes in Book Four

The Last Dark.

Glossary

Abatha: one of the Seven Words

Acence: a Stonedownor, sister of Atiaran

Ahamkara: Hoerkin, "the Door"

Ahanna: painter, daughter of Hanna

Ahnryn: a Ranyhyn; mount of Tull

Aimil: daughter of Anest, wife of Sunder

Aisle of Approach: passage to Earthrootstair under *Melenkurion* Skyweir

a-Jeroth of the Seven Hells: Lord of wickedness; Clave-name for Lord Foul the Despiser

ak-Haru: a supreme *Haruchai* honorific; paragon and measure of all *Haruchai* virtues

Akkasri: a member of the Clave; one of the na-Mhoram-cro

aliantha: treasure-berries

Alif, the Lady: a woman Favored by the *gaddhi*

amanibhavam: horse-healing grass, dangerous to humans

Amatin: a Lord, daughter of Matin

Amith: a woman of Crystal Stonedown

Amok: mysterious guide to ancient Lore

Amorine: First Haft, later Hiltmark

Anchormaster: second-in-command aboard a Giantship

Andelain, the Hills of Andelain, the Andelainian Hills: a region of the Land which embodies health and beauty

Andelainscion: a region in the Center Plains

Anele: deranged old man; son of Sunder and Hollian

Anest: a woman of Mithil Stonedown, sister of Kalina

Annoy: a Courser

anundivian yajña: "lost" Ramen craft of bone-sculpting

Appointed, the: an *Elohim* chosen to bear a particular burden; Findail

Arch of Time, the: symbol of the existence and structure of time; conditions which make the existence of time possible

Ardent, the: one of the Insequent

arghule/arghuleh: ferocious ice-beasts

Asuraka: Staff-Elder of the Loresraat

Atiaran: a Stonedownor, daughter of Tiaran, wife of Trell, mother of Lena

Audience Hall of Earthroot: maze under *Melenkurion* Skyweir to conceal and protect the Blood of the Earth

Aumbrie of the Clave, the: storeroom for former Lore

Auriference, the: one of the Insequent, long dead

Auspice, the: throne of the *gaddhi*

aussat Befylam: child-form of the *jheherrin*

Bahgoon the Unbearable: character in a Giantish tale

Banas Nimoram: the Celebration of Spring

Bandsoil Bounds: region north of Soulsease River

Banefire, the: fire by which the Clave affects the Sunbane

Bann: a Bloodguard, assigned to Lord Trevor

Bannor: a Bloodguard, assigned to Thomas Covenant

Baradakas: a Hirebrand of Soaring Woodhelven

Bareisle: an island off the coast of *Elemesnedene*

Bargas Slit: a gap through the Last Hills from the Center Plains to Garroting Deep

Basila: a scout in Berek Halfhand's army

Benj, the Lady: a woman Favored by the *gaddhi*

Berek Halfhand: Heartthew, Lord-Fatherer; first of the Old Lords

Bern: *Haruchai* slain by the Clave

Bhanoryl: a Ranyhyn; mount of Galt

Bhapa: a Cord of the Ramen, Sahah's half-brother; companion of Linden Avery

Bhrathair: a people met by the wandering Giants, residents of *Bhrathairealm* on the verge of the Great Desert

Bhrathairain: the city of the *Bhrathair*

Bhrathairain **Harbor:** the port of the *Bhrathair*

Bhrathairealm: the land of the *Bhrathair*

Birinair: a Hirebrand, Hearthrall of Lord's Keep

Bloodguard, the: *Haruchai*, a people living in the Westron Mountains; the defenders of the Lords

bone-sculpting: ancient Ramen craft, marrowmeld

Borillar: a Hirebrand and Hearthrall of Lord's Keep

Bornin: a *Haruchai*; a Master of the Land

Brabha: a Ranyhyn; mount of Korik

Branl: a *Haruchai*; a Master of the Land; one of the Humbled

Brannil: man of Stonemight Woodhelven

Brinn: a leader of the *Haruchai*; protector of Thomas Covenant; later Guardian of the One Tree

Brow Gnarlfist: a Giant, father of the First of the Search

caamora: Giantish ordeal of grief by fire

Cable Seadreamer: a Giant, brother of Honninscrave; member of the Search; possessed of the Earth-Sight

Cabledarm: a Giant; one of the Swordmainnir

Caer-Caveral: Forestal of Andelain; formerly Hile Troy

Caerroil Wildwood: Forestal of Garroting Deep

caesure: a rent in the fabric of time; a Fall

Cail: one of the *Haruchai*; protector of Linden Avery

Caitiffin: a captain of the armed forces of *Bhrathairealm*

Callindrill: a Lord, husband of Faer

Callowwail, the River: stream arising from *Elemesnedene*

Cavewights: evil creatures existing under Mount Thunder

Cav-Morin Fernhold: former Forestal of Morinmoss

Ceer: one of the *Haruchai*

Celebration of Spring, the: the Dance of the Wraiths of Andelain on the dark of the moon in the middle of spring

Center Plains, the: a region of the Land

Centerpith Barrens: a region in the Center Plains

Cerrin: a Bloodguard, assigned to Lord Shetra

Chant: one of the *Elohim*

Char: a Cord of the Ramen, Sahah's brother

Chatelaine, the: courtiers of the *gaddhi*

Chosen, the: title given to Linden Avery

Circle of Elders: Stonedown leaders

Cirrus Kindwind: a Giant; one of the Swordmainnir

clachan, **the:** demesne of the *Elohim*

Clang: a Courser

Clangor: a Courser

Clash: a Courser

Clave, the: group which wields the Sunbane and rules the Land

clingor: adhesive leather

Close, the: the Council-chamber of Lord's Keep

Clyme: a *Haruchai*; a Master of the Land; one of the Humbled

Coercri: The Grieve; former home of the Giants in Seareach

Colossus of the Fall, the: ancient stone figure guarding the Upper Land

Consecear Redoin: a region north of the Soulsease River

Cord: Ramen second rank

Cording: Ramen ceremony of becoming a Cord

Corimini: Eldest of the Loresraat

Corrupt, the: *jheherrin* name for themselves; also the soft ones

Corruption: Bloodguard/*Haruchai* name for Lord Foul

Council of Lords, the: protectors of the Land

Courser: a beast made by the Clave using the Sunbane

Creator, the: maker of the Earth

Croft: Graveler of Crystal Stonedown

Crowl: a Bloodguard

croyel, **the:** mysterious creatures which grant power through bargains, living off their hosts

Crystal Stonedown: home of Hollian

Currier: a Ramen rank

Damelon Giantfriend: son of Berek Halfhand, second High Lord of the Old Lords

Damelon's Door: door of lore which when opened permits passage through the Audience Hall of Earthroot under *Melenkurion* Skyweir

Dance of the Wraiths, the: the Celebration of Spring

Dancers of the Sea, the: *merewives*; suspected to be the offspring of the *Elohim* Kastenessen and his mortal lover

Daphin: one of the *Elohim*

Dawngreeter: highest sail on the foremast of a Giantship

Dead, the: spectres of those who have died

Deaththane: title given to High Lord Elena by the Ramen

Defiles Course, the: river in the Lower Land

Demimage: a sorcerer of Vidik Amar

Demondim, the: creatures created by Viles; creators of ur-viles and Waynhim

Demondim-spawn: another name for ur-viles and Waynhim; also another name for Vain

Desolation, the: era of ruin in the Land after the Ritual of Desecration

Despiser, the: Lord Foul

Despite: evil; name given to the Despiser's nature and effects

dharmakshetra: "to brave the enemy," a Waynhim

Dhorehold of the Dark: Forestal of Grimmerdhore

dhraga: a Waynhim

dhubha: a Waynhim

dhurng: a Waynhim

diamondraught: Giantish liquor

Din: a Courser

Dire's Vessel: Giantship used by the Swordmainnir to convey Longwrath

Doar: a Bloodguard

Dohn: a Manethrall of the Ramen

Dolewind, the: wind blowing to the Soulbiter

Doom's Retreat: a gap in the Southron Range between the South Plains and Doriendor Corishev

Doriendor Corishev: an ancient city; seat of the King against whom Berek Halfhand rebelled

drhami: a Waynhim

Drinishok: Sword-Elder of the Loresraat

Drinny: a Ranyhyn, foal of Hynaril; mount of Lord Mhoram

dromond: a Giantship

Drool Rockworm: a Cavewight, leader of the Cavewights; finder of the Illearth Stone

dukkha: "victim," Waynhim name

Dura Fairflank: a mustang, Thomas Covenant's mount

Durance, the: a barrier Appointed by the *Elohim*; a prison for both Kastenessen and the *skurj*

durhisitar: a Waynhim

During Stonedown: village destroyed by the *Grim*; home of Hamako

Duroc: one of the Seven Words

Durris: a *Haruchai*

EarthBlood: concentrated fluid Earthpower, only known to exist under *Melenkurion* Skyweir; source of the Power of Command

Earthfriend: title first given to Berek Halfhand

Earthpower: natural power of all life; the source of all organic power in the Land

Earthroot: lake under *Melenkurion* Skyweir

Earthrootstair: stairway down to the lake of Earthroot under *Melenkurion* Skyweir

Earth-Sight: Giantish power to perceive distant dangers and needs

eftmound: gathering place for the *Elohim*

eh-Brand: one who can use wood to read the Sunbane

Elemesnedene: home of the *Elohim*

Elena: daughter of Lena and Thomas Covenant; later High Lord

Elohim, **the:** a mystic people encountered by the wandering Giants

Elohimfest: a gathering of the *Elohim*

Emacrimma's Maw: a region in the Center Plains

Emereau Vrai: Kastenessen's mortal lover, now victim to She Who Must Not Be Named

Enemy: Lord Foul's term of reference for the Creator

Eoman: a unit of the Warward of Lord's Keep, twenty warriors and a Warhaft

Eoward: twenty Eoman plus a Haft

Epemin: a soldier in Berek Halfhand's army, tenth Eoman, second Eoward

Esmer: tormented son of Cail and the Dancers of the Sea

Exalt Widenedworld: a Giant; youngest son of Soar Gladbirth and Sablehair Foamheart; later called Lostson and Longwrath

fael Befylam: serpent-form of the *jheherrin*

Faer: wife of Lord Callindrill

Fall: *Haruchai* name for a *caesure*

Fangs: the Teeth of the Render; Ramen name for the Demondim

Fangthane the Render: Ramen name for Lord Foul

Far Woodhelven: a village of the Land

Father of Horses, the: *Kelenbhrabanal*, legendary sire of the Ranyhyn

Favored, the: courtesans of the *gaddhi*

Feroce, the: denizens of Sarangrave Flat, worshippers of the lurker, descended from the *jheherrin*

Fields of Richloam: a region in the Center Plains

Filigree: a Giant; another name for Sablehair Foamheart

Findail: one of the *Elohim*; the Appointed

Fire-Lions: living fire-flow of Mount Thunder

fire-stones: graveling

First Betrayer: Clave-name for Berek Halfhand

First Circinate: first level of the Sandhold

First Haft: third-in-command of the Warward

First Mark: Bloodguard commander

First of the Search, the: leader of the Giants who follow the Earth-Sight; Gossmer Glowlimn

First Ward of Kevin's Lore: primary cache of knowledge left by High Lord Kevin

First Woodhelven: banyan tree village between Revelstone and Andelain; first Woodhelven created by Sunder and Hollian

Fleshharrower: a Giant-Raver, Jehannum, *moksha*

Foamkite: *tyrscull* belonging to Honninscrave and Seadreamer

Fole: a *Haruchai*

Foodfendhall: eating-hall and galley aboard a Giantship

Forbidding: a wall of power

Forestal: a protector of the remnants of the One Forest

Fostil: a man of Mithil Stonedown; father of Liand

Foul's Creche: the Despiser's home; Ridjeck Thome

Frostheart Grueburn: a Giant; one of the Swordmainnir

Furl Falls: waterfall at Revelstone

Furl's Fire: warning fire at Revelstone

gaddhi, **the:** sovereign of *Bhrathairealm*

Gallows Howe: a place of execution in Garroting Deep

Galt: a *Haruchai*; a Master of the Land; one of the Humbled

Garroting Deep: a forest of the Land

Garth: Warmark of the Warward of Lord's Keep

Gay: a Winhome of the Ramen

ghohritsar: a Waynhim

ghramin: a Waynhim

Giantclave: Giantish conference

Giantfriend: title given first to Damelon, later to Thomas Covenant and then Linden Avery

Giants: the Unhomed, ancient friends of the Lords; a seafaring people of the Earth

Giantship: a stone sailing vessel made by Giants; *dromond*

Giantway: path made by Giants

Giant Woods: a forest of the Land

Gibbon: the na-Mhoram; leader of the Clave

Gilden: a maple-like tree with golden leaves

Gildenlode: a power-wood formed from the Gilden trees

Glimmermere: a lake on the plateau above Revelstone

Gorak Krembal: Hotash Slay, a defense around Foul's Creche

Gossamer Glowlimn: a Giant; the First of the Search

Grace: a Cord of the Ramen

Graveler: one who uses stone to wield the Sunbane

graveling: fire-stones, made to glow and emit heat by stone-lore

Gravelingas: a master of *rhadhamaerl* stone-lore

Gravin Threndor: Mount Thunder

Great Desert, the: a region of the Earth; home of the *Bhrathair* and the Sandgorgons

Great One: title given to Caerroil Wildwood by the Mahdoubt

Great Swamp, the: Lifeswallower; a region of the Land

Greshas Slant: a region in the Center Plains

Grey Desert, the: a region south of the Land

Grey River, the: a river of the Land

Grey Slayer: plains name for Lord Foul

Greywightswath: a region north of the Soulsease River

griffin: lion-like beast with wings

Grim, the: (also the na-Mhoram's *Grim*) a destructive storm sent by the Clave

Grimmand Honninscrave: a Giant; Master of Starfare's Gem; brother of Seadreamer

Grimmerdhore: a forest of the Land

Guard, the: hustin; soldiers serving the *gaddhi*

Guardian of the One Tree, the: mystic figure warding the approach to the One Tree; formerly *ak-Haru Kenaustin Ardenol*; now Brinn of the *Haruchai*

Haft: commander of an Eoward

Halewhole Bluntfist: a Giant; one of the Swordmainnir

Halfhand: title given to Thomas Covenant and to Berek

Hall of Gifts, the: large chamber in Revelstone devoted to the artworks of the Land

Hamako: sole survivor of the destruction of During Stonedown

Hami: a Manethrall of the Ramen

Hand: a rank in Berek Halfhand's army; aide to Berek

Handir: a *Haruchai* leader; the Voice of the Masters

Harad: one of the Seven Words

Harbor Captain: chief official of the port of *Bhrathairealm*

Harn: one of the *Haruchai*; protector of Hollian

Harrow, the: one of the Insequent

Haruchai: a warrior people from the Westron Mountains

Healer: a physician

Heart of Thunder: Kiril Threndor, a cave of power in Mount Thunder

Hearthcoal: a Giant; cook of Starfare's Gem; wife of Seasauce

Hearthrall of Lord's Keep: a steward responsible for light, warmth, and hospitality

Heartthew: a title given to Berek Halfhand

heartwood chamber: meeting-place of a Woodhelven, within a tree

Heer: leader of a Woodhelven

Heft Galewrath: a Giant; Storesmaster of Starfare's Gem

Herem: a Raver, Kinslaughterer, *turiya*

Hergrom: one of the *Haruchai*

High God: title given to the lurker of the Sarangrave by the Feroce

High Lord: leader of the Council of Lords

High Lord's Furl: banner of the High Lord

High Wood: *lomillialor*; offspring of the One Tree

Hile Troy: a man formerly from Covenant's world; Warmark of High Lord Elena's Warward

Hiltmark: second-in-command of the Warward

Hirebrand: a master of *lillianrill* wood-lore

Hoerkin: a Warhaft

Hollian: daughter of Amith; eh-Brand of Crystal Stonedown; companion of Thomas Covenant and Linden Avery

Home: original homeland of the Giants

Horizonscan: lookout atop the midmast of a Giantship

Horrim Carabal: name given to the lurker of the Sarangrave

Horse, the: human soldiery of the *gaddhi*

horserite: a gathering of Ranyhyn in which they drink mind-blending waters in order to share visions, prophecies, and purpose

Hotash Slay: Gorak Krembal, a flow of lava protecting Foul's Creche

Hower: a Bloodguard, assigned to Lord Loerya

Hrama: a Ranyhyn stallion; mount of Anele

Humbled, the: three *Haruchai* maimed to resemble Thomas Covenant in order to remind the Masters of their limitations

Hurn: a Cord of the Ramen

hurtloam: a healing mud

Huryn: a Ranyhyn; mount of Terrel

husta/hustin: partly human soldiers bred by Kasreyn to be the *gaddhi*'s Guard

Hyn: a Ranyhyn mare; mount of Linden Avery

Hynaril: a Ranyhyn; mount of Tamarantha and then Mhoram

Hynyn: a Ranyhyn stallion; mount of Stave

Hyrim: a Lord, son of Hoole

Illearth Stone, the: powerful bane long buried under Mount Thunder

Illender: title given to Thomas Covenant

Imoiran Tomal-mate: a Stonedownor

Inbull: a Warhaft in Berek Halfhand's army; commander of the tenth Eoman, second Eoward

Infelice: reigning leader of the *Elohim*

Insequent, the: a mysterious people living far to the west of the Land

Interdict, the: reference to the power of the Colossus of the Fall to prevent Ravers from entering the Upper Land

Irin: a warrior of the Third Eoman of the Warward

Ironhand, the: title given to the leader of the Swordmainnir

Isle of the One Tree, the: location of the One Tree

Jain: a Manethrall of the Ramen

Jass: a *Haruchai*; a Master of the Land

Jehannum: a Raver, Fleshharrower, *moksha*

Jerrick: a Demimage of Vidik Amar, in part responsible for the creation of *quellvisks*

Jevin: a healer in Berek Halfhand's army

jheherrin: soft ones, misshapen by-products of Lord Foul's making

Jous: a man of Mithil Stonedown, son of Prassan, father of Nassic; inheritor of an Unfettered One's mission to remember the Halfhand

Kalina: a woman of Mithil Stonedown; wife of Nassic, mother of Sunder

Kam: a Manethrall of the Ramen

Karnis: a Heer of First Woodhelven

Kasreyn of the Gyre: a thaumaturge; the *gaddhi's* Kemper (advisor) in *Bhrathairealm*

Kastenessen: one of the *Elohim*; former Appointed

Keep of the na-Mhoram, the: Revelstone

Keeper: a Ramen rank, one of those unsuited to the rigors of being a Cord or a Manethrall

Kelenbhrabanal: Father of Horses in Ranyhyn legends

Kemper, the: chief advisor of the *gaddhi*; Kasreyn

Kemper's Pitch: highest level of the Sandhold

Kenaustin Ardenol: a figure of *Haruchai* legend; former Guardian of the One Tree; true name of the Theomach

Kevin Landwaster: son of Loric Vilesilencer; last High Lord of the Old Lords

Kevin's Dirt: smog-like pall covering the Upper Land; it blocks health-sense, making itself invisible from below

Kevin's Lore: knowledge of power left hidden by Kevin in the Seven Wards

Kevin's Watch: mountain lookout near Mithil Stonedown

Khabaal: one of the Seven Words

Khelen: a Ranyhyn stallion; mount of Jeremiah

Kinslaughterer: a Giant-Raver, Herem, *turiya*

Kiril Threndor: chamber of power deep under Mount Thunder; Heart of Thunder

Koral: a Bloodguard, assigned to Lord Amatin

Korik: a Bloodguard

Krenwill: a scout in Berek Halfhand's army

kresh: savage giant yellow wolves

krill, the: knife of power forged by High Lord Loric; awakened to power by Thomas Covenant

Kurash Plenethor: region of the Land formally named Stricken Stone, now called Trothgard

Kurash Qwellinir: the Shattered Hills, region of the Lower Land protecting Foul's Creche

Lake Pelluce: a lake in Andelainscion

Lal: a Cord of the Ramen

Land, the: generally area found on the map; a focal region of the Earth where Earth-power is uniquely accessible

Landsdrop: great cliff separating the Upper and Lower Lands

Landsverge Stonedown: a village of the Land

Landwaster: title given to High Lord Kevin

Latebirth: a Giant; one of the Swordmainnir

Law, the: the natural order

Law of Death, the: the natural order which separates the living from the dead

Law of Life, the: the natural order which separates the dead from the living

Law-Breaker: title given to both High Lord Elena and Caer-Caveral

Lax Blunderfoot: a name chosen by Latebirth in self-castigation

Lena: a Stonedownor, daughter of Atiaran, mother of Elena

lianar: wood of power used by an eh-Brand

Liand: a man of Mithil Stonedown, son of Fostil; companion of Linden Avery

Lifeswallower: the Great Swamp

lillianrill: wood-lore; masters of wood-lore

Lithe: a Manethrall of the Ramen

Llaura: a Heer of Soaring Woodhelven

Loerya: a Lord, wife of Trevor

lomillialor: High Wood; a wood of power

Longwrath: a Giant; Swordmainnir name for Exalt Widenedworld

Lord: one who has mastered both the Sword and the Staff aspects of Kevin's Lore

Lord-Fatherer: title given to Berek Halfhand

Lord Foul: the enemy of the Land; the Despiser

"Lord Mhoram's Victory": a painting by Ahanna

Lord of Wickedness: a-Jeroth

Lord's-fire: staff-fire used by the Lords

Lord's Keep: Revelstone

Lords, the: the primary protectors of the Land

loremaster: a leader of ur-viles

Loresraat: Trothgard school at Revelwood where Kevin's Lore is studied

Lorewarden: a teacher in the Loresraat

loreworks: Demondim power-laboratory

Loric Vilesilencer: a High Lord; son of Damelon Giantfriend

lor-liarill: Gildenlode

Lost, the: Giantish name for the Unhomed

Lost Deep, the: a loreworks; breeding pit/laboratory under Mount Thunder where Demondim, Waynhim, and ur-viles were created

Lostson: a Giant; later name for Exalt Widenedworld

Lower Land, the: region of the Land east of Landsdrop

lucubrium: laboratory of a thaumaturge

lurker of the Sarangrave, the: monster inhabiting the Great Swamp

Magister, the: former Forestal of Andelain

Mahdoubt, the: a servant of Revelstone; one of the Insequent

Mahrtiir: a Manethrall of the Ramen; companion of Linden Avery

maidan: open land around *Elemesnedene*

Maker, the: *jheherrin* name for Lord Foul

Maker-place: *jheherrin* name for Foul's Creche

Malliner: Woodhelvennin Heer, son of Veinnin

Mane: Ramen reference to a Ranyhyn

Maneing: Ramen ceremony of becoming a Manethrall

Manethrall: highest Ramen rank

Manhome: main dwelling place of the Ramen in the Plains of Ra

Marid: a man of Mithil Stonedown; Sunbane victim

Marny: a Ranyhyn; mount of Tuvor

marrowmeld: bone-sculpting; *anundivian yajña*

Master: commander of a Giantship

Master, the: Clave-name for Lord Foul

master-rukh, **the:** iron triangle at Revelstone which feeds and reads other *rukhs*

Masters of the Land, the: *Haruchai* who have claimed responsibility for protecting the Land from Corruption

Mehryl: a Ranyhyn; mount of Hile Troy

Melenkurion: one of the Seven Words

Melenkurion **Skyweir:** a cleft peak in the Westron Mountains

Memla: a Rider of the Clave; one of the na-Mhoram-in

mere-**son:** name or title given to Esmer

merewives: the Dancers of the Sea

metheglin: a beverage; mead

Mhoram: a Lord, later high Lord; son of Variol

Mhornym: a Ranyhyn stallion; mount of Clyme

Mill: one of the Seven Words

Minas: one of the Seven Words

mirkfruit: papaya-like fruit with narcoleptic pulp

Mishio Massima: the Ardent's mount

Mistweave: a Giant

Mithil River: a river of the Land

Mithil Stonedown: a village in the South Plains

Mithil's Plunge, the: waterfall at the head of the Mithil valley

Moire Squareset: a Giant; one of the Swordmainnir; killed in battle by the *skurj*

moksha: a Raver, Jehannum, Fleshharrower

Morin: First Mark of the Bloodguard; commander in original *Haruchai* army

Morinmoss: a forest of the Land

Morninglight: one of the *Elohim*

Morril: a Bloodguard, assigned to Lord Callindrill

Mount Thunder: a peak at the center of Landsdrop

Muirwin Delenoth: resting place of abhorrence; graveyard of *quellvisks*

Murrin: a Stonedownor, mate of Odona

Myrha: a Ranyhyn; mount of High Lord Elena

na-Mhoram, the: leader of the Clave

na-Mhoram-cro: lowest rank of the Clave

na-Mhoram-in: highest rank of the Clave below the na-Mhoram

na-Mhoram-wist: middle rank of the Clave

Naharahn: a Ranyhyn mare; mount of Pahni

Narunal: a Ranyhyn stallion; mount of Mahrtiir

Nassic: father of Sunder, son of Jous; inheritor of an Unfettered One's mission to remember the Halfhand

Naybahn: a Ranyhyn; mount of Branl

Nelbrin: son of Sunder, "heart's child"

Nicor, **the:** great sea-monsters; said to be offspring of the Worm of the World's End

Nom: a Sandgorgon

North Plains, the: a region of the Land

Northron Climbs, the: a region of the Land

Oath of Peace, the: oath by the people of the Land against needless violence

Odona: a Stonedownor, mate of Murrin

Offin: a former na-Mhoram

Old Lords, the: Lords prior to the Ritual of Desecration

Omournil: Woodhelvennin Heer, daughter of Mournil

One Forest, the: ancient forest covering most of the Land

One Tree, the: mystic tree from which the Staff of Law was made

Onyx Stonemage: a Giant; one of the Swordmainnir

orcrest: a stone of power; Sunstone

Osondrea: a Lord, daughter of Sondrea; later high Lord

Padrias: Woodhelvennin Heer, son of Mill

Pahni: a Cord of the Ramen, cousin of Sahah; companion of Linden Avery

Palla: a healer in Berek Halfhand's army

Peak of the Fire-Lions, the: Mount Thunder, Gravin Threndor

Pietten: Woodhelvennin child damaged by Lord Foul's minions, son of Soranal

pitchbrew: a beverage combining *diamondraught* and *vitrim*, conceived by Pitchwife

Pitchwife: a Giant; member of the Search; husband of the First of the Search

Plains of Ra, the: a region of the Land

Porib: a Bloodguard

Power of Command, the: Seventh Ward of Kevin's Lore

Pren: a Bloodguard

Prothall: High Lord, son of Dwillian

Prover of Life: title given to Thomas Covenant

Puhl: a Cord of the Ramen

Pure One, the: redemptive figure of *jheherrin* legend

Quaan: Warhaft of the Third Eoman of the Warward; later Hiltmark, then Warmark

quellvisk: a kind of monster, now apparently extinct

Quern Ehstrel: true name of the Mahdoubt

Quest for the Staff of Law, the: quest to recover the Staff of Law from Drool Rockworm

Questsimoon, the: the Roveheartswind; a steady, favorable wind, perhaps seasonal

Quilla: a Heer of First Woodhelven

Quirrel: a Stonedownor, companion of Triock

Ramen: people who serve the Ranyhyn

Rant Absolain: the *gaddhi*

Ranyhyn: the great horses of the Plains of Ra

Ravers: Lord Foul's three ancient servants

Raw, the: fjord into the demesne of the *Elohim*

Rawedge Rim, the: mountains around *Elemesnedene*

Reader: a member of the Clave who tends and uses the *master-rukh*

Rede, the: knowledge of history and survival promulgated by the Clave

Revelstone: Lord's Keep; mountain city formed by Giants

Revelwood: seat of the Loresraat; tree city grown by Lords

rhadhamaerl: stone-lore; masters of stone-lore

rhee: a Ramen food, a thick mush

Rhohm: a Ranyhyn stallion; mount of Liand

rhysh: a community of Waynhim; "stead"

rhyshyshim: a gathering of *rhysh*; a place in which such gathering occurs

Riddenstretch: a region north of the Soulsease River

Rider: a member of the Clave

Ridjeck Thome: Foul's Creche, the Despiser's home

rillinlure: healing wood dust

Rime Coldspray: a Giant; the Ironhand of the Swordmainnir

Ringthane: Ramen name for Thomas Covenant, then Linden Avery

ring-wielder: *Elohim* term of reference for Thomas Covenant

Rire Grist: a Caitiffin of the *gaddhi*'s Horse

Rites of Unfettering: the ceremony of becoming Unfettered

Ritual of Desecration, the: act of despair by which High Lord Kevin destroyed the Old Lords and ruined most of the Land

Rivenrock: deep cleft splitting *Melenkurion* Skyweir and its plateau; there the Black River enters Garroting Deep

River Landrider, the: a river of the Land, partial border of the Plains of Ra

Riversward: a region north of the Soulsease River

Rockbrother: Swordmainnir name for Stave

Rockbrother, Rocksister: terms of affection between humans and Giants

rocklight: light emitted by glowing stone

roge Befylam: Cavewight-form of the *jheherrin*

Rohnhyn: a Ranyhyn; mount of Bhapa after Whrany's death

Roveheartswind, the: the *Questsimoon*

Rue: a Manethrall of the Ramen, formerly named Gay

Ruel: a Bloodguard, assigned to Hile Troy

Ruinwash, the: name of the River Landrider on the Lower Land

rukh: iron talisman by which a Rider wields the power of the Sunbane

Runnik: a Bloodguard

Rustah: a Cord of the Ramen

Sablehair Foamheart: a Giant, also called Filigree; mate of Soar Gladbirth; mother of Exalt Widenedworld

sacred enclosure: Vespers-hall at Revelstone; later the site of the Banefire

Sahah: a Cord of the Ramen

Saltheart Foamfollower: a Giant, friend of Thomas Covenant

Saltroamrest: bunk hold for the crew in a Giantship

Salttooth: jutting rock in the harbor of the Giants' Home

Salva Gildenbourne: forest surrounding the Hills of Andelain; begun by Sunder and Hollian

samadhi: a Raver, Sheol, Satansfist

Sandgorgons: monsters of the Great Desert of *Bhrathairealm*

Sandgorgons Doom: imprisoning storm created by Kasreyn to trap the Sandgorgons

Sandhold, the: the *gaddhi*'s castle in *Bhrathairealm*

Sandwall, the: the great wall defending *Bhrathairain*

Santonin: a Rider of the Clave, one of the na-Mhoram-in

Sarangrave Flat: a region of the Lower Land encompassing the Great Swamp

Satansfist: a Giant-Raver, Sheol, *samadhi*

Satansheart: Giantish name for Lord Foul

Scend Wavegift: a Giant; one of the Swordmainnir; killed by Longwrath

Search, the: quest of the Giants for the wound in the Earth; later the quest for the Isle of the One Tree

Seareach: region of the Land occupied by the Unhomed

Seasauce: a Giant; husband of Hearthcoal; cook of Starfare's Gem

Seatheme: dead wife of Sevinhand

Second Circinate: second level of the Sandhold

Second Ward: second unit of Kevin's hidden knowledge

setrock: a type of stone used with pitch to repair stone

Seven Hells, the: a-Jeroth's demesne: desert, rain, pestilence, fertility, war, savagery, and darkness

Seven Wards, the: collection of knowledge hidden by High Lord Kevin

Seven Words, the: words of power from Kevin's Lore

Sevinhand: a Giant, Anchormaster of Starfare's Gem

Shattered Hills, the: a region of the Land near Foul's Creche

She Who Must Not Be Named: an ancient bane slumbering under Mount Thunder, now composed of many lost women

Sheol: a Raver, Satansfist, *samadhi*

Shetra: a Lord, wife of Verement

Shipsheartthew: the wheel of a Giantship

shola: a small wooded glen where a stream runs between unwooded hills

Shull: a Bloodguard

Sill: a Bloodguard, assigned to Lord Hyrim

Sivit: a Rider of the Clave, one of the na-Mhoram-wist

skest: acid-creatures serving the lurker of the Sarangrave, descended from the *jheherrin*

skurj: laval monsters that devour earth and vegetation; long ago, the *Elohim* Kastenessen was Appointed (the Durance) to prevent them from wreaking terrible havoc

Slen: a Stonedownor, mate of Terass

Snared One, the: ur-vile name for Lord Foul the Despiser

Soar Gladbirth: a Giant; youngest son of Pitchwife and Gossamer Glowlimn

Soaring Woodhelven: a tree-village

soft ones, the: the *jheherrin*

Somo: pinto taken by Liand from Mithil Stonedown

soothreader: a seer

soothtell: ritual of revelation practiced by the Clave

Soranal: a Woodhelvennin Heer, son of Thiller

Soulbiter, the: a dangerous ocean of Giantish legend

Soulbiter's Teeth: reefs in the Soulbiter

Soulcrusher: Giantish name for Lord Foul

South Plains, the: a region of the Land

Sparlimb Keelsetter: a Giant, father of triplets

Spikes, the: guard-towers at the mouth of *Bhrathairain* Harbor

Spoiled Plains, the: a region of the Lower Land

Spray Frothsurge: a Giant; mother of the First of the Search

springwine: a mild, refreshing liquor

Staff, the: a branch of the study of Kevin's Lore

Staff of Law, the: a tool of Earthpower; the first Staff was formed by Berek from the One Tree and later destroyed by Thomas Covenant; the second was formed by Linden Avery by using wild magic to merge Vain and Findail

Stallion of the First Herd, the: *Kelenbhrabanal*

Starfare's Gem: Giantship used by the Search

Starkin: one of the *Elohim*

Stave: a *Haruchai*; a Master of the Land; companion of Linden Avery

Stell: one of the *Haruchai*, protector of Sunder

Stonedown: a stone-village

Stonedownor: one who lives in a stone-village

Stonemight, the: a fragment of the Illearth Stone

Stonemight Woodhelven: a village in the South Plains

Storesmaster: third-in-command aboard a Giantship

Stormpast Galesend: a Giant; one of the Swordmainnir

Stricken Stone: region of the Land, later called Trothgard

Sunbane, the: a power arising from the corruption of nature by Lord Foul

Sunbirth Sea, the: ocean east of the Land

Sunder: son of Nassic; Graveler of Mithil Stonedown; companion of Thomas Covenant and Linden Avery

Sun-Sage: one who can affect the Sunbane

Sunstone: *orcrest*

sur-jheherrin: descendants of the *jheherrin*; inhabitants of Sarangrave Flat

suru-pa-maerl: an art using stone

Swarte: a Rider of the Clave

Sword, the: a branch of the study of Kevin's Lore

Sword-Elder: chief Lorewarden of the Sword at the Loresraat

Swordmain/Swordmainnir: Giant(s) trained as warrior(s)

Syr Embattled: former Forestal of Giant Woods

Tamarantha: a Lord, daughter of Enesta, wife of Variol

Teeth of the Render, the: Ramen name for the Demondim; Fangs

Terass: a Stonedownor, daughter of Annoria, wife of Slen

Terrel: a Bloodguard, assigned to Lord Mhoram; a commander of the original *Haruchai* army

test of silence, the: test of integrity used by the people of the Land

test of truth, the: test of veracity by *lomillialor* or *orcrest*

The Grieve: *Coercri*; home of the lost Giants in Seareach

Thelma Twofist: character in a Giantish tale

The Majesty: throne room of the *gaddhi*; fourth level of the Sandhold

Theomach, the: one of the Insequent

Thew: a Cord of the Ramen

Third Ward: third unit of Kevin's hidden knowledge

Thomin: a Bloodguard, assigned to Lord Verement

Three Corners of Truth, the: basic formulation of beliefs taught and enforced by the Clave

thronehall, the: the Despiser's seat in Foul's Creche

Tier of Riches, the: showroom of the *gaddhi*'s wealth; third level of the Sandhold

Timewarden: *Elohim* title for Thomas Covenant after his death

Tohrm: a Gravelingas; Hearthrall of Lord's Keep

Tomal: a Stonedownor craftmaster

Toril: *Haruchai* slain by the Clave

Treacher's Gorge: ravine opening into Mount Thunder

treasure-berries: *aliantha*, nourishing fruit found throughout the Land in all seasons

Trell: Gravelingas of Mithil Stonedown; husband of Atiaran, father of Lena

Trevor: a Lord, husband of Loerya

Triock: a Stonedownor, son of Thuler; loved Lena

Trothgard: a region of the Land, formerly Stricken Stone

Tull: a Bloodguard

turiya: a Raver, Herem, Kinslaughterer

Tuvor: First Mark of the Bloodguard; a commander of the original *Haruchai* army

tyrscull: a Giantish training vessel for apprentice sailors

Unbeliever, the: title claimed by Thomas Covenant

Unfettered, the: lore-students freed from conventional responsibilities to seek individual knowledge and service

Unfettered One, the: founder of a line of men waiting to greet Thomas Covenant's return to the Land

Unhomed, the: the lost Giants living in Seareach

un-Maker-made, the: in *jheherrin* legend, living beings not created by the Maker

upland: plateau above Revelstone

Upper Land, the: region of the Land west of Landsdrop

ur-Lord: title given to Thomas Covenant

ur-viles: Demondim-spawn, evil creatures

ussusimiel: nourishing melon grown by the people of the Land

Vailant: former High Lord before Prothall

Vain: Demondim-spawn; bred by ur-viles for a secret purpose

Vale: a Bloodguard

Valley of Two Rivers, the: site of Revelwood in Trothgard

Variol Tamarantha-mate: a Lord, later High Lord; son of Pentil, father of Mhoram

Verement: a Lord, husband of Shetra

Verge of Wandering, the: valley in the Southron Range southeast of Mithil Stonedown; gathering place of the nomadic Ramen

Vernigil: a *Haruchai*; a Master of the Land guarding First Woodhelven

Vertorn: a healer in Berek Halfhand's army

Vespers: self-consecration rituals of the Lords

Vettalor: Warmark of the army opposing Berek Halfhand

viancome: meeting place at Revelwood

Victuallin Tayne: a region in the Center Plains

Vidik Amar: a region of the Earth

Viles: monstrous beings which created the Demondim

vitrim: nourishing fluid created by the Waynhim

Vizard, the: one of the Insequent

Voice of the Masters, the: a *Haruchai* leader; spokesman for the Masters as a group

voure: a plant-sap which wards off insects

Vow, the: *Haruchai* oath of service which formed the Bloodguard

vraith: a Waynhim

Ward: a unit of Kevin's lore

Warhaft: commander of an Eoman

Warlore: Sword knowledge in Kevin's Lore

Warmark: commander of the Warward

Warrenbridge: entrance to the catacombs under Mount Thunder

Warward, the: army of Lord's Keep

Wavedancer: Giantship commanded by Brow Gnarlfist

Wavenhair Haleall: a Giant, wife of Sparlimb Keelsetter, mother of triplets

Waymeet: resting place for travelers maintained by Waynhim

Waynhim: tenders of the Waymeets; rejected Demondim-spawn, opponents and relatives of ur-viles

Weird of the Waynhim, the: Waynhim concept of doom, destiny, or duty

were-menhir(s): Giantish name for the *skurj*

Whane: a Cord of the Ramen

white gold: a metal of power not found in the Land

white gold wielder: title given to Thomas Covenant

White River, the: a river of the land

Whrany: a Ranyhyn stallion; mount of Bhapa

Wightburrow, the: cairn under which Drool Rockworm is buried

Wightwarrens: home of the Cavewights under Mount Thunder; catacombs

wild magic: the power of white gold; considered the keystone of the Arch of Time

Wildwielder: white gold wielder; title given to Linden Avery by Esmer and the *Elohim*

Windscour: region in the Center Plains

Windshorn Stonedown: a village in the South Plains

Winhome: Ramen lowest rank

Woodenwold: region of trees surrounding the *maidan* of *Elemesnedene*

Woodhelven: wood-village

Woodhelvennin: inhabitants of wood-village

Word of Warning: a powerful, destructive forbidding

Worm of the World's End, the: creature believed by the *Elohim* to have formed the foundation of the Earth

Wraiths of Andelain, the: creatures of living light that perform the Dance at the Celebration of Spring

Würd of the Earth, the: term used by the *Elohim* to describe their own nature, destiny, or purpose; could be read as Word, Worm, or Weird

Yellinin: a soldier in Berek Halfhand's army; third-in-command of the tenth Eoman, second Eoward

Yeurquin: a Stonedownor, companion of Triock

Yolenid: daughter of Loerya

Zaynor: a *Haruchai* from a time long before the *Haruchai* first came to the Land